THE PROPHETS OF ETERNAL FJORD

The Prophets of
Eternal Fjord

KIM LEINE

Translated from the Danish
by Martin Aitken

LIVERIGHT PUBLISHING CORPORATION

A Division of W. W. Norton & Company
New York • London

The translation of this work was funded by the Danish Arts Foundation, an organization to promote the arts in Denmark and Danish art abroad.

DANISH ARTS FOUNDATION

For information about permission to reproduce selections from this book, write to Permissions, Liveright Publishing Corporation, a division of W. W. Norton & Company, Inc., 500 Fifth Avenue, New York, NY 10110

For information about special discounts for bulk purchases, please contact W. W. Norton Special Sales at specialsales@wwnorton.com or 800-233-4830

Manufacturing by Courier Westford
Production manager: Louise Mattarelliano

Library of Congress Cataloging-in-Publication Data

Leine, Kim, 1961– author.
[Profeterne i Evighedsfjorden. English]
The prophets of eternal fjord / Kim Leine ; translated from the Danish by Martin Aitken.
pages cm
ISBN 978-0-87140-671-2 (hardcover)
1. Greenland—History—18th century—Fiction. 2. Clergy—Fiction.
I. Aitken, Martin, translator. II. Title.
PT8177.22.E47P7613 2015
839.813'8—dc23
2015013260

Liveright Publishing Corporation, 500 Fifth Avenue, New York, N.Y. 10110
www.wwnorton.com

W. W. Norton & Company Ltd., Castle House, 75/76 Wells Street
London W1T 3QT

1 2 3 4 5 6 7 8 9 0

Dedicated to the
Government of Greenland
(1979–2009)
and its pioneers

Translator's Note

In eighteenth-century Danish the third person pronoun was often used as a marker of politeness or of distance if addressing inferiors. This convention disappeared around the beginning of the nineteenth century, but it explains why characters in this book are sometimes addressed by others as 'he' rather than 'you'.

THE PROPHETS OF ETERNAL FJORD

PROLOGUE

The Fall

(14 August 1793)

The widow has come up here of her own accord, no one has forced her. She has beaten the lice from her finest clothes and put them on. She has washed her hair in the urine tub of the communal house and tied it up. Silently observed by her heathen cohabitants, she scraped the sooty grease from her cheeks and consumed the good meal that had been put out before her. Then she came up here, carried along by a lightness of step. Now she sits on the brink of happiness, expectant and with warmth in her cheeks, at the edge with her legs tucked decorously beneath her in the way of all widows, the way she sits at home on the little side bench under the window opening. In one hand she clutches the crucifix and feels comfort in the solid warmth of its gold. Far below her, a drop of at least a hundred fathoms, she hears the waves as they break, the sea colliding with the cliff, dissolving into white spray, retreating with a rush. But she sees it not, for she has closed her eyes, turned her gaze inwards. She has fought back the fear, forced her breath and heart to settle into dogged rhythm, and she moves her lips, repeating the litany over and over. *O God the Father, Creator of heaven and earth, have mercy upon us. O God the Son, Redeemer of the world, have mercy upon us. O God the Holy Spirit, Sanctifier of the faithful, have mercy upon us. O holy, blessed and glorious Trinity, one God, have mercy upon us.* She feels the wind gusting from below, breathing life into her garments, and she clings to the damp turf of the cliff so as not to be prematurely blown over the edge. She remains there, seated, repeating the litany and waiting for her helper. *By thine agony and bloody sweat; by thy Cross and Passion. Good Lord, deliver us!*

Now she hears him, the creak of his boots behind her, stealing up with hardly a sound, embarrassed almost, as bashful as a young suitor. She hears how he tries to suppress his laboured breathing and she can hardly resist smiling to herself in recognition. *We beseech Thee to hear us, good Lord!*

She senses he has come to a halt, just a few short paces behind her, and she imagines him standing looking at her, as he did the first time they were together, considering where best to strike, and how hard, for she knows that he will kill her, though he has no wish to harm her. It is a comfort to her that he should be so close, now that her life is about to end. She is calmed by the thought and feels herself relax, lowers her chin towards her chest and takes a deep breath. *Son of God, we beseech Thee to hear us!*

The air is mild. The upward swirls smell of mussels and seaweed left uncovered at the tideline. Gulls scream in the distance. Instinctively, she opens her eyes. Incorrigibly curious by nature, she cannot do otherwise, not even now, at the furthest edge of all things, where her mind by rights should be above the trivialities of life on earth, and disposed to the heavenly. But she must see what the noisy gulls are at, and she spies the ship on its way north, a two-master, its sails filled, dazzling white as gulls' wings, and the flock of screaming birds drifting like an amorphous cloud around the masts. No, she is not yet ready to meet her maker, not this day, and yet she knows it is too late to change her mind, too late for herself, too late for the one who stands behind her. Everything has been arranged and made ready. The fall has already begun, began many years ago.

She hears in the calmness of his breathing that he has not noticed the ship. He is far too preoccupied by what he is about to do. Is he as afraid as she is? Does he want it not to happen? If she can make him see the ship, she thinks, perhaps everything will be changed and this murderous rendezvous will be postponed.

She feels his hand at her throat. She cowers and whimpers. But what he wants is the crucifix. Deftly, he flicks the cord over her head and wrenches the golden cross from her hand that held it so tightly. Take it, she says in silence, I have no longer need of it. And what good has it ever done me?

She turns her head slightly to the side in order to catch a glimpse of him, knowing only too well that it is foolish of her, that it will merely hasten on the deed, render it even more inevitable, and the moment she senses the dark shadow at her shoulder she gives a start and splutters out loud: *Christ, have mercy upon us!* Then the sudden kick of the boot against her spine. Her head snaps back, her body thrusts forward, and she plunges over the precipice, falls, flailing and twisting, dragging a vertical scream in her wake like an uneven line drawn in charcoal.

†

He takes a step forward, places his boot cautiously on the soft, yielding moss, leans over the edge and sees the body, peacefully bobbing face down in the surf. He removes his hat, clutches it to his chest and mumbles: *O Lord, let thy mercy be showed upon us. Amen.*

PART ONE

The Schoolmaster's Son

Copenhagen

(1782–7)

The weather is cloudy and rather damp on Morten Pedersen's arrival in Copenhagen on the first day of June 1782, ten days after his twenty-sixth birthday. He sits bobbing in the barge and looks back upon the forest of masts in the roadstead. It is half past six in the morning. He has been up all night, pacing the deck of the packet boat from Christiania, to the seamen's hindrance and annoyance. As he jumps onto the quayside at the Toldboden, his clothes are soaked with the dampness of the fog that lies like a bung in the Øresund. He feels a slight cold and knows he will soon have a cough, but he is not unduly disturbed by the prospect. His constitution is strong; the process of selection among his siblings was such that he considers himself to be a survivor, moreover equipped with a not inconsiderable portion of fatalism. The journey has taken three days. The wind has been up for much of the way, but he has not succumbed to seasickness. He feels he has managed his first sea journey like a man and has been expecting some form of acknowledgement from the crew, at the very least a handshake and some words of parting. He has imagined whispered comments about the young, stout-hearted Norwegian who has remained so steadfast. But without a word they manhandle his chest ashore and leave him to his own devices. Other barges bump against the wharf behind him. Figures jump onto the quayside, others emerge in the grey light of morning, hauling their bundles, sacks and chests.

Where to, master? A porter has left his barrow and approached him.

9

He produces an envelope and opens it, hands him the paper with the address on it. The porter will not have it. He looks at him enquiringly. Aha, Morten thinks to himself, an illiterate.

Nørregade, says Morten, endeavouring to pronounce the word in Danish. The printer Schultz's house.

This way, master, says the porter, and leads him to the gateway where a customs officer unfolds his passport and studies it before handing it back.

Copenhagen bids the student welcome, says the customs officer, perhaps with sarcasm.

And now he strides in towards the city in the wake of the little barrow. The sea has made his legs unsteady, now and then he lurches. The bustle of the city is overwhelming. Peasant carts with wares for the serving houses and market places come thundering, wagons with barrels of ale, carriages with shadowy figures behind the panes and coachmen elevated upon the box, marching soldiers with stamping boots and eyes that stare emptily ahead. Men lugging great bundles of slaughtered geese, hens or rabbits slung over their shoulders. Boys waving broadsheets, squawking snippets of the verses they have learned by heart that same morning. The cobbles are as slippery as soap, coated by some indefinable substance. Morten loses his footing, but grabs the arm of the porter, who turns and pulls him upright, then thrusts him harshly towards the pavement. A carriage drawn by a team of horses rattles past. People shout after it, the coachman yells back and lashes the whip. Morten does not understand what they say. He knows the language only from the sorenskriver and the pastor at home in Akershus, and theirs is not the Danish spoken here. Nevertheless, he understands that the porter has saved him from being struck down by a carriage wheel. A concern as to how much he is now to give the man in gratuity interrupts his thoughts. He discovers he has placed his feet in the gutter and springs abruptly back onto the pavement, only to realize that one boot is already sopping with a fluid whose more exact constitution he does not wish to dwell upon. Women stand in doorways and gateways, displaying ankles and garters, and smiles that dispatch cold shudders of fear into his being. They follow him with eyes that size him up, and smirk once they have him appraised. Bumpkin.

The porter enters a gateway. Their footsteps reverberate from all sides. They stand in a large courtyard. He pays the porter, a sum far in excess of what is expected, and the man now calls him honourable student, perhaps with a hint of scorn, perhaps in jest, then says something more in the same tone that Morten cannot understand. A moment later a man appears and presents himself as the Procurator Gill, a Norwegian like himself, who by agreement with his father has arranged for his lodgings and is to manage his financial affairs for the duration of his time in Copenhagen. The house and premises belong to a book printer by the name of Schultz, and he has been assigned a small room above the printing shop. A maid from the printer's household delivers a key and informs him that he is to partake of his meals in the company of the print workers. She shows him where. He follows on her heels across the yard. Men clad in work garments cast cursory glances in his direction without greeting. He hears a machine hammer out a metallic rhythm. The men's movements display skill and efficiency. He returns to the Procurator Gill, who hands him a piece of paper with his address on it before bowing courteously and taking his leave. The maid leads him on to the main house on the other side of the courtyard, where the lady comes out and bids him welcome.

Madame Schultz stands and considers him. Indeed, she says after a moment, he seems harmless enough. Does he drink?

Morten shakes his head and is taken aback. No, Madame.

He shall be welcome, the Madame says kindly.

Morten bows deeply, the way his father has instructed him to bow to those who rank above him in the intricate hierarchy of the royal city. Most likely bowing to this woman is an error, and he is in doubt as to whether Madame is the correct appellation, but now it is done and he stands alone in the yard with his hat in his hand. He goes up the stair to his little room, removes some items from his chest and arranges them

variously on the desk and inside the small cupboard. He undresses and
hangs his clothes, still moist from the sea journey, over the chair. Then
he lies down to sleep, but is wide awake. He listens absently to the clatter
of horses' hooves and iron-clad carriage wheels against the cobbles
outside the window. Only four days have passed since he awoke in the
alcove of his chamber at home in Lier, outside Drammen, and heard the
familiar sounds of his parents below and of the animals in the stalls. He
rose, put on his travelling attire, packed the last of his things and went
downstairs to breakfast, before walking in to the village accompanied
by his father, the schoolmaster, who remained standing, waiting until
the mail coach departed for Christiania. It seems so implausible, Morten
thinks to himself on the bed of his new room, that he should make the
same journey in the opposite direction. As implausible as to imagine one
might journey back in time.

He is the youngest of a flock of seven, of whom he is the only
surviving boy. Always, a sibling lay in the alcove of the parlour to
dwindle away with a patient smile. He sat with them often, his warm hand
wrapped around another that was cold. Then the hand would stiffen,
and with it the smile. The emaciated body would be carried out into
the barn, the alcove washed down, the room aired. And then another
would take its place. The process of death was a permanent state, a
perpetual occasion of solemnity during which it was forbidden to run or
laugh. Unfathomable silence. This is how he remembers his childhood.
Unceasing self-control, a studied gravity that eventually became fixed
in one's features as death churned on and on. At last only his elder sister
Kirstine was left. They watched each other surreptitiously for a couple
of years, but both eluded the alcove. Now she lives with a pastor's family
in Nakskov.

When eventually Morten finished Latin school he assisted his father
as a teacher. A year or two passed. Then he announced that he intended
to study medicine. He cannot recall whence the idea came. His father
said no, he was to enter the priesthood. His father had wanted to join
the clergy himself, like his grandfather and his great-grandfather before

him. Now Morten would fulfil his ambition. The means were there. And so he resigned himself to his fate, happy to at least be allowed to leave.

†

He is now settling in to his new life in royal Copenhagen. Each day he eats with the people of the printing shop, a fare lacking in meat and consisting mostly of meagre gruel in every conceivable variation. He learns to devour without tasting and to make sure he grabs as much bread as he can so that his shrunken stomach may be filled. He sits in the window seat of his room, reading his Greek grammar, eyes now and then darting to the busy street where horse-drawn wagons and carts trundle by with goods for the markets, and soldiers on leave drift about and accost young girls, who hurl back gutter slurs. He returns to his grammar, though always with an ear on the lechery and drunken rant-ings of the street. Two sides of the same coin, and a continuing struggle within him between desire and duty, his wish to become a physician and the imperative of becoming a priest. He attends what few lectures are given in the natural sciences at the university and elsewhere in the city, usually private events. He studies Linnaeus's great nomenclature. He learns to draw flowers by sitting in the reading room of the university, furtively copying drawings from the *Flora Danica*, cautious on account of the church's ambivalence to the book, which on the one hand depicts the work of the Creator, and yet on the other makes itself its master by classi-fying it into families and species. He walks from the city and sits down at a roadside with his sketch pad resting on his thighs, pencil hovering over the paper, and to a certain extent he feels he becomes one with his image of the young Linnaeus in some similar situation. What interests him is life as it is found, the whores and the flowers, the bustle of the city, the rivers of filth that run through its streets to be expelled into the canals. And yet he attends dutifully the lectures in theology. He learns to spell his way through the Bible in the two original languages. He converses with fellow students in undergraduate Latin. He writes letters home in faltering Latin, which he nonetheless hopes will impress his father, and signs them *Your obedient son, Morten Falck.* The surname stems from a branch of the family that has fared better than his father, the schoolmaster. But when he receives his father's replies they are written in Danish and addressed to *stud. theol., Morten Pedersen.* He feels aggrieved. Not a single one of his student comrades bears a name ending in *-sen*, at least not officially.

The situation of his room, directly above the printing shop, means that his rent is low on account of the noise. From morning to evening, and not infrequently in the night, when a message arrives from Høegh-Guldberg's cabinet with an ordinance for urgent attention or a proclamation to be pasted up across the city, the compositors slam their type loudly in the letter cases, and the incessant rattle of the printing press causes plaster dust to descend from the ceiling and all the joints in his room. Early in the morning, long before the watchmen have retired, drowsy messengers come to collect printed matter to be sold in the streets or distributed in some other way, and these voices belong to boys before the onset of puberty, voices that make them eminently suited to their work and to terminating his sleep. Horse-drawn carts clatter in and out of the gateway, the iron cladding of the wheels resounding against the cobbles of the printer's yard, echoing from all its walls. Carriages arrive with ordinances to be printed immediately, bundles of official notices and announcements, smelling sweetly of rolled pulp and the oil-based chemicals of printer's ink, are loaded onto carts and taken out into the city. So much on which to dwell, so much that is new and fascinating, things he has never before imagined, and his Greek and Latin gather dust. When he can afford to send a letter, he writes to his sister Kirstine in Nakskov and tells of his life in the royal city. She writes back and tells of hers in the market town, in the home of the pastor in which she lives, and he understands it to be as far from their life in Lier as Copenhagen itself.

Morten lies on his bed and is kept awake by the eternal rattle and hum beneath him. He hears Schultz ordering his people about. He hears the syncopated rhythm of the press, the tramp of the printers' and compositors' wooden shoes, their coughing and hacking, and their arguments whenever the ink becomes smudged, the making up of a text has gone wrong, or if some object has contrived to become stuck and thereby halt the press.

†

But all that keeps him awake in the beginning later lulls him to sleep. On occasion he sails with the packet boat from the Toldboden to visit his sister in Nakskov. The elderly provost in whose home she resides is a distant relative of their mother's. The oppressive silence of Nakskov's rectory makes him sleepless, and when finally he succumbs, the sycamore outside the window rouses him, dabbing its branches against the pane of his room. He attends service with his sister and sometimes sees the count on his way through the market town, drawn by a team of six horses, servants standing at the rear of the carriage, coat-tails flapping, one hand holding on to the vehicle, the other to their tall hats.

The provost fulminates from the high pulpit. An imposing, red-haired man, stout as a smith, he holds forth on perdition and the lake of fire and brimstone, as though these were places and states under his personal and daily supervision. He then offers to issue loans to tenants who wish to purchase their freedom, and ends by discharging a volley against the Swedish enemy, who, under the protection of Beelzebub himself and his hordes of fallen angels, has robbed the town of its former glory. And in his concluding prayer he prays fervently for the royal household, his voice a tremble as he speaks the names of its members.

After the service, the congregation file past and deliver their thanks for the sermon. Morten approaches. There is something the matter with the way the old man extends his hand, the expressionless stare of his eyes.

Is the provost blind? he blurts out.

Ssh, his sister breathes. It is forbidden for us to mention. But Magister Gram has been without his sight for two years now.

How, then, can he carry out his office?

No one dares get on the wrong side of him, she whispers. Besides, he knows the Bible and Luther and Pontoppidan inside and out, so I imagine he will remain in his living until the Lord calls him home.

And which lord might that be? he enquires, pointing first up, then down, prompting his sister to put her hand to her mouth and giggle.

Kirstine takes his arm and shows him how the land is in flux. The wilderness is in retreat, and the marshlands also, and ponds with attendant insects that have spread disease for centuries. The forest is long gone and where it lay are waving fields of cereal crops that yield a fifth more in grain than only ten years ago. Ancient trees are felled, hedgerows planted. All is neat and tidy. Even the cows in the meadows seem scrubbed and dispirited.

Strolling through the town, they are met by smiles and greetings. Some approach and wish to talk with her. The young girl from the rectory is liked by all. It makes him proud. She speaks Danish, but when they are alone together they converse in their own sing-song Akershus dialect with its consistent stress on the first syllable of each word. They walk along the beach; they kick at the seaweed and search for Baltic amber; they gather shells. She confides to him that she suffers from homesickness. She has lived here for two years now and yet she does not feel settled. The old pastor is indeed a trial for any man or woman, but her unhappiness cannot be attributed to him alone. Rather, it is more due to his wife, a quiet and self-effacing woman on the exterior, and yet an ill-tempered and cantankerous tyrant when his sister is alone with her. It is intended that I receive instruction in the duties of the housewife and be of service in the home, she explains. Yet the true reason for my presence here is known to me.

Morten looks at her.

One of the provost's four sons is to enter the seminary himself, says Kirstine. My father and the Reverend Gram have corresponded.

Aha, says Morten. And what is he like, then, your intended? May we see him?

He is gone to Fyn on horseback to visit some family. He is both affable and decent. I find no fault with him. It's not that.

No?

People of today ought to be able to arrange their matters according to their own desires, instead of the will of their parents, she says.

Dearest Kirstine, he replies. If the gentleman in question is an honest and good-natured soul, then you ought to take him. Who knows what else might be presented?

It is true, I know. As I said, I have nothing against him. It is this flat and filthy land I cannot tolerate. Where there are no hills, the smells and filth collect around the houses like fog. It causes me to feel that I myself am unclean. One cannot wash it away.

Perhaps he will find a living in another place, Morten says by way of comfort. You can put it to him once he begins to court. State your conditions, barter with him. If he is a decent man he will listen to what you say. Perhaps he might even be moved by the prospect of a living in Norway.

Oh, but these people, says the sister impatiently. They are so proud of their dismal little town. One cannot utter a single word against it without their jumping on one, filling her ears with regard for the rich soil, the glorious history of the town, and the splendid aspects of the land. I have learned to hold my tongue on the matter.

There is time yet, says Morten. Perhaps it will all sort itself out. He is somewhat irritated by her and cannot fathom why she should make such a fuss. It seems to him akin to complaining that the wind lies mostly in the west or that winter is longer than summer. He thinks she ought more properly to be content at the prospect of becoming a pastor's wife. And how can a person long to be back in Lier, the most insignificant spot in all the kingdom? He cannot grasp it.

His visits to Nakskov extend no more than a few days at a time. Often he leaves earlier than planned, consumed by headache at Kirstine's complaints and his own desires to be home, a yearning for the city. If the packet boat does not sail, he boards the coach to Nykøbing in the early morning, changes to the northbound mail coach and spends the night in Vordingborg, where he lodges at the Kronhiorten, eating a meal comprising hunks of rye bread and cracklings, and sleeping above the stable, wrapped in stinking blankets. The next day he continues on to Køge and Copenhagen, munching on apples and pears he has stolen from a garden. Seated in the mail coach he wedges his boot against the seat opposite and endeavours to steer his way through an edition of *Gulliver's Travels*. He reads of how the hero, abandoned in the land of giants, is cared for by a young woman twelve times his size. Morten rests the book upon his thigh, his index finger inserted between the pages. He has removed his wig and placed it on the seat beside him. He puts his brow to the pane of the pitching, heaving, lurching carriage and stares dreamily out upon the fields that ripple by. A maiden twelve times one's own size, he thinks to himself. A mouth twelve times larger than normal, a tongue, hands, breasts, vulva. A veritable mountain land-scape of a woman! He opens the book once more. Gulliver is marooned in countries whose people are either abnormally small or large, or else aberrant in other manners. But perhaps, Morten thinks, the aberration is in Gulliver himself; that is, in the author who has created him, and thereby in the reader who abandons himself to the story.

He thinks of Rousseau and his words on the subject of human liberty, to which Kirstine alluded: *Man is born free and everywhere he is in chains!* Gulliver, too, is enchained to the man he is. Wherever he goes, he remains the same, unable to adapt, thus forever running into trouble with the natives of the various lands at which he arrives. Such a person will he, Morten Falck, never become, he will not stiffen into some fixed form and become old before his time. This he resolves now, in a mail coach travelling north along the bay of Køge Bugt.

The journey is soon at an end. He glimpses the towers of Copenhagen and the wetland expanses of Amager, converses with his fellow passengers, one of whom passes round a hunk of yellow cheese, some bread and a bottle. He has felt anxious on behalf of his sister, a tiny lump of pain beneath the ribs, but his concern is revealed to be founded upon mere geography and hunger. As he nears Copenhagen with his stomach full, he feels cheerful once more.

And then he is home. He walks through the gateway of the printer Schultz's house in Nørregade with a whistle on his lips, turns right in the courtyard, ascends the stair, enters his room and deposits his sack in a corner. He lays his head upon the stained pillow of his bed above the printer's machine that ticks and rattles, shudders and groans, knocks and bangs. He sighs with well-being. Gulliver slides from his hand. He sleeps.

†

The royal city is ninety thousand people squeezed inside a rampart, enclosing them within an area that may be wandered through on foot in less than an hour. A city ravaged over centuries by epidemics, fires and a series of inebriate, insane, inbred and incompetent sovereigns. Yet still its population steadily rises and the pressure upon the ramparts increases with each year that passes. Morten notes that although most have but a short life ahead, followed by a painful and humiliating death, the people of the city see little hindrance to amusement. On the contrary. The city's squares and places are alive with entertainers, gateways and street doors customarily occupied by prostitutes, and all would seem to indicate that they have no reason to be idle.

Morten Falck strolls through the narrow streets whose buildings on each side seem to lean towards each other, allowing only a thin band of sky to show between their roofs. He walks across the expansive public squares, the great concourse before the new palace, a colossal and imperishable edifice of Norwegian granite. He wanders over the bastions and crosses the Langebro bridge that swings open whenever a ship has need to pass. He returns in an arc to Christianshavn across the dyke from Amager. A troupe of entertainers has erected a booth on the square in front of the orphanage. He remains standing to see if the strongman Karl Johan von Eckenberg will appear. Von Eckenberg always attracts large audiences, dandies, fine ladies in crinoline who shade beneath parasols, wealthy traders from the merchant houses, ship owners, sea captains, sailors, officers and enlisted men, right down to such inmates of the correctional facility as have been granted parole. And with good reason. Von Eckenberg is splendid.

Morten is fascinated by the strongman. He knows his repertoire inside and out, yet never tires of watching him. His feats are an expression of something true and profound, he feels, not simply of dexterity and skill. What this profundity consists in, however, he is unable to pin down. And for this reason he continues to attend the man's performances.

He is fond of three feats in particular.

First drum roll. Karl Johan von Eckenberg ascends a wooden construction, some ten ells in height. He positions himself upon a cross-beam and gives a signal to his assistants on the ground by means of a near-imperceptible nod. Beneath him now are brought forward a horse and two liveried riders onto a platform with a rope attached to each corner. Von Eckenberg takes hold of the other end of this rope, winding it around his forearm and wrist, and with one arm he lifts the platform with horse and riders one foot from the ground, while with the other hand he puts a postal horn to his lips and trumpets a fanfare.

Second drum roll. Karl Johan von Eckenberg, now descended from his platform, places himself between two chairs, his body extended horizontal, one ell above the ground. Whereupon eight good musicians, dressed in red double-breasted jackets, tricorne hats, knee-length stockings and shoes with polished buckles of brass, clamber one by one onto this sinewy and scantly muscular, though very long, body that is supported only by its neck and heels. Balancing on von Eckenberg's chest, stomach, hips and legs, they now proceed to perform a minuet by Brentner, while von Eckenberg himself stares up into the sky with brown, mournful eyes and resembles one who is thinking back upon his childhood, his blessed mother or a love of his youth.

Third drum roll. Karl Johan von Eckenberg's third feat is performed between the same two chairs, though after his having risen, accepted due applause and enjoyed a moment's retreat inside his wooden booth. Refreshed and ruddy-cheeked, he returns, his brown eyes now sparkling. He bows and positions himself once more between the chairs, whereupon two assistants place a solid stone slab upon his stomach. A third assistant, dressed like a smith or perhaps an executioner, steps forward with a sledgehammer, raises it above his head and hesitates. In the name of Jesus, strike! von Eckenberg commands in a loud and melodious voice. The hammer falls and the slab is broken into two parts that drop away at each side. Karl Johan von Eckenberg rises and bows to his audience. A boy goes round with a hat while acrobats caper. Coins are thrown onto the cobbles from windows above.

But one day the strongman is no longer there. His booth on the square is dismantled and removed, and there is no trace of the troupe of acrobats. Morten asks around with the street traders and they say von Eckenberg has injured himself during a performance and was carried away in a state of weakness. He can find no one who knows what has become of him.

†

Occasionally, Morten allows himself the luxury of hiring a carriage to one of the city gates and paying the driver a supplement to take him a couple of land miles into the countryside, to some outlying village: Gladsaxe, Husum, Ordrup, Herlev. Here he alights, sends the carriage home and proceeds back along the highway. He passes through villages where the stench of soap-making and tanning hangs like some infectious fog, greasy and sticky in the air. He walks by the fields where cows peacefully graze, and past dwellings where silent peasants stare at him from beneath their hats.

In the city he devotes himself to his books, although abandoning divinity in favour of natural science. Driven by scholarly thirst, he seeks out and attends lectures whose subjects are anything other than the doctrines of the Trinity and transubstantiation. Thus, he immerses himself in one professor's lecture on the hierarchical classification of all life on Earth, as elaborated by Linnaeus. There is booing, but also applause. The lecture, held in the Comedy House on account of the university's unwillingness to provide a venue, opens his eyes in a new and surprising manner. The world is a connected whole! A banal realization once revealed, and yet a total reorganization of his consciousness, his picture of the world and of himself: I am a part of a connected whole.

One of his friends, Laust, who studies medicine, invites him to the Academy of Surgery on Norgesgade, popularly called Bredegade, where he attends lessons on blood vessels and bones and nerve channels and glands. It is a journey inwards, whereas botany and zoology are journeys outwards, although just as staggering and just as eternal. And in such eternity, man is at the middle. So placed by the Lord.

In the company of Laust he earns a small sum hauling corpses from the canals, or else they bribe a watchman to procure bodies and deliver them to the faculty's vaults, where the professor stands ready with frigid eyes and a scalpel. With the instrument poised between three fingers as though it were a quill pen, the yellow skin of the corpse a parchment upon which he intends to jot down his thoughts, he informs the students of what they must pay attention to during the autopsy that will follow. He makes his incisions with casual exactness, exposes the greenly glistening muscles of the dead, layer by layer, allowing their shameful smells to be released into the air as the students snigger uneasily or exchange jokes in Latin, and the iridescent tinge of the intestines becomes, little by little, reflected on their own faces. But not on Morten Falck's. He stands with the morning's bread and warm gruel pleasantly wallowing inside his stomach and gazes in wonder upon these humans whose humanity is gradually removed from them as they become divided into their constituent parts according to the Latin nomenclature. Nerves, muscle fibres, the finely separated layers of cutis and subcutis, adipose tissue and organs, creamy yellow, salmon-pink, violet as a beet, as lustrous as varnish. The professor divides limbs from torsos, his knife descends into the tissue, splitting joint capsules, laying bare arteries and veins whose names he cheerfully lists. Morten thinks it sounds as if he is hailing them, as if at a morning roll call of a classical Roman college. *Arteria carotis*! *Nervus olfactorius*! *Musculus mastoideus*! He listens to the professor's explanations, which are always attended by a doleful clang of sarcasm, but also of solidarity with the deceased. As we are, so were you, and as you are, so will we become. After the shock of the vaults a number of students abandon the course in favour of other studies, devoting themselves instead to the law, retiring to the estates of their fathers or else departing to the south on Grand Tours, where many end their days as drunkards tormented by fever. Morten Falck, the only one among them who knows he cannot complete the study and become a physician, remains.

He is a regular guest of these dissections, even after Laust falls ill and must abandon the course. With his botanizing pad and his pencils he sits in the dim light and draws detailed anatomical sketches. The professor praises them and arranges for the room, a damp crypt whose origins are lost in the gloom of the Middle Ages, to be properly lit with modern lamps. He encourages Morten to enrol as an alumnus. Yet admission is restricted by quota, and objections of a finger-wagging, admonitory nature issue from the schoolmaster's house in Lier, and Morten knows that the relative financial ease in which he exists is conditional upon his divinity studies being completed with a minimum of diversion. He has been a matriculated student for two years now, the time in which many complete their studies, but as long as he remains and does not abandon his course, his father's patience with low marks and deferments appears to be almost boundless. He reports to the Procurator Gill on the first weekday of each month, and receives his allowance alongside detailed accounts of his progress at the university.

The printer's house, a solid, four-storey building erected in accordance with the most recent regulations, that is to say after the last fire in 1728, and therefore not held together by hazardously inflammable timber frames, is situated at the back of the courtyard. Its main entrance is by Studiestræde, though the family often uses the rear gateway. Morten has never been inside the door of the printer's home. For a poor student and tenant of a modest room diagonally above the gateway, it is not a place into which he may expect to be invited. Schultz's three daughters frequent the courtyard. They skip and sing, and play at Scotch-hoppers and tag. He hears the slap of their soft laced shoes against the cobbles, their giggles and disagreements. They grow up outside his window. At first, they are little girls he hardly notices, high voices and shrill laughter echoing in the cobbled yard. He hears the swish and snap of their skipping rope, and sees their dresses unfurl and fall into place, unfurl and fall into place, revealing their feet and legs in brief glimpses, long curls bobbing at their shoulders, their rather round and prominent brows, their clear, deep-set eyes, the harmonious triangles of nose and mouth exuding good humour and light-heartedness. And then they skip no more. They retire into the shade of the sycamore in the middle of the yard, where there is a bench. Here they sit and read, all three in the same book, the eldest of them flanked by the younger, who lean in from either side, legs swinging to and fro. Morten Falck passes them frequently on his way to the lunch room. He senses their eyes as they follow him and he hears their giggles. He has no idea of their names. He never speaks to them and has no reason ever to do so. There is something about girls yet to reach puberty that annoys and repels him, all that smugness and gaiety, the unquestioned assurance that a wonderful life awaits them, the clean white dresses, the soft and prissy shoes, the ribbons in their hair, all that as yet remains bound up and kept inside, the things of which they are ignorant. In a few short years they will be drawn into the stall and impregnated, swell and give birth, amid ejaculations of blood and slime and stifled gasps, into handkerchiefs splashed with anaesthetic alcohol and perfume. The corpses in the faculty cellar are preferable to the maidens Schultz, Morten tells himself with newly acquired cynicism. There, at least, no false hope resides, only honest, uncompromising decomposition.

†

One of the girls sticks out from the trinity, the eldest. All of a sudden she has shot up and is a full head taller than her sisters. Morten sees that she has become a woman. She must be the same age as the Crown Prince, he calculates. Confirmed and ready to depart the nest, Miss Schultz moves about the yard as awkwardly as a lame foal. She is apportioned little time alone without the mother appearing in the doorway and calling her name.

Abelone!

THE SCHOOLMASTER'S SON 25

Obediently she rises from the bench and goes into the house. Morten tries to imagine what duties the mother calls upon her to carry out. To sew her bridal gown, perhaps. Or to learn to keep house, to fold napkins, make table plans and write invitations. Perhaps she is simply to be kept from the eyes of the print workers and other men, among them the young student, and from the thoughts to which such attention might give rise.

Abelone.

If one wishes to protect the virtue of one's daughter, he thinks to himself, one ought properly to keep her name a secret. Now he knows it and it feels as though he has already been under her skirts to peep.

Abelone.

Morten Falck is twenty-eight. He knows a thing or two about love. He has studied the subject on his nightly wanderings in the city, in gateways and backyards, in the narrow alleys of Øster Kvarter, further out by the ramparts, in the no-man's-land between the rampart path and the steep and grassy embankment where the lighting is poor or else wholly absent. He has conducted observations upon the nature of love and its manifestations in the dim passageways and nooks and crannies of old, run-down houses. He has with caution pushed open doors and spied with bated breath. He has seen girls the same age as the sisters Schultz draw up their skirts, bend over and, without a word, at most a suppressed moan, receive a gentleman's erect member. His cynicism has been honed by his spying. He has learned that love is mysterious; sometimes it seems even more humiliating than death as presented in the vaults of Norgesgade. The sums he receives from the Procurator Gill have not been sufficiently generous to allow him to partake of amorous activity himself in any gateway or serving-house yard, but with the supplement of his payment for dragging corpses to the autopsy bench he may on occasion permit himself to purchase the services of a common prostitute. Afterwards, he feels disappointment and shame, slight nausea and the desire to do it again. He learns that not only death smells foul. He feels himself dirty, is relieved each time it is done. He thinks to himself that now he has done it he need do it no more. And yet he does it again. His lust accumulates in the fluids of his body and relentlessly they flow towards the same point. He pays a girl a few marks and an arse is placed at his disposal. He plunges into the darkness and warmth, into the living, yielding flesh that parts and comes together, parts and comes together. He sways slightly on the balls of his feet, he stares down upon the flesh that ripples back and forth and slaps against his own, upon frills and pleats, buckles and buttons, a pale neck patiently lowered, hands that clutch a table edge. His lips draw back from his teeth, he rears his head and groans as if in pain, and then the evil has left him and he steps back, neatens himself, nods a farewell and is gone, liberated for some short measure of time. And always it returns, like water in a gravel pit.

One day he is strolling as usual along Vimmelskaftet in the direction of Amagertorv. The stalls are many and close together, the tables display finery, colourful fabrics, cages of live hens ready for the slaughter, staring cockerels, skinned rabbits in heaps, bundles of weasel and fox furs. The sun beats down upon the rooftops, flies swarm. Vimmelskaftet is a suffocatingly hot bottleneck in which a person can hardly proceed forward or back. And for this same reason he loves to wander here, in the city's trading centre, taking in the sickly stench of meat, human as well as animal. He pushes his way through hordes of ladies with baskets on their arms and women with bobbing crinoline beneath their skirts. Drunken youngsters wave copies of the latest satirical songs and bray out their sample verses. Peasants and fishermen tramp along in bast shoes, drawing their barrows behind them, laden with wares or piles of empty sacks. In this obstruction of traffic the people of the city meet, some by necessity, others for pleasure or the sake of curiosity. A counsellor of the chancellery swings his cane, an officer of the military parades his pigeon-blue uniform, an alehouse potman unloads a barrel from a cart and tips it onto his shoulder. Two whores stroll arm in arm, twirling parasols that are faded and frayed, rustling dirty tulle skirts that draw a wet trail of gutter behind them. Fine ladies pinch their noses demonstratively as they pass, but the officer halts and bows gallantly, removing his hat in a sweeping, ironic gesture. The whores laugh and curtsy and say, Good afternoon, Løjtnant Holm, how is he today, and will he not soon be away to fight the Swede?

Morten follows the two women. He desires to see them find customers. They walk up Store Købmagergade, cross over Kultorvet and continue along Rosengården to the rampart at Skidentorv, where they seat themselves on a bench by Hanens Bastion. Morten passes leisurely by and lifts his hat and is ignored completely. I see, he thinks to himself, offended, the ladies are obviously too fine for a student! He returns home in ill humour. The young Miss Schultz is seated under the sycamore. Her sisters are playing hopscotch, their skirts flapping about their legs. He remains standing and watches them, then shifts his gaze towards the young lady beneath the tree. Their eyes meet. He approaches her, removes his hat, presses it to his chest and bows.

Miss Schultz, I am a tenant of your good father.

I know who he is, she says with a smile. He has lodged here for some years. He is a student, I believe?

Theology, he says, and for the first time is happy to put his studies to good use. Under Mr Swane's tutelage.

She smiles. Is that so? I was confirmed by the same gentleman.

The clear, bright voice of a young girl. He has heard it many times before, but now it speaks to him.

What a coincidence, he says. Perhaps he will marry you, too.

She pulls a face. I am not betrothed.

Oh, but I am sure you will be before long, Miss Schultz.

Does he think so? One can never tell. Some never become betrothed. She looks up at him, an inquisitive expression, as though he were already ordained and stood before her to receive her confession. But why should one marry at all? My mother refuses to say.

The question takes him by surprise. He has never before exchanged a word with the young lady, and now they are almost in intimate conversation. It is the accepted opinion, he replies uncertainly, that young women such as Miss Schultz find benefit in being married, that they may find purpose in life and avoid idleness. A spinster is no encouraging sight.

But to bear children, she says bleakly. It makes it even more discouraging.

To give birth is the privilege of woman, he says, embarrassed, and surmises that her mother must have neglected to instruct her in suitable and unsuitable topics of discourse.

He looks at her. She has grown rather a lot this last year, though remains lean and boyish of build, hardly yet marriageable, he considers, his eyes darting about the girl's budding endowments. The sun is filtered through the leaf of the sycamore, dabbing her dress and her blonde curls. He thinks he smells a hint of perspiration mingled with the aroma of bluing or whatever else is used to wash the dresses of young girls. Then someone calls.

My mother! She jumps to her feet, but remains for a moment. Goodbye.

He bows. She vanishes through the main door, past Madame Schultz, who fixes him in her gaze. The door shuts. He goes up the stair to his room, lies on his side on the bed and picks at the wall with his fingernail.

The thoroughfare that runs between the city's outermost houses and the rampart, popularly known as *voldgaden*, the rampart path, is cobbled only in places. Mostly, it is unmade. In the time of Christian IV cobbles were laid throughout its length in a grand endeavour to improve the sanitary standard of the city, but these stones have long since been broken up under cover of night and used for other purposes. What remains is a mire of mud, the contents of latrine buckets emptied arbitrarily by the area's inhabitants, and waste products from the brewing of ale and the distillation of aquavit. The area teems with rats and stray dogs, whose behaviour is erratic and aggressive due to the alcohol content of the discarded mash. The regular epidemics of typhoid, pox and plague that have ravaged the city through centuries must in Morten's opinion have their source here in this no-man's-land between the eating establishments, alehouses and inns on the one side and the dark rampart on the other, where people are driven either by desperate lust or desperate need to earn some rigsdalers. The city ought properly to employ a physician to clean up the filth, and this physician might appropriately be himself, Morten Falck. He smiles at the thought. Yet he is compelled to admit that he is fond of the filth and of the opportunities it provides.

He frequents the place with caution and with squinting eyes. The only illumination is from the occasional window on the city side which allows the sound of laughter and song. Fleeting shadows appear from the gloom and vanish again. Thieves, watchmen, cock-bawds, it is impossible to tell. The whores, the cheapest in town, occupy the scattered islands of light. They stand in the doorways and chew tobacco, lifting up their skirts without change of facial expression whenever a pair of breeches passes by. The watchman comes with his mace rested against his shoulder. He exchanges some words with the women, then continues on his way.

Morten conducts observations of human nature. He stands in the shadows, resting in the security of his cynicism and disillusionment. He watches the transactions of suppliers and customers, and the purchased service is often delivered on the spot. There are many men about the town on such an ordinary night, many of them fine gentlemen, as far as he can tell, whose lust cannot be contained within the respectable confines of wedlock. He wonders what lies were told on their leaving home and what replies were uttered in return. Was the lady of the house aware of his intentions, and is he aware of her knowledge? Is there a contract, a mutual understanding? And is the lady happy that such places and persons are found to take care of those aspects of marriage she finds displeasing? Morten smiles to himself. In the dim light ahead he hears there is something afoot. He tiptoes forward, holding his breath. The sounds become clearer, the rustle of damask, the slapping of flesh, a man's voice issuing instructions as to what services he wishes to receive for the monies paid, and in what manner. Slowly his eyes become used to the dark. The girl is of tender age and kneeling. It looks as if she is praying and perhaps she is. The man is standing, leaning back against a tree. He looks as if he is studying the firmament above the rampart or else dictating a letter to his secretary. He wafts his face with his tricorne hat to cool himself in the sticky air of evening. Morten Falck observes it all, not because it arouses him, he tells himself, but because he wishes to learn. Soon you will be dead, he muses, and I shall make fine illustrations of your dismembered bodies.

But what do these women do about their own lust? he wonders. Or rather, he knows. They go to church with it. To the priest. To me. And therefore it is important for me to be one to whom nothing in this life remains unknown. That is why I am here. He finds a measure of comfort in the thought.

The indecencies occur not only at the ramparts but across most of the city. The watchmen earn good skillings by turning a blind eye when these encounters between vendors and customers take place with all their repetitive predictability. Toothless hags sell themselves for a few coins and will do anything for any gentleman who cares to beckon.

There would seem to be no lower limit to the age of a whore. He sees men of middle years standing back against a wall in a yard, while small, pink tongues flutter about them in the dark. The child prostitutes are often fit to drop and pale with fatigue. They entice their customer with exaggerated gestures, just as their procurers have taught them, but which appear grotesquely false to any other than he who genuinely wishes them to be sincere, the fine gentleman with a clean conscience. Most likely they consume greater quantities of semen than proper food during the course of a day. The watchmen chase them away with their maces, and yet they soon return, like the rats. It happens regularly that the watchman finds a child who is barely alive, or else dead. In these instances, they are put onto a cart and driven away. Morten does not know what becomes of them. Their bodies do not appear in the faculty vaults, for which he is grateful. His enquiring mind has its limits. Once he asked a watchman about it, only to be threatened with detention should he not keep his curiosity to himself.

He tires of spying in gateways and courtyards and along the rampart. He puts it behind him. It no longer feels important. He is twenty-eight years old. Miss Schultz will soon be sixteen. The Crown Prince, Frederik, assumes the regency and is driven about the town in an open carriage to be hailed. His father, the king, retreats into his madness, which is not of a tyrannical character in the manner of his forebear's megalomania, but quieter and more unassuming. Morten and the young mistress exchange pleasantries beneath the sycamore, sometimes being permitted to converse a while before Madame Schultz appears in the doorway to call her in. He imagines, purely for the sake of experiment, the young lady bent over the bench, her dress drawn up and corset snatched apart, her arse beaming against his thrusting loin, his member vanishing into the hirsute and rankly smelling darkness between her buttocks. But the scenario does not appeal to him and is practically impossible to establish, a fact that is only to his relief. Perhaps I am in love, he thinks to himself.

He strolls in Kongens Have, a haven of grassy lawns, trees and fountains to which the general public enjoy restricted access. Miss Schultz and her two sisters accompany him with their mother's permission. On the gravel, midway along the wide central axis, they stand and look towards Christian IV's picturesque Renaissance palace. A succession of fountains spurt and sparkle, one behind the other. The trees are pruned and topped off. They resemble green toadstools whose stalk-like trunks have been placed with such monotonous precision that one feels gripped by some disorder of perspective. But the dizziness he feels is perhaps on account of other circumstances, such as the young ladies in his company now seating themselves on the green of the lawn. Their dresses are spread about them; they are like daisies descended from above to take up their places in the grass. He glimpses the toe of a shoe. Morten halts a few paces away. To demonstrate tact, he averts his gaze. He knows why Madame Schultz has allowed him to be out with her daughters. It is not because he is a suitor, for in her eyes he is not, nor even in his own. It is because he is taken to be a harmless and reliable student of divinity, and because the Madame clearly trusts in her fellow human beings, and in him in particular.

The splash of the fountains feels comforting now. A cool dampness is felt to drift across the lawns. A girder of rainbow appears above the neatly trimmed grass and dwindles among the topiary of the trees. He wipes his brow with a handkerchief, which he returns to the pocket of his waistcoat. Shoes crunch the gravel, a walking cane, a slim young gentleman clad in a green tailcoat and chalk-white stockings passes by in the company of a lady, by no means entirely young, whose lower body and legs are enclosed within a birdcage of crinoline, for which reason one cannot help but think first and foremost precisely of her lower body and legs. Her dress ruffles about her, the playful breeze toys with the pleated trim that has absorbed the dark colour of chlorophyll from the grass across which it has been drawn. She smiles while looking straight ahead with a firm expression that appears to Morten to be false or melodramatic, but which nevertheless has prompted her gentleman to assume a rather fawning posture. The white-stockinged man seems almost to be silently begging for some favour. Miss Schultz and her sisters have wind of the drama. Breathlessly they watch the couple and take in the scene. Each time the gentleman comes up alongside her, the lady increases her pace, yet when he lags behind she walks more slowly until he catches up with her again.

Once they are out of earshot, the three girls begin to twitter. They debate and argue as to the nature of the relationship between the young gentleman and the more mature lady. Morten can tell as he listens to them that they are by no means unused to reading novels of chivalric romance. He wonders if he should lend them his *Moll Flanders*, which he read in the winter. He considers it might shake them up a bit.

What opinion has the student? says Abelone Schultz. I see he stands there smiling, as if in possession of better knowledge.

Whatever I might imagine of the relationship between these people, I shall wisely keep it to myself.

They tease him and call him Magister Stick-in-the-Mud. But when they walk on, Abelone puts her arm in his.

A finery stall in Østergade sells intimate garments and perfumes for ladies. He purchases two flacons, one of lavender, the other of bergamot, and presents them to the maid of the printer's house with a message that they are a gift to Miss Schultz. It is her sixteenth birthday. He has composed a brief letter and attached it to the parcel: *Dear Miss Schultz, please accept this humble gift and may it remind you of the most obedient of all your admirers*, id est stud. theol *Morten Falck*.

The following day the gift is returned by the printer's maid. He puts it aside. He has allowed himself to be carried away. He has revealed his intentions. The time is unripe. He must be patient. He regrets nothing. Now she knows, and the family Schultz know, where he stands. It feels liberating. It is as though he has kissed her, then passed his hand over her hip.

He watches the door of the printer's home. Abelone is in hiding, but her sisters are there, and Madame Schultz, too, spends time in the courtyard, fussing and yet in good humour. A person of cheerful disposition. He likes her and he is certain she is not unkindly disposed towards him. The two younger sisters conspicuously refrain from looking up at his window, where he sits reading in the window seat. It is plain from the manner in which they ignore him that they are keenly aware of his presence.

†

Morten's mother writes to him often from Lier. She, too, uses his former name, Morten Pedersen, until, in an angry letter, he instructs her to employ his new one. She does so. His father, however, continues to refer to him as *stud. theol. Pedersen*, and it is in this name, too, that he receives letters from the Procurator Gill. Yet it is his mother who writes most, once a week at least. She must spend considerable sums on the postage, both to himself and to Kirstine in Nakskov. She names with caution one or another girl who now has been confirmed or has reached a certain age, who is of sound constitution, diligent and meticulous, an obedient daughter to her parents, of good moral standing, etc. She keeps a careful eye on the parishes whose incumbents are of poor health and whose vacant living he might seek once he has become ordained. Their own pastor is not of advanced years, so the prospects are slight, but he has been kind enough to promise to put in a good word for Morten when the time comes for him to apply for a parish. *Your father is once more of ill health, she writes, and has now lain for two days without rising while complaining of aches and sounds inside his head. Should he write to inform you of his imminent demise, however, take heed that he is as fit as a confirmand, and the numerous ailments of which he inclines to suffer are but imaginary.*

The letters darken his mood; they make him itch and give him headaches, and he is consumed by the urge to get drunk or go to a prostitute. He frequents a drinking establishment with Laust, who has returned after his illness, a spontaneous melancholy that almost did away with him. Now he is descended into the opposite ditch, throwing his money about, hiring carriages and insisting on paying for everything wherever they go, inviting his friends to the Comedy House, where he has rented a box. Morten sits in his velvet-covered seat. The large audience and the lamps cause him to sweat. On the stage the singers stamp about, making fearful grimaces, throwing out their arms and roaring at one another. A classical Italian opera is performed. The audience comments loudly on the action, boos and cries of bravo compete to drown each other out. There is a ceaseless coming and going, a slamming of doors, a scraping of chairs, chatter and the chinking of ale glasses that makes it impossible to follow what is going on. The music rises and falls, someone fires a pistol, a soprano shrieks and falls dead, gunpowder smoke drifts into the orchestra pit, the painted backdrop is hoisted up by a noisy pulley, another descends with a clatter, one hears the stage hands tramping back and forth, groaning and out of breath, the first violin shouting out the time to his orchestra and endeavouring to conduct them with his bow. Morten looks down from his vantage point upon dozens of swelling bosoms. The ladies are powdered white, beauty spots decorate marble cheekbones and the occasional breast. They fan themselves to stave off the heat. The stalls are like a warm and sunny field full of flowers and fluttering butterflies. He has the most recent of his mother's letters in his breast pocket. He thinks to himself that it is a peculiar mingling of worlds. Imagine if my ageing mother were here. He smiles to himself. The world of the theatre must be as distant from his mother's as anything could ever be. He wishes that she could enjoy it, though most likely she would be shocked and would perhaps even faint with fright. She is not the kind of person who can forget who they are and rise above themselves. She is enchained, like almost everyone else.

Afterwards he drives with Laust to a serving house, where they sit and pretend to be fine gentleman until they are ejected and make towards the ramparts, pursued by a trail of prostitutes, who stride along, arm in arm, bawling raucous drinking songs.

Then Laust is gone again. Morten hears rumour that some accident has befallen him, but learns of no details. He writes to his father, a customs officer on Fyn, though without reply. He attends a single performance at the Comedy House, but it is costly and rather dull without the festive Laust to hurl insults or excessively intimate compliments at the ladies, without a box to separate him from the rabble, and he stands alone in the throng of the stalls, unable to hear or see a thing, and thinks of Rousseau and *Man is born free and everywhere he is in chains!* He cannot expel the sentence from his mind. It is as though the philosopher has placed his hand upon his shoulder and wished to speak to him in person.

†

The winter of 1784–5. The royal city is inundated with farm labourers and lads who have run from the villeinage of the Stavnsbånd to seek their fortunes. January brings strong frost. The hearses are busy, and the corpses that arrive at the vaults beneath the academy are well preserved, delicate almost, unsmelling and as white as snow. After Laust's disappearance, Morten has stopped collecting bodies around town, but he earns a small sum from his drawings, which are more detailed than ever before, and some now hang upon the walls of the academy's teaching rooms.

Morten sees the carriages come to the printer's house with young men, who bound up the step to be welcomed inside. Suitors. He is little concerned with the matter. At the eleventh hour he has found interest in his theology studies and spends many hours each day at the university's library. Moreover, he has taken on work teaching small boys a couple of days a week at the Vajsenhus orphanage. Now when he goes to the Procurator Gill on the first weekday of each month it is to bring money to his account, rather than to request a withdrawal, and he receives a receipt as evidence of growing savings. He lives cheaply and sensibly and goes seldom into town. His excursions outside the city gate are made on foot and rarely further than to Valby Bakke, where he sits near Frederiksberg Palace and gazes out across the semicircle of frozen lakes and the rampart, the thoroughfare of Vesterbrogade to his right, and behind the ramparts the steeples and spires and hundreds of smoking chimneys. He has no idea what he might do when his studies are completed this coming summer. Perhaps he will continue to teach. Perhaps seek a living. But finding a living is difficult, the competition is stiff. And where would he want to go?

Winter. The frost is beneficial insofar as it freezes the city's filth and excrement, making it easier to walk about without becoming soiled in the gutter or bespattered by carriage wheels. The stench of the latrine buckets is less penetrating. On the other hand, a thick and immovable blanket of coal smoke enshrouds the city, and people die by the hundreds from lung disease or else they simply freeze to death. He himself is in good health. He has hardly had a cold since his arrival here and the various epidemics of fever sicknesses have passed by his door. The print room beneath his chamber is kept well heated, for otherwise the ink becomes stiff; and, besides this good fortune, his room is equipped with a small tiled stove, which he may light as need arises. He fetches the coals from the printer's coal bunker and pays a fixed sum each month. Apart from this, he spends much time at the university, which, though not exactly warm, nevertheless maintains a tolerable temperature. For his sake, the cold and the winter may continue. It reminds him of his childhood and the native place from which he hails and which now more often seems distant to him.

One evening he proceeds shivering along Vestergade in the direction of the rampart. In this district of the city live many ale brewers and distillers of aquavit, and every other stairway contains a drinking establishment whose enticing yellow light beams into the snow. He goes inside at one place where the window is illuminated, driven by an acute need for human company. There is music and some singing, men play cards, a fire roars in a tiled stove, tobacco smoke gathers below the ceiling joists. The atmosphere appears relaxed. At a table a boy is seated alone. He sits down opposite him and orders a mug of ale. He meets the youngster's gaze, but neither says a word in greeting. He looks foreign. A Gypsy, Morten guesses. Perhaps a Jew.

Morten receives his ale. He sips.

Is it cold? the boy asks in the dialect of Sjælland.

Yes, the night is cold. Bitterly cold.

The boy stares at him wearily. His eyes droop towards his mouth. His Adam's apple ascends and descends. Morten wishes he could move to another table. He hears himself say: Will you join me in a mug?

Aye, says the boy quickly. I shan't say no to that. He winks to the host and shouts out his order. On this here gentleman's bill, he adds, and points demonstratively. Morten nods to affirm, but avoids looking up at the man. He regrets having come here. He has no idea why he should enter into conversation with this young scoundrel. Then a man rises and embarks upon a long ballad, and he leans back and listens to the song, a saccharine tale of unrequited love.

When it is over the boy says: A student, eh?

He nods, but refrains from turning to face him. He feels he is being scrutinized.

Priest, says the boy.

Morten turns. How can you tell?

The boy grins sheepishly and wipes his mouth with the back of his hand. It's a skill I have. An art.

An art? says Morten. What more can you say of me?

I can tell the pastor's fortune, says the boy. But it'll cost him copper.

Ah, a vagrant trickster, Morten thinks to himself, who earns his bread from the credulity of others. How much does this fortune telling cost?

That depends on the prophecy. The boy smiles with cunning. A long life and good luck in matters of love and with wealth to boot is dearer than haemorrhage, the workhouse and imminent death. It stands to reason.

Morten gestures for their two mugs to be filled. He asks the host if he serves food. Herring, says the host. All right, two portions of herring. The boy casts himself over the meal. His mouth full of boiled cabbage and the rich, salted fish, he divulges to Morten that he travels with a troupe of acrobats and tells fortunes for his living. The Lord has given me the gift to look folk firmly in the eye and to read them as if they were a book, even though I can't read and can only scratch my mark.

And you can read me? Morten enquires.

Hm-m, says the boy between two mouthfuls, and nods. I can see right the way in and out the other side. Easy, it is.

And what can you see?

The same as all the others, the boy replies jauntily. The pastor's nothing special, if that's what he thinks. But if he wishes to have his fortune told, it'll cost him three marks. It's the usual price in winter, otherwise I take five.

First I shall test you to see if you are worth your money. Can you tell if both my parents live?

The boy studies his food, as though Morten's secrets lay hidden there. He fills his mouth again. They live. And your sister, too, is in good health. But some brothers departed this life a long time since, God rest their souls.

So far, so good, says Morten. He feels his mouth to be dry. Can you see what my sister is doing?

Oh, she's playing the two-headed beast with her pastor. The boy breaks into a peal of laughter.

Morten feels himself grow pale. Kirstine? he says.

I don't know her name. But I can see a white dress and black vestments. I hear church bells, a dreadful clamour, not for me at all. Priest weds priest, a dainty sight, indeed! And the bridal gown is white on the outside, but inside it's black and stained with filth. He spits out these latter words as though with malice.

His hair drops into his eyes, black and greasy. A dribble of spit glistens in the upwardly curled corner of his pretty mouth, and in the spit a crumb of bread has settled. The breadcrumb moves as he speaks. Morten reaches out and removes it with the tip of his index finger. Their eyes meet, and then he asks:

Is she happy?

The boy smiles. I think she's in good humour. She laughs, at least, but even skulls seem to laugh when the flesh is picked from them, so what would I know? I'm a seer. I look through people, not within them. I'm no soothsayer. People around her are happy. I can tell by looking at them. They've got what they want, but I don't know about her. Her face is like water when you piss in it. The weather's nice, the sun's shining on the church, white, white, shining on the dress, white, white. I can't wait for summer, can you, Pastor, when the lark twitters and a person can go wherever he wants? Then I'll be able to travel again with my people and sleep in the woods.

What about me? says Morten. Can you see my future?

I can see a whole lot of strange people dancing in the fells. Not Christian folk, though. They don't look like Christian folk. Black and dirty they are, but they're your friends and you're dancing with them. And I can see fire.

Fire?

Flames and balls of fire. The pastor's a man who likes to play with fire. But the fire doesn't touch him. He comes out of the fire without so much as an eyebrow singed.

The boy has finished eating. He has drunk three mugs of ale. Now his chin drops to his chest. He begins to snore, shoulders drooped, his body slides back against the wall. Morten sits a while and studies him. Then he tosses some marks onto the table and walks home. It has begun to snow.

†

He does all that is expected of him. He goes to the lectures; he pores over his Latin and Greek and Hebrew, and reads his works of theology. He teaches his boys at the Vajsenhus. He courteously acknowledges Miss Schultz when encountering her in the courtyard. She looks at him as though she were waiting, as if she has prepared something to say to him if they should meet, but he does not take the time to converse with her. The printer clearly imagines that Morten is pining away with unrequited love for his daughter. He pats him sympathetically on the back and says, My dear theologicus, give it time, give it time, for all things come to he who waits. Morten nods and does his best to look like a valiant suitor. The truth is, it is merely a role he takes upon himself. He thinks only infrequently of the young mistress, although he knows he ought to devote himself to her rather more, that it would be the natural thing to do. But the young mistress is so pure and untainted. It is hard to imagine that there is anything else beneath her skirts and underskirts than more skirts and underskirts, and much that is pleasant to the smell.

He realizes he has an unopened letter from his sister. How long has it been in his drawer? He can hardly remember when he received it. Perhaps a few weeks before. Since then, his mother has written and told him of his sister's plans, of the happy news. The ceremony will already have taken place. He knew it even when he sat before the boy in the drinking house. He prises open the seal without tearing the envelope. A long letter, several pages, with writing on both sides. *My dearest brother Morten, by the time this letter reaches you.* It sounds like a suicide note, a thing one might write with the noose hanging ready from the hook in the ceiling. It *is* a farewell, and the noose is around her neck. The priests stand ready, one at her side, the other at the altar, and the church bells chime. He puts the letter aside without reading to the end.

A week later. The same day of the week. The same snow, though somewhat milder. The boy sits in the same drinking house as before. He seems unsurprised when Morten sits down opposite him at the table.

Evening, sir.

Good evening, my child.

The boy flashes a wry smile.

Does he come to have his fortune told again?

No, not for that. Morten purchases two mugs of ale and shoves one of them across the table. He looks more awake today. He has an odd twitch about his eye. What is it? Sarcasm? A muscular spasm? And that mouth! It is the mouth he has returned for. It is a riddle, a question unanswered. And Morten does not consider himself to be a person who leaves any question unanswered.

Thanks, says the boy, and raises his mug to drink.

You remember me?

You're my benefactor. You gave me money.

That's right.

But it was a lot. You've got more owed.

Well, we'll see about that. As I said, I haven't come to have my fortune told.

I can show you something you've never seen, says the boy.

And what might that be? Morten stares at him intently.

The gentleman will be *sehr vergnügt und überrascht*, says the boy, switching seamlessly into German.

I have seen many things, says Morten. It would take rather a lot to make me *vergnügt*, and even more for me to be *überrascht*.

The boy laughs. He does not force the matter. He sits with his trump card, whatever it might be, and is in no hurry to present it.

All right, what is it? Morten asks.

It is what I earn my way by in the winter. There are many gentlemen such as yourself, Pastor.

I'm not one of your gentlemen. My needs are quite normal.

The smile is unchanged, confident.

Then show me, says Morten.

Five marks, says the boy.

Out of the question. Shame on you! Three.

For you, three, says the boy. He rises, pulls down his breeches and looks at Morten with a cheeky grin on his face.

Should I not have seen such a little cock before? It's hardly worth a skilling.

Silence descends at the counter. Eyes are upon them. The fiddler stops tuning his instrument.

The boy draws up his shirt and his face opens wide in a grin.

Morten jumps to his feet and staggers backwards. His eyes dart up and down as he stares at the figure before him.

My dear girl! he blurts.

Coins rain down on them and the hermaphrodite receives the jubilations of the drinking-house customers with a courteous bow and a chivalrous sweep of his arm. Morten hurries outside, leaving his mug and his plate, fleeing over the encrusted puddles of the gutter with his coat-tails flapping. Laughter erupts in his wake.

†

The printing press clatters and rumbles below the floor; the compositors slam the lead in the cases and exchange banter. He awakes with all his clothes on, though only one shoe. The rattle of harnesses, clopping hooves and carriage wheels in the street. The bells of Vor Frue Kirke sound every half hour. There is a knock at the door. He gets up and rubs his face. Outside stands the printer's maid with a note in her hand. He sits down to read it, then crumples it up.

Some days pass. He hides himself from Miss Schultz, sneaks away to his lectures, sneaks home again. And then he is back in the drinking house. The host accords him a nod of recognition and brings him a mug of ale.

A portion of herring, sir?

No, thank you. Not tonight.

He looks around, but cannot see the boy. He has decided to call him *the boy*, though it is perhaps the girl he desires. Or a third gender, if such a thing makes sense. Perhaps it is merely the biological inadmissibility that interests him so. He has the feeling that what happens tonight, the choices he makes, will decide the rest of his life.

He feels a cold draught from the door behind him, senses the change of mood at the other tables, and knows what it means. The boy appears in his field of vision and sits down opposite him.

Peace of God, he says.

Morten nods. The boy smiles. He snaps his fingers to the host, who comes with ale. Morten stares at him. He can see the girl embedded in his features. But it is the boy who speaks.

My benefactor. You have a fine and noble heart, I can see that. You don't need to be ashamed.

I am not ashamed. I merely wonder what sort you are.

Come with me to the ramparts, says the boy, and I'll show you. The cost's ten marks. When the gentleman's done with me, he'll have peace in his soul. He'll be a good citizen then, and court his girl as duty commands.

The grassy banks are scantly illuminated with light from the windows facing the rampart path. A watchman blocks their way. Morten gives him a few skillings and they are permitted to pass. The boy leads him to a shed. He taps a signal on the door. A bolt is drawn aside and they enter. In a small room a wife sits knitting in the dim glow of a candle. She does not raise her head to look. They go on to the back room into which is crammed a bed and a stove and nothing else.

Does he want light? says the boy.

Yes, he replies. Much light. His pulse throbs in his head. His mouth is dry. Nothing shall be unknown, he tells himself. *Man is born free and everywhere he is in chains!*

An oil lamp is lit. The boy undresses. He lies down on the bed and looks up at Morten. There is something knowledgeable in his eyes for which he does not care, and the person they know about is him, Morten Falck, the schoolmaster's son. He stares at the naked body. It is at once a grotesque and titillating sight. He expels an unexpected moan and tries to disguise it with a cough. A hand unbuttons his fly and his member springs forth. The girl laughs in acknowledgement. She strokes it gently, but remains lying on her back.

If he wants to lie with me it costs five marks extra, she says.

My needs are quite normal, says Morten, and expels another moan.

She giggles. So I see, sir. Normal indeed. Her voice is utterly changed. It is the voice of a young girl.

She raises herself up onto her elbow and kisses the underside of his member. Her tongue darts forward, a glimpse of red. It twirls around the head, then retracts between her teeth. Morten sees that she, or the boy, is erect. He bends forward and touches the hard, boyish cock. It feels completely normal. He investigates the scrotum. Both testicles are present and of ordinary size. As far as he can see, there is no sign of female genitals beneath, and the sexual urge is fully that of the male, he notes. His hand jerks the penis, the girl releases him and falls back on the bed. He kneels down beside her and takes it in his mouth, drawing back the foreskin from the head, tongue rotating as he presses the knob against the roof of his mouth, nodding slowly, as though he were pondering the matter. At the same time, his right hand reaches up and fondles the girl's breast. She arches upwards. A warm liquid fills his mouth. He swallows. The girl flops back down on the bed and rolls onto her side with a stifled moan.

He gets to his feet and studies her. One arms rests over her eyes. It looks like she is sleeping. He smoothes his hand over her hair.

Then he places two rigsdalers on the pillow and neatens himself, bids the wife a friendly farewell on his way out and returns across the no-man's-land.

†

He is back in the city, on his way home, away from the ramparts and the strange part of himself he has left behind. He cannot grasp what has occurred, only that it has made him glad. The snow falls quietly without a breath of wind to disturb it. The white streets glisten in the faint glow of the train-oil lamps that light up the windows. Morten Falck tramps along Studiestræde. Some streets away he hears a watchman sing, a rambling melody from medieval times, though he is unable to pick out the words. The hour must be well past midnight. The pretty tune makes him giddy. He dances a few steps in the virgin snow, twirls a pirouette, draws a circle in the blanket of white with the toe of his boot, sees its powder whirl at his feet. He stops and glances around. No one has seen him. He continues on his way.

Noble sir!

The watchman steps from the shadow of a gateway and raises his hand.

Morten halts, stiffening in mid-pace.

Noble sir, the watchman says again, is he inebriated?

No, Morten replies. He considers the man's bulbous nose, the blood-shot eyes. But you are! he feels an urge to say.

The watchman stares at him unkindly. Should I light his way home?

Thank you, but that won't be necessary. My lodgings are only two streets away.

Before the watchman can say any more, he turns down Nørregade and walks briskly on towards the printer's house.

Nothing shall remain unknown, he tells himself, the greasy taste of hermaphrodite sperm still in his mouth. I wish to know everything before I marry.

†

February passes, March comes. The snow falls without abatement. It swirls around the steeples and piles up in the gutters and along the walls of the buildings. Peasants and fishermen bring their wares to the city with runners on their carts. The nostrils of the horses expel white columns of frosty steam. The beasts labour, stumble in the slippery streets, whinnying and snorting, depositing excrement in fear. The steam of their breath freezes into beads and garlands of lace in their manes and forelocks. Morten finds it a torment to see the poor animals mistreated. The stables in the city are filled to the brim. Peasants are unable to come home at night or else they lie drunk in the serving houses, leaving their horses tethered to a fence or a stake. Each morning the watchmen discover those that have succumbed in the night, hanging by their heads in the tethers, thin legs splayed to the sides. If the owner turns up he is handed a fine. The carcasses are transported out of the city, to the melting houses of the soap and glue makers, who work around the clock on account of this sudden abundance of raw materials.

But the cold has its advantages. The stench of the gutter, a plague for most of the year, is almost gone. Even when the nightmen come and slop out the buckets there is hardly a smell. Rats and mice have become less of a pest. The eternal gnawing and scratching in the filling of the wall behind Morten's bedstead quietens, and the bugs vanish into cracks to become dormant. The city smells only of coal and wood smoke, of which Morten is fond, especially when it is mingled with the frosty air. But it is not healthy. It makes him cough, as the whole town resounds with the coughing of its inhabitants. For a fortnight he lies with fever and spits mucus into a bucket at his bed. One of the printer's maids comes with soup and hot elder syrup and aquavit. She changes his damp sheets and will wash his clothes. There are more messages from the young mistress. He no longer crumples them up. He gathers them in a pile in the drawer of his nightstand. He gives the girl the flacon of lavender to bring to Miss Schultz, and this time it is not returned. He thinks about the boy, or the girl, in the little shed out at the ramparts, the wife who sat knitting without glancing up, the warm liquid in his mouth. Is it something he has imagined in his fever? Or is the fever a punishment for having sinned against nature?

His temperature subsides. He feels the fever leave him. He coughs investigatively. His chest and ribs are sore from all his hacking, but the thick mucus of before is gone. He will not die. His sins are forgiven.

With cautious, testing steps he crosses the yard to eat with the print workers. They greet him kindly and make room for him on the bench. Several have also been ill; one is there no longer. He enquires about the printer's household. Have they been struck? No, the printer and his family are privileged and may retire to the country, where they can stay isolated from the poisonous and invisible filth of the city air, so all are thankfully in good health. And now they have returned. They glance at him and smile. He stares into his soup.

One day she is in the courtyard as he comes unsteadily from his lunch. Her gaze is firm and bright. She smiles. He nods, hesitates, unable to walk forward or back, and raises a hand in greeting. She goes back inside the house. He sees the heel of her ankle boot as she jaunts up the step and imagines a fragrance emanating in concentric rings from her dainty feet. He thinks of his hand against her skin, against silken garments drawn aside to reveal the animal within, her warmth merging with his cold, her mouth opening, a darting tongue. A faint smell of lavender hangs in the air of the yard. Either he is hallucinating or else she has opened his gift.

Sitting in his room, the steeple of Vor Frue Kirke visible in the upper rectangle of the window, he struggles to write her a letter. No words are forthcoming besides the salutation. *Dear Abelone. My dear Miss Schultz. Dearest Miss Schultz. Beloved Abelone. My beloved Miss Schultz. Dear friend.* He feels his mind to be unready after his illness. His judgement cannot yet be trusted to strike the proper tone and form of address that will reveal to her his intentions without being inappropriate.

The mistress encourages him to touch her. She demands payment for placing her skin at the disposal of his trembling fingertips. He draws her rags aside and his fingers explore. He whimpers and cannot find what he is looking for. He does not know what he is looking for. Love, perhaps? A quintessence of the female principle, concealed at the point where her legs meet? A wild animal? He looks up at her, but her face is like water, indistinct in the dingy corner of the serving house. He grabs her harshly, tears the rags from her body and forces his member inside her. Her buttocks part, and he feels her warm anus thrust against his pelvic bone. She looks up at him over her shoulder and laughs shamelessly. She lies spread across a table, her hands fumbling to grip its edge. He studies her closely. It is Miss Schultz, not the other one. Or is it? Is this love? he asks himself, then falls on the floor and wakes.

Dear Miss Schultz. I am now sufficiently restored as to be able to sense once more what is occurring and what has occurred during this recent time.

My gratitude to you is greater than I can express in words. I wish, therefore, to do so in action!

What then? What action? He crumples the paper in his hand. There are no more sheets. The ink pot is nearly dry and broken quill nibs lie all about, together with his crumpled attempts at formulation. He goes outside, crosses the yard and knocks on the door of the printer's house. The maid ushers him in. He stands and waits in an anteroom on the ground floor, then is led upstairs to the printer's office. He has no idea what intention has brought him here.

Schultz sits behind his desk, surrounded by heavy folios and stacks of books with gilded letters on the spines. He issues a sound to convey that he is aware of Morten's presence and requires him to wait, but does not look up from his papers. Morten goes to the window and looks out. The view is an altered version of his own. The same walls, the same rooftops and chimneys, the steeple of Vor Frue Kirke protruding from the bare branches of the sycamore. He sees the window of his room, a surface darkened by reflection and allowing no view inside. The yard is white with snow, circular tracks of horse-drawn carts wind around the tree. Faintly, he hears the sound of the press.

It gladdens me that he has risen, says Schultz behind him.

He turns, then seats himself on the chair to which the printer's hand is extended.

I feel nearly fully restored.

We were worried about him. The printer's eyebrows are raised high on his forehead, as though he has uttered something amusing or else expects Morten to do so. My eldest daughter especially has been concerned for his well-being.

I hope I have not been the cause of unnecessary anxiety.

Not at all! Solicitude is in a woman's nature and it is only healthy for young girls to be given a proper sense of life's realities, to learn of the harshness that exists outside the protective walls of the home. Nevertheless, it is a good thing Mr Falck did not succumb. It would not have been beneficial to my daughter's aspect on life.

Nor to my own, says Morten. The printer nods. They laugh. Morten makes note of two things: the printer has called him Falck and referred to his daughter as a woman.

No, I am genuinely happy to see him, says Schultz. It pleases me, really. We have become used to having him here with us. If he were no longer here, something would feel amiss. Anyway, was there something he wished to ask?

I have run out of paper and ink, he says. And quill nibs.

Aha! The student is at work on his thesis? When does he intend to conclude his studies?

This summer, if all goes well.

If he wishes to have the thesis printed and bound, he must come to me. A well-composed text will surely make an impression on his principals.

Thank you. I shall remember it.

There is a lull in the conversation, during which neither speaks. Schultz sits reclined in his high-backed chair considering him. His hands are folded on his stomach. He has dark eyes, Morten notices, and his powdered wig is placed on the desk. His own hair is gathered in a thin, grey pigtail at his nape.

Approach my bookkeeper, Kierulf. He will equip the student with whatever he might need.

Morten makes a third note: the printer mentions nothing of payment for these supplies.

He returns to his room with ink, pens, quality paper, envelopes and sealing wax enough to last him months. The desktop is scarred with deep grooves made by the penknife he has used to absently dig into the wood. He retrieves a blotting pad and spreads it out over the desk. He moves the desk to the window facing the yard so that he might look out over the rooftops as he works.

Dear Abelone.

He does not crumple the paper. Now he can stand to look at it. He studies his handwriting, the swirls of the quill. His hand is fully restored like the rest of him, though it has become rather more slanting, a touch more pointed. Through the window he watches the afternoon turn grey. He sees that beyond the frost-covered pane it has begun to snow. He puts on his coat and boots and goes into town.

The cold has subsided. His feet remain warm inside his well-greased boots. The city is oddly still. Perhaps it is the silence that follows upon serious illness or perhaps it is because of the snow that falls in large flakes. He walks down Vimmelskaftet towards Amager Torv, but then turns left along Klosterstræde, wanting to look around the narrow streets of the Klædebo quarter, perhaps purchase a little something for Miss Schultz, a token of his gratitude for all that she has done for him, for his being alive, and for the feelings she arouses within him. And then he is in Vester Kvarter. He cannot recall having passed the Rådhus, and yet he must have done. Hanens Bastion. And now he is in the same drinking house. The host seems to recognize him and brings ale. He seats himself and listens to the music and the talk at the tables.

Later, the boy appears. He sits down at his table.

Now it'll soon be spring, Pastor.

He says nothing.

Then we can get away from here.

Where will you go?

All over. Anywhere. I like to be journeying, to see what's round the next corner.

I could go with you, says Morten and laughs.

The boy laughs, too. A fine gentleman like the pastor can't go with one like me.

Morten smiles. He says nothing. The potman brings them their frothy mugs. He looks up at the man and sees himself reflected in him. I must be radiant, he thinks. Am I lost or saved?

Does he want a turn like before? says the boy.

No. I just wanted to see you one last time. To see if you were real.

Skål, Pastor, says the boy. I'm sure we'll meet again.

I doubt it, he says, and leaves half a rigsdaler on the table.

†

He resumes his studies, working his hardest to complete them. Eventually spring arrives. The days grow longer, the weather milder. The gutters thaw and the nightmen shovel the filth ahead of them through the city to the canals. The cobbles are shiny and clean, then comes new waste from the latrine buckets and night pots, mash from the brewing houses and distilleries. The warmth, the stench and the rats come seeping back with an epidemic of the fever that weeds out the city's most impoverished. Four of the boys he has taught at the Vajsenhus expire with them. His own constitution is strong and sound.

†

In June 1785 he graduates *non contemnendus*, i.e. with the lowest grade required to pass. And yet it is better rather than worse than he had expected. He has been afraid of a *rejectus* and has already composed in his mind a letter of apology home to his father. He has neglected his theology. Not until this last half year has he studied systematically. But for his probationary sermon in Vor Frue Kirke, where he speaks for Professor Swane and a select congregation upon David's Psalm 43, he receives a *laudabilis*, the highest mark possible. His performance surprises not only his examiners, but also himself. He has felt a man's gaze upon him, a very old man seated in the front row, with grey-blue eyes, angular hawk nose and a smiling, vivacious mouth that seems to repeat and chew upon each word he hears. He does not know who this man is, but his presence has a stimulating effect upon him and after a while he addresses only him. Afterwards, they are introduced. He is Poul Egede, pastor of Vartov and bishop of Greenland, son of Hans Egede. Moreover, he is principal of the Seminarium Groenlandicum, a position he has inherited from his father.

He bows deeply before the bishop. An honour, he mumbles.

Has the Magister considered joining the holy mission? Egede enquires, sizing him up with lively, aged eyes.

The thought has occurred to me, says Morten. Are there prospects with the Mission?

In Greenland, says Egede. He reaches out and squeezes Morten's upper arm tightly, then smiles and retracts his claw-like hand. You are Norwegian?

It is the first time a person of his status has addressed him informally, as an equal. He tells him where he is from. Egede asks him about his family and his plans for the future, and he tries to hide the circumstance that he has no plans whatsoever. He thinks to himself: This is a sign. He agrees to consider entering the seminary as alumnus the following autumn. Heartily, Egede wishes him a pleasant summer and wags a finger at him to indicate he does not intend to forget the matter.

Somewhat dazed after the examination, the unexpectedly excellent mark and his conversation with Egede, he leaves Vor Frue Kirke and wanders out of the city by the Vesterport gate. He walks and walks. A shower passes and drenches him. He dries out. He feels the grit beneath the soles of his boots, the wind blowing in his face, full of the smells of stables and the fresh aroma of cut grass. He has no idea where he is. He asks a man with a horse-drawn cart. Rødovre, learned magister. He is still in his vestments. He removes his wig, sits down on a stone by the road and watches the swallows flitting above the field, twisting sharply in the air, ascending towards the heavens. He feels the blue consume his eye. He is content, yet empty. His divinity studies are completed. The letter of apology to his father need not be sent. What is he to do with himself? He has devoted no thought to the matter.

Curtains of rain approach from the west, a thunderstorm rumbles and crackles, the wind bends the trees. He walks back and the weather catches up with him. The dirt track becomes a mire, soil washed from the fields. His ruff collar wilts and the potato starch runs in rivulets down his cassock. And yet he feels himself free. On his return home he takes off all his clothes and drapes them over the furniture. He lies down naked on the bed.

Greenland?

†

Midsummer's Eve, 1785. Two coaches trundle through the city, one in front of the other, each drawn by hired carthorses with blinkers and rattling, creaking harnesses. The coaches arrive at the Nørreport gate and must wait a whole hour to come out into the countryside. Many respectable families have felt the urge to take the air outside the ramparts.

Morten Falck sits in the same carriage as his host. The printer has lit his clay pipe. He calls out greetings and lifts his hat to other families in other coaches. He is in an excellent mood, recalling excursions of his youth, handing out pamphlets of cheerful ballads and prompting the others in the carriage to sing along. With them are some of the men from the printing shop. They sit leaning back in their seats, eyes veiled with fatigue and the blasé aspect of the city dweller. But Morten is attentive. He notes everything: the pretty mistresses in the other carriage with their mother Madame Schultz, and the young men who ride by, the suitors, pert backsides bobbing in the saddle as they issue their courteous greetings. At the gate, acrobats and other entertainers perform; punch and ale is served; wives go about and sell pastries and confectionery. Schultz splashes out on punch to all his men, including Morten. He drinks some of the sugary liquid. It fizzes like fresh ale and goes straight to his head. Shortly after he finds himself bawling along to one of the printer's raucous ballads. The printer smiles at him encouragingly. He pats him on the knee. Morten turns his head and looks at Miss Schultz. He is about to propose a toast to her, but thinks better of it. Instead, he calls upon the print workers to drink in honour of Madame Schultz and her sister, who also wishes to take the country air. He stands up in the coach, swinging his mug. Smiles and good cheer, sunshine and laughter. He plops back onto his seat and promptly falls asleep.

When he awakes they are out of town. The carriages make slow progress. They are in the middle of a procession stretching as far as the eye can see. He realizes the printer is talking to him.

Has the Magister visited the spring before?

No, I did not know of its existence until the printer was so kind as to invite me. We have our own little spring back home. They say its waters have healing properties.

You must drink a cup, says the printer. Spring water is without a doubt healthy for both mind and body. It cured me of the melancholy of youth.

Morten nods. He notes, too, that the printer now addresses him as an equal. It is exactly what they say of the spring at home. I remember I drank from it as a child. However, I believe it is now silted up.

But the Magister is a man of science, says the printer, and, moreover, a theologian of the modern age. Does this notion of healing springs not run counter to both?

Not at all, he replies. Partaking of water from a spring can be nothing if not healthy for a person who has spent a long winter inside the ramparts.

The printer laughs. He is satisfied. Morten realizes he is being assessed. He hopes he has said nothing inappropriate during his brief intoxication at the city gate. Schultz leans forward. What is more, he whispers, they say the spring of Kirsten Piils Kilde can make the secret wishes of young people come true.

I shall bear it in mind, says Morten. Absently, he wonders if the printer's words are a subtle hint. His head feels heavy. He jumps down from the coach to follow along on foot for a while. The mistresses Schultz and their mother smile down at him. He lifts his hat and bows. Presently he climbs aboard again.

The printer complains about the dullness of their route. He would prefer to go by Strandvejen, which affords splendid views across the sound on one side and to the woods on the other. But Strandvejen is in poor condition, he is told, potholed and broken up. The driver suggests they go by way of Gentofte and Ordrup and pick up the coast road a little south of Klampenborg. He knows an occasional shortcut where the traffic will be less. The printer approves the plan, out of consideration for the ladies' behinds, he says. Madame Schultz turns and scolds him.

Tsk, I shall have to wash his dirty mouth! She laughs. The girls roll their eyes and fan themselves excitedly.

Morten dozes, but wakes again as they reach the point at Hvidøre. The coach turns north along Strandvejen, which indeed is pitted with holes. The driver growls a command to the horses to slow them down. Morten looks out across the glittering Øresund. He looks at the ships, their sails flapping lazily in the slack wind, the dismantled fleet that lies packed together further south. On the other side of the water the hostile coast, at once threatening and enticing, the same clouds drifting over its hills as swept across Denmark only a short while before. Morten thinks upon the matter drowsily, his head nodding slightly this way and that, until his thoughts become a muddle. The nature of the earth is conveyed to the mind, he thinks to himself, whereupon the mind reflects upon the earth, which in turn rises up once more into the mind, and so on, an endless sequence of matter and spirit. A chatter of voices and peals of laughter from the carriage in front, a snorting of horses, hooves clacking on cobble, the rattle of traces, gulls screaming out across the sound. Morten straightens up. He wipes drool from a corner of his mouth and looks about. They have arrived.

Singing, they drive through the red gates of the Dyrehaven, the royal hunting grounds to which Copenhagen's public in its yearning for nature has been admitted since the days of Frederik V. Here, too, they make slow progress due to the sheer number of carriages. Eventually, the driver stops and begins to unload. The party jumps out and finds a spot close to the spring, where they spread out their blankets upon the grass and hand out the contents of their picnic baskets. The printer and his wife seat themselves. Schultz sends his store man to find them some coffee, which in his opinion is as beneficial to the health as the waters of the spring, not least when it contains a splash of aquavit. His daughters gather round them, three daisies in the grass. They pester their father so that they might be allowed to explore. Please, Daddy, dearest Daddy, we shan't go far. Only if they keep to the area around the spring, says the printer, and only if they are each accompanied by one of his men to look after them, armed with a cane. The fairground of Dyrehavsbakken is a den of pickpockets and tinkers, Jews and Gypsies and scoundrels of the dark, and the bailiff in Kongens Lyngby and his appointed officers meant to uphold the peace have already drunk themselves silly, I shouldn't wonder, Schultz opines gruffly, in which state they will not be of use to anyone.

Morten bows to Abelone. Miss Schultz, allow me to perform the duty of accompanying the mistress and ensuring her safety.

Abelone exchanges glances with her mother and receives a nod. The Madame coos and instructs her to take care. Her sister, who is seated at her side, seconds her caution. Abelone rises and crooks her arm under his elbow.

They stroll about and watch the entertainers, the jugglers, the sword swallowers with their flaming breath, the Turkish percussionists, the buxom female singers who play the harp and stringed instruments and display their sumptuous cleavage. Young Jews with shaved heads wander among the throng with trays folded out at their midriffs, from which they peddle Dutch cigars, percussion caps, blacking and fuses that may be ignited and thrown to fizzle and crackle under people's feet, making them dance with fright. A tightrope walker clad in a leotard performs dizzying tricks high above the ground. More than once he would seem about to fall and the audience gasps, some scream. Miss Schultz grips his arm, puts her hand to her mouth, her eyes fixed upon the figure in the air. Morten is inattentive to the tightrope walker and watches instead a thief at work, emptying the onlookers' pockets. When he comes nearer their eyes meet. The boy stiffens, observes Morten with a canny, measuring eye. Then his pretty lips part in a smile. He bows with an elegant sweep of his hand and vanishes. Morten watches him go. His mouth fills with the greasy taste of sperm.

Abelone looks at him, her cheeks blushing. Magister Falck, she says, are you unable to stomach such excitement?

Er, no, he squeaks, and runs a finger inside his collar.

You're not unwell, I hope? she says. You look so pale. Have you seen a ghost, Morten?

I could do with some refreshment.

Abelone pulls on his arm and leads him to the spring.

She runs over to her mother to fetch cups, then returns and considers him inquisitively. You really are pale, she says.

It's nothing. He blames it on the punch, the long drive, the heat, on becoming faint from standing with his head leaned back. I feel better now. He accepts a cup and stares at it.

A cup from which no person has drunk, she says. Otherwise the spring water will fail to have effect.

The area around the spring, which is built up with boards in the way of a well, resembles a camp hospital. The sick and infirm sit about on stools and lie upon stretchers or else they come limping, supported by helpers. Behind the spring, further up the bank, lie heaps of abandoned crutches and bloodied and pus-soaked bandages thrown away by pilgrims ecstatic at abrupt recovery. The smell of sickness and infected wounds pinches the nostrils. Abelone holds a handkerchief in front of her mouth. She nudges him forwards. On the platform above the steps music is played and there is singing and dancing. He sees twirling skirts, hears laughter, the beat of a drum, a bear growling and straining at its chains. He feels dizzy and fatigued, the sun beats down upon his neck as if all of a sudden he were in the circles of the Inferno itself. Abelone tugs on his sleeve.

Look, it's our turn now, Magister.

The attendant of the spring, a peasant woman in a bonnet and a white embroidered apron, asks if they have brought with them a cup *from which no person has drunk*. They hold out their cups and a boy fills them with water from the spring. Then they are pushed onwards to stand at a short distance to drink. The water tastes rather muddy, as well water often does, and has an unclean appearance. He empties his cup. Abelone dashes hers against a stone, causing it to shatter, and asks that he do the same. He must throw his own cup three times before it breaks. Finally, they each give a coin to the spring, remove themselves from the crowds and stroll, arm in arm, towards the woods.

Did you remember to whisper a wish? she asks as they walk away.

Indeed, he says. I feel better already. And you?

She laughs. Now we are cleansed, Magister Falck. Now we can do exactly as we please.

They wander along the shore, arm in arm still, though occasionally Abelone lets go and dances across the sand, jumping aside with a little shriek when the waves come lapping in, before returning to join him again. The foam licks away her footprints. She chatters without pause. There is a self-confidence about her now, something playful, challenging even. He is not sure, but she makes him feel ill at ease. What does she want? Does she even know? How does a man do these things, and in what order? Why is there not a handbook on the subject?

She walks backwards before him. The hem of her dress is wet. She laughs and points. He turns round. Their footprints are a curve marking the border of waves that have come and gone.

These two people, she says, look like they have just come from the inn, to judge by their uncertain path.

I am intoxicated, he says. By love.

But she seems not to hear him, for which he is grateful. What is he to say or do now? Force her down into the sand so that his kisses might wash over her like the waves? What expectations of the choreography of love has her reading of novels imparted to her? He sees the printer in his mind's eye as he lay with his head in his wife's lap but a short while ago. His shirt frill was open, he puffed on his clay pipe, Madame Schultz's fleshy, yet no less beautiful hand rested familiarly on the hair of his chest. When Abelone informed them they would walk along the shore, he raised his glass of punch and winked his eye at Morten. Whatever that was supposed to mean.

They stand still and look out on the Sound.

The ships are pretty, she says. Their sails are as white as the gull's wings.

Yes, he says. The wind must have got up out there. They sail at some speed.

Where do you think they are bound, Morten?

Her voice is altered. Has he kissed her? He is unsure, but he must have done, a fleeting brush of the lips. It is why she calls him by his Christian name.

Oh, all sorts of places, he says. Tranquebar, Serampore, Canton, Godthåb, the Gold Coast. Most likely they are merchant ships to our colonies.

It's so hard to grasp, she says. There are people out there on the ships. Now they are here. And in a few weeks or months they will be in a foreign place we have never seen and never will. Is it not strange to think?

Certainly, he says. Strange indeed.

And some of them will perhaps never return home, she says. Is that not true?

Indeed, many perils await these seamen. They put their lives at risk so that we may purchase our porcelain and cotton fabrics and coffee, and spices to put in our cakes. They are brave, one has to admit.

But how exciting it must be, she says. I am sure it is all worth it, even if one were to end at the bottom of the sea, though not until the journey back, of course, after having seen the world. If I were a man I would be the captain of a ship. You smile, Magister, she says, offended. Why may a woman not harbour such dreams?

Why indeed?

If my intended husband should get the idea of journeying out into the world to make his living in the colonies, I would go with him.

He says nothing. He ought to speak now. A better opportunity will hardly arise. She has played the ball into his court, a cautious, loose ball that comes rolling gently towards him and stops at his feet. And still he says nothing. He stands beside her with her arm tucked under his own and looks out upon the water. He senses the dense, sweet smell of lavender, and this time it is no hallucination.

They continue along the shore. They are silent. She has let go of his arm. She has distanced herself ever so slightly. He wishes he had brought his pipe, for then he would know what to do with himself.

Your mother will be worrying soon.

About what, Magister? My virtue? I am sure it is in safe hands in your company.

He looks at her. She walks on, faster all of a sudden. With every stride she sinks further into the sand. It is plain that she struggles to keep up her pace. She hoists her skirts slightly and he sees the twist and spring of her step in the yielding sand, her ankles as they are raised and brought forward in turn. He wants to say something. It vexes him that he has no aptitude for quick and humorous remarks. Something by which the mood may be turned again. A series of poor jokes passes through his mind only to be rejected. He is silent.

And then she runs, away from the shore, into the scrub, towards the road. He sees the flap of her white dress between the trees. She calls out and he tries to catch her words. She glances back over her shoulder. He runs after her.

Miss Schultz! He cries and can tell by his voice that he is annoyed, but also anxious. Be careful!

Of what does he warn her? Wild animals? Robbers? Thugs?

The woods are unsafe! he shouts.

He listens. A branch snaps. Leaves rustle. He runs, finds tracks in the earth, but cannot see the mistress Schultz.

He is uncertain as to where he might be, in which direction the shore is or the Dyrehavsbakken and the spring. He must have run further than he thinks. Deep into the woods. He has become alarmed by his own words of caution, and imagines poachers and wild men armed with knives. If she lies injured somewhere the guilt will be his alone, no matter what might have happened. He stands still, hears the blood rush inside his ears. He takes a few steps and a wood pigeon flaps suddenly into the air in front of him. Before he is recovered from the shock, he sees something white in the corner of his eye. It is she. He runs after her. She laughs out loud, an echo among tree trunks.

He can see her legs amid the flutter of her dress, and what he sees are legs of flesh and blood, not merely tulle skirts and fragrance. His own move at a steady pace. She is a drum roll, he a march. He comes nearer. How troublesome it must be, he thinks, to run in a long dress through a wood. How absurd! Women are not built for the wilderness, at least their clothes are not. If she were dressed like a man or a Hottentot she might perhaps be quicker than he. But she is clumsy as a peacock among the trees. He runs faster now. She glances over her shoulder and lets out a shriek, then a shrill laugh, and bares her teeth in spite. Her arms flail, her hair falls loose. He sees her galloping feet beneath the hem. His breathing is steady. He knows he can run still faster and catch her up whenever he chooses. And then he will do what is to be done. He senses he is erect, his member slapping the fabric of his breeches as he runs. The wild animal is he, robber and thug armed with a knife, he ought to have warned her against himself. He is no longer timid and she senses it and thus her laughter is now tinged with anxiety.

They come to a clearing in the wood and she bounds through grass that reaches to her midriff. He increases his speed, leaping onwards with long, elastic strides, and catches up with her almost immediately. He grips her arm and twists her around. She struggles, howling with laughter, spluttering with rage. He forces her to the ground. She kicks at him, lashes out with her fists, spitting and giggling and thrashing as he climbs on top of her. And then she is calm. Her bosom is like a bellows, but she is stiff and tense. She stares at him with eyes that are barely human. He releases everything, groping and fondling, tearing at the fabric, hearing the rip of seams. Flesh comes into sight, then more. He dips down, kissing, licking, slobbering, and she observes him with curiosity. He feels her hand at his neck, fingers worming in his hair. He kisses her and she turns away. She squeals a protest, but he pulls her back by her hair, kisses her again. He senses her muscles relax beneath him, her body become soft and womanly once more. He is certain she can feel his erection. But does she know what it means? They remain lying for a moment, gasping into each other's faces.

You are a pig, Magister Falck, she breathes. I knew this was what you were after. I knew it all along, have always known it. And then she rolls aside and in a single movement pulls her dress up over her head and is in her underskirt in the grass.

†

The betrothal is proclaimed from Vor Frue Kirke a week later and thereupon announced in the *Adresseavisen*. For the time being, Morten remains in his lodgings. He mentions nothing to his betrothed about Egede and his plans for him, as indeed he mentions nothing to Egede about his engagement. He enrols at the seminary in all secrecy. He writes a letter to his sister informing her that he is to be married. Only a fortnight later he receives a reply with an invitation to spend the rest of the summer with his betrothed at the rectory in Nakskov. He realizes that every occurrence, and every decision he makes, cancels out the next.

They board the packet boat on a windy day in July and are blown through the Øresund and out into the Smålandshavet. Abelone is seasick. He sits at the bulwark with her and supports her brow as she empties her stomach into the waves. For this reason they lodge frequently on the way, at inns in small market towns, in good, separate rooms paid for by the printer. After a week they arrive by mail coach in Nakskov, where his sister receives them with sobs of joy.

It soon becomes plain to Morten what is happening. The reverend pastor Johannes Gram, Kirstine's husband, places his hand upon his shoulder in a friendly gesture that is quite unlike him. Morten knows him as an introvert who says nothing more than is absolutely necessary. He possesses the solemnity of the former, now deceased pastor, his father, though not his fiery temperament. He is in the habit of rehearsing his sermons in part to the audience of his family and becomes offended should they pose too many questions or put forward comments of a less than wholly positive character. Now he chatters away. He calls Morten his *dear colleague*, *dearest Magister* and *beloved brother-in-law*, and invites him to drink wine with him in his study when Morten would rather walk with the ladies in the woods. He has noticed an envelope on Gram's desk, with the printer's name on it. A sudden suspicion prompts him to enquire: Do you know my future father-in-law?

Gram pushes the letter hastily away beneath some papers. Morten finds he exudes an unpleasant and sickly smell, and he shudders at the thought of the man lying naked with Kirstine in the night.

The printer Schultz has been most kind, says Gram. He has sent me a copy of Martin Luther's sermons, which are as good as unprocurable.

The brother-in-law picks a volume from the shelf behind him and hands it to Morten. As he is about to leaf through its pages, Gram removes it from his hand and puts it back in its place.

It is a very precious work.

Of course.

Let me fill your glass, my dearest Magister.

When they have drunk most of the decanter, Gram says Come, dear colleague, let us go for a drive. I have something to show you that you may find of interest.

They go outside. An open carriage is brought forward, drawn by a single chestnut gelding. A young stable boy stands and adjusts the harness. Gram climbs aboard. Morten does likewise and sits beside him, facing forward. The carriage sets in motion, a wide arc over the cobbles and through the gateway, and oscillates gently along the road between the fields. Morten feels the sour wine slosh in his stomach. At the perimeter of the rectory's land he sees two women dressed in white, strolling side by side along a path. They turn and look out from under the brims of their hats as the carriage passes them by and a cloud of dust swirls in its wake. They wave with their parasols. Morten and the Reverend Gram raise their hands in greeting and return their waves. Even at a distance of several hundred feet he can see that the ladies look solemn.

They are getting to know each other already, says his brother-in-law with a chuckle. Most likely they complain about us.

Yes, they are delightful indeed, says Morten, adding in a moment of sudden inspiration: Two of the three women I love most dearly.

Gram turns his head and looks at him enquiringly. And the third?

My mother.

Aha. Hm. Yes, of course.

It is mid-afternoon. They drive with the sun on their right. Gram does not say where they are going and Morten does not ask. He tries to picture the map of Lolland and to place the carriage, the Reverend Gram and himself upon it. There is no water to be seen anywhere and no sea breeze to be felt. They must be in the middle of the island. The gelding has chosen a casual pace to which it adheres without variation in bends or on slopes. Morten sits in a slipstream that smells of horse and pollen from the warm fields. The landscape is monotonous, mostly cultivated, broken only by a rather large number of passage graves and tumuli that seem to comprise the only raised areas of ground. Gram tells him that his father, God rest his soul, worked all his life to persuade the manor owners to reform their agriculture and convince the suspicious farmers that it was in their interests to keep abreast of progress. Now drainage has soon done away with the last of the island's bogs, large areas of fallow land and pasture have been cultivated, woodland and scrub cleared, and improved cereal types developed. It is good farmland. For the same reason, they are no longer plagued by biting and stinging insects as in former times, and epidemics have thereby become seldom. Leprosy has not been seen in generations. Most of the farms have moved out of the villages, plots have been joined, the farmers enjoy prosperous circumstances, have become independent, thinking Christians, no more the darkened slaves of medieval superstition as in olden days, and soon the Stavnsbånd, that last relic of former aristocratic rule, will be lifted by royal decree.

Morten nods during his brother-in-law's lecture. Gradually, it occurs to him that he is listening to a sales pitch.

A person can lead a good life here, Gram concludes, adding with somewhat cryptic reflection: providing he has the aptitude for happiness.

They enter a small market town and arrive at a large pre-Reformation church in red stone, a cathedral almost. Gram jumps down from the carriage. Morten follows.

This parish has been vacant since the winter, when Magister Pade left us, says Gram. Let me show you the church, beloved brother-in-law.

Together they approach the edifice that towers before them. The stable boy goes off to find the warden and presently an elderly man appears with a bunch of keys. He bows deeply to the two priests, then they are let inside. The interior of the church is enormous; there must be room here for a congregation several hundred strong. The gallery for the use of the finest families comprises a row of white-painted cubicles with gilded frames and small entrance doors upon which are inscribed the names and monograms of the noblemen to whom they belong. However, the overall impression is one of decay, dilapidation and abandonment. The pulpit is placed on high, under the white arches of the ceiling, so that the congregation must lean back their heads in order to see their priest and thereby demonstrate their Christian humility. Gram nudges him forward, encouraging him to take a closer look. To reach the pulpit one must open a small gate into something that resembles a sentry box and then clamber up a steep staircase that is almost a hen-coop ladder. The wood creaks and yields under his weight. It smells ancient. He hopes the stair is not pre-Reformation too, though it feels as if it is. Then he emerges into the vast space and looks out upon its empty pews and organ gallery, as well as the face of the Reverend Gram turned towards the heavens, coloured faintly green by the light that falls from a stained-glass window. It is a face of aggressive expectation. Morten becomes aware that he is expected to speak, to test how the acoustics of the church interior will receive and modulate his voice. He imagines all the faces when the church is full, the ordinary members of the parish in the pews, the finest ranks upon the gallery.

What should I say? he mumbles.

The Lord's Prayer is always an option, his brother-in-law replies from below in a voice that is loud and clear.

He opens his mouth, then closes it again, mute as a codfish. The text that each and every person in the kingdom is able to speak in their sleep, has vanished from his memory.

Very well, says Gram, once he has climbed down again. Let us inspect the Latin school at the back.

†

His brother-in-law is kindly disposed to him that evening as they sit in the living room of the rectory with Abelone and Kirstine. Gram tells the ladies of their excursion into the neighbouring parish. Only now does it occur to Morten that they have visited Rødby Kirke and Latin school.

Some days later he is finally able to spend time alone with Abelone. They have all gone by carriage to the narrow spit of land that reaches out into the Langelandsbælt and which the locals call the Elbow. Morten and Abelone walk arm in arm along the shore. Kirstine sits behind them among the shrubs and reads a book, protected from the elements by her white garments and shawl and a wide-brimmed, veiled hat. Her husband naps under a parasol, a pair of thin legs protruding beneath a large belly. He has consumed a solid lunch of pie, cheese, sweet ham and no small amount of wine.

The strait is grey in colour, with occasional stabs of sun from an unsettled sky. Rain clouds come and go without releasing their contents. By evening, when the air cools, there will be a downpour. Across the water lies the island of Langeland. The fields of Spodsbjerg are plainly visible to the eye, flax-coloured panels bordered by stone walls and hedgerows. A number of sails can be seen, ships on their way to or from the countries of the Baltic.

What a marvellous view, says Abelone.

Indeed, says Morten, accommodatingly. It is a beautiful spot.

Do you think you can live here, Morten? It cannot be beautiful all year round. Your sister says that in winter it is quite a harrowing place.

I imagine, he says, and laughs. It seems your father and my brother-in-law, the Reverend Gram, have already found a living for me.

Is it not what you want? What we want?

Certainly!

Finding a living is no easy matter in our day.

This is true.

Johannes Gram is a man of influence. If he lets a word drop to the provost, you will doubtless be given the parish.

Yes.

Have you other plans, Morten? Have we other plans?

No. I just find it all so, I don't know, so real. So sudden.

Things happen so quickly sometimes, says Abelone, absently. Such is the way. I feel I am years older since the spring. But I am glad. You have made me happy. Are you not happy, Morten?

I am, he says. I am happy.

I love you, she says.

He half turns towards her with a smile and pats her hand. He reminds himself that he must remember to say something similar at some appropriate time, without making it sound false or like an automatic reply. I love you. Hm, a difficult sentence indeed.

They return to the others. His sister, too, has fallen asleep and lies with her book at her breast. Ants crawl on her hand, which lies flopped in the sand. He crouches down and sweeps them away without waking her.

In the evening he reads aloud for them, a German translation of Rousseau. *Man is born free and everywhere he is in chains!* The words receive sarcastic comment from the Reverend Gram. Kirstine makes apologies and retires early on account of feeling indisposed. Abelone follows shortly after, leaving him alone with his brother-in-law. A tall grandfather clock stands ticking against the long wall. Gram brings them glasses and a decanter. They get drunk while hardly exchanging a word. Morten reads his book, his brother-in-law Luther's sermons.

This Rousseau may be inserted in a certain orifice, as far as I am concerned, Gram eventually proclaims, and staggers to his room.

†

Luncheon in the great dining room some days later. It has been raining since the excursion to the Elbow and they have kept indoors, reading and playing cards. Gram's ageing mother has arrived home from a journey to Altona to visit an old female friend. She is an affable woman who, in season and out, cheerfully allows her son to bite off her head. At one point during the meal he abruptly clatters his cutlery down upon his plate, rises to his feet and bellows: Mother, you are the dullest person I know! I am ashamed! And with that he marches to his study and does not show himself for the remainder of the day. It is a scene that repeats itself with variations during the days that follow. The reason for their difference is a mystery to Morten, who notes only that seemingly innocuous, everyday remarks invariably cause his brother-in-law to explode.

My son has a strong temper, says the mother with a chuckle. He takes after his father.

†

The weather changes and they can once more stroll in the woods and along the shore. Things begin to repeat. The woods, the shore, the sea, the same people who greet them as they walk through the town, the heavy meals followed by leaden afternoon naps, the drowsiness when waking up before evening, the effort to summon the energy to go for yet another stroll, only to remain in the chair and read or pass the time with a game of patience. Then another evening of reading aloud for each other, punctuated by the continuing disagreements between the pastor and his mother. He conducts not a single conversation of a personal nature with Kirstine during the entire visit. Indeed, he avoids it on purpose, terrified of what she might confide to him, and he to her.

They depart with the packet boat on the tenth of August and take lodging in a single room at an inn in Vordingborg under the name of Falck, where they spend a week together, much of it without leaving their alcove bed.

We are good at this, she says. At being on our own together. Let us never forget it and let us never allow anyone or anything to change it.

He finds it an odd thing to say. As though she has a premonition that some dreadful event will occur.

Back in Copenhagen. He is with Abelone and she is happy to be home again. They stroll arm in arm in the town and amble through Rosenborg Have with the two sisters. They see the great regatta in the city's canals. They make excursions to the countryside in the company of Madame Schultz. When again he is alone with Abelone, she asks him to show her the sordid quarters around Nikolaj Kirke and the ramparts, and to explain to her what goes on behind the walls.

He tells her. He conceals nothing. She listens with interest.

But why, Morten?

Why what?

Why do they do it?

It is their only way of earning a living.

But the men, I mean. Why do they do it?

It is the men's lust, he says. It is their savage nature, a fearful thing. An innocent girl such as yourself cannot understand it.

Innocent, ha! Do you not think girls may possess a savage nature? Let me show you savage!

She wishes to be taught, and in teaching her he becomes himself a student. This is quite another matter than death's exact and static revelations. It is muscles responding to the touch, glands releasing substances more fragrant than the deathly fluids in the vaults of Bredegade. It is eyes widening and beads of perspiration on the lip, sweat that can be tasted, a pulse throbbing at an artery in the neck, gasps of breath of so many nuances as to be language on their own. And he is an attentive pupil, a sensitive teacher.

Miss Schultz is fond of the inadmissibility of copulating while still being fully clothed, with the exception of small apertures through which a thing may stick out or be stuck in and received. They can spend hours arousing each other with words and small, innocuous touches of the hand, until one of them can withstand no longer and they begin to snatch and tear at each other's clothing. Often she slaps him hard in the face from sheer excitement, or else happens to bite him.

The opportunity of being together presents itself only seldom. Madame Schultz watches over her daughter and nothing can be concealed from the two sisters. But they are nevertheless betrothed and as such are allowed to walk in the town without a chaperone. The things she says to him during these walks would be enough to make an old whore blush, he says, and she laughs heartily.

Who is the innocent one now, Magister Falck?

When she sneaks up to his room in the evenings, presumably with her sisters' knowledge, she insists they enter the roles she has devised for them. They play the mad King Christian and his prostitute mistress Støvlet-Cathrine. They play brothel. She commands him to treat her badly and to pay for her humiliations with a few meagre coins. He plays along, and yet he is unnerved. Perhaps it is not men's lust that is the worst, he thinks to himself.

†

At the end of August he moves into a small room in the attic of the Seminarium Groenlandicum. He writes a letter to Abelone by which he breaks the betrothal. *My dear Abelone, my heart, friend of my soul, love of my life!* It is no easy letter to compose. *Our visit to Nakskov prompted me to look into the future*, he writes. *And there I saw that whether I content myself as a rural provost or else follow a call to the colonies of Greenland, what we have enjoyed together will be destroyed for always. It will destroy you, as it will destroy me. I have not the heart for such, my beloved Abelone. Let us therefore be parted, so that what we are may continue to be, and our love be preserved in its original form.*

He details the tribulations life in a Greenlandic colony will impose. It is no place for a young woman of her fine standing, a place in which the worst of vices flourish and where the majority of those who venture there succumb to cold and sickness. He cannot defend it. *The scurvy, Abelone. Alas, to see you removed of your sparkling white teeth. The mere thought of it is more than an honest man can bear!*

It pains him to write such a letter, which he composes in a serving house in Vestergade, drinking several mugs of ale as he ponders. The headache with which he awakes the next morning is not caused by drunkenness. He knows, of course, that the explanations he has proffered are but claims and poor excuses. He cannot fathom why he is so unable to marry her. All he knows is that he does not desire it. Yet to state as much would be unthinkable.

Some days later he receives a frosty letter of business from Schultz. The printer makes it clear that while fully entitled to pursue the breach legally, he has for the sake of his daughter's reputation, which already is tarnished by Falck's treachery, as well as in concern for her weakened state in general, decided to let the matter pass. *In the expectation of the Magister that he repair from the countenance of my family, and preferably as soon as possible travel to the far and frigid place in which he intends to work, I remain his respectfully, Thøger Schultz, Printer.*

The unfriendly letter lifts his spirits. It is a liberation, a clear signal that opens up the gates of his life, much like those that allow a person out of a plague-ridden city into the open countryside and fresh air.

But Miss Schultz will not permit him to retreat so easily. She manages to find him, and in the middle of a lesson in which he is receiving instruction in the Greenlandic affixes, she bursts in and announces in the presence of all the alumni: Morten Falck, you lecher! You owe me five rigsdalers for having lain with me!

The classroom is deathly silent. The remaining Greenlandic affixes are scattered to the floor and the only thing to be heard is old Egede's nervous titter.

Miss Schultz . . . what kind of garb is this? says Morten, staring in bewilderment. He has risen to his feet. Abelone is clad in a loose, pleated, gaudy dress with train, cut low to make her bosom swell. Her shoulders are bare, her hair let down, and in her hand she awkwardly grips a little parasol that rests against her shoulder. You look like a woman of the street!

He receives a triumphant smile in return.

Egede ushers them into his office and leaves them to their own devices. Morten hears him chuckle and click his tongue as he returns to the classroom. Abelone flops down on a chair, abandons her parasol and bursts into tears. I just wanted to show you I'll do anything for you, she sobs. If I can shame myself in front of a whole audience of priests, then I can surely accompany you to the furthest corner of the world, don't you see? She weeps. She wrings her hands. Take me with you. Let me be your companion, Morten. I have said I will go with you anywhere in the world, have I not?

Indeed.

Then let me go with you, my dearest. I can be a good friend and a faithful wife. I can teach the children of the savages. We can keep each other company in the dark nights and read Rousseau.

Impossible. The rules do not allow accompanying spouses.

Do you remember the summer? Do you remember how you ran after me, the way you bundled me to the ground and took me by force? And then ever since, have we not had fun together? What we have shown and confided to each other cannot be given to anyone else. It will be lost if we are no longer together, can't you see? Lost for always.

He considers her. She extends a hand, a leather glove. He accepts it reluctantly, feels her fingers through the material, the softness of her flesh, the bones. He lets go again. He is embarrassed by what has happened, the thought of what the other alumni will say, and when his eyes meet hers he can tell that she knows what he is thinking.

It is you who are narrow-minded, she says. You think only of your reputation. How will you fare among the savages, Morten? You will perish from shame at what they will do to you.

Yes, he says, perhaps you are right. And for that reason I attend the seminary here, to prepare for life among the savages.

I can be your own little native, she says eagerly, her tone altered at once. I can be as wild as the savages, if only you allow me the chance.

I know you, he says. I know what you are. You are a good and gentle girl of fine standing. Savagery is but a game for you.

And for you! We are alike, even if you refuse to admit it. I understand you. Perhaps I would have done the same if I were a man. But we can liberate ourselves from it all. We can be free together.

You are young, he says. You will mature and change. Such is life. I am ten years older than you. I know what I am doing.

And this has only just dawned on you?

Her words are almost a scream.

Your father has written to me, he says with hard-won composure that must appear stony to her, which is his intention. I think it hardly likely that he would deliver you into my charge.

Indeed, he is angry. Furious. He took his sabre and thrashed at a chair until the stuffing flew in the air, and said, Look, here is your theologian! A smile appears amid the tears; she sniffles and lets out a giggle. But I don't care. I want to go with you, if you will have me. You can do with me as you wish, anything at all. When do you think you will receive such an offer again, Magister Falck?

How will you get a passport to board the ship? You are not yet of age.

Practical matters! Of no importance! We bribe the captain with my dowry. Take me with you!

No.

Do you not love me any more? She extends her hand again, but this time he does not accept it.

This is leading nowhere.

Some floorboards creak in the corridor. He hears muffled voices, as though in everyday conversation, sounds from the street, the sounds of a sunny day. A shaft of golden light falls upon Egede's desk. He sees that the shadow cast by the quills in his pen holder have moved the breadth of a finger since he sat down with Miss Schultz. She sits diagonally opposite him, a theatrical harlot. She cries quietly, blinking her eyes, tears streaming down the sides of her nose, halted briefly by the down of her upper lip, which also is made golden by the sun, then to release and fall onto her exposed bosom, where they trickle and dry. She ignores them. She wrings her hands.

I shall take my life, she says faintly. I know where my mother keeps her laudanum.

He sits quite still. Go now, he thinks to himself.

I can have you prosecuted, she says.

I know. You have the power to destroy me.

My sisters know. They know everything. They can give sworn statements.

Yes.

My father's staff know, too. I'm certain of it. They can bear witness against you. And then you will be neither a priest nor a missionary, unless you wish to preach in the gaol.

No.

She looks up and their eyes meet. How calm you are, Morten. How can you be so calm?

I place my fate in your hands, he says, unperturbed.

At long last, she takes a handkerchief and wipes her eyes, dabs her cheeks and bosom. She sniffles once or twice. I am glad to have come to speak with you one last time.

Yes, I too, in spite of the circumstances. I am sorry. Forgive me.

She looks up at him briefly and winces. I shall not forget you and I will not hate you. You cannot make me hate you. I shall keep what is ours inside my heart and cherish it. No one can take that from me, not even you.

Thank you.

She rises to her feet; he likewise. They stand before each other. They shake hands, she turns and leaves the office in a rustle of tulle.

Shortly afterwards Egede's face appears in the doorway. He wears a crafty smile.

Oh dear, Magister Falck, I fear you have missed your affixes!

†

He receives the call to Sukkertoppen in January of 1787, half a year before he is to leave. Egede takes him under his wing. They stroll in the garden of the seminary. Egede tells him of his experiences in Greenland, of his father and mother and siblings, of the sly and sullen heathens, of his childhood in Lofoten. They converse in Norwegian. Egede is proud of his Norwegian and Morten has not the heart to tell him it hardly resembles the language at all.

He meets one of Schultz's print workers in a serving house and learns that Miss Schultz has suffered a breakdown and become worryingly ill. The man does not know her illness, but the mistress has been taken from the city in a weakened state, apparently to some family in the country. They say she is not right in the head, the worker whispers. She called herself Støvlet-Cathrine and was improper towards us in the printing shop, tore her clothes to tatters in everyone's presence, we had to hold her still until Madame Schultz came and put a blanket around her. The man shakes his head. I can't forget the sight of her loveliness, so pure and fresh, and then the madness in her eyes. I can't put it from my mind. Was the Magister not betrothed to the young mistress?

It fell through, says Morten.

Oh, I see. How sad, says the man. But such a madwoman could never make a pastor's wife, it stands to reason. *Skål*, Mr Falck!

Man is Free!

(June–August 1787)

Morten Falck steps down into a ship's boat at the Toldboden to be rowed through the forest of masts to the roadstead that is the Rheden. He stands erect in the stern. He is thirty-one, has belonged to the city for almost exactly five years, has become a part of it and it a part of him. The sea air wraps around him. He is leaving. He does not know if he will ever see the city again. He does not know if he will survive the journey. He feels exhilarated and strong.

The boat comes alongside a ship, and he is ushered up a rope ladder. A hand reaches down from the bulwark. He takes it and swings his leg over the gunwale to stand on the deck of the brig *Der Frühling*. The weather is clear, though here on the water the air has a chill. The sun is above Amager, twinkling in the swell of the sound. The wind makes the masts creak and click and rushes in the rigging, its tone an ebb and flow. The ship strains at its anchor rope; the keel groans. From the main mast waves the double-pointed swallowtail flag that bears the emblem of the Royal Greenland Trade, two crossed harpoons. He turns and takes it all in with his eyes. It is quickly done. His environment these next six to ten weeks is captured in a single glance.

A seaman shows him to his cabin below deck. The ship is a former whaler fitted out for the route to Greenland, which is to say to withstand drifting ice, to carry a small number of passengers as well as goods to the colony, and to bring home raw materials and barrels filled with train oil.

His fellow passenger on the voyage is a cook bound for Godthåb. The cabin is a cubbyhole containing a stool, a hinged table that may be raised or dropped, and a bunk whose bedding is a mattress of straw.

Would there be anything else, learned magister? the seaman enquires. Can I bring you something? A blanket?

This will be fine, thank you. I have my own blankets.

And unlike yours, they are free of lice, he thinks to himself. But the mattress is undoubtedly alive with all manner of vermin and he considers it will be a battle against superior forces to endeavour to keep them from his person. Thus, he will not waste energy on what cannot be changed, but instead concentrate on what perhaps might. It is something Egede has impressed upon him, the first rule of the missionary.

The man bows and withdraws. Morten looks about. The cabin is neat and clean. Hm, he had prepared himself for a pigsty. Regrettably, it is without a source of natural light. The place will be too dim for him to remain undisturbed in his cabin to commit his observations, he assesses, and he will therefore be obliged to do so in the open. He is unwilling to ruin his good eyesight by the poor glow of a lamp or tallow candle. But so much the better! Of necessity comes virtue, and with virtue unexpected gifts will often follow. He can look forward to lots of fresh sea air.

He tests the bunk, then seats himself on the stool and examines the mattress, prodding gently. The lice seep forth like water. He withdraws his hand in a hurry. Here I must sleep, he thinks with a shudder.

He raises the table and presses down on it with caution. The leaf yields perilously. He must keep his books in stacks on the floor. The table is unfit for writing. Never mind! Reading and contemplation will be on the deck and in the bunk, as the case may be. He is vexed for a moment by the cabin not being as he had expected, but then he dismisses it from his mind.

He goes up on deck to make sure his travelling chests are brought safely on board. And then there is the matter of the particular conveyance for which he has been obliged to purchase an additional passage from his own pocket, the greater part of his savings, as if it were a passenger like himself. Which in a way it is. It should be here presently, sailing on a barge from Kastrup by a farmer and his two sons. Morten looks out to the south-east, but the many ships at anchor obstruct his view. This is what he is most anxious about. Not the seasickness or the scurvy, nor the danger of drowning, or sea monsters, pirates or the many other perils of the ocean. He is most concerned that his precious cargo will not arrive in time.

He crawls over luggage and sacks, barrels, bundles of clothing and coils of rope to stand in the bow and crane his neck, then negotiates further obstacles until at the quarterdeck, where the bustle is less pronounced, and positions himself at the wheelhouse. The ship's wheel is lashed to a number of wooden dowels. He sees the ropes by turn become tense and then release as the ship strains nervously. Captain Valløe, a clean-shaven, corpulent man in a uniform that defies exact specification, approaches and greets him heartily.

Magister Falck!

He nods.

Has the Magister received his cargo?

Not as yet. But my chests are being loaded, I see. Is the ship fully manned?

All bar my first mate. He's dashing about to have the last of the documents stamped. We shall set sail early this afternoon, I imagine.

It looks like she is impatient to depart. Morten Falck points at the wheel that strains at its mooring.

We all are, Mr Falck. The sea calls.

Hm, he says, and thinks: Such banality! How is the wind?

The wind is good. The wind is as the wind should be. We're nearly fully laden and await only the Magister's companion. He smiles wryly, puts his hand to his hat and straightens it.

I'm certain she is on her way, he says. Perhaps the captain might send a man up in the mast to see?

Captain Valløe ignores his request. He stands before him with a silent grin on his face. Then, after a moment: What does the Magister want with a cow in Greenland?

A milch cow, he corrects him. A Holstein.

Such a beast will piss and shite, says the captain in his accent, whose hard g's and d's and open vowel sounds indicate that he is of German descent. It'll have to be kept alive and have its muck shovelled. I'm not keen on my ship being turned into a floating cowshed.

I shall be dealing with these things myself, Morten replies. He needs only sail his ship.

The captain looks at him along the length of his pipe stem. Do you know about such matters?

I was brought up in the country. However, I know nothing of maritime travel and will confidently leave that in the hands of my good and capable captain.

The captain has several objections. He believes that if there were any advantage in shipping farm animals to Greenland, then his hold ought to be filled with them, and yet he has never seen as much as a cat in those climes. And how does he intend to keep it fed?

Hay and straw, says Morten. We shall bring with us compressed fodder with which to feed the animal.

A shipload of hay? says the captain. And where might this be kept?

On deck, he says. Where the cow, too, will have its place.

It'll be salty hay it'll munch, says the captain.

Morten Falck is fully aware that his plan is not without its weaknesses. Thus, in order to avoid further questions of a practical nature, such as what the cow is to drink, a matter to which he has forgotten to attend, he leaves the captain's presence and goes to direct the loading of one of his travelling chests. The trunk is too big for his cabin, so, after he has removed some items he needs for his journey, the crew carry it into the hold. He lies down to read and keeps the door open at the foot end of the bunk so that some light may enter.

A little later he hears cries at the side of the ship. The folk from Amager with his cow. They have brought with them broad leather straps to place under the belly of the animal and appear to be reassuringly used to shifting cattle in such manner. Two boats accompany them, fully laden with bales of hay and straw. Five seamen haul the cow on to the deck, where it lies and tosses its head a moment, though otherwise turns not a hair at its treatment. Morten pays the peasants the skillings owed and leads the cow to its place amidships. A makeshift byre is erected around the animal from the straw bales once they have arrived on board. It looks bizarre and gives rise to jocular comments from the crew, but seems to work well enough. Rope is lashed around the bales to keep the structure from blowing away. He spends a long time tethering and tightening. He keeps the leather straps, which he has purchased, and will use them to steady the beast in heavy sea, as well as to bring it ashore at their destination. He orders the bales of fodder for which there is no room on deck to be carried into the hold, much to the captain's annoyance. But he is allowed his way. He hopes they will be sufficient to sustain the cow for the duration of the passage. He stays with her, talks with her, feels to see if her muzzle is moist. A healthy creature. He knows how to treat a cow and how to speak to them. He pulls on the hocks, nudges the animal gently, and within a moment it lies down obligingly, its belly swelling over the deck. It munches on some hay and descends into rumination while he stands and watches. All would seem well. A thought has become action. A cow to cross the North Atlantic. He puts his hands to his nose and sniffs. They smell of childhood.

They kept a small number of cows in the shed at home in Lier. He would go to them early in the morning if he could hear they were unsettled. He would find the milking girl seated with her brow against the belly of a cow, her pale feet buried in a heap of steaming dung she had shovelled together in order to keep them warm. Sluggish, binary spurts of milk striking the bottom of the bucket. His elongated shadow on the floor of the shed. The cows turning their heads, the girl turning hers, drowsy with sleep, strands of hair fallen down in front of her eyes.

Come here.

He steps closer.

Open your mouth.

He does so.

And then she would twist a teat and send a jet of warm, fatty milk in an upward-reaching arc into the air, and, if he was lucky, it would all be squirted into his mouth. The girl would laugh. Afterwards they drank themselves full of fresh cow's milk, sharing an udder and sucking until they could suck no more. If his father had found out he would have dealt a caning and the girl would perhaps have been sent away. Later, he realized the milk had most likely kept him from the deathbed in the parlour.

Roselil. He remembers her name all of a sudden. He thought of her as an adult, though she could hardly have been more than a year or two older than him. Dark as a raven and filthy dirty. A tinker, whatever that meant. The family had probably been itinerant pedlars or swindlers, who had left her there for a few years to be fattened up. Certainly, there was something foreign about her. She slept in a corner of the shed and often he crept out and lay down with her. She smelled sweetly of cow dung and buttery excretion, and of the lard she rubbed into her hands to stop the skin from cracking. Her skilled milking hands.

Then one day she was gone and he remembers how empty the place was then, despite other girls succeeding her, with wispy pigtails and silly faces and utterly vacant eyes. He cannot recall them individually, much less their names.

So he calls the cow Roselil. This mingling together of cow and human, of the affection he feels for the cow and that which he holds for the recollection of the milking girl, does not bother him. It is a matter of circumstance, the cow a living embodiment of a memory he respects and appreciates. He pats the animal, and when he sniffs his hand it smells of Roselil.

Shortly after, the first mate gives the order to raise anchor. The sails are hoisted. They unfurl brightly in the sunlight and catch the wind in a series of abrupt flaps. The ship heels slightly, they are on their way up through the sound. A representative of the Trade is to accompany them up the coast of Sjælland. Bottles are opened and a thick stew served in the mess. Later in the afternoon they reach Elsinore, where the representative is helped into a barge, roaring drunk and singing at the top of his voice. The crew stands at the bulwark and bids him farewell, whereupon he is rowed ashore, together with the pilot. The wind has dropped. They cast anchor to the north.

The days pass. The wind turns to the north-west and dies down again. The crew scrape and tar and carry out repairs to the ship both inside and out. Morten strolls in the town. He views the halls of the castle, eats his meals at an inn, walks down to the harbour, where the barge is moored, and is sailed out to the ship again. Life at sea is easy. Perhaps he should have sought a career in the navy? He reads his favourite works, pores over Bayle's lexicon and spells his way through a couple of articles in the French text, reads an issue of *Minerva* that bores him, re-reads Voltaire in the German translation, his preferred foreign language, and laughs heartily at the frightful adventures of the foolish *Candide*. But Rousseau remains his favourite author. *Man is born free and everywhere he is in chains!* These two main clauses continue to affect him deeply, the recognition of an *and* rather than a *but* to join them together. The two statements are in no way opposed. Man is born free. *And* he is in chains. He shudders with each reading.

Given his theories on man and nature, Rousseau, he considers, must be at least partly responsible for his present situation, beneath the deck of a small ship, on his way to a living as a missionary among savages. He yearns to meet people in their natural state, free and unspoiled. Perhaps also he yearns to find some natural state within himself.

One night he is awakened by unfamiliar movements of the ship, the crew bustling about on the deck above. He ascends and watches the lights of the pleasant town of Elsinore grow small in their wake. The captain is on the quarterdeck. The wind is with us! he exclaims and smiles, a corner of his mouth drawn askew by the stem of his pipe.

Ahead of them first is the Kattegat. The ship's deck becomes unsteady under Morten Falck's boots. He attends to the cow. It is lying down, munching. When he approaches, it turns its head and looks at him trustfully. She is a beautiful heifer with black-and-white markings and great, dark eyes. He smiles at her. The byre is clean but for some wet hay he can remove in the morning. On the foredeck he stands sheltered from the wind by the fore staysail and looks out to sea. Behind them, the past draws back into the darkness along with the last of the lights in Elsinore. Ahead is nothing, only the sounds of the sea and the wind. He feels like he has emerged from a great void and is on his way into one that is even greater.

He milks the cow each morning, when the sea is usually calm. Roselil seems to be well and gives a good yield of milk. No one, he considers, not even the sceptical captain, will deny that fresh milk is good for a man's stomach and frame of mind on a long sea journey, when ship's biscuits mould, meat barrels smell like latrine buckets, and the herring is alive with mites. He charges a sum for the milk he cannot drink himself, five skillings a half pint, and the crew pay willingly. They tease him with good-natured jibes and ask to what use the money might be put when they arrive? To frequent the Comedy House, perhaps? Or to purchase fine clothes? Or perhaps he intends to pay the savages to allow him to turn them towards the Christian faith? But the only thing that worries him is whether there will be sufficient fodder to keep the cow alive.

Each time he goes inside the byre to Roselil, she stamps her feet on the deck, turns her head and rolls her eyes. Are you glad to see me? he says and gives her a pat. The cow's devotion opens once again the old wound which he had forgotten, his loss of the dark-skinned tinker girl. He sits down on the stool, rests his brow upon the warm belly, pulls on the teats, two by two, and listens to the soothing squirts of milk, the sound gradually altering as the bucket fills. He is quite aware of what this action calls to mind and in part replaces. It is not something of which he is ashamed.

The crew have seen it, too. They call the cow the pastor's mistress, though plainly in jest.

They receive their daily cup of milk. The captain, who shows himself to be a good-humoured and convivial man, states appreciatively that it may be on account of the milk that so little sickness is with them on the voyage and that the crew are so content. As yet, not a single fist-fight has occurred, nor even a heated argument. He will speak to the ship owner on the matter, and perhaps a milch cow will soon be the custom on long sea voyages. But how will the poor creature fare when we reach the cold? he wonders.

We shall see, says Morten. However, it is my conviction that where people can live, so too can cattle, and where cattle cannot, people would do wise to avoid.

You may be on to something there, the captain mutters.

Late in the evening on the third day they pass Skagen on the port side. He stands and looks out towards the beacon of the vippefyr just south of Grenen, Jutland's northernmost tip. He remains for several hours until it vanishes from sight beyond the stern. Then the final scraps of land retreat into the darkness and they are alone. The wind from the Skagerrak strikes them like a punishing hand. They must beat to windward, causing the vessel to heel considerably. Roselil is unsettled. She tries to crawl up the slope of the deck, tossing her head. More than once she succeeds in bringing herself upright, only to fall back onto her belly again. He is helped by a seaman to secure the leather straps under her abdomen. He tightens them well, and they pat her soothingly and feed her with hay. Their efforts seem to alleviate much of her discomfort, though still she rolls her eyes in fear.

He, too, feels unwell. He is ravenously hungry, yet nauseous. His stomach swells, though he has eaten hardly a thing. He belches incessantly, but is unable to release at the other end, which he feels would be of some considerable relief. He sticks his fingers down his throat and spews bile. He drinks a little milk, which comes up again. He is ashamed of his condition, having felt assured that he could never succumb to seasickness. The crew slap him on the back and ask him how he is feeling. Fresh wind and salt on the lips becomes me well, he replies and staggers away.

I am aware that this will become worse than the present pitching and rolling, Morten says to the captain one day. But how much worse, I wonder?

My dear Magister, the captain replies with a smile. This is fair weather. Has he never sailed on the open sea?

I have sailed by the packet boat to Nakskov, he says, and once from Christiania to Copenhagen. I have experienced harsh weather in the bay of Køge Bugt. But I have never felt such unpleasantness as this.

This is neither Køge Bugt nor the packet boat to Nakskov, Magister. Ships go down each year on this route to Greenland.

I am informed of the dangers of the voyage. I am not afraid.

He ought to be. Most certainly. A prayer or two would do no harm.

Very well, he says. As soon as my constitution has returned, we shall say prayers in the forecastle.

†

The opportunity occurs only a couple of days later. He speaks of the Saviour's forty days in the desert without food or water, a fitting allegory, he considers, under the circumstances. The men thank him kindly when he is finished. They joke that the sun of the desert has done them good, and return to their work.

They are eating medister sausage with cabbage soup when the watch calls through the hatch that they are nearing the Norwegian coast. There is a rush on to the deck. Some dark rocks become visible in the grey and then Morten Falck sees farmhouses, open clearings in forest, clusters of sombre dwellings. He swallows. It looks not at all like his native Lier and yet a sudden surge of homesickness nearly causes him to burst into tears.

The captain decides that since the storm has blown them so far in to the coast they might as well take the opportunity to forage. They go ashore at a small settlement and spend a few days on land. Morten Falck purchases bales of hay and straw, and throws what is ruined over the side. He has barrels filled with fresh water especially for the cow. The crew are helpful, though he has to promise them free milk in payment. When night comes, he goes into the forest to sleep. One early morning he sits against a tree and seriously contemplates whether to be absent when *Der Frühling* sets sail again and instead settle once more in the country of his childhood. Such abrupt national sentiment catches him unawares, this pure-seeming fondness for moss-covered rocks, pine forest and dry stone walls, the embroidered garments of the peasants, and their dialect, regardless that it is so far from his own. The sound of cow and sheep bells in the forest. The feeling of pine needles between the fingers, and of sticky resin, its fresh and pungent odour. For a long time, ever since he was quite young, in fact, he has learned to think of himself as a privileged subject of King Christian and has not at any time questioned the matter. But I am not a Dane, he thinks to himself now. The thought of leaving the country again is dreadful, and yet he does. He tries to think of his sudden feelings on land as a fit brought on by seasickness and terror at the thought of being wrecked and drowned.

He sails out with the ship's boat and clambers aboard. He attends to Roselil, who munches on fresh grass and seems contented. Then he descends into his cabin and lies down to read. When he arises the next day the land has sunk into the sea. They continue towards north-west. He enquires of the first mate as to their position and route. The man takes him into the captain's saloon and spreads a chart out on the table. He takes care to explain. His finger draws a diagonal line upwards and to the left.

We'll sail here, to the fifty-ninth, he says, then follow the latitude in a westerly direction, cutting between the Orkneys and Shetland, continuing south of the Faroe Isles, if the wind and currents are willing to take us that way, to Staten Huch, here, his finger tapping at a headland, Greenland's southernmost point, which we'll sail close to or keep away from, depending on how the ice has pleased itself to lie this year.

Morten Falck goes down into his cabin and notes it in his diary.

His thoughts often dwell on the strongman von Eckenberg, although the reason eludes him. Indeed, there is much that catches up with him out here on the sea. He was young when he saw the strongman perform, sensitive and impressionable. Most likely he has forgotten the greater part of what he saw in the royal city at that time, or else he has seen

through it as but superficial, vacuous frills. But von Eckenberg remains
in his mind. He lies in his bunk in the creaking belly of the ship and
thinks of this modest gentleman with his mild countenance and brown,
mournful eyes, of how he meticulously waxed his twisted moustache
after each turn and stepped to the mirror to neaten himself undemon-
stratively. Occasionally, a strangely enchanted mood descended on
the audience – when he blew on his horn, when the musicians played
their minuet, when the stone slab split into two. This, Morten thinks to
himself, ought to be the effect of a priest upon his congregation. This is
how the savages will receive the Word, if I convey it to them as skilfully
as Master Eckenberg performed his tricks for pitiful convicts, seamen
and merchants. But am I a Master Eckenberg?

They sail in to the Shetland Isles and remain a few days in the bay
of a fishing community. Morten Falck grasps the opportunity to collect
fresh grass for Roselil. It is much needed, as the stock of hay has depleted
faster than he has calculated, and much of it is rotten on account of the
salt water. A cow can consume astonishing amounts, but on receiving
new and succulent fodder the animal descends into a vegetative state of
contented rumination. Her yield of milk has been on the decline, but
now she once more delivers nearly a whole bucket each day. The crew
tease him and complain that they have been cheated of the fresh steaks to
which they have looked forward to being served once he was compelled
to slaughter the beast.

A couple of days after setting sail again, the wind gathers, something
the captain had told him would happen sooner or later west of Scotland.
The waves loom tall, catching up with the ship from behind and swelling
past. It feels as if they are being sucked backwards, then forced into
the air, before the deck abruptly disappears beneath their feet. But the
captain is glad. The weather is with us, he says. If the wind remains
where it is, we shall be at our destination earlier than usual.

Or else at the bottom of the sea, Morten says to himself.

Der Frühling, a heap of mouldering, waterlogged oak from the forests
of Norway, with a ballast of wet sand whose nauseating smell seeps

throughout. The vessel is held together by a quarter Danish mile of rope, some thousands of wrought-iron nails, the pressure of the water against its sides, and the prayers and curses of its crew, among them Morten Falck. He curses and spews, spews and curses. Then one day he wipes his mouth and says the Lord's Prayer. He prays for forgiveness and absolution from his sins. Please do not let me die, Lord, without first having served Thee and atoned for my sins, committed in the wantonness of youth. Save me, Lord! Forgive my outrageous abandonment of Miss Schultz!

He knows it is imagination and hallucination, and yet it is as though the gusts of wind carry with them a fragrance of lavender.

He endeavours to read, but is overcome by nausea and feelings of guilt, and must leave his book until later. The oblong shape of the cabin and the sheer confinement of its space causes him to think he is lying in his coffin, about to be lowered into the grave. The rank smell of his own corpse sears in his nostrils. He hears the seamen shouting on deck and tilts himself out of the bunk to totter unsteadily into the air, only for them to usher him back below.

Down below, where you belong, priest!

He seats himself on the top stair and inhales fresh air through a crack in the door. It feels good. He hears Roselil lowing without abatement and thinks of how terrified she must be. But he cannot attend to her.

As the worst sea is upon them, his crisis ends. The seasickness is gone. He devours a large portion of dried fish, boiled with barley oats, is made deliriously thirsty by the salty meal and drinks several cups of the ship's beer, spews one final time and feels restored. The storm rages for a day, then dies down sufficiently for him to attend to the cow.

Roselil? He opens the gate into the makeshift byre and expects to find her dead or dying. She lies in her own filth, yet lifts her head to look at him as he steps inside. She stands up willingly to be milked, though her flesh trembles and she provides only half a bucket. Nevertheless, there seems to be little wrong with her. He mucks out and washes her, rubbing vigorously with a rag of linen. She settles and sighs contentedly in sleep. He takes his blanket and sleeps next to her. Stars and a violet night sky are visible between the masts.

The sea remains troubled. *Der Frühling* meets the waves as they rise before her bows, mounts them, rolls over their crests or else remains suspended within an elastic duration of time that is drawn out or squeezed together, at once compressed and elongated, eternal and momentary, then to emerge as the swell crashes down upon her decks, the sea breaking open to spew out its foam, rushing away over the sides and surging into her wake. The ship wrenches itself free and steers towards the next wave with the deepest of groans from its hull or masts. The cow lifts its head and lows.

The *Frühling* loves the sea, says one of the men. That's why she pitches the way she does.

Morten regards him with puzzlement.

She wants her nose into every hole, says the seaman.

The weather calms. Morten feels he has been on the breaking wheel for a month. An icy rain drums against the deck and will not be stopped by the good leather coat he wears, but continues through his clothing, pointed diagonals of cold that pierce the skin like small projectiles. He spends much time with Roselil, dries and warms her with blankets, rubs her hide, feeds her fresh hay. She still provides milk, though the yield has diminished. He no longer demands payment for the milk the crew receive, but reserves two cups a day for himself, heats it up, adds aquavit and drinks the mixture while it is still scalding.

Then the rain turns to snow. Midsummer snow! The captain announces that they now follow the sixtieth and presumably have the Faroe Islands on starboard. But the snow falls so thickly they can hardly see the point of the jib boom.

You'll have to take my word for it, says the captain.

With the snow the air becomes milder, or at least feels as such. Whether it is true or not, the cold no longer goes to the marrow. Roselil has also settled and gives more milk. But the deck is covered in slippery slush that makes moving about perilous to any man's life. He spends many hours each day in the mess, where a lamp swings from the ceiling and a stove burns. He reads his Voltaire, his Bayle, German poetry, some Montaigne and Rousseau. He sleeps a lot and the more he sleeps, the greater becomes his fatigue. Time is frivolous and unreliable. He blinks his eyes twice and half a day has passed. His entire childhood and the years in Copenhagen swirl by, scene by scene, and half an hour has idled away. He begins to wander, from bow to stern, from port to starboard. He abandons himself to the peripatetic joys in which he so delighted in Copenhagen.

The crew grow mad at this wandering priest who insists on making use of the ship in all its length and breadth, which is to say one hundred times twenty-five feet. One hundred ship-lengths are thus the equivalent of some half mile, he tells the captain, which is the minimum a grown man should commit himself to walking each day if he is to maintain a healthy constitution and keep ever-encroaching melancholy at bay during a long sea voyage.

If the Magister falls overboard, it will not be beneficial to his constitution, says the captain, even less for good humour, be it the Magister's own or anyone else's. A ship is not a place for strolling. Can he imagine the men going about like that?

He asks permission to climb the rigging.

Mind he doesn't fall down and do his learned self a mischief, says the first mate, and laughs.

He clambers up the shroud of the mizzen, straddles the top and wedges himself between backstays and mast. But the sails obstruct his view and the danger of falling down constrains his movement. He realizes the deck is the better place. Besides, there is nothing to spy, other than the monotonous sea and the no less monotonous sky above it. He remains in the rig for some time until he feels discomfort in his groin from the narrow top on which he sits, and climbs down.

†

The weather improves. He spends most of his days seated at the deck hatch, making notes for a treatise on the satisfaction of physical and spiritual needs on long sea journeys. He intends to send the work, if ever it is complete, to a magazine such as Mr Lyne Rahbek's *Minerva*, an enlightened libertarian publication, if regrettably rather dull. He believes it will make instructive reading for travellers unfamiliar with the sea, and begins to draw up a list comprising two columns of healthy and detrimental aspects of life on board a ship. Clean air, he writes in the first column. Peace in which to write and philosophize. Satisfaction of natural curiosity. Comradeship. Learning to live frugally. He moves the pen to the column on the right, ponders a moment, then scribbles what enters his mind: Drowning. Scurvy. Spiritual sloth. He puts down his pen and paper, presses the bung into the ink pot and stares out at the horizon. There are things a man yearns for while at sea, things that cannot be written about, unless for initiated eyes only, but which any reader cannot help but think upon when reading an article concerning privation on sea journeys. Lack of female company, he then writes in the right-hand column. Lecherous thoughts. Self-abuse and, even worse, inappropriate relations with members of the crew.

Morten Falck has thought frequently of the hermaphrodite Gypsy boy while he has been patrolling the ship. The cabin boy is approximately the same age, run away to sea after his confirmation, though not an orphan, but from an impoverished environment somewhere in Jutland, so Morten has learned. He often sits opposite him when the men are gathered to eat in the mess, where the mizzen mast creaks and groans in its cylinder. His gaze meets the boy's across the soup, he smiles at him and the boy smiles back. The freckled and pimply face of the adolescent sticks out among the weather-beaten seamen. They make him blush with their stories, but Morten notes that the boy's presence also makes the men feel embarrassed. When they look at him they begin to boast and exaggerate, behaviour to which they are otherwise disinclined. They tell boisterous tales of escapades at sea and conquests on land.

When Morten Falck sits with Roselil, at her milking or merely keeping the ailing beast company, the boy often appears in the byre and offers to muck out. Morten gives him a cup of milk. My father had a cow, the boy tells him. It had no name, but I called her Karoline. A pretty name, says Morten. I call mine Roselil.

May I call her Roselil, too? the boy asks.

Of course you may. It's her name.

Is it her real name?

What do you mean?

What you're called is what you are.

And what are you? asks Morten Falck.

Carl Asger, the boy replies solemnly. My name's in a book.

†

A number of the men have never been to Greenland. There is talk about the natives and what they might expect. It is the captain's twelfth voyage across the fjord, as he rather boastfully refers to it. The savages are decent enough folk, he says at the dinner table. More decent than many of the white people there, I can attest to that. But some of their habits are disgusting and abhorrent. They wash in their own filth and eat rotten meat.

Like us, says one of the crew, holding up a mouldy green slice of pork. The men laugh.

But they like it, says the captain. They don't use salt to preserve their meat. They prefer it rotten. The worse it smells, the better.

One man asks about the föhn winds of which he has heard terrible stories.

What are föhn winds? asks another.

Warm winds from the south, says the captain and releases a squealing fart.

The men roar with laughter. Morten Falck looks down into his pea soup. Something is moving about in it. A dung beetle, fighting for its life: he sees the flailing legs. He assumes it to have landed there by accident, perhaps on account of greed, and now it struggles so as not to drown in the same substance on which it intended to gorge. He fishes it out with his spoon, then hesitates, not knowing what to do with it. The insect solves the problem itself by springing down and scuttling across the table, where a seaman's hand squashes it flat.

They say the savages can kill a white man with their farts, says the ship's boy.

The captain replies solemnly: So very true, my boy. I've seen it with my own eyes.

The men around the table gape in anticipation.

One of my hands, says the captain, Iver, his name was. God rest his soul. He put his face too close to the backside of one of their women, and she bent over and blew the head off the poor man.

The ship's boy pales. The men fall about laughing and thrash their spoons on the tabletop.

Why did she do that? asks the ship's boy.

You see, boy, the native women are not to be trifled with. They will eat a lad such as yourself for breakfast. But you've no need to be afraid. I can outfart even the strongest of savages. He lifts his arse and lets out a thundering wind. The men roar still louder, tossing back their heads and hooting, howling at the ceiling like wolves and stamping on the floor in their heavy boots.

Thank you for the meal, says Morten Falck, and goes up on to the deck. He hears the mirth continue below. Shortly after, the boy comes and sits down beside him on the hatch.

You shouldn't believe everything they tell you, says Morten Falck.

I find it exciting, says the boy. I know they're only stories, but they're exciting anyway. When I get home, it'll be me telling far-fetched tales.

The deck inclines to starboard, the bow chops calmly through the oncoming waves. Tiny showers of atomized sea water pass over them and cling to their clothing.

She doesn't care for the swell, says the boy with a nod towards Roselil. Should I go in and keep her company?

Let's go together.

When they are sat with the ruminating cow, the boy asks: Does the pastor receive confessions?

We held a service and confessed our sins at the outset of the voyage, he says. Did you not take part?

Yes. The boy avoids his gaze.

Then why do you wish to confess now?

If something new happens, does the old confession still count?

On the ship, you mean?

I sin every day, says the boy. With the cook. We share a bunk, as the pastor knows. It's my fault. I make him lustful. But I don't know if it's wrong enough to have to confess to a priest.

Morten Falck says nothing. He does not desire to listen.

The cook calls me a wanton little devil, even if I don't much care for it, says the boy, and downs his cup of milk. But he says he can tell I like it, I can't run away from that. He has told the carpenter. And now Jensen wants me in his bunk as well. They fight about me.

Morten Falck gets to his feet. Say your Lord's Prayer and trust in God, he mumbles, and returns to his cabin.

†

In storms the crew go about the deck like ghosts. They bend their necks against the wind and rain, the sleet and the ice, and work stoically in the manner of sleepwalkers. He hears them talk behind the bulkhead when he lies in the cubbyhole of his cabin, though never are their voices laughing, nor do they sing, which he would have thought was in the seaman's nature. To bawl out shanties in season and out. The only one among them who occasions to sing is the ship's boy, pious popular ballads from his native home or psalms, sometimes an endless satirical song from a broadsheet, entire novels in verse. His voice is dainty and he has a good ear. The men hang upon his lips as he sings. And all the time the ship keeps its course along the sixtieth latitude towards worse and colder weather.

After a storm the sky unfolds above the ship, as blue as royal porcelain. The air grows cold and still, exceptionally cold for the time of year, with frost in the night. The crew is sent into the rigging to chop ice. A pale yellow moon wanders its curved path across the colour spectrum, from violet to blue-green to orange to red. The sails flap in the lazy yet freezing gusts that send showers of ice on to the deck from shrouds and rigging. Morten remains standing, impervious to the frozen shards that rain from above. He abandons himself to quiet mortification of the flesh and daydreams of the place to which he is bound, and the one from which he came. He learns to appreciate the bitter wind that buffets his chest.

An atmosphere of sexual excitement arises on board, triggered by the circumstance that the ship's boy is now passed around among members of the crew. He seems to have become aware of the effects at his disposal, Morten muses, albeit he is unable to control them. Arguments flare, fistfights loom, tin mugs and plates fly through the air. The mood at table is leadened by poisonous insinuation and lowered eyes. Tales of farting are no more. Only the ship's boy seems happy. He takes liberties, shirks his work, teases the men and makes inappropriate innuendos. Morten knows that it is his duty as ship's pastor to bring him to reason, but he considers his words will make no difference. He is weak, he knows he is weak, he permits himself to be weak. In the night he hears stifled cries and laughter from other parts of the ship. He pulls his coat over his head and tries to sleep.

One day of wind and rain he hears a commotion on deck. Running and shouting, the tolling of the ship's bell. He ascends the stair and sees some of the men standing at the portside bulwark. He approaches as the ship's rowing boat is put into the waves and four men man the oars. They do not row far. A pair of ship-lengths and they retrieve something from the water and haul it aboard. They return to *Der Frühling* and the boy is pulled on to the deck. He lies motionless on his back, mouth gaping, arms splayed to the sides. The men gather around him. They stand in their heavy boots. Now they are calmed. They have regained their dignity. Morten crouches down and puts his hand to the boy's chest, then places his ear to it and listens, his fingers feeling at the artery of the neck. He gets to his feet and shakes his head. Someone tosses a sweater over the boy's face.

It began early this morning, the first mate tells him. The boy behaved like an unruly child at breakfast, commenting obscenely upon his shipmates and flicking lumps of porridge at them from his spoon. The cook lost his temper and lashed out at the boy with his ladle, striking him on the side of the head. The boy screamed and called him a lecher and worse, whereafter he ran up to the deck, the cook after him with his ladle. They chased around the ship until the boy climbed the main mast with the cook on his heels, balanced his way out along the yard like a tightrope walker, and when the cook refused to retreat but crawled out after him, he plunged into the waves and was gone. A time passed before he floated to the surface.

Now perhaps we can find peace to sail the ship, says the first mate, and spits into the sea. A dirty strumpet like that has no place on a vessel.

In the afternoon the captain asks him to manage the funeral. He has been sitting in his cubbyhole, trying to read. Now he ascends to the deck. The weather has turned and is clear and still. The ship's carpenter is at work knocking together a coffin, instead of the burial shroud more normally appointed to shipboard deaths. The young boy will be sent off well and good, he says, so they can be sure he does not remain on board. He drills a number of holes in the lid so that the coffin cannot stay afloat. He smiles at Morten Falck. He sticks a finger in one of the holes and winks at him with a grin on his face.

Presently, some of the men carry the boy out, clad in the same clothes in which he drowned, and place the body in the narrow casket with sacks filled with lead weights. The coffin is lowered into the rowing boat that lies chopping at the ship's side. Morten Falck climbs down after it with his Bible in his hand and remains standing erect as the seamen row away. Some hundred ells from the ship they pull in their oars and raise them aloft. They fix their eyes expectantly on Morten Falck. The waves glug beneath the keel. The coffin rocks with the movement of the boat. The wind rushes between the blades of the oars.

Morten Falck clears his throat. Almighty God, he pronounces with vigour, but finds that the open space and exposure to the elements in the little boat causes his words to swirl away and become almost inaudible. He raises his voice. Father of our Lord Jesus Christ, we hereby commend unto Thee Carl Asger Jørgensen as we commit his body to the deep. The Lord bless him and keep him. May his demise serve to remind us all, we who remain in sin, to reflect upon our own death and to prepare our house. For the sea shall give up her dead and they shall be delivered unto their judgement, as they themselves shall be permitted, each and every one, to make their grievance. Amen. He reaches into his pocket and retrieves the handful of soil the captain has given him for the purpose, and casts it on to the coffin. From dust thou hast come.

But when he has rattled off his words, they continue to look encouragingly upon him.

What now?

Usually we sing when one of us is committed to the waves, says one of the men. Perhaps the Magister would sing one of Kingo's lovely hymns?

He chooses 'Vain World, Fare Thee Well'. His voice is strong, but he is no practised singer. The seamen join in, their crisp voices drifting out across the sea. *Lord Jesus shall shine as my sun every day, in heaven for aye.*

The coffin is manoeuvred carefully over the side. They shove it away with their oars, remain seated and watch. Morten Falck stands upright. The coffin heels slightly. But it does not sink. One of the men curses.

That bugger, the carpenter. I'll drill holes in him when we get back on board.

There's not enough lead in it, says another. We should have given the lad a cannonball between his legs. It would have been fitting.

The coffin drifts to sea, away from the boat. They pursue it, prodding with their oars, trying to force it to sink, only to see it bob up again and continue valiantly on its way.

Let Jørgensen sail his own boat, says the man from before. He's welcome, the poor lad.

Back on the ship, the men and the carpenter squabble. Their bickering swells this way and that and they come perilously close to blows. Eventually the captain intervenes and calm is restored.

Morten Falck spends some quiet days sitting with Roselil. He leans his forehead against the warmth of the cow's belly, which bubbles and seethes disturbingly from eating fermented hay. The dwindling stocks of fodder and water concern him, too. He drinks some milk, but finds it tastes of salt. It is not a good sign. He enquires of the captain as to the possibility of having her brought beneath deck, but Valløe refuses.

We've had muck enough down below.

The still weather continues. It gets on the seamen's nerves and makes the captain irritable. The cook has retired to his bunk with a bad stomach and the carpenter has descended into the hold, where he entrenches himself and refuses to come out until the ship reaches land. The rigging is filled to the last jib and yet the vessel rocks gently on the sea with no forward movement.

On the third day of the same weather someone shouts from the mast. He has seen something on the port side. The first mate studies the object in his telescope.

It's Jørgensen, he says. The lad won't let us get away.

The carpenter is plainly drinking himself into the grave down in the hold. He bellows out hymns, hurls bottles that shatter against the wall, and emits long and lamenting howls. Morten Falck descends and speaks to the man through the barricaded hatch of the hold. For his effort he receives invective, yelled in a voice demonically inebriated. Morten Falck refers the content of this exchange to the captain, who curses and orders the crew to break down the hatch and bring the bloody coffinmaker out so that they might deliver to him the thrashing he ought to have received from his mother. Four men go down and return shortly after with the man in their charge. They douse him with buckets of seawater, whereafter he is lashed to the mast.

First problem solved, the captain mutters, and lights his pipe. Now for the next.

He fetches his flintlock and loads it, then wants to know if the unfortunate ship's boy is still in sight. The first mate points to the port side, where the coffin is seen bobbing on the water. The captain nestles the firearm in the hollow of his shoulder, aims and delivers a round. He hands the weapon to the boatswain, who reloads and hands it back. The captain repeats the procedure a number of times. Eventually he takes the telescope from the first mate and looks through it for perhaps a minute.

That's the second, he mutters, and returns to his cabin.

†

In the evening a pale and composed carpenter eats with the rest of the crew. No mention is made of the deceased. The captain announces that in spite of several days in the doldrums the vessel has reached the thirty-fifth longitude and that an area of low pressure is on its way from the south-west. If not, he will eat his hat. They may expect to round the cape of Staten Huch within a couple of days. He places the aquavit on the table and tells them that if they wish to drink to do it now, though the carpenter can keep his hands to himself.

They drink. And Morten drinks with them.

In the night he senses life in the ship. He sits up, careful not to strike his head against the ceiling. But there is no ceiling. His hands fumble and find straw. He opens his eyes and sees the cow next to him. He must have lain down here in a state of drunkenness. He totters, stiff-legged, from the byre and notes that the sails are taut and filled by south-westerly wind. *Der Frühling* heels and makes good headway. Roselil wakes and lows. He crawls back into the byre and speaks comfortingly to her. The captain puts his head in and says that now they had better make sure to hoist the beast below before she is washed from the deck.

Two days later, in the afternoon, he hears cries and hastens to the deck. The boatswain stands pointing into the fog. A dark and looming density has emerged. The sea sounds different. Breakers at the shore, says the boatswain. Morten Falck stands for a long time, staring into the haze. He smells seaweed. A cloud of gulls swirls around the masts. He sees eider-fowl in plough formation appear and vanish among tall and foaming waves. But there is hardly a wind. Nevertheless, they sail at speed. Several knots, says the boatswain, and conditions are with them. The current is northerly and strong. A cliff comes into sight and retreats again. Some snow. Tufts of grass. It makes him strangely wistful.

Greenland!

†

At the cape the wind becomes a hurricane and all hatches are battened down. He is compelled to remain in his bunk, since no one is allowed on deck without express permission. He is buffeted back and forth between the bulkhead and the planks of his bed. When he wishes to sleep he must call on a crew member to lash him down with a rope of hemp, and he is exhausted enough to close his eyes now and then for an hour.

Time unfolds like a serpent, flicks its tail and curls up like a cat, distance is abolished, space consumes itself only to emerge again, over and over, dreams repeating in endless loops, fast-slow-fast, then are absorbed into crystal-clear moments of awakening, a soup of conscious-ness sloshing back and forth inside the cabin. One of the crew looks in on him, shakes his head and laughs, hands him a bowl of porridge with sugar and butter and forces him to eat. His inner fluids find a level. He hauls himself along the corridor, where salt water rains in from the hatches and the floor is awash with the slippery sea, to the bucket on which he crouches to empty his bowels, then hauls himself back to his bunk. He stares drowsily at the lamp that swings from its hook in the ceiling, squeaking out its sharp, thin discord. It is the Devil himself, scratching on a pane with long, yellowed nails. He sees his mischievous, malicious eye cast a sideways glance at him. He leaps from his bed, tries to walk, but strikes his head against a beam, his knee against an edge, and returns to his bunk. His legs feel as if they are melting away like hot tallow. He collects himself, forces himself to be sick and watches his vomit drift like thick plasma across the floor. He feels slightly better. He sits up. He stands. He lies down. He goes to attend to Roselil.

She is tethered in the hold and lies trembling with cold and seasickness, coated in excrement. She turns a weary, sallow eye towards him as he approaches. She no longer has the strength to low. Long, viscous drools hang from her muzzle. He is overwhelmed with sympathy and the emotion restores him somewhat. He sits with her, indifferent to her excretions soiling his clothes. She turns her head towards him in gratitude as he pats her and speaks. Roselil, he whispers, Roselil, Roselil. He rubs her muck-encrusted belly and udder to make her settle. Some drops of milk seep from inside her. He tries to squeeze out some more, but she has stopped producing. Muscles and fat have retracted, ribs protrude, skin hangs loose. But his hands bring comfort. He feels his own body relax. He sleeps a while.

And then he is back in his cabin, which creaks and heels like scenery in a theatre imitating a vessel in distress. A new bowl of porridge is brought to him. He eats, then dozes off and falls to the floor. He is tied down in the bunk and sleeps.

†

Sixty-three degrees north latitude, fifty-two degrees west longitude. 25 July 1787. Morten Falck fixes the horizon in the sextant he has borrowed from the first mate and writes down the position in his diary with a slightly trembling hand. He studies the coast through a telescope. Some days have passed since the last storm, the weather is clear and mild, and the fells south of the colony of Godthåb have been in sight for a night and a day. Roselil has been brought up on to the deck again, the captain predicting that they will have fair weather for the rest of the voyage. Only rotting, sopping wet straw remains, and the barrel of fresh water they have opened for her smells badly. But she has begun to eat and to produce milk, though as yet it is discoloured and poor in taste. Roselil will survive, he feels quite certain of it now. And at Godthåb she can come ashore and munch upon fresh grass.

Morten Falck stands in the bow. He peers into the telescope, endeavouring to pick out portents of his destiny in the blurred contours of the land, suggestions of what this country and its inhabitants will do with him, and why at all he might be here. Will his bones end up somewhere beyond those crags? Will he have the chance to accomplish anything meaningful? A short life is a fair price for good work carried out. But what could be said of him if he expired now? He left in the lurch a woman who loved him and abandoned those he loved himself. He has achieved nothing yet that might offset the bad he has done. But he intends to do so. He wishes to accomplish something to justify his misdeeds. And Greenland is the means he requires to find meaning in his life. He has resolved to start work the moment he steps ashore, and not to idle. The natives must feel that someone has come to do them good!

He stands leaning against the bulwark, one foot wedged firm so as not to fall overboard. His upper body sways gently, but measured against the horizon he stands absolutely still. He maintains this vertical protest, which is directed in part towards the present horizontal disorder of the world, in part to his own inner doubt. He yearns for solid ground beneath his feet. And he feels a tinge of anxiety that the voyage will soon be at an end and a new reality will require his undivided attention.

Cries go up in the stern. Some members of the crew come running, pointing, and he turns his head to see what all the commotion is about. A shot rings out on the starboard side. From the sea in front of him a shadow emerges. It is as though it remains suspended in the air several ells above the surface, at the same height as the top or even higher. A raised finger, or rather a full fist, completely contrary to reason, as if a seaman's yarn had materialized in front of his eyes. This is not happening, he tells himself, and blinks, only to see that indeed it is. The dark upright mass is as yet before him, and he is clearly not alone in his vision, for now the entire crew stands and points.

Then the body descends, or the apparition, as the journal-writing part of his consciousness has already named it. At the instant it vanishes into the waves he has forgotten what it looked like. The men scurry back and forth, trying to ascertain where it will become visible again. Three times the beast rises up and each time he refuses to believe what his eyes behold. This is happening, he tells himself. Nothing shall remain unknown, I shall fix all details of it in my mind, so that I might later commit them to paper. And once I have written down what I have seen, I will understand it.

Afterwards, the men are eager to discuss the monster. They are in good cheer and somewhat boisterous. The captain gives them a glass to fortify themselves. Magister, one of them addresses him. What sort of beast was that, does he think? Has he seen the like in his books?

A whale? he suggests.

I've seen many a whale, says the man, and shakes his head. This was no whale.

Then it was a whale he has never seen before, Morten Falck notes. Next time he encounters it, he can tell his comrades he has seen it before and knows what it is. Then he will be held in esteem.

But it laughed at us. Did the Magister not see? And wiggled its tail, the hussy.

So what opinion have the men formed of what creature this was?

Oh, it was just the Greenlander women bidding us welcome, says the man with a chortle. It waved to you, too, Magister Falck. Gave him a wink, it did. Just he wait and see how they'll be lined up ready when we come ashore. All those lovely girls.

I had the impression you preferred young boys, he replies unkindly.

He descends to his cabin to make an entry in his journal and ends up composing a detailed description of the beast. Still wilder lapses of memory as to the whale's appearance shove aside what he actually saw or thought he saw or categorically denies having seen. Moreover, he finds himself becoming physically aroused as he writes, his member straining against the fabric of his breeches. He tears the page from his diary and discards it, dips his pen in the ink and hastily scribbles: *Leaping marine animal of great size and bulk observed July the 25th at 63rd parallel north, 52nd meridian west. Presumably whale.*

He reads the entry. He sees that hand and content are at odds. He wishes he alone had seen the monster. He would then have been able to write *presumably hallucination* instead.

Der Frühling anchors off Godthåb, seat of the country's southern inspectorate. He has become used to the deck and to keeping himself upright when the ship rolls and heels. Now as he steps ashore from the rowing boat into the old colony harbour, it is he who rolls and heels. The ground looms up before him, compelling him to halt or else trip a couple of paces so as not to fall. Then it rises like a slow and increasing swell beneath his feet and he must crouch down. All this is a disturbance of the fluids and the ossicles of his inner ear. He has exposed them on drowned individuals with his lancet in the vaults under the academy on Norgesgade. And yet his giddiness surprises him. On the surrounding rock are people, people with dark faces, eyes that stare emptily. They find no mirth in his stumbling and staggering, but chew on something and gape. They must think him drunk.

These natives, he notes, are not nearly as native as he had anticipated. Rather, they resemble hardened Danes more than even the colony folk themselves. Clad in knitted coats and anoraks, caps pulled down over their brows, shoddy footwear, stinking clay pipes in their mouths. Their proud smiles vex and offend him. Wide-bellied and smug they are. He addresses them in their own language, sentences he has learned at the seminary under Egede's tutelage, but they appear not to understand and reply in Danish.

What? What says the pastor? We don't understand the pastor's tongue.

He finds them slovenly, aloof, unreliable, dirty, foul-smelling. They possess an ability, he notes, to stare utterly without expression at any person who speaks to them. It is like tossing a stone into a pond without making a ripple. Seemingly there is nothing within, no thought, neither joy nor anger, no bed of emotions. The stone descends into emptiness and gloom and the surface closes about it in silence.

The colony is situated on a peninsula, which, seen from the top of one of the fells to its rear, which he ascends the day after his arrival,

resembles a crippled hand extending amputated fingers into the sea. The
Trade and the inspectorate command perhaps a score of houses, the
Mission has the church, a provided residence and a storage house. There
are a number of small dwellings built with peat and comprising some
European features, such as doors, window frames and even gutters. Here
live the christened natives, mostly families with an abundance of children, who play more or less naked outside. The place appears peaceful
and cosy, at least from a distance. But much of it is in a miserable state.
The savages live further from the colony, in tents made of hide, or in
communal dwelling houses close to the shore. One sees a number of
them on the water, passing in their skin-covered vessels on their way in
to the fjord or out to the sea. On the opposite side of the peninsula, in the
bay between two promontories, lies the Moravian station of the German
brethren and their large congregation of Greenlanders. He visits them
and finds this stronghold of Pietism in Greenland to be properly clean
and well organized, and the natives there to be far more hospitable and
accommodating, and less corrupted, than those on the Danish side.
Unfortunately, there is bad blood between the Brethren community and
the Danish mission, a circumstance issuing from the elder Egede's days,
so although they inhabit the furthest wilderness and live only a quarter
Danish mile away from each other, the two communities keep largely
to themselves.

The colony itself is dirty and unproductive, plagued by drunkenness and libidinous behaviour on the part of the Danish-Norwegian
employees, as well as the land's inhabitants. It would seem they are
resolved upon breeding and drinking themselves to death. In truth, he is
prepared for such wretchedness. The reputation of the country's oldest
colony has been poor ever since its foundation, when two dozen convicts
were dispatched here as cheap labour. During the first ten years, nine-
tenths of the district's natives perished, and old Egede himself returned
home disillusioned and without his wife, who succumbed to one of the
epidemics. Presumably the place is in better shape than it was then,
though this is to say little indeed.

His gait still unsteady, he pays a visit to the inspector, hoping to find there a modicum of culture, some small measure of homeliness and comfort. But Inspector Rømer proves to be a cantankerous Aalborgenser, heavily burdened by paranoia and a dermatological condition that causes the skin of his face to fall away in white flakes and blights his hands with weeping sores. Morten Falck recognizes that the man is plainly reacting pathologically to the place, both mentally and physically. He smells of damnation and rotten teeth, and is convinced that the colony crew and the natives are plotting to do away with him. He sends Morten Falck a look that is at once hostile and frightened.

The Magister has spoken to Basbøl, I take it? he says in a voice that is a rasp hardly with sound.

No. Who is Basbøl?

Ha, Rømer croaks, lifting his brow as if to say, All right, play your games, but take note that I have seen through you. He coughs, or else he laughs or emits a choked lament, Morten Falck is unsure. Priests have never done anything but cause trouble in this land. They come here with their notions of guilt, their cross and their ministry, and keep the natives from their work. He scratches his eyebrow and a puff of dusty skin descends slowly through the air. Oh, I know perfectly well why you are here, sir.

And why might that be? I can assure Monsieur Rømer that I merely wish to pay my respects, as is befitting for any new arrival.

Indeed. The inspector laughs silently to himself and pours himself a brandy, sits and scowls and scratches his eyebrows, until Morten Falck, having given up expecting anything at all sensible from the man, gets to his feet and leaves.

Later, he learns that the inspector is a hardened alcoholic and is rumoured to lie with small native girls in bouts of drunkenness that he is wont to display, whether the hour be late or early.

Morten Falck writes letters home to his parents, his sister and to the Bishop Egede. He draws up a more official report to the Mission-skollegium in which he bemoans, inter alia, the filthy conditions in the colony, and in particular the inspector's antics, which he finds to be of poor example to the natives. Encountering Rømer at the harbour, he informs him that he has lodged an official complaint.

The inspector bursts out laughing, though utterly without sound. He shall find his bloody match, he shall, the honourable Magister, he wheezes. Wait until winter, then the Magister's demons will come crawling from their hiding places. And then it'll be me reporting him.

I follow my calling, Morten says, and intend to behave like a decent human being.

You listen to me – priest! Rømer squeaks. I was here before he came, and I shall be here when he goes again, whether it be in his coffin or as a passenger on ship. I've found my modus vivendi, and it's the only way for white folk in this place. This land is not made for innocent babes such as the noble Magister. Either he grows up in a hurry and trims his sails or else he goes under. Farewell, Mr Falck!

In the bishop's residence, which normally stands empty, he greets his colleague in Holsteinsborg, the colony north of Sukkertoppen. Mr Oxbøl is an old man and has been in the country a lifetime. Morten Falck finds it comforting to speak with the old missionary, as the inspector's prediction has put him ill at ease. The old man seems to be bright of mind and body and would moreover seem disinclined to drinking. Yet he is plainly an uncompromising soul, Morten senses, and realizes that he is in for no gentle chat. Nevertheless, the man appears solid as the rock on which he stands, and moreover well clad and proper in appearance.

However, Mr Seidelin, Godthåb's own missionary, is clearly given to debauchery and intemperance, for which reason Morten Falck is compelled to pen a second report. His official residence stinks abominably, and Morten must enter the man's bedchamber and rouse him in order to speak with him.

Have you no help in the house? he asks when Seidelin finally rises to his feet.

The priest shuffles over to a chair on which stands his night pot. He unbuttons his breeches and passes water with his back to his guest.

Certainly I have, and many of them, he says, laughing over his shoulder, his urine splashing everywhere except the pot. But they've no conception of what it means to keep clean. They're used to living in filth and disorder.

Your catechist had to give the service today in your place. You should be ashamed.

Oh, but I cringe with contrition, says the priest, buttoning his fly. The same goes for us all in this terrible place. He yawns and stretches his limbs. But we have a good time of it, I can tell him that!

He returns to *Der Frühling* and is relieved again to be in the company of decent men, yet is filled with doubt and apprehension. If his own colony is ridden with only half as many ills as he has seen in Godthåb, he will have more than enough to attend to. But he feels far from convinced that he is the right man for the job. He is not even properly devout. Salvation and the liberation of man through the Passion of Christ are to his mind at best metaphors, at worst empty phrases. Prayer cannot fortify him; he finds it to be mere words learned by rote, whose content he does not believe. He must place his faith in detached rationalism, he tells himself. He will sweep the darkness from the colony, from the minds of the heathens and the benighted colony folk. He will teach them, illuminate by common sense and instruction. He sees the pastor Seidelin in his mind's eye, pissing in his chamber pot as he looks over his shoulder and laughs. Ten years, he thinks to himself, despondently. What will ten years do to me? He lies down on his bunk and picks up his Rousseau.

The weather is still, though quite damp. Much of the land remains hidden from sight, only the skerries and islets through which they pass are clear. They sail in the sheltered waters, the captain familiar with them from previous journeys on which he has entered sunken rocks and other perilous hindrances on his private charts. There are many birds. The boat is launched and a number are shot for dinner. One day Morten Falck sees the back of a whale curve the surface ahead of the ship, many hundredweight of flesh, bones and blubber passing silently through the sea, leaving behind only clouds of atomized water in the air. The sight gladdens him. The whale is one of God's creatures; in this, at least, he believes. And life is all around him, even here. There must be a meaning in it. His reading of Rousseau has returned to him some of his vigour and optimism, as it always does. He looks out upon the vast expanses of green that cover the land. After his wanderings at Godthåb they already feel familiar and homely. He longs to be upon them, to lie on his back in tall grass and gaze at the sky. He recalls the Dyrehaven where he lay with Abelone. The sound of humming bees, the swallows that flitted about on high, her happy laughter. He feels a stab of guilt. They come to him still, these pangs of remorse, and always they cause him to yield, and he must cough in order to conceal it should others be present.

Man is born free and everywhere he is in chains!

He has read these words so many times they seem almost to have lost substance, as the Lord's Prayer may become devoid of its content and work simply on account of the ritualized repetition of its constituents, their rhythm and ring. He has made use of the quote quite automatically whenever he has encountered a problem or felt anxious about a matter, and the words have fortified him like a strong dram or a splash of cold water in his face. But now he baulks at them. It is as if the sentence dissolves in front of his eyes, to reappear in a new guise. It startles him. He recognizes what it is the words wish to tell him. He has always thought of them as a cynical expression of resignation to life, an interpretation that once fuelled his own blasé cynicism as a young student in Copenhagen. And yet such an interpretation is incorrect, he realizes now. The words are a cry, a fanfare, a direction, full of optimism and joy! Man, be thou free! Cast thy chains away!

Indeed, he thinks to himself. This is what I have done and what I shall do. The betrothal was a chain constraining us both. I broke that chain and cast it away, as I have wrenched myself from all else in my life, from my family, my homeland. How simple it is! He can hardly comprehend that he has failed to grasp the meaning until now. My entire youth, he muses, wasted on a misinterpretation. It took a sea voyage for me to understand Rousseau's utterance, to understand myself, why I am here and not in a rectory on Lolland.

Is the Magister unwell?

He feels a hand on his shoulder. Captain Valløe. The captain looks at him with concern. It would seem he burst into laughter, or perhaps cried out.

He turns to face the captain and takes his hand. I should like to thank the captain for all that he has done! he exclaims excitedly. For everything, yes, indeed, everything!

Valløe smiles. Come down into my cabin, Magister, he says, and we shall drink a toast for a successful voyage.

Roselil has recovered after the long journey. At Godthåb she was taken ashore and allowed to graze on the rough tussocks outside the colony. She produces a small amount of drinkable milk again, and both he and the ship's company partake of it every day. As he reminds the captain, they have suffered very little scurvy on the voyage and Valløe cheerfully agrees that such a cow is a blessing.

They near their destination. A time is drawing to a close. It is the sixteenth of August and they have been underway for two and a half months. The men hang in the ropes and peer into the fog. Morten Falck holds prayers on the deck. He allows the crew to confess their sins. All have been troubled by impure thoughts. They have taken the name of the Lord in vain, have spoken ill of their fellow men and abandoned themselves in self-abuse. All the usual. He demands no more of them. He places his hand on their foreheads and gives them the benediction. Your sins are forgiven, he says, cast away your chains, go forth into the world and do good. They become as children, smiling gently and becoming calm. Their faces light up. The miracle of the blessing. These are good, Christian people, he thinks to himself. And finds it sad that he will soon be removed from them.

Voices sound in the fog. Women? The laughter of women? One of the seamen shouts and points. Kayaks and skin boats approach. The oarswomen of the latter wear their hair tied up in a knot. Morten finds them a funny sight. They look over their shoulders as they row, faces shining like copper coins. Are they singing? Savages! At last, he thinks, at last he is to meet the true savages, whom he shall guide in the time to come, and turn towards salvation and freedom in Jesus Christ, the Lord. This is quite another matter than the laziness of the hybrids he encountered at Godthåb. He feels overwhelmed with gratitude for having been permitted to be a part of this, for being designated such a role in life, and he must descend into the cabin and lie down to rest one final time on the bunk, where the lice seep forth and mingle with those that inhabit his clothing.

He hears the salute from the shore, a feeble splutter of the colony cannon and voices that cry hurrah. He hears the anchor cast, the rope run over the side. He feels the vessel turn and settle. Boots trample back and forth on the deck above him. The unloading commences. The rowing boat is swung out and gently buffets the side of the vessel. He hears Roselil low at the top of her lungs. The colony bell tolls without pause.

He lies on his back on the bunk. He has folded his hands. He looks up at the ceiling. This cabin, this ship, is still Danish ground. Invisible threads run all the way back from here to Denmark, and further still, to the home of his childhood. As yet he remains unreleased. There is still a chain. But once he steps ashore it will be broken and he will be free.

The Assumption

(15 August 1793)

Falck has ascended to a cliff top south of the colony and stands looking out across the sea. It is early morning. All night the fog has had its clammy arms and pasty fingers far inside the fjords, but now sudden lagoons of sunlight and clear sky appear, magnificent visions emerge only to vanish again, as surprising as illusions.

He stands with his telescope directed towards a point in the south where he has spied a two-masted ship, a brig or a ketch, several nautical miles distant. The fog has slipped from it like a silken cloth. The vessel glints in occasional shafts of light and has plainly found good wind, bursting with vigour, its sails full and taut in the sun, blowing her straight towards him. He sees the sparkle of the bow, he sees figures gather on the deck, then disperse in unknown industry. He sees the wake squirming from the aft, foam fanning out and settling. It is as dream-like as an apparition and it dizzies him. He shifts his stance, so as not to lose footing, and then the ship is gone. He seeks it in the telescope, issues a groan of annoyance, sweeps the lens from left to right, field by field, systematically searching back and forth. The ship is gone. He lowers the telescope from his eye and squints towards the banks of fog, blinding white reflections of sun. He stares at the place he believes the ship appeared until his eyes begin to water. But there is no ship. Was it a ship? Or was it an illusion, a wishful invention brought forth by accumulated months of need, the need to see a ship?

His cartographic position is sixty-five degrees and twenty-four minutes north, fifty-two degrees and fifty-four minutes west. By his own calculations and enquiries with various ship's captains he has arrived at this position and has recorded it in his diary. An intersection of two imaginary lines, a cross, the furthest outpost of his longings. It is this place close to the colony that affords the best views of ships arriving from the south.

Below him, restless waves wash on to a stony beach and retreat, wash up and retreat. Gusts of wind nudge gently at his back. To his right eye, the left seeing only a milky haze following a gunpowder accident some years before, he puts the telescope, a dented, tarnished ship's telescope purchased from an English whaler. By means of the telescope what is distant may be brought near or vice-versa, and in this out-of-the-way place one or the other is generally required. The lens is loose. He has tried to fasten it to the casing with putty, but without success. Therefore it works satisfactorily only when viewing the world from above, which is another reason why he has clambered his way up to the cliff.

The colony is a quarter Danish mile from the vantage point. One hour of scrambling, groaning and sweating across the rocks, hiking across gurgling stretches of bog. Here he has spent more than half the ten years for which he signed up when he was appointed to his living by the Missionskollegium. He is thirty-seven years old, a man of middle age, as old as his own father.

> *Lier, Akerhus diocese, Saturday,*
> *this twenty-eighth day of August 1791*
> *My dear son, Morten. It is with sadness that I must inform you that*
> *the Good Lord called upon your dearest mother this night and took*
> *her unto Him. Your old father is now quite alone on this Earth, as*
> *both your sister and your self are gone from the country.*

He shivers in the damp, mild gusts that come sweeping over the fell to enter in through the stitches of his threadbare clothing. He stabs his tongue against a front tooth that will soon yield to scurvy. His intestines are in an uproar. He senses the ominous ripple of diarrhoea in the bowel, the quivering alarm of the sphincter. His feet are soaked in bog water from the walk up. The sensation is a pleasant one, taking the edge off the bodily infirmities that yell all at once as a reminder of his mortality. The tepid water squelches between his toes as he wriggles them inside his leaking, oil-tanned boots. The sense of giving oneself up to decay, of dissolving away, puts his thoughts at rest. To abandon oneself to the Lord, to dissolve like a crystal of sugar in the great cosmos. He raises the telescope again, puts it to his good eye and gazes out into the fog.

Where is the ship?

Sukkertoppen, this fifth day of May 1792

Most esteemed Dr Rantzau,

Having during these past years made unsuccessful application to the Trade with a view to securing more comfortable quarters of residence and premises for Service, and since now it has become impossible for me to endure dwelling any longer in this damp and cramped chamber, and therefore to continue to carry out the duties of my position, I am compelled to request that a successor to said position be secured this coming year, as in the absence of such I shall be compelled to leave it vacant. The esteemed Doctor will I trust take into account that five years of existence in such a chamber may outweigh further years in more adequate lodging and with such other comforts as many of my fellow ministers most surely enjoy. Further to justify this humble request is the matter that I have suffered the anguish of scurvy not only all this winter but also and unusually all the summer before, and without respite. And now my teeth fall one by one from my mouth, causing me much difficulty to chew the hard bread available to us in provision.

Your humble servant,

Morten Falck

What he expects of this year's ship, if indeed a ship will come at all this year, are numerous matters, firstly including that he be summoned home by the Missionskollegium with the blessings of the most esteemed professor Rantzau, and that revocation be formally executed with all necessary documents and signatures. He sent his request by last year's ship, prompted then by an accumulation of everyday ills in the way of sickness and fatigue. Now it may rescue him from chains and process and the shadows of the misdeeds he unwittingly has committed in this place.

And then there is the widow.

He does not wish to think of the widow.

Yet he senses that the widow thinks of him.

Is he now bound to her for all time? Will she ever release him?

These six years of misfortune and adversity have conspired against him and made him melancholy and cantankerous, they have ruined his digestion, relieved him of half his teeth and the sight of his left eye, and tested his faith. Falck yearns for home.

Home, he thinks to himself, defined as some place, no matter which, as long as it is not here. Preferably on the other side of the Norwegian Sea. A place where trees grow and may be touched, with woods one may enter and leave again. The longing for woodland in this treeless landscape is immense, like the hankering for a fresh apple or the feeling of squashing a strawberry against the palate, the pealing of church bells on a Sunday morning, or the willow warbler, whose song sounds like a fluttering leaf. He longs for a place with doors that may be closed, where walls keep out draughts and damp, a place where sunlight slants down upon the floor. And when, as now, he allows himself to indulge in such futile diversions as to consider the future, his tongue stabbing at the wobbling tooth in his mouth, he imagines securing a living in a small and inconsequential parish in some cosy corner of Denmark, or else in the place from which he hails, in the parish of Lier, the diocese of Akerhus, some few hours by the mail coach from Christiania. His father lives yet, at least until the ship comes with word from home. Kirstine is still a pastor's wife in Nakskov. But his sister has appeared before him some months previously in a procession of the dead, a vision that cut into his heart, but which also made him joyful. She is blessed now, he thinks to himself. He wants to go home to see her grave, and his mother's in Lier. He wants to go home to a living in his native parts, a cosy parsonage nestled among woods and undulating hills, pastures divided by dry stone walls, a view of the fjord, a boat dragged up on the shore, trout nets drying in the sun, a parlour with a wife and children, three boys who honour him and a girl who loves him, offspring and descendants who will remember him without shame.

The tooth feels looser now. He tries to leave it be, but the pleasure of pestering it with the tip of his tongue is too great.

> *My dear brother Morten,*
>
> *Since the day of Christmas Eve here at Nakskov the air has been heavy and unhealthy with fog, and hardly a day with any glimpse of sun. It accords ill with our own climate in Lier, where almost the whole time the air was clear, there was sunlight and pleasant weather. As for myself, we enjoy here the necessities of life and more, as indeed your own eyes have seen, yet I do, and shall always, long for Lier, our good father and blessed mother, the churchyard with the pretty graves of our siblings. I found greater pleasure in our modest circumstances there than in this vainglorious and self-righteous town in which I find not the slightest enjoyment and still after seven full years of marriage do not feel at home. May God mind my tongue!*
>
> *Dear Morten, I ask myself often if we shall ever again see our childhood home and our father. Will I see you, beloved brother?*

A ship may be laden with the future, and it may be laden with the past, mail decreeing this or another action, notifications of the past year's events at home, condensed into half an hour of feverish reading.

Besides release from his living, he hopes for a replacement, a priest who perhaps at this very moment stands and spies towards the land as he did himself six years before. A new man in the appointment would alleviate his predicament.

Journal for this fifth day of March 1791:
Greenland is the night that separated the evening when I retired to sleep cheerful and young, from the morn when I awoke a palsied old man.

Falck moves his lips in prayer for the ship, imploring his sighting to be real and not an illusion. He prays for its crew, that they may be protected from all manner of disaster, for the letter that is to release him from this confinement, for the good colleague who is to succeed him, that he may have been spared descent into tantrum and sickness or the urge to commit himself to the sea. He prays for himself by praying for others – or does the opposite hold? – for his father, his sister, for the natives of this land, christened or heathen, for all the circumstances of life over which he has been compelled to accept he has not the slightest influence. He presses the telescope to his eye once more, stabs at the tooth with his tongue, tightens his sphincter against renewed onslaught. *Let not Thine, but mine be done.* No, the opposite! He stares into the fog. No ship. *Amen!* A gust of wind carries with it a haze that collects and condenses. It rains. The skerries vanish from sight and with them the purpose of standing here to stare.

He snaps the telescope shut and returns it to his pocket. He glares angrily at the sea, the leaden bulk of water merging with the lighter nuance of fog, the two elements that together comprise the damp climate he has now inhaled for six years. His coat grows heavy with rain. The cold spreads down his neck and out into his shoulders. He hears the rain as it falls. A grey patter. His hearing, at least, is intact. He takes off his hat, strikes it against his thigh, straightens his hairpiece and settles the hat once more upon his head.

I ought to go home.

Go, my legs!

But his legs do not obey. He remains standing, increasingly wet, on the dismal, rain-soaked cliffs. There is also the problem of his bowels. If he begins to walk after standing still for so long, a chain reaction of nervous impulses will shoot through his organism into the core of his latent peristaltic unease. The musculature of the colon is unamenable to argument, it senses any conspiracy and its revenge is harsh and prompt.

Falck stands immovable in the wind and rain. Once, he made a decision that led him to this cliff. When was it? he asks himself. Why did he do so? Is there forgiveness for the harm one causes the self?

†

On the outskirts of the colony he passes by the huts of the natives, constructions of peat, clay, shale, driftwood and whalebone, as well as unhewn and broken planks discarded by the Trade. There are perhaps a dozen such dwellings, which seem almost to have emerged from the ground like molehills. Jagged scraps of discarded glass have been pressed into the recesses made for windows and let in a measure of light. But the homes are abandoned, the paths dug out between them fallen into decay, hides and joists removed from the roofs. The rain falls directly down into them, washing away through openings and depositing earthy sediment on the slopes down to the fjord. The dampness envelops these former homes with cold and stagnant odours, reminding him of those who lived here and the life they led, a stench of heathens, their filled urine tubs, their lice-infested beds, their always-simmering pots. The smells arouse Falck's nostrils, bringing to his mind fresh meat and naked, sweat-glistening bodies, improprieties shamelessly perpetrated in the semi-darkness, libidinous moans in the nooks and crannies. His bowels contract, he presses a hand to his stomach, then breaks suddenly into a canter, halts, canters off again. Presently it subsides. A cold sweat is upon his brow. He wipes it away with his hand and assumes a gait more suitable for clergy.

Only from one of the peat dwellings, the one closest to the colony, does smoke still rise. Pale faces of children at the window holes. He puts on a smile and waves awkwardly. They stare back solemnly, perhaps they are afraid, or even hateful? Who knows what these people think or feel? He certainly does not. He will go in to them later in the day with his catechist, to preach Christian love and propriety, freedom through salvation, the usual lesson. He hopes it may re-establish some semblance of day-to-day normality.

Further on, his path takes him past a cluster of tents in which there is more life. More heathens. They have come from the south in boats fully laden. A sure sign the ship is indeed on its way. Smoke rises up from the holes in the top and coils into the fog. The tent openings are drawn aside: he glimpses people in the murky interiors. They are clad in a strange jumble of hide and colourful Danish linen, which they have bartered from the employees of the colony or ships' crews. He cannot explain it, but their presence makes him feel rather intimidated, the unfathomable darkness they represent, their intimacy with death and unworried aspect on life. He never crawls inside one of the peat dwellings without first making the sign of the cross and pronouncing the Lord's Prayer. And these newcomers are even more foreign and disconcerting than those who permanently inhabit the colony.

Natives journey here and settle each autumn when the ship is due, in the hope of trading. Usually they are more numerous, the tents often approaching five score, but these past winters have been harsh and unknown numbers have perished, either directly from hunger or by the rampant culling of widows and children.

A woman and a man are seated on their haunches in front of the tent. They gape at the pastor, unsmiling and without expression. They exchange some words he cannot understand, a slippery babble of sounds. He wonders if it is he they are talking about, and walks on all the more quickly, pursued by their stares. Do they know about me? Do the natives talk about what the pastor does? About the pastor and the widow? He squelches ahead in his boots and hums a psalm to cheer himself up.

Down at the bay, drawn up on to land, lies the *Taasinge Slot*, dark and brooding, a Danish whaler wrecked years before. Its masts and parts of the woodwork have been taken away and used for firewood and building materials, despite the colony manager having issued a ban on removing so much as a rivet. Predictably, this merely hastened the destruction. The ship was found drifting some nautical miles south of the colony without a soul on board, yet still laden with numerous barrels of good oil, and was towed here with much difficulty. The colony manager has written to its owners, but it is clear now that the whaler has entered into a pact with the land and will never leave it.

He looks up at the captain's cabin beneath the quarterdeck, where the frames of the windows are intact, though the glass removed. He sees part of the ceiling inside. It is less than a year since he lay there within, clinging to the widow and a keg of aquavit, determined to die. He finds it to have been a happy time.

Sukkertoppen, this seventh day of August 1793

My dear sister Kirstine,

Autumn is soon upon us and all of us, Danes and natives alike, now await the arrival of the ship.

So many boats put into the colony with blubber at present that it resembles market days at Christiania. However, it is the trade that brings them, and company with the other savages; certainly not the pastor or the good Mission or the Salvation of the Lord.

My own longing to see this year's ship is as great as any other's. As I have already confided to you, it is my deepest hope that within a few weeks I shall be putting to sea, this same autumn once again, to be reunited with my beloved sister, if indeed she be above the soil, and to kiss her and pull her to my breast and thus make this letter superfluous. We shall then confide in each other, Kirstine. I shall be your father confessor and we shall be each other's comfort and solace. You shall listen to my account and I am confident you will forgive me everything!

Alas, how great a burden it is to remain separated from those one loves. I think and fear that you will find me quite changed in body and soul after these last six years, and I fear even more that my nightly vision of my sister Kirstine has spoken true.

Falck descends into the colony proper, where greasy smoke from the boiling of blubber infects the air and conspires with the eternal fog to inflict upon the permanent inhabitants a chronic hacking, bloodied phlegm and viscous, soot-infested mucus. At the blubber house he remains standing for a moment, his gaze turned to the harbour. He sees the Trader over by the colony house in dialogue with his overseer. Falck ducks, then scurries across the open space between the blubber house and the store to reach the water's edge from where the Trader cannot see him. Here, he almost collides with the smith, Niels Hammer, who comes trudging round a corner carrying what looks like a large bundle of sticks or switches on his shoulders.

Mind where you're going, Hammer! He leaps aside so as not to be knocked down by the brawny, heavily burdened smith.

Hammer drops his bundle. It lands with a swish on top of others of the same material, long, white sticks whose kind cannot readily be ascertained. He turns and looks Falck up and down. He does not smile, though his eyes flicker mischievously beneath his brow's protruding buttress of thickened bone.

Magister Falck. You're as soaked as a crow.

The smith hails from Lofoten and speaks the sharp, resounding tongue of northern Norway, a fact that occasions him to speak in a manner as though they were childhood friends, which is to say inappropriately familiar and steeped with sarcasm. Falck, quite as Norwegian himself, replies in Danish.

Spare me your observations, Hammer.

He tries to get round the man, makes to his right, then left, but each time the smith steps in his way. He senses the foul stench of sweat, rotten tobacco and badly digested aquavit, and steps backwards.

Is there anything you require of me?

Is there anything the pastor requires of me? the smith rejoins facetiously.

A confession, perhaps? Falck suggests snidely. But his sarcasm cuts no ice with the smith, a notorious and unscrupulous fornicator. The

Ten Commandments alone do not suffice to capture the sins of Niels Hammer, and for two consecutive years now Falck has worded written reports on his criticizable habitus and the damaging influence of his presence on Danes and natives alike, christened or otherwise. But these reports seem without effect, perhaps because the pastor's own reputation is hardly any better, and because due to an incalculable number of other complications he is unable to report the smith for the unspeakable outrage he has committed against the Madame of the colony house. A fact of which the smith himself is eminently aware and for which reason he feels he may do as he pleases. The worst thing, however, is that Falck is wracked with guilt-tinged anxiety at having reported one of his flock.

What are these things? he asks, striving to be friendly and pointing at the heap of pale sticks.

Baleen, says Hammer. To be shipped.

Aha, says Falck. I see. Interesting. Indeed.

Whalebones, the smith adds, sensing that Falck has no idea what he is talking about.

I am familiar with the meaning of the word, Falck says.

Only now, though, does he realize what the items are. He puts his boot upon them, feels their spring as they yield beneath his sole. The bundled whalebones are bristly and as though decayed. There is something inadmissible, shameless and pastily naked about them that is at once repulsive and inciting. One can hardly avoid imagining the process of refinement to which this material will be subjected by the textile manufacturers of Denmark, and the final product that will come of it, the delicate, elastic stays of waist-cinching corsets. The journey which they are to make comprises one of the modern world's strangest metamorphoses from nature to culture: from the plankton-filtering mouth of the humpbacked whale they bob along on the sweat-drenched shoulders of this smith to sway in the hold of a ship, are subsequently immersed in the cleansing chemical tubs of the factories, then cut and shaped and sewn into lace and fabric, finally to fulfil their destiny nestling against the waists of women, constraining undesirable flab.

The smith stares at him, the light sparkling in his keen blue eyes. He scratches his throat with hands the shape of shovels. Did I say something wrong? Morten asks himself. Did I make a sigh or cut a grimace? Why does he still stand here?

Indeed, he says, and clears his throat. I hear the ship will be here soon.

Der Frühling, Hammer replies. She's out there somewhere, chopping in the fog. I saw her on my fire-watch this last night. A man sees a lot of things when he's out in the night, Magister.

Indeed, says Falck again. Very interesting, Hammer. He is about to say something that might lead the conversation in a different and less uncomfortable direction, but the smith is too quick for him.

So the pastor might be leaving us then?

I go wheresoever the Lord calls me to go. It is no matter for your interference.

The Trader says he'll send you home in chains for what you did.

Like I said, be good enough not to interfere in matters that do not concern you, Hammer.

There'll be those sorry to see you go, I shouldn't wonder, the smith says, more good-naturedly now.

And those less than sorry. Is that it?

The smith chuckles. The Magister's in the mood for jest this morning.

I may be leaving and I may not, Falck says frankly. It depends on one thing and another. If I am called home I shall go. If the Trader wishes to initiate proceedings I shall yield. I place my trust in the Lord.

Things will be quiet here without our pastor. The smith grins.

If I were you, I wouldn't count my blessings. And what of you, anyway, Hammer?

Me? This is my home. A land for proper men, Magister. I'm like a fish in water. My bones will rest in Greenland's earth.

I see. Still, I'm sure you are aware that such a wish may come true even before we anticipate. Life is brief and death is always at the door. Have you prepared for that, Hammer?

I'm prepared, the smith says. My bones are drawn by the soil. I suppose that's why I have this confounded arthritis in my hands. Do you not think so, Magister, him being both clergy and physician?

In my capacity as physician I would say it was more a matter of his trade and the cold of winter, the damp of summer, the heat of the workshop, and not least excessive consumption of distilled spirits.

There's nothing like a wee dram to warm a man, Magister Falck. I know the Magister sets store by it too, now and then.

You don't say. Well, there's a thing or two I know about you as well, Hammer. He would be wise to bear it in mind.

You know everything about me, Magister. I am a sinner before the Lord, Hammer says with unveiled pleasure.

Falck wishes to move on, but the smith blocks his way.

Will the Magister not see the body?

He looks away. What body?

The widow. I've laid her in the timber store. I thought the Magister might wish to see her one last time, make sure she's ready to go into the ground like a good Christian.

He struggles to maintain his composure. Thoughts swirl in his head. My successor will attend to it, he mumbles.

The smith studies him. Then he nods and changes the subject. Does the Magister know what I'm looking forward to when the ship comes?

It really doesn't interest me in the slightest, but let me guess. He looks forward to bartering and drinking and fornicating in the company of the crew.

That as well, the smith admits. They're a good bunch of lads and have been a long time away at sea. They've not seen an underskirt in months and I've not had word from the homeland for a year, so who can blame us for wanting to enjoy ourselves? But do you know what I most look forward to?

He feels weak and rather poorly. No, what do you look forward to most, Hammer?

When the ship is unloaded and I can cook me stew with meat that is not musty, the smith says, and he is rapt.

An innocent wish, indeed, says Falck. If he thought more of the joys of the table and less of fornication it would be a step in the right direction. But now he must excuse me.

Barley soup with cherries, the smith fantasizes. Pancakes with maple syrup.

Yes, well, says Falck. He feels as though his bowels are listening in on the transports of the smith.

Blood gruel, salted goose meat, bread-and-ale porridge with sour cream, matured herring that melts on the tongue.

That's enough, Hammer! Get a grip, man! He senses the sweat start out on his forehead and hears the squealing lament of his stomach. At once he sees the Trader coming briskly towards the harbour, followed by his overseer Jens Dahl and two native constables of the Trade. The Trader wields his stick, pointing to left and right, the overseer hastening in his footsteps, pitching in with obsequiousness. They do not seem to have noticed Falck, so he scuttles away, past the smith, ducking between the boathouse and the warehouse, scrambling in a zigzag over the rocks behind, as agile as a spider, sliding down the other side and crouching to wait. He hears Kragstedt's drawl drift away towards the harbour, Dahl's chatter and the greeting of the smith. Kragstedt utters some words in a commanding tone and Hammer answers back. They laugh.

His boots squelching and his coat-tails clinging to his thighs, Falck scurries further, to the flat area where the Mission house lies slightly apart from the main buildings of the colony. Again he crouches and remains in hiding until long after the Trader disappears from sight. And then he is inside. He slams the door shut behind him. Now he is safe. He flops down on the bed and stares up at the ceiling. She is dead. Good, he thinks. Indeed! It is consummated. I am free.

The Mission house is a sagging, half-timbered building clad with planks. The mortar rots in damp weather, which is to say most of the year, crumbling away at double the speed in the short spells of dryness. In winter the frost cracks branch and diffuse to eat away at the house as it is battered by storms this way and that. In the spring the process of disintegration continues, advancing rather more quickly than the year before. Half-timbered houses are ill suited to this land, as ill suited as the people who inhabit them, little more than ice-cold encasements in which a person can but sit and brood over his wasted life, yet when they catch alight they blaze like tindersticks.

Falck's accommodation comprises one half of the Mission house, a room measuring eight ells on each side, draughty and cold, and with a single window to let in a measure of light, the glass of which, however, is of such poor quality that everything outside appears as indistinct as a painting in which the colours have run together. Which is just as well. Morten Falck appreciates anything that may serve not to remind him that he is where he is.

The fixtures of this room are as follows: an alcove bed with a mattress of straw in need of replacement, some fox hides and two reindeer skins sewn together, all infested with mould and damp; a small desk with a drawer; a wooden chair whose back he wrenched asunder in a moment of unthinking rage; a leather armchair that looks as if it suffers from psoriasis; five bookcases filled with books, many of which cannot be opened on account of their pages having stuck together. A great monstrosity of a wrought-iron stove takes up much of the space. It smokes so infernally that he prefers to fill a bucket with glowing coals from the kitchen and place it on the slate beneath the desk, from whence it gives off sufficient warmth. The ceiling sags in the middle and he has felt obliged to support it by means of a plank jammed between ceiling and floor, taken from the *Taasinge Slot*. This has been Falck's home for six years. He is fond of it.

He rises to neaten himself, expelling all thought of the widow from his mind. He senses again the movement in his bowels. He regrets not having used the privy on his way. But then he would have been like a fox in a trap and Kragstedt would have been waiting for him when he was done, perhaps with the shackles at the ready. And so he endures, he takes off his clothes, tossing his coat, waistcoat, trousers and stockings over the washing line he has drawn between the walls and which may or may not allow his clothing to be dry by morning. He frees his long hair from the hair bag, winds it in his hand and squeezes the water from it. Then he gathers it on top of his head and puts on his hairpiece once more, stands for a moment and looks down at himself. His torso, especially his shoulders and chest, are mottled blue and black by the wet garments. He looks like an erect corpse, covered with death spots.

As he is crouching down on all fours to settle his bowels, naked but for his hairpiece, the door opens and the catechist Bertel Jensen enters. He remains standing and observes him. If he has received word of the widow's death it cannot be seen by his expression.

Did the pastor catch the plague when up in the fjord? the catechist enquires in a hopeful tone.

It is only the colour from the wet clothes, Falck says. I was on the cliff and got soaked.

Ah, the pastor was spying for his ship.

Close the door, Bertel, for goodness' sake. Otherwise I shall catch both plague and the pox, as well as a cold for good measure.

The catechist turns and shuts the door demonstratively. Falck gets to his feet and clutches pensively at his stomach. He raises his hands to the helmet of coarse horsehair that encapsulates his skull, making a slight adjustment. His bowels emit a series of shrill tones of varying intensity. He grimaces, then collects himself.

My dear Bertel, he says. Are we friends today?

The catechist spits on the stove. But the stove is cold and the antici-pated sizzle fails to materialize. The phlegm runs down its side and drips to the floor.

Falck sighs. Be good and help me put on the vestments.

The catechist glares at him, but nevertheless obediently takes down the cassock from the hook and holds it out ready. Falck retrieves a pair of long, yellowed underpants from the line and feels to see if they are dry. They are not. He puts them on, then finds a fatigued sheepskin doublet and woollen stockings and puts them on, too, hopping from one leg to the other. Bertel stands with the cassock, staring, fishlike, the corners of his mouth downturned. Falck wriggles his way into the garment. It is dry and warm. Thank goodness. Small demons of cold are driven from his body and cause him to shudder. Immediately he feels better and clearer in his head. His stomach settles. He turns to meet Bertel's gaze and sees a reflection of the transformation he has undergone. Now he is the pastor.

The ruff, he says. Is it stiff?

Bertel takes down the box from one of the shelves and lifts out the collar, holding it gingerly in his hands, as though it were of brittle glass. Falck takes it from him, feeling to see if the potato starch is dry. Flakes of the substance crumble away. Dry enough, he decides. He fastens it around his neck, turning it until the button is at the nape, then wiping the stickiness from his fingers.

The crucifix.

Bertel finds the brass cross and holds it out with the chain taut in his hands. Falck bends down and puts his head through the loop, feeling the intimate weight of the cross against his chest. He puts on his buckled shoes. Last of all, he retrieves the Holy Scripture and Pontoppidan's catechism. Both straddle the same clothes line, spine upwards, so as to remain dry.

Now he is ready. The catechist stands empty-handed and stares at him, tensely silent, as though the sight of a pastor in full vestments awakes sentiments inside him that Falck is unable to fathom.

Is there anything wrong, dear Bertel? You are very quiet today.

A rare smile curls the catechist's lips like a ray of sunlight and is gone again. You reminded me of someone else, he mutters, and averts his gaze.

Falck is glad of this kindness, a straw at which he may clutch. He commits the error of grasping it, whereby it naturally snaps. Another pastor, perhaps? he says. One with whom you have worked in your long service?

Naluara. I don't know. It is one of the few words Falck cannot help but recognize, he hears it said so many times each and every day. He is familiar, too, with its *true* meaning: *You can kiss my arse!*

What a lot has happened since we first met, says Falck with a sigh. And you were away for how long, a year and a half? Where were you in all that time, Bertel?

Here and there, Bertel says.

I thought you were dead.

I thought the Magister to be dead. I thought the cannibals up the fjord had devoured him. Bertel cannot suppress a malicious grin. Falck senses now for the first time the anger that is brewing inside him.

We shall speak no more of it, he says.

Is the Magister sent home now?

Yes, my time here would seem to be over. The place has need of new blood.

Bertel considers him, then nods, turns and goes out. Falck follows him.

Are my catechumens gathered?

You mean we are to catechize today? Bertel enquires, his expression exaggeratedly sheeplike.

Indeed, says Falck vaguely. I should imagine so. Are we not?

Bertel shrugs. *Naluara*. I am not the pastor.

Falck stands to consider his catechist and wonders if indeed he knows of the widow's death. He can hardly avoid learning of it before the day is over. Once we were good friends, he thinks to himself, and could speak with each other on any matter. What went wrong?

Bertel Jensen is in the region of thirty years old, a man of fair, freckled skin and an insipid gaze. A so-called mixture, a people frowned upon by natives and Danes alike. It has occurred to Falck that it is perhaps the fair aspect of his being, his Danishness, that he despises so, in the way all others seem to despise the mixture of blood. The two genea-logical features of the catechist's appearance, the Danish and the Eskimo, seem layered upon each other in staggered arrangement like some racial palimpsest. The white man, his father, has scrawled upon the pure and splendid Eskimo heredity and thereby, besides the fair skin and the freckles, allotted him a meagre, round-shouldered appearance, spindly, disharmonious arms, bandy legs and an angular, fox-like face with narrow, shifty eyes. In Denmark he would promptly be taken for some unspecific member of the common class, most certainly not a man of the Lord.

He has now worked with the catechist for six years. That is to say that for the last year and a half he had vanished, only to reappear a fortnight ago without wishing to say where he had been. But Falck himself has been away from the colony for most of the past year. With the exception of a couple of family members, Bertel is the person with whom he has enjoyed the closest, lengthiest and most regular relationship in all his life. So much more does it hurt him, then, that they cannot become friends again as they were in the beginning.

Is there any reason why we should not catechize today? he enquiries warily.

Why should there be?

Has something happened? Speak to me, Bertel.

What should have happened? The catechist is neither to be led nor driven.

Very well. Naturally we are to catechize, Falck decides. We shall continue our usual work until my departure. We shall pretend it to be a day like any other and we shall put this gloom from our minds for an hour. What do you say?

The catechist nods, then turns away.

The colony bell sounds over by the colony house. Together with Bertel he stands outside the Mission house and observes the crew come walking up from the harbour: the smith, the new cooper and carpenter, who came with a whaling ship in the summer, the constables, the Trader's overseer, all cap in hand to honour Madame Kragstedt, the colony manager's wife, who stands, pale and stiff, in the doorway to bid them welcome. They stand on the step and bow deeply, receive a curt nod in return and step inside. Falck feels sorry for the Madame. He knows Kragstedt insists she maintain the role of first lady of the colony, and he knows that she would do almost anything to escape it.

After the Danish men come the Greenlandic constables and servants. They stand likewise clutching their caps, though below the step. With her maid, Madame Kragstedt steps down to them and spoons up small portions of porridge into bowls. They devour, then bow humbly and retreat. The two women retire into the house again. Falck sees the door close behind the Madame. He swallows his spit.

He turns to Bertel. Are you hungry?

Yes? the catechist replies inarticulately, a rising interrogative as though he cannot quite comprehend that Falck should ask such a ridiculous question. I haven't a crumb to eat at home.

Falck smiles at him. Well, a crumb or two ought to be within my capabilities.

They go into the tiny kitchen where the stove stands cold and covered with soot. Falck finds a hunk of bread and cuts away paper-thin flakes of it until all the mould is gone. Then he divides what remains in two and hands the larger piece to Bertel. Each takes a knife and scrapes lard from the jar. It is salty and burnt, and quite rancid. They spread it onto the bread, thick embankments of it which they devour, and then more. Falck senses his stomach settle with the fare, yet he knows his intestines soon will wreak havoc again. His head feels heavy. Bertel licks his fingers, meticulous as a cat, then wipes his hands on his breeches. Falck pours ale from the jug into two cups, which they empty in long gulps.

That was the last of my soft bread, says Falck. Now we must make do with hard tack.

My son was fond of hard tack, says Bertel. He enjoyed it with train oil and crowberries. Or syrup, if we could get any.

Falck is embarrassed by the mention of Bertel's son. He has no idea what to say and therefore says nothing.

And your wife? he says. Have you heard from her?

I should ask the pastor himself, says Bertel and looks at him directly. He was the last of us to see her.

Sofie was well when I saw her, says Falck. She and the little one. They are taken well care of there.

Whatever did happen? Bertel then says, a visible struggle with his pride.

Yes, whatever did happen? says Falck. What happened was what might have been expected. He sighs. But I hear no one has suffered unduly. I don't think you need to be worried.

I shall go there, says Bertel. As soon as I am finished with my matters here. They say the Magister corresponds with the prophets, that he has a whole bundle of letters from them.

Oh, one or two, perhaps, he says. Maria Magdalene wrote as recently as a fortnight ago.

> *Igdlut Settlement, Eternal Fjord,*
> *this twenty-ninth day of July 1793*

To Magister Morten Falck
Sukkertoppen Mission
Dearest Morten, my friend and confidant,

Alas, how sadly it all has ended. Nevertheless, we are in good spirits and no one among us is worse off for being relieved of earthly goods we cannot in any circumstance take with us into the hereafter.

I am, however, more concerned for you, my dear friend, than for any other following these events. As you surely have learned by now, your wife departed for Holsteinsborg in the company of my own husband. What may have happened to her there, I know not. Perhaps you have reports of such. She is an unhappy person.

My dear husband is now returned to me. He has humbly asked my forgiveness, which I have granted him, since the Lord has spoken, as He has a habit of speaking to me, and has told me I must forgive him. He is my husband. I love him. May it also be an example to you, Morten, that so must you also forgive, as He has forgiven you. But who am I that I should instruct you in what to do and what not? The Lord will guide you!

People were spread to the winds, but some are already returned. We now live once more in our old peat dwelling at the shore, where we can hear the babble of the stream, and we are both pleased by these circumstances. Who knows, in some years we may even be in number again. Our cause is good and just. Neither blunderbuss nor grapeshot nor chains may stop it. Sooner or later, the Dane, who stole this land away from us, will recognize this!

We place our trust in the Lord, praised be His name!

I wish you well, dearest friend of my heart, on your continuing voyage through life. Do not forget us here in the Eternal Fjord! I remain

Your friend, Maria Magdelene

People have arrived for prayers, he sees, as he leaves the kitchen with Bertel. The majority of Greenlanders and mixtures of the colony who are christened have come, perhaps a score of people for whom Falck harbours an oddly unhappy and fearful fondness. Unhappy, because their attitude to the colony's pastor at best would seem to be mild indulgence. Fearful, because in his years here he has been more dependent on them than they on him, an imbalance that may quickly be further tipped in his disfavour, as indeed would seem to have happened. In addition to the colony's natives are some outsiders wholly unfamiliar to him. According to Bertel they are visitors from the southern part of the district.

So it is a peculiar congregation that seats itself on the benches of the Mission house parlour, reeking of blubber and skins tanned with urine. The men are clad in linen smocks, probably illegally bartered, the women in their own costumes, breasts visible in the neckline. One of them has pulled down her upper garment at the neck and brought out her breasts to feed a child. She rocks gently back and forth. The faces are foreign in appearance, eyes keen and alert, the children unusually quiet, even the feeding baby, which looks askew upon Falck from the breast. He feels himself to be unpleasantly observed. On one of the rear benches he sees a face he knows, but which ought not to be there. The widow. He gives a start and looks away.

No! he exclaims in silence.

The blessed Poul Egede urged him to quickly become skilled in the language so as to be able to hold his services in Greenlandic. It was indeed his intention. But when he arrived in the country and made use of what he had learned at the seminary, no one understood but a croak of what he uttered, or else bizarre and highly embarrassing misunderstandings occurred, befitting some burlesque, whereby the congregation were brought into commotions of roaring and unstoppable laughter. Since then he has employed an interpreter, which is to say Bertel.

He knows the catechist cannot content himself with merely translating the words, but often elaborates as he sees fit, taking great liberties in the process. Everything considered, he has no idea of how his sermons are received in their translated form, nor of what effect he has on the congregation by virtue of his own person. It is one of countless matters over which he no longer has control.

The service is held in an immense and almost incredulous silence, most particularly when one of the christened members of the congregation comes forward to receive the blessing and the communion in the form of broken-off pieces of ship's biscuit and a sip of the sour wine Madame Kragsted has given him for the purpose (in a fit of raging hunger he has himself consumed the holy wafers dispatched here by the Kollegium, and has washed them down with the entire stock of altar wine). They conclude by singing two of Brorson's hymns and a single from Kingo's book. The congregation loves to sing, joining together so as almost to raise the roof and to make the timber frame tremble in its bed of crumbling mortar, though they hardly understand a word of any verse.

After the service Bertel goes through the Ten Commandments with the two catechumens who have come, a young girl, a daughter of one of the Danish-Greenlandic seamen, and her unmarried mother. The catechist reads aloud the text and has them repeat it by turn. The outsiders have been allowed to remain seated and observe the instruction. They sit with their hands in their laps and listen and show no sign of restlessness, now and then pinching a louse from their hair and flicking it with practised, playful elegance in the direction of the coal bucket, where it expires with a sizzle. Falck permits himself to drift into a light sleep.

Amen! Falck jumps in his chair and blinks. Church is over. The people rise from the benches and file out. The stench of ammonia and fermented blubber lingers in the air behind them.

He remains standing in the empty parlour that has resounded with hymns and prayer. Soon it will all be in his past. He senses the bread and lard moving through his bowels, a thick mash of masticated sustenance on the march towards his terrified sphincter. He feels it pass through his small intestine, seeping into the large intestine on the right side of his abdomen.

He presses his hymn book against his stomach and goes outside. Bertel stands and considers him out of the corner of his eye. The widow is beside him and now he sends her a glance. She smiles. He refuses to be thrown by her presence. He is a man of the church, with its entire authority behind him. Moreover, he remains in spite of everything an adherent of rationalism. He ought to be stronger than she. He feels his large intestine writhe like the Midgard Serpent. In a moment he will be stricken with the cramps. Perhaps he should go behind the house and crouch behind a rock. Oh, he thinks to himself, to bend down, draw up the cassock and deposit his load in the heather. No, he will wait! They have a long day ahead of them and he must make himself master over his body, lest it become master over him. He forces himself to approach Bertel. He holds the book in front of him, now against his chest, the embossed cross of its cover turned outwards. The widow retreats, releases herself from her form and runs away like water. He stands and looks as she goes. Bertel stares at him in anticipation.

Since we have much time before us this day, I will first challenge you to a game of chess, he says eventually. As we did in the old days.

Bertel nods. I accept the challenge, Magister.

They walk together to the catechist's house. It is a solid house built of shale, peat and red-painted planks, with a small and pretty window in a white frame. A chimney from a ship's stove protrudes from the roof. There is no smoke from it.

Inside is cold and dark. The place smells of old straw and the bleakness of a man alone. The house comprises a room some few paces in length and breadth, yet stuffed with furniture, two large bunks, a table with four chairs, a soft armchair, boxes filled with books, many of them originally from Falck's own shelves. Bertel finds the board and sets up the pieces upon it.

Falck flicks through a couple of books. Some illustrations give rise to recollection and he smiles to himself. Do you read? he asks.

Bertel shakes his head. Not any more. The boy read. I think he read every book in the house.

Yes, he was bright.

I wanted that he should become a priest, says Bertel.

He would have made an excellent one, as clever as he was.

He didn't wish it. He said he wanted to be a sea captain. Bertel smiles with bitterness. I was angry with him about it. I should have listened.

Falck says nothing. He points to one of Bertel's extended fists. The hand turns and opens.

White, says Bertel. And I am black.

Next time you will be white, says Falck encouragingly.

He who wins has white, says Bertel. It is usually the way.

Falck opens with a pawn. Bertel moves his corresponding pawn forward so they stand directly opposed. Falck brings his knight into play and Bertel does likewise. He knows that Bertel will continue in such a manner, maintaining symmetry in a battle of nerves. They will direct their pieces forward and back without end, watching each other, brooding upon each other's moves, retaining a balance that sooner or later, imperceptibly, will begin to tip, and then will follow a brief struggle of life and death in which Falck most regularly will be the loser.

Why did I teach you this game? he says with a sigh as Bertel captures one of his bishops.

Your move, Magister.

But I have lost.

You must play to the finish, Bertel insists. I am entitled to my endgame.

Falck moves a rook this way and that. Have you heard that Oxbøl, the old missionary at Holsteinsborg, is dead? He looks up at the catechist.

I have heard.

They say he suffered an act of violence and died of his injuries. Have you heard anything about it?

The catechist shakes his head. Play the game, Magister.

Perhaps he struck himself too hard on the forehead when realizing what a wicked person he had been, and then died from the concussion, Falck muses out loud. I wonder if they have apprehended his assailant? Anyway, one may be thankful not to be mixed up in that affair, at least, he says with a nervous laugh.

Bertel emits a sound of impatience. Falck moves his knight to a position where it would seem to be reasonably safe.

May a person not ask where you have been this last year and a half? Falck enquires.

That would be my own business.

Did you visit your old mother?

Yes, I visited her.

Then you were at Holsteinsborg, he says triumphantly.

Only for a short time. I was in many places.

Did you meet your sister? he ventures to ask.

Bertel sends him a malicious look.

Very well, he says quickly, drawing in his horns. In any case, I am glad that we are together again. As long as it lasts.

Bertel says nothing.

They play four games. Falck almost has the upper hand in the second, but at the same moment he realizes he can win, his nerves fail him and he loses. After that he resigns himself and is beaten twice in a row.

Thank you for the contest, says Falck as they rise to leave. Bertel puts the pieces away. He nods and smiles smugly.

Should we go and preach to the savages? he suggests.

They follow the shore to the communal dwelling house of the natives. The fog shows no sign of lifting, and even if the ship lay at anchor in the bay, he would be unable to see it.

†

Some hours pass. The afternoon comes; the light changes within the compartment that is the colony, walled in on three sides by low, steep rock faces. He parts from Bertel's company and stands on the rock that protrudes between the Mission house and the colony harbour. At least the rain has stopped. Sunlight slants down on the fjord, bundles of diagonal shafts penetrating the clouds. He narrows his eyes in the hope of spying the ship, but sees nothing. He could go out to the point again, where most certainly he would see it, if a ship was there.

He catches sight of Kragstedt down at the warehouse. He ducks and gallops like a long-legged insect in a wide arc behind the colony and arrives at the colony house unseen from the harbour. He straightens himself up and slows to a more dignified pace. He passes the whipping post that has been unused for a number of years and yet serves admirably as a deterrent, stained with blood and bodily fluids that have seeped into its wood, together with the recollection of the man who last hung there. Falck shudders and gives it a wide berth, continuing around the fence that encloses the vegetable garden where, in a layer of imported Danish soil, the Trader's wife grows turnips and celery for use in her kitchen, the only vegetables to have proved hardy enough to survive the sixty-fifth latitude.

He goes to the door and knocks. Madame Kragstedt must have seen him coming. She answers immediately.

Come in, dear Falck.

She has appointed him her saviour, a hero who arrives, charging, to snatch her up on to his steed and redeem her from – what? A flood, a blaze, an irate mob? He does not feel himself to be a knight and does not care to be the Madame's saviour. He has enough to do saving the remnants of his own life. He edges his sick and rumbling organism past her in its encasement of black cassock, making sure to keep one or two paces of distance between them. At least he will not have to speak of the widow with Madame Kragstedt. She is to all intents and purposes without contact with the outside world, and is to his own knowledge unaware of his connection with her.

She closes the door behind them and the latch clatters loudly. She sends him a radiant, carnivorous smile that fails to conceal the fatigue, the despair and the encroaching madness. Please enter, Magister. I am alone.

Dear Magister Falck,

I trust you are well and in good cheer. My husband has now told of what occurred, at least in part. But of this, the least said the better.

I miss you, Morten! Am I to suppose that you are avoiding me? You have not yet paid me a visit since your return here, although a week and a half has now passed.

As for myself, I arise each day in solitude, melancholy and slothful, such has become my fate in this place. However, I have now read the book you recommended to me last year, for which reason I hope you will pay me a visit this afternoon, or whensoever you may find the occasion and inclination, so that we may talk of the unfortunate woman whose name my pen cannot express without my feeling shame and perplexity on behalf of my gender. But more of this when we meet, Magister Falck. You are awaited with longing by

Your devoted and most grateful, Haldora Kragstedt.

He stands in the parlour of the Trader and his wife. He inserts an index finger beneath his starched collar and runs it back and forth against his itching neck. A sticky mixture of sweat and potato starch collects on his finger. He wipes it discreetly on his sleeve. He hears the Madame's footsteps behind him, a padding of slippers. She closes the door to the hallway and glides past him like a ship, a rush of red satin, her dress swelling like a sail. As she halts by the tall chest of drawers, an item apparently spared by the fire, her dress shudders with nervous delay before settling.

I take it the Magister will not decline a little glass in my company? She looks back at him over her bare shoulder and smiles.

Certainly not, Madame.

She casts an enquiring glance across the room. How is your eye, my dear?

It bothers me not. There is nothing wrong with it other than being more or less blind.

I feel such guilt about your eye, and cannot forget your service.

Forget it, he says. I am trying to.

She turns round again. She is becoming when seen from behind, when the observer is relieved of looking upon her tired face with its scar that runs across her cheek like the flaming trace of a hand. She is tall, half a head taller than her husband, and the measure of Falck himself. Her shoulders and arms, which apart from the straps of her dress are exposed, are pale and freckled. But the arm at which he looks bears the mark of the accident too, he notes now, the skin seeming almost to have been crumpled down to the elbow. Apparently she sees no reason to hide her scars, perhaps because they serve to draw attention away from others that are much worse. Her hair, which has grown out again, is chestnut brown and displays a lustre: even in the semi-darkness of the colony house parlour it captures the tiny gleams of light from the gaps between the curtains, and is loose about her shoulders, according to the style of the day. He knows that the Madame frequently receives catalogues from Paris, richly illustrated, and small paper dolls that parade the latest collections. Presumably she spends no small part of her husband's income following fashions practically no one in the colony understands or appreciates.

You stare, Magister, she says, turning towards him with two glasses filled with a liquid the colour of tea. Surely not at me?

She blinks like a mechanical doll, her head moves jerkily and he imagines he hears the ticking of clockwork. Her eyes scintillate: their lustrous shine resembles something applied by means of a varnish brush.

He bows gently. Why, yes, dear Madame. At you indeed. He takes a glass and downs its contents, then hands it back.

Madame Kragstedt has put down her glass, she has taken only a small sip. Another, Mr Falck?

Only if you insist.

They are finding their former tone. He feels the familiar diffusion of warmth inside him, the serenity, the apathy. This is where he wishes to be. He had completely forgotten.

Her satin rushes and swells. He is handed a full glass, downs half the dram and seats himself at the dinner table, which he sees must have been knocked together after the fire. He empties the second glass. The Madame disappears behind a screen. He hears a splashing of water before she appears again. Washing her hands seems to have soothed her.

The Trader's brand-new house, built of solid Norwegian timber, is dry and warm. The colony crew resides in a pair of rooms at the other end: five men who drink and bawl and piss out of the windows, carousing until well into the night, to the considerable detriment of the Madame's highly strung nerves. The living is cramped on this colossal coast. The parlour smells intensely of camphor and other ethereal oils, which the Madame, on his recommendation, either imbibes or else applies to her exterior in order to prevent the unwanted displacement of bodily fluids and to assuage her irksome nerves, the unmanageable ebb and flow inside her mind. A solid tiled stove takes up one end of the room. Under the windows, on the south side of the house, stands a long bench, also new, and in front of it a table with six chairs, no longer those of before, which were upholstered with ox leather, but thin and rickety, made from what materials were available. New furniture is presumably on its way with the next ship.

Here at this long table the crew eat dinner each day, and it is where Falck has seated himself. The curtains are drawn, as heavy as Persian rugs. An unpleasant grey light bristles in through the cracks at the sides, fanning dustily out over the surface of the wall. Previously, no less than eight medallion-backed Louis Seize chairs stood lined up along the opposite wall, four to the right and four to the left of a tall grandfather clock, the echo of whose tick he still hears. Now all of it is no more, a considerable fortune gone up in flames on account of his, Morten Falck's, carelessness. Fortunately, the Madame is unaware of the fact, her husband likewise. The only person who knew is dead. A small ship's chronometer has replaced the grandfather clock and hangs on the wall, ticking frenetically.

Behind the colony house still stands the small annexe that saved the Madame's life last winter, entered through the same door in the corner of the parlour as before. Everything is disconcertingly as he remembers it, though in a bare and roughly hewn variation. The annexe was built so as to preserve the lady's modesty, that she may be spared the men's latrine and their lecherous looks and fantasies. Is there a slight whiff in the air of the parlour, a faint odour of female evacuations issuing from the concealed privy? Hardly. And yet he senses himself sniffing the air as he sits, imagining the Madame's effluvium.

He empties his glass. Madame Kragstedt fills it up. He drinks half. She downs several in succession and does not shy from slamming the empty glass down hard on the table. Now and then she disappears behind the screen and he hears vigorous rubbing and much splashing of water.

Magister Falck, she says when she appears again. Do you sense something?

Sense what, Madame?

A smell, she says. A foul smell.

Now he sees that her nostrils vibrate.

No, Madame, he says in a firm voice. I smell nothing.

I cannot refrain from thinking there is a smell of smoke. It has become a nervous obsession.

Understandable, he says, relieved that she has not referred to the smell of the latrine. And now it is as if he, too, can smell it, though he knows it is surely his imagination. It must have been hard on you, Madame.

I shall most likely come to terms with my fate.

She sits down opposite him. They smile to each other, but say nothing. They have always been good at being silent together, he thinks to himself. We should have done away with the Trader while we were at it and then married. We could have been silent together for the rest of our days and none of this would have happened.

He rises and crosses the room to study some copper engravings and gouaches hanging on the rear wall, ten views of Copenhagen: Rundetårn, Vor Frue Kirke, Nytorv with the Rådhus and the fountain, Børsen, Knippelsbro, Toldboden, the palace square with its colossal new edifice, a mountain of stone, at once ethereal and imperishable. Moreover a couple of prospects from the rampart and one from the hill of Valby Bakke.

Madame Kragstedt comes over to him. They were in the storage house, she says over his shoulder. He feels her fingers flutter upon his arm. A gift from my husband's brother-in-law, a copperplate engraver. We hadn't found the time to unpack them.

How fortunate, he says. They consider the works together. The Madame slips her hand under his arm and holds his elbow tight.

As you know, I spent much of my youth in the royal city, she says.

It is a grand city, he says, with beautiful buildings. Such lovely pictures bring back memories. Especially the large gouache with the panorama of Frederiksberg. I have sat many a time at the exact spot where the artist must have stood, and painted his work.

Let's have some fun, Magister Falck, if you will humour a poor woman who is far from home. Let us imagine these engravings to be windows. We are husband and wife and this is our residence in Copenhagen.

He squints at her. He sees that her hands are shaking. Very well, he says. She rewards him by replenishing his glass, sweeping by in her long dress. He takes on the role, addressing her in a jovial, gentlemanly tone. Haldora, my dear wife, I thought we might promenade in this fair weather. Would you care to accompany me?

Oh, yes, she says, and grips his arm, rather overdoing her part and continuing theatrically, her face turned to an imaginary audience: But the sun is so strong, dear husband. Allow me to fetch my parasol. She scurries away into the bedroom and comes rustling back with a bamboo cane that she holds against her shoulder. Where will you take me, dear husband?

The Madame is a sorry sight with the scarred skin of her burns and her eye that cannot be closed, and the half-manic looks of play that she sends him. For a moment he almost regrets having come here, but dismisses the thought from his mind.

We shall stroll in the countryside, he says in an actor's voice, to see the good peasants tending their fields and harvesting their crops.

They walk around the parlour several times, arm in arm, sweeping out an occasional hand to indicate to each other the rural idylls through which they pass. The Madame laughs, a laughter over which she does not have complete control. It is an old game of theirs, which they played often prior to the accident, but Falck realizes he no longer finds pleasure in it. However, their promenade seems to have calmed the Madame somewhat, and when they return to the table and seat themselves some natural colour has returned to her cheeks, as if they really had been in the countryside.

I wonder if I will ever see my beloved Copenhagen again, she says rather sadly, appearing at once to be quite normal.

You are young, Haldora. Naturally you will see it again.

In this country days move slowly and the years quickly. I feel each winter to be like entering a long period of confinement from which I may never again emerge. She sends him a melancholy smile, though remaining calm and contemplative.

It is a country that takes its toll, he concedes.

And gives little in return, she adds. At least if one happens to be a woman. As a man you may go wherever you please, over the land, upon the sea, into the fjords. I saw you just before on your way to the savages. I cannot even imagine what it must be like. It is a world that remains closed to me, like many others that are closed to us women. Tell me what it is like, Morten. Tell me what you saw inside the fjord!

I thought we agreed that we would not mention it, Madame Kragstedt, he replies rather primly.

Indeed. Forgive me. I shall not speak another word of it. But then tell me something else instead. Tell me about the savages you visit.

He describes their conditions fairly precisely, though omitting the peculiarly erotic atmosphere that so often resides in the communal dwelling house, and how he is affected by it. He tells her of their nakedness, of the warmth inside, and provides a vague description of their odours.

Her eyes consume him greedily as he talks. But what do they do when they wish to be together as man and wife? she ventures, her voice trembling noticeably.

They are uncivilized, Madame Kragstedt. They live in accordance with their nature and not with Christian modesty.

So they hide nothing, she says, and all is nakedness and physical urges without shame?

They are most decent, whenever I visit. They are not stupid, not at all like animals. One does well not to underestimate them. He tells her of a discussion with one of the native men, who believed the Danes could learn from the Greenlanders and quickly had him on the defensive. The story makes her laugh.

It would appear they are no easy match, she says.

They are cunning and say what they mean. They can be ruthless. A person could easily fall foul of their ways.

How strange, she says. If only fate had decreed that one should be born among them, one would be sitting there now without a thread and gnawing on a bone. What of their women, Morten? Would you say they were more liberated than us, their European sisters?

You ought not to make the mistake of envying these people, he says. They live a hard and brief life, and often suffer an unnatural and untimely death.

But their freedom, she says. Surely freedom is worth some years of life, do you not agree, Morten?

What freedom? Freedom to do what? To copulate at will, without hope of any afterlife? Do not forget that we ourselves rose up from savagery some hundreds of years ago, to find freedom in the Lord Jesus. We ourselves were once at the very stage from which we now as good Christians strive to save these native people.

Hm, she says, and studies his face. You are right, of course. There is the afterlife to consider. But sometimes a woman may feel her life to be without purpose. As you may recall, in the time after my arrival at the colony here I took part in many practical tasks. I gave instructions to the crew, kept the servants on a short rein, and taught their children. I supervised the soap-making, the cleaning, the laundry and the bluing of the clothes in spring. I arranged excursions to the fells, where we gathered berries and angelica for winter. It was a happy time. But now I do none of it. I cannot, for I sense their eyes upon me and it is a trial merely to receive them when they come to eat.

I know, he says. I remember how busy and glad you always were.

And now I potter about here, confined within a cage of Pomeranian fir or whatever it may be. Only seldom do I venture out. I am stuck here, a rarity about whom the people talk. I feel they can look in and observe me through the timber, with all their unsavoury thoughts about me.

The crew hold you in esteem, Haldora. I have never heard them utter anything but respectful opinions about you.

If only one had been blessed with children, things would have been easier. I have drawn the Lord's attention to their absence, but my prayers remain unheard.

Heard, certainly, if not fulfilled, says Falck. The ways of the Lord are unfathomable.

Do you think it has something to do with what happened? With what we did? Can a person be punished with eternal barrenness for such sins?

There are certain physical changes, he says, that may occur after an accident of such nature. But there is no question of punishment, and you, Madame, have nothing for which to blame yourself. We have spoken of this many times already.

Yes, we have spoken on a number of occasions. But the reason is that I cannot expel it from my mind.

The Lord is forgiveness, he reminds her. Do not forget.

But who would even bring children into the world in this place? The poor creatures would not survive the first winter. And afterwards, when the child had been taken back again, one would be lonelier than ever before. So it was when my maid's boy passed away. How terrible it was. I was so fond of him and would have taken him as my own, but it was not to be. Alas, Morten, this country is so unmerciful. I have a premonition that I shall not leave it alive.

There, there, he says comfortingly. Have you taken your laudanum today?

I have stopped. The drops make me lethargic.

But you must take them, he says admonishingly. After all, there is a reason for my prescribing them in the first place.

Yes, she says. I do feel I need them. I will take some straight away. She goes over to the bureau and takes out the little bottle containing the laudanum and imbibes a measure. Then she fills their glasses once more and returns to the table.

Madame Kragstedt's bustle creaks beside him as she seats herself on the bench. He has been thinking about his mother. His sister. And the widow. She is down there, he tells himself, in the warehouse. I can go and see her whenever I choose. Then he looks up and pushes his thoughts aside, focuses once more on the Madame.

You are pensive today, he says. For what reason? Is it that novel?

Yes, the novel, she says, abruptly seeming to shake off her gloom. She becomes enthusiastic. It is an interesting novel, quite singular. Whether it is a good novel, I do not know, though certainly it is thought-provoking. It is about freedom, of which we have just spoken. The woman in it is – how should I put it?

Moll Flanders? A whore, yes.

Well, indeed. You are forthright, Magister Falck. And yet she is free. Can one say that a person is free in her situation?

It is many years since last I read it, he says, avoiding the issue.

She believes herself to be free. She is a strong woman. And she ends up rich and apparently contented.

She is a character in a novel, he says. The product of a male author's imagination.

This Defoe, is he French?

No, I believe he is English. The edition I gave you is translated into German from that language.

I see. That would explain why much of it appears so nebulous. I shall read it again. I wish I had mastered the English language, then perhaps many things would be so much clearer to me.

I will send you an English dictionary and the novel in the original, he promises. It will make a healthy diversion in the dark months.

Thank you for your concern, she says, rather curtly. I shall expect to receive it in a year's time.

She places the pipe rack in front of him. He thanks her and picks up a small pipe whose bowl is of whalebone, the long stem and bit of amber. He loosens a sheet of tobacco from the thick block, tears it into strips with his fingers and twists them into the chamber. Madame Kragstedt asks if she may be allowed to light it for him. She strikes the tinderbox and holds the burning char cloth over the hole. He puffs. The flame dips, rises, dips again. He blows smoke towards the ceiling. Madame Kragstedt extinguishes the char cloth. She laughs.

Has the Madame considered taking up smoking? he asks. It is healthy for the constitution and makes good recreation.

I think I have had enough fire and smoke, she says curtly.

Forgive me, Haldora.

No matter. It was not your fault.

He pretends not to have heard. If he answered he would inevitably give himself away, he imagines. They say nothing for some time. The Madame disappears behind the screen and makes splashing noises. He lets his gaze follow the smoke to the ceiling, where it spreads outwards and remains in a cloud beneath one of the joists. He thinks of what is above, a store full of groceries, tea, coffee, tobacco, ale, aquavit and salted hams. He has been up there several times, that is to say in the previous colony house. It was reached, as it is in the new one, by a steep ladder and a hatch in the gable end, where a pulley has been fixed to the wall, so that wares may be hoisted to the loft. He thinks he can smell the sweet aroma of hops, the pungent whiff of ammonia from the legs of lamb that hang from the beams there. If only he could get hold of the key. He dismisses the thought from his mind. He has been to the loft for the last time.

Madame Kragstedt brings him yet another glass. She squeezes by and seats herself. The irregular ticking of the chronometer reminds him of the warbler at home in Lier.

Magister Falck must know that I am rather displeased with him.

He looks at her, ridden with guilt. He feels his pulse pounding in his neck. He swallows. With me, Madame? For what reason?

Her cheeks redden. Oh, please do not play innocent, Magister, she barks irritably. I am displeased because you are abandoning me. Leaving me here in this wilderness.

I see, he says with relief. I was not aware that you knew of my plans.

If you thought it a secret, Magister, then I must correct you. The whole colony knows that you are waiting for the ship like a lecherous youngster waiting for his sweetheart. Oh, forgive me, my tongue!

He places a comforting hand on her arm. My time is done, he says. My present circumstances, my health, my finances, are not such as to allow me to remain. If I can get away with body and soul intact, I may still be able to secure a living at home.

Oh, Morten, what about me, how shall I survive without you? Perhaps you think I, too, can apply to be released? But I am stuck here in this filthy whore hole! She clasps her hands together, her knuckles white. The scar on her face is almost violet.

Oh, dearest! He rises and sits down again beside her on the bench. Cry as much as you wish, my dear.

She puts her head to his shoulder and sobs. He holds her, feels her skin through the fabric of her dress, her ribs shaking with tears, chest heaving, the quivering flesh of her abdomen, her trembling spine.

Thank you, she says, and dries her face in her handkerchief. She smiles, then laughs a little. You are the only man I have met who is not afraid of a woman's tears.

Do you mind if I pour myself one last glass? he asks.

Please, take as much as you want, she says in a thick voice. Drink from the bottle if you so wish. But pour me a glass, too.

In the hall, which is not spacious enough for two, she stands and studies him.

Madame, he says in anticipation.

She does not move, but stares at him with a look on her face as if she is considering where and how hard to strike him.

He reaches for the door, but her hip is in the way of it opening. She moves aside, but in the wrong direction. It is as if she is playing a game, and part of the game is that he is not familiar with its rules. If he opens the door now he will force her against the wall. He turns slightly, so that she may squeeze past him into the parlour. They exchange glances. She presses her lips together. He laughs nervously. But she does not move. Her face is vacant, her mouth without expression, eyes empty and black as coal from the laudanum.

Is something the matter? he asks.

Kiss me, for goodness sake, she hisses irritably.

He leans forward and kisses her on the cheek. Not so much a farewell as an au revoir, he says.

She has placed her hands on his shoulders. They rest gently upon the muscle. He feels a slight warmth from her palms. Then she kisses him on the mouth. He laughs and tries to push her away. Her tongue protrudes from between her lips. She looks grotesque.

They change places. She edges past him and stands in the doorway of the parlour.

Go now! It is almost a scream.

All will be well, Madame Kragstedt. Have faith in the Lord and all will be well. He stands for a moment at the door before stepping out. She sends him her twisted smile, the tip of her tongue protruding inappropriately from between her lips.

†

Jesus Christ, our Heavenly Father!

It gushes from him the moment he pulls up his cassock and sits down on the privy seat, a mud-like mass, almost without smell, an inexhaustible landslide of brown. His intestines writhe in agony, and yet there is a considerable element of joy at being able to release, to discharge this spray of filth and empty the bowels. He groans, bites his hand and chuckles. His sphincter blares and squelches, and then there is silence. He feels more is to come and shifts his weight from side to side, bent double, his head between his bony knees, his hands massaging his stomach, but nothing is forthcoming. It is as if something is stuck inside him, a thick log of excrement blocking his passage. But most likely a fold of the intestine, he considers. He recalls images of the corpses he dissected and drew as a young man, and he sees now his own colon in his mind's eye and the blockage that has occurred. He imagines its slow release and the sudden slop that comes with it. The thought of it helps. A new deluge is evacuated and his anus trumpets a fanfare.

And then silence again. Is it done? Experience tells him that it is never done, that there is always more to come. He remains seated and kneads his stomach, digging his fist into the saggy flesh, systematically following the garland of intestines. Nothing happens. The colony's privy is situated on a promontory a short distance from the warehouse buildings. Beneath him, lapping waves lick the slime of faeces from the rocks. An icy wind wafts his behind, causing his genitals to contract. It feels pleasant, and a short exposure is most probably even healthy. Thank you, Lord!

Magister Falck, is that you?

He stiffens. The voice comes from the cubicle next door, on the other side of the partition.

Mr Kragstedt?

I thought it sounded like your voice, says the Trader. Are his evacuations pleasing?

Indeed, Falck replies. Most pleasing.

I saw you come running from the colony house. Have you attended
to my wife?

Yes, she wished to converse with me.

Excellent, Mr Falck. You are such a helpful person. I, too, wish to
converse with you and have waited some time. I almost have the impression the Magister has been avoiding me.

Certainly not, Mr Kragstedt. I have been busy with a number of
matters. A priest has much to which he is compelled to attend. As a matter
of fact, I was intending to come and see the Trader this very afternoon.

Well, then, Kragstedt says. And now here we are, each on his own
perch.

Indeed, says Falck.

I trust my wife offered him a little pick-me-up?

The Madame is most generous.

Yes, she is quite exceptional. Did she confess her sins?

No, she did not ask to confess. Her soul is pure.

Oh, come now. There is always something, surely, says the Trader,
no longer sounding quite as convivial. It is a simple fact of life, Magister,
that sins accumulate faster than dung in a cowshed. A person must muck
out in the mornings.

Perhaps the Trader wishes to confess his own sins? Falck ventures,
the same attempt at malicious irony that failed in his earlier confrontation with the smith.

The Trader ignores him. I often get the feeling the Magister knows
my wife's secrets better than I do myself, he says.

There are matters a person can only confide to a man of the cloth,
says Falck. It is a pastor's job to bear such burdens, that they do not
come between spouses.

Hm, the Trader grunts. Falck hears a rustle of clothes behind the partition, the rattle of buttons and buckles. As I am sure the Magister realizes, his carrying on with the prophets ought to result in proceedings.

I see, Falck says to the wall.

You have incited the natives to revolt against the Trade and His Royal Majesty's trusted representatives.

It was not my intention to do so.

You have disregarded your duties as a priest, the Trader thunders.

Yes, it is true. Falck groans as a new deluge departs his rectum. Yet he senses a light in Kragstedt's anger. It occurs to him that if the Trader really did intend to put him in chains he would not be issuing this tirade while seated on the privy, nor would he have kept him on tenterhooks these past two weeks.

You have been a poor example to Danes and natives alike!

I cannot argue with the Trader.

So what do you suggest we do about it, Magister Falck? He hears the glee in the Trader's voice and feels deeply relieved. His excrement runs like thin gruel.

My fate is in the Trader's hands, he says, releasing a sigh. What will you do with me?

I can think of any number of things, including wringing the honourable Magister's neck.

Indeed, he says, and finally feels himself to be purged. I am certain I have deserved it. Thank you, Mr Kragstedt.

But a man in my position cannot always do as he sees fit.

Of course not.

And therein lies the difference between me and the Magister. I take my responsibilities seriously.

Indeed.

A silence descends for some seconds behind the wall, a tantalizing silence. The Trader would probably prefer to be argued with so that he might fulminate some more, but Falck will not give him the satisfaction. Word has it from our bishop, says Kragstedt, that the Mission station here in the colony will be closed down in the autumn.

Closed down? Falck exclaims.

By royal decree, says Kragstedt with ill-concealed contentment. The Mission's activities will be curtailed along the entire coast. Which is to say that whatever else may happen, the Magister will be returned home by the next ship.

A storm of conflicting emotions rushes inside him.

Does the Magister understand what I am saying?

Yes. I understand. At least, I think so.

Since your connection with the Trade will be terminated, I find it best that we settle our accounts today. I shall wait for him outside.

The planks of the floor creak, the door of the adjoining cubicle opens and slams shut. Falck remains seated. His relief is short-lived. He is not to be put in irons, and yet he is greatly in debt to the Trade, a matter which financially may have him enchained for a considerable number of years to come. He realizes that Kragstedt has made sly use of his threat of arrest, the fear and anxiety Falck has borne within him this past fortnight, and his subsequent relief at the threat being lifted, as a means of softening him up in order to claw back his money.

Exactly how much he owes the Trade is a matter of which he has no conception. All he knows is that the debt has accumulated over six years and that he has long since lost control of it. A disgraceful circumstance of being called to the Mission in the colonies is that all expenses accrued by virtue of the office are accountable wholly to the missionary himself. He ought to have kept his own ledger in the years that have passed, but has never got round to it. He considers himself to be a practical man, not a bookkeeper, and the very sight of a ledger causes his vision to blur. He has shirked the responsibility, has received groceries on tick, tobacco and aquavit, to begin with also coffee and tea, wares that are not a part of the normal provision. But for the last two years the Overseer Dahl has refused him credit and he has had to make do without such items, which are a small, yet comforting, luxury of life in the wilderness. He fears the reason has to do with the size of his total debt. There may be a ceiling, some astronomical sum, of which he has now fallen foul.

He gathers a handful of moss and wipes himself, then studies the result with interest. Indeed, there is blood. Good! With blood there is cleansing. He gauges the amount to be the equivalent of a minor bloodletting, something he often performs on others, but never on himself. He pulls up his drawers and lets the cassock fall around his legs. Stepping outside, he sees the Trader standing on a rock some distance from the privy, his brass-buckled boots planted firmly apart, hands on hips.

Jørgen Kragstedt looks cheerful and contented, he thinks to himself and wonders whether it will be to his advantage. The Trader has not yet changed into his commandant's uniform, is still in his working clothes, a worn leather waistcoat with buttons of tin, a linen shirt and a homespun coat. His head is bare, his brown hair gathered tightly at the neck in a little pigtail, an appearance which lends him an air of civil authority that Falck finds more foreboding than any wig. The Trader is a picture of raw strength and physical health, and the situation seems to become him well. His double chin rests gently upon a white scarf. He looks down at the pastor with a smile as he clambers up to join him.

Falck straightens his back. He stands close to the Trader, but one step below him, due to the slope of the rock, something Kragstedt most likely has anticipated. The situation makes him think of his father, who he has seen stand before the sorenskriver in Lier on many an occasion. He can see the remnants of the Trader's last meal between his healthy teeth. Going by the smell of him, and the stains on the front of his shirt, he has partaken of smoked salmon and a rich meat soup, probably containing good and solid dumplings.

Falck senses his stomach rumble. What are we waiting for? he hears himself ask, a faint echo of the enterprising Morten Falck of old.

After you, Magister, says the Trader, and sweeps out his arm.

They descend from the rock, walk past the whipping post and enter between the buildings at the harbour. The Trade office is located in one of the warehouses. For a brief moment they stand and look out to sea. The Trader believes the ship will cast anchor in the bay within twenty-four hours. The natives have gone out in their kayaks and boats, he says. And they are never wrong.

Overseer Dahl rises politely as they step inside. He greets Falck rather formally, making him fearful that dreadful circumstances are about to befall him. It is plain that the Overseer has been expecting him. He is shown a chair and sits down on it. His mouth is dry. He looks around the room, but sees neither shackles nor chains.

Dahl picks up a thick ledger from the desk and opens it. He licks his finger and skims through the pages. Then he turns the book round and indicates a column.

Here.

His finger runs down the page and turns it over. Years, dates and sums of money flash by as though in a tombola, page after page of entries and figures, and then his finger stops and stabs at the bottom.

And here.

Falck bends forward. He squeezes his bad eye shut and stares at the figure. It is worse than he had anticipated, though not quite as bad as he had feared. Neither shackles nor chains, at least not yet. Only the debt.

One hundred rigsdalers? he says, looking up at the Overseer, then at the Trader, who has remained standing. One hundred rigsdalers exactly? Why not one hundred and seven or ninety-five? How can it be explained?

The exact figure was slightly larger, as the Magister may ascertain by examining the account, says Dahl. Mr Kragstedt has instructed me to round the figure down to the sum mentioned.

Easier to remember, says the Trader. The Magister has been given a rebate for the sake of old friendship.

Perhaps Magister Falck would like to be alone in order to study the figures for himself, Dahl suggests politely.

He turns the pages. I don't understand, he says. These are ordinary goods for which my contract stipulates I should not be charged. Butter, bread, oats.

And nor has he been, says Dahl, not until a certain limit. However, purchases in excess of the ordinary provision must be paid for, as the Magister would know if he cared to study the terms of his tenure.

All these extra rations have gone to the needy, he protests. As the Overseer will be aware, times have been hard, there have been shortages, and since the Trade has declined to take any responsibility at all for the hungry, the Mission has donated small amounts of oats and butter in order that they should not perish.

How very touching of the Magister, says Kragstedt drily. I am sure he will receive his due rewards in the next world, but this is a business, not a charitable institution, and neither is it the gateway to Heaven. He chuckles at his wit and the Overseer emits a cackle. Oats and butter cost money, and in the final account, Magister, it is all the property of His Royal Majesty. I take it he would not steal from the king and share the spoils with anyone who happened by?

I was unaware it had to be paid for, Falck replies meekly. These are provisions for charity. I find it unjust.

The instruction is quite unambiguous, says Dahl. Moreover, the tariff for luxuries has gone up.

What tariff? What instruction?

A copy has been put up on the wall of the store, says Kragstedt. It has been there a whole year. Has he not seen it?

No, as a matter of fact I have not. I am not in the habit of reading the Trade's announcements. I must assume they concern neither me nor the Mission.

Oh, but they do, Magister. Indeed they do. Dahl, would you be so kind as to show Magister Falck the instruction and the tariff? It seems he has been too busy to take note of them.

Certainly, Mr Kragstedt.

But Falck cannot tear himself away from the columns of figures, now that he sits with them at his disposal. He flicks back and forth through the pages, studying entries for aquavit, tobacco and coffee going back years. The ledger is an almanac of excesses for which he is now being held accountable, on top of the help he has provided to the needy out of the good of his own heart. There is something not right about this account, he knows it. He sits bent over the columns. He feels himself grow warm under his wig, removes it and puts it down on the desk. He sees the lice come crawling from among the white powdered horsehair. He runs his hand through his own hair. It is damp with sweat.

This expenditure, he says. I admit that it may be excessive, but much of it must surely fall under the old tariff?

Correct, says Kragstedt. If the Magister had settled his account earlier, the old tariff would have been considered valid. But now the new one has come into effect, and therefore his debt has risen accordingly, and with retroactive effect. Wholly in accordance with the instruction, of course.

And this column here, Falck says. What is this?

Interest, says the overseer.

Interest! He tears at his hair. What interest? At what rate?

The rate according to the tariff, Dahl replies imperturbably.

I don't understand it, he says, turning the pages. It cannot be right. I intend to submit a complaint.

Very well, says Kragstedt. He's within his rights. Nevertheless, he shall have to sign to the effect that he has been made cognizant of the account and has studied it, if not accepted its validity.

The Trader dips a pen in the ink pot and hands it to him. The Overseer considers him inquisitively with the trace of a grin. Voices can be heard outside, laughter, running footsteps, heavy boots dancing a jig on the quayside. Probably the cook and the smith. Laughter again. Kragstedt and Dahl exchange glances and a smile.

Here, says the Overseer, and places his index finger where the signature is required.

No, he says, and pushes the pen away. I wish to initiate investigations first.

What investigations, Magister Falck? Kragstedt looks at him in puzzlement.

Furthermore, I wish also to speak to you, Mr Kragstedt, of certain matters of a personal nature. Concerning the Trader's wife.

Kragstedt retains his composure. If he does not sign, I shall have to consider it embezzlement of public money. I would be compelled, no matter how reluctantly, to have the Magister arrested.

It would not be the first time.

Think it over, Magister, Kragstedt implores. This can only cause him further problems, besides the ones he has already brought upon himself. If he signs this document, I shall give him my word as a gentleman of honour that he may continue to live well and without accrual of further debt until his departure. Gratis and with full access to all shelves of the warehouse. What do you say?

He dips the pen once more, tapping away the excess ink against the edge of the ink pot and handing the quill across the desk, eyebrows raised in a question mark, face lit up in a smile.

Be good and keep your honour for yourself, says Falck. It is my right to ask for some days of respite.

He looks up at the Trader, who stands pensively on the other side of the desk. His thumbs rest in the waistband of his breeches, his paunch full and heavy.

I dare say, he replies. In which case, naturally, I must take my own precautions.

Falck senses the terror creeping up on him. He expects at any moment to hear the sound of shackles and chains. What on earth have I done? he asks himself. Why am I so stubborn? But instead he hears the voice of the Trader:

I have something in my possession that would seem to belong to the Magister.

Kragstedt steps up to the shelf and finds a folder, which he opens. It contains a stack of papers full of writings and drawings. He flicks through them and chuckles. He holds up a sheet with a sketch of a naked woman. Falck feels himself at once grow cold.

Not bad. The Magister is a proper artist.

How . . . ? Falck blurts out, only to choke on his words and remain silent.

We found this journal, as we might call it, among the Magister's things when we collected him up the fjord. If I am not mistaken, this would be his mistress so lovingly portrayed here. The Trader hands the paper to Dahl, who studies it with a smile of acknowledgement before handing it back. This journal makes very interesting reading, Kragstedt says. Wouldn't you say, Dahl?

Very interesting indeed, the Overseer echoes.

The Magister's college and Professor Rantzau himself will no doubt find it both instructive and titillating, says the Trader.

Falcks says nothing. His arms rest like lead upon the desk.

The Trader cannot resist twisting a knife in the wound: Such a shame about your mistress, Magister.

She was not my mistress, he mutters under his breath. She was my wife.

The Trader appears not to have heard him. It was your good friend the smith who found her last night. It seems she jumped from the cliff, unless someone pushed her. It grieves me on your behalf, Magister. I know he was attached to this unfortunate person. The Trader does not appear to be grieved at all, neither in voice nor appearance. Rather, he would seem to be in his element.

Falck sits with his head in his hands. Outside, the sun appears in a fleeting glimpse. A shaft of its light creeps on to the desk and illuminates a column of the ledger, then fades away and leaves the paper grey. It is all over, he thinks to himself. Everything is over. The only thing he wishes now is to come away to the Mission house and close the door behind him.

He clears his throat. I want my groceries back. Good bread, pork, oats, a jug of ale, aquavit. My catechist, Bertel Jensen, must also be provided for.

Of course, says the Trader promptly. Overseer Dahl will make sure he gets what he needs. The Magister can carry it all home with him once he has signed.

And my papers, Falck adds. My journal.

His journal will remain with us, Kragstedt replies. You have my word, Falck, that these papers will not be seen by any unauthorized person.

He looks at them in turn, Dahl in front of him, the Trader to his right. He takes the pen, dips it in the ink and taps it against the edge of the ink pot.

Where do I put my name?

The Overseer points again.

Here.

It is as if both of them hold their breath as he places his signature beneath the final column with a cramped flourish:

Hereby attested by Morten Falck, Priest of the Mission at Sukkertoppen.

This fifteenth day of August, AD *1793.*

†

He returns home, staggering slightly. The defeat, the humiliation and the shock have made him weary, but as the Saviour has taught him, in humiliation there is liberation, in misfortune and grief a catharsis. If it is true, he has good reason to be glad. Indeed, he feels happy and, for the first time in years, free. Moreover, the sun now shines on the dampness of his perspiring back. In a canvas sack he carries the groceries Dahl has issued to him, among them a bottle containing one and a half pots of aquavit, his other hand bears a jug of good ale.

The grass is wet, the path muddy. The hem of his cassock drags in the dirt. He lifts it up, stumbles and drops the sack in the mud, almost spilling his ale. By some dexterity not a drop is lost. Thank God. He continues on his way, only a couple of hundred paces to the Mission house, yet today his path seems longer. He walks in the shadow of his debt and the poverty which by a few swift strokes of a pen has been imposed upon the remaining years of his life. In exchange for a measure of aquavit and ale. Thereupon more humiliation. Supplication. Ridicule. Self-contempt. Without prospect of becoming decently wed. An early death. At this moment he feels contented by the thought, relieved of responsibility and hope, and thereby free to abandon himself to the bottle that nestles in the sleeve of his vestments and the jug he balances in his hand. From dust thou hast come, he mutters to himself, to dust thou shalt return, and from dust shalt thou rise again. How can they treat a man of God in this manner? What has happened to the world that such a thing is possible? But he wishes not to dwell on it. He thinks of the bottle, of how he will remove it from his sleeve and twist the cork from its neck. The pungent vapour of alcohol in his nostrils. He will take his time, for he is in no hurry. He has the evening, and the night as well.

He puts down the muddied sack in the kitchen and finds the fire steel and flint. He takes a handful of dried heather and makes a pile in the stove, stacking the peat around it and on top. With numb fingers he strikes the steel. A fan of sparks leaps to the tinder, igniting it at once. He gets down on all fours and blows cautiously, a thin jet of hard air. A crackling blue flame flickers, rises up yellow through the peat and gradually reddens. He remains on the floor and watches it, feeling its warmth against his face. The cramped room is soon unbearably hot and in order to endure it he must keep the door open to the rain that now falls heavier than before. He stokes the fire with the poker. The smell of the pork makes the saliva well in his mouth, though he is unsure if it is due to hunger or nausea. Yet he knows it will help to eat. The thought of the aquavit calms him.

He adds dried peas to the meat, some water from the trough, and stirs with a ladle. He leaves the pot to boil, goes to his room and removes his cassock, the ruff and his wig. All of it is wet. The ruff, a gift from his father, has again lost its shape, has become limp and sticky to the touch and now resembles a pamphlet picked out of the gutter. The horse-hair wig has absorbed so much rain as to double in weight, the powder coagulated into thick, mealy lumps on which the lice feed lustfully. He puts on a shirt and breeches and takes the ruff with him into the kitchen. He stirs some potato starch into cold water and dips the collar until it is soaked. With a brush he removes the worst of the dirt. Its white has long since gone, but he has no more blue with which to restore it, and he does not allow the girl who washes for him to touch an item so essential to his work. It must be crimped, and this is a job he manages himself. He finds the collar iron and heats it in the fire. He shapes the ruff carefully, taking care not to singe the material, burning his fingers instead. Soon it is returned to its intended form. He carries it back to his room and places it in its round wooden box, which he leaves open in order that the damp may leave it.

The peas are almost boiled. Dahl has endowed him with a lump of rancid butter, which is better than nothing, and he recalls the conviction of his dear, deceased mother that a person ought to consume at least a pound of dung each year. He puts a spoonful into the peas. The instant smell of ammonia from the fetid substance fills his nostrils. He can barely wait until the food is cool enough to eat and pours himself a cup of ale, which he downs in one. He belches, the yeasty aroma of the flat brew prickling in his nose. Alcohol issues out into his brain and body, concentric rings of well-being that prompt him to relax. He fills the cup again and sips at its contents. And then he eats.

He potters about in the house, in his room, in the kitchen, the parlour, putting things in their place, cleaning the stove, humming a psalm, opening the flue so that some of the after-heat may seep into his habitation. He shovels a few glowing embers into the bucket and tops it up with fresh coal from the alcove in the kitchen. Coal produces only a minimum of smoke once it has burned down to embers, and for this reason he uses it in his lodging instead of the cheaper bricks of peat. He carries the coal bucket to his room, shakes it slightly in order that the hot coals may be dispersed among the cold, then puts it down on the thick slab of slate under the desk. There should be enough to last the evening.

He places the aquavit on the desk along with a glass. For the moment he leaves it untouched. But it is there, in all its power and glory. He hums to himself and performs a few more domestic rituals, turns the clothes on the line, tidies his bed, goes back and forth between his room and the kitchen, shakes the coal bucket again. It will soon be hot.

Outside, daylight yet remains, but rain, fog and cloud have descended upon the colony. The colony house has vanished from sight. Indeed, he cannot see a single structure from the somewhat removed situation of the Mission station. The fog is good. It will help him forget where he is. He goes back to his room.

He plucks an issue of the *Christiania-Kureren* from the clothes line, a publication his father sends him annually, a year's subscription at a time, which he reads on the appropriate date, though with a delay of exactly one year, providing the issue in question has not been ruined by damp. He tears half a page from it to use as a spill. He dwells on an obituary notice, now several years old:

Christiania, the twelfth of January 1789. Our beloved mother, Birgithe Christine Falck, née Rasch, widow of long since deceased postmaster Falck of Christiania, has peacefully departed this life in Akershus, aged 88 and one half years. Notice hereof is hereby given to kin and friends by her sorrowful bereaved. Andreas Falck. Carl Falck.

A notable age. She must have come into the world in the year 1700, when Tordenskjold was still a boy and Frederik IV was king. His father has circled the notice. The deceased hails from his side of the family, the side from which Morten has taken his surname.

He rolls the paper, the notice and his name together and puts it to the coals, lifts the tiny flame to the lamp and ignites the wick. He sits, holding the spill between his index finger and thumb, watches the flame consume the printed characters, *lly depart, 88 and on h, ful bereave, Carl Fal*, sees his own name vanish and then lets go at the last moment, as the flame turns to ash and gently descends to the floorboards. He steps on the glow and takes out his correspondence.

He lifts the bottle of aquavit from the desk, weighs it in his hand, pours half its contents into a cup and lays out writing paper, pens, ink and sand. Evening is drawing in, the colony bell has struck nine. Now the fire-watcher will sing the hours. He tests the nibs of the pens with his fingers. They are all soft and in need of sharpening, preferably they should be replaced. With his sharp letter opener he cuts thin shavings from them, tests them again with the tip of his finger, one after another, makes his selection and dips it in the ink, turns to the most recent page of his diary and writes for an hour or so of his visit with Madame Kragstedt. He drinks a little of the aquavit, then puts down his cup and adds a short addendum concerning the widow and his encounter with Kragstedt and the Overseer Dahl.

He takes out his lead pencil and sits down to draw, a distraction that never fails to settle his mind. He takes his little mirror and endeavours to produce a self-portrait. The result is a brooding, disabled-looking individual of suspicious intent. He looks at the drawing, looks in the mirror. The drawing speaks true; it knows something he did not. He crumples it up and tosses it into the coal bucket, takes a new sheet and draws a woman, naked and smooth-haired. She reclines with legs apart and the beholder is confronted first by the sight of her vulva, the glistening moistness of whose labia he labours upon, and beyond her genitals her abdomen, languishing breasts, her chin, mouth and eyes, her gaze. It is a satisfactory drawing, in its composition as well as in certain other respects, yet he is unable to keep it. Someone, perhaps Bertel, has been rummaging among his papers. The thought of him possibly having read his diary, especially his entry of the previous night, concerns him. He ought to begin the habit of destroying all that he writes of such nature. Libidinous drawings are perhaps not the most damaging of items, but they must nevertheless be disposed of. To the bucket with the drawing. The jug of good ale is empty, the bottle of aquavit considerably depleted. He is flushed with warmth from drinking and writing and drawing, perhaps also from an impending fever that is most likely of sexual origin.

He goes to the window, cools his heated brow against the pane and looks out towards the colony house that lies somewhere in the fog. The glass is uneven and has drooped in its frame like a caramel mixture, probably as a result of too little lead. The raindrops spatter against it. He picks out the roofs of the boathouse and the blubber house at the shore. There are no people to be seen. But the fire-watcher is about, perhaps the smith again, almost certainly patrolling at the warehouse and along by the promontory from where he will spy for the ship they await, and look out for thieves on the prowl. The crew are most likely as always in their room, passing round the ale jug and the aquavit bottle, slapping their playing cards down on the table, blustering their bids and keeping the Madame from her sleep. And then there are the mixtures in their small houses, the silent servants of the colony, among them Bertel, and the native folk in the Greenlander dwellings. They are many who inhabit the place. And Kragstedt himself, enshrouded in the blue-grey smoke of his long-stemmed pipe, or else retired to bed.

There is a knock on the door. He gets up and opens it, stares blankly into the night.

You? What do you want?

She does not reply.

He steps back, a single pace. She enters, takes off her clothes, hurriedly and yet as a matter of course, and climbs into the bed, drawing the covers over her. The woodwork of the alcove fails to creak, he notes, the straw of the mattress is silent. She looks across at him. She says nothing.

Now that you are here, I am glad, he says, then adding with a sigh: I suppose there is nothing I can do about it.

He stands and looks down at her, wearied by alcohol and defeat. Her naked body beneath his foul-smelling covers. She blinks her eyes. He bends down, stares at her, puts his hand under the covers and touches her between her legs. She is there. She is to the touch as she has always been, still and passive, cold as a rock. He retracts his hand. He can sense the smell of her, or perhaps only the recollection of it.

Sleep, he says. I have work to do. A pastor's work. He smiles. *Palasi* work!

She turns over towards the wall. He tucks the covers around her. She is now a parcel waiting for him. Indeed, he has missed her.

He seats himself once more at the desk. There is still some aquavit in the bottle. He puts his finger through the ring and pulls out the cork. The sound is like a kiss. He puts the bottle to his mouth and drinks a little, corking it again with a vigorous shake of his head, a gasp and a shudder – *huuh!* – only then to promptly open it again and drink some more. Now he is drunk. Drunk, but still not merry. How much aquavit does merriness require? And why drink otherwise? One drinks to become merry. *And he said unto them: Drink, and let your hearts be merry!* He follows the Lord's commandment, for he is a true Christian. He drinks again, small, measured mouthfuls. And now there is none left. The aquavit is inside him. It has changed places. Now it is he who is the bottle.

He puts the bottle down on its side. It rolls towards the edge of the desk. He observes it with interest. It drops and skitters across the floor without breaking. The widow sits up and looks at him. After a moment she lies down again. She is used to his excesses. He retrieves the bottle, places it once more in the middle of the desk and releases. Again, it travels towards the edge and drops to the floor with a clunk. The widow emits a sound of annoyance. He chuckles quietly to himself, feeling at once mischievous and almighty. He picks up the bottle and repeats his experiment, and then again. The bottle rolls, the bottle drops. Why does it drop? How does it know in which direction the floor is to be found? He shakes his head, the room mimicking the motion, though in reverse and with a kind of elastic delay, as though space were a frame attached to his head by means of threads. It continues to travel after he has stopped. An excellent observation. It must be committed to paper! He snatches up the pen, but is unable to coordinate his movements sufficiently to dip it in the ink pot and is forced to abandon the enterprise. Besides, he has no more paper left. He resumes his bottle game. Everything strives downwards, he thinks to himself. Everything bears within it a yearning for the depths, for the darkness and the filth that is there at the bottom of all things. Everything that is human or is created by man bears within it an inherent aversion to light, to purity, to ascension, to the heavens. We may rise up but briefly, in the faith, in will and in prayer, in sense and knowledge, perhaps even in love, yet always we will strive downwards again, to the filth in the gutter. This is the phenomenon Dr Newton calls gravity, without which all the gutters of the world would run in arbitrary

directions and their dirt would consume us all. Thank you, Lord, for
your wisdom!

Falck retires. He undresses and crawls under the covers to lie with the
widow. Her skin is warm. He squeezes her hand, wraps himself around
her body, presses his mouth to the soft, yielding flesh between her shoulders and neck. She turns her head slightly and whispers something he
does not understand. He smiles. Then he says:

My wife.

I forgive you.

Do you forgive me also?

Now we shall sleep.

He knows that she is not real.

PART TWO

Colony and Catechism

The First Commandment

Visionaries

(c. 1785–8)

The First Commandment, as it is most plainly to be taught by a father to his family:
'Thou shalt have no other God before me.'
What does this imply?
Answer: That we should fear and love, and trust in God above all things.

The settlement named Igdlut comprises a handful of peat dwellings scattered around a bay some way inside the inlet the Danes call the Eternal Fjord, approximately two days north of the colony. A score of individuals inhabit the place, among them Maria Magdalene and her husband Habakuk. The fjord, measuring thirty Danish miles in length, comprises several perpendicular elbows, giving the illusion that at each turn it will come to an end, only for it then to continue – the eternal fjord. The settlement of Igdlut, whose name means 'the dwellings', lies near the first of these turns. The bay is several hundred paces in extent, and its bed is of sand, allowing a person from the vantage point of the tableland to plainly pick out the shoals of fish as they pass through its waters. It is an excellent landing place for boats. The surrounding slopes rise steeply, their scrubby vegetation often difficult to penetrate, but some twenty or thirty fathoms up from the shore lie the monumental plateaus, staggered in height and separated from each other by low and rugged rocks. When Habakuk's mother died last year they buried her there at her request, in an unmarked grave, her head faced towards Jerusalem. The spot affords a view extending all the way to the mouth of the fjord and the open sea in the west, and to the jagged fells and dogged, creeping glaciers that wind towards the water in the east.

In the spring they fish for capelin, *ammassat*, that run into the fjord in shoals so tightly organized the fish may be scooped on to the shore with sieves fastened on poles, until the rocks teem and glisten with the flapping catch. In July it is the trout, sometimes the salmon, speared with a stake of split willow armed with barbs, or else long perches made of wood to which are fastened the sharp, hooked bones of the seal. In autumn the men depart to the north to hunt the reindeer. The settlement possesses a flintlock. Habakuk, the leader, acquired it some ten years ago when working for the Trade up at Holsteinsborg. The rifle has maintained the people of the settlement ever since, but now it is in poor repair and Habakuk never uses it without fear that it will backfire and turn him blind.

Habakuk and his wife Maria Magdalene inhabit one of the dwellings furthest inside the bay, at the mouth of the river. They have lived here for some years, though originally they hail from Holsteinsborg. On occasion they talk of how pleasant it might be to live upon one of the plateaus, with a fine view to all sides. Yet to be settled so far away from the shore and the river would be troublesome. No one lives on the fell, people would shake their heads at them if they should ever move there, and they would be looked upon as peculiar. So they have remained at the shore. It is where we Greenlanders belong, as Habakuk is wont to remark to his wife. The sea is our mother and there we must remain.

Maria protests: But there comes a time when one must leave one's mother and we are no longer children.

He scrutinizes her and then she knows it is best to remain silent, for otherwise his mood will be foul for the rest of the day.

Both were christened as adults. In the first years of their lives they lived as their parents, in heathenism and ever on the move. They speak only seldom of this previous time, prior to their christening, it feels as if it were another life entirely, a dark and provocative issue on which it is best not to dwell. And yet Maria Magdalene thinks upon her youth, a nomadic life, summers spent in the skerries with her family, winters close to the colony. They lived in tents made of hide and in earthen huts, makeshift and temporary. They existed in their filth, but the filth had its function, it was natural and of no inconvenience to anyone. Only when a person becomes Christian, she thinks to herself, does filth become filth, a substance to be avoided and removed, a foul-smelling and shameful thing.

Home was where the family was, and where the creatures of land and sea which they hunted were to be found. No loyalty existed towards any place in itself, no particular feelings of home attached to certain rocks, plateaus or bays, no urge to settle. Such things came only with Jesus and the Baptism. It was as if the three dashes of water with which the priest wetted one's forehead imparted a whole new set of emotions. They listened to the stories about Jesus and learned from the catechist to burst into tears. And the tears created the emotion that lay behind the tears, as though in reverse and by delay. They had not existed before. But now they occurred in any conceivable situation. Laughter belonged to the heathen life, tears to the Christian. And so it was that they became attached to one place, the same tent rings and dwelling walls, the same constellation of ridges and valleys, and the enervating rhythm of daily life. When they went away to hunt, they told each other and people they met of their home by the colony. And when they did so, they burst into tears. They realized that they longed to be home. A completely new emotion. And always it was a relief to return, to slot back into familiar surroundings as though into old clothes, to walk the same routes across the same rocks, to greet the same people.

She recalls how the winter would twist and tighten its grip upon Holsteinsborg. Kællingehætten, the great peak behind the colony, made aflame by the low sun, the Northern Lights flickering blue above snow-clad slopes, the moon spreading its metallic sheen across the fellsides. She ran in her kamik boots over the snow, young and cheerful, almost weightless. The missionary Oxbøl received her in his big house, and he gave her lessons in private, for she was quick to learn. He had taken it into his head to teach her to read and write. This was before she knew Habakuk.

Mind what you learn from the priest, said her father. He is forever after the young girls.

She was familiar with the rumours concerning the old pastor. He had lain with several girls she knew; two of them had become pregnant and the skerries were said to teem with his illegitimate offspring, without him ever bothering to have them taught or christened. Now the majority are grown up and the priest himself remains vigorous and productive. She often encounters his progeny whenever she is away from the colony, light-skinned and freckled and unreliable. The lake of fire and brimstone awaits Oxbøl, there is no forgiveness for the likes of him, and most likely he knows it too. But back then she was unworried by the pastor's intent. His wish to teach her to read and write had become her own. The urge to read was like a hunger. And she learned quickly. She read the catechism and the Gospel, she read issues of *Kjøbenhavns Posttidende*, used by the Trade for wrapping paper, and she read books from the pastor's library. When he tested her on the catechism, he was compelled continually to interrupt.

I must impress upon you not to answer my questions in your own words, as though in ordinary conversation, but to follow the exact wording of the text.

But if you put it into your own words, it shows you have understood the meaning of it.

That may be so. But this is the Holy Word of God and it is to be learned, not understood. You must bow to the Word, woman, and desist from making yourself His equal.

He made me in His image!

That's enough, Maria, Oxbøl would splutter, exasperated. Or else I shall be unable to confirm you.

Nonetheless, in the autumn she was confirmed.

Now I'm christened and confirmed, she said to him, so now we may no longer sleep together. It's a wonder you haven't got me pregnant.

He sat in his chair and studied her with his foxlike eyes and a wry smile on his bloodless lips. You could be my wife, Maria.

You're an old man, I don't want you, thank you very much. Besides, I am engaged.

And what is his name, this fortunate young man?

His name is Habakuk. Oxbøl can marry us.

Oh, thank you. Thank you, indeed. I am most touched. Have you been seeing this suitor while you have been coming here?

We've been seeing each other since the winter.

You're no better than all the rest, the priest spat.

Lauritz Oxbøl, the Lord will punish you for your sins, she said, sending him a carefree smile.

Hm, the priest muttered, and drummed his fingers on the table.

And your bastards will return and take vengeance.

Let them come. I am not afraid of them.

She kissed him before she left. She was actually fond of the old philanderer. He was a hard master, who said what he meant. It was a trait she appreciated.

Habakuk was employed as a blubber-cutter at the Trade. He was tall and dark and always wore a tricorne hat he had purchased from a seaman. They had attended confirmation classes together, where they got to know each other.

You're the priest's mistress, Habakuk said. I bet he's taught you more than the Lord's Prayer.

And so they became lovers. Habakuk's parents were settled at Holsteinsborg and had been christened in youth. Habakuk himself had received schooling for a couple of years, taught by Niels Egede, son of Hans Egede, Greenland's apostle. He could both read and write, and the first letter she ever received was Habakuk's formal request of marriage. She took him to Oxbøl, who grudgingly married them in the new Bethel church. Afterwards, Maria crept back to read what the priest had written in the register. It said:

15 August 1775, Assumption Day. On this day were joined together in the

Bethel Church Habakuk, a blubber-cutter, and the woman Maria Magdalene, both of Holsteinsborg. With His blessing I did wish the newly wedded couple a long life together in happiness and unity. Amen. Lauritz Oxbøl, Missionary.

Maria laughed when she read this. The priest had been so disagreeable while wedding them, and yet the entry recording the marriage belied the fact entirely. He must have been biting his tongue, she thought to herself. She tore the page from the book and put it in her pocket. Now it hangs in a frame on the wall inside her home.

But the missionary Oxbøl was loath to release her. He sent for her at odd times of the day and he was a powerful man, so she was afraid not to answer his call. And she became pregnant. A pale and freckled child with untrustworthy eyes was delivered into the world. Habakuk was not pleased. He went to the colony manager and lodged a complaint. The colony manager wrote to the priest and the priest wrote back and had Habakuk dismissed from the Trade. After which they packed their belongings and came to Eternal Fjord.

And now they are here, at the settlement of Igdlut, where live a score of christened individuals and approximately the same number who remain heathen yet wish to become Christian. Maria Magdalene and Habakuk have provided instruction in collaboration with the catechist, the unchristened have learned the catechism and sing the hymns of Brorson in such a manner as to nearly raise the roof of the earthen hut in which they gather. They have wept at the sufferings of the Lord until dissolved in tears and mucus, and they live a life as devoutly Christian as any other. But no priest has visited them in years. Maria hopes this will change. She has learned that the missionary at Sukkertoppen, a Magister Krogh, whom she has never met, has ended his days and that a new pastor is on his way. Perhaps this one will be more interested in what goes on in his district than the one who hanged himself.

That autumn both the trout fishing and the reindeer hunt fail. The winter is hard. They must boil and eat their leather belts and kamik boots – a humiliation Maria has not experienced since childhood. All the children of the unchristened perish; some are strangled so that they may be spared the suffering. The mothers go into the fells with them, singing, and return, silent, with their clothing. The catechist at the settlement speaks to the parents and tells them that killing their own children is incompatible with the Christian life. But he can do little in the face of their problem and inwardly most are grateful for this departure of hungry mouths. Two young hunters are lost, failing to return from hunting trips. The elderly walk quietly away into the fells or on to the ice, they turn their heads one final time and look back upon the settlement with weary eyes, then vanish beyond the point or over the ridge, never to be seen again. When spring comes only half a score of adults remain. The catechist holds prayers for the dead and the missing; and those who have survived feel a strong sense of togetherness, yet remain fearful of what the future may bring. There is talk of them perhaps having to move out to the colony at Sukkertoppen, where at least they will not be allowed to lie around and die.

But the catch of capelin turns out to be good: optimism returns. They sail out into the skerries at the mouth of the fjord and collect the eggs of the long-tailed duck, black guillemot and common murre. They harpoon seals as yet heavy with the fat of winter; glistening chunks of blubber-covered meat are laid out, steaming on dried skins, and a feast is held which lasts for several days.

In the skerries they encounter a young woman who has also come from Holsteinsborg. Habakuk enquires how things stand there. They are the same. The old pastor, Oxbøl, is he still alive? As far as she knows. And has he given you instruction and christened you? asks the catechist. He has instructed me, she says, and here is the result of it. She indicates her little girl, pale and freckled and sickly in appearance. He let the Spirit of the Lord come upon me, but he did not christen me. So all is unchanged at Holsteinsborg; they cannot return there. If they are to leave, then it must be to Sukkertoppen, which indeed lies closer, but is also the poorer.

The young woman and her daughter return with them to Igdlut and move in with Habakuk and Maria Magdalene, installing themselves on the sleeping bench for visitors. The other women of the settlement dislike her; they find her haughty and presumptuous on account of her having lain with the priest and because she can read the scriptures and write her name. Moreover, she is a mixture and the fact makes them ill at ease. Indeed, some of these same feelings taint their opinion of Maria Magdalene, not least the suspicion that she considers herself above them, but due to Habakuk, who is the settlement's oldermand, they have swallowed their resentment and treated her well. Instead their bitterness is turned towards the stranger. Voices whisper and the situation is made no better by the woman sticking her nose in the air and plainly thinking herself better. On two occasions she accompanies Habakuk and some of the other men into the fjord to catch trout. They return without a single fish, though smiling smugly all over their faces.

Maria Magdalene's feelings towards the woman are mixed. She has some sympathy for her on account of her shrewdness and for being an outsider, yet she, too, is galled by her arrogance and feels pangs of jealousy when she returns from the fjord in the company of the men. She has words with the woman. You give rise to unease and envy, she warns. The other women hate you.

But she will not listen. She is as contrary as a child and seems to be permanently consumed by anger, which she is determined to take out on others. She replies that if the women cannot hold on to their men, it must be their own fault.

I wanted to help you, says Maria Magdalene. But now I understand that you do not want to be helped.

The women seethe in silence; they put their heads together and mutter. Maria hears them agree that they are ill-served by having a stranger live among them who nourishes herself so heedlessly on their meagre resources. When the winter comes she must be gone. And if she will not leave of her own accord, they have decided, they will kill her. She is unchristened and one cannot be punished for killing a heathen. Maria broods upon it and must concede that in her heart she wants them to do it. Why will she not leave? It is her own fault if anything should happen to her. Naturally, the men are aware of what is afoot, but remain passive. They are contented by the upheaval; they amuse themselves with the stranger and take her with them into the fells and lie with her, or else they creep over to her place on the sleeping bench when the lamp has been extinguished, whereafter the darkness is penetrated by giggles and pleasured moans. But when the winter comes, Maria considers, and life turns harshly upon them, then they will be quite as eager as the women to get rid of her. So for the time being they grin smugly, stay frivolous for as long as they can, and refrain from pondering the consequences. Maria speaks with her husband, only for him to sweep her concerns aside. The woman is a heathen. She has lain with almost everyone; it is no wonder the women frown upon her.

You lie with her too, Maria accuses.

He flinches slightly, then smiles, puts her hand to his mouth and kisses it. She is but a heathen, a bit of fun for us men. Surely you cannot begrudge your husband a bit of fun? It is you I love, you who are my wife.

They are going to kill her, says Maria.

Oh, I am sure it will not come to that.

You have no understanding of women at all, says Maria. You have no idea how vengeful and wicked they can be. You think women are better than men.

Let us speak no more of it.

She must leave, says Maria. I tell you, I won't have her living here any more.

Now you are the vengeful one, says Habakuk.

But that evening the stranger does not come to lie on the bench. Maria discovers that she has moved into one of the other dwellings.

Habakuk has bought himself peace for a time. After a while, Maria asks him about the woman's plight. It seems they neglect her; she exists on chewed bones and rotten food. They force her to give up her child to another woman. One evening, when five of the women are alone with her, four of them hold her down and the fifth thrusts a tent pole into her groin.

Here's your priest! they shriek. Can you feel how pleased he is to see you?

She clenches her teeth and her face contorts into a lump of pain. Yet she makes not a sound. Maria takes no part in these goings-on. But she is present. And she does nothing to stop them.

They cease when she begins to bleed. They draw away, frightened by the sight of blood, and leave her to lie in peace on her bench. She continues to bleed, then comes the fever. She curls into a ball without making a sound and assumes she is dying. Maria hopes she will die. It would be best. And yet she attends to her every day and brings her water and soup. It is her duty as a Christian. Eventually the woman gets up. She staggers about on her spindly legs and gloats. The women respond by placing red-hot coals on her skin when she sleeps. They tear out tufts of her hair. Maria offers to let her move back into her house. She declines.

These are my lessons, she says. And better at least than those of the Missionary Oxbøl.

Then one day, when most of the men are away, the women drag her down to the shore; and those who do not drag her, kick her and scream their encouragement to the others. They tie a rock around her neck, then row out into the bay and throw her overboard. They row ashore again and gather together to watch. Maria Magdalene sees it all from outside her house. She does not intervene. The woman does not sink. She hangs suspended with her head down, legs flailing in the air. The women stand on the shore and yell that she must die! Some of them wail hysterically. They gather stones on the beach and hurl them at her. *Diavulu!* they shout. Die! Their missiles rain down and penetrate the surface with loud splashes and plops. Some are well-aimed and strike their target. Maria hears it all. The woman still flails. It seems her head cannot be entirely underwater, for strangled, spluttered screams issue from her mouth and lungs. The women retire to their dwellings. They cannot endure the sight of her struggle to remain alive. Maria hears them break into a shrill-sung hymn.

She goes down to the shore and wades out to the little island on which the boats lie drawn up, and launches a kayak into the water. As she approaches the woman she can see that she has been kept afloat by pockets of air in her clothing. Maria keeps a distance, she is afraid that the woman will grab her and cause her to capsize. Their eyes meet. Her gaze is oddly calm. She reaches out her hand and the woman hesitantly accepts it. She cuts the rope and the rock sinks to the bottom. The woman heaves herself on to the stern sheets. She grips the boat tightly, coughing and vomiting.

Those useless idiots, she says. I could have told them myself that rock was too small.

Maria takes her home with her. She gives her dry clothes and hot soup. She must force her to eat.

Why do you want to die so much? she asks angrily.

Because I'm good for nothing, the woman replies through chattering teeth. I can spread my legs for men; it's all I can do. I'm full of the Missionary Oxbøl's semen; it runs in my blood and when I sweat, I sweat semen. Once, I wanted to be christened and die in order to find peace, salvation. Now all I want is to die. Salvation is not for me.

You cannot stay here, says Maria. You poison the entire settlement. You're a bad person. I want you away from here.

The woman looks at her with a smile of resignation. You are like me, she says. You are my sister.

What do you mean? I'm not like you at all.

You have lain with him, too, she says. He told me. You were his great love.

The Missionary Oxbøl's only love is the Missionary Oxbøl himself, Maria says. He will find punishment in time. She turns and begins to mend some clothes.

Behind her the woman chuckles and talks deliriously to herself about old Oxbøl. She calls him Pater Oxbøl and speaks in detail of the things he forced her to do and of what she would like to do to him in return. Maria regrets having brought her ashore.

When Habakuk comes home, she tells him what has happened. He is at once dismayed and angry.

How dreadful!

How barbaric!

The poor woman!

You're as guilty as them, says Maria. You can do penance by helping her.

I will do whatever you believe is best, says Habakuk.

The next day two kayaks paddle out through the fjord. They lie deep in the water. Each carries a passenger in the stern, their backs to the kayak man. One is the woman, the other her little daughter. The women of the settlement stand on the promontory and watch them leave. In the evening the catechist holds prayers. We are all of us guilty before God, he says. Let he who is without sin cast the first stone! When he has finished, the women break into their shrill song. Maria Magdalene sings with them.

Outside, it begins to snow.

†

She has not told anyone about it. But she cannot keep it secret for ever. Sooner or later she must at least speak to her husband. Or a priest. But where to find a priest? Especially now, after the colony has been moved to its present location, the clergy have neglected their district. Of course, she could speak to the settlement's catechist. But he is too pious to her unsentimental mind and would doubtless only fall down upon his knees and endeavour to talk her into following his example; and there they would moan and wail and invoke the wounds of Christ and the like. Such matters are not for her. She loves the Lord, she has respect for the Passion, but she has no desire to wallow in wounds and blood and bodily fluids like the Brethren.

She must wait until her husband returns. He is away hunting the reindeer and has not been home for some weeks. He has taken a mistress with him, another young woman, to cook and sew and keep his bed warm. She herself is too weak to go on such demanding trips. And keeping him warm at night is something she increasingly neglects, as Habakuk frequently has complained. If you were as expert in attending to your husband's needs as you are in the Gospel, then I would be a happy man, he says. As such, it is only right and fair that he take a mistress with him. But she wished that he did not.

She doesn't even know when it began. It was sometime during the winter when they were still snowed in and their meat reserves were dwindling. She had these strange dreams in which a figure clad in white appeared to speak to her. To begin with she thought it was Oxbøl coming to her, that it was a nightmare, and she would wake up with the bedclothes soaked in sweat. Oxbøl is not a man with whom she wishes to spend another night. The dream recurred twice and she began to sense that it was not the old priest at all. The figure spoke, but she was unable to catch the words. Perhaps they were uttered in some foreign language, Greek or Hebrew, it was hard to tell. Though she is relatively well-read, the biblical languages are not her strong point. She can rattle off some rhymes in Latin, but that is all. When Habakuk is in a playful mood he will often refer to her as his little papist. No, the figure did not speak Latin. Nor was there anything threatening about him. She had felt there was, the first time, but then her impression changed. If anything, the figure was beckoning to her. But what was he trying to say?

Then the dreams stopped. Most probably this was common, she told herself, that dreams become particularly vivid after some dreadful occurrence. First there was the woman who had arrived and caused them such trouble. Then came the truly dreadful occurrence. Their eldest son, the pale and freckled boy, had been practising firing the bow his father had made for him, and a wayward arrow had struck his sister in the eye. The boy had run away and hidden; the girl lay on the shore, screaming. Some of the other children came running up to their house to raise the alarm. When they came to the girl, the arrow was broken, whether by her own hand or her brother's they never found out. But Habakuk grasped the short and jagged shaft and tugged. It was a real arrow with barbs, and the point was a sharply honed piece of metal from the Trade, the type that breaks off and lodges itself crosswise in the flesh. Habakuk pulled on the shaft, Maria had to hold the girl's head tightly, and she could feel her husband use all his might as he twisted and turned the arrow to remove it. The leather bindings succumbed, but the arrowhead remained where it was. They hoped the wound would close and encapsulate the metal inside the orbit of her eye. But the girl died in the night. The boy, her older brother, returned the next day. He acted as if nothing had happened, ate his food, slept on the bench, and they left him in peace.

It was some days, or rather nights, after this accident that Maria Magdalene again dreamt about the figure clad in white. She thought perhaps it was the Lord wishing to comfort her in her grief. But she did not want His comfort. If You were any good, You would have saved my daughter and spared my son from becoming a murderer; now it is of no consequence. Each day she went about the place in the presence of her son, the murderer. She gave him food, mended his clothes, stroked and caressed him, and could not help but hate him and his freckled face and foxlike eyes. And the boy could sense this; he drew away from her. They had no other children who had survived the first year of life.

Habakuk has now begun to talk of moving up on to the high ground. He pretends not to remember it was her idea. It would be unusual. Maria has never known of anyone settling more than a stone's throw from the water. And yet there is something majestic and alluring about the plateaus. The fog does not reach there. A person can sit and watch it come creeping in the evenings and lay itself upon the water from shore to shore, pearly and lustrous, and so dense one feels able almost to step upon it and cross the fjord on foot. In the mornings one may watch it drawn out to sea again. Living at the shore a person cannot see a hand in front of their face in the fog, one is blinded and incarcerated and cannot judge from where a sound might issue.

We would be closer to God up there, says Habakuk.

Maria smiles to herself.

And then the white-clad figure returns and speaks to her again. It is the middle of summer. The son has gone into the fjord with his father and Maria is glad to be rid of them both. The settlement is all but depopulated, apart from the catechist and two elders who survived the last winter and now live in fear of the next.

This time she both hears and understands what he says: *Maria Magdalene, do you believe all this to have come from nothing?*

He has taken her up onto one of the plateaus, they must have wandered there in the dream, though she cannot recall having done so. Now he stands and sweeps out his hand to indicate the fjord and the fells and the sky. She scrutinizes him, taking note of his appearance, for she has decided to commit the dream to writing as soon as she wakes. Now she sees that it is He. The Saviour. She is in no doubt. He resembles the illustrations she has seen of Him in several ways: the beard, the long wavy hair, the brown eyes, the pale skin, the coat. But the look He gives her, the expression on His face, is not as she would have imagined. His eyebrows are raised, His lips curled in a wry smile. Is the Lord tormenting me? she thinks to herself.

And then He is gone. She stands alone, high up above the settlement, which is enshrouded by fog. It is the middle of the night, yet light. A pair of ravens tumble in the air and caw. The next day she writes it all down on a piece of hide from which the blubber has been scraped. She puts the document away under her mattress. She has need of someone to consult about the dream and wishes her husband would come home soon.

Some days later the dream recurs. She is standing at His side, as though she were His equal, and He sweeps out his hand and repeats the same, perhaps mischievous question: *Do you believe all this to have come from nothing?*

No. Of course not.

But no exchange comes of it. She would like to ask Him about various matters now that He is here, she would like to ask His forgiveness for being angry with Him for the death of her daughter; to ask His advice concerning her son, the boy with the freckles. But every time she is about to speak He waves his hand dismissively. He does not look at her. He looks away, out across the fjord and the fells.

Do you believe all this to have come from nothing?

No, I have already said.

She ventures to examine His chest; she bends forward and draws His coat aside. And there she sees the wound. It is not bleeding, but neither is it healed. A flaming, open gash. The entry point of the Roman lance. It reminds her of her daughter struck by the arrow. She wakes up crying.

Maria Magdalene, He says to her one night, *go forth and say to your people that their lives are sinful. They shall gather in number and leave the colony and the Danish drunkards and philanderers, and they shall worship the Lord.*

It is the longest pronouncement she has heard Him utter. She writes it down, word for word, in the morning. Now she has covered the entire parchment with his words. That same day, Habakuk returns from the hunting.

He hangs his head and appears remorseful. They have killed several large animals; they come with the skinned carcasses and deposit them on the ground, hind quarters with legs poking up into the air, red muscle marbled by yellow-white tallow and tendons. The winter is secured. But Habakuk is silent. After he has washed the blood from his hands he goes into the house and lies down on the bench. She boils him a portion of entrails and barley oats, but he pushes the plate away and turns to face the wall. The boy comes in. She gives the food to him instead and he gulps it down. She can see that he has grown. When he has eaten, Habakuk asks him to leave.

Something has happened, he says.

Yes, she says. Something has happened. But what?

He tells her. They hunted every day, but without fortune. The animals were too far away; they were too timid, and whenever he came within range to shoot, he missed. Something was wrong; they could sense it. He stopped sleeping with his mistress, thinking that perhaps the Lord was angry with him on such account and that sleeping alone would better his fortune in the hunt. Yet still they killed nothing. Then one of the men suggested they resort to hunting magic. They made small effigies of reindeer out of dwarf birch and heather, and pronounced spells over them. In the days that followed they killed many animals. But no one among the men was pleased. They were afraid they would be punished with sickness and accidents.

Maria is horrified. You have worshipped idols!

Yes. The Devil made us do so, am I right?

Then Maria tells him about the dreams. She shows him the parchment with everything the figure in white has said to her. They resolve to follow the commandments to the letter in order to avoid punishment. They lie separated from the rest of the dwelling house by means of a hide draped from the ceiling. It allows them some privacy. They hear the other members of the household come in bringing meat with them, which they begin to boil. The room quickly becomes stiflingly hot. Maria and Habakuk take off their clothes and lie down naked on the skin. They listen to the talk going on in the house. They whisper and make plans.

†

In the autumn they move up on to the high ground. To begin with they live in tents. They lift the joists from the old dwelling at the shore and carry them up the fell. They dig fresh peat and allow it to dry. They erect the walls. The wives tan the bowels of seals, which they use for windows; the men salvage the carcass of a humpback whale and lay the bones on the shore for the beach fleas to cleanse, after which they will be used for rafters and struts. They sail along the coast, which is awash with wreckage from sunken vessels, and collect what driftwood they find: planed planks, blubber barrels, wooden chests, rope and great rolls of canvas. Inside the fjord the inhabitants gather together whatever they possess in the way of European building materials, boards, hasps and latches, iron hooks for their pots, but the spoils of the shipwrecks turn out to be plentiful enough for their efforts to be superfluous. They know that plundering wreckage constitutes a violation of Danish law and that they risk chains and the pillory should they be discovered, but they tell each other that this is our country, what drifts onto our shores belongs just as much to us as to the Danes, and they can come and claim it if they dare. Habakuk constructs a long bench with room enough for each of the three couples who are to live with them to have their own spacious dwelling area. They erect a flagpole made from a jib mast, and hoist up a bowel skin decorated with a stylized impression of people dancing, hand in hand, in a ring. Their fluttering flag can be seen from afar.

Habakuk holds prayers on the plateau, in front of the new house. He tells of his wife's latest dream in which the Lord once again has appeared before her. The Lord is pleased, he says. He rejoices in His children. He says they have chosen the path to salvation and independence, a path they cannot walk with the Danish philanderers and topers of the colony. We are ourselves now, says Habakuk, and the Lord Jesus Christ is with us!

Yes! they reply who sit listening to him. But what are we to do if a boat should come from the colony and they say that we have corrupted the faith and stolen the wreckage that rightfully belongs to His Majesty the king? For this is, indeed, what we have done!

As long as we give heed unto the Word of the Lord, nothing bad can happen to us, says Habakuk calmly, taking his time to look them each in the eye. This land belongs to us, what washes on to the shore is ours to take without permission, and no one has the right to tell us what to believe in. The Lord is with us! He speaks to my wife and I pass His word on to you.

The autumn gives up trout, salmon and reindeer in abundance. The winter stores are filled by the time the cold arrives and the fjord ices over. People come to them from all corners of the district; new dwellings are built on the high ground, of peat and wood and stone. New storage pits are dug in the ground for winter stockpiles and are quickly filled. Blubber and brushwood and peat are burned for heating, but also driftwood from the shores of the skerries. The dwellings are good and warm; children are born and their mothers have milk. Then winter comes and the settlement hibernates and lies dormant. Thick, fresh smoke rises in silence from a score of chimneys high above the fjord. When spring arrives no one has perished from hunger, and they even have meat in reserve when the capelin fishing begins.

That summer boatloads of new settlers arrive almost by the day. They laugh in astonishment at the sight of the plateaus on which stand houses of all shapes and materials. What is this? they exclaim. These people must be insane! And then they go ashore and build something even stranger.

†

Maria Magdalene dreams. She has dreamt these houses and these people, now she dreams even greater things. She dreams houses on all the rocks and thousands of people living well and in peace and harmony. She dreams a school and Habakuk says to the people: The Lord has said there must be a school for our children, so that they may learn to read and write. And so they build a school and the children learn to read and write. And Maria Magdalene dreams of a hospital for the old and sick, and Habakuk passes it on; and they devote a house at the top of the plateau to those who are infirm, and employ some elderly women to look after them. And Maria Magdalene dreams, or perhaps merely has the idea, of a communal store and a list of those who have plenty and those who are in need, and all of it is carried out; and a widow's pension is set up for those who are left on their own, and a sick-benefit scheme for those who for a time find themselves unable to work, and a fund for those who lack the aptitude to go on the hunt, but who are able to carve figures out of driftwood and soapstone. And Maria Magdalene dreams of a church. And she says to Habakuk, The Lord has spoken to me. He says we must build a church and it shall be made of the land's own building materials, though we may use driftwood, too, and it shall lie upon the very highest point of the highest plateau. And thus they begin the laborious work of gathering driftwood and slate and peat for a church. The building work lasts a whole summer; hundreds of people take part. It is a fine church, facing west, to the mouth of the fjord, to travellers arriving by boat, and in front of it an arch is erected with the jawbone of an Arctic whale.

What have you dreamt this night? Habakuk asks his wife.

I dreamt that we are to live in peace and tolerance with one another, she says.

He seems disappointed. Is that all?

It is the greatest of all dreams, she says.

The Second Commandment

A Meal

(August 1787)

The Second Commandment, as it is most plainly to be taught by a father to his family:
'Thou shalt not take the name of the Lord thy God in vain.'
What does this imply?
Answer: That we should fear and love God so that we may not curse, swear, conjure, lie or deceive by His name, but call upon the same in every time of need; to pray, praise and give thanks.

Bertel is awoken by something cold and smooth passing across his belly. It is the hand of his wife, fumbling in sleep. He pushes it away, gets out of bed and goes over to the boy. He is sleeping peacefully. His feet have scuffed the cover from his body; his shirt has twisted around his torso and ridden up under his arms. Bertel puts it gently right again and pulls up the cover. The boy sniffs a little and turns on to his side. Concern and love. A difficult mixture. He has inherited his father's freckles and pale skin, as well as his irregular teeth, dishwater-blond hair and the bunged-up snoring, about which Sofie has always complained in relation to his own person. In addition, the good head on his shoulders. A fine candidate for the clergy. Bertel smiles to himself. Then he tears himself away and goes down to the harbour to look at the new arrivals.

 The ship lies calmly swinging at anchor in the bay, half-concealed in the fog. The colony bell tolls – perhaps it was what caused him to wake – and the crew are busy making ready for the welcome. He seats himself on top of a barrel, begs a spill from one of the native constables and lights his pipe.

Presently he sees a ship's boat on its way ashore, four seamen at the oars, the captain standing upright in the bow. The Trader stands ready to receive him, his young wife under his arm. She says something to him, then laughs, a chirping twitter, bright and foreign. What a strange bird she is, Bertel thinks to himself. The natives gather at the shore, hoping to do trade with the seamen. He notes that the women have neatened themselves; they are clad in whatever European clothing they own in order to make an impression on the Danish seamen. Bertel grimaces. The thought of his own mixed blood fills him with nausea, and when the native women jostle to mingle with the white men, he feels rage.

The boat is laden with wares and luggage. One of the colony's own boats has put alongside the ship to be filled up. Bertel goes over to Dorph, the cooper who lives with his sister-in-law, the only member of the Danish colony crew with whom he is remotely on speaking terms.

What is that hanging from the boom?

The cooper laughs. They say it is a cow.

A cow? Bertel stares. He has never seen a cow before. The beast hangs suspended from the cargo boom, and sways high above the deck. It lows in suffering. He has seen cows in the illustrated magazines that Sophie brings home with her from the Trader's house, where she is maid. He never thought he would see one in real life.

Or maybe it's the Holy Spirit, says Dorph. The way it floats about between the masts and won't come down.

You should not talk of the Holy Spirit like that, says Bertel by way of correction, though he nearly bites off his own tongue on seeing the glare the cooper sends him in reply. Know your station! it says. He realizes Dorph could lodge a complaint for having been addressed in such a manner by a native. Most likely the pulley is stuck, he says, to smooth things over. He can see the crew gathered on the deck; they look up at the cow and parley.

But who would bring a cow, and what's it to do here? the cooper says.

The cow belongs to the new pastor, says the Overseer Dahl, noting something on a slate. It is a milch cow. Its milk is highly nutritious, it restores the sick and keeps those who are well in vigour.

Does it help against pains in the chest? Bertel enquires.

Milk is like medicine, says the Overseer, for once deigning to look at him. It helps against this and that. If it survives the unloading we might all have a glass.

If it is the pastor's cow, then I shall ask for a glass for my boy, says Bertel.

I'm sure he will receive all the milk he wants, Bertel Jensen, says the Overseer. After all, he is to assist the pastor in his duties, so it's only natural he keep his catechist in good health.

Dorph asks the Overseer if he thinks the ship has brought his marriage licence. I have waited years as it is, he complains.

I know nothing of any marriage licence, Dahl says dismissively. He shall have to wait until the mail is brought ashore.

But I live in sin! the cooper exclaims dramatically.

Don't we all? Dahl retorts. Dorph is not nearly as put upon as he thinks. Nevertheless, I wish him all the best in the matter. He withdraws with his slate.

The boat lays to, and two men clamber on to the quayside. The captain follows them, bringing with him some of the light and fresh weather of the sea. He straightens up and smiles. He is clad in a long coat and white stockings to the knee. His hair is quite short. Bertel recognizes him from previous arrivals, a corpulent man with a pockmarked face and agreeable countenance. The Trader and his wife walk forward to greet him, the former raising his hand in salute to the tricorne hat he has donned for the occasion. Kragstedt is in full commandant's uniform, silver-buckled shoes and a short wig. At his belt is a sabre. Madame Kragstedt wears a floral dress trimmed with gold flounces. Bertel is quite familiar with the garment, Sofie having recently brought it home with her to mend. She put it on and together they jumped into the bed, there to play the Trader Kragstedt and his wife. Bertel smiles at the thought. He catches Madame Kragstedt's eye and is glanced by her brilliant smile. Bertel looks down at the ground. The captain slides one foot forward in front of the other in the way of the true galantier and bows, takes her hand between his thumb and index finger and raises it to his mouth, touching it lightly with his lips. Apparently a joke, Bertel thinks to himself, for all three laugh. But then they know each other from the year before. The Danes and all their peculiarities, understood by them alone. They walk back together along the quayside, the men's sabres swinging at their rears as they cross the planks, the Madame's dress a billowing rustle. They ascend the little slope to the colony house, where the bell still tolls. Kragstedt barks out an order to the ringer, a native employee of the Trade:

Enough, man, or we'll all be deaf!

The bell goes quiet. They enter the house.

The winch seems to be working again. The cow is lowered in stages into the ship's boat, whereupon some men follow, clambering over the bulwark and descending by way of the rope ladder. The oars are put into the water; they move up and down like the wings of some mechanical bird. Bertel sees a man in a black coat and wide-brimmed hat with a high crown standing in the bow, his gaze fixed upon the land. He must be the new priest. He begins to boss the men about. His agitation apparently concerns the animal that now lies tethered in the bottom of the boat. One of the seamen loosens the ropes around the cow's legs, shouts and commands are heard from all quarters, the cow kicks its hooves and the boat rocks perilously. And then it is brought ashore onto the quayside, where the priest speaks soothingly to it while holding its muzzle and scratching behind its ears. Folk stare, especially the natives, who gape, literally, in disbelief.

A reindeer! They exclaim. Why has this fool taken a reindeer across the sea? Where are its antlers? Look, its teats are as big as a sack of blubber!

Bertel does not dare to approach the priest as long as he is standing with the cow, which tosses its head and lows. Without realizing, he has removed his hat and stands clutching it before him, in hesitant subservience. The cooper steps up to the priest. He takes the cow by the rope and leads it over to the blubber house to be tethered. The beast strains against the rope and lows. The priest asks for water to be brought and the cooper fetches the fire bucket. The cow lowers its head and drinks. It urinates, a gushing torrent upon the planks of the quay. The priest addresses the cooper. Bertel cannot hear what is said, but the cooper removes his hat and bows courteously. The priest looks about him. Bertel sees that he sways slightly, rocking backwards and forwards.

Bertel Jensen, he says with a bow. Catechist. And the Magister is our new priest, I take it.

The priest looks at him and extends his hand. Bertel takes it in his. Morten Falck. I am to replace the missionary Krogh. Where is the missionary?

Kicked the bucket, honourable Magister. Passed away, I mean.

Of what did the good priest die? Was he ill?

It was more an accident, Magister, says Bertel, hesitating.

What kind of an accident? Falck looks him in the eye.

He hanged himself, says the cooper, now returned. Inside here, in the blubber house, honourable Magister. When they cut him down, the body fell right into the boiling tub, but we fished him out again with a boat hook. Sizzling more than a suckling pig on a spit, he was.

My goodness! says Magister Falck. I must remember to find a more suitable place should I wish to accompany Mr Krogh.

If the Magister's thinking of doing himself in, it best be done away from the colony, Bertel blurts out.

But the priest takes it with good humour. He pats him on the arm. A joke, dear Jensen. I assure him, I have no immediate plans to do such a thing, but am fit and healthy in body as well as in mind.

I see, says Bertel, and catches the priest's eye. Would that be on account of the milk?

The priest wanders off along the quayside, then returns. Bertel studies him. He is a tall man, stout and broad-shouldered. His eyes are blue, but the thick pigtail that hangs down his neck would indicate that his hair is dark and crinkly.

So this is Sukkertoppen's famous colony? says the priest in a jovial tone. Not much to look at.

The district's a good size, says the cooper. Several days in any direction. Bigger than Jutland's mainland from Skagen to Flensborg.

Indeed, says Falck. A colossal land and only a handful christened.

There's plenty to be getting on with for a pastor, says the cooper. Idol worship, murder and heathen darkness all around. The Magister Krogh had to give up, God rest his soul.

The soul of a suicide finds no rest, says Falck.

Perhaps he just stole a march on something worse, says the cooper. The Magister was losing his senses, kept hearing trumpets and hymns, and saw dead people wander across the heavens.

Indeed? How interesting. A shame I did not have the opportunity of making his acquaintance.

The cooper suggests they move the cow on to the land, where it may munch the fresh grass. They loosen its tether and find a place below the colony house where they fasten its rope to a rock.

Do not be afraid, says Falck to Bertel. She will not kick. She is as good as the day is long and appreciates human company. He pats the beast on the back and Bertel does likewise. He feels the hide tremble and withdraws his hand. It feels greasy. He wipes it on his shirt.

It looks sad, he says. Most probably it knows it is to die soon.

Falck looks at him angrily. She most certainly is not to die, excepting the fact that we all must, sooner or later, you take heed of it. Perhaps this cow will survive us all. Her name is Roselil, by the way.

Hello, Roselil, says the cooper, petting the animal in a way Bertel finds rather intimate and odd. Oh, I've not seen a cow since I was a boy. A man could start missing his home.

Bertel knows he should refrain from comment, but priests have always made him want to utter inappropriate things. Who is to make sure the natives don't kill the cow and put it in their cooking pots? he blabbers.

This seems to give the priest pause for thought. Does he think there is a risk of it?

There's a lot of meat on a beast like that, says Bertel. He senses he has the pastor's full attention and can allow himself to say what he wants. The savages are most bloodthirsty and cold-blooded, and cunning to boot. They won't hesitate a moment if they get the chance to do it in.

I shall ask the Trader to post a watch, says the priest pensively.

Perhaps it would be best to slaughter it straightaway, Bertel suggests, before the savages get there first. Then we might all have fresh steaks.

The priest pales. Bertel bows with a smile, then walks back to his home. He has spoken far too much, but cannot help but gloat over having alarmed the priest.

Sofie is up now, making porridge for the boy, who lies on his bed, flicking through one of his magazines.

When you get up I'll show you something, says Bertel.

The boy looks up at him over the page. Show me what?

Wait and see. But I promise you, you've never seen anything like it before.

Bertel goes up and kisses Sofie on her neck. She twists and shoves him away with her shoulder, then glances up and laughs. She bares her teeth and growls at him. He pretends to be afraid. The boy looks across at them from the bed. But when Bertel looks back at him, he retreats behind his magazine.

I must be off in a minute, says Sofie.

Of course, to wipe the Madame's arse.

There's a big dinner on, I have to wait at the table.

I'll give the boy his porridge. You go.

She puts down what she has in her hands and sticks her feet into her kamik boots. She kisses him fleetingly, then the boy, and is out of the door. A pot on the stove spits clumps of boiling porridge.

Where is Mother going? asks the boy.

To help out at a dinner at the Trader's. A ship has come.

He could bite off his tongue. But now he has said it. The boy becomes ecstatic and rushes over to the window in his bare feet. He eats not a mouthful of food until they have been down to the harbour to see the ship and greet its crew, who tramp up and down the quayside. Afterwards they walk up to the place where the cow stands tethered.

A cow, says Bertel. A real live cow. Who would have thought such a thing?

A heifer, says the boy. I think it's a heifer.

Yes, I suppose you can tell by its teats, says Bertel.

It's called an udder, says the boy.

The milk can be drunk, Bertel tells him.

I know. You can make porridge from it, and cheese and butter.

It seems no one can tell you anything you don't know already, says Bertel.

The boy grins. I read it in a book.

And what are you going to be when you grow up?

A sailor, says the boy, and laughs. A sea captain.

I think there are two of us to decide on that, says Bertel, and gives the boy's ear a playful tug. What do you want to be?

A priest, says the boy dutifully and looks up at his father. His blue eyes sparkle.

That's right, says Bertel. Think of it, the first Greenlander to be ordained into the clergy! You'll show them we're no stupider than them.

†

Two days later. A knock on the door. A young woman is standing outside. She gives him a folded piece of handmade paper.

From the priest, she says.

And who might you be?

She says nothing.

Do you work for the priest?

She shakes her head. He asked me to give you this, that's all.

He unfolds the paper and reads the cramped handwriting:

Dear Bertel Jensen, I am not quite well and would be indebted to him if he came hither! Morten Falck, missionary.

What is the matter with the priest? Bertel asks. He is not drunk, I hope?

He might be ill, I don't know. He looks like a ghost.

Bertel studies the woman closer. Where do you come from? I don't think I have seen you before.

From up north.

Holsteinsborg?

She raises her eyebrows in the affirmative.

What are you doing here in the district?

I am here with my daughter, she says. I live in the communal house.

With the savages? Has the priest at Holsteinsborg not christened you?

I am unchristened, but the old Missionary Oxbøl has been diligent in his teachings.

Indeed, I know all about the missionary and his teachings, Bertel replies curtly.

The woman looks over his shoulder into the parlour. I can look after your boy, she offers.

But you have a daughter of your own.

Milka. She is five years old, a pleasant girl. We can come here in the daytime, the children can play together. I can clean and cook.

We have no need. This is an ordinary house, we have no servants here. My wife and I take care of our own domestic matters. And my boy needs peace and quiet, not friends.

She lowers her gaze. Bertel is annoyed at her, and at himself for the pangs of guilt he now feels. She is a mixture like him; most likely her life is hard if she is alone with a child. He wants to shut the door, but it would entail shutting it in the woman's face and he cannot bring himself to do so. There is something about her that makes him wonder.

Do I know you? he asks.

She shrugs. *Naluara.*

Is there anything else you want?

Perhaps the priest has need of a housekeeper, she suggests.

Yes, perhaps. I can ask him. But he cannot take you in to live. You understand that, of course?

I can read and write, she informs him. Oxbøl taught me.

He would seem to be your benefactor, the Missionary Oxbøl.

He is the girl's father.

Old Oxbøl? Bertel stiffens. He doesn't know what to say. You let the priest lie with you? he enquires reproachfully.

Maybe it was that Holy Spirit of his. It didn't feel like it, though. Is the Holy Spirit made like you men?

Mind your blaspheming tongue, woman. I ought to beat you for that.

I won't hit back, she answers impertinently.

No, and I would advise you not to. Anyway, now that you're here, hm. I shall speak to the priest. Go now.

I'd rather be here.

Tired of the clergy, is that it? Thinking to try one of your own kind instead?

Being catechized can be painful, she says. A girl risks becoming with child.

The new priest is not like that. I'm sure you would be one to ruin him, though. He lets out an involuntary chuckle. It's worth a try, I suppose. Let me speak to him. Perhaps he will take you on.

At last she leaves. He watches her as she walks away. Her strong posture, her buoyant stride. Where have I seen you before? he thinks.

He finds Falck sitting on the step in front of the Mission house in his vestments, marble-white feet protruding from beneath the hem of his cassock. He is staring at something up on the fell, but when Bertel looks he sees nothing.

Magister Falck? he ventures, and can tell by the sound of his voice that he has now returned to his subservient role, though his hat remains upon his head.

Slowly, the priest turns his gaze towards him.

Can I be of assistance, Magister?

God bless him, Bertel Jensen.

Is the Magister ill?

Not ill, exactly. But then not quite well either, it would seem. It must be some sort of land sickness after the long sea voyage. This entire continent pitches and heaves worse than any vessel in a storm. And the Trader's hospitality doesn't help.

Bertel says nothing.

Is it always like this? Falck enquires.

Like what, Magister?

Drunkenness and gambling, frivolity from morn to eve?

I wouldn't know. *Naluara*. What the Danes get up to is not my concern.

One can only hope things will get better once the ship sails again.

Bertel stands in anticipation without replying.

And today I am invited once more, Falck sighs. How shall I stand it?

The Magister could say no, Bertel suggests.

Indeed he could, says Falck. Nevertheless, it is important to get to know people, to get off on a good footing with those with whom one is to associate in the years to come. And good people they are, too, it seems, better certainly than those at Godthåb. But I have neglected him. I have neglected my good catechist. Not a moment's work since my arrival. He must think badly of his new priest.

Bertel could say that the new priest is no different than the former, but he elects to remain silent.

He shall come with me, says Falck all of a sudden, perking up. He shall accompany me to dinner at the Trader's.

Me? I've never eaten in the colony house. I've never been inside.

Well, then it is high time. Falck reaches his hand out towards him. Help me to my feet. I feel better already.

Bertel follows him inside where Falck puts on his wig, breeches and boots. It is the first time he has spoken to the pastor since his arrival two days before, and now he is helping him dress. He mentions the woman who is seeking a position as housekeeper. Falck is receptive. He needs someone to wash his clothes and keep the place tidy. Bertel says he will send her over, so that the priest might speak to her himself.

Excellent, though I already made her acquaintance when I sent her off with my message to you. Who is she? Falck enquires.

I don't know her, Magister. But she has been taught the scriptures and she has a daughter.

Is she on her own? Who is the child's father?

Dead, Magister, says Bertel. Sometimes the lie is the more profound truth, he thinks to himself.

Ah, a widow. Poor soul. Send her to me, by all means. It will be a pleasure to help the unfortunate woman. Perhaps we may even make a good Christian out of her.

Perhaps, Magister Falck.

The priest beams. Bertel stands waiting while he makes himself presentable. As they leave the house, Falck says: Enough ceremony. From now on we are friends, Bertel. What do you say?

What's the Magister's name, then?

Falck is slightly taken aback. He stutters and says: Morten, my name is Morten.

Have you anything against me calling you Magister Falck?

Call me what you want, dear friend. But now you must show me the delights of this place, Bertel Jensen.

Together they stroll through the colony. Bertel explains to him its situation at the southern end of an island extending some two Danish miles to the north. He points to the peaks and tells him their Danish names. He takes him to a clifftop with a view out over the sea and in towards the mainland with its rugged peaks covered by snow.

Falck makes enthusiastic noises. He asks many questions whose naivety amuses Bertel, questions concerning the cold, the darkness of winter, the opportunities of getting about, the doings of the natives, but he answers readily. And Falck enthuses. This is all so much better than I had hoped, he says. We shall work well together. I am certain everything will turn out splendidly.

They come by the communal dwelling house of the heathens. There are people everywhere, children, women, men, all are occupied by some or another task that must seem to the priest to be strange and incomprehensible. Bertel explains to him about the natives' kayaks and boats and hunting equipment, the particulars of their houses and how they are arranged inside, the ways in which they prepare their food. Falck is all ears.

And these people, he says, none is christened?

Most are familiar with the Word, some receive instruction in order to receive the Baptism. But since the former pastor's demise things have been at a standstill.

Indeed, says Falck briskly. There is much to do. These ignorant souls, they are as lambs, waiting only for a shepherd to lead them into enlightenment and freedom.

Perhaps, says Bertel. Could be.

And out in the district, Falck continues. How do matters stand there?

There are many people, says Bertel. In the south and in the north and inside the fjords. Most likely they will have heard of the Lord Jesus from their own kind, and there will be some who have been christened and who teach them as well as they can, but there's probably several hundred who've never seen a priest.

Excellent! Falck exclaims with enthusiasm. We shall go to them and teach them, you and I, Bertel.

They are on their way back to the colony. Falck turns towards him with his hand outstretched.

For our fruitful collaboration, he says.

They shake hands. The priest's feels solid and strong.

I thank the Lord for having sent me here, says Falck. I feel certain it will be a blessing to me, and perhaps my presence may even bring some good to this land.

I'm sure, says Bertel.

Falck begins to talk of a tour of the district as early as this autumn. How is it to be arranged?

The Magister will need to get hold of a boat and a crew, and all the equipment as well, says Bertel.

Has my predecessor, the unfortunate Magister Krogh, not left anything that might be of use?

The Magister never went anywhere, he did his work here in the colony.

You mean he never left this island?

He did once accompany the Trader on a trade journey, but he didn't seem to care for it much. His sea legs were no more, he said, after the long voyage from Copenhagen.

Then how did he envisage returning home again? Falck says, beginning to laugh.

Well, he never did, did he? Bertel rejoins. He hanged himself in the blubber house.

Falck's laughter immediately subsides. Hm, so very true. How sad! Let us hope the good Lord has mercy upon his soul.

†

As they enter the Trader's home a loud clatter is heard, followed by shrieks of laughter. Madame Kragstedt sweeps towards them in her expansive dress.

Magister Falck! she exclaims, radiant with joy. Come inside. You can say prayers over what is left of the soup. Our maid has just dropped it on the floor.

I have brought my catechist, says Falck. Madame and Bertel Jensen know each other, I assume?

The Madame hesitates for a moment, before her face lights up in a smile. Why yes, of course, my maid Sofie's husband, we have indeed bumped into each other now and then. It can hardly be avoided in such a little place as this. She glances uncertainly from Falck to Bertel. Does the Magister wish for his catechist to join us at the table?

Naturally, Madame. We are all equals before the Lord, are we not?

They enter the room. Beneath curling veils of tobacco smoke sit perhaps a dozen men around the dining table. Captain Valløe greets Falck exuberantly and makes room for him at his side on the long bench. They step around the soup that lies in a puddle on the floor, and Sofie, who is on all fours, picking up the shards of broken porcelain. She glances up at Bertel, a look of distress, and mouths something to him which he fails to grasp. He shakes his head and nudges a shard towards her with his foot. Falck stops and looks at Bertel.

My wife, says Bertel.

Indeed, says Falck, and puts out his hand to the disconcerted Sofie. Good afternoon, madam.

Er, says Sofie, staring now at the rivulet of soup that runs between Falck's feet.

He steps out of the way. A pleasure to meet you, Madam Jensen.

A voice at the table erupts into laughter. Madam Jensen, indeed!

They seat themselves. Drinking glasses are put out before them. The mate fills the first of them, but as he is about to fill the second a hand extends to grip his wrist. Kragstedt's hand. The aquavit is for the Danish crew only, he says. The law forbids the provision of spirits to the natives on all but the flag days.

The mate puts the cork back in and removes the bottle.

Would he care for a glass of beer? Madame Kragstedt enquires kindly.

Rather a glass of water, he says. He feels the warmth rise in his cheeks. A glass and a jug are put out in front of him. He pours himself a glass and drinks a mouthful. He hears little of what is said, but sits and watches his wife on her knees wiping up soup from the floor. Then he is distracted by Falck's wig, which he has placed on the table next to his plate. He sees that it is teeming with lice. A dish of meat, peas and cabbage is handed across the table. He takes some and puts it on to his own plate and begins to eat. Several of the other dinner guests have likewise removed their wigs and deposited them untidily next to their plates. All are ridden with lice. Bertel cannot take his eyes away. He shovels the food into his mouth without tasting it.

To his left sits the smith, in conversation with the colony's cook, who is sat opposite him. Bertel grasps little of what they say, though understands that it has to do with varieties of aquavit.

My old man was a drunk, the cook says. Færch, his name was, but they called him Jøns.

We have been talking about the drift towards religious revolt, Madame Kragstedt says to Falck. Rumour has it that a whole flock of christened natives have abandoned the true faith and given themselves up to idolatry. Does the Magister know about it?

If it is so, they must either be brought back into the fold or excommunicated, Falck says. But no, he has heard nothing of any such drift.

He drank himself to death, says the cook. It was the best day of my dear mother's life, God rest her soul. But before he went he managed to get the stable girl up the spout, and when the boy came out she called him Jøns.

Perhaps the good Bertel Jensen might know? says Madame Kragstedt.

At once all eyes are upon him. He swallows a mouthful of cabbage and peas and washes it down with a gulp of water.

Any man partial to the aquavit will always share with others, no matter how little he's got, the cook drawls, only to be shushed.

I know, it's funny, isn't it? replies the smith, who likewise has failed to notice that all attention has turned to the catechist.

Well, says Bertel with hesitation. They say there's a man and his wife – their names are Habakuk and Maria Magdalene – who claim to receive visions and messages directly from Christ.

Captain Valløe clicks his tongue. Little more than a handful of wayward natives, I shouldn't wonder. I'm sure it's of little consequence.

I've heard say they're attracting followers, says the Trader. It's not healthy for the Trade if too many people lump themselves together in one place, especially if it's far from the colony.

There can't be that many of them, surely? Falck looks at Bertel.

I wouldn't know, he says, and bows his head over his plate. *Naluara*.

Won't it affect the hunting if too many people gather in one place? Valløe asks.

That's what I mean, Kragstedt replies. They say they go off along the coast and steal wreckage. That's enough on its own to warrant chains and the whipping post.

Perhaps it's down to hard times, suggests the Overseer, who has not spoken until now. He is seated to the Trader's right. Every year when we journey out we find settlements with everyone dead to the last man.

How dreadful! Valløe exclaims. Christian people?

No, heathens mostly. The Trade looks after the Christian Greenlanders in times of shortage. It's said the way of the Danish crown in the colonies is exemplary. We make sure people are taken care of. A lot of other nations could learn from us. The English especially are known for hard-handedness in their overseas dependencies. We needn't look any further than the table here. The Overseer nods in the direction of Bertel. In this country we invite them in and let them dine with us.

Laughter ripples around the table. Bertel chews on a piece of meat and wonders how he might make his excuses and beat a retreat as quickly as possible.

They should certainly consider themselves lucky that the Dutch or the English do not rule the country, says Madame Kragstedt.

So very true, my dear, says the Trader. That would be a different kettle of fish entirely, none of your laissez-faire.

One of the seamen from *Der Frühling* addresses Bertel. He enquires as to where he might buy hide or some whalebone.

I didn't hear that, says the Overseer, wagging an index finger at the man. You know perfectly well that all trade with the natives is forbidden.

And yet they leave the Mission and the colony, says Valløe, returning to the subject from before. How does the Trader explain that?

The religious urge often defies common sense, the Trader replies. That's the way it is, unfortunately, even with the savages.

I have some good skins from the winter, says Bertel. Thirty good fox skins. You can buy them off me, if the Trader will permit.

My older brother was a great big hulk of a fellow, says the smith, drawing the cork from the bottle and pouring himself a glass, before passing it across the table to the cook. He never bloody put up with anything.

But they're afraid of the whipping post. That, they are, says the Overseer with a chuckle. No matter that it's hardly used.

Mr Kragstedt, says the seaman. Would the Trader make an exception and allow me to purchase these skins?

Well, says Kragstedt. All right, I shall let it pass.

And how much would he then sell these skins for? the seaman asks.

They cost five marks each, says Bertel.

So then what do you think he did to my old man? says the smith.

He is shushed once more, though seemingly he fails to be aware of it.

There's not been any problems here since we put up the whipping post last year, Dahl continues.

Five marks, says the seaman with a smile. That would be too much.

It's the going rate, says Bertel. I can't undercut the Trade.

Well, I'll tell you, the smith slurs. He gave him a good hiding. Not long after, he kicked the bucket.

Mine was a brutal bastard and all, says the cook. He beat us with his belt buckle, he did, the bloody swine.

The smith and the cook descend into raucous laughter. The bottle passes between them.

Do be quiet, says Madame Kragstedt. The smith pulls a face and the cook cackles.

The going rate is the going rate, I can see that.

Bertel is sweating. His tongue rotates the tough meat inside his mouth.

You could send a boat up, Valløe suggests. Talk some sense into them. If they won't listen, then bring this Habakuk back here. I'm sure your inspector would sign and post-date an arrest order if we turned up with the sinner in chains.

That may yet be the outcome, says Kragstedt. But as you say, it would require an arrest order from our honourable inspector in Godthåb, and he would need an order from Copenhagen. It would be a very lengthy process.

But if the Trader permits, says Bertel, you can have the lot for ten rigsdalers.

That's a good deal, says Kragstedt to the seaman. You'll save a whole mark per skin.

I had the pleasure of speaking to Inspector Rømer, says Falck.

Hm, says Kragstedt. A pleasant and charming man, would the Magister agree?

Good, says the seaman. I'll buy his skins.

Indeed, says Falck. I mentioned him in a letter to my patrons.

That won't help you any. The man has taken root like lichen on Greenland's rock.

As for these visionaries, says Falck, do you not consider, Bertel, my friend, that it would be best to proceed with caution?

What does the Magister mean by that? the Overseer interrupts across the table.

I would consider it appropriate, says Falck, that I – in my capacity as missionary of this colony – should assume responsibility for the salvation and discipline of these stray sheep, and journey to their place of settlement, wherever it may be.

Igdlut, says Bertel. Their settlement, inside the fjord.

What fjord?

The one the Danes call Eternal Fjord.

And the leader of these people, says Kragstedt, his name is Habakuk?

And his woman is Maria Magdalene, says the Overseer. They call themselves prophets by the mercy of God.

I will travel there, Falck determines. I will speak to them. I'm certain they will listen to me. The Word of the Lord is compelling when properly imparted.

The Magister would do well to take care, says the Overseer. They may be armed with flintlocks and ammunition purchased from the English. And the natives are excellent shots.

The Lord will be with us, says Falck. I am not afraid.

Then good luck, says Kragstedt. I'll make sure you get what equipment you need, Magister. Such an expedition requires nothing in writing from His Excellency, so you'll have no problem there.

Prophets, Madame Kragstedt muses. How magnificent it sounds. The prophets of Eternal Fjord. Bertel sees that she takes Falck's hand and holds it tight, as though in a vice.

Now, about those skins, the Trader says to the seaman. I'm afraid I shall have to cancel that transaction.

Cancel? says the seaman.

A soup bowl is no inexpensive item, says Kragstedt. That was good French porcelain, that was. Been in my wife's family for three generations.

The Madame places a hand upon his arm, only for Kragstedt to brush it away unkindly. He gives Bertel a wry smile and leans forward. Thirty fox skins is fair compensation for such a fine bowl. It's in your favour, and you've even had a meal into the bargain.

Captain Valløe roars with laughter. He shakes his head vigorously and holds up his hands in deference. Kragstedt, you old shyster! I wouldn't want to trade with you, that's for sure.

But the skins are mine, says Bertel, and almost chokes on the indigestible lump of meat he endeavours to swallow. He glances around the table, appealing for support, and his eyes meet the pastor's own. But Falck smiles fleetingly and looks away.

It's not fair, says the seaman, and Bertel thinks he will come to his aid.

I made a deal in all honesty and in the presence of witnesses: the skins are as good as mine!

Yes, but now that they have been transferred, you must bargain with me, says Kragstedt, and the price is still ten rigsdalers.

A good deal, says the Overseer and laughs. Several of the other men join in. A toast to our Trader!

Bertel fetches the skins the next day and delivers them to the warehouse. The Overseer receives them, examines their quality one by one, indicates an occasional flaw and writes out a receipt. Bertel stands with his cap clenched in his hand and accepts the worthless piece of paper in return.

The Third Commandment

A Wrought-iron Gate

(1788)

The Third Commandment, as it is most plainly to be taught by a father to his family:
'Thou shalt sanctify the Sabbath day.'
What does this imply?
Answer: That we should fear and love God, so that we may not despise the preaching of the Gospel and His word; but to keep it holy; willingly to hear and learn it.

Some two years following her arrival in the country, Haldora Kragstedt decides she will have a vegetable garden. She has made mention of it to her husband before, only for him to laugh incredulously.

A vegetable garden? Why not a wheat field or an apple orchard?

Glancing up at her, he thought better of his facetiousness. My dear, a vegetable garden? Come, let me show you something.

He took her outside, made her wait in front of the house and fetched a spade from the warehouse. He handed it to her.

What am I to do with it?

Dig a hole, said Kragstedt. For your vegetable garden. He laughed. Don't look so glum. Let me.

He lifted the spade and thrust it down into the ground. A metallic clatter sounded out, whereupon he stepped up on to the edge of the blade and pressed it down with the full weight of his body. It sank a couple of inches. Then he angled it upward, wrenched away a small edge of peat and thrust the spade into the ground once more. The same occurred.

You see? he said, stepping back.

Stones, she said.

No, not stones. *Stone*. The bedrock of Greenland. How will you bring forth a vegetable garden in a land in which one can hardly bury a body?

The wilderness should be cultivated, she said. Isn't that what we are doing here?

We?

We, the white people. Is that not the purpose of all this? She nodded her head in the direction of the warehouses.

Not even white people have solved the problem of cultivating rock.

Then we must order some good Danish soil, said the Madame.

Have you lost your senses? her husband spluttered.

Not yet. But you must remember, dear husband, that I am a woman. It is my task to make things germinate and grow. She passed a hand across her abdomen and said in that gentle and instructional tone that always made him feel so ridden with guilt: As long as I have no child to care for I must find pastimes, or else I fear I shall indeed lose my senses.

And now, but two years after this exchange, she still has no child to care for. But the soil is there, having sailed with the good ship *Der Frühling*, along with some bags of assorted seed. As soon as the frost leaves the ground, she has the good-hearted cooper dig up some score cubic ells of peat and fill the hole with the soil. Afterwards she stands beside him at the edge of the black rectangle. Her heart races in her breast with excitement. The cooper, too, is touched by the moment.

We have moved a piece of the homeland to this place, he says.

Indeed, she echoes. We should put up a flagpole.

I'll ask the carpenter to make one, says the cooper. We shall raise the flag and sing songs.

And see the cabbage sprout, says Madame Kragstedt.

Pastor Falck approaches. Well, I never, he says and is clearly impressed. He fetches his Bible and holy water and blesses the vegetable patch. Madame must make sure to fence it in properly, says Falck, so that my cow does not trample her plants.

She and the pastor sow the seeds: turnip, beet, celery, carrot, garden cabbage and kohlrabi. They water the ground and remain standing and look upon it in reverence. Madame Kragstedt enjoys the sensation of sticky soil between her fingers and the natural fatigue that has settled in her muscles.

The next day she has the carpenter make an enclosure of fencing. By evening it is done. Will the Madame want it painted?

Yes, the Madame will want it painted.

The carpenter bows. He promises to begin the flagpole as soon as possible.

I haven't felt as happy in years, she confides to the pastor, who is now seated in her parlour.

You have found your calling, he says and smiles.

We had a vegetable garden at home in Køge. I suppose that's why such feelings arise in me now. The muscles of her jaw tense; she is about to cry. But instead of holding back the tears, she releases them. The pastor can surely endure some snivelling. She feels her cheeks warmed by the moisture. She laughs and dries her eyes with a handkerchief.

The pastor remains seated and studies her. He waggles his foot and sips at his glass. The Madame yearns for home, he says.

What it needs now, she says, is a gate.

A gate? For the vegetable patch?

At home in the apothecary garden there was a wrought-iron gate that made an entrance to the vegetable patch. Do you think the smith will make me one, Magister?

I suppose it is his job, says Falck.

A wrought-iron gate? says Niels Hammer, the smith. What would the lady want with such a thing?

To open and close, she says. When going in and out.

Indeed, I am familiar with what a wrought-iron gate is used for, says the smith. But why not an ordinary wooden gate? Iron isn't exactly in abundance in this place.

She has made a detailed drawing of it, together with Pastor Falck: a stylized vine wreathed around her family crest and motto.

The smith studies the drawing and snorts.

I'm aware it is a complicated pattern, says Haldora. Do you think it exceeds your abilities, Mr Hammer?

The smith snorts again. Presently, however, he begins work on the gate, all the while muttering about how meaningless it is to waste iron of prime Norwegian quality on a gate leading in and out of nothing in the middle of a wilderness.

We are civilizing the wilderness, she instructs him.

All well and good, but I fear we shall need more than soil and a gate.

†

She comes to the workshop every day to see how the work is progressing. She sits on a chopping block and watches the smith as he stands, bare-chested, clad only in his apron hide, pounding at the iron, making the sparks and slags fly. Curious, she asks him about the things he makes, and he explains to her, hesitantly, about barrel hoops, rivets, lugs and hinges, pots and pans to be hammered out, guns to be mended, bullets to be cast, the many iron parts of the blubber boiler to be repaired; among them, he says, fixing her with a malicious gaze, the heavy chain in which the unfortunate Magister Krogh hanged himself. And as if that were not enough, I'm now making a wrought-iron gate for the Madame, so that she may go in and out of the wilderness and close the door behind her.

Haldora laughs. The smith does not. He swings his hammer. A shiver runs down her spine as she thinks about the fact that he is also the colony's executioner, he who punishes the mutinous with the cane or pinches them with glowing tongs, in the worst cases chopping off their limbs or even releasing their souls from their bodies. Not that she has seen him in that function yet. Her husband, the colony manager, is a patient commandant who prefers to resolve conflict amicably.

The smith endeavours to negotiate with her to simplify the pattern of the gate, but with a smile she insists it be made exactly as indicated. She sees immediately whenever he tries to cut corners and is upon him with a wagging finger and admonitions issued in a tone of sarcasm that clearly annoys the smith excessively, much to her delight. She enjoys being in the workshop, taking in the foul smell of iron as it is made malleable in the furnace, to be twisted and shaped like caramel; the sizzle and hiss of the water when the iron is hardened; the fire; the flickering shadows; the body of the smith bent over the glowing metal.

What do these letters mean in the middle? the smith would like to know.

Semper felix, she says. It's Latin and means always happy.

I see, says the smith. And all the letters are to be in place, even though none but the lady understands them?

All of them, Mr Hammer.

The man and the hammer, the iron and the fire. The rush of heat whenever the door of the furnace is opened is almost unbearable, yet she does not turn her face away from it. Her eyes seem almost to draw in the fire and something inside her that needs to be scorched is set alight. She is aware of the impropriety of her being here so often. And yet it is hard to distract oneself from it and she must keep an eye on the work of the unwilling smith. Mr Kragstedt, her husband, is away most of the time in the summer months. As far as she knows, he is presently at Holsteinsborg, the wealthy neighbour colony to the north. He harbours dreams of founding a similar guild of whale hunters in the Sukkertop district, for then they would soon be prosperous indeed, he says. It is a matter to which he is highly devoted. She wonders what he will say when he returns home and sees her vegetable garden. She looks forward to showing it to him and hopes the gate will be finished and that some of the seeds will have begun to sprout when such time comes. It would seem to be feasible. It is well known that the ancient Nordics, besides keeping animals, cultivated cereals and vegetables further south in the country, albeit well inside the sheltered fjords, though they were never in possession of genuine Danish soil.

Morten Falck is also gone away. The only person with whom she feels able to converse, and then only barely meaningfully, is the cooper, Carl Dorph. But he is of strong faith and wont to spout nauseating pieties and complaints that he has not yet received licence to marry the native woman with whom he shares his bed and who is mother to his child. She tells him she will put his case when her husband returns home; perhaps there is something he can do. Then she goes down to the workshop and seats herself. The smith stands, working the bellows. He scowls. The muscles in his back tense beneath the sheen of sweat that glistens like oil upon his skin.

She withdraws. She goes up to the vegetable garden that has yet to show sign of life. Then she walks back to the colony house and sits at the window, reading one of the novels Falck has lent her from his book collection. She finds her writing implements and notes down some matters to remind herself that she is to discuss them with the pastor on his return. He has become a good friend and she considers that he must be somewhat in love with her. She can tell from his eyes when she opens the door for him and he enters her parlour. Sooner or later, most likely this coming winter, they will end up kissing each other and inflicting upon each other a slight harm. She often finds amusement in imagining how it will happen and what will be said. She will pour him aquavit and it will loosen his inhibitions. Swiftly, rather desperately, he will draw her towards him and kiss her. Thus! She will push him away, admonish him. He will be ridden with guilt. They will act out their roles. And then she will lend him her lips again. His hand will brush against her breast and she will take it and press it to her bosom. The hand will cup, it will clench and squeeze, and tingling pleasure will radiate from within, downwards, upwards, inwards into the very core of the obscure seat of woman's desire. But the pastor understands and relieves her of her shame.

No more fantasies now! She returns to her novel. After a time, her new maid arrives. She is at some loss as to what use to make of the girl in the middle of the day, apart from the fact that she usually reads a little of the catechism for her. It was Kragstedt's decision to take her on as a sort of chambermaid alongside Sofie, who is their regular help, or perhaps rather as a kind of pet whose purpose it is to keep her company while he is away. She has not yet become entirely used to her. Today she amuses herself by reading aloud to her from her novel. The girl sits, nonplussed, wearing an inward-looking expression, and clearly does not understand a word. Afterwards, she asks her to help her loosen her corset and undress, whereafter she retires to bed and sends the girl away. She reminds herself that tomorrow she must remember to ask her name and whether she has any family. Falck recommended her. She launders for him and cleans in the Mission house, a job that is quickly done, and the rest of the time she is at the Madame's disposal in the colony house, though she must not clean or launder and thereby encroach upon Sofie's domain, and Sofie plainly dislikes her. Servants, she thinks to herself. They are no easier to manage here than they were back home in the apothecary's residence in Køge.

†

The next day is Sunday and the smith has rested his hammer in observance of the holy day, or rather to avoid being fined, so that particular pleasure is denied her today. The chambermaid comes and helps her dress. As the hours pass, she sits and reads, goes for short walks, considers the peat dwellings of the natives that are left empty for the summer. She hears the screaming of gulls and watches as they fly against the wind, suspend themselves in the air, then release to dip down and sweep over the waves in full control, before ascending in a single extended arc to hang suspended once more. If one were a seagull, she thinks, one would be free.

When she returns to the colony, she sees the smith standing talking to the pastor's cow, which is called Roselil.

I see you have found a sweetheart, she says teasingly.

The smith turns slowly to face her, but says nothing in reply. She notices the empty bottle in his hand and feels a stab of unease.

Later, when she is down by the vegetable garden, studying the black earth that still is devoid of shoots, the smith appears again. In the corner of her eye she sees him walk up and knock on the door of the Overseer's house. He holds the same empty bottle in his hand. Overseer Dahl comes to the door. The smith has pulled his hat from his head and stands with it clasped in his hands.

What does he want? Haldora hears the Overseer enquire.

The smith holds up the bottle.

No, I cannot and will not give him aquavit today, Hammer. How many times do I have to tell him?

The Overseer did not give the full half-pint yesterday, says the smith, his voice meagre and pathetic.

Then why did he not come and complain straight away? It would be most unlike him to let such injustice pass without comment.

Because of my many burdens, says the smith. Now that the carpenter and the cooper are both ill, I must do their work, besides my own. And yet I receive only wages and provisions for one.

Today is Sunday, says the Overseer. Instead of seeking pleasure he ought to observe the holy day and read in his postil. It would become him better than filling himself with aquavit.

Haldora finds herself thinking the Overseer is correct in what he says. And yet she feels for the smith and considers Dahl to be self-righteous and insensitive.

Now she sees the smith clutch at his throat and cough, as though on a theatre stage. I've such a tightness here, he whimpers. I think there is a cold coming on, perhaps a boil in the throat. Who knows how long a man may have left in this vale of tears? It is only wherefore I come to ask the Overseer for a small and insignificant half-pint of the aquavit, to chase the cold away, so I don't end up in bed like the carpenter or under the peat like the old pastor.

Indeed, we can't have that, can we? Dahl quips back with a sarcasm that is lost on the smith, though not on Haldora, who prods gently here and there in her dubious vegetable garden while she eavesdrops.

Dahl sighs. All right, Hammer. A half pint and not a drop more, does he hear me?

Thank you, your Excellency, says the smith, and Haldora hears how he has already discarded his subservience and adopted a more brazen, sneering manner. She looks forward to tomorrow, Monday, when she might take him to task and order him about.

She straightens her back and watches the two men as they walk towards the warehouse where the colony holds its stock of ale and aquavit.

I'm docking this from next week's provision, she hears the Overseer say. Just so he knows.

They disappear from view and she walks back up to the colony house, rather excited by this minor dispute. Through the walls a short while later she hears the carpenter and the smith talking in their room in the other part of the house. Their voices are woollen, she cannot make out what they are saying, but from the tone of the smith's voice she can tell that he is not in the best of humour. A lengthy exchange follows. She feels, perhaps, that they are speaking of her. She hopes the carpenter, decent as he is, will defend her. Then a door slams and all is quiet.

She settles down to write a letter to her sister, only to lapse into daydreams. The chambermaid comes in and looks at her enquiringly. Not now, she says, and sends her away with a wave of her hand. When she is gone, she wishes she had not, but is loath to go out and call her back. Sunday. Once it was the best day of the week, a day of outings and trysts with young men, whose desires she found mysterious and inciting. But that was at home. That was when she was still young and unknowledgeable and thought that life would be just as her father, the apothecary, encouraged her to believe. It is a long time ago. Now she has travelled from youth at home to adulthood abroad.

Her husband Jørgen loves this wilderness. He came to Godthåb as a ship's boy aboard the schooner *Aurora*, allowed her to sail again without him and was taken on by the Trade. He told her the story during the time when they were engaged, and she has heard it told many times since. It is more than twenty years ago now. He worked his way up; for, as he is wont to say, the only qualification needed to advance a man's station in the colonies is not to be dead. If only he makes certain to remain alive, then sooner or later he will be king. Or Trader, as Haldora tends to add. Indeed, but that is but a station. You mark my words, my dear.

He speaks often of Greenland's future development. It is a land of enormous opportunity, as he likes to lecture her, and immeasurable resources. Only ambition and will are lacking, and someone to organize matters into a system. Most who are posted here are satisfied to stick it out for the apportioned number of years, earn a wage and serve the king. Survive. Advance a couple of rungs.

My dear Haldora, he says, occupying the middle of the room. What this country needs is for the small administrative units, the colonies, to be dismantled in favour of centralization, with a view to the industrial exploitation of what the land has to offer. Of course, a certain autonomy, he mutters, pacing back and forth beneath the rafters of the ceiling, will be required, a degree of, erm, detachment from the mother country; self-rule, if you like. A new governor would have to be appointed . . . indeed, of course!

At this juncture, Jørgen Kragstedt sends his wife a smile, which she returns. This is a discussion they have conducted many times before.

Had he asked her what she needed, she would have said: a child.

So he refrains from asking.

†

The marriage came about during his time in Denmark awaiting his position as colony manager. Her father, the apothecary Knapp in Køge, was family to his mother far removed, and Kragstedt had frequented the residence in the summers of his childhood, long before Haldora was born. Her father it was who had taken it into his head that they should be brought together, before she even realized that he existed at all. He was invited into the home on a number of occasions; a heavy man with red hair, a feature she found slightly repulsive, though not sufficiently to cause her to object. She had yet to become herself again, following the death of an older sister in labour. Decisions were made, steps taken. It was the easiest way.

The proposal itself occurred during a walk. Woods. A village. The manor. Fields. The lake. It was a very long walk. Eventually they were standing on a bridge that led over the millstream. The sound of gushing water and the paddles of the mill wheel released her from the exact and no doubt stuttered articulation of the proposal. She said yes. He stood with his hat under his arm, his upper body slightly bowed. His scalp was freckled. He looked at her enquiringly, anaesthetized by the noise of the mill. They walked home, arm in arm, neither having heard what the other had said, though both assuming the matter to be happily resolved. When they arrived home, her parents embraced them and wept. And thus they were betrothed.

The dowry never materialized and Kragstedt spoke of taking the issue to the courts. But then so much else happened. He was given his position, preparations were to be made for the voyage, and they married so quickly that it gave occasion to gossip. Then they departed. Her parents and sisters sailed as far as Elsinore. A year after their settling at Sukkertoppen they received word of her father's bankruptcy and sudden death. Two sisters are still living, and her mother, too, but she has no one close by in whom she feels she may confide. Now, however, she has begun to regard Magister Falck as one who might fill the void in her life. She has no idea if she will ever see Denmark again.

She catches sight of the smith, who stands gazing at the enclosed garden, the black soil. She draws quickly away from the window and the smith fails to notice her presence. But then she hears someone on the main step and a knock at the door. She goes into the hallway, stands in the dark and listens.

Who's there?

Niels Hammer, Madame. The smith. If you don't mind, it concerns the Madame's gate.

She opens the door, opens it wide. The smith stands looking up at her with bloodshot eyes, his head bare, hat pressed to his chest. He gapes. Haldora glances down at herself. Is there something amiss with me? she wonders. She realizes she perhaps ought to have draped a shawl over her bare shoulders and gathered her hair, which hangs freely down her back.

The smith clears his throat. The thing is, you see, Madame Kragstedt, the thing is I need your help.

My help?

The smith laughs nervously. With the gate. The drawing. He flaps his hand in the air: The drawing has become blurred. On account of the dampness, perhaps. He groans softly, then pulls at his whiskers. Haldora smells the fumes of alcohol that waft towards her and recoils. The smith steps up to her, only to think better of it and retreat downwards again. Would the Madame do me the favour of casting her eye on the drawing and explaining to me certain things about which the pitiful smith is unclear?

We have already spoken of this several times, she says admonishingly. I thought him to have understood. Did he not assure me of it just the other day?

That may be so, but a man can become uncertain. He throws out his hand in apology. I wouldn't wish to make a mistake so the whole thing should have to be scrapped. All I want is to do it just the way the lady wishes. He stares at her, his eyes devour. She stares back, without causing him to lower his gaze.

Does he have it with him? The drawing?

In the workshop. He jerks his head nervously in the direction. If the Madame would come with me down to the workshop, she will see what I mean. I can't describe it properly in words, it's kind of . . . He throws out his hand again and expels a slight, explosive snort. It's the iron, Madame, a resistance in the iron, in the transfer from the paper. I'm sure the lady understands that I can hardly bring the iron and the drawing and the hammer and the anvil up here to show her. Can the lady not see? He closes his mouth and bites his lip.

Haldora smiles at him. The sight of this fawning and subservient muscle of a man makes her feel strangely at ease. She could extend the toe of her boot and he would take it in his hand and kiss it with reverence. The thought makes her feel rather elevated, omnipotent and extravagant. She feels goodness and mercy absorb into her soul. She smiles. Yes, I can see that. But can it not wait? Today is Sunday. Tomorrow I can visit him as usual and we can go through the whole thing again.

If the Madame would have me excused, I've all manner of things to be getting on with tomorrow. With the carpenter and the cooper being laid up in bed, I've been saddled with their work as well as my own, as if it weren't enough to be smith. The way things are, I've got no choice but to work on the gate on the rest day, and run the risk of a fine into the bargain.

She considers the smith as he stands there in his Sunday best, heavy and drunken. If truth be told, he has said what she hoped he would say. There is no other way but to go with him. She leaves the door ajar and goes back inside, where she puts on a shawl and her boots, sticks a couple of pins in her hair and gathers it under her hat. When she comes out on to the step, the smith stands rocking on his heels and smooths back his hair with his fingers.

Lead me to his workshop, she says in a commanding tone.

Following on his heels down to the harbour, she registers that the air has become chaotic. It must be the change of tide, she thinks to herself. Gulls scream, swooping down and rising sharply, one of them absconding with something hanging in its beak, a whole flock in pursuit. The smith throws open the door of the workshop. She hesitates a moment before stepping inside. The door snaps shut behind her. She stands in the room's bitter cold.

Has he not lit the furnace? she asks. I thought him to be at work.

She turns to face him. He is standing with his back to the door, observing her. He smiles gingerly. She stiffens, aware of herself in her flaming red dress, her bare arms beneath her shawl.

The lady is like a piece of Heaven, says the smith in a thick voice.

He moves forward. She retreats a pace and is stopped by something against the back of her thighs. She puts a hand out behind her and raises the other in front of her face to fend him off.

Do not hurt me, she breathes.

Pardon? says the smith with the French pronunciation, and laughs.

Tell me what you want, Mr Hammer.

He breathes heavily and she can see that he swallows. She knows that she should not be hesitant and passive, that she ought instead to speak to him in an ordinary tone about the wrought-iron gate, and thereby drag him out of that which is about to overcome him. But she is herself in a state of terror and giddiness, as though she were standing on the edge of an abyss looking down. She wants to jump, but dares not.

I want to lie with you, Madame Kragstedt. He speaks calmly and deliberately.

He knows what he wants, she thinks to herself. The thought has formed inside him, and the thought is the mother of the action. It is too late now to stop him with talk.

Indeed? she says. I imagine he does. She feels her lips quiver, her teeth chatter.

Is the lady cold? He sounds almost kind and caring.

Yes, it is cold in here. She fumbles behind her back, her hand finds an object and explores it, identifying it as a tool. Hammer's hammer. She tries to force herself to be calm.

The smith stands stock-still, looking at her. He seems to be taking pleasure in the situation, as though he were thinking: Who is the master now? He moves away from the door, takes a couple of steps forward, reaches out and touches her breast.

The Madame is becoming. It's neither right nor fair that her husband should have her splendours to himself.

She feels his hand on her breast; it squeezes investigatively, quite unroughly. She looks down at the hand. It is huge and coarse, marred with scratches and sores, the fingernails yellowed and broken. It squeezes her breast again, cautiously, and more than once. The smith looks up and she meets his gaze.

I hope the lady doesn't mind me having a feel, he says

She shakes her head stiffly.

My father used to say you're all that way, all women. Lustful. It's why women and not men become whores. I can't say if it's so, but it's certainly true that only women submit to their lust and sell their bodies for copper. What would be the lady's opinion on the matter?

Her mouth is as dry as paper. She tries to wet it in order to speak. Is his father still alive? she stutters through chattering teeth.

There'll be no talk of my father here, he snaps.

No.

She feels his hand against her cheek. It feels like a dead thing, timber or a piece of iron. Her face must be warm.

The lady blushes, says the smith. It becomes her. Madame Kragstedt is beautiful, beautiful as an apple. He laughs. What nonsense!

His hands begin to explore up and down her dress, trying to find a way inside. But the fabric resists, more than she herself, layer upon layer of confining garments to be peeled away if he is to reach the goal of his desire: her skin. The hands move feverishly, he issues sounds of annoyance and comes closer, pressing himself against her. She smells his sweat and the aquavit on his breath, but also the bitter scent of her own skin and the rancid smell of stale sweat embedded in the fabric of her clothing as it becomes warm. He lowers his head and kisses her. She feels his wriggling tongue wet against her cheek and ear. He takes a step back and spits.

Ugh! he exclaims. What's that?

Powder, she says. Does he not like it?

He stares dully as she grasps the hammer and wields it in an awkward, circular movement that sends a flailing shadow across the ceiling and ends in a thud against his head.

He steps backwards, a single pace, and sways. She is filled with a primitive sense of at last having overcome her paralysis, and withdraws in an arc to the right, edging her way towards the door, facing the smith with the hammer raised above her head. Hammer's hammer. Now it has struck him back. She almost finds it amusing.

Don't hit me! He staggers and shakes his head and looks like he is about to collapse. He retreats another step and grasps the frame of the door.

If I have to, I will, she says without emotion. Let me out and I shall refrain from striking him again.

I'll open the door, he says. Look. I'm opening it now.

He has turned his back on her. She could easily, and with justification, deal him a solid blow across the neck and put him out of commission for good. But she does not. She hears the bolt drawn back, the heavy sound of the iron, and as the thought of what he might be doing becomes complete in her mind, he swivels around almost in a pirouette, with such grace it would have been comical in any other context. But in his hand is the long iron bolt, jutting outwards like a sword. He raises it in the air, extends his arm to its full length and brings the iron down hard on her forearm.

She hardly registers the pain, only that the blow causes her to drop the hammer, which falls to the floor with the dullest of thuds. She sinks to her knees. The smith swings his booted foot and kicks the hammer away from her, propelling it across the floor and out of reach.

Now you have made me angry, he says calmly, and she can tell from his voice that he is smiling. Now I must punish you, Madame Kragstedt. Whatever happens now, the Madame has brought it upon herself.

In the name of the Lord, she stutters, and now it is she who whimpers. Have mercy, please. I have not caused him any harm.

She remains on her knees, half in pain, half in humility and prayer. Her hand clasps the point of the impact. Her arm hangs limp. She wonders if it is broken. She hears the smith lay down the bolt.

Why did the lady do it? he asks. Why did she strike me? I wasn't going to hurt her, only lie with her. He lowers his hand to grasp her chin, raises it slightly, forcing her to look at up him. Now I shall have to tie her up, otherwise she will strike me again.

He finds a short length of rope and ties her wrists together. She cries softly from the pain in her arm, and her sobs cause him to pause and gaze at her.

I'm sure it's not as bad as it feels, he says.

She watches him fasten another rope around the stone on which the anvil rests. Now I shall tie you here, he says in a kind voice. There's no use fighting. If the lady screams, I shall have to gag her. What a pity for that sweet little mouth, to stuff it with dirty cloth.

She shakes her head and tightens her jaw.

Good, says the smith. Now we can begin.

He takes his time as he lifts her gown, running his hands through the fabric. How on earth are we to free the lady from these garments? he says.

She sees the difficulty of it. She is lying on her back with her arms above her head, bound to the stone. The heavy gown of damask has shoulder straps and cannot be pulled down. He tries to draw it over her head, but to no avail. He looks at her enquiringly.

Release me, she says, and I will undress myself. It is no easy matter to undress a woman.

He guffaws and shakes his head. He heaves at the dress, but succeeds only in twisting it awry. He produces a pocket knife.

No! she exclaims. Not like that. At the back is a corset, hidden.

He rolls her on to her side and fumbles with small fasteners that hold the rear of the dress together. She feels it release.

What is this? he says. This crossed lacing?

The corset of the gown, she says. There is a knot.

His hands search up and down her back until finding it. But the hands of a smith are crude and clumsy and he cannot untie it. He inserts a finger between the corset and the skin of her back and tugs at the lacing, but must abandon and release it, causing it to snap into place again in a way that makes her jump. He returns to the knot.

I don't want to ruin such expensive clothes, he says. But this knot is too tight for me.

She says nothing.

Then she feels him press his face against her back. She wonders what he is at, but then realizes that he is trying to loosen the knot with his teeth. He straightens up and curses. She glances over her shoulder. He draws a hand across his cheek, then sits down with a wince.

A bad tooth, he says. He opens his mouth and prods the tooth with his finger. That wretched knot has made it come loose.

I can give him aquavit with which to dab it, she proposes. My husband does so to good effect. But you must release me first.

I've got my own aquavit, he snaps. The lady can keep her old wives' twaddle to herself.

He grasps the corset and tugs at it once more, hard and repeatedly. The pain that shoots from her arm causes her to whimper. Then the silken cord snaps audibly and the dress is released.

Ha! exclaims the smith. He takes hold of the two sides of the corset's drawstring and pulls them apart. The gown opens, seams split as the lacing is wrenched. He pulls the garment over her head. She thrashes her legs, feeling she is about to be suffocated. Then the gown is at her arms, and he gathers it in a thick heap at the point where she is tied to the anvil stone.

The smith wipes his brow. He considers the next layer. And what on earth is all this? he says.

She turns her head to see what he is looking at. My tournure.

And what good does it do?

It expands the skirt at the rear. It is considered becoming.

He sniffs contemptibly, then unfastens the rectangular horsehair cushion, relieving her of it and casting it aside.

The next layer is her silk chemise. His rough hands pause to stroke it. The silk catches on his skin like burrs. His breathing is heavier now. She knows its sound. Then the chemise is pulled up to the same place as the dress.

Another corset? The smith curses under his breath. He tries to insert his fingers, only to find it too tight. He pulls and tears, but the corset will not yield.

Why must gentlewomen use such inconvenient garments? he asks.

It is a corset, she hears herself say. It is what the fashion dictates. And men like to see women who are narrow at the waist and broad across the hip.

He shakes his head and grins. It must be why gentlefolk have so few children, he says. The iron's gone cold before it's struck.

He looks at her, his eyes settling on her breasts that rest in the cups of the corset. He seeks her gaze. She stares away, though is afraid to close her eyes for fear that it may provoke him. She says nothing.

Women of the lower classes do not have this custom of constricting themselves and stuffing cushions under their skirts, he says. We common men are not so easily fooled. We know what's underneath. It might be contended that makes our women freer than yours. He pauses, and when she remains silent he continues in pensive mood: But then I suppose we are all of us constricted, one way or another. And no matter how we may plead and beg to be released, there's no one there to listen. Such is life.

She senses — still in this remote manner that is so unquestionably a result of her mind having separated itself from her humiliated and suffering body — how his little speech begins to carry him away with indignation. She refrains from comment, but nourishes a faint hope that he is losing himself in thought, perhaps soon to forget what he is about, and that the iron will grow cold. But then he is at her garments once more.

How does a lady manage to tie this every day? he asks.

My chambermaid helps me. Sometimes my husband.

Perhaps I should call for your husband, so that he can help me. He laughs amiably. But I remember now that he's away.

On his return he will commence proceedings against you and have you severely punished, Hammer, she says, aware that her tone is hardly convincing.

Punishing me would mean acknowledging that I have made him a cuckold. Not many men would do so of their own will.

She says no more.

It would seem he has tired of corsets and knots. He takes out his pocket knife again and proceeds to cut open the lacing. It yields with an elastic snap for every slice of the blade, and retracts through the garment's brass lace holes. He pulls the fabric away, puts it to his face and inhales deeply. When he removes it, she sees that he smiles with delight.

Woman! he exclaims.

He tosses the corset into a corner, then looks down at her. Only the chemise remains.

He slits it open from top to bottom, a single, clean cut, as meticulous as a tailor, the blade following the sleeves all the way to the wrist. The garment falls away. He rolls it up into a ball and casts it aside. Now she is naked. She wonders that she is not cold. But she is warm, glowing even. She is on her back with her arms above her head, looking up at the smith who is looking down upon her. Her chest heaves, she lies tense so as not to move her injured arm. She has gathered her legs and drawn them slightly upward. But she cannot hide the thick bush of her pubic hair that completely hides the vulva and the pubis, continuing like an arrowhead towards her navel where it dwindles to a thin though pronounced black thread. She has always felt shame at this rampant shock and considered it a reminiscence of something wild and untamed within her, something that she has always repressed. Right up to this day. And therefore I lie here now, she thinks to herself.

The smith bends forward and buries his face in her belly, snorting and grunting, then pressing his mouth to her breast, extending his tongue, seizing the nipple with its tip and licking its circumference, sucking and releasing with a slobbering sound of pleasure, playing with its elastic resistance, clasping both her breasts roughly now in his hands; his calloused hands that grate against her sensitive skin, the yellowed horn of his nails digging deep into the tissue.

Soft as a newborn mouse, he gasps in a dreamy tone. When I was a boy I would find the nests of the mice in the barn and take up the soft and tiny young. I adopted them like they were my own children. I caressed them and looked after them. So soft they were, so soft. And you,

Madame Kragstedt, are so beautiful and perfect, once your garments are removed, like a small animal, warm and beautiful and afraid.

As he takes hold of her and turns her on to her side, he sees the metal shavings that she has hardly noticed dig into the skin of her back. He tries to brush them away, and snorts in annoyance on discovering how deeply they have pierced. He draws back his hand and she sees it is bloodied. There is a knock on the door.

He is on his feet in an instant. She realizes the door is unlocked now that he has taken out the bolt and used it upon her.

Tentative knuckles against the oak door.

Quickly, he lifts the great anvil from its base, swings it across the place where she lies and puts it down so as to block the door. He squats down on his haunches and places a hand over her mouth.

Who's there?

Is the Madame with you?

She recognizes the voice. It is the catechist, Bertel Jensen.

Go away! the smith shouts at the door. There is no lady here!

The maid says she went with you, says the catechist. Is all well with her?

How should I know? The Madame is not here, I say. Go away, and look after your own people instead!

The door is rattled cautiously, but will not open on account of the anvil. Silence descends. She thinks she ought to scream. The Lord has sent her this native catechist and now she must demonstrate her willingness to be saved by screaming. But she does not scream. She hopes only that the man will go away and leave her alone with her shame and fear.

Hammer returns. He is gone, he says in a soothing, conspiratorial tone, as though they are both of them together in this, and both afraid of being caught. Then he takes off his shirt, loosens his braces and steps out of his threadbare Sunday breeches. He kneels, his member jutting, heavy and swollen. She cannot take her eyes from it. His nakedness chafes her nostrils. He smells like a horse. He bends down and whispers into her ear as though they are in cahoots.

We must be quiet.

She tries to utter agreement, but cannot. Her chest convulses in spasms. She feels her mouth contort.

No, don't cry, he implores. It will be no good if the lady cries. I shall be gentle with her. The lady will think it's her husband come to court her.

She lets go of herself and begins to sob, then feels his hand across her mouth again. Their eyes meet. His member brushes against her stomach, hanging half-erect in a downward arc. She feels its warmth, how full of yearning it is to be put inside her. He wriggles into place and forces her legs apart. He thrusts a thumb into the fold next to her sex. It makes her jump and stretch out her legs. She sees how the smith's muscles tremble across his chest and shoulders.

I've never had a true lady friend, he says. A sweetheart, I mean. It's mostly just been bend over and pull up your skirts, woman! But this, this is different. The Madame should know that I am grateful indeed.

She feels his member thrust against her opening. But she is dry and will not allow him to enter. The enquiring, melancholy eyes look upon her again. She sees that he is at a loss.

Then his face lights up. He turns and reaches to the bench and retrieves a round, wooden container. It is a grease tub, she realizes, smelling the rancid fat as he pulls off the lid. He scoops his fingers inside and smears the contents first upon his member, then her vulva. She gasps.

There. Now the lady is as sweet as a jar of honey.

She gasps again as the smith enters her. She clenches her teeth so as not to scream and turns her head to the side, feeling the smith pressing her to the floor, the metal shavings digging into her back. Now he begins to writhe and she senses the final hindrance give way inside, his member moving freely, her inner form treacherously yielding to his shape. He takes hold of her ankles, bends her legs upwards, pressing her further into the floor and the razor-sharp fragments upon it. His grip is a vice. He thrusts his head backwards and she cannot help but look at him; she can see that he is losing the last remnant of awareness of what he is doing, becoming at one with his action, as she becomes at one with her pain. And then it is he who cries out, while she tightens her jaw and utters no sound.

It is dark when he loosens her ropes. She cannot get to her feet on her own and must reach up to take the outstretched hand he offers. He passes her her clothing, item by item, and she dresses. Her back is an open wound, but there is little pain from it, only a warm, burning sensation. The smith sees it, too.

Dab the sores with some of your husband's aquavit, he says. She wonders if it is meant to be a joke.

She makes do with putting on the damask gown and her boots. The smith accompanies her back to the colony house, carrying the rest of her garments gathered in his arms. Reaching the door, he hands them to her in a bundle that she snatches from his hands. For a moment they stand staring at each other. The smith has removed his hat. He is bareheaded before her, clenching it to his chest.

The Madame has no need to despair, he says solemnly. No woman has ever cared for it. It is painful to them, our old pastor told us so. I know very well that women are not lustful at all. So it is. Goodnight, Madame Kragstedt.

†

The chambermaid comes to her that same evening, silent and knowing. She extracts the metal shavings from her back with a pair of tweezers, cleanses and dresses her wounds. It takes most of the night. She promises she will say nothing to her husband when he returns.

Sleep with me tonight, says Haldora.

They retire to the chamber and snuggle up to each other beneath the down. The girl has an odd smell and the thought occurs to her that she might bring lice into the bed. But she doesn't care. She clings to her and falls asleep with her arms wrapped around her.

Some days later she ventures outside for the first time since the encounter with the smith and finds the wooden gate of the vegetable garden replaced by one of wrought iron. The gate is perfect, the pattern exactly as intended, and all the letters are present and correct. *Semper felix*. Her family motto.

She opens the gate and enters the vegetable garden, then falls to her knees. All over the little patch, green shoots have appeared in the black soil.

THE FOURTH COMMANDMENT

A Visitation

(1788)

The Fourth Commandment, as it is most plainly to be taught by a father to his family:
'Thou shalt honour thy father and thy mother.'
What does this imply?
Answer: That we should fear and love God, so that we may not despise or provoke our parents or superiors; but to give them honour, to serve, obey, love and esteem them.

A morning in autumn, early dawn, September. The first sun bathes the fells of the mainland and warms away the fog. The fjord is still.

Seven people leave the colony by kone boat and kayak; four oars-women, three men. One of them is Rasmus Bjerg, constable of the Royal Trade. It is not without reluctance that he embarks upon this long, hazardous and in his view pointless journey. But the Trader has ordered him and there is nothing to be done about it. He sits in the stern, making use of the time by taking apart his flintlock and cleaning its components with linseed oil. He assembles and disassembles and assembles it again. It is a nervous compulsion; he cannot prevent himself from taking the firearm apart when it is assembled or from putting it together when it is apart. He retracts the cock, pulls absently on the trigger, and the cock strikes the pan with a snap that causes the women to jump. He retracts it once more, pulls again on the trigger.

Constable Bjerg, says Falck, who is standing upright in the bow, erect as a mast. For God's sake, man! You'll drive us all to madness.

Very well, Mr Falck. He puts the firearm down. His fingers itch to pick it up.

One of the mixtures from the colony, Didrik is the kayak man and leads the way. He sails some boat-lengths ahead of them, quite without sound. Bjerg wishes it was he who sat in the kayak, so that he might make more use of himself, employ his strength, propel himself through the water and be free. But he has never learned to sail a kayak. He has tried on more than one occasion and was almost drowned. They say that if a person does not learn it as a child, he will never sail such a vessel safely. Most likely it is true. Didrik certainly looks like he is at one with it, gliding swiftly along, parting the water in silence.

Constable Bjerg sits face to face with the oarswomen. They work in seamless harmony, leaning on their oars, rocking back and forth. In the follow-through of each stroke they perform a flicking motion of the wrist that causes the boat to dart forward abruptly, and the two passengers, he and Falck, to sway slightly at the hip. The blades of the oars ripple the surface of the water and the ripples dance like tops. His eyes follow them. Then he stares at the oarswomen, amusing himself by resting his gaze upon them one by one. They dislike it. Like animals, he thinks to himself. They don't care to be looked at either, at least not dogs; a dog can be provoked into attack by staring into its eyes. But these women are good-natured. He wonders if they are like other people under all their garments of skins. Like other women. He would like to find out. Their hair is tied up in a knot on top of their heads, bound with twine studded with coloured beads of glass. Their feet, in sealskin kamik boots, are placed against the crosspieces in the bottom of the boat, he sees the little kick they make with every pull, the almost imperceptible lift of their behinds from the thwart. They sit, two-by-two, one pair in front of the other. Their cheeks are large, polished surfaces mounted on high cheekbones; their mouths are small, teeth ground down, though not rotten, more honed by chewing on a diet of bones. Their upper garments are bulky jackets trimmed with leather straps laid crosswise to present their breasts, though not so as to give rise to arousal. Rather, the breasts are items of utility. It is said they wash in their own filth, yet they look clean enough to Rasmus Bjerg. Appetising, almost. A man is put in good humour by observing them.

Constable Bjerg, Falck says again, this time rather more sharply.

He realizes he has picked up his flintlock and sits tapping it against the powder keg. He grins sheepishly and puts it down. *Pardonnez-moi, monsieur le prêtre*, he says. Bjerg has learned a small amount of French on board large ships.

Give me that gun, says Falck.

It is my gun.

It is the Trade's gun. Give it to me. Then he will have no cause to be tempted.

Bjerg passes it over the heads of the oarswomen. They both stand, the boat rocks slightly. The constable sits down again, but Falck remains upright, spying ahead across the water. The women break into song. Their shrill, metallic voices cut to the marrow.

It is rather late in the year for a journey into the district, he says.

I beg your pardon? says Falck.

Autumn is upon us. Snow might fall at any time.

I'm sure we've plenty of time to do what needs to be done, says Falck.

He looks back and picks out coils of smoke from the houses of the colony, and one or two peat dwellings of the natives. To the left, steep, forbidding fells rise up, to the right are skerries of low-lying islets, and far into the mainland some snow-covered peaks. He wonders if it is where they are destined.

The fog still lingers in the bays and where the sun has yet to reach. It is as though the rocks are shrouded in gauze or tulle. It makes him think of death. There are people who live entire lives here, he says to himself, and is unable to comprehend it.

Rasmus Bjerg is twenty-two years old, the youngest man in the colony. He hails from the Horsens area, his father is a freeholder, but with five elder brothers he is so far removed from allodial rights that remaining at home was pointless. He went to sea immediately following the confirmation. He receives letters from his parents and thus assumes that they are still alive, but he has not seen them in many years. At one point he sailed the trade triangle, transporting slaves from the Gold Coast to the West Indies, though mostly he has worked ships conducting lesser trade on minor routes. This is his first time in Greenland. He finds it to be dark, insular and oppressive. He misses the open sea, the discipline of life on board, the comradeship, the freedom of going ashore, the lack of ceremony, the fistfights and the heartfelt scenes of reconciliation, the long voyages and all the routines. He misses a girl whose name was Ulrikka and whom he does not expect to ever see again, but to whom he would like to write, if only he could put words together on paper in a manner that is decent and proper. He is capable of writing and has written letters to his parents, but never to a girl. Perhaps the priest will help him, if he can bring himself to confide in him.

He leans back against the tent of skins and the sleeping bags that are stuffed away in the stern. His arm dangles over the side, his fingers trailing, making little whirls in the cold water. The boat is heavily laden with goods, among them ten flintlocks of poor quality, a keg of gunpowder, lead, casting moulds, fuses and flints, twenty copies of the New Testament translated into Greenlandic, transported in a box lined with lead, and other merchandise. What Falck and the others are unaware of is the envelope Rasmus Bjerg carries in his inside pocket. It contains a warrant issued by royal decree for the arrest of Habakuk and his wife Maria Magdalene. Kragstedt has invested Rasmus Bjerg with the authority to do what must be done, and to do so with force should it be deemed necessary. He wonders what it will feel like if he is compelled to shoot another human being. He is confident that he wishes to do so, it being the secret desire of any man to kill another, and yet he is afraid at the prospect. The slaves died in droves and were tipped over the side as casually as the contents of chamber pots, but he has never actually seen a person be killed. And now he has the authority to do so. If necessary. It is a strange thought.

The song of the women rings out across the fjord; the oars creak in time. Are they smiling at him? They appear stupid. They laugh too much and he is already rather tired of them. When they sing he can see into their mouths, all the way in to their flapping uvulas. Is there even a human thought in their heads? He sees their fat knuckles tighten and release on the handles of the oars, he sees their small feet brace as they take the strain. If he were to lie with one of them, which would it be? He studies them by turn. It is hard to tell the difference. The black slave women were hard to tell apart, too, but most likely on account of their features being obliterated, as it were, by the blackness of their skin. These Eskimo women are pale and yet they still look so utterly similar. It is as if the knot in which their hair is tied up has drawn their facial features upwards as well, lending them an odd expression of constant astonishment about the eyes. It must be strange to kiss one of them. How would they taste? He refrained from doing so with the slave women, though the opportunities were plenty and the crew all urged him: Get some practice in on one of the savages, Bjerg, so you know what to do when you get married. But the thought repelled him. He would often be put to work hosing below deck, a task that did little to stimulate feelings of any romantic nature. These women who now sit facing him, rocking gently back and forth, are not slaves and one cannot do with them as one pleases. As far as he knows they are, moreover, good Christians. And yet they are so very different from him, as different from him – and from the girl named Ulrikka of whom he still thinks from time to time – as the pitch-black women who lay like herrings in a barrel in the hold of the *Fredensborg*.

They make their way gently north; his head lolls; noon passes, then afternoon, with no change. He sleeps a little, the nodding of his head travels into his dream in which he is seated in a boat that is taking in water and no one else has noticed. He opens his mouth to raise the alarm and not a sound comes out. He wakes and lifts his feet abruptly from the bottom of the vessel. But the boat is dry.

Falck calls out to Didrik. He points ashore. Bjerg scans the landscape. He sees some nodules on a plateau; they look like molehills. A settlement. Didrik waits for the boat to catch up with him and takes hold of the gunwale. The women rest on their oars.

No people there, says Didrik. It would be a waste of time, Mr Falck.

Falck nods and stares at the land. Bjerg wishes they would go ashore; he feels a desperate need to stretch his legs.

Onward, says Falck. We shall put in soon enough.

They pass through a narrow sound that runs diagonally to the north-west, and the heavy swell from the open sea presses down upon them. They cross between small islands; the land becomes more varied. Here and there they see dwellings or what is left of them, but no sign of people. Eventually they go ashore on to a small island. All disperse immediately to crouch behind rocks, then assemble again a little further inland. Didrik says something to the women and they light a fire and make tea in which they soak some hard tack. Constable Bjerg stretches out in the heather and observes them. A packet of lump sugar is passed around. The women speak in lowered voices. Their cheeks bulge with the sugar. He is annoyed by their laughter.

When they have drunk their tea and eaten their hard tack, the men walk along the shore and look at what signs are left of humans: some tent rings, a pair of huts without rafters. No one has lived here for years, says Didrik.

Have they all gone to join these prophets? Falck wants to know.

Some, says Didrik. Many are dead. Some have gone north to Holsteinsborg or other big places.

Dead? Why dead?

Scarcity. A failed *fangst*. Hunger. Has the Magister not heard of these things?

Bjerg detects a derisive tone in the man's voice. He wonders if it is aimed at the natives' inability to survive, or the priest's ignorance.

Falck pokes at the site of an old fire. It would seem they resorted to preparing their garments as meals, he says pensively.

It is quite common among the savages, says Didrik. In the winter they eat their clothing; in the spring they must sew anew.

Ugh! Says Bjerg.

Falck looks at him. Hunger is a hard master, Constable Bjerg.

Forgive me, Magister, says Bjerg, but I am revolted by the thought of eating a shoe, even if it were my own feet that had been inside.

There are many graves on the island, marked by whale bones or decayed planks. Didrik translates the Greenlandic words that have been scratched into them. *Rest in peace* is popular and probably much welcomed.

So these are christened people? says Falck.

Christened and heathens, says Didrik. Death has poor eyesight, as we say. It cannot tell the difference.

Falck sighs. He takes a box under his arm and wanders up the fell. His botanizing box, he tells Bjerg. I enjoy looking for flowers and all manner of plants, and to make drawings of them in my sketchbook. It is my pastime.

Rasmus Bjerg walks inwards across the land; the slopes bring him to an elevated position. He turns and looks back. The camp seems very distant now, after only half an hour's trek; the boat is a mere wood shaving; the people resemble busy beetles. Smoke rises from the fire. From the shore the water stretches upwards and resembles a wall. The horizon extends at eye level. How peculiar! He cups his hands to his mouth and calls out. The beetles halt; they scan the fellside, but cannot see him. He calls again. They wave. He ducks. Spotted! He laughs.

He descends through a valley, eating berries from the bushes and arriving at the shore a little north of the camp. Here he meets two of the women who are out gathering berries and mushrooms. He gives them a wide berth, has no desire to speak to them. He is not even aware of whether they understand Danish. They straighten up as they hear him coming, shade their eyes from the sun and watch him as he passes. He affords them a formal greeting and walks on. They call out to him. He does not understand what they say, but he can tell they are up to something. He turns hesitantly. They wave him back and he approaches them. The flintlock slaps at his thigh.

What do you want? he demands to know, putting on a severe tone.

They speak to him and gesture for him to sit down with them. One of them smokes on a pipe made from a piece of hollowed-out animal bone. The smoke smells of heather and herbs. She takes the pipe from her mouth and hands it to him. He sits down. The heather embraces him, soft and warm. The bowl of the pipe is red-hot; he holds the stem and puffs a little, expels the smoke and coughs. The women laugh. They chatter, without including him in any way in their conversation. He allows them to sit and smoke. The smoke has a wearying effect on him; the only thing he feels inclined to do is to sit here and listen to the women's nattering that sounds like a stream running over a bed of shingle in his mind. An iceberg drifts on the sea. It must be colossal, as big as a palace, he thinks to himself, as big as the white palace of Christiansborg in Copenhagen, which he has seen more than once, most recently on the day he shipped out to Greenland. He draws their attention to the iceberg, pointing and pronouncing the word in Danish: *is-bjerg*. They say a word in their own language, a word with a rippling ring to it: *iluliaq*. He tries to say it. They laugh. One of them takes hold of his mouth, presses it together and pulls his lips outwards. *I-lu-li-aq*, she says. *I-lu-li-aq*, he repeats. She nods with contentment, or perhaps in resignation.

They introduce themselves to each other. *Rasimusi*, they call him. His surname is impossible for them to pronounce, though in his opinion it is the shortest and easiest surname imaginable. Their own names are Rosine and Amanda, good Danish names they were given at their christening. He knows they have other names, but perhaps they are secret; perhaps they are ashamed of their heathen background. He does not enquire and would have been unable to do so, even if he had been inclined.

Now we know each other, he says, and hands the pipe to Amanda. Now we are almost betrothed.

They laugh obligingly, though probably they do not understand a word he says.

On his way back he encounters Mr Falck, who is returning from his botanical expedition. He seems happy and refreshed from his walk. He shows Bjerg his sketches. Look, he says, and takes out one of the plates. Annual stonecrop. *Sedum annuum.* Do you see, Constable Bjerg, it was still in flower!

Bjerg glances at the drawing. Falck has given it colour, a striving green plant with a dozen yellow petals.

Do you see how it reaches for the light, Constable Bjerg? It strives towards the sun. In the morning it inclines to the east, in the evening to the west, even when the weather is cloudy. In fact, one can look at these plants and tell which direction is south. Provided, that is, one knows the time of day.

I see, says Bjerg. His mind is elsewhere.

In the dark months that lie ahead I shall make proper drawings of these sketches, Falck declares happily. I may even produce a gouache painting or two. Have you heard of the *Flora Danica*, Bjerg? No, of course not, but nonetheless let me confide to you that I intend to prepare a *Flora Groenlandica*, a comprehensive atlas of botany containing illustrations of the wild plants that are native to this land. It shall be my life's work, along with my work in the Mission, of course. I have been in this country a year, but only now have I been able to purchase and have made the necessary equipment that will allow me to journey about as I wish. It is high time I began!

It's late, says Bjerg, who understands not half of what the priest has said. We'd best get back to camp.

They decide to spend the night on the island, though find it unnecessary to put up the tent. Instead, they crawl into the two sleeping bags, the men in one, the women in the other. Bjerg lies listening to the tide, the clacking of the pebbles on the shore. He hears a stomach grumble, apparently Falck's, and the light breathing of the women on the other side of the fire. He thinks of the woman, Rosine, who put her fingers to his mouth to make it pronounce the Greenlandic word correctly. It is the first time a woman other than his mother has touched him there. He embroiders slightly upon his recollection of the hand; he makes it caress his cheek and puts his lips to it. The woman, or the girl, Rosine, has at once become visible, has stepped forward from behind her native mask. He cannot understand how he was unable to tell her apart from the three others. Amanda, too, is easily recognizable with her round paddings of fat at the cheekbones, her wide grin, and eyes that slant and seem to tell of cunning. He thinks that if he were to lie with one of them, it would be most uncomplicated to lie with Amanda, who is clearly the elder and more experienced. But it is Rosine he thinks about, Rosine's hands touching his mouth.

†

In the morning Falck holds prayers. He hands out sacramental bread, passes round a cup of wine and bestows a blessing upon them. After that, they sail on.

Their destination is the settlement at Eternal Fjord and the Christians there, who it seems have embroiled themselves in ignorance and false doctrine, but first they must sail through the rest of the district to see if there are people left at all. The kayak man does not believe it to be worth the effort: everyone is either dead or has joined the prophets. They find several abandoned settlements, tent rings, foundations, recent graves. Most places seem not to have been inhabited this year. In a bay they cross some days later the water is but a few fathoms deep and as clear as bottle glass. Bjerg hears the priest call out and the women stop rowing. And then he sees them. On the light-coloured bed of sand at the bottom are a number of dead, outstretched on their backs, arms spread to the sides, long heathen manes loosened from the bead-studded bands that would normally have held them in place. They rock gently in the current. Their faces are gone. He sees small fish dart into the sockets of their eyes.

Falck says the Lord's Prayer and they continue on. Bjerg studies the women, who study him. If they feel the same dread as him, they conceal the emotion expertly. He looks upon the relentless fells, the sky and all that surrounds them with different eyes than only an hour before. What is it we are doing here, exactly? he asks himself.

Evening. The women have made a fire. Slices of pork sizzle on the pan. Having conducted a cursory reconnaissance, he returns and informs them that the place is suited to their long rest. There is driftwood on the shore, plenty of fresh water, and he believes there will be hare.

Very well, says Falck. Let us put up the tent and make ourselves more comfortable.

Bjerg takes his flintlock and follows the river inland to a lake that collects water from three fells. His progress is slowed by small streams and his feet are quickly soaked. The kayak man, too, has gone hunting with his own rifle. Bjerg can see him on the other side of the valley. There are many ptarmigan. He hears them clucking along the esker. He will resort to them if he should fail to catch a hare. He walks on. The silence is monumental, broken only by the sound of running water. The fells are ancient. He looks up at them and feels small, exposed and solitary. They must have been here since the days of Noah, he thinks. Clouds pull themselves from the peaks and drift across the sky. There is something unfathomable about nature, a thing that has always frightened him somewhat. To die here must be dreadful; to lie in the open and be decomposed into bones at nature's own unhurried and inescapable tempo. He thinks to himself that nature may decide to do him harm and prevent him from returning to the camp. The thought is unbearable.

When he gets back he says he has pains in his stomach and lies down beside the fire. He had imagined that Rosine would give him tea and sit with him to keep him company, and perhaps teach him some more words in her own language. But she is not there. In the evening Didrik returns with a clutch of hares. The women, too, have returned. They skin the animals and put them on spits of wood and roast them over the fire. Falck, who suffers from chronic stomach trouble, advises him to stay away from the meat and instead to eat a portion of the thin gruel he has boiled. The priest hands him a plate whose contents he sups before lying down to sleep in order to forget how hungry he is.

From the sleeping bag he watches Rosine, who is seated with the other women, meticulously turning a hare bone between her fingers. She sucks on it, her tongue darting forward, pointed and pink, teeth flashing, mouth glistening with fat. She glances across at him, he smiles, she says something to Amanda, who comes over with some meat. Disappointed that Rosine would not come herself, he devours it greedily.

But she watches him. Her dark eyes study him. Amanda says something to her in a harsh tone. It sounds like *panik*, perhaps her Greenlandic name, he thinks to himself. She lowers her gaze.

They pass Old Sukkertoppen, the original site of the colony. A handful of houses, whose relocation proved unviable, remain, but the Danes are all gone. A few Christian families of mixtures and a small number of heathens live there still, from fishing and small-scale hunting, and a very elderly catechist and his wife. Despite this score of inhabitants, the European slant makes the place appear even more forlorn than the abandoned settlements they have seen on their way. Grey, timeworn cladding, blind window holes, crumbling stone foundations, sagging roofs, a churchyard, a whole field of white crosses. There are names on them: Jens, Peter, Søren, Kristian, Maren, Gunhild, Karoline, Olga. *Rest in peace.* The words sound more like a heathen invocation now than Christian piety. The grass has grown up around the crosses and is buffeted by the wind.

Further north they encounter some small groups of individuals, people from Holsteinsborg who have begun to seep southwards in search of a place to spend the winter. The hunting is good, they say, and there is little competition. Bjerg finds them a sorry sight, they look more like they are heading south by compulsion than free will. Falck tests their knowledge of the Saviour and the good Word. Yes, they know of it, they mumble. The pastor at Holsteinsborg has preached the Gospel to us and many have been christened. But it is not for us, they say, there are too many problems in the colonies and they prefer to try their fortunes on their own. Perhaps they will enter the Eternal Fjord, if all else fails. It is said they know no shortage there.

Falck warns that they should stay away from the so-called prophets and their game. His Majesty the king, who owns this land, has heard tell of their antics and has been much grieved and angered by what has occurred. The blasphemers of Eternal Fjord are soon to be consigned to history. Habakuk says it is the pale faces in our country who will soon be gone, they rejoin, laughing in a mocking manner that offends the priest.

They are now at the northernmost margin of the district. A light, sandy brink projects from the shore; behind it, a round valley and jagged peaks. Bjerg points out that there is at least one tent at the place. Falck is gladdened. Let us hope for no more of these inveterate transients from the north, he says, but for people with whom one can speak of the Saviour and the love they may find in Him. He jumps over the side and wades ashore, squelching in the soft clay bed into which the boat glides with a sigh.

Bring the tent and pack, Falck commands from the brink. I will go and greet the inhabitants. He disappears from sight.

The women are disgruntled. They are tired of all this travel to no avail. They cannot be bothered with any more heathens, living or dead. They will not go ashore. Bjerg has no idea what to do to make them fall into line. Fortunately, Didrik steps in and speaks to them; his voice is soft and kind. After a short while they climb out of the boat and drag it on to the land in unison.

The women carry their items ashore, while Bjerg and Didrik follow on after Falck. From the brink they can see him outside the tent. He paces back and forth.

It seems no one is home, says Bjerg.

Didrik gives him a look. He laughs. Perhaps the priest does not find it agreeable inside.

A path has been trodden down in the heather between the brink and the camp. In front of the tent lie the remains of a kayak and a kone boat, both relieved of their skins, the frames bare and white.

So, did our priest say hello to the inhabitants? says Didrik as they approach.

Falck shakes his head. He draws the opening aside and steps back. Bjerg bends down and enters, then Didrik and Falck likewise.

There are four people in the sleeping area. They lie neatly, head to toe, arms at their sides, almost like the negroes on the slave ship. All substance has dissolved away under the skin and there is an intense austerity about the parchment-covered cheekbones, chins and foreheads. These are faces Bjerg imagines might await him on Judgement Day.

Poor, unenlightened heathens, says Falck. This is what comes of trying one's own fortunes. Why on earth did they not come to us? We could have taken care of them.

I know one of them, says Didrik. She received instruction from Magister Krogh some years ago. He indicates one of the figures. She was a young girl, perhaps fourteen years old.

Did the magister not christen her? Falck asks.

I think she changed her mind. Some relatives came and persuaded her to go with them.

How sad. How stupid! Falck sounds as if the loss is personal.

Bjerg reaches out to the train-oil lamp and runs a finger along its edge, loosening a fatty crust. He pokes in the cooking pot and lifts out strips of some undefinable substance.

Falck studies them, feeling them between his fingers. Garments of skin, he says. The national dish of the hungry.

Bjerg has had enough of death for one year. He goes outside and sits in the heather with his back to the tent. He hears Falck inside say, Such peace, Didrik, this is as good a farewell to life as anyone could wish.

Death was certainly better than what went before it, says Didrik.

How do you consider they died? It would seem to have occurred at one and the same time. Could they have eaten poisoned food, intentionally perhaps, in order to end their days?

They froze to death, says Didrik. They ate the clothes from each other's bodies and then there was no more blubber for the lamp. It looks like it happened two years ago, when there was a long cold spell.

But where is the fifth? Falck asks. Someone must have arranged them like this.

They find the fifth inhabitant a short distance from the tent, face-down on the ground. Bjerg sticks the toe of his boot under the corpse and turns it on to its back. The well-preserved face of a female stares up at them, a bare breast, a bird spear protruding from between the ribs.

Lord Jesus, Bjerg whispers. Is there no limit to this land's cruelty?

They pull the tent down, wrap the dead in its skins and commit them to the ground as best they can, then build a cairn of stones from the shore. Falck says a prayer over the grave. Lord, have mercy upon these innocent children of a heartless land. The wind picks up with the changing tide; the words flap away from Falck's mouth. Bjerg clutches his cap. The women are called to observe the ceremony, but they are reluctant, giggle and utter inappropriate comments about dinner. As soon as Falck is done, they hurry back to the camp. They eat hare. Bjerg makes do with gruel and this time it is more than sufficient. In the night the women's subdued jabber is like a dripping tap. He shushes them, but when they lower their voices it annoys him even more. Next to him, Falck mumbles in his sleep. Now I am closer to Thee, Lord, he says more than once. The smell of the sleeping bag's dark, close interior is appalling. He lies up against Falck's backside and must focus his thoughts for fear that the physical contact will give him an erection. Eventually, he leaves the sleeping bag and walks until he is over a hill. He lies down in the heather and curls up against the cold, preferring to freeze than to lie marinating in the sweat and bodily smells of other men.

He hears someone approach, light footsteps rather than heavy boots. He lies with his eyes closed, on his side in the heather, pretending to be asleep. He is furious with her. He does not know why, but the emotion is there. He acknowledges an urge to do her harm, so refuses to open his eyes and receive her. Instead, he lies motionless, savouring his malice and lack of willingness to oblige her. She places her hand on his arm and squeezes gently. He feels her fingers sink into his woollen sweater and grip the muscle of his upper arm. He breathes deeply, his jaw hanging

open like an idiot's. He is asleep. And yet he smells her. Her naked
body, clad in the skins of dead animals, her skin against the skins, sweat
mingled with remnants of blubber and the urine used in tanning, the
smell of smoke from the fire. He lies still and senses all this as she sits
on her haunches and studies him, assessing the authenticity of his sleep.
Someone calls out to her from the camp. He recognizes the voice of
Amanda.

Panik.

He hears the rustle of her feet once more behind him as she hurries
away. She has abandoned him. He would like to have looked now, to
catch a glimpse of her back, but he is facing away from her and does not
wish to run the risk of her seeing him stir. So he remains quite still. He
wonders how she will deal with the disappointment after she has returned
to the camp, imagines her squeezing into the tightness of the sleeping
bag, the women folding themselves around her, the women folding
themselves around him, their hands exploring under his garments. He
imagines her hurt at having been rejected. Perhaps they will whisper,
poke fun at her and make things worse. He gloats at the thought. It will
only do her good. He tears tufts of heather from the ground, causing
the soil to fly. He grinds his teeth and groans in annoyance. Now he is
close to her.

†

The Eternal Fjord. Last evening the clouds descended on to the fells,
and when this morning they drifted away, the peaks were collared
with snow. It is the first time Bjerg has seen glaciers at close quarters.
They snake between the fells, down towards the fjord, where they are
curtailed, ending in vertical walls of blue ice. One hears them rumble;
sometimes the reiteration of a former swell passes by and raises the boat
several ells, then lets it down again, utterly without sound. The fells on
both sides are jagged; they rip apart the clouds, reflect in the sheen of
the fjord, so clearly that a person can fall into doubt as to what is up and
what is down. For this reason, Didrik prefers to sit in the boat, other-

wise he fears he will be seized by the kayak sickness so dreaded by all Greenlandic hunters. He amuses himself by teasing the women. They chatter away in their own language, secure in the linguistic incapacity of the two Danes. Didrik is rather more popular than Bjerg cares for, and he is aggrieved by the fact that the kayak man is so able to make the women shriek with laughter.

When they sail on the next day, the fjord has drawn in the fog. They must go close to the land in order not to lose their bearings. Falck is unsettled by it. He keeps asking Didrik if his course is certain. Didrik points diagonally upwards. There is the sun, he says. Bjerg can see it. The place into which he points is slightly brighter than the rest of the bell jar they are in.

Bjerg would not mind them getting lost and ending up somewhere else entirely, far from the prophets. The sealed arrest warrant burns in his pocket. The closer they get to the time and place at which he must step into character as an executive authority, the less he feels like one. He has not the slightest inkling of what awaits him inside the fjord, whether there are many people or few, whether they are savages or more like the christened Greenlanders in the colony, or whether one or the other would be most to his advantage. Perhaps they have prepared themselves for some sort of attack; perhaps they have entrenched themselves, cleaned their rifles and laid plans. He is not ready for such a contingency. He has never been a soldier and has no intention of beginning now. At the first sign of violence he intends to lay down his arms and wave the white flag. Moreover, he considers that people should be allowed to believe in whatever they wish and he suspects that deep down the priest is of precisely the same opinion.

The ice creaks and sighs. Now and then it is a loud whistle or a supernatural wailing note. They stare solemnly into the fog; the women look over their shoulders. Falck believes the sound to issue from the wind as it is pressed between the fells. Bjerg cups his hands to his lips and blows.

Exactly, says Falck. All great natural phenomena can be duplicated on a smaller scale, as you so admirably demonstrate, good constable.

Then all of a sudden they think they hear hymns. The women pull in the oars. Everyone pricks up their ears. They sit and listen.

If I'm not mistaken, says Didrik, it is one of Count Zinzendorf's.

I think you may be right, says Falck.

Again they listen. Didrik mouths the words, *das ist in Jesu Blut schwimmen und baden.*

What hideous piety, says Falck with a laugh. Indeed, it is Zinzendorf. It seems he has found his proper place at long last. Row, he commands the women, it cannot be far now.

It went straight to the stomach, that song, Magister, says Bjerg.

Indeed, says Falck, the poor nobleman was no great poet. His hymns are as long as this fjord. How scandalous that the products of his sick mind should find root in this country.

I find many of the hymns to be things of beauty, says Didrik. We Greenlanders are fond of a good hymn with emotion to make us cry.

That may be so, but you would be well advised to keep the Count's perversions as to the Lord's bodily fluids, not to mention his libidinous piety, out of the ministry. Such things have an inflammatory effect on receptive souls. Use Mr Richardt's hymns instead, if pietism really is necessary, his works are pleasing and quite harmless.

They keep on rowing, though without the settlement appearing. Falck thinks they must have rowed past it, but Didrik remains certain it lies somewhere ahead.

But the singing, says Falck. It sounded so clear and close by.

Then they are out of the fog; the fjord is visible again, the same fells and glaciers as the day before, only closer now. Didrik points. Some irregularities in the landscape can be made out in the distance. Houses. Smoke is rising up from them. Falck stands in the bow and peers ahead. Bjerg hears him mutter something about spectral reflections of sound, natural amphitheatres creating echoes and acoustic illusions.

Can I ask the Magister a question? Bjerg enquires.

Of course, says Falck, turning round to face him. Ask away, my boy.

All these phenomena, whistling noises and hymns and tall waves when there is no wind, does it not indicate that the fjord is bewitched?

Bewitched? Bewitched does not exist. What are you trying to say? When something occurs that we do not understand it is not a case of witchcraft but a law of nature as yet unknown to us. Medieval darkness and superstition is not something to which we would care to return, am I right?

Indeed, learned magister, Bjerg mumbles, but I still think it peculiar.

On second thoughts, perhaps you might be on to something, dear Bjerg, albeit unwittingly, says the priest kindly. He laughs to himself. This fjord contains an accumulation of mysterious and unfathomable natural phenomena, that much is true. And this fact precisely, in combination with pietistic fogs, has made fertile soil for the uprising we now, by the fresh winds of reason, are about to disperse. Do you understand, Bjerg?

Yes, Mr Falck. We're nearly ashore.

They look in at the land and see staggered plateaus separated by rock, high above the shore. At each level are houses of stone, timber or peat. Smoke curls from their chimneys. At the highest point is a larger structure with a kind of gateway in front and a cross uppermost on the gable end. A church. Most probably there are at least as many houses as yet concealed from them as those that are visible. Bjerg estimates their number: at least threescore. The inhabitants here must be several hundred strong, the greatest concentration of Greenlanders in the country's history.

Jesus, Bjerg blurts out, thunderstruck. It looks like a whole peasant village!

Falck, too, is astonished. It reminds me of Norway, he says. Of a settlement up on the ridge at Drammen. But I have never seen one as big as this at home.

They are received kindly on the shore and are helped to unload their goods and draw the boat up on to the land. Bjerg looks around; he carries the flintlock on his shoulder. He is overwhelmed by their sheer numbers;

his ears are assailed by their palaver. They are clad both in coarse frieze and in skins; most wear European as well as Greenlandic garments. Pipes are smoked, passed from mouth to mouth. Fresh water is brought and they are given cups from which to drink. Bjerg notes that the oarswomen are welcomed heartily, presumably by relatives they have not seen in a long time, and he feels pangs of jealousy. He realizes the women are no longer under his command, as he at least imagined them to be during the journey. It was a mistake to bring them here. Already they disappear up the slopes with their friends. He sees Rosine go with them; she has merged in, stepped back behind her mask. He has lost her.

It occurs to him that he has committed a second error. He has allowed the people to carry the goods ashore, among them the powder keg and the box of flintlocks. He watches as they are taken to a structure at the shore, presumably a storehouse. Now he has equipped them with weapons and ammunition enough to start a war. He stops a man. Take me to the person in charge.

The man looks at him kindly, though without comprehension.

Nalagak? Bjerg ventures in unhelpful Greenlandic.

The man smiles emptily.

Habakuk, says Bjerg. I wish to speak to Habakuk or his wife.

Falck comes over to them. All in good time, constable. Let us first find our accommodation and see what is what. He sweeps a hand. Such a magnificent, majestic place, don't you agree? One quite understands them in their choice of location.

I am to arrest Habakuk and his woman, Bjerg says in a low voice. By decree of the king.

He produces the warrant and hopes he is not committing another mistake in handing it to Falck. The priest takes his time to read the document. He studies the seal, scrutinizes the signatures. Then he hands it back to Bjerg.

We must first speak with them, he says quietly. Perhaps they may be talked into coming along of their own accord. Who knows?

The settlement of Igdlut is short of dwellings; people have arrived in their droves all summer and not everyone has yet managed to build their own house; they sleep cramped together on the sleeping benches of others. Bjerg orders the tent to be raised at the top of the main plateau, close to the church building. Here they arrange themselves. Didrik stays with them. He seems to be worrying over some matter, is silent and brooding. Bjerg has noticed that he and the priest have conducted whispered conversations, or heated discussions, with much gesticulation, shaking of heads and pulling of faces. When Bjerg approaches them, they fall silent and wait for him to go. Then they begin again. They see little of the women; it seems almost as if they are hiding. Bjerg mentions his concern to Falck. Will the oarswomen be at all inclined to return with them to the colony? Let us perform our duties as well as we are able, Falck responds, and leave it to the good Lord to take care of matters over which we have no control, Bjerg.

What's wrong with our kayak man? he asks.

Oh, a conflict of conscience, says Falck. I told him about your document.

Was that wise, Mr Falck?

That remains to be seen, the priest replies. We shall place it in the hands of the Lord.

The Lord's soon got plenty to be getting on with, says Bjerg with annoyance.

Tomorrow I shall conduct a service in the splendid church building, says Falck. I expect you to be in attendance. Then we shall have to see what happens.

Shall I take the gun?

My dear Constable Bjerg, surely you would not even contemplate taking an instrument of death into God's house?

I would.

Well, be that as it may, I would ask you to refrain. We shall employ the power of the Spirit and the word, not gunpowder and bullets.

They are strong in number, says Bjerg, and we are only three, or rather two.

Exactly, says Falck. He bends over some papers Bjerg assumes are notes for his sermon.

Bjerg wanders about the settlement and looks around. People greet him politely, though seem in no way approachable. He addresses a few, but receives only vapid smiles and nods. A number of them are seated on the rocks facing the fjord, eating salmon laid out before them. He is invited to join in. He selects a piece, removes the flesh from the bones and devours it. The fish is fat and juicy and tastes of salt. He can hardly remember having tasted anything as good in years. He reaches out for more and looks up at them with an enquiring expression. They speak all at once. *Takanna.* He does not know the word. But he understands that he is welcome to take another piece.

He sees Rosine some distance away. He stays close by in the hope that she will notice him. But she does not, or perhaps pretends not to. Who can blame her, he thinks, the way I have behaved. He scolds himself for his stupid pride. He would so very much like to speak to her, to take her hand in his and tell her he is sorry, to call her by her proper name. *Panik.* He feels so abysmally alone among all these strangers who treat him with such kind indifference. Tomorrow they will be indifferent no more. Something will happen. He has no idea what. But he cannot go back to the colony without at least having tried to carry out the arrest warrant.

Early in the evening he lies half asleep in the tent and is woken by a rummaging at the opening. He sits up. A head appears. Amanda. She says something to him, *Rasimusi,* and then something else that sounds like *kraajid!* She beckons to him.

Are you asking me to go with you? Is it about Panik?

She nods eagerly. He follows her out.

They walk upwards, following the ridge at an angle, though always ascending. Their path is made difficult by the vegetation, tall bushes and branches of creeping willow catch on their clothing and slow them down. They descend into a gorge, leap across a stream, scramble up a slope. His boots are not suited for climbing and more than once she must reach down and help him. Then, eventually, the ground levels out, a new plateau on which grows only moss and lichen. There are no dwellings here. They continue higher still and come to a narrow pass with boulders at the bottom. Amanda puts a hand on his shoulder. Now, he thinks to himself, now she wants me. We will take off our clothes and join together. We will kiss and caress. I want to see her and commit it all into my mind, to touch everything, and I will imagine her to be Rosine. It will not be perfect, but it is better than nothing.

Amanda looks at him. She smiles. There is something oddly nervous about her, something urgent. Her eyes widen and she points.

Are we to go down there? he asks.

She shakes her head, then gives him a shove in the back. He stumbles forward and turns. But she is gone, vanished in a matter of seconds.

He turns round once more and strides off in the direction of a tarn that is half-encircled by the steep crags at whose foot it lies, plunging rock extending like two arms that almost meet at the opposite shore. The lake is thus pleasantly sheltered from the wind, a natural dip in the rugged landscape. At the shore he sees a figure seated in the sand. He stiffens and squints. He walks on, slowly and without haste; her figure grows closer; the rounded neck he has studied and stared at in the boat, and behind it her face, eyebrows arching above a look of astonishment.

Panik? he says.

She bursts into laughter. Then shakes her head.

Rosine, he says.

Rasimusi.

He sits down beside her. They shuffle closer. He puts his left arm around her waist, cups the fat of her hip. She places her left hand on the knee of his breeches, the palm facing upwards. He places his own hand on top of it. They lace fingers; they squeeze each other's hand.

Panik? He tries again.

She shakes her head energetically. It seems he is not allowed to use her proper name.

And there they sit. He has no idea what they are to do. But he wishes for nothing more than this. It is sufficient. They look out over the body of water that lies in the shadow of the dark fell. It is a foreboding place. The snow-clad peaks to the south of the fjord sparkle in the sunlight. The fells they see furthest away to the south-west must be those close to the colony. He could tell her about it, if only they could speak.

He turns his face towards her and she looks up at him. Her smile is a stiff mask. She is quite as nervous as I, he thinks to himself. He draws her towards him and she relaxes, rests her head against his shoulder. He kisses her, feels her soft, spongy lips against his own, which are tough and weathered. She says something and tugs at the sparing tufts of his beard. He pinches the lobe of her ear. She says something else, firmly this time. He breathes into her ear and apologizes. Did it hurt? She is appeased and they kiss, both of them now at once. He feels the tip of her tongue as it darts; he chases it with his own; their tongues come together and wrestle gently inside her mouth. She gives him a playful shove. They sit beside each other, he with his arm around her, she with her left hand in his right.

Lovely view, he says. A good place to live.

When they return towards the settlement Amanda is there, waiting on the slope. She gets to her feet and goes with them the rest of the way. Bjerg hears her interrogate Rosine and he hears that she replies in a positive tone. They arrive at the dwellings. Hardly a soul is out; the people have turned in for the night; the air is thick with smoke from their fires. Bjerg wonders where they are leading him, what their plan is for him. He walks with them; whatever is to happen will happen. He loves Rosine, he knows this now. Nothing can happen to change it.

They come to a house which Amanda enters. Bjerg hears low voices inside. Rosine stands beside him. He cannot make her look at him.

Then Amanda comes out again. She gestures for them to come inside. There is a small entry where he must bend his neck. He kicks off his boots and steps into a room some few paces in length and breadth, illuminated by a train-oil lamp that spits and splutters. Two old people, apparently chased from their beds, are putting on their clothes. They smile and greet him and edge their way out towards the door. Bjerg removes his hat and bows politely. The old folk vanish. Amanda says something to Rosine, who sends her a calm, trusting look. Then Amanda, too, is gone. The door closes quietly behind her. They are alone.

Bjerg looks at Rosine. He senses that she has known all along that this was to happen. It must mean something, but what it means is not apparent to him. Her knowing what is to happen has a calming effect on him. It relieves him of some of his burden.

And then they are naked beneath the reindeer skin. He explores her and takes his time. It surprises him how clean she is, though she has always been so in his fantasies. There is a faintly acrid smell about her, an olfactory echo of urine tubs and fermented meat. He is aware, too, of some effluvium reminiscent of ammonia, but not even that repulses him. Rather, it strikes him as pure and clean, like the chemical fumes of textile manufacture. Her skin is warm and smooth; it smells spicy and dry and of smoke. Her cunt is sweetly odorous. She pushes him away when he tries to kiss it. He tries again and she strikes him about the head and admonishes him in a whispered voice.

This is what we Danish men do, he says, as though he were an experienced lover. It is our favourite meal.

She lets him do it. It feels soft and downy against his mouth. It opens and is smooth and moist. He explores her hands. They are rough and callused and he remembers that they comprise one fourth of the power required to transport six people in a heavily laden boat over more than one hundred nautical miles. Poor little hands, he breathes, kissing her palms and sucking her fingers. He fumbles at her breasts, buries his face in the folds of her skin, sucking and licking. Glancing up, he is confronted by her impassionate and curious gaze. But when he goes down again, to touch and lick her cunt, to feel inside it, she makes a brief sound of protest. It is not what she wishes.

What do you want? he asks. Tell me what to do?

She tugs at him. He sits up and she opens her legs, slaps the opening of her cunt twice with the palm of her hand, then roughly parts her labia. This is not her first time, he thinks to himself. He positions himself between her silken legs and enters her. She forces his head down towards her and utters sounds of gratification. When he comes, he bursts into tears. He lies awkwardly with his head between her breasts and gasps for air. She runs her fingers through his hair, dries his moistened cheeks and makes maternal noises.

You are my first, he says. I have not had a woman before. I want no other than you, my darling. I belong to you. Do with me as you please.

†

When he returns to the tent the next morning, the flintlock is gone. He searches through his things, in all his pockets, but the arrest warrant is gone, too. He sits on the bed. Without the warrant and the gun he is without authority. He is nothing. He is just a boy. But no matter. A burden is removed from his shoulders. Now he can do what he wants.

He hears the ship's bell and goes outside. There is a fog, but the plateau itself is bathed in sunshine. The fog is a gleaming white and as thick as custard; it follows the fjord as it weaves inland and he feels the bitter cold that accompanies it, but also the warmth of the sun that will soon chase it away. Behind the settlement and on the other side of the fjord, the profile of the peaks stands as sharp as a knife against the blue autumn sky. People come wandering up the slope; they follow the paths that have been trodden through the moss; a long train of families with children, clad in their finest garments. Bjerg stands in the opening of the tent in a worn sweater of Icelandic pattern, shrouded by the night's vapours, and feels like the most uncivilized of them all. He catches sight of Rosine, walking arm in arm with Amanda. They do not look up at him. Soon we can present ourselves together for everyone, he tells himself. I shall ask Pastor Falck to give us the blessing in the church. The thought makes him feel like a benefactor and he is moved to imagine Rosine's gratitude.

He goes inside and puts on a different pair of breeches and his blue coat, its sleeves are embellished with galloons to signify his royal authority. He loosens his pigtail, tightens it again, spits on his fingers and smooths his short fringe as well as he is able. He unties his oil-tanned boots and scrapes off the worst of the mud before putting them on. There is no mirror, yet he feels at ease with himself, a handsome young man. She will take note of me, he thinks, she will feel proud that I belong to her, just as I am proud that she is mine.

There must be more than a hundred people outside the church. The bell still peals in its little tower between the church building and the gateway of whale bones. It is a brass bell, he sees, it looks like the kind used to mark the hours on board a ship. Probably something they have plundered from a wreck. The churchgoers turn to look at him; a path opens in their midst, leading to the church door, where Pastor Falck stands in full vestments. Bjerg sees that the priest is pale. He clutches his Bible and looks like he is freezing. Bjerg notices now that the air has chilled during the last hour. Cold gusts sweep down from the high ridge behind the settlement and a grey carpet of cloud extends between the peaks.

Where on earth have you been? Falck asks.

Where is our kayak man? Bjerg asks.

There has been much commotion in the night, says Falck. Have you not sensed it?

I was up on the fell, says Bjerg.

All the more fortunate for you. Your arrest warrant has caused a great deal of anger. They have been looking for you everywhere.

The warrant is gone, says Bjerg matter-of-factly. I don't know where it is and I don't care.

On a low rock stand a man and a woman, side by side; she in colourful garments embroidered with pearls, he in a simple black anorak and breeches of skin. They smile kindly, solemnly, and exude authority.

Habakuk and his woman, says Bjerg.

They have not shown themselves until now, says Falck. They are cunning. Now everyone understands that they must choose between us and them.

Bjerg feels at once uncomfortable in his blue braided coat. He feels naked without his flintlock, even though it would probably only make things worse. He senses a feeling of excitement and restless joy among the throng. They laugh and chatter; some young men perform somersaults and leapfrog to much amusement and jubilation. Still more people come wandering up the slope; the crowd swells.

Did Didrik take the warrant? Bjerg asks.

One would assume so.

It is treason, says Bjerg. It may cost him his life.

Indeed, says Falck. But one must understand that Didrik was plunged into strife when he heard about the order. Rather a peculiar dilemma, if one thinks about it. Falck wipes his brow with a handkerchief he has hidden in his sleeve. His loyalty to the king on the one hand and to his people on the other. These two matters are usually one and the same, but not in this instance.

I feel a similar conflict myself, says Bjerg.

Falck turns and looks at him. What do you mean?

I have, well, er, committed myself to a certain person, he says.

Aha! A brief grin passes over Falck's face. Our pretty oarswoman, I take it?

Bjerg nods.

You have been courting, Constable Bjerg. So that was what you were up to while the entire settlement was out looking for you. And probably with her mother's blessing, I shouldn't wonder.

Her mother?

Amanda is Rosine's mother. Didn't you know?

So that's why she calls her *panik*, says Bjerg. I thought it to be her name.

Falck laughs. It seems she is an eager matchmaker, this Amanda. Are you happy with each other?

I love her, Bjerg hears himself say.

I see. Well, you are young. I feel a certain yearning myself now and then, a budding devotion, whose object I need not divulge here. But I understand you, indeed.

I cannot commit violence against these people, says Bjerg. Besides, they have taken my gun as well. No one would expect me to contain the settlement with my pocket knife, surely?

Be at ease, says Falck. I shall preach for them. We shall practise the grace of free will that was given to us by the Lord at our christening.

Eh? says Bjerg and looks at the priest in puzzlement.

We shall let them decide for themselves. First I shall preach, then Habakuk likewise, and then we shall see which of us wins most favour with our congregation. It will be a duel of words. The Lord will ensure the victory of the just.

The man who has been ringing the little ship's bell steps down. The people fall silent. Falck opens the door and all heads turn at once to the two upon the rock. Habakuk nods. The congregation moves into the church. Bjerg stands beside Falck as people file past. Amanda sends him a sly look; Rosine stares straight ahead. She looks almost cantankerous, he thinks anxiously. Behind them come a number of men, among them Didrik. He looks at Bjerg with animosity and Bjerg feels even more ill at ease.

Falck reaches out and puts a hand on Didrik's shoulder. He halts.

Dear Didrik, you must help me. You must be my interpreter. Will you?

The kayak man nods. I will translate.

The church is quickly filled. There are still some fifty people outside who cannot come in. Bjerg follows Falck through the nave to the choir, where there is a step up. There is no pulpit and no decoration. The church could almost have been a warehouse.

Falck asks him to stand at the side, to his right. Didrik stands next to him. Voices rise to a hum, benches creak and scrape on the floor, a couple of children begin to cry. Then all goes quiet. Bjerg sees Habakuk and Maria Magdalene seated in the front row. He sees that they are holding hands. Further back he sees Rosine and Amanda, her mother and, with any luck, his future mother-in-law. But he senses that something is about to happen. There is a strange feeling in the air.

Falck clears his throat. His voice a-tremble, he thanks the community for the hospitality it has accorded him and his company. Didrik translates. Falck praises the settlement, which in his opinion is much better organized than any colony he has seen, and Bjerg notes that he looks directly upon the two front rows as he speaks. His praise would seem to be well received, many smile and nod in acknowledgement of his words. This bay, Falck continues, this little community, for such it is, indeed, must surely be one of the most splendid spots on the entire earth. A hum of approval ripples through the congregation.

However, says Falck, and pauses. He looks at Didrik and the kayak man translates the word. *Kisjeni.* A silence descends.

However, His Majesty the king was saddened to hear that some of his children have submitted to heresy and false doctrine and have abandoned the only true doctrine, says Falck. He goes on: It is not because our king wishes in any way to determine in what we are to believe, most certainly not. Rather, it is because you are his children, every one of you, and he weeps to hear that his children have offended against the Lord, such that they cannot join him in Paradise. You must understand that the king loves you all, Falck urges. He does not care to lose a single one of you, and if in any case he does, he grieves for a very long time. The king grieves now.

Bjerg observes how the congregation as one is gripped by pangs of conscience. They bow their heads or look away. Some dry their eyes with the sleeves of their garments. A child cries incessantly. Habakuk and his wife stare up at the priest and are unmoved.

I should like to tell you a story about our king, says Falck. The tale concerns how the king, out walking in his city one day, sees a child drowning in one of the canals. He jumps into the water without a thought for his own life, but when he reaches the child, the child does not wish to be saved, but kicks and lashes out, shouting oaths at the king and beseeching him to leave him alone. But the king refuses to give in and eventually he succeeds in bringing the child on to land, where all his escort stands full of admiration and fright at what they have witnessed. Then the child's mother and father come running. They kiss the robes of the king and fall down upon their knees and thank him. It is no matter, says the king. I would do the same for any one of my subjects. Even the child began to cry when he understood that his life had been saved by the king himself, and together with his parents he was given accommodation in the palace and received work in the king's gardens, and the family was contented thereby.

Someone at the front begins to sob, Bjerg hears. Didrik must have translated the story well. Bjerg, too, has a lump in his throat from listening to such a touching tale. He pictures the king at Frederiksholms Kanal, heaving the idiotic boy on to the cobbles; how everyone is overwhelmed with gratitude and impressed by what has occurred. Rasmus Bjerg feels for a moment that he is himself the king. He sees that Falck, too, is moved and has produced several handkerchiefs with which to wipe his face. Weeping spreads throughout the congregation.

So now I say unto you, says Falck, taking his time to look his audience in the eye, that the king has confided in me that he cannot be here in person today, and therefore he has appointed me to save you from drowning. I say unto you: return, turn away from this false doctrine and feel the love and forgiveness of the Lord!

He is finished. He steps down from the rostrum, bows politely to Habakuk and his wife, then returns to his place next to Bjerg.

How did I do? he whispers.

The Pastor has converted me, at any rate.

Excellent. Let us hear what the good Habakuk has to say.

Habakuk steps up onto the rostrum. He is a tall, well-built man; his hair is worn in a bowl cut and hangs like a mop over his broad, chiselled forehead. Falck beckons to Didrik to come and translate what he says.

Friends, fellow settlers, Habakuk begins. I will not speak at length and I will not tell stories. Everything the priest says is true. His Majesty the king is saddened. He wants us back where we were before. Do you remember what it was like? He looks out across the assembly and smiles.

Bjerg hears Falck sigh. He feels himself already forgetting what Falck has said and understands that the same is happening in the congregation.

The king is so saddened, Habakuk goes on in a sarcastic tone, that he now requires my own and my wife's presence in his palace in Copenhagen! He waves a piece of paper in the air. Bjerg sees it is the arrest warrant with the red seal.

But we are not to live with the king and look after his gardens, says Habakuk. As all who were present at last night's meeting will know, this is not an invitation to dine at the king's table, but an order to put me and my wife in chains and ship us away to a dungeon in Denmark.

An angry murmur.

I think it best that the priest and Constable Bjerg leave now, says Didrik.

Certainly not, says Falck. We shall remain here. No one will harm us.

His Majesty wishes to remove us, to take us away from our home, our country and our people, and he most surely hopes that everything will then settle and that the rest of you will bow down and return to the fold as the Missionary Falck of Sukkertoppen has asked you to.

Someone shouts from the congregation. Down with the king, Didrik translates.

But we will not bow down to the king, says Habakuk. Again, a shout: Down with the king! He is not our king, says Habakuk, and now he must raise his voice in order to be heard. He is their king. He points at Falck and Bjerg. The angry murmur increases. They come here with their guns and their warrants and their chains and their stories of children drowning. But we are not children, we are grown men and women and this is our country! We shall do as we please in our own country!

A shrill voice cries out: Down with the priest! The words are repeated by others. The commotion is becoming unpleasant; it echoes now from the crowd outside the church. But Habakuk lifts one hand and it is as if the noise is a ball he catches in mid-air, for at once everyone falls silent.

We Greenlanders are polite and friendly people, he says, and hospitable, as the priest has noted. Sometimes we may be too hospitable for our own good. We welcomed the priest and his constable among us, they have eaten our food and slept on our soil. They have done so because we are hospitable people. But our hospitality has been abused. These people have not behaved as guests ought to behave. They have harmed a person in our midst.

Falck and Bjerg exchange glances. Bjerg feels at once stricken by terror, though he has no idea where such a feeling should come from or why it should present itself.

Habakuk beckons to someone in the congregation. Some people come walking up the aisle. At first, Bjerg cannot see who it is, but then he recognizes Rosine and Amanda. Together with them are two elderly people. Bjerg recognizes them to be the couple who lay on the sleeping bench in the house in which he spent the night with Rosine. Now Didrik goes over and stands next to Rosine.

Habakuk takes Rosine by the hand and speaks to her in a kind voice. She replies almost inaudibly. He straightens his back and looks directly at Bjerg. He smiles as though in triumph.

This woman, he says in Danish, tells me that you, Rasmus Bjerg, committed an outrageous offence against her own and her husband's dignity.

A hundred faces turn and two hundred eyes fall upon Bjerg. He stands paralysed. He registers that those in his immediate vicinity step back from him.

Is the Constable not aware, says Habakuk, that violation of marriage contravenes the laws and regulations set out by both the Bible and the Royal Greenland Trade?

Falck speaks. Violation of marriage? How so? It may be the case that Constable Bjerg has acted inappropriately, that he has taken liberties and has allowed himself to be led into temptation, in brief that he has erred. But the dear little Rosine cannot be married, surely?

She is now, says Habakuk, and smiles. I married her myself yesterday in the name of the Lord and to this young man. He points at Didrik, who glares furiously back at Bjerg.

You have no authority, says Falck calmly.

I have the authority invested in me by my own people, Habakuk snaps. And now we wish the priest and his constable to take their leave.

You are a sly scoundrel indeed, says Falck. Your sin, sir, surpasses by far Constable Bjerg's human error. You and those who dance to your tune will burn in Hell for an eternity of eternities! Come, my dear Bjerg, come with me.

There is only one way out, and it leads them past Habakuk and the small group gathered around him. Bjerg fixes Rosine's eyes in his gaze, yearning for one last look from her. He still feels her skin against his palms and the salty taste of her sex on his tongue. She stands with Didrik. Amanda is beside them. He sees, or senses, that all three laugh at him with malice, and the feeling of it is more than he can contain. He expels a scream and hurls himself at the kayak man. The surrounding congregation steps back; they are given space in which to fight. Bjerg has floored him; he fumbles around for something to grab, finds a wrist, only for it to twist from his grasp. He takes him by the collar, then feels the other man's hand clutch at his hair and heave. He senses a searing pain in his scalp and thinks that if he does not do something fast the skin and its attached hair will be torn from his skull. He thrashes his fists, but the men are too entangled, they roll this way and that on the floor of the church. He endeavours to thrust his knee into Didrik's groin. Seemingly, he succeeds, for Didrik emits a cry and curls into a ball. Bjerg twists free and as he glances up he sees the ring of people surrounding them begin to close in. They will string me up in their gateway! he thinks to himself. He reaches swiftly into his boot and pulls out his pocket knife, locks his arm around Didrik's neck and hauls him to his feet. He holds the blade of the knife against his throat, turning it slightly in the light so that all may glimpse the steel. They step backwards.

I arrest you in His Majesty's name, he splutters, for assaulting a king's officer and putting his life at peril.

He begins to drag Didrik towards the church door. A path opens up in the congregation before them. The people stare at the two men, then all eyes turn to Habakuk, who smiles and nods and waves his hand dismissively. Let them go. And for that reason no one tries to prevent him as he bundles the kayak man away.

In the king's name, Bjerg repeats, and then again. In the king's name. He waves the knife in the air, then puts it to Didrik's throat once more. Mr Falck! he shouts. Please follow me! We have a long journey to row!

With puzzlement he realizes they will be allowed to go. Some even offer to help him with his prisoner. Down at the boat they find a thin rope and tie the man's wrists together behind his back, then throw him into the vessel. He remains lying there, protesting vociferously. Bjerg cannot understand why no one attempts to free him.

Falck has followed on at a trot with a handful of men to help them put out. He has Bjerg's flintlock with him.

I took it to prevent you doing yourself harm, he says.

So you knew what would happen?

Only in part. Someone was kind enough to send me a warning. I think it came from Maria Magdalene. But I had not reckoned on them turning against us in such manner.

But now they will let us sail away with this man?

I suppose they consider it a small price. He is not one of their own. Perhaps they feel obliged to give something up to the king.

And who is going to come with us?

We are on our own, I fear, says Falck. The two of us and our prisoner. The women prefer to remain here, and who can blame them?

Are we to row all the way home?

I'm afraid it is all most unfortunate, says Falck. I cannot help but feel it would have been better had we not come here at all.

What about our merchandise? says Bjerg. And the firearms?

I think we should be grateful for being allowed to leave at all, don't you agree?

They enter the boat and are shoved away from the shore. They glide out into the bay, seat themselves on opposite thwarts and begin to row. A fresh breeze comes down from the ridge and blows them gently away through the fjord. With two of the oars and part of their tent skin, they organize a makeshift sail that is useful as long as the wind is behind them. They row until darkness begins to fall, then pull the boat ashore, turn it upside down and sleep beneath it. They loosen the ropes around Didrik's wrists and take turns to keep watch on him. But he shows no signs of wishing to escape. When they row on the next day, he is at one of the oars. He watches Bjerg from the corner of his eye, as though expecting him to leap on him again at any moment, notwithstanding that he no longer seems to be angry with him. They survive on berries and mussels and a bird shot by Bjerg. It begins to snow. A wind comes in from the north; a strong, icy wind that causes waves to break and the boat to heave and pitch. But at the same time it pushes them onward at speed. In increasingly tempestuous winds and showers of sleet and rain, frozen to the bone, exhausted, hungry and coughing convulsively, they reach the colony three days later.

Kragstedt laughs when he sees them. You almost frightened the life out of us, the state you're in, he says. We were beginning to think you'd joined the prophets.

Four of us did, says Falck. This movement is greater than us, Kragstedt. How is your wife?

My dear wife is not quite well, the Trader replies. She has been on the decline since the spring. I think she is soon prepared to submit herself to the Magister's medical skills.

The constable delivers the prisoner to the Trader and briefs him on what has occurred.

We shall carry out proceedings against him in my parlour, the day after tomorrow at two o'clock, says Kragstedt. He turns to the smith. Hammer, take the prisoner to the blubber house. And keep watch on him.

Bjerg is overcome by intense feelings of release on retiring to the crew's quarters and flopping down on his bunk. He sleeps for fourteen hours, though his sense of humiliation and loss is unrelieved.

†

Rasmus Bjerg at the Trader's long table, two days later. The blood sausage is fat; the cabbage soup thick and rich; the steam billows from the tureen each time the lid is lifted. The missionary Falck is seated at his right, next after him Dorph the cooper. Opposite is the smith Niels Hammer, then the Overseer Dahl, the cook, and Madame Kragstedt. The carpenter is absent. The Trader himself sits at the head. Outside it is raining; the wind whistles in the chimney. Grey daylight seeps into the parlour. They eat in silence.

Falck has provided what for all parties involved is a considerate report of their journey and events at the settlement of the prophets. Kragstedt clicks his tongue in dismay and regret. He is infuriated at their leaving merchandise there without receiving payment. And now it is too late in the year to sail and enter the fjord again, regardless of the fact that it would hardly serve any purpose. We must await the next ship, he says, and then we shall rid them of their faithlessness with gunpowder and grapeshot.

I hereby volunteer to take part in the punishment, says Bjerg. I feel in no small part responsible for the failure of our mission.

Heard, says Kragstedt. Note is taken.

Violence is hardly likely to lead anywhere, Falck points out. It will merely instil in them an even greater sense of community. Moreover, they are well armed.

Indeed, we've been very obliging on that count, says Kragstedt with a glare in his direction. But as far as I can see, prayers and preaching have failed to achieve the desired result.

Falck does not reply.

The Overseer speaks. I know these people, they're terrified of losing face; it's a fate worse than death for them. If we restore the whipping post and announce that it is intended for Habakuk and his woman once we get hold of them, it will surely have some considerable deterrent effect.

That's a good idea, says Hammer. I'll forge the shackles and make it ready.

All right, says Kragstedt. Our prisoner in the blubber house might fittingly inaugurate it.

May I point out, Trader Kragstedt, says Falck, that the man has not yet enjoyed his right to a fair and decent trial?

You may. But he will have one to enjoy, as the Magister puts it, in just a moment.

Very well, says Falck. I should like to represent him as his defence.

Out of the question, says Kragstedt. The Magister is himself a party in the matter.

We are all parties in the matter, Falck protests. All of us have suffered in one way or another as a result of our failure, either personally or financially.

The accused is guilty by his own confession, Kragstedt interrupts. The only issue to be addressed is the punishment.

I must protest, says Falck. This is disgraceful!

Shut up, Magister!

Bjerg stifles a nervous snigger. The smith and the cook grin smugly and hang their heads. The Overseer prods at his food. The cooper looks ill at ease and moves crumbs about on the table.

Falck rises with a scraping of his chair. I refuse to be part of such a mockery, he says. I shall compile a comprehensive report on what occurred and whichever authority it may concern will then have to pass judgement.

That's your entitlement, says Kragstedt. We can hope the letter will arrive in, let's see, just over a year's time. Or perhaps you were thinking of approaching your old friend Inspector Rømer and asking for his help in the matter? I'm sure he remembers the Magister from the time he paid a visit on him down at Godthåb and wrote reports on him.

Falck looks for a moment at the Trader, who spoons his soup imperturbably. Then he turns on his heels and marches to the door. Madame Kragstedt emits a strange whimper. She jumps to her feet and darts out into the hall. Bjerg hears them speak in hushed voices. Kragstedt's fingers drum on the table. The Madame returns. She seats herself.

Kragstedt places a hand of comfort on her arm, only for her to pull away. The men sit bent over their soup. Kragstedt glares furiously at Bjerg, who instantly lowers his gaze.

Gentlemen, says Kragstedt. An unpleasant task has fallen upon us and I suggest we make short shrift of it.

Heard, mutter the smith and the cook in unison.

We have a confession, the Trader continues. Is that not correct, Hammer?

Indeed, says the smith with a grin. A full confession.

And what is the wording of that confession?

The smith produces a document, which he reads aloud in a toneless voice. *I, Didrik, a hunter, do hereby declare that on this past Sunday, the twentieth of September, I did assault a king's officer, one Rasmus Bjerg, constable of the Sukkertoppen trading station, with the intent of causing him bodily harm and thereby preventing him from carrying out an order of the king.*

Is the confession signed? The Trader takes the document from the smith's hand and studies it.

Signed in his full name, Mr Kragstedt.

Was he shown the document, and were its contents explained to him before he signed?

Yes, Mr Kragstedt. The man speaks Danish well. He acted as interpreter on the trip into the district.

Excellent, excellent indeed. We shall now proceed to fixing the punishment. I suggest twenty lashes and a stand at the whipping post of three days and nights. The gentlemen will now by turn state whether they agree or wish the punishment either reduced or increased. The Trader looks around the table. Is that understood? The men nod.

Overseer Dahl?

I have no objections to the suggested sentence, says the Overseer.

Hammer?

The same here.

Constable Bjerg?

Who is to mete out the punishment? he asks.

Usually the smith has the pleasure, says Kragstedt. Perhaps you wish to relieve him of the duty?

If the Trader permits.

Very well. The exercise will do you good, I'm sure, Kragstedt says with a laugh.

Thank you, says Bjerg. He feels his heart pound.

Karlsen? Kragstedt turns to the cook. Do you have any objections to the sentence?

I suggest the punishment be reduced to ten lashes and a stand of two days at the post, says the cook.

On what grounds, Karlsen?

The weather, says the cook. It's getting cold. Tonight it will snow. Three days and nights would be the same as death, and the man is hardly likely to learn his lesson if he pops his clogs.

All right, says Kragstedt. Your objection is noted and seems indeed reasonable. Let us then say twenty lashes and a stand of two days and nights at the whipping post. Any protests?

The men say nothing. Madame Kragstedt holds a handkerchief to her face. Her shoulders tremble. Bjerg cannot help but look at her. Whatever can be the matter with the lady? One ought not to allow women to be present in cases concerning corporal punishment, they are far too nervously disposed to hear of such matters. The Madame gets to her feet and disappears through the door into her chamber.

Proceedings are concluded, Kragstedt declares. Pass round the sweet wine. There will be pudding.

†

Bjerg and the smith decide to construct a new whipping post that will be visible from afar. The constable helps Hammer drag a heavy beam of oak from the warehouse and holds it steady while he drives an iron wedge with an eye into it. To this eye they attach ropes of a suitable thickness. The chains and the irons he will forge later, says Hammer. For the moment this will suffice. They dig a hole in the ground, one shovel deep, until they strike the rock. They erect the post and pile up stones to support it.

A fine flagpole, says the smith and laughs. Now all we need is to hoist the flag.

They fetch the prisoner from the blubber house, where he is sitting cross-legged, staring into space. When they grasp him under the arms, he gets to his feet voluntarily and offers no resistance as they lead him to the whipping post. Bjerg smells strong fumes of alcohol on the man's breath. The priest must have stupefied him. They tie him to the post and leave him out in the rain. A while later an audience of natives has gathered on the rocks behind the colony house. They stare at the prisoner with empty expressions. He moans softly and protractedly. It sounds like he is crying.

Kragstedt comes. He is in uniform, with his sabre and tricorne hat. He looks satisfied, happy almost. The Madame is not with him. He approaches the prisoner and studies him at length. The man coughs, a hollow rattle, his arms are raised and his head hangs down.

More people come. The Overseer, the catechist, the cooper, even the ailing carpenter has left his sickbed to witness the punishment. The prisoner begins to sing. Bjerg listens to the words; he sings in Danish. *My Heart Always Wanders*. One of Brorson's carols, he recalls, and a strange feeling passes over him. How often he heard it sung in the church at home in Horsens.

Constable Bjerg, says Kragstedt firmly, fixing his eyes on him. Perform your duty!

The smith shows him how to tear off the shirt of the prisoner so as to expose his back. He grips the linen and rips it apart. It makes a loud searing noise. Great drops of rain splash against the man's bare skin. He continues to sing, unabated.

Bertel Jensen, says Kragstedt to the catechist. Since our pastor has elected not to participate, perhaps he would be so kind as to say the Lord's Prayer.

The catechist steps up and obediently positions himself before Didrik with his head bowed. He rattles off the prayer, then returns to his place next to his wife. The prisoner now sings a hymn: *Vain World, Fare Thee Well*. Bjerg thinks of Rosine; he sees the gloating faces in the church and the rage he felt on realizing they had tricked him wells up inside him once more. He sees Rosine, naked, her arching back, her expressionless face as he writhed, so helplessly abandoned to ecstasy. The smith hands him the whip. The Trader gives the signal with his sabre.

One!

He strikes. It is not a good stroke.

Vain world, fare thee well. I purpose no more in thy bondage to dwell.

Two!

He flicks the whip backwards at the moment it strikes home and senses immediately how much better it seizes.

I spurn thy allurements, which tempt and appal.

Three!

The whip stings. Its lashes fall like hail.

'Tis vanity all!

The sabre is raised, the sabre is lowered. Four!

The whip licks the bare torso.

It is naught but bubbles and tinctured glass.

Five!

Bjerg sees a man's back. He sees Rosine's arched back. He swings the whip.

O, honour and gold!

Six! says the sabre.

Bjerg stands in a hailstorm of lashes. They circumvent him and seize the exposed back before him.

False are your affluence, your pleasure and fame.

Seven! Kragstedt intones.

Now he sees the blood break through the skin. He smells it. Some of it accompanies the whip as it returns; he feels it spatter against his face.

Your wages are envy, deception and shame.

Eight!

The blood flows; it gathers at the waistband of the man's breeches. Bjerg strikes harder. He regrets not having used his full force from the outset.

Your garlands soon wither, your kingdom shall fall.

Nine!

The whip unfurls and retracts. It is a hand with many fingers, clawing to tear the bloody flesh.

'Tis vanity all!

Ten!

Now the blood splashes and sprays. The onlookers step back, so as not to be soiled. Kragstedt halts the proceedings.

Water! he commands.

The smith fetches a bucket and douses the prisoner's back. The man screams.

Keep singing, says Hammer. There are many verses yet in that hymn.

Eleven! says Kragstedt and his sabre slices the air.

Stop this atrocity!

Out of the corner of his eye, Bjerg sees a dark figure come striding up to him. Falck. The pastor puts out his hand.

Give me the whip.

Mr Falck, says Kragstedt. I must request you to step back. You are in the way.

Falck darts forward and snatches the whip from Bjerg's hand. Enough! he says. The blame is yours for this man's error.

Bjerg suddenly feels weak. He stands with his arms at his sides.

The prisoner sings: *O carnal desire! Thou tempting, consuming and treacherous fire.*

Give back the whip, Mr Falck, says Kragstedt. Or I shall make sure you receive a taste of it yourself.

Falck stares at him. Come and take it, costermonger, if you are man enough.

I warn you, Magister. You are interfering in the execution of a sentence sanctioned by the king.

And you are a poor husband, Falck rejoins, leaving your wife without protection when you are away.

Priest, you are plainly drunk.

Then fare thee, farewell!

Rather drunk than sober, if it is to be on the Trader's conditions.

Hammer approaches the priest. Falck sees him and steps back. I will not give you the whip, smith.

That will not be necessary, says Hammer. He walks up and takes it from him, then hands it back to Bjerg.

I yearn for the solace from sorrows and harm, of Abraham's arm.

Eleven!

By the time the twenty lashes have been delivered, the prisoner has ceased to sing. He breathes irregularly and with a choked sound, and hangs limply in the ropes. Blood from the wounds in his back trickles into the mud. The people disperse.

In the night, Bjerg hears hymns sung from the whipping post. They peter out before sunrise. Yet the silence is quite as unbearable as the song. He rises from his bed and goes there.

Here, he says. Drink this.

Didrik empties the flask Bjerg holds to his mouth.

He goes home again, but cannot sleep. He returns to the man and sits down in the rain. He feels he is closer to Rosine by sitting with her husband. He rattles on about the journey, his falling in love and what he felt in the church when everyone turned against him.

At six o'clock the fire-watcher comes by. He bends down over the prisoner, emits a grunt of dissatisfaction and informs Bjerg that the delinquent has expired.

Rasmus Bjerg walks home. He lies on his bed and stares up at the ceiling.

The Fifth Commandment

An Expulsion

(Autumn–Winter 1788)

The Fifth Commandment, as it is most plainly to be taught by a father to his family:
'Thou shalt not kill.'
What does this imply?
Answer: That we should fear and love God, so that we may not hurt or afflict our neighbour in his body; but we should help and further him when he is in bodily need.

Haldora Kragstedt sees a woman in the large mirror of her bedchamber. She studies her profile, how she turns to the left, turns to the right, smoothes her hands over her gown, and she feels a tinge of nausea, acidic fluids that make her insides seethe and gurgle. Somewhere within her, in the contorted recesses of her female body, beneath the corsets and the physical exterior, the bulging abdomen and the extravagant flourish of pubic hair, the smith sits moping. She sees him, curled up and sleeping. He is inside her; it is not some feverish dream. He is real. He has entered her. Now he will not go away again. A whole life together with the smith, she thinks, the smith feeding from my breasts, the smith lying in my bed, seated at my table. To kiss the smith goodnight every evening for twenty years. There must be something to be done.

She has experimented with the laudanum she receives from her husband so that she might sleep and gain colour, though in small doses, so as not to become addicted. She downed the flacon in one gulp and slept like a log for a night and half a day. The smith sits there yet. She applied the substance locally, squirting it into her vagina, a difficult manoeuvre and moreover utterly without effect. Now she has ceased to take the medicine, which has triggered a rather promising bout of diarrhoea and a cheering sensation of being encased in pain from top to toe, as if she were wearing a heavy coat of chain mail. But the smith remains seated. He takes nourishment from her and grows. Still he sits, curled up, his cheek resting on his knees, in the deepest sleep. But soon he will begin to move. He will stretch out his legs, extend his arms and step into character. The thought of it is unbearable. She has tried to incite Kragstedt to brutality; she has flung herself over the table and hurled filthy obscenities at him, with her bare, shining arse in his face, only for him to gape incredulously from within a fog of distraction.

Whatever is the matter, my dear? he enquires. Is it the impending months of darkness? Are you bored? Desist, you make me shameful. Stand up, arrange your clothing. The maid might come in at any moment.

She glares at him in fury. He pats her cheek. She says something about his manliness, or lack of it. He smiles absently, bent over his ledger. She smashes porcelain. He drums his fingers and looks out of the window. I think, he says, that if we establish a whalers' guild at the old colony the catch would be most lucrative for the district. What do you think, my darling? I have already spoken to a number of skippers from Holsteinsborg and they agree with me. Have you now taken up handicraft? Well, that is certainly a sensible way to while away the winter.

She finds her knitting needles, takes a selection of various lengths and thicknesses with her to the privy and blindly jabs them up inside her. She detests touching herself – the smell, the sticky fluids of her body – but she must. She inserts a needle, more carefully now, feeling for the soft, elastic bung that is uppermost, then thrusting sharply. She screams with pain, then bites her lip and looks down. There is some blood, a few small drops running down the implement. She cries with joy. That evening a further three clear, red spots on the towel. In the morning the bleeding has stopped. The smith remains seated. He is utterly secure. He grows.

She has considered the possibility of confiding in her husband, but realizes it would lead to changes in their life together whose magnitude she cannot imagine and does not even care to address. Either Kragstedt would do something about it and have the smith, the child's father, punished, thereby making the matter common knowledge, not just in the colony, but elsewhere too, among those at home, family and friends, indeed almost anyone. Her humiliation would be his defamation. They would never be able to return home again. Or else, and rather more probably, he would do nothing, the consequences of which would be less dramatic, but quite as unbearable within their marriage. And besides, she would then not be able to do what she intends to do now.

She goes to the source himself, to the smith, so that he might expel the smith, with a glowing hot chisel, for instance, or whatever his instruments might be called.

He stares at her. And the child is mine?

She goes through the workshop like a fury, finding sharp implements that seem suitable. He follows her and removes them from her hands.

Whose would it be otherwise?

The Trader's? He is your husband, after all. And it feels like yet another assault that he, a man who ought to be led to the gallows, should have the nerve to speak so confidentially to her, so sensibly and reprovingly.

She finds an iron rod of one ell's length and holds it up in front of him, waves it about in the air. This, she says, with an angry smile.

He takes it from her and puts it down on the pile. He sighs. Madame Kragstedt, what you are asking me to do, I cannot. I am no barber surgeon and I am no quack or abortionist either. If the poor child got in there, then it must surely in the name of Jesus be allowed to be born.

Never! I should rather swallow a spoon of gunpowder and a burning taper.

It would hardly become you well, Madame.

Then take me. He is hereby permitted to do with me as he did before.

The smith looks upon her with pity. Do not speak like a whore, Madame Kragstedt. It does not become the lady.

What is the matter with him? He sounds like his postil has gone to his head, or perhaps he has succumbed to the prophetic reveries that flourish in the district?

Please be so kind as to leave the workshop, Madame.

Is there nothing he can do? He is the one who got me into this predicament!

He stares at her. He exudes repugnance and disgust, as though she had brought a foul smell into his workshop. Then he says: Charcoal is said to be a means against unwanted circumstances, though you never heard it from me, Madame.

The door slams shut like a peal of thunder as she leaves.

She eats charcoal, munches a lump of it as though it were an apple. It tastes of salt, stings the tongue and burns in her throat. She sits down to wait for the effect. It occurs in the evening; she becomes dreadfully ill. She bends over the toilet and opens her mouth and her vomit comes out, a thick green plume. She falls to her knees and convulses. She puts her cheek to the seat and feels her body become limp and devoid of feeling. She drifts away. Kragstedt must have found her lying on the floor, or perhaps it is one of the colony crew. She rocks in his arms when she wakes. They are on their way home. He tells her that she must no longer be compelled to use the crew's privy, it is a cold and despicable place. I shall have one built for you behind the house. She lies in bed for several weeks, trembling with stomach cramps, wrenching tar and bloody green gall from the knot of her insides into the white enamel washbasin. She sees how her skin becomes yellowed, retreats from her fingernails and tightens over her bones, and she thinks that if I do not die, then *it*, at least, must surely perish. But it does not perish. And she does not die. They survive together. The smith is rooted within her. He will not leave her, at least not yet. He seems to be the only part of her to thrive.

The young native girl tends to her while she is confined. Sofie, their maid, refers to her as her sister, though they would seem not to be related at all, and despite the fact that she still seems to care little for her. Haldora cannot see the reason in it. The girl looks after her personal needs and spends most of her time with her in the bedchamber. Late in the evenings, however, she leaves and returns home, to wherever that may be. Sofie says she has a child to take care of, and that she hails from somewhere in the outlying district where she has experienced terrible things. Now she has come here to become a good Christian. She attends the priest and receives instruction from him. Sofie inserts a suggestive pause at this point and Haldora wonders if there might be anything inappropriate about the relationship between Falck and the girl. She feels revolted by the thought of a native together with a white man, as though it were a kind of sodomy. But of course it would not be the first time such a thing occurred. Perhaps she will ask him about it at some future opportunity.

From early until late the girl is at her side. Haldora speaks to her; she finds comfort in confiding in this unwitting and savage individual, who presumably does not understand a word of what she tells her. At any rate she utters not a peep. She gives her some of her clothes, a shift, some stockings, a pair of shoes. They lie together in the bed; they hold each other tight and it soothes her to feel the warmth of another human being who is not her husband and not the smith. Sometimes they fall asleep and wake with Kragstedt standing in the door, staring at them with a question mark on his brow.

She seems like good company, the little native pet I found you, he says.

Haldora Kragstedt withers away during the summer and autumn, but her belly swells. She feels the smith begin to move within her, at first a bubbling sensation in the intestines, then movements more distinct and abrupt. The girl puts her ear to her abdomen, her eyes vacant as she listens. Ba-dum, ba-dum, ba-dum, she says. She presses her hands to the Madame's belly, burrowing her fingers into the flesh, bundling the smith back and forth. Then she holds up her thumb and index finger and shows Haldora how big she thinks the child to be.

Child, go away! says Haldora and makes a downward scooping movement with her hands.

The girl shakes her head. She smiles. No, no, child not go away! Child ba-dum, ba-dum, ba-dum!

I should never have taught you Danish, Haldora says.

You didn't, says the girl. The Missionary Oxbøl did.

†

Some weeks after Morten Falck has returned home from his long autumn trip, she writes him a note and sends the girl over with it.

The priest appears from out of the snowstorm, tired and coughing after his visitation, a detailed and lengthy account of which is soon forthcoming.

It sounds like the Magister has had some adventure, she says.

I erred, he says. The Lord would have it that I erred. A poor man lost his life because of my error. It is no easy matter with which to come to terms. I incline to think I was guilty of arrogance. Now I have received my punishment and bow my head in humility. He doubles up in a fit of coughs.

She thinks that she at least is not alone in pangs of conscience. She heard the screams of the man they punished. She felt it was she who screamed. She heard the lashing of the whip. It was she on the receiving end. She felt the sticky tongues of the instrument tear the skin from her back. Bound to a pole, she thinks to herself, with one's shirt ripped to shreds and all the body's most intimate functions placed on display. This is how it feels to be involuntarily fertile.

Madame's husband tells me you have been unwell and melancholy for some time, says the priest.

She has risen from her bed to receive him in the parlour. They sit at the dining table, he on the bench, she in a leather-upholstered chair, a blanket wrapped around her, her robe gathered in makeshift manner like a dressing gown. The chambermaid comes in with a jug of ale and pours two glasses. Madame Kragstedt notes that she exchanges glances with the priest, and that he smiles and nods to her.

This is not easy, she says.

No, indeed, he muses out loud, and then sighs. What is not easy, Madame Kragstedt?

To tell the Magister of my troubles.

Hm, I see. He sips his ale and watches the girl as she leaves.

I know not where to find strength to tell of them, Mr Falck.

Are you ill? he asks. You do not look well, Madame Kragstedt.

No, I am not ill. Unfortunately. I wish I was.

Do not say that. Good health is a blessing that may be swiftly removed from us. He gets to his feet and wanders about the room, studies a picture on the wall, examines the grandfather clock, pulls the curtain aside and looks out of the window. He sighs again, heavily.

The Magister received instruction in the medical sciences when he was a student, did he not?

Yes, a little, but no more than that. I am familiar with the human anatomy, both the female and the male.

Have you experience in surgery, Magister?

Some. Not much. He sits down again at the table. He looks at her. What sort of surgery do you have in mind, Madame?

The sort that removes something unwanted, she says.

The priest falls silent. He looks rather pasty, she thinks. And seems not to be in the slightest bit interested in her problems.

I have removed tumours, he says, some as big as cauliflowers. But the patients were already dead, you understand. The procedures were dissections, so I am not sure they would count.

She closes the gate on her secret, abandons the idea of involving him in it. She sits with her elbow resting on the armrest, forehead cupped in her hand. Her hair hangs down over her shoulders. She feels her tears trickle down her cheeks, tiny rivulets. She takes out a handkerchief and blows her nose.

All at once the priest becomes aware of her distress. He comes over, kneels at her chair and takes her hand in his.

Madame Kragstedt? Oh, dear.

Yes, she says, and breaks into laughter.

What on earth is the matter?

I have got myself into trouble, she sobs. I haven't a clue what to do about it.

He draws up a chair and sits down, still holding her hand. Tell me.

It's terrible.

You cannot shock me, he says.

Are you certain?

Try me! He sounds like he is full of expectation.

It happened when you were away on your trip this spring, she says, and my husband was in Holsteinsborg.

He listens attentively to her account, sits squeezing her hand, looking up at her, saying nothing.

And now the detestable man goes about as if he were virtue itself, she says, devoted to his postil and saintly, as though elevated above me. He knows all too well that I will not report him.

His salvation is already wasted, says Falck comfortingly. The Lord will take care of him. Forget about him, Madame Kragstedt.

How can I forget about him when I have him here inside me? She presses her hands to her belly.

Does your husband know about this?

My husband has been concerned with his own business this past year. He has been away a lot. He has many responsibilities. Now he wishes to set up a whalers' guild and become wealthy. My chambermaid knows, and perhaps my housemaid Sofie.

He asks her about dates, about intimate matters of which she has never before spoken with anyone, at least not with a man. All that is private and by which a woman is burdened.

Take off your robe, he says, and his voice is kind and casual, as though he had said glove instead of robe.

She draws the garment aside and lets it fall to the floor, then pulls the shift over her head. There is no corset. Now she is naked. She feels his fingers against the bare skin of her back, squeezing the raised areas of the skin in which the metal shavings were embedded and which the chambermaid spent most of the night extracting. She groans. He clicks his tongue disapprovingly.

The wounds are long since healed, he says. A number of splinters remain beneath the skin, but they are encapsulated and are of no consequence apart from the purely cosmetic aspect. There will, however, always be visible signs of your mistreatment.

She nods.

Sooner or later your husband will discover them. Should I not speak to him?

No. Later. She gathers the robe about her and ties the cord around her waist. The shift remains on the floor. She goes over to the sideboard and pours two glasses of aquavit, returns and puts one of them in front of the priest; the other she empties in a single mouthful.

To the Madame's health. He raises the glass and downs its contents, then returns it to the table. He asks where the chambermaid might have got to; she could make herself useful now.

Most likely she is outside. She is in the habit of sitting on the step and smoking her pipe. It is what we pay her for, so it seems.

He goes out and calls for her. When he returns he says that if the Madame is up to it he would like to perform a closer examination of her inner parts.

She is already in agreement with herself that he is the only person in whom she can trust and that she will do as he says. Do whatever you feel to be necessary, she tells him.

He orders her into the chamber and onto the bed, and she lies down on her side with her robe apart and feels his expert fingers wander across her abdomen, squeezing, pressing and prodding, while he emits occasional small sounds of satisfaction. The girl sits cross-legged at her side, her back against the wall. She stares at the priest's large hands. He draws the robe away and inserts two fingers into her vagina. She whimpers patiently and feels his fingers squashing her womb upwards. With his other hand he presses against her pubis. Now he has hold of the uterus and rocks it gently back and forth.

This is a manoeuvre I learned from Professor Schiøtz, he says, and smiles at her from the gap between her legs.

He withdraws his hand, straightens up and wipes his fingers with his handkerchief. Madame Kragstedt, you are pregnant.

How far gone am I, do you think?

Approximately five months, judging by what the Madame has told me and by the size of the embryo. It is a ripe time.

Ripe? For what?

For removing this . . . tumour. Is that not what you wish?

Then you will help me?

I shall consider it. He looks at her solemnly. Abortion is a serious matter, particularly for me, an ordained priest, but no less so were I a surgeon, which of course I am not.

I have not asked you to . . .

On the other hand, he says, cutting her off, this pregnancy, which has been forced upon you, is highly detrimental to your constitution. Allowing it to proceed to childbirth would involve placing your life in peril.

I would end my days.

Exactly! A life would thus be saved by terminating another.

I shall not press you, Magister Falck.

Ha, a fine time to say so! It would have been better had you not come to me at all with this matter, dear Madame Kragstedt. You have put me in a veritable dilemma.

Forgive me, Mr Falck. But you are the only person in whom I can confide.

Now at last he removes himself from the vista of her gaping, seeping vagina and seats himself on the edge of the bed. He takes her hand with fingers still damp from the examination. She feels an urge to pull away, but the priest holds tight.

Madame Kragstedt. Haldora, if I may. So much has happened this past year, in my life as well as in yours. The muscles of his face tremble. His jaw appears to ruminate.

The Magister has had much to attend to, she says in a comforting tone.

Indeed, so very true! I have suffered defeat and have already failed in my calling. But you, Madame, are a harbour of security and normality and all that I feel to be slipping away from me in this peculiar land. In short, you are an indispensable friend to me.

And you to me, Mr Falck. Morten.

Thank you, thank you indeed. He leans forward and kisses her on the cheek, presses his face against it and expels a protracted sigh. It is as if he vanishes completely into his own thought. The native girl is still seated beside them, she realizes. She has put on the expressionless mask of the savages. She meets her dark gaze across the top of the priest's wig.

Falck straightens up and collects himself for a moment. How can you be certain the child is not Kragstedt's?

The same way I am certain it is not yours, Morten.

Aha. Yes. I see.

My husband has had much to attend to this past year.

Had he attended to his most important responsibility, this would never have happened, says Falck irritably.

Her bare belly is still exposed, and her pubic hairs that travel up like a black cord towards her navel. She senses her own odour, yet feels no urge to cover herself. She is beyond all modesty and shame. Can you help me to remove it?

Hm, says Falck. He taps the side of his nose rhythmically with his index finger, the same one that a few moments ago was inside her. I do not know, Madame Kragstedt. I shall do what is best for you and it shall be my only consideration.

Thank you. I trust you.

But the child is yours, too, he says. You must not forget that.

I have spent months considering the matter, she says impatiently. I wish it removed from my person.

I shall speak to the smith, he says. I shall study my medical handbook. I shall ponder upon it. I may even pray. And then I will come back to you, Haldora, whether as a surgeon or as a priest. But always as your friend, Madame, remember this!

I saw the priest was here, says Kragstedt that evening in the bed-chamber. What did that bird of misfortune want here?

To offer me salvation, she replies.

I see, Kragstedt snorts. Perhaps he should try and save himself first. They say he conducts himself inappropriately with his housemaid.

I don't believe such gossip, she says. Our missionary is a good man.

I don't contest it, he says peaceably. If you find pleasure conversing with him, then by all means.

They are silent for a while. She hears Roselil lowing down by the warehouse. Is there something the matter with the pastor's cow?

Kragstedt laughs. Most likely it misses the smith; he looked after it while the priest was away. I think she may have become attached to the dear man. He's got the knack of her, they say.

I see, she says. Let us hope it is to their common good.

Oh, come now, he mutters, at once annoyed by her tone. The smith may not have studied theology, but he is a good man for the Trade, always civil and easy to get along with.

I'm sure. I have no prejudices.

Smiths have a reputation for being difficult, he says. I recall a few bad examples myself. We should be grateful having a man like Hammer, who sits and reads his postil both early and late. He has even stopped drinking.

Indeed. God bless him, she says.

They lie next to each other in the bed, beneath the same down. A blue blanket is folded over the down's upper edge, forming a border that runs under their arms and across their stomachs. Kragstedt has folded his hands and rests them on his chest. Every time he breathes, the mattress creaks. In the night he keeps her awake with his snoring. She lies and stares up at the ceiling and thinks about her childhood and lost youth. She must have been a flighty girl, she thinks, always dreaming about court balls and suitors of high rank who would come sailing or on horseback. By behaving dismally she would play jokes on the young men who came to court her. She cringes at the thought now, not for her own sake, but because she feels sorry for them. They would take their leave, bowing with embarrassment, and say Au revoir, Miss Knapp, and she would feel ill at ease, furious and despairing. Once she allowed the miller to kiss her and feel beneath her skirts, not because she was afraid to say no or because she really wanted to be fondled, but because she knew he possessed this peculiar, male desire and it made her curious. How old was she then? Fourteen, perhaps, or fifteen. She remembers his searching hand, how it squeezed her thigh, how it trembled like a frightened little animal, the moisture of his mouth, his gaze, which at first was firm, then crumbling and distant, and finally wretched and distressed. He was old, had children her own age and smelled like the bridle of a horse. She pulled away from him and ran home. She had felt that he was like a tightly coiled spring or the cock of a flintlock. It made her frightened. But also curious. What would happen if one refused the spring to be released, or the cock to strike the pan? Now she knows.

Kragstedt is asleep. She leans over him and blows out the light, feels her swollen breast brush against his arm. She falls back onto the pillow. Outside, the fire-watcher calls the hour and announces all is well. She recognizes the smith's fine singing voice.

†

Two days later Falck returns. He has spoken to the smith, who has admitted everything and acknowledges that he has committed a great sin, though he does not in any way appear to be burdened by conscience and most certainly has no plans of confessing the matter to the Trader. A most inveterate person! But enough, we must leave those who are lost to their own damnation. The priest seems to be in splendid humour; his cough has gone, the colour has returned to his cheeks, he strides about and holds forth on techniques of performing an *abortus provocatus*. There is the medical way, he says, which the Madame has already tried, a method we shall pursue no further, and then there is the surgical way.

We shall use neither. He sends her a sly smile. Or rather, we shall use both.

So you have decided? You will help me?

It is a challenge, he says, theologically as well as scientifically. Not to mention for me personally. Yes, I will help you. It will be a form of redress for my studenthood, when I was prevented from following my wishes and was compelled instead to obey my father and study for the priesthood. I have found a certain method by which to remove the child.

What method is that?

Fire, he says with a nervous grin. Fire is the ultimate purification. Think of Purgatory, cleansing the soul of sin and releasing it from tellurian before it slips into Heaven. We shall need the help of your chambermaid, a garment of linen torn into strips, a spoonful of gunpowder, some melted blubber, i.e. train oil, and these instruments forged by our friend the smith at my request. He shows her a bent metal rod and an instrument comprising several loose parts that can be joined together. We call this a duck's bill, he says, or a speculum to be more precise. He hands her the instrument and allows her to study it. It is cold and heavy and rattles in her hands.

She gives it back. She looks at the priest, whose eyes shine brightly and whose facial skin has taken on a pale silver appearance with a blush of red on his cheeks. He looks like a young suitor come to court. I understand. But where does the fire come in?

A recurring problem with such operations, says the priest, is that the surgery will often result in fever and haemorrhage, or indeed the patient's death, while medicaments may enforce lengthy periods of confinement, as you have already experienced. What we shall do is to place a little detonator, a fuse in the Madame's, erm, in the relevant locus, and the controlled detonation then performed will, erm, well, I'm sure you follow my meaning, being a person of intelligence.

Will it not hurt? she asks.

Yes, indeed, very much so. It will require both confidence and strength, as well as great courage. But the pain will be short-lived.

Moreover, I shall premedicate you with a hefty dosage of laudanum. You may even sleep through the whole operation. Are you prepared for this, Madame Kragstedt?

I am prepared, she says calmly.

Where is your husband?

He went away yesterday and will be back in a couple of days.

Splendid. Let us begin immediately.

He has the girl make up the bed with a linen sheet, and removes the down. Madame Kragstedt clambers up and imbibes the laudanum that Falck has measured out to her, then lies down and waits for the familiar drowsiness and serenity to come creeping. She notes that Falck has begun to tear a second sheet into strips and to soak them in a bowl of train-oil. He lays each one out on a towel, then produces his powder horn and sprinkles the black substance onto each in turn.

We must burn all this when we are done, he says in a conspiratorial whisper. I hope you understand.

Yes, of course.

What we are about here constitutes a criminal act. We can both be put in gaol for it.

She looks down at herself. She must have fallen asleep. She sees the priest's head, wigless, between her legs. She thinks she sees the lice upon his scalp, but tells herself it is the medicine. As yet there is no pain, just a dull sensation of someone interfering with her below. Bent over the priest's shoulder with a light in her hand stands the girl, her other hand extended and holding an object of some description. Both are staring at the same point between her legs, utterly absorbed, the light from the lamp flickering in their faces.

It would be better for you to look up at the ceiling, Madame Kragstedt, he says. There is nothing of interest to you here.

She puts her head back on the pillow. She is in a wood where the light falls in bottle-green bundles. She wanders in the space between the treetops and the brown leaves on the earth. She is not alone, for her deceased sister walks at her side; they stroll, arm in arm, chatting and giggling. Her sister is to become engaged; her suitor is at their home speaking to their father. She lists all the things that must be bought, first for the wedding, then for the household. The house is there, a fine house in a provincial town; there are servants, horses and how many children? Many children. And how shall these children be obtained? By being together as man and woman, of course, says the sister. Haldora laughs. It is the most foolish thing she has ever heard. To dine together, to stroll arm in arm, to kiss? However might such things result in a child? What nonsense! To share the bed, whispers her sister, to do unmentionable and delightful things together. To let him come close to you, to enter inside, prising you apart so that you become open, an act of transformation whereby the man becomes a slave and the woman his master.

Oh, that, says Haldora, recalling the miller.

When the priest has confirmed you, I shall tell you all about it, her sister says.

Lie still, dear Madame Kragstedt.

Apparently she has been laughing in her sleep. Now she looks up at the Trader's ceiling, sees the heavy oak beams that bear the weight of the ceiling planks, or the floor of the loft, if one is above. The hams are above, smelling of ammonia, she thinks to herself, the Trader's ale and aquavit settled in their fat-bellied barrels, the sacks of cereal and oats are there, and the sweet-smelling hops and the tobacco with its spicy aroma. Though I cannot see it, it is there anyway. The world is more than the little bubble about my own person; it is large and great, and hangs together. There are so many people in the world, and my sister Jensigne is one, even though she is dead, and my father, dead, is another, and my mother and my living sisters, and I, too, am here, albeit they cannot know that I am here still, and have no idea that I am lying in this bed about to have gunpowder detonated inside my vagina, and no one else could care less, including myself.

She sees that the priest is sweating, that he bends forward and peers squintingly into her wide-open vagina at what lies inside.

More light, he says.

The girl brings the lamp closer. If only he does not singe his hair, Haldora thinks.

More light! says the priest again.

The girl turns up the lamp. It begins to spit.

Thank you, says the priest. That's better.

She feels that he is stuffing something inside her, presumably the linen rags. The girl holds the speculum that keeps the vagina open, at the same time balancing the spitting lamp in her other hand.

Madame Kragstedt, says Falck, rather strained. I shall now insert this probe into the cervix. You will most probably feel some pain, but you must endeavour to remain completely still.

The pain comes in a single stab, a searing bolt of lightning that leaps from out of the numbed darkness. It takes her utterly by surprise and causes her abdomen to jolt at once.

Lie still, Madame Kragstedt. Clench your teeth.

Another stab, and again her body jolts in response, though not quite as violently as before. Falck mutters something under his breath. He is manipulating a long piece of steel wire by which he would seem to be inserting the linen rags into her uterus. He mutters again, clearly in annoyance.

Are you having problems? she enquires in a voice she hardly recognizes.

Not at all, no problems, dear Madame, just an unexpected narrowness. I shall have to be a little rougher, I'm afraid.

I see.

It is essential you remain quite still, Madame Kragstedt.

Call me Haldora, for God's sake, she says.

Very well. Haldora, dear friend, you must lie completely still for a moment. I shall now penetrate.

She grips the linen underneath her and turns her head to the side. Yet now when the jab comes, her abdomen reacts utterly of its own accord, an upwardly arched spasm. The instrument Falck is attempting to insert inside her flies through the air and lands on the sheet at her side. She

hears an exclamation, a commotion, a shattering of glass followed by
a protracted hissing sound, then a bang and a flash of light. Falck leaps
into the air with a cry, hands to his face, hair aflame. I knew he should
mind his hair, she manages to think, but perhaps now he will be rid of his
lice. She senses a searing pain, but it is as though she sees the pain rather
than feels it; it is removed from her, and inconsequential compared to
the stabbing endeavours of the priest as he sought to enter her uterus.
But then she realizes that the burning sensation she feels is literal. There
is a spitting and a sizzling between her legs and the room is quickly filled
with a nauseatingly foul stench. She leaps from the bed and staggers
into the parlour, where she sees the girl come running towards her with
a shovel. On the shovel is a pile of snow, and the Madame squats down
and presses her scorched genitals upon it. Steam and smoke rise into the
air. Falck groans inside the chamber. He appears in the doorway and
fumbles his way to the table. He sits down on the bench.

Water! he moans.

The girl fetches the bucket. He bends over it and splashes his face.

It was an accident! he wails. The cursed lamp! The gunpowder
ignited before I was ready. It exploded in my face. Madame Kragstedt,
are you all right?

With the girl's help, she is picking charred strips of linen from her
vagina. They smell of burnt flesh and saltpetre. There is some blood,
and when the final rag is removed the blood runs red and clear onto the
snow beneath her.

†

The smith is expelled in the night, at two o'clock, according to the
fire-watcher's melodic calling from the harbour. She has ached increasingly down below and blood has emerged, with dark, elongated lumps in it
that Falck has studied with the one eye by which he is able to see. He
has wound a cloth around his head, his face is marred here and there by
burns, and much of his hair has been singed away. They have all drunk
a fair amount of aquavit and the priest has recited the Lord's Prayer

more than once and told her about his childhood in Norway, his years in Copenhagen, and eventually about his enchantment with the native girl who launders for him.

But he insists that he has not laid a finger on her. Rather, he is besotted by what she represents, he explains. Her freedom, perhaps. Falck sighs. I don't know what it is.

They sing a couple of hymns. They kiss each other and weep. The girl comes and lies down to sleep next to her. The Magister steals glances at her.

There you both are, he says. The two of you.

He goes into the parlour and sits.

She calls out for him when she feels her abdomen contract. It comes in waves and she presses as hard as she can, while Falck kneads her stomach. But the smith will not come out; he clings to her. For the first time she feels a kind of tenderness for the child, the way it fights so hard to remain in a world in which it is unwanted, and she is overcome by guilt.

But then she feels it come. Falck, who has monitored her bleeding, becomes excited. They press in unison and presently she hears a sudden squelch, followed by a small plop. The priest bends down and picks something up off the floor. He exits into the parlour, huddled over whatever it is that has fallen out of her. For some minutes everything is completely silent. Then he returns, spattered with blood, eyebrows raised. He nods.

What was it? she asks foolishly.

Nothing, says the one-eyed pastor. It was nothing at all. I ask the Madame to forgive this ignorant clergyman, but you have been wrongly diagnosed.

Wrongly diagnosed?

Indeed, Madame. You are not pregnant at all!

Am I not? Then what was it? Why?

This has not occurred, Madame, says Falck. It was a dream. Not a pleasant one, but a dream nonetheless. And none of it means anything at all.

I understand, she says.

Lie down and go back to sleep, Madame Kragstedt. I am certain your next dream will be much nicer than the one you have just had.

And she dreams of Jensigne in her confinement. She sits with her; they hold each other's hands. Her sister sleeps most of the time and when she is awake she is usually confused. But one day she wakes up and looks at her with very attentive eyes. They are alone; the family is downstairs. Haldora sits for a long time, holding her sister's hand. I am with you, she says.

THE SIXTH COMMANDMENT

Holy Wedlock

(1790)

The Sixth Commandment, as it is most plainly to be taught by a father to his family:
'Thou shalt not commit adultery.'
What does this imply?
Answer: That we should fear and love God, so that we may live chastely and modestly in words and actions; and that each should love and honour his spouse.

Morten Falck passes a golden hour. He has clambered up one of the low yet steep peaks behind the colony, has found himself a ledge facing south and sits baking in the sun. He has removed his wig, shaken the lice from it and put it down beside him, loosened his hair bag and allowed his hair to hang freely about his shoulders. He feels it benefit from the air and the sun, like the rest of him. He draws the broad brim of his hat down onto his brow and squints his eyes. His face is warm and he feels as if the inside of his skull is illuminated by a blinding white light. This must be the kind of peace one feels immediately before death, he thinks to himself. But he does not feel that he is to die. Not yet. And it is easy to reconcile oneself with not dying, at least today.

His botany box is beside him. His sketchboard with a sheet of drawing paper on it is on his knee, but he has not yet drawn anything. He has not drawn from nature all through this past winter, ever since he lost the sight of his left eye, and has satisfied himself with sketching the women of his eternal fantasies as one way of staving off his loneliness. And now he lacks the heart to be confronted by his partial blindness and the recognition that his poor vision perhaps has rendered it impossible for him to produce his botanical studies. He has been forced to acknowledge that the dream he had on his arrival here, the dream of compiling a *Flora et Fauna Groenlandica*, will never be realized. With only one eye he is unable to accurately judge distance and perspective. The world consists of coloured surfaces arranged in front of and behind each other like theatrical scenery, the seamless transitions between them are gone. In isolation they remain detailed enough, but he is unable to gauge how far away they are. It causes him difficulty when he is out on his hikes. He must often feel his way forward with his foot and at all times proceed with caution, so as not to step awkwardly and break his ankle.

Instead of taking his sketch pad he has begun to bring along with him into the fells a stone-breaker. Within the fjords he has discovered several strata of precious metals and on a trip north he observed sediments of graphite in the fellsides, and moreover coal in the region of Disko Island, in part already exploited, though clearly unsystematically and on a hand-to-mouth basis. In a cloth bag at home in the Mission house he has put away some nuggets of gold he washed from the gravel of a riverbed, likewise in the Disko area. Approximately four ounces in all, rightfully belonging to the Trade, and thereby ultimately the Crown, though this is a fact he has no intention of heeding. The gold is his pension, sufficient for him to establish a living on his return home.

Morten Falck smiles to himself.

He has now been in the country for three years this autumn. The time has passed quickly; terrible events have occurred, but much good as well. Death has stared him in the eye more than once, and he has stared back almost without blinking. He has matured. His years in Copenhagen were no more than an extended childhood. Many carry on as such throughout their entire lives. But not he. With a shudder he thinks of how things would have been had he married the young Miss Schultz and settled in a parish in Denmark. Sweet Abelone, he thinks, such harm we would have done each other. Much rather his damp dwelling, the daily struggle against spiritual darkness and a lost eye. This, at least, is how things appear to him seen from a sunny ledge behind the colony of Sukkertoppen.

The widow has cleaned for him when he arrives home. The place is neat and tidy; his clothes are laundered and lie smooth and folded in the chest. The widow herself is not there. Most likely she has gone over to the Trader's house. But he can smell her. He is still in the process of her catechism, preparing her for the mercy and salvation of the Lord. If she is proficient, he has promised her that she may be christened and confirmed in the autumn. And she is proficient. He has taught her all through the winter and she can rattle off the articles and explanations quicker than even the brightest orphanage boy at the Vajsenhus. The only thing is, she asks too many questions. She insists on arguing with the Lord, which is to say His local vicar on earth, the Missionary Falck. And in the event that she senses an opportunity to get the better of him, she never hesitates to do so. He is an easy prey. Sometimes he feels he is a mouse teaching a cat as to proper eating habits. He has solemnly explained to her the importance of humility when appearing before the Lord. The Lord detests arrogance, he tells her, hearing to his annoyance an echo of his father, the schoolmaster, though insisting nonetheless: When appearing before the Lord, one must be as a washed and obedient child.

It was the Missionary Oxbøl who made me dirty, she says. I was obedient to him and look what came of it.

The Lord will deal with Oxbøl, he tells her for the umpteenth time. He is sick and tired of hearing about the old priest's repugnant habits. Time and again he is put forward as a counter-argument, an example of the bankruptcy of Christian principles in this land.

No one can ever wash the old priest from me, she says mournfully.

But most certainly, he says, that is exactly what the Lord can and will do. He will cleanse you of your sins. He will make you pure and new as an infant. You must trust Him.

That sounds fine, she says. If he can wash the priest's blood from me I will do whatever He wishes.

He takes her hands and says the Lord's Prayer. She follows him, word for word, her lips a whisper. Afterwards, she appears calm and clarified. The saving of this woman's soul in particular has become important to him. So far he has instructed and christened five adult Greenlanders, of whom three are now dead. If she can obtain salvation, he thinks, then he shall have committed one good deed in this place. But she is full of bitterness and anger and is always on her guard. The slightest physical contact is carefully weighed and considered, each word he speaks is turned and examined.

You must trust me, he says. I am not Oxbøl.

You are a Dane, she replies.

We each have a job ahead of us, you and I, he says firmly. I must win your confidence in the name of the Lord and you must cast off your arrogant garb.

Take off my clothes?

He is compelled to apologize and put it differently. The meaning is not literal, he says, the words are a parable, a metaphor, you understand. We all of us must undress before the Lord, but it is not a matter of the flesh, as perhaps in the case of your former priest. But all she does is stare at him.

And he imagines, beyond the metaphors and the parables, his relationship with the widow becoming more intimate. That she will undress literally. That they will marry. That he will take her daughter unto himself. That she will provide him with a batch of strong sons who might carry him to the grave upon their shoulders. Sometimes she gives him a scrutinizing look. He feels she can see right through him and that she does not care for what she sees. I am not worthy of her, he thinks.

An insistent knocking on the door wrenches him from his thoughts. Outside stands the cooper.

Good afternoon, Dorph, he says.

The peace of God upon you, Missionary Falck. Might it be possible to have a word with the pastor?

Of course. Let us sit down here on the step. The sun is lovely and warm.

They sit down. The cooper is a corpulent man with a large and doleful face, full of righteous outrage at this vale of tears and his own unreasonable plight. Speaking with him always leaves Falck with a slight headache.

I just wanted to ask the missionary if he has heard news?

I'm afraid not, Dorph. There has been no ship and the Inspector, as you know, does not interfere in such matters. When the ship comes in a fortnight we shall see if there is anything for you.

It will be the same as other years, says the cooper, and hangs his head. Seven years I have waited for that marriage licence, without anyone having bothered to send an official rejection.

I sympathize with you, Dorph. I do indeed.

I live in sin, says Dorph. Falck sees the man's lips begin to tremble with rage. How long must my children live as bastards? How long must people be allowed to call my beloved wife the cooper's mistress?

There, there, says Falck, and pats him on the arm.

I am a good Christian! the cooper sobs.

One of the best, says Falck. The Lord sees your devotion.

Is there nothing you can do, Mr Falck?

Such as what?

He could marry us.

Hm, says Falck, somewhat uneasily. However much I wish to help you, going against the authorities is hardly the way.

Is it not the pastor's duty to bless a man and woman's cohabitation that has given four children to the world? the cooper says irascibly.

No, it most certainly is not. I would remind you, Dorph, that it was entirely of your own free will that you took a native woman to be your partner, despite, as far as I am informed, having been warned against it by Magister Krogh. You chose to turn a deaf ear.

It was love, says Dorph, and submits like a lamb.

You might call it that and I am in no doubt that such love is genuine.

But at the time you allowed yourself to be governed by your lust and now you are paying the price. A glance at the cooper makes him regret that he has spoken harshly to him. A ship will come soon, he says in a more conciliatory tone. Then we shall see if it brings a marriage licence with it.

Marriage is instituted by God, says Dorph, not by a mad king.

Yet subject to the authorization of State, Falck rejoins with a wagging finger. Do not forget that the two parts make up the whole. The cooper's shoulders sag. He stares at the ground. I give you my word, Dorph, that you shall not remain unmarried. Your plight is most unsatisfactory and I shall do what I can to help you.

God bless the missionary, says the cooper, contented, and returns to his home. Falck remains and chews his lip.

The other woman in his life is Madame Kragstedt. He has spent many hours in the warmth of her parlour during the winter. He has read to her from Voltaire and Rousseau. *Man is born free and everywhere he is in chains!* He reads his boyhood's *Robinson Crusoe* to her, in the German translation, savouring the language's vowels as they ring in the Trader's rooms. She is Robinson, he Friday. She bursts into tears at her bondage, her childlessness and insufferable boredom within the timber walls of the colony house. They stroll, sauntering, arm in arm, out of royal Copenhagen and into the countryside, around and around the parlour, conversing light-heartedly upon the things they observe along their way, be they door frame, window frame or ceiling joist. He draws her attention to the farms that lie between scattered copses of beech, undulating fields dotted with grazing cattle. She indicates bulrushes, daisies, buttercups and foxtails. Around the folding screen, past the stove, then back again. He bends down and picks her a posy of wild flowers. She chirps with delight and carries them as she would a child, against her breast, stroking their petals gently with her free hand. Before he returns to his rooms, he kisses her on the cheek. He feels her sharp talons clutch at his side and releases her. If Kragstedt dies, he thinks to himself, I shall ask for the Madame's hand in marriage. It would be the decent thing to do.

If I am not already wedded to the widow by that time. The women in his present circumstances are new, his ambivalence old and familiar.

The smith's workshop is open. He goes inside. Hammer stands stripped to the waist, clad only in his loincloth, working a glowing lump of iron. He straightens up on seeing the priest in his doorway, but Falck gestures for him to carry on. He pumps the bellows and the fire flares up. He puts the iron into the flames, turns it several times, removes it and places it once more on the anvil, to be hammered again. The clash of metal has a musical aftertone. Falck wanders about the workshop. The smith ignores him. The heat from the furnace burns the side of his face that is turned towards it, the other remains chilled. The work of the smith fascinates him, alchemically magical, fire and darkness, something one ought to shy away from, but which nonetheless he is drawn towards. A transubstantiation, spirit implanted into the iron, which takes on the shape of the thought by the intervention of fire. The muscles of Hammer's shoulders ripple in the glow. Falck pictures him on top of Madame Kragstedt's naked body on the filthy floor. This is where it happened, he thinks. Here on this very spot.

The iron spits and sizzles as Hammer immerses it in the water tub. He removes it, studies it with an appraising eye, and puts it down on the anvil. He slams the door of the furnace shut. The room becomes dark and abruptly cold. He gives the priest an enquiring look.

I wish to ask Hammer about a matter.

Ask away, priest.

Is it conceivable that you would confess your sins to me?

The smith butters a hunk of the colony's black bread with butter he digs from a wooden bowl with his sheath knife. No, thank you, Mr Falck, it would be of no interest, I'm afraid. I've already told the priest all I have to say.

You have committed serious sins, Hammer. You ought to make peace with the Lord.

The Lord wants nothing to do with me, nor I with Him, and that's that. We leave each other alone. I know what I've done. I know what awaits me when I lay my head on the pillow for the last time. He sends Falck a glance. Why is the priest so interested in my sins?

The inferno, Hammer. Hell. Are you prepared for it?

I imagine it's much the same as here, the smith replies with his mouth full, sweeping out the hand in which he holds his buttered bread. Just a bit bigger and hotter and populated with old friends. I'm sure they need a smith in Hell as much as they do in Sukkertoppen, don't you think so, priest?

I wonder if he will be as uppish when lying on his deathbed, Falck says.

If the priest will excuse me, I think he ought to mind his own death and let me mind mine. Mr Falck is hardly unblemished himself, as far as I've heard.

I shall pray for you, Hammer, says Falck. Though I cannot promise that it will help.

Shut the door behind you, the smith says sourly, and turns his back on him.

†

Together with Bertel he makes a trip into the skerries for a week, boarding the Trader's boat that is outward bound and going ashore on an island where a number of natives have settled for the summer. The Trader sails on to Godthåb in the south. Falck is drawing up a comprehensive report on the state of the Sukkertoppen district for the Missionskollegium. It is to contain statistics of christened, unchristened and those who remain more fiercely recalcitrant, among them self-appointed shamans, *angakokker*, as well as a description of living conditions in the colony itself and its outlying settlements. A perlustration, a natural survey in the tradition of Hans Egede. A *Cultura Groenlandica*. He has penned a brief account of his failed visitation to the prophets two years previously and received from the bishop a written exhortation to renew contact with the apostates and lead them back to the true faith, if necessary by the use of force. *What words fail to convey, the flintlock must proclaim,* as

Bishop Wedell so succinctly put it. An unveiled incitement to violence. He intends to omit any mention in his report of the Eternal Fjord and the community of the prophets, and highlight instead the more positive things that occur. The small number of heathens he has christened these past two years become several score in the report, when including newborn infants. He does not mention that after their christening most have since joined Habakuk or that the colony is on the decline for lack of hunters, kayak men and servants within the Trade.

A number of Habakuk's followers are present in the skerries this summer. He recognizes several, among them two of the oarswomen from the trip with Constable Bjerg. He preaches in the open air and baptizes the children of Christian parents. The converted and heathens alike gather to listen to him, but he knows not to place importance on the fact. He is their entertainment. People gather, eat, swap wives, sing smutty songs, tell tales of the winter, and listen to the priest. He is a clown and little more. The shamans maintain their hold. He meets one of them and speaks amicably with him, a quick-witted man with poor eyesight and a withered leg, who makes a living doing what his physical limitations have compelled him to do. The shaman confides to him that he has considered becoming Christian and decided it would be bad for business, for which reason he sees himself remaining a heathen for the rest of his days. Falck teaches him the Lord's Prayer. The shaman teaches him a magic formula. They part as friends. He writes nothing of any of this in his report.

In the evenings he plays chess with Bertel. The catechist has carved a set of pieces from narwhal tusk. Sometimes they sit playing until well into the night. He asks himself if he will ever become friends with the catechist, the person with whom he spends most time of all. But there is something about Bertel that evades such confidence, and the fact pains him rather. He has told him about his childhood in Norway, about his parents and his sister, the brothers who died as children, his journey to Copenhagen and his time as a student at the university. He knows nothing of Bertel's own background, apart from the fact that his wife Sofie has told him that his mother is still alive and living at Holsteinsborg. When he asked him if he knew who his father was, his eyes flashed with rage.

On their return to the colony, *Der Frühling* lies already anchored in the roadstead. The colony mills with activity, natives have come in droves from the furthest corners of the district, and the ship's crew are a danger unto themselves and all those around them. He greets Captain Valløe, who tells him news of major and minor events at home. The captain enquires about his cow and he takes him with him to where Roselil stands grazing. He offers him a glass of milk. Valløe shakes his head in disbelief. Who would have thought? A cow nearly at the North Pole.

He reads his mail, which includes a letter from his father telling him his mother is confined to bed with a cold. Despondent and fearful of the worst, he puts the bundle of letters aside. His sister would seem to be all right, which is a comfort, at least.

The cooper comes and knocks on his door that same evening. The long-awaited marriage licence remains unforthcoming. Dorph is despairing and angry. He clenches and unclenches his fists as he speaks, and more than once Falck must ask him to calm down. When eventually he gets rid of the man, he goes over to Madame Kragstedt and converses with her for an hour or so. The Trader has not yet returned from his trip and she feels burdened by the social duties that accompany a ship's arrival. Falck asks the Madame's advice concerning the cooper.

It would be a good Christian deed to marry Dorph to the woman he loves, she says.

Your husband would likely not agree, as long as there is no licence.

I shall speak to my husband, she says. Let us go over to the cooper and bring him the good news.

Now?

If we ensure the couple are married before my husband's return, he will be unable to do a thing about it. Bonds forged in Heaven cannot be broken by any mortal authority. Madame Kragstedt rises and throws a shawl over her shoulders. Her cheeks have gained colour and she glows with industry.

I have not seen the Madame thus in a long time, he says.

She beams a smile.

The cooper's house lies some half-hundred paces away on the other side of the Mission house, halfway up a low, rocky incline. A child sits on the step. Voices and clattering are heard from inside.

Is your father home? the Madame asks the child.

The boy stares at them emptily. It occurs to Falck that he is not right in the head. A retarded child, hardly to the benefit of the cooper's situation. He exchanges glances with the Madame, then steps up and knocks on the door. The cooper himself opens up.

Mr Falck? Madame? Dorph retreats backwards inside out of deference.

May we come in, Mr Dorph? Madame Kragstedt enquires.

Of course, says the cooper. Come in, only the lady and the pastor must mind their heads. The ceiling is low.

They enter a room that smells of warm bread and tobacco smoke. An old native woman sits at a table, smoking a pipe. The cooper's woman sits in the alcove with the youngest at her breast. Falck sees how the Madame stares at her breasts, which are swollen with milk. The woman stares back. She does not cover herself up.

Kutaa, she says.

Good evening, madam, says Falck. He is aware of how odd it must seem for him to have appeared with Madame Kragstedt, who for her part seems almost to have fallen from the sky, such is her wonderment at the small, though pleasant parlour.

The cooper draws out two chairs and says something to the native woman, who gets to her feet and goes outside. Falck and Madame Kragstedt seat themselves, side by side, the cooper facing them.

What can I do for Madame Kragstedt and the Magister? Dorph enquires. Can I offer anything?

No, thank you, Dorph, says Falck. We shall not be staying long.

He looks around. The room is crammed with homemade furniture. The walls are adorned with pictures, faded maritime motifs. On a hook in the open fireplace a kettle hangs above glowing coals. To the right a door leads off to a small sleeping chamber. Two girls peep out from the top bunk. Their eyes are narrow, curving half-moons, their hair is bowl-cut. He becomes aware that Madame Kragstedt is clutching his hand as it rests on the table. The cooper stares at the two of them joined. Whatever must he think? Falck wonders. He clears his throat and pulls his hand away.

I have spoken with Madame Kragstedt, he begins rather uncertainly. And she has it very much at heart that you should have your wish, Dorph. In, erm, brief, that your circumstances be made orderly.

We have decided to allow him to be married, Madame Kragstedt interjects.

I see, says the cooper, looking at the two of them by turn. Well, that's exactly what I said the pastor should do, Mr Falck.

Indeed, and now it shall be done. He already knows he is committing a serious error and the cooper's tone annoys him.

When would this happen? the cooper enquires with suspicion.

Will he have time tomorrow? Madame Kragstedt replies.

Already?

Yes, why not tomorrow? says Falck. A Sunday would be fitting.

I shall have to ask first, says Dorph.

Ask whom? says Falck, following the cooper's eyes. He laughs. Do you mean to say you have not yet proposed?

It was never relevant until now, says the cooper. Flustered, he rises and looks across at his bride-to-be, who continues to breastfeed in the alcove.

In that case I think you should make good your intention and ask for her hand, says Falck.

Now? The cooper looks petrified. How?

How what?

How does one say such a thing, in their language?

Do you not speak the native tongue? You mean, you cannot speak with your own wife?

She's not my wife, the cooper rejoins, irked.

Your future wife, then.

I've never learned, says the cooper with a sigh. Besides, there's never a lot to say. You know, between a man and his woman. What's there to say?

Falck shakes his head in disbelief. I'm afraid I cannot help you there, Dorph. You must manage on your own. If you really want this woman, I'm sure you'll find a way. He gets to his feet. Now Madame Kragstedt and I shall go outside and await the result of your proposal with much anticipation.

Stepping outside, the Madame puts her head in her hands. Oh, Lord, she says. I'm not sure whether to laugh or cry.

Regrettably, I am far too familiar with the stupidity of man to be taken aback, says Falck. But our cooper is certainly a case.

The boy is still seated on the step. He looks at them, smiling blankly, his eyes bright blue. He is the only one of the cooper's children to have been born with predominantly Danish features.

How sweet he is, says Madame Kragstedt, staring at him. What is your name, little boy?

The boy does not reply.

I think the child to be deaf, says Falck. Perhaps he suffers from aphasia. He is most certainly dumb.

Inside they can hear Dorph's voice. Then all is silent. They listen, but cannot hear any reply from the woman. Dorph's voice is heard again. To Falck's ear, the cooper sounds like he is holding a sermon. He looks at Madame Kragstedt. She looks back at him.

It reminds me of the time Kragstedt proposed to me, she says. We failed to comprehend each other too.

They remove themselves slightly from the house. The boy stares at them.

Ah, here we have it, says the Madame.

The cooper appears in the door. He looks exhausted, but is smiling.

She said yes, he says. That much I do understand of their tongue. She wants me!

†

The certificate of marriage he draws up the following day reads thus: *Notice be hereby given that Carl Julius Dorph, cooper of the colony at Sukkertoppen, and the Greenlandic woman Maren Jensdatter on this day were married. What therefore God hath joined together, let no man put asunder. Witness this signature, Morten Falck, missionary, Sunday the 2nd of August, AD 1790.*

Around this text he has drawn two laurel branches striving upwards so as almost to converge at the top of the page. The cooper places the certificate in a glass frame and hangs it on the wall of their home, in between the maritime scenes.

I thank you, at long last, he says, taking Falck's hand immediately after the ceremony.

There is something self-righteous about his tone that Madame Kragstedt hears, too, prompting her later on to draw Falck aside: This is a good deed you have done, Morten Falck. The Lord will remember you for it.

†

Dainty! Dainty indeed! says Jørgen Kragstedt, waving the marriage certificate in his face.

A week has passed. The Trader has returned, only a couple of days before *Der Frühling* sets sail.

Thank you, says Falck. I spent much time and effort on it.

Of course, you know it is invalid? says Kragstedt. The marriage is without royal approval.

The marriage is valid, says Falck. The ceremony was performed with a hand upon the Holy Bible and in the presence of witnesses, among them Madame Kragstedt herself.

All right, let us say it is valid. And now I annul it. Kragstedt tears the document into four pieces, crumples them together and tosses them into the air. They are caught by the wind and carried along the ground. He smiles at Falck provokingly.

I shall merely draw up a new certificate, says Falck. It is not the document itself that decides whether the cooper is married.

If you dare write another certificate, I shall tear that one up too. Moreover, I intend to write to your principals and inform them of how their representative is carrying on here in the colony.

The marriage has been entered, says Falck calmly. There is nothing either you or I can do about it.

The marriage is annulled, the Trader answers back shrilly. I have told Dorph about the error and I can inform the Magister that he fully understands. Now all we need is for it to dawn on you.

And perhaps your wife, says Falck with a smile.

I strongly advise you not to turn my wife against me. The consequences for the Magister would be immeasurable and long-lasting.

Falck goes down to the cooper's workshop, where he finds Dorph filling the bowl of a pipe he has carved out of bone. On the bench next to him are shavings, a maul and various clamps. The cooper does not look up.

I shall write you a new certificate, says Falck. The Trader has no right to intervene.

It would seem otherwise, says Dorph.

Do you believe in the mercy of the Lord? says Falck in a voice louder than he had anticipated in the tiny space.

The cooper flinches. He puts the pipe down and looks at him. I believe in the mercy of the Lord, he says. But in this mortal life the Trader and his principals are the masters, and it is here in the mortal world I sin with my woman and make my children into bastards. It is in this world I wish to be married, not in the next.

You are married, says Falck. I shall draw up a new certificate.

Just as I finally got round to asking her, Dorph whimpers, the marriage turns out invalid.

It is not invalid! Falck is tiring of the man's obstinacy. Can't you understand that you are married in the name of God and that no man can put asunder what He has joined together?

If the missionary speaks to the Trader, says Dorph, and makes him concede that the marriage is good, then I shall believe him.

I will speak to him, says Falck.

The next day he goes to the cooper's house with Madame Kragstedt and the new certificate. The Madame assures the cooper that there will be no further issues with the Trader. She has spoken to him, she says, and he has seen his error. Falck is uncertain as to whether the Madame's assurances are supported, but since the Trader has departed south by *Der Frühling* on yet another visit to the inspectorate at Godthåb, and will thus not be seen for several weeks, he hopes matters will settle of their own accord. The cooper, at least, is happy, if only in his own surly and mistrustful way, and he accepts the presents Madame Kragstedt brings, an embroidered rug for the alcove and an oil lamp, with a measured bow. She asks him about the boy who always sits on the step. He is an idiot, says the cooper with a sigh, but the dearest I have. The Madame falls quiet.

Dorph puts the certificate in the frame and hangs it up on the wall. Falck sees his lips move in a silent Lord's Prayer.

†

A week later he invites Madame Kragstedt on a hike. They walk from the colony, past the dwellings of the natives and on over the low-lying rocks, down to the shore at the eastern end of the island that faces in towards the mainland. He helps her as they climb the slopes and waits for her when they descend.

Try putting on skirts and a corset, then let us see who is the most agile, she says with a laugh.

That would be you, Haldora, I am sure, he says.

It's so long since I walked. During my first time here I walked a lot. I loosened my corsets and strode freely, either alone or in the company of my husband. I haven't the courage any longer. I didn't realize I missed it so much.

We shall walk together, he says, as often as you want.

The Madame looks at him; she sends him a pretty smile that is almost relieved of the aftermath of rape and abortion.

They strive to follow the coast in a northerly direction, but find it less than easy. The island has no natural beaches and its coast is intersected by coves and inlets separated by steep, wet inclines. The Madame's boots often become stuck in cracks; she plumps into puddles and slips on the smooth rocks. Yet she insists they go on. Eventually they find themselves confronted by a drop of several hundred fathoms and retreat. They sit down some distance from the abyss.

I can hear the sea, she says. You never hear it in the colony, even though we live at the shore.

There are always waves on the open sea, he says.

She has let down her hair. It blows in the wind. He feels it brush his cheek.

Inland, to the east, they can see tall fells, snow and glaciers. He tells her of the landscape there.

I am like a blind person, she says despondently. I need someone to tell me what the world looks like.

Can you not say to your husband that you would like to accompany him on his trips? Falck suggests.

He will not take me.

Have you asked?

I can feel it. And I would only get in the way of his activities.

But you are his wife.

Exactly.

Perhaps he is afraid you will catch a cold, he says.

Yes, she says, rather curtly. There is an explanation for everything.

Before getting to their feet again to walk back, she leans towards him to be kissed. He kisses her as usual on the cheek.

Thank you, Morten, she says. What would I have done without you?

You would be compelled to take a lover.

You are better than a lover, she says. You are a friend.

When they return to the colony the Trader is standing outside the colony house, watching them.

Jørgen, she says, are you back already?

Yes, is it inconvenient?

No, my dear, it is lovely to see you. The missionary and I have had the most marvellous walk in the wilderness.

Magister, says Kragstedt.

Trader.

They look at each other. Falck thinks he perceives a smile on Kragstedt's lips.

Go in and get some warmth inside you, says the Trader. The Magister and I have a matter to discuss.

Madame Kragstedt goes up the steps. She glances briefly at the two men, then disappears into the house.

Falck endeavours to sound friendly. What might the Trader want?

To talk to you about that confounded cooper. Come, let us go down to the warehouses.

They pass between the buildings and amble out on to the wooden jetty. As they reach the end, Falck says: The Trader wished to speak to me about the cooper?

The happy husband, indeed. I hear there is a new document?

That is correct. Though the document in itself is of no consequence. Its value is merely symbolic.

Exactly, says the Trader. And that is why I have relieved him of it, so that he will not go about and be reminded the whole time that you have made him believe he is married.

They have turned and proceed now back along the jetty. Kragstedt is half a pace in front. Falck stops. The Trader continues a few paces, then turns and looks at him.

I accuse the Trader of blasphemy, says Falck.

Have you any idea how much harm you have caused that poor man, Magister Falck?

I have written a full report on these events, says Falck. And I understand that I shall have to furnish it with an addendum, putting you, most honourable Trader, in a very bad light indeed.

Such a report, supposing the Magister is telling the truth and that he intends to submit it, will be his letter of resignation, says the Trader.

The document carries signatures, says Falck. Among them Madame Kragstedt's.

He sees the Trader clench his teeth. Kragstedt narrows his eyes into a glare.

Where is this document?

Where is the marriage certificate?

Hm, says the Trader. I suggest we make a little exchange.

As you wish.

You have won a battle, Kragstedt says. I give you credit for that. But you will lose the war. Mark my words.

Give my regards to your lovely wife. Falck cannot stop himself.

†

Sunday, and the sun is beaming down. It is eight o'clock in the morning and a crowd has gathered outside the Mission house, both christened and heathen, as well as the entire colony crew, with the exception of the Overseer Dahl, Constable Bjerg and the Trader. The cooper, Dorph, arrives in polished boots, black-tailed coat and white stockings; his military whiskers are brushed back, he is without wig, his hair dark and frizzy and gathered tightly at the neck, from where it fans out between his shoulder blades. He carries his two daughters in his arms: they cling to him. The cooper fixes his gaze upon Magister Falck, who stands waiting at the Mission house door. The bride is more humbly clad in a pale-blue linen dress and kamik boots edged with dog fur. She bears the infant on her arm. The eldest child, the blue-eyed angel boy, is absent.

Falck greets the cooper and his wife. We are waiting for Madame Kragstedt, he says, then we shall proceed.

I hope all will be in order this time, says the cooper, and puts down his two daughters. And that the Trader will not ruin everything again.

Bear in mind that this ceremony is merely confirmation of what is already a fact, says Falck. You have been married for several weeks, but now we are allowing the whole colony to witness the nuptials. The Trader would not have the nerve to go against his own people; it would be foolish of him indeed. Ah, the Madame arrives.

They turn and see Madame Kragstedt on her way from the colony house. Her long red gown billows about her person, edged with a colourful drawstring border that resembles a garland of flowers. On her head she wears a rust-red cap with a veil of muslin that falls all down her back and mingles with her thick, mahogany hair. The crowd falls silent. They turn their heads and watch as she approaches. She passes the smith with a confident smile and approaches Falck and the happy couple.

Welcome, Madame, says Falck, his eyes consuming her. Where is your husband?

My husband is sleeping, she replies in a low voice. I gave him a measure of laudanum in his wine last night, as you advised.

Excellent, Madame Kragstedt. Let us hope his sleep will be long and refreshing. He addresses the crowd, projecting his voice: Welcome to the house of the Lord on this splendid Sunday, heathens and Christians, Greenlanders and Danes, adults and children! You shall now be witness to the performance of holy rites, the joining together of two people who love each other. Let us take this delightful sunshine to be a sign of the Lord's approval of this marriage, and let no man, however powerful, break this pact.

Amen, says the cooper.

He steps aside and the crowd moves to enter the Mission house. At the same moment the colony bell begins to peal.

Who rings the bell? Falck demands angrily. I have expressly asked that it not be rung today on account of the Trader.

I think it is our own Constable Bjerg, says Madame Kragstedt. Perform the ceremony before my husband comes and intervenes.

The wedding proceeds peacefully. When it is done Falck addresses the congregation in the tightly packed room: This little ceremony you have attended has not in itself joined these people in matrimony, rather it is mere confirmation in public of a union that has already taken place in the presence of witnesses. We have chosen to repeat the service today for the pleasure and edification of the colony's inhabitants, and so that all shall know that the cohabitation of our cooper and his Maren has been blessed by the Lord and may not be broken by any living man.

Magister Falck!

He has already seen the Trader in the doorway. Now everyone turns to look. Kragstedt approaches. His clothes are untidy, his hair dishevelled. He stares out over the Mission house room with eyes that are bloodshot. Under his arm he carries the colony's flag in a bundle. In his hand is a pistol.

I have taken down the flag, he says in a thick voice. Our sacred flag shall not be tarnished by this unlawful act. Now everyone will go home and in the name of His Majesty King Christian the Seventh I hereby arrest you, Magister Falck!

He waves the pistol slackly. Those closest to him step back in fright.

That pistol is not loaded, says Falck. No one is going to help you carry out your orders.

The Trader sways slightly. He wipes his face with a corner of the flag. Falck grips his shoulder to steady him. He wrenches himself free and points the pistol at him.

You are the Devil himself! he says. You have destroyed my marriage. You are turning people against me.

At this juncture the congregation breaks into song, led by Bertel, who conducts them with great, sweeping movements of his arms. They sing in harmony. The Trader retreats a couple of paces, staggers to the door and leaves. Several hymns are sung. Then, little by little, the Mission house empties, leaving Falck alone with Madame Kragstedt. They go outside together. The Trader is sitting on a rock; he stares at them listlessly. The Madame approaches him; she squats down and strokes his cheek.

My poor husband. Now we shall go home and I shall have Sofie make you a nice cup of cocoa.

The Trader leans towards her and rests his head against her shoulder. She pats him on the back and glances at Falck. He goes over to the cooper's to take part in the celebrations. A little later he sees the Trader and the Madame go, hand in hand, back to the colony house. On the cooper's wall hangs the third marriage certificate Falck has drawn up. In his own opinion the most artistically successful of them all.

†

An early morning about a week after the most recent of the weddings, he sees the Trader's boat glide out of the bay and head to sea. Two men are seated in the vessel. In the telescope he recognizes the Trader and Rasmus Bjerg. He asks around and is told that the Trader has departed south to Godthåb, probably to speak to the inspector.

I don't hope the Trader drowns on his way, says the cooper.

Indeed, says Falck, neither do I. On the other hand, he adds, God's judgements are unsearchable.

Amen, says the cooper.

Some peaceful days follow. It is nearly autumn. He feels at home now in this cycle: short, hectic months of summer followed by darkness and tranquillity. Every morning he stands upon the rocks outside the colony and scans the sea for the Trader's boat. But the Trader does not appear. September passes, October presents itself in silence. But not Kragstedt. The Madame tries on her black dress. Falck helps her adjust it, his mouth full of pins. He reads aloud to her from *Candide*, seated opposite her, the Madame's feet resting in his lap. The widow appears so as to be of service to the Madame, or for Falck, but they send her away.

One morning a notice appears on the door of the warehouse. People stand reading it and discussing its contents. Falck's heart sinks. He has seen the Trader's boat, moored at the jetty.

He goes down to the warehouse and sees that the notice is signed by Inspector Rømer. He narrows his eyes and reads:

By order of law: Be it hereby notified to inhabitants of the Colony and to crew appointed to the Trade, that:

The marriage of cooper Carl Julius Dorph and Maren Jensdatter is declared invalid.

1. *Cooper Carl Julius Dorph shall, with effect from the date on which the present notice may be read in the Colony, consider himself discharged from his services as cooper of the Trade, thereby relieved of all attendant privileges, including dwelling, provision, and warrant to move freely within the Colony and its surrounding district.*

2. *Any person showing disobedience in respect of the present notice, and of Colony Manager, Trader and Commandant Jørgen Kragstedt, will likewise be considered to be discharged and will be liable to prosecution and punishment.*

Dieterich Rømer
Inspector, Southern Inspectorate, Godthåb
27 October 1790

It is in large part as he had anticipated, with the exception that there is no mention of his own role in the matter. He had been expecting – and had come to terms with – his dismissal. The fact that the Trader and Inspector Rømer, his two worst enemies in the country, completely omit to name him in writing is almost the hardest part of it. The burden of guilt as regards what has occurred, and what will occur, rests thereby entirely on his own shoulders.

In the evening he drinks what aquavit is left in his bottle, then whatever he can find in the way of wine and ale. He wakes to a pounding noise and thinks at first it must be his hangover thumping in his head, but then it is repeated. Outside stand several men with torches in their hands. Their voices are a clamour and for a moment he is afraid they have come to drag him away and place him in chains on the Trader's orders. Then he begins to grasp fragments of what they say. Something has happened. The cooper. The blubber house. In the name of Jesus!

He pulls on his coat and steps into his boots and follows the men down to the harbour.

The smith stands guard at the blubber house. He opens the door for the priest and lets him in. A large torch has been placed in a holder on the wall inside the door. It lights up the cooper's heavy frame from below, the body hanging by a chain over the boiling tub, face twisted in sanctimonious despair.

He swings still, says the smith at his side, looking up. It must be less than half an hour since he jumped.

What are you waiting for? says Falck. Get him down, for goodness' sake!

By an intricate muddle of ropes and knots, the cooper has made it nigh impossible for his body to be returned to the ground. A posthumous joke, though no one laughs, apart perhaps from the cooper himself, wherever he may be.

It's Magister Krogh all over again, says the smith, labouring to loosen the rope that holds the cooper aloft, the rope which in turn is attached to the chain by a myriad knots. The carpenter, the cook, Constable Bjerg and two of the colony's native constables struggle to steer the cooper's body away from the blubber boiler, while Falck supervises the removal from a safe distance. And yet the cooper slides from their hands and plunges into the tub. Falck turns away in disgust as the smell of boiling human flesh fills the room of the blubber house. Boat hooks are called for, the men curse. Eventually they haul him up, though are unable to touch him because of the heat, and he is deposited on the stone floor with the same sound as a dead fish. Falck steps forward and squats down at the body. The cooper's face is swollen from the hot oil, he stares up at the ceiling with an affable, greasy grin.

Outside the blubber house stands the cooper's wife. Falck approaches her. She carries the infant on her arm. The retarded boy is with her. He calls out for his father in Greenlandic, a manic, braying voice. Someone holds him back to stop him from running inside.

Falck pats the wife on her shoulder. He does not know what to say. He feels an urge to vomit. Then Kragstedt is there. He looks content.

Now look what you have done, he says. May I be the first to congratulate the Magister.

THE SEVENTH COMMANDMENT

A Salute to the Mad King

(1791)

The Seventh Commandment, as it is most plainly to be taught by a father to his family:
'Thou shalt not steal.'
What does this imply?
Answer: That we should fear and love God, so that we may not rob our neighbour of his money or possessions, nor acquire the same by spurious merchandise or by fraudulent traffic; but to assist him in improving and protecting his property and livelihood.

Darkness has crept over the land. When the sun retreats to the south, the ice projects silently from the north. The frost is like a barber's blade against the cheek. The edge of the ice lies a day's march away, say the hunters, the only ones to defy the cold, clad in ragged kamik boots and worn-out anoraks of canvas whose most vulnerable points are lined with old issues of *Københavns Adresseavis*.

The snow crunches beneath Morten Falck's thin leather soles as he hurries home from his weekly pilgrimage to the Trade office, where the overseer has handed out his allotted provision. The Trader himself was absent, a fact for which he is thankful. Kragstedt avoids him as far as possible for the moment, and Morten Falck avoids Kragstedt. He has not visited the Madame for some time. The intimacy that had occurred between them had become oppressive and the easiest remedy was to slide apart. He has seen the Trader and his wife stroll from the colony, arm in arm, returning ruddy-cheeked, and he has felt pangs of jealousy on this account. He misses his visits with the Madame, the warmth of the Trader's parlour, their discussions of the novels they are reading, the good aquavit, the grandfather clock measuring the stagnancy of time. He misses the confidentiality of another human being. And yet he sets store by solitude.

However, he does pay visits to the Trader's loft. He secured the keys while seated in the Trade office one afternoon, waiting for the overseer to come. They were there in front of him and he took them, that is to say his hand took them. Once home again with his modest provision in a bag, a week's food and drink, he took out the keys and pondered what to do with them. Eventually he decided to use them for their proper purpose: to open a door. Since the autumn he has thus been well provided with groceries. Roselil still gives some small amount of milk. He has thought of having her butchered. The expenditure and the bother involved in keeping her is more than her scarce quantities of milk can compensate for. But he has not the heart to have her put down. The smith has gradually adopted her and will under no circumstance hear talk of her slaughter, though he will not pay for her maintenance either.

He shuts himself in the kitchen, prepares oats and pork, and takes the meal into his room to eat, devours it and wipes the plate clean with bread. His stomach grumbles its disgruntled thanks. The time is just past four; his catechism and instruction are completed; he has no visits to pay this afternoon, unless he is called upon. Previously, the widow would have been at his door at this time to receive his personal instruction. He smiles glumly. It is several months since her disappearance. He has no idea where she might be. He doubts that she has gone to the Eternal Fjord and he is certain that she is not to be found at Holsteinsborg. Apart from that, she could be anywhere. Her christening has been postponed and postponed again, either because some other matter prevented it or because of her own sudden reluctance. Sometimes he wonders if she even wants to become a good Christian.

Did I love the widow? he asks himself, noting that he already thinks of her in the past tense. Judging by the pain and longing he feels now that she is no longer with him, he did. But what was it, then, that I loved? A sullen, recalcitrant woman who often succumbed to outbreaks of rage. Once, she sliced holes in his mattress with a cleaver, thrashing and tearing at the straw until he was forced to lie on top of her and hold her tight. What are you so angry about? he asked her. Who is it you want to kill? You, priest! she replied in her own language, the language of rage and honesty, a wicked grin curling her lips. *Illit, palasi!* And with that she wrestled free, dropped the cleaver and left. A mystery. That was what he loved, or perhaps loved. He sighs. The daughter is abandoned in the communal dwelling house, where most probably she is neglected by the natives.

A light glances the window and is cast briefly against the ceiling. The fire-watcher's lantern. He hears the man's heavy footsteps as they pass. The smith. An incorrigible sinner not even twenty degrees of frost and year after year of debauchery can do away with. Inspector Rømer's words come back to him: *I was here before he came, and I'll be here when he goes again.* Apparently, the worst sinners are those who do best in this wilderness.

He sits skimming through the day's issue of the *Christiania-Kureren*, dated 27 January 1790 or exactly one year ago to the day. There is a piece on the previous year's disturbances in Paris. He has read on ahead, which is not his custom, and has absorbed in disbelief, partially excited, partially horrified, reports of the persecution of the royal family, the annexation of church property, the storming of the Bastille. And now his year's issues come to an end. Compared to these events the dissolution of the Stavnsbånd in Denmark was little more than a triviality. He wonders where it will end and imagines prison cells full of noblemen awaiting their fate, palaces razed, bodies floating in the Seine, burning buildings and red flags waving on the barricades. A new order, which perhaps will spread to the rest of Europe. The papers seem to expect it will happen, some even hope. In the Danish and Norwegian press it is a time of suggestion. How will life in peaceful little Copenhagen be affected, or back home in Lier? Will there be anything left to return home to? Does he even want to return home? In the summer he felt like a fish in water up here, now he is no longer sure.

There is a knock on the door. Bertel's wife, Sofie, who is still employed in the Trader's household, stands outside with a letter for him. Come in, he says, and close the door, my dear. She enters, looks about her, and he can tell she thinks the priest's home to be humble and rather sorry compared to what she is used to.

He tears open the letter and is surprised to see that it is an invitation:

In anticipation of the approaching birthday of His Majesty, our beloved King Christian the Seventh, and the annual celebrations of such an occasion, it would please Madame Haldora Kragstedt and the undersigned if the Magister would favour us with the pleasure of his person's presence and company in the Trader's home this coming Sunday the 29th of January at 12 o'clock noon. Food and wine will be served to the Colony's Danish contingent, and subsequently a dram of spirits to such Greenlanders as are employed by the Trade. Moreover, at the request of my good wife, and as a novelty this year, treats will be handed out to the Colony's children. Your humble servant, Jørgen Kragstedt, Commandant, etc.

Falck broods at length over the letter. He reads it several times. Is its tone to be understood as sarcasm and thereby as a deterrent against presenting himself? Or is it correct and neutral, and perhaps identical to the invitation all others in the colony have received? Has the Trader resolved to let the past lie or has his wife talked him into reconciliation?

He crumples the letter in his hands and throws it on to the floor. Only then to pick it up and smooth it out. Sofie sits waiting in his armchair, he realizes. Her feet are on the table and she is watching him. He smiles at her. She returns her feet to the floor. I shall attend, he decides. Or rather, I shall not. Hm. I shall write a similar letter to the Trader in reply, in exactly the same tone, and if the Trader's letter is meant to be sarcasm my reply will appear quite as sarcastic. If it is meant sincerely, then mine, too, will be taken as such. The only problem is that he has no idea what to put. I shall attend, he thinks. Or shall I? No! Or perhaps.

Thank the Trader for his invitation, he says. I shall be happy to attend, of course.

She curtsies, a gesture the Madame must have taught her. He has never before seen a Greenlander curtsy. Or is this, too, some form of sarcasm? I spend too much time in my own company, he tells himself. Sofie has gone.

Say hello to your husband! he shouts after her. And your fine boy!

A poor decision, if timely, is better than a good one that is not. Some statesman's motto he has read somewhere, perhaps the Count von Bernstorff's. He is decided and feels relief. Thank you, dear Count! Now he is alone. Now he may permit himself to drink, though the bottle is as good as empty.

Again he thinks of the widow. He recalls the lingering smells of the dwelling house in her clothes. Like heathen skin, he thinks, that he ought to have stripped from her body, removing her from her natural state and replacing her into civilized, pale nakedness that he might have covered with his kisses and copulated with in the good Danish tradition as practised by his colleagues, among them Pastor Oxbøl at Holsteinsborg. But then he might not have found her so alluring now. Anyway, it came to nothing, and now he regrets it, as he knows he would have regretted it even more had he done it.

She had lain with so many men and was not reticent in speaking of it. He allowed her to confess her sins and listened to what he told her of the lusts and vices of her lovers. He absolved her of her sins. She looked at him enquiringly and smiled. Why is *palasi* crying? I am not crying, he said. Go now and come back in the morning. She could not get it into her stupid head that he was not like the men she told him about in her confessions. At moments of weakness neither could he.

Two of the large communal houses are inhabited in the winter, besides them some smaller dwellings of peat and planks in which live mostly christened Greenlanders employed by the Trade. According to his most recent survey, the still-heathen count thirty-five souls, children and adults, an improvement on the previous year when the colony was all but depopulated. Famine has made people hesitant; they take their precautions and elect for the relative security of the colony rather than freedom in the outlying settlements and the ever-looming threat of hunger.

He thinks much upon the two prophets inside the fjord and their well-organized settlement on the high land. He had been petrified standing in the church and speaking against Habakuk, and the man's ability to address his people impressed him.

†

Morning, the 28th of January. Bertel has laid out the chess set when Falck arrives.

Brr, such cold! he says. But here is nice and warm.

Bertel takes the thick coat Falck wears outside his cassock and hangs it on a nail.

The boy lies on the cot, reading. Sofie has gone up to the colony house to help the Trader's wife get things ready for the occasion of the king's birthday. The boy's breathing is laboured and punctuated by wheezing, yet he seems wholly absorbed in his reading. Now and then he turns a page.

Falck and Bertel sit down facing each other and begin to play. On his way here Falck decided on an opening, but some few moves into the game his plans are already crumbling and he is as usual forced on to the defensive.

I have been invited to dinner, he says.

Bertel moves a piece.

At the Trader's.

Falck's move is foolish and Bertel punishes him promptly.

I'm not sure about it. I feel most inclined to make my excuses.

The boy coughs.

Though I should not like to appear inaccessible.

Your move, Pastor.

And the Madame may wish to see me. We were once good friends, the Madame and I.

Check, says Bertel.

Is something the matter? Falck asks.

Yes, your queen is in danger.

Falck leans over the board. They play, silent in the light of the lamp.

What are you reading? Falck asks the boy.

He holds up his book. Falck nods and smiles. It is one of the volumes he has given him from his library.

The lad is clever, he says to Bertel. He will make a fine catechist like his father.

He won't be a catechist.

So you say.

He is to be a priest. Bertel makes an assault from his right flank.

Priest, indeed. I must say. Or bishop, perhaps? Falck smirks.

Why should a Greenlander not become a priest? Bertel says rhetorically.

I suppose it is possible, says Falck peaceably, though he senses that his look is one of doubt. A priest, is that what you want to be? he asks the boy over on the cot.

The lad looks up from his book and shakes his head. A ship's captain.

Ah, a ship's captain. You wish to journey out and see foreign lands?

He nods earnestly, then returns to his reading.

Checkmate, says Bertel.

Falck laughs.

†

They go to the communal house together. To enter they must descend on to all fours and crawl. Morten has drawn his cassock up to his chest and holds it gathered in one hand to save it from becoming dirty, which is to say dirtier than it is already. Everything becomes dirty so fast. Bertel crawls in first. From the ceiling in the entry hang remnants of clothing and skins, curtain by curtain, and various objects of bone, wood and metal. Hunting implements, perhaps, or heathen amulets. The entry is long and narrow. Morten follows Bertel's boot shafts and concentrates on the words of his Lord's Prayer.

Shrill laughter greets him as he pokes his head into the dwelling-room. Immediately it ceases again. Eyes watch him in the dim light. Their laughter has always scared the wits out of him. But it is not him they are laughing at, it is a secret mirth, most likely unfit for other ears, and in this instance he is grateful that his poor Greenlandic spares him from grasping their obscenities.

He seats himself on the strangers' bench and pulls off his coat, though still he is too warmly dressed. The long room is dark, thick with the stench of filled urine tubs, human odours, sizzling oil lamps, flesh boiling in dented pots over the fire. He knows these houses; he has become used to the smells and the nakedness, the sound of squelching breasts and hands slapping at lice. But the heat is hard to endure when clad in a wool cassock.

Faces lurk behind the lamps, cheekbones shine like copper. There must be some thirty people at least. They sit tightly beside each other, behind each other, women, men, children in a naked, perspiring huddle. He greets them unspecifically. A number return his greeting in a friendly manner. *Kutaa, palasi.* Hello, Priest. His eyes adjust to the dark. He sees the naked bodies glistening, copper-red in the light of blubber lamps. Some are occupied eating soup from bowls of tin; women comb each other's hair; men sit cross-legged outermost on the benches and are deloused by their daughters. The pots boil vigorously, bones protruding from the scalding liquid; steam fills the room with moisture. Falck wishes he could take off his cassock, divest himself of his priestly dignity and merge naked and perspiring into the midst of these bodies. But he knows he cannot, that it is not possible.

They were indulging in something when he and the catechist arrived, he senses it and can tell by their faces, something that hangs yet suspended in the air above the benches. He knows it still takes place, especially when visitors come from outside. New blood, new flesh. Lamps are extinguished and bodies come together in the dark, fresh seed is sown. A mixture of entertainment and necessity. The priests have fulminated against it ever since Egede's day, but the practice is seemingly impervious to such criticism. Combating it is perhaps inadvisable. Falck at least has no intentions of opposing such an entrenched feature of their lives. He pretends it does not exist.

Let us speak of the Baptism, he begins uncertainly. Let us speak of why Christian people have devoted themselves to the Lord.

Bertel translates. A silence ensues.

Why should we be christened? says one of the unfamiliar men who sits scraping the sweat from his upper body and arms with the broad blade of a woman's knife.

So that you may become good people, Falck replies, and so that you may know God and find peace through Jesus Christ.

But we are good without knowing God, the man retorts, flicking his wrist to send a fan-like spray of perspiration from the blade, causing a blubber lamp to flicker and sizzle. The acrid stench of steaming sweat claws at his nostrils.

Indeed, he says accommodatingly. But some of you are not good. You live in sin. You commit evil deeds. You kill defenceless children and women.

Unruffled, the man continues to scrape the sweat from his skin; there is something affectionate about the way he proceeds, as though it were a form of self-satisfaction. Falck cannot look away from it.

But the Christians in the colony, do they know God?

Yes, they are christened, they know God and the Saviour, His only begotten son. Falck knows what comes next.

The man smiles. But these people are bad. They drink and curse and are lecherous, and they too kill others who are innocent. Is this not right?

It is true, some of them are bad. God has forsaken them.

They have children by our women, then want nothing to do with them.

They will be punished in the life to come.

Are all people like this in Denmark?

The discussion is not proceeding in the direction Falck had wished, but he knows from experience that it does not pay to evade an issue or lie. One must forge ahead, concede what must be conceded, and hope to emerge unvanquished. Many are, he says. Man is weak. But there are many good people, too. Our king is good.

The man looks at him attentively, not unkindly. He is on his own territory and feels secure. He has raised an eyebrow. Falck senses he is up against a highly astute man who is amusing himself. Perhaps we should send some of our people with your ships to Denmark, to evangelize in your country and teach your king to turn his people to righteousness?

If first they would be christened, then indeed, Falck replies slyly. Then they could go to Denmark and teach the people there to be good Christians.

But Priest, the man counters, flicking the blade once more and causing the lamp to spit, many have journeyed to Denmark and have never come back. What has happened to them?

I don't know.

They are dead. Are they not?

Yes, I'm afraid they probably are.

Greenlanders cannot tolerate the air in Denmark, says the older-mand in the corner. It is like poisoned water to them, and since they cannot help but drink it, they become sick and die. With the Danes it is much the same. They cannot abide the air in our country. They become maddened by it; they drink and whore and die like flies. You do not look so well yourself, Priest. Why is this so? Did God make us so different?

We are all equal before the Lord, he says half-heartedly.

Bertel says something to the oldermand, who says something to his wife, who in turn spoons a portion of soup into a bowl. She comes over and places it on the floor in front of him. He can see that the soup is full of barley groats, indicating to him that Kragstedt has shown mercy upon the natives and is sustaining them with Danish groceries.

Eat, Priest! says the oldermand. You look like you need it.

Both he and Bertel scoop the soup into their mouths.

It's unfair of him to judge Christian people on how the colony folk behave, he says to Bertel when presently they sit digesting the meal.

Why? says Bertel.

Because they are scoundrels, says Falck.

Exactly, says Bertel.

Hm, he says. Are you not supposed to be on my side?

Is the priest not supposed to be on our side? Bertel retorts.

Of course, he says. You know I am.

Danes look after Danes, says the catechist. That's how it's always been.

Instead of discussing matters of theology and arguing with Bertel, he tells a story from the Bible. The natives always have good appetite for a story. The scriptures speak to everyman, such is their divine nature. They are all ears, and watch the priest attentively as he speaks in Danish, then turn to Bertel when he translates.

Today it is the story of Jonah. He makes the most of the unwilling prophet's arguments with the Lord, he waves his hands, alters his voice and play-acts. The natives laugh. On the floor a flock of children sit, open-mouthed, gaping up at him. Then Jonah flees from the Lord. He runs back and forth, stooping beneath the low ceiling, sweating grotesquely in his cassock. He sails upon the great ocean and a terrible storm begins to blow. His arms flail like the wings of a windmill; the wind blows from his mouth. This is something they know and understand. What kind of boat was it? they want to know. Was it a rowing boat or a sailing boat? Was the wind onshore or offshore?

On this matter the scripture is silent, he says, out of breath.

And what kind of whale swallowed the prophet?

On this, too, the scripture is silent.

A humpback, perhaps? No, not a humpback, for a man cannot pass through the neck of a humpback. It must have been a sperm whale; they can swallow a whole boat.

They love the details and when he is unable to account for them they make them up themselves. And yet they readily accept what is unreasonable, such as Jonah surviving in the belly of the whale. It is all a part of the conception, things happening that cannot happen in reality, like when the shamans with their hands tied behind their backs fly to the rear side of the moon or descend to the bottom of the sea.

A discussion arises concerning Jonah's behaviour. Of course he should run away, some opine. What God asks of him – to go into the town of Nineveh and tell the inhabitants there that they are going to perish – would place his own life in jeopardy. Before he knew it, the messenger himself would be dead. But the Lord gives him strength, say others, only Jonah will not trust Him. Who would, after He sent him out in a storm and into the stomach of a whale! They roar with laughter. Falck feels his sweat run down his chest and hopes that he will not catch a cold once they are outside again.

The palm tree at the end of the story presents a problem. A tall plant with big leaves is how Bertel translates it. They cannot picture it. A fern? A bush? Falck draws a sketch on his pad. At the foot of the tree he places a stooping, emaciated figure.

Aha, they say at once. *Palasi!*

No, he says. Jonah.

But he looks exactly like *palasi*, they reply impishly.

Perhaps you are right, he says kindly and laughs along with them. Perhaps it is *palasi* under the tree.

What about God? they ask. Where is He?

It is forbidden to make images of God, Falck tells them. It would be blasphemous.

Discussion continues. There is growing agreement that Jonah's God is unreasonable and intransigent, unamenable to negotiation. Our spirits, they say, are not spiteful like your God.

It is a comment he cannot ignore. He protests. No, God is love! He shows us what is good.

Even before his utterance is complete, he knows what they will say. And the reply comes promptly:

But you Danes are not good. God must be terribly angry with you!

†

As usual, he receives his few catechumens in the Mission house and prepares them for christening. That is, he endeavours to gain an impression of the degree of their ignorance or stupidity, in the Christian sense, and the extent to which it will be feasible at all to venture towards consecration in Christ through baptism.

Again he misses the widow. She was bright; she could follow his thoughts even when he began to babble and could tell him what he was trying to say and what she would say in counter-argument. It would annoy him dreadfully, but now he misses it. She had a good grasp of the Gospels and could be merciless if he should refer incorrectly to a passage in the scripture.

Magister Oxbøl said, she would say.

Just forget Magister Oxbøl for the moment, would be his reply. It would be best if you forgot all about what he taught you and allowed me to instruct you instead. Then perhaps you would more fully understand that God's love and the old priest's are not necessarily the same.

But when he tested her in the articles and their explanation he would invariably hear some echo of the Missionary Oxbøl's voice.

He asked her, Do you wish it?

She looked at him in bewilderment, her expression exaggerated like an actor's. She knew exactly what he meant.

Do you wish to be christened? To be betrothed to the Lord?

I am a poor widow, she said. I would rather be betrothed to you, Morten Falck. That other one has been dead for many years, and if he is not, then he is too old for me.

He sighed. Answer me properly. Do you wish it?

Yes, I wish it.

Why?

So that they will not kill me.

Who?

She jerked her head silently. Them over there.

Her fellow natives in the dwelling house. He was aware of the delicate situation she was in. Unproductive members of the communal houses were often done away with. Fortunately for her, the hunting had been good that winter. But now she was living on borrowed time. If she became christened she would be protected by Danish law and then they would not dare harm her.

If you behave, I shall prepare you to be baptized in the spring, he said. But you must make every effort to deserve it. Not for my sake, but for your own. If you should be christened with serious sin on your conscience, then you will be lost.

Priests! she spat disdainfully. You are like nosy old women, always wanting to know everything about a person before giving your absolution. God knows me, I've told Him everything. He understands me.

The baptism, and preparation for it, is like a bath, he explained to her. One is cleansed of sin when kneeling down to repent.

Perhaps that's why you Danes never wash yourselves with water, she said. Old Missionary Oxbøl's cock smelled like a rotten salmon, but even then he was not ashamed to stick it inside me.

How disgusting! he exclaimed. Be quiet! It's your tongue that's like a rotten salmon. I will not have such talk in the Mission house.

Shall I go into the Pastor's chamber? she said and smiled.

Yes, do so. Wait for me there. I shall give you some linen to wash and we shall talk of these matters later, without such rudeness.

The widow in his little parlour, which she filled with the smell of smoke and urine tubs and boiling pots, a blend of odours whose single elements repulsed him, but which as a whole led him around by the nose. His entire longing and lust was contained in that smell. It remains here still, long after she has vanished.

In one matter, at least, he is inclined to agree with old Oxbøl: he feels that from a theological standpoint it would be wrong to baptize the widow. She is a heathen through and through, vivacious, steeped in carefree heathen sin. It was only when discussing Christianity that she became sullen and recalcitrant. The Christian phrases were a thing she could put on like clothing by virtue of her natural shrewdness, yet he was in no doubt she divested herself of them as soon as she was back in the dwelling house. But perhaps, he thinks to himself, once again in doubt, perhaps salvation might have been attained gradually, as an after-effect of the christening, rather than the other way around. Perhaps she might have learned to love Jesus and to love me, the way I, perhaps, loved her. Now it is too late to find out. I have let her down. I have allowed a soul to slip from my hands.

Perhaps he will never see her again.

†

He wakes up late on the morning of the king's birthday. The day has crept in, freezing cold and dark, the remnants of dawn an effervescence on the horizon. There is some wind; he sees the snow whirl upon the ice, chasing across the islets. Towards noon the sun appears, a bombardment of frigid colour, before burning out like a tinderstick, daylight gone.

The colony has seen a frenzy of activity. The flag has been hoisted, the colony bell has tolled, and a stifled semblance of a speech has been made in honour of the king, given by a Trader clad in full uniform in front of his house and attended by his shivering wife, the Danish crew and a handful of natives come to receive their cup of aquavit. The little canon has spluttered a tenfold salute, the carpenter has blown a fanfare, the modest gathering has barked its hurrahs in time with the Trader's sabre, and now everyone has scuttled back inside, the flag has been taken down and all is dark.

Before his attendance at the Trader's house, Falck washes from head to toe. He does this in the blubber house, the only place in the colony, apart from the colony house, where the copper is always on the boil and where it is warm enough for such excesses. The cow is sheltered in the blubber house in the winter. He goes to the booth and greets her. She rubs her muzzle against his coat, nudges him, and he speaks to her:

What do you want, Roselil? If you don't tell me, I can't give it to you. He laughs, takes the hard tack from his pocket and extends his hand. She crunches it between her teeth, munches for a moment, licks her lips and looks at him once more in expectation. I see the smith has been spoiling you, he says.

He takes off his clothes, digs his hand into the soap tub and rubs the fatty substance into his skin. The carpenter, who also wishes to be clean for the occasion, douses him with buckets of hot water. He scrubs his body and limbs until the blood rushes to the skin and turns it pink. The soap is made of seal blubber and lends him the same bitter smell as greets his nostrils when entering the communal houses, the same smell that issued from the widow's warm skin garments.

Naked and steaming, he changes places with the carpenter, who is tall and awkward and forever stooped forward on account of his bad back. He fills the leather bucket and pours the water over the man. The carpenter groans with delight and scrubs himself vigorously, working the soap into a lather. When they are done, they scrub the floor, then ascend to the drying loft where their clothes are hung.

A bath is a good thing indeed, says the carpenter. One should do it more often.

Falck agrees.

He puts on his laundered and ironed cassock; his hairpiece has been hanging outside in the frost for a week and should now be relieved of louse eggs. He has washed and starched the ruff himself and shaped it into neat crisp folds with the collar iron. Sofie, Bertel's wife, takes care of his laundry for the time being: she is the widow's replacement. He pays her too well, a manifestation of the unfathomable, chronic guilt he feels with regard to Bertel, and he knows they despise him for it. The washing is done here in the blubber house where the copper is and where there is a loft for drying. His clothes are impregnated with the rancid smell of train oil and are slightly sticky to the touch, but such inconveniences are usual and the same for everyone, including the Trader and his wife, for which reason he is unbothered by it.

Once I saw a sailor who kept a bird in a cage, says the carpenter. I wonder if the Magister, having read so much, would know what bird it might have been?

A parrot? says Falck. Many sailors take them from the colonies to sell them at home.

No, it wasn't a parrot, it was a small bird with green and blue feathers and a bright yellow beak.

A canary, says Falck.

I can't ever forget its song, so pretty and sorrowful it was. It had a mate that didn't survive the voyage, so it was all alone.

How sad.

Anyway, this one died too. The climate didn't agree with it. So that was that.

Something about the carpenter's tone makes Falck stop and look at him. The bird dying could hardly have been much of a surprise to its owner. Are you trying to tell me something, Møller?

Sometimes I think the Madame is like that canary. The Trader has her locked up in a cage. I suppose he's frightened she'll fly away.

Madame Kragstedt will not fly anywhere.

Of course not. The Trader looks after her. He doesn't want anything to happen to her.

Such as what?

Everyone knows what happened a couple of years ago when the Trader was away.

Do not speak ill of your neighbour, says Falck.

I'm just saying, that's all, so the pastor is informed.

It is more than two years since that occurrence, says Falck. If you had knowledge of it, you ought to have said so before. What more do you know about the matter, Møller?

The Madame was harmed. She was like a ghost to look at for a long time after. The pastor himself was away at the time, the only ones here were myself, the smith, the cooper and the Overseer.

Do you know who harmed the Madame?

The carpenter evades his gaze. No one knows for sure. But the cooper and I spoke of it.

Falck scrutinizes him. He realizes he doesn't want to hear any more.

He didn't hear it from me, says the carpenter, but the pastor might wish to speak with the smith.

Have you talked to anyone about this, Møller?

Yes, to the cooper.

And no one else?

To you, Magister Falck.

Yes, all right, Falck snaps. That's not what I meant.

No one else, Magister. The cooper thought the smith should have been put in chains.

The cooper is dead and has his own account to settle with the Lord. The smith's salvation is none of your business, Møller. Speak to no one about this, do you understand?

Indeed, says the carpenter. It may be not my business and I'll take it with me to the grave, but now at least I've spoken and no one can come and say different. The matter is yours, Magister Falck.

When they open the door they see that the steam from the blubber house turns to ice as it collides with the freezing air and falls to the ground as snow.

✝

At the Trader's table the talk is of sickness and how to stay well while stationed at such an outpost.

Good health, says the Trader, is usually an art of omission. It is more a question of what a person refrains from doing rather than what he actually does. Would you not agree, Mr Falck?

He swallows the food in his mouth and takes a sip of wine. Most certainly, Trader.

I, for instance, refrain as far from possible from being outside in bad weather, says Kragstedt, and thereby I never catch a cold. I refrain from drunkenness and lechery and am thereby unstruck by those ailments of body and soul that result from such behaviour.

So it was sarcasm, Falck thinks to himself. Or sheer obtuseness. He concentrates on the food.

Do you not agree with me, dear? says Kragstedt, turning to his wife. The Madame says something in a brittle voice that Falck fails to hear.

Hard work, says the smith. That's the best cure for any illness. To sweat the poison out.

In Germany they have discovered an elixir of youth, says the Overseer. There's a lengthy article on the subject in my journal. It's a kind of antidote for the ills of ageing.

Then we must order a barrel of it, says the Trader, to a scatter of laughter.

The substance is being tested on mice, the Overseer continues. Their short lifespan makes them suitable for experimentation.

Revolting, the Trader mutters. Magister Falck, what do you say about this? Have not all the Lord's creatures the right to be shown respect and not be subjected to unnecessary suffering?

Well, it's only mice, says the cook. We've quite enough of them back home. I don't think the Lord will miss a couple.

I'm not so sure about that, Detlef, says the smith. Mice are in many ways better than us people. I'm very fond of mice.

Are you thinking about the same kind of mice as the rest of us, Niels? says the cook, lifting a forkful of food to his mouth. Sniggers are heard, followed by the subdued clatter of cutlery. Falck notes that Madame Kragstedt sits as though paralysed.

We eat animals, the pastor says. If these experiments can help humans to live longer then they are a good cause, worthy of the Lord's approval.

But are not our years, in the opinion of the church, dealt out to us by God? the Trader enquires.

No, as a matter of fact they are not. Such thinking is but blind faith. The Lord has equipped us with free will. Our actions, along with our inborn constitution, determine how long we shall live and how healthy we are.

Which brings us back to the beginning, says Kragstedt smugly.

Madame Kragstedt has begun to breathe more easily, Falck sees. She sends him a look and smiles cautiously. She passes him the wine and he holds up his glass and allows her to pour.

Skål, Morten Falck.

Skål, Madame Kragstedt. To your health.

Her cheeks blush slightly. Has she been drinking? he wonders. Was her husband's comment aimed at her rather than me? She has begun to look older. Small pillows of fat have appeared under her eyes, her chin is more pointed, her mouth appears sponge-like, her skin is blotched.

Yes, a toast to His Majesty the king, says Kragstedt. They rise and raise their glasses. Long may he live, with or without elixir.

If indeed he is still alive, says the smith once they have sat down again. You never know.

In that case let our toast be to his splendid son, the Crown Prince, Kragstedt says.

They say the king is not right in the head, says the carpenter.

Mad as a hatter, says Constable Bjerg, who has been silent until now. But his son is said to be all there, and fortunately he's the one running the country.

They've all been mad, ever since the days of Christian the Fourth, says the smith, the same as all the other fine gentlemen who stroll in the parks or sit with their hands in their lap. If they don't look out they'll be run over by the people, just like the Frenchmen, and then they'll end up in the hole, counts and barons alike.

Enough, says the Trader, no more of such talk, not today when we are gathered to celebrate our dear, distracted king. I would also like to propose a toast to my wife.

Again they rise amid a scraping of chairs and give three cheers, while Madame Kragstedt remains seated and looks as though she is trying to tear up her napkin.

Later, when Falck leaves, the Trader comes up to him and puts a hand on his shoulder.

Thank you for coming, Mr Falck.

Thank *you*, he says, slightly overwhelmed.

Let us put the past behind us, what do you say? I would like to ask your forgiveness for the difficulties I may have caused you.

We have both made errors, Falck replies with a stutter. Serious ones, even. Forgive me, dear Kragstedt.

They remain standing for a moment in the hall. The Trader's heavy hand feels warm against his shoulder.

†

He returns in the darkness. The widow is in his bed in the alcove; he can see the curves of her hips beneath the blanket. He sighs and sits down with the *Christiania-Kureren*, lights the lamp. The widow clatters in the kitchen with the pots and pans. Go away, he urges wearily.

He pulls out the drawer and takes out the sketches he has made of her by memory. Most are facial studies, an attempt to capture her in as few strokes as possible. There are detailed nudes, too, drawn meticulously and with feeling. He has never actually seen her naked. What he has drawn is what he wanted to see: a wild woman he has captured and attempted to tame. The sketches are not very good. His hands have begun to tremble; his pencil is no longer as sure as before. He tears the paper into pieces and tosses them into the coal bucket, where they flare up and dwindle. Now she is gone. Now there is the bottle and the *Christiania-Kureren*.

But the bottle is nearly empty. There is not enough for an evening in festive company with himself. Either he must fetch new provisions or else go early to bed. He takes off his clothes and crawls beneath the reindeer skin.

Yet he is too angry to sleep. Angry at whom? He has no idea. The widow, perhaps. Or the Trader. Or himself.

He climbs out of the alcove again, hopping about on one leg as he puts on stockings and boots. And then he is outside. The fire-watcher's lantern is nowhere to be seen, and no people are about. Most likely they indulged in the Trader's punch after he left and are now sleeping. The windows of the colony house are dark. Above his head flows a phosphorescent river, an undulating S in the sky, greenly iridescent, blue, white, the firmament meanders and squirms, flicking its tail, as though it has become unstable and is being sucked through a hole, drowning in its own maelstrom of galaxies uncontrollably expanding and dissolving into long, billowing ribbons, utterly silent. He has never before seen it this magnificent. The snow absorbs all light; he is illuminated from below and above, a figure in a magic lantern. He hurries, so as not to be discovered.

He knows the way and would be able to walk the path with his eyes shut, up to the ladder, up to the hatch, to breathe his alcohol fumes into the lock. He stands there now, in the long loft of the colony house. His nerves settle. He closes the hatch behind him and lights the lamp, places it on top of a barrel and listens. But not a sound can be heard from the Trader's rooms below.

He narrows his eyes towards the long shadows that sway like seasickness upon the planks of the floor, breathes in the smell of the food store and tarred timber. Five heavy barrels stand beneath the sloping walls, three smaller casks of aquavit in front of them, moreover barrels of grain and oats stacked in pyramids, bales of sticky hops and shag tobacco, sweet and aromatic. A pair of hams and a leg of lamb hang suspended from a beam in their sacking of flax. The pungent smell of salted, fat-covered meat makes his mouth water and his stomach rumble ominously. He puts a tentative foot forward. He is directly above the sleeping chamber. One creak from a loose plank may wake the Trader or his wife. But the house is solid. He can hardly hear his own footsteps.

He opens a barrel, scoops a hand inside and tastes, only to recoil in disgust: gunpowder! Now it is spilt and he scuffs it with his foot so as to disperse the substance and avoid its discovery. The loft is full of barrels and crates he recognizes from *Der Frühling*. He needs a dram to steady his hand and clear his head.

He rummages about, rather casually, as though he were at home, humming quietly to himself as he lifts the lid of a keg and notes that this time he has discovered a spicy aquavit. He considers he might remain here seated on the floor and drink a little; it will leave room for more of it in his flask. He finds the cup on its hook and dips it into the barrel, drinks a few mouthfuls, thinks about the young Miss Schultz, the eunuch, the widow. He thinks about Madame Kragstedt asleep and snoring but a few ells beneath him, about Roselil and the milking girl on the farm back in Lier, the way she glanced over her shoulder at him and laughed, her upper lip curling back to expose the pink flesh of her gums, her squirting milk at him, him catching the jet in his mouth, or else being drenched, her throaty laughter at his injured expression. He fills the cup again, forgets where he is, sits and stares out ahead into the dim light.

Then at once he stiffens. Voices. He hears footsteps, the creak of a door. Someone speaks beneath him. Madame Kragstedt. Instinctively he rises to his haunches, ready to snuff out the light and conceal himself behind a barrel if anyone should venture to the loft. The Trader's voice replies. He relaxes. There seems to be no alarm. A door creaks again and shuts. The Madame has gone to the privy. He feels the good aquavit warm his blood, pictures with arousal the Madame's figure bent forward on the lavatory below, her stockings around her ankles, shift drawn up, the spray of her urine.

He collects himself. He is cold. It is time to fill his flask and return home.

He wonders what the Trader wants with so many kegs of aquavit. It is – not to put too fine a point on it – a sin, the vice of greed, to hoard so much provision without sharing it with others. He ought to take the Trader to task, reprove him, lash him with some biblical quotes. His anger returns. He feels it now to be a personal affront that he should be compelled to sneak up here in order to secure his winter sustenance. This time he will take with him enough to ensure that his trips back and forth become less frequent.

The keg is heavy and unwieldy. He tries to hoist it on to his shoulder, only for it to jar against the ceiling, and he realizes he must carry it in his arms. At the same time he needs to hold the lamp and the ham he has lifted from its hook. He staggers somewhat, momentarily unsteadied. The aquavit sloshes inside its wood, the ham slaps at his hip. He veers to the side, but recovers course. A plank creaks underfoot and yet he has no fear of being heard. Stooping forward, he proceeds cautiously towards the hatch. The lamp swings unmanageably in its cradle, striking against the ham. He wriggles his hand, attempting to shift the lamp so that it may hang from the crook of his arm. But the manoeuvre fails, the lamp falls to the floor. He hears a shatter of glass, looks down and sees that the flame has escaped its chamber and now ignites the gunpowder he has scuffed across the floor and which remains on his boot. He dances a jig to stamp it out, but succeeds only in causing it to spread. He pauses, the keg of aquavit cradled in his arms, and tries to focus his thoughts. But the fire spreads like spilled water across the planks, a blue breaking sea. The gunpowder flares, flames rise and crackle, and then he hears voices, downstairs at first, then outside. He recognizes the Trader's hoarse modulation as he roars out the alarm; the cry of the smith, who has the fire-watch; and he heads for the hatch, the cumbersome keg still clutched to his chest.

Jørgen? he hears below him. Jørgen! It is the Madame: she sounds so forlorn, solitary, as helpless as a captured bird.

Kragstedt shouts back. Return to bed! Hardly the soundest advice, Falck thinks, jiggling his legs to be free of the flame.

The gun! he hears Kragstedt holler. Bring the gun and I'll give the bloody thieves the fright of their lives! He hears footsteps running, more voices.

Now it's the whipping post and chains, he surmises, tap dancing towards the hatch. Behind him the fire spreads, flames lick the first barrels, the timber stanchions, then strive towards the hams at the ceiling, and he is cold no more. Orange tongues of fire, flashes of blue, red leaping flame. I know you, he realizes, the eunuch warned me about you.

Below, the Madame calls out again. Jørgen, I smell smoke!

Smoke, indeed, he says to himself, the whole loft is full of it and I am suffocating. But now he is at the hatch, he opens it and is too late, he sees, for the Trader and his men are already ascending the ladder with loaded flintlocks and eyes flashing with rage.

Who's there? the Trader demands. Halt in the name of the king!

Which is easier said than done when one's boots are on fire and one's arse is as hot as a frying pan. He senses the rush of air that is sucked into the loft, as though the room were taking a deep breath, and he sees how it causes the fire to blaze up behind him. He sees the carpenter, the abstainer, the soberest man in the colony excepting the natives. Their eyes meet, a millisecond of recognition, perhaps another of bemusement, before the carpenter throws up his arms in front of his face at this sudden encounter with flames and smoke, and Falck is about to speak; to say he is sorry would be the most appropriate utterance, but as he bends down to climb through the hatch the pressure leaps inside the loft, which is now a powder room, and he feels an abrupt force against his back: the hatch is the gun barrel, he the grapeshot, and as the roof is blown from the colony house he is projected high above the snow-clad fells towards the shimmering Northern Lights, out into the universe and inwards into the depths of his own being; he dissolves into the aurora, is torn from his own flailing body, a human cannonball, and his keg of aquavit blown out into the winter's night, expelled into a place where even the silence has no name.

†

When he wakes up he is safe and sound in a cot, naked though wrapped in skins. The ceiling is low; he would bump his head if he tried to sit up, which he has absolutely no intention of doing. A lamp burns; the room is warm. It is a tidy chamber, though small, a cosy den. The only thing wrong is that it leans rather drastically to one side.

And now he understands. He is back in his cabin on board *Der Frühling*. His voyage is incomplete, he has yet to reach his destination, he has dreamed a nightmare of four years. Or is he on his way home? And why does the cabin lean thus? Is the ship about to sink?

The widow leans over him.

Awake?

He moves his lips. He does not know if any sound comes out.

She holds his head and gives him some water. It is the strongest water he has ever tasted. He splutters. The widow laughs.

Spit it out. There is plenty here. A whole keg.

Go away, he breathes. You are not real.

Go away yourself, Priest, if you can. This is my chamber.

He sleeps. When he wakes up she is gone. I knew you were not real, he says to himself. Such relief.

It dawns on him where he is. The *Taasinge Slot*, the wreck. This must be the captain's cabin. He must have dragged himself here, half-conscious. He remembers the loft, the burning gunpowder, the boots of the men on the ladder. The darkness. The aurora. And then a deeper darkness that ought to have been death, followed by one of the lower levels of Purgatory, but apparently it was not.

Behind his eyelids the light is removed. He opens his eyes, but still it is dark. He fumbles for the tallow candle, but succeeds only in knocking some objects to the floor. He falls back on to the cot. In reality he is lying halfway up the wall on account of the leaning vessel.

And then the widow is with him again. She sits up against the bulkhead, cutting hunks from a ham and putting them in her mouth. He groans. When will this nightmare end?

Slept well? There is both kindness and sarcasm in her voice. It is a surprisingly delicate dream.

Good ham, says the widow. But the priest won't be able to chew it with such miserable stumps instead of teeth. Here. She takes a lump from her mouth and puts it inside his. He presses it against his palate and sucks on it. It is salty and tastes of the Trader's loft.

The widow removes her outer garments, then climbs into the cot with him, shuddering with cold.

Warm me up.

It is you, he says.

I live here, she says. I have lived here for some time.

How have you managed?

My brother looks after me.

I didn't know you had a brother.

Neither did I. We only just found out.

I see.

Soon we will leave, you and I, she says.

Together? Where will we go?

To Habakuk and Maria Magdalene. They are waiting for you.

I must remain in my calling, he says. My work is incomplete.

You have done enough, she says. The colony house is burned to the ground. The carpenter is dead. The Madame has lost her mind. What more do you need to do?

He says nothing for some time. He allows the information to settle.

Do they know who caused the blaze?

I know, she says.

When his thoughts become clearer she tells him what happened. Every man, woman and child in the colony took part in extinguishing the fire. She saw the charred body of the carpenter, burning hot, the snow melting around it. Constable Bjerg was badly burned, but survived. She saw him come running from the crew's quarters, pursued by a flaming tail of fire. The smith was unharmed and seemed even to be in his element. He poked at the carpenter's corpse and said it was as good as fried!

And Madame Kragstedt, says Falck, what about her?

The Trader ran backwards and forwards in front of the burning house, the widow says. He called out for his wife, but everyone was sure she had perished. The house was consumed. No one could get anywhere near because of the heat. Joists collapsed, windows burst in loud explosions. Each time a keg of aquavit went up there was a rushing sound followed by a bang that caused everyone to duck. The Trader stood with his hands at his sides, staring up at the house. The smith said something about intruders in the loft. He was of the opinion some of the natives had been out plundering.

Falck says nothing.

Then someone screamed. At first the widow thought it was the fire, so inhuman was the sound. Then it came again and everyone turned and looked in the same direction. It was the strangest sight, says the widow. From the steep incline behind the colony house a figure came floating across the snow. It appeared in the light from the flames, twirling like some great flake of soot, but then she saw that the figure was flailing; it screamed again, as hoarsely as a raven. It sought out the house, as though it wanted to go in, and then everyone could see who it was; they shouted to her and the smith ran up and took hold of her, dragged her away and fell on top of her. I kneeled beside her, says the widow, but I could not bring myself to touch her, for she stank so foully and was covered from head to toe in some slimy substance, and then of course I realized what had happened.

The Madame was in the privy when the house exploded, says Falck, and recalls her footsteps below him as he stood in the loft. She was covered in excrement.

She had been on the lavatory reading, says the widow. She would do so often when I worked at the house, sometimes for hours on end. The Madame is fortunate to be such an avid reader, though she did not seem happy.

What book was she reading? Falck asks.

†

He must have suffered serious concussion; he feels dizzy; his head aches and he is pained by a sense of everything taking place at staggered intervals. His mind is addled by the kind of distraction whereby one finds one's own utterances to be clear, while others seem to speak in a delirium. Apart from that, he is fine. He discovers the keg of aquavit she has recovered and brought to the wreck. He drinks a little. He offers the widow a cup. She drinks.

I knew you would be glad for the aquavit, she says. It was heavy to carry. I almost gave up.

It was kind of you, he says.

The blubber lamp hangs by a cord from the ceiling, the peat wick burns unevenly; she attends to it the whole time, straightening it with the trimmer. In the evening she gives him boiled stockfish, which he devours ravenously. She chatters away, though he does not understand a word.

This is the new home the Lord hath prepared for me, he thinks to himself. Thank you, Lord.

He is unclear as to whether the matter of Madame Kragstedt and the fire was something he dreamed, so he asks the widow and she tells him the story again, about how the Madame came floating down from the incline like an angel covered in filth from the privy tub.

How awful, he says.

But he does not think it awful at all. He finds it banal and tedious.

†

Everyone is asking about you, says the widow. You must go back to the colony; otherwise they will find out what happened. Madame Kragstedt is out of her mind; she goes about in the warehouse where she and the Trader are living until the new colony house is built, searching for her things. My brother would like to see you back, too. His son is ill. Perhaps you can help.

Your brother, says Falck. Have I met your brother?

You can meet him later today, she says. He is coming here to collect you.

The captain's cabin of the *Taasinge Slot* is warm. The horizon leans like seasickness in the portholes, half the planks are broken away and the gaps filled with whatever materials were at hand. I am content here, he protests. I wish to remain here for the rest of my days.

The widow smiles and shakes her head.

This is my home, she says. Yours is in the colony.

I thought you said you were going to take me to Eternal Fjord.

I will. But the time is not right.

The door opens. A man steps into the diagonal cabin. He stands with one foot on the floor, the other against the bulkhead.

Magister Falck.

Falck lifts his head in the cot and stares at him.

Bertel? Is that you?

Yes, it is me. And here you are, Priest. What a cosy little arrangement.

The widow steps up and kisses him.

Magister Falck, Bertel says again. Everyone is looking for you. I don't know why you are hiding here, nor do I wish to know. But I think it best that you come home.

He sits up, supporting himself on stiffened arms, and glances from one to the other. Do you two know each other?

I told you, I found out I had a brother, says the widow.

THE EIGHTH COMMANDMENT

Questions and Answers

(1791)

The Eighth Commandment, as it is most plainly to be taught by a father to his family:
'Thou shalt not bear false witness against thy neighbour.'
What does this imply?
Answer: That we should fear and love God, so that we may not deceitfully belie, betray and backbite our neighbour, nor raise an evil report; but we should excuse and speak well of him and direct all things for the best.

Bertel decides to try his luck fishing while there is still ice on the fjord. He gathers his tackle, lines, hooks, ice pick. Outside, on the roof of the house, he has left a pair of sealskin mittens, now frozen stiff. He cuts them into strips and puts them on the hooks for bait.

The boy wants to go with him.

You are not well enough yet, says Bertel. Promise me you will stay in bed. We'll go out in the spring and then I will teach you to fire the gun.

Why not today? I promise to wrap up warm. There is an accusing tone about his voice, as if it is his father's fault that he must stay in bed all winter.

Bertel is in dejected mood as he makes his way across the ice, but the cold air freshens his thoughts and quickly brightens his aspect. On his feet are the skis he has covered with sealskin, the hairs of which are faced to prevent him from sliding backwards. He makes good speed, rounding the promontory where the wreck of the *Taasinge Slot* lies, then entering the bay where sometimes the wolf fish gather in the shallow waters. The sun makes the sheer fell light up like a torch. He chooses a spot where he knows there is a good current and where the ice is therefore thinner, and begins to hack his way down to the water. With his bowl he scoops up the mush of ice that collects as he works, dousing the edges of the hole with water until a hard, smooth rim is formed. When the hole is nearly an ell in width, he drops in his line and hooks. A bundle of nails from the Trade is his plummet. He feels it touch the bottom, then stands and jerks the line, his back against the cold and his skin hat pulled down to cover his neck.

A raven circles at the fell, drawing figures of eight in the air; it turns with such ease, now and then raggedly cawing out, watching him. He smiles and realizes he is praying to it, the spirit of the raven, praying for a catch, a heathen practice in which he ought not to indulge, even in secret. He says the Lord's Prayer out loud to make up for it, only then to add: Great Raven, give me a big fish and I shall leave its guts for you.

Presently he feels a tug on the line. He can feel what kind of a fish it is; each species has its own way of taking the bait; some do not struggle, others, the small ones especially, fight as though possessed. This one resists, then resigns and becomes but dead weight. He heaves it on to the ice without difficulty and is contented. A wolf fish!

It is a good fish, almost an arm's length, perhaps ten pounds in weight; the head is large and knobbled, the eyes stare emptily into death. Ever since he was a boy and his uncle told him that if they manage to bite they will not release until they sense the bone is crushed, he has been afraid of the strong jaws and sharp, fang-like teeth of the wolf fish. Swiftly he stabs the knife into its head and watches the sullen mouth stiffen. He makes a long incision in the belly and allows the liver, stomach and intestines to spill out on to the snow as he has promised. Then he fastens the line to the lower jaw and drags his catch off across the ice with a cry over his shoulder of *takanna!* – dinner! He looks back and sees the raven descend in decreasing circles, then land.

COLONY AND CATECHISM   357

A man does wisely, he thinks to himself, to stay friends with the raven. He hastens to say the Lord's Prayer once more.

At home he hangs the fish by the door. Later he will boil it. His mouth waters at the thought of the thick layer of fat beneath the skin, how it will open between his teeth and the juices seep into his mouth.

The boy is lying with his book open, exactly as before.

You have not been up, have you?

No.

Stubborn. Defensive.

Have you been out, boy?

Silence.

He is afraid of being found out, yet he also wants me to know that he can defy me, Bertel thinks to himself.

He goes up to the bed and pulls the covers aside. The boy is fully dressed, the bedding wet with melted snow. The boy grins cheekily, eyes fixed firmly on his book.

You have been out to see them put the roof on the new colony house, he says, taking the boy's chin in his hand, turning his face to make him look at his father. Then he strokes the boy's hair. Was it exciting?

They fired the cannon, says the boy. Three times.

Yes, I heard the salute. Did they hit anything?

The boy laughs. They laugh together. Then Bertel shows him the wolf fish and they help each other prepare it. For the first time in a long while, the boy eats up.

All will be well again, Bertel thinks.

Question: How may the world be categorized?
Answer: Into the spiritual world and the physical world.

Spring, light, renewed hope. But also: thaw, wet floors, soaked stockings, dripping ceilings, cold feet and coughs. The boy has a fever; he lies staring up with eyes that are moist. On the now-returned Falck's instruction, Bertel lays a cold compress on his forehead, a warm compress on his chest. He is not entirely convinced of the wisdom of such opposing remedies, but he is reluctant to do otherwise. He knows the priest has studied medicine; he speaks often of the lectures he attended and of how he only pursued theology to appease his ageing father. Bertel has no choice but to trust in his judgement.

How are you feeling? he asks the boy.

Well.

Oddly enough, the answer makes him feel even more anxious.

He asks Falck to come and attend to the boy again. The priest does not appear to be in the best of health himself. Besides his bad eye, which resembles fish meat, white and matt and presenting a lattice of tiny red veins, Morten Falck is rather sickly of appearance and has acquired the peculiar habit of frequently tipping his head to one side, as though he were listening out for something. He speaks much of his cow, the only decent being in the entire colony, he says, which presumably is why she is allowed to maintain such good health. The cook is laid up again, this time definitively so. Falck considers the man has but weeks to live at most. The Kragstedts have moved into the new colony house, though the Madame continues to wander about in search of her former belongings and seems unable to grasp the fact that they were destroyed in the fire. She speaks in torrents of nonsense; the Trader sits brooding in his chair facing the wall. Hammer has moved out into his workshop on a permanent basis; he labours at his anvil day and night, but no one knows what he is working on, perhaps not even himself. Constable Bjerg seems to have recovered from his burns, though appears consumed by religious longing and speaks of travelling into the fjord and joining the prophets, no matter that it would hardly be good for him.

Even I, says Falck with a cough, who have always considered myself to be an enlightened and rational individual, have had certain, er, experiences of late.

What kind of experiences? Bertel asks.

Have you not heard or seen anything? Falck replies. Trumpet calls? Hymns? People who, er, ought not to be there?

I have enough with mortal matters, says Bertel curtly. But Magister Krogh did speak of such things before he did away with himself.

I saw my poor deceased mother last week, says Falck with melancholy. I wonder what it means? And the gold I washed from a river in the north has disappeared.

Gold? says Bertel.

Stolen, says Falck. While I was staying on the wreck. I don't suppose you would know anything about it, Bertel?

I didn't steal the priest's gold! Bertel snaps. I didn't know he had any. Was it not rather careless of him to leave it lying about in the Mission house?

Indeed, says Falck sadly. It is my own fault, I know. There was a whole new life there, Bertel, it was enough to get me settled back home, a fortune. And now it is gone.

He sits down next to the boy and senses their spirits lift. He asks him about his reading and the boy shows him the book he is on. Falck flicks through the pages; the boy stops him to point out an illustration and read a passage aloud. Falck calls him Professor Bertelsen and they agree it is a fine title. He opens his medical bag.

The boy sits up, pulls his shirt above his chest and follows Falck's instructions. They exchange banter and chuckle. Falck lets him borrow his stethoscope and pulls up his own shirt. The boy listens intently.

I can hear the pastor's heart.

Oh, thank goodness, I must still be alive then, says Falck.

Wait, I can hear something else, too, says the boy.

Falck sits with his back hunched towards him as he moves the chestpiece about. He looks at him over his shoulder. What do you hear, Professor Bertelsen?

Music, says the boy and laughs. A whole brass band. It think it must be the royal musicians.

Bertel stands watching as they jest and speak of things he does not understand and is excluded from. He feels a stab of jealousy.

Falck takes back the stethoscope. He taps his fingers against the boy's back, then his chest. He listens to his lungs, retracts the eyelids and studies the mucous membrane, feels his throat and under his arms. Bertel tries to infer something from the priest's facial expressions.

Well? He looks enquiringly at Falck as he returns the stethoscope to his bag.

A minor case of consumption, says Falck. When the summer comes with warmer weather, it will subside.

He has been sick every winter for years, says Bertel.

Childhood is a perilous voyage, says Falck with a mournful smile. Once the beard begins to show on the chin, it will usually be overcome.

That will be a while yet, says Bertel.

Give him salt, Falck instructs.

Salt?

A tablespoon every day, to facilitate the flow of the bodily fluids. Moreover, plenty of fresh water. And fatty food, he adds. Do you make sure to eat what your father prepares for you?

The boy nods.

Liar, says Bertel.

The boy looks away.

He will hardly eat a thing, says Bertel. Not so much as a spoonful.

A little later Falck returns with a jug of fresh milk. He makes the boy drink a glass of it.

I don't like it, says the boy.

Hold your nose when you swallow, Falck says, then you won't taste it.

The boy pulls a face, but does as he is told.

Falck pats him on the shoulder. Professor Bertelsen, you must promise me to drink a jug of milk every day, otherwise you will not be as clever and wise as your father. Will you promise me that?

The boy nods.

He takes the salt as Falck has prescribed, swallowing it dutifully, though gagging with revulsion. But when Bertel pours him a glass of milk in the evening he will not have it.

The priest has told you to, says Bertel.

My stomach hurts, the boy complains.

That's because it's empty, Bertel tells him. If you drink a little or eat something it will get better, just like Pastor Falck said.

But the boy has turned his face to the wall and refuses to either eat or drink. Bertel sees the hint of a victorious smile on his face and knows this is a battle he cannot win.

Question: What may be noted in general about the true movement of the planets?

Answer: Any planet exhibits a double movement; that is: (1) Its orbit around the sun, and (2) Its rotation around its own axis.

He gets Lydia, his sister, to come and mind him while he is away with Mr Falck. She brings her daughter with her, the boy's cousin, he reasons, and at the same time his father's sister and her own mother's sister, Oxbøl's child and grandchild. An incestuous mess. How strange to have these new people in one's family, he thinks. And yet he is in many ways glad to have met his sister. He sees that they resemble each other, in appearance and temperament, and that both resemble their secret father, old Oxbøl. She is the only person who knows who his father is, apart from Sofie, who has guessed. They are together in a shameful matter, something that has hitherto been silence and great solitude. Now they speak of it occasionally, he and his sister, and for this reason life has become somewhat easier.

The visit livens the boy up, and a couple of days later he rises from bed. The children sit at the table. The boy reads aloud for his cousin, explains to her the trajectories of the planets and that of the Moon around the Earth. The girl stares at him with a smile that is at once febrile, gormless and inbred. Her head nods with fatigue.

Are you listening to what I say? the boy asks.

Yes, says the girl. Her elbows lean against the edge of the table. They keep falling down. She puts them up again and rests her chin in her hand.

If you don't listen, you won't learn anything and then you will be no better than the savages.

I'm listening.

What was the last thing I said?

Something about water?

The properties of water, says the boy. What are the properties of water?

I don't know what a property is.

What does it do?

Make you less thirsty.

The boy sighs. Go and lie down, you're tired.

The girl shuffles over to the cot and pulls a blanket over her head. She coughs in her sleep. The boy remains seated at the table, turning the pages of the book in the lamplight. Bertel lies secretly watching him, with curbed affection. He has become long-limbed during the past year, but skinny too. If only all that reading could put some weight on him, he thinks.

His sister appears not to care much for her daughter. She gave her over to the natives while she was in the Trader's household and could fill her belly every day. Now that she is no longer in their employ, the girl's presence seems to annoy her. Bertel cannot understand her. He has considered adopting the child and thinks it would be good for the boy to have company. But he finds it unpleasant to think of who the father is and that his own inherited characteristics, so to speak, are doubled within her.

In May the girl falls ill with the fever and dies quickly and without drama. She is discovered by Sofie in the morning, stretched out at the foot end of the sleeping bench with her arms at her sides and wrapped in a blanket. The boy has prepared her. He sits huddled at the opposite end of the bench with his knees drawn up to his chest, arms folded around his legs, staring out of the window with his fringe falling down over his tired eyes.

Why didn't you say anything? Bertel asks him.

She was dead. Can you wake the dead, perhaps?

The girl is buried the same day. She was unchristened, but had attended Falck's instruction, so the priest prays for her and they are allowed to put her to rest close to where the carpenter lies. A handful of people stand at the grave. The sound of the hard soil as it strikes the small, bony bundle at the bottom of the hole is harrowing. Bertel looks across at his sister. She stares into the grave with wide eyes and looks as if she might jump in at any moment.

Now I suppose he will be glad, she says.

Who? asks Bertel.

You know who I mean. Her father. Our father.

Oh, him.

Yes, him. He hates his children. He hates us. It is our curse.

They stare at each other for some time without speaking.

He is old, says Bertel. He will die soon.

Ha! He will never die.

The Lord will punish him for what he has done, says Bertel, borrowing Falck's standard response to any malice he can do nothing about.

The Lord would seem to prefer to punish his children, she says, her eyes seeking the grave again. And we are many. You know that, don't you?

Question: What is a spirit?
Answer: A single being with intelligence and will.

The boy starts to feel better. He stops coughing; his fever recedes and he even begins to eat the hard tack that Bertel soaks for him in boiling water and sugar. He seems cheerful. Bertel takes him out hunting for ptarmigan on the fell and they ascend two of the peaks behind the colony. He speaks chummily with him, but for some reason he is unable to strike the same chord with the boy as Falck.

This is our country, he says to him on the fell. Beyond those peaks

lies the old colony where I grew up, and the fell the Dutchmen called
Zuikerbroot, from which the colony takes its name. I will show you the
place sometime. Further north lies Holsteinsborg and to the east is the
mainland, which is very inhospitable because of steep mountains and ice,
but which teems with reindeer.

The boy gazes out over the sea. What lies on the other side?

A foreign country, says Bertel. Foreign people.

Can a person sail to it?

People can sail everywhere, says Bertel.

The boy nods.

Do you still want to be a ship's captain?

I don't know, says the boy in truth. Perhaps, if I get better.

If you become a priest you could journey across and preach to the
savages who live there, Bertel says, trying to make the prospect sound
attractive.

Like Mr Falck? says the boy, and laughs. Then he says: Is it true my
grandfather is a priest?

Who told you that?

Milka said so.

What does she know about it? Bertel snaps. That stupid girl. Your
grandfather's name was Jens, like your own.

But Milka said her father and yours were the same man, and that is
why our skin is so fair.

Milka was just a silly child, says Bertel. With little reason. I tell you,
your grandfather's name was Jens. He was a true Greenlander, a great
hunter.

But we don't look like Greenlanders.

Enough nonsense! No one should be ashamed of what they are.

They exchange not a word for the rest of the day. When they return
home the boy climbs silently into bed and opens his book. He does not
eat what Bertel puts in front of him. Bertel regrets having lost his temper
and can do little about the boy punishing him in this way.

†

Late in the month it is time for the spring voyage. Together with Falck he sails into the skerries and seeks out the natives who have settled for the summer on the outermost islands, where they hunt the smaller whales and seals. Sofie does not wish for his sister to mind the boy, so she has asked permission to have him with her in the colony house, a request the Madame has granted. Bertel cares little to think of the boy being in the Danish household all day. He does not trust Kragstedt and the Madame's mood is unstable following the accident. Sofie says she often shouts at her for petty matters, and that afterwards she repents and falls on her knees, weeping, begging to be forgiven, which is every bit as bad.

If we could afford it I would hand in my notice, Sofie says. I cannot abide the Madame any longer and I think it would do her good to have someone else instead. Your sister doesn't go there either, after the accident.

Bertel has thought upon the matter. If she stopped working for the Trader they would have to make ends meet on twenty rigsdalers a year, as well as doing without the food she brings home with her from the colony house. If they were on their own, he would say she should give notice, of that he is in little doubt. But the boy has need of the extra butter in his diet and the sugar and meat that is left over from the meals.

Sometimes I think we would do better to join them, says Sofie.

Join who?

Habakuk and his wife. It is said they share everything there. No one is allowed to go to bed hungry.

You shouldn't believe everything that's said. They probably say the same things about us. My sister was not treated well when she was there, you remember that, I hope? They very nearly drowned her.

Perhaps it was her own fault, says Sofie. She can be difficult, your sister, in case you were unaware of it. Besides, that was before their new faith.

Their false doctrine, says Bertel, correcting her. If you, who are christened, were to join them, the Church could punish you and put you in the pillory.

But life here in the colony is harsh, she complains. We are not free, we Greenlanders, we are like slaves.

If you stood chained to the whipping post you would soon have another conception of freedom.

Question: What may be noted in general about the movement of the Earth?

Answer: The Earth moves once around the Sun in one year and revolves once every twenty-four hours around its axis, like the wheel around its axle as the wagon is propelled forward.

The trip into the skerries lasts three weeks. He and Falck are alone. They travel by whatever boats happen to come by that have room for them. They have taken the chessboard along. In good weather they sit outside the tent in the evenings with their game between them. He can see that the colour is returning to the priest's cheeks. His own outlook brightens; he sails out in the kayak to shoot birds with small arrows like the old natives; his wrist recalls the fine technique he learned from his father, or rather from his stepfather, Jens. Magister Falck gathers eggs of the long-tailed duck, skua and black guillemot, and for dinner they boil the eggs and pluck a bird to roast over the open fire. Bertel savours being away from the colony and its problems. A small measure of ill-feeling still lingers between him and the priest, who seemingly continues to suspect him of stealing his gold. He hears it in Falck's voice when he speaks of his lost fortune, how he washed the nuggets from the shallows, how much he had anticipated selling them for on his return home, the things on which the money could have been spent. Bertel ignores him. If the priest wants to suspect him of being a thief, then let him!

When they return to the colony in June he sees how the boy has changed. He has gained weight and is almost ruddy with good health. He greets his father joyfully and shows him the schoolbooks he has been given by Madame Kragstedt. It would seem the Madame has taken it upon herself to educate him, and according to Sofie it is at least as beneficial to her as to the boy.

But I am the boy's teacher, he says. I don't want him going there to become fine and mighty and confused.

The Madame will be sorry to hear it, says Sofie.

The boy is furious when Bertel informs him that he must cease his visits to the colony house. You want to decide everything! he shouts, with tears of indignation. You don't care if I'm happy, as long as you can decide!

I only want what's best for you, says Bertel, astonished.

Then let me go to school with Haldora.

Haldora?

Madame Kragstedt.

Hm. Soon you'll be telling me the two of you are to marry.

You can't decide over me, says the boy. If I want to go there, I will.

You must understand, Bertel tells the boy, who now turns his back on him in the cot, they are not like us, they are our guests here, they do not belong. In a few years they will be gone, but we will still be here.

He's so happy to go there, Sofie says, smoothing things over. What can be wrong about it? And he eats well. You can see for yourself how much better he looks.

And you, he says, turning to face her. Do not make yourself master of your own husband! He lunges forward and strikes her on the cheek. Immediately he is overcome by remorse and wants to apologize, but feels it would make him look weak in the boy's eyes, so instead he says: Make us some dinner. I'm hungry. For the rest of the evening Sofie is as cold as ice and shuns him. He has never struck her before.

The next day the boy lies in bed. He refuses to get up, refuses to eat and narrows his eyes when Bertel speaks to him.

He is upset that he cannot go to the house, says Sofie.

Thanks for your help! he says, and she steps back in fear that he will strike her again.

The boy's protest lasts for three days. Then Bertel submits.

If you are home by three o'clock each day and show me what work you have done with Madame Kragstedt, he says, then you may go there.

The boy gets up. Bertel is annoyed by the triumphant, conceited look on his face, but makes an effort to be especially kind to him that evening.

The next day at three o'clock the boy has yet to return home. Bertel sits waiting for him. At four o'clock he still has not come. When the clock says half past four he can no longer endure it. He puts on his cap, walks up to the colony house and knocks on the door.

Sofie opens up. He can tell she feels guilty.

Where is he?

Dearest, he is enjoying himself so much with the Madame. She is teaching him to write.

Call him out. Otherwise I shall come and get him myself.

She vanishes inside. He hears voices from within, Madame Kragstedt's and the boy's. The boy's laughter, a chuckle. Eventually he appears in the doorway. He ignores his father completely, edges past him and walks home.

Question: What are the bodies that belong to the animal kingdom?
Answer: To the animal kingdom belong all such bodies on Earth as
have organic structure, life, senses and discretionary movement.

In the evening, when Bertel asks him what he has learned from the Madame, he relents somewhat and shows him his exercise books. The Madame is teaching me script, he says.

You write neatly, says Bertel.

I'm to write something for tomorrow.

What will you write about?

My family.

I see, he says, rather curtly. Does the Madame wish to know about your family?

It's one of the exercises in the book.

None of your nonsense about a Danish grandfather, do you hear? says Bertel.

Yes, father, says the boy obediently. He remains seated at the table until late in the evening, writing in his exercise book.

Tomorrow he is to be home by three, Bertel says to Sofie.

Every morning his wife rubs between her legs and puts her fingers to her nose to pensively sniff. I think I am with child, she says. I have not bled for two months.

He feels happy. How long have you known?

I'm not certain of it yet. But if there is a child it will come at the beginning of the new year.

He kisses her. Thank you, he says.

You must not hit me again, she says.

No, I shall never hit you again. The Lord is my witness and my judge. Forgive me.

Dear man, Sofie says, and places a hand cautiously on his cheek.

In the afternoon the boy fails to appear at the appointed time. At four o'clock Bertel goes from the colony and sits down on the rocks to stare out at the sea until his temper has cooled. On his return the boy has still not shown up. Not until evening does he come, together with his mother. He has put plates out for them. They eat their porridge in silence. The boy sits down to write, apparently unmoved by the tense air. Bertel feels his anger gradually subside.

What are you writing about tonight? he asks.

About a person I admire, the boy replies. It's my exercise for tomorrow.

And who might that person be? Bertel enquires in the frail, forlorn hope that it is he.

Moses, says the boy.

A good choice, Bertel says, relieved that he has not chosen someone living.

But later, after the boy has fallen asleep, he steals a look at his exercise book and sees that he has not written about Moses at all, but about Crown Prince Frederik.

The Prince Regent is a good and loving person. He cares inordinately for his children, including those who inhabit his colonies, among them Greenland and the colony of Sukkertoppen. Whenever someone in his great kingdom dies, His Royal Highness weeps heart-rendingly and prays for their soul.

Bertel closes the exercise book. The boy has lied to me, he tells himself. It is a sin he must confess and repent for the sake of his salvation. He leaves the exercise book open on the table, but when the boy rises the next day he picks it up without any sign of a guilty conscience. Perhaps he has forgotten that he lied, Bertel muses. He says nothing.

The next day the boy remains at the colony house until evening. Bertel refrains from questioning him and risking more lies. Perhaps it is I who am in need of absolution, he thinks to himself, since I have such an effect on my son that he feels he must lie to me. He considers speaking to Mr Falck on the matter, but the priest is keeping himself to himself at the moment. Days may pass without a sign of him, and when eventually he appears he resembles a wild man and stinks of aquavit. He asks his sister if she lies with him, but she denies it. The priest lies in the ship and drinks, she says. He has a whole keg of aquavit there.

Where did he get it?

He found it after the explosion, she says. It flew over the fell.

Then it belongs to the Trade, says Bertel.

She gives a shrug.

She still lives in the communal house. It is there she always returns, there she feels most at home – or perhaps it is the only place where she feels safe. He realizes that he does not know her at all. She grew up with an aunt, her mother having died giving birth to her. They lived like all other natives, wintering inside the fjords, remaining in the skerries for as long as possible in the months of summer. When she told him she was a daughter of Oxbøl's he felt annoyance, hatred, compassion, disgust, a chaos of emotions. She had already guessed they had the same father; she had sensed it, she said, and Sofie had known for some time. It is about time you found out too, brother. His own mother is still living, further north at Holsteinsborg, where the old priest still wreaks his havoc. He cannot understand how she can endure to live in the same colony as Oxbøl. But it is several years since he last saw her. Most of his life he has avoided the place in which he was born and grew up. He receives the occasional greeting from his mother, by the kayak messenger that serves the two colonies.

Bertel wonders who it was who decided he should become a catechist. His father — that is, the man who in official respects was named as such, the hunter, Jens — enjoyed seasonal employment by the Trade at Holsteinsborg. Most probably he was aware of who the biological father was, and so presumably they found the catechism to be in some way appropriate. Whatever the reason, at the age of fourteen Bertel Jensen became a pupil of the catechist at Old Sukkertoppen, which is now all but depopulated. Later he came to the new Sukkertoppen and has remained here ever since.

Question: What are the planets?
Answer: Round, dark bodies having many mountains and valleys upon their surface, surrounded by atmospheres and presumed habitable by living beings.

Bertel dismisses his speculations as to the past. The present demands his attention. He goes over to the carpentry shop where he meets the smith. He shows him the materials he has collected and asks if he may use some tools.

What will he make? asks the smith.

A kayak. For my boy.

Ah, Madame Kragstedt's little fancy man? says the smith and laughs. He can use what he likes as long as he clears up after him. And if he breaks anything he must make sure it's replaced.

I won't break anything.

I said if he does.

He doesn't bother to reply. He waits until the smith has gone. Then he goes about the work. He has built kayaks before, though some years ago. And this kayak is small; he must spend much time and exert himself mathematically to scale down from adult size. He begins with the hull. For the frame he uses old wood he has had stored to dry. It takes him a week to construct the skeleton. Then he carries it over to the communal house where some women clad it with skins. They seal the vessel with seal fat, which they rub in from bow to stern. When they have finished they leave it to dry in the wind for some days, returning frequently to rub in some more. In the meantime he carves a double paddle out of a plank of larch, drills small holes in it and equips it with fittings of finely filed and polished narwhal tusk, which he lets into the wood with dowels made of the same material. The native women have fixed amulets to the cords that criss-cross the deck, some stumps of bone and a small leather pouch of indefinable contents. He dares not remove them, but recites the Lord's Prayer over the vessel in the hope that it may appease both heathen and Christian powers.

On the boy's birthday at the end of the month the kayak is finished. He goes over to collect it early in the morning and places it in front of the house. The coating of fat makes it shine and he pictures the vessel gliding through the water. Then he goes inside and says in a casual tone, Someone seems to have left something for you outside.

The boy goes out and stands gaping at the kayak. He walks around it. Sofie scurries to join him. She claps her hands together and emits high-pitched cries of astonishment. You kept this quiet, she says.

Bertel is gladdened. He cannot stop chuckling. He sits on his haunches and watches the boy. What do you think of it?

Is it for me? the boy asks. There is a trace of suspicion in his voice.

Who else would it be for?

Who made it?

I did.

Really? says the boy.

Didn't you think your father could do such things?

The boy smiles wryly. Can I try it out and see if it fits?

I had your mother measure your backside when you weren't looking, Bertel says. Let's go down to the shore. You can try it out in the element in which it belongs.

He spends the whole day teaching the boy to keep his balance. By afternoon he has become proficient enough for them to paddle out together, each in his own kayak. They paddle alongside each other. When the boy becomes uncertain, Bertel extends his paddle so that he may grasp it tightly, or else he lays it across the decks of both kayaks, so that they may drift side by side.

When they return home in the evening, Bertel says: I'm thinking of making a trip south next month. Do you want to come with me?

Just me and you? asks the boy.

The two of us on our own. I've bought an extra rifle. I can teach you to shoot.

Is he old enough? Sofie asks with concern. He is not even confirmed yet. Wouldn't it be better to make some shorter trips around the island instead?

But the boy is all for it. Father, he asks, can I go and tell Madame Kragstedt so that she can come and see my kayak?

Yes, do so, my boy.

Later he discovers the Madame has given the boy a present: a folding writing set of mahogany with three pen shafts of varnished bamboo, a dozen nibs and a small gilded knife with which to sharpen them. It is the finest writing set Bertel has ever seen, a preposterous gift.

It's a travelling set, says the boy. I can take it with me on our trip, Father.

Bertel lifts the little brass ink pot from its hollow and turns it between his fingers. He puts it back in its place. It's much too fine, he says. It might break.

Sofie's pregnancy is confirmed, she tells him when he enquires. She has not bled since the spring and can tell by her breasts that she is with child. She asks him not to say anything to the boy until some months have passed and she can no longer conceal it.

We're doing well together, says Bertel.

Yes, she says. They lie on the bed, their legs entwined.

Do you remember to say the Lord's Prayer? he asks.

Every morning.

You must remember to thank the Lord as well.

I thank him each and every day. I thank him for my capable husband and my clever and beautiful son.

He lies with his arms around her and senses her drift into sleep. He wriggles cautiously on to the other side to do likewise.

Question: What are the four major parts of the Earth's land masses?
Answer: Europe, Asia, Africa and America.

Before he departs with the boy, he asks Sofie to return the writing set. It is inappropriate, he says, to give the boy such a precious gift. It must be worth more than you are paid there in a year.

But Madame Kragstedt says she is so very fond of our boy. I think she has become attached to him in a way neither of us can understand.

All the more reason to return the gift. Can't you see that she is trying to ingratiate herself? I shouldn't wonder if she wished to adopt him as her own.

Perhaps it would not be the worst thing to happen, says Sofie. He would still be our son. And his opportunities would be much improved.

My boy is not going to grow up in that madhouse. Return the gift, say whatever you like to the Madame, but I will not have such an expensive item in my house.

Then he sets out with the boy.

†

They sleep under the open sky; they sleep with the natives they meet along the way; they sleep in some of the small timber huts that have been erected by the Trade. All the time he is alert to make sure the boy does not overly exert himself or become cold and wet. In the evenings he rubs his legs and feet with snow. The old winter snow that still lies in the clefts and in places of permanent shade is coarse and good for stimulating the circulation.

It's odd, says the boy, that cold snow can warm you up.

It is one of the things a person may learn from our people, he replies. The Danes do not understand such matters. They think the snow is cold.

At a summer encampment in the far south of the district they witness a shamanistic seance. The hands and feet of the shaman are bound by leather thongs. His drum is on the ground in front of him. The audience is invited to check the bindings, and the boy, too, is allowed to test them. Then a skin is hung up in front of the light-hole and the lamps are extinguished. There is grunting and groaning, the drum begins to play. It is as if it hangs suspended in the air, now at one end of the room, now at the other. A strange voice speaks to them, scolds them, curses and derides the Danes. The drum is struck loudly throughout. Then it becomes silent. A couple of children whimper, an infant sucks manically at the breast, otherwise all is still. In a voice that is almost normal but for a slight bleat, the shaman asks that his bonds be loosened. The skin is removed from the light-hole and the lamps are lit. The man is seated in the same place as before, with hands and feet bound. When it is over, the mood becomes buoyant. Soup is served and stories told.

Bertel lies down on the sleeping bench and clutches the boy tightly. You must not tell anyone about this, he says into his ear. He feels the boy tremble. There, there, he says, nothing happened.

I miss my mother, says the boy.

We go home tomorrow, says Bertel.

He can sense the boy is unwell as they paddle north. He is plainly weak and cannot paddle for any stretch of time. Bertel tries to tow him, but it is awkward and unworkable. They make slow progress. When finally they reach Sukkertoppen he must carry the boy up to the house.

What have you done? Sofie says when she sees him laid out on the bench, gasping for breath.

He doesn't know what to say.

Question: What is the air?

Answer: A fluid, elastic body encompassing the entire globe until a certain altitude and allowing us the sense of hearing.

He goes to Falck and the staggering priest comes to tap his fingers routinely against the boy's chest and back, conversing with him lightly and casually.

Is it the consumption again? Bertel asks him.

Yes, the consumption returned. Falck has gone outside; they stand by the step and talk. It would seem your trip was rather strenuous, he says.

It was not strenuous until he became sick, says Bertel defensively. We had a fine trip together.

As you will, but the fact of the matter is that he is suffering from exhaustion and has caught a chill that has awakened his former condition.

Can you help him?

I could open a vein and let his blood, but whether it would help I have no idea.

Do so, says Bertel.

Falck goes home to fetch his medical bag. When he returns, he speaks with the boy and explains to him what is going to happen. The boy does not protest. Falck produces a thin metal tube from a case, an instrument he refers to as a *straw*, which is cut diagonally at the tip. He takes the boy's feet, leans forward and studies them, his bad eye tightly closed, runs his hand over the ankles, taps them briskly with his fingers. Then he asks Bertel to grasp the boy's lower leg and to press down hard. He inserts the diagonal point of the tube into a bulging vein at the ankle joint. Bertel sees how the skin parts obligingly around the metal and droplets of blood appear. The boy emits a stifled whimper. Dark blood now begins to drip from the instrument's opposite end into a cooking pot. Falck massages the calf, long downward strokes, milking. The blood runs faster. When a cupful has collected he removes the tube and wraps a cloth around the ankle. He studies the blood in the pot. It glistens with a hint of green; its pungent odour offends the nostrils.

Gall, he explains. The boy is full of it. I shall perform a second bleeding in a couple of days if needs be. And remember to give him the cow's milk each morning.

Bertel does not tell him that the priest's milk is thrown away in the evenings. None of them can stand the taste, least of all the patient himself.

The bloodletting has settled the boy; he sleeps heavily for twelve hours and smiles when eventually he wakes. He asks for his writing set.

Later, says Bertel. When you are well again.

The boy studies him inquisitively. His gaze is unkind.

Later he goes up to the colony house and asks Sofie to retrieve the writing set. They stand in the hall. The Madame hears them; she comes out to see Bertel. Her expression is taut.

Let the boy come here, she says. I shall look after him and make sure he recovers.

I know what the Madame wants, says Bertel, and it is not in my boy's interests.

If he wants the writing set back, he must let the boy come to me.

Does the Madame think children are wares that she may purchase when the fancy takes her? Is this how she endeavours to make up for what has happened to her, and for the fact that she cannot have children of her own?

Silence. Both women, Sofie and the Madame Kragstedt, glare at him.

Forgive me. He utters the words very quietly. I am doing only what I believe to be best for my boy.

He turns and goes back home.

That evening Sofie informs him that she has been released from her employment. But she has the writing set with her. The boy is happy to see it returned. He sits up all evening, coughing and wheezing, writing in his exercise book.

If the boy becomes well, I will join them inside the fjord, Sofie says. I'm tired of this.

†

A couple of days later Bertel tries to find Falck so that he may perform a second letting of the blood, as he has promised. The boy has a high fever; the writing set lies idle on the table beside the cot. It is all they can do to force water over his lips. But the priest is not at home and when Bertel goes down to the wreck and calls out for him there is no sign of life inside.

In the night a crisis occurs. The boy is tormented by spasms, between which he lies limply and without response to their voices which repeat his name. Sofie cries. He is dying! she sobs, and peers out from between her fingers.

Be quiet! Bertel snaps angrily. You're only making it worse.

The next morning Falck appears. His wig sits askew upon his head and his cassock is dirty. Bertel sees that the priest's hands are shaking. After a perfunctory examination he leaves without a word, only to return an hour later, calm now and smiling, clad in his daily garments.

I must perform an operation upon the infected lung, he tells Bertel. A cleansing, a removal of the purulent matter, the poison that is spreading to the body and giving him the fever. If I am successful, he will recover.

Do what you can, says Bertel.

Question: What are the peculiar properties of water?
Answer:
1. *Its fluid nature.*
2. *Its perceptible density.*
3. *Its transparency, such that other bodies may be visible in clean and still water.*
4. *The unity of its particles in drops and beads.*
5. *The hardness of its particles. If one casts a stone at an angle against its surface, the stone will be cast back in the same manner as in the case of solid bodies.*

Falck produces a new pipe from his bag. It is made of copper and as thick as a finger. Like the one he used to let the boy's blood, it is cut diagonally at its tip, ending in a sharp point.

The smith has made this instrument according to my instruction, he says.

They roll the boy onto his side and pull him to the edge of the cot. He seems to be unaware of what is happening. Yet Falck speaks kindly to him; he strokes his hair and tells him, in almost a jovial tone, that he will now do something to make him well. Then he proceeds to tap his fingers against his back, investigating, inch by inch, the resonance of the lungs.

Here, he says, indicating an area, is where the evil lies.

He picks up his copper instrument and a small hammer and turns the point to the place in question. He instructs Bertel to hold the boy firmly, a superfluous instruction insofar as he is unconscious, then taps the point in with the hammer. The boy whimpers. Bertel thinks the sound is like the call of a seal.

Falck kneels down and puts the copper pipe to his lips. He begins to suck, then abruptly removes his mouth from the instrument. A murky fluid drips into the pot. It smells sweet and sickly.

Look, he says, almost enthusiastically. There we have the mischief!

The pus runs slow and thick. Falck must speed it up by sucking on the pipe. He spits and rinses his mouth with water. The pot fills. Sofie empties and returns it. All three stand in silence, staring at the matter as it flows. And then it ceases. Falck withdraws the pipe a little, then inserts it again at another angle. The boy emits a hollow whimper, but remains still. The fluid begins to trickle again; this time there is more blood in it. Falck repositions the instrument a number of times, sucking and spitting, before finally he withdraws it completely. He instructs Sofie to dress the wound. Then they turn the boy over onto his other side.

He must lie with the sick side down, Falck instructs them. In that way we allow it to settle and the good lung to work most fully.

Should I give him salt? Bertel asks.

I fear we are beyond salt, Falck replies. My advice is to pray for him. He gathers his things. Send for me if anything happens. I shall be at home.

The boy does not wake that evening. Bertel sits up all night with Sofie. They listen to his breathing, which at first is lighter and more eased, then later a succession of protracted gasps. Sofie cannot stand it and goes outside. He hears her sobbing on the step and feels angry. He wishes she would not come back, that she would simply go away and disappear.

He must have slept a little, his chin resting on his chest. When he looks up he sees the boy's clear, inquisitive gaze. Sun slants into the room. The boy is very pale. He must have lost a lot of blood during the priest's operation.

Are you awake?

The boy swallows. He says nothing.

Do you want something? Some water?

The boy looks at him in bemusement.

He fetches a cup of water and lifts the boy's head. His lips part slightly, but the water runs out onto the pillow.

Shall I read something for you? Bertel asks. He picks a book at random and opens it.

No, thank you. Clearly articulated.

Bertel takes his hand, but the boy draws it back. He stares without abatement at his father, the same inquisitive gaze.

Madame Kragstedt sends her love, he says desperately.

The boy does not react.

Your good friend, Haldora.

The corners of his mouth quiver slightly. Perhaps it is a smile. Then his eyes close. He sleeps.

The priest does not present himself. Bertel asks Sofie to look for him, but she cannot find him anywhere. Presently, his sister comes. She relieves him at the bedside while he goes to the wreck to find the priest in his berth, stupefied by drink. He goes home again. The boy passes away quietly, shortly after eight in the evening.

†

With a sense of alleviation he sits down at the table, opens the writing set from Madame Kragstedt and writes: *Jens passed away peacefully in sleep some short time after the Trader's bell rang eight p.m. He was my best friend on earth. Now all fear is past.*

He remains seated and skims through the boy's book. Outside, the fire-watcher sings: *At the hour of midnight was our Saviour born.* Between the pages lie small scraps of paper on which he has written with a pen from his set. They must be passages from the book, Bertel thinks to himself. He reads them, one by one. Darkness falls. The fire-watcher sings: *The clock has struck three!* It becomes light: *Black night departs and day begins to dawn.* The hours pass. He reads the boy's notes. He hears the smith: *Jesu, Thou Morning Star!* He hears the colony bell strike the hour. He hears the priest's cow as it lows. He hears the people talk, and life go on. Next to him lies the boy, with marbled skin, as stiff as wood. He wonders if it is true that he is now in a better place. It does not feel like it. It feels as if he is simply gone forever, and that he will never see him again.

†

The boy is buried beside his cousin. Bertel performs the ceremony himself. He buys wood from the Trade and joins the coffin. He puts the boy inside it, folds his hands, combs his hair. He reads at the grave and casts the soil. He stands alone, mumbling over his Bible in the sunshine. The women – Madame Kragstedt, Sofie and his sister – form the three other corners of a rectangle around the grave. They stare in silence down into the hole, and he considers that like himself they are consumed and mortified that life at any time may be consigned to a hole in the ground, and are filled with guilt that the boy should lie there instead of any one of them.

When he lies beneath the covers that night with his back to Sofie, she tells him that tomorrow she will be leaving. If you've anything to say, say it now.

The next day he goes down to the blubber house and strikes the priest's cow hard on the temple with the smith's hammer. Its legs buckle beneath it. It tosses back its head and jerks its limbs. He places his boot upon its muzzle, then strikes again. The cow is still.

He pretends not to notice Sofie as he returns to the house. She is packing her things, placing them in large bundles by the step. At the shore some natives are making ready a kone boat. He lifts his kayak from the frame and puts it down in the grass. He goes inside and puts on his kayak coat. He glances around the room. There is not a single item he wishes to take with him.

Sofie looks at him enquiringly when he comes back outside. He walks straight past her, lifts up the kayak and carries it down to the shore.

His sister comes running. Where are you going?

I don't know.

Are you coming back?

He looks at her. I don't think so. Perhaps.

We have lost the most precious thing of all, she says. But we still have each other.

Give your priest my greeting, he says.

Then he climbs into the kayak and paddles out towards the open sea.

Question: *What is the human soul?*

Answer: *The spirit that is united with the human body, such that the body is enlivened and by the soul's influence may conceive of such things that are outside the body and think upon them.*

The Ninth Commandment

The Taasinge Slot

(1792–3)

The Ninth Commandment, as it is most plainly to be taught by a father to his family:
'Thou shalt not covet thy neighbour's house.'
What does this imply?
Answer: That we should fear and love God, so that we may not by any stratagem attempt to obtain our neighbour's inheritance or home, nor acquire the same under the pretext of justice; but to be subservient in preserving the same in his possession.

Morten Falck has discovered that a person may simply let go. Life makes no claim upon a man, but trickles away through the orifices of the body and is gone. It is easy.

In the captain's cabin of the *Taasinge Slot*, where the horizon inclines in the portholes like the seasickness and where half the planks have been broken up, he sits and allows his beard to grow. He writes letters to Kragstedt, to Haldora, to his sister in Nakskov, to the Missionskollegium in Copenhagen, to his parents at home in Lier. *Do not believe what you hear, my dear Kirstine, and forget me not! With peace in my mind I go to rest. I have been happy and am now reconciled. Your loyal and devoted brother, Morten Falck, former Priest of the Mission, the Colony of Sukkertoppen.*

The widow takes care of their dispatch, or at least assures him of it. She comes to him daily. She sits on the cot and is bored. She considers

him with curiosity. He offers her aquavit from the keg, but she declines.
What do you want from me exactly? he asks.

I like to look at you, she says. You look strange, Priest.

You enjoy watching me die. That is what.

She gives a shrug.

So much has happened. Bertel's boy is dead, Sofie gone away, Bertel
himself vanished. What has become of Bertel? he asks. Your brother.

No one has seen him since last autumn, she says. Most likely he is
dead, the lucky fellow, and sitting with his boy at this moment at the
table with Abraham and the others.

He grasps what she tells him and understands that he ought to be
saddened, perhaps to cry, at least to say something priestly concerning
the colony's state of total disintegration. But he feels nothing and
remains silent about it.

And Roselil? he says after a while. Is Roselil dead too?

Your cow is dead, she says. I've told you many times. It was almost
a year ago. Someone hit her on the head with a hammer.

Good, he says. I am glad to hear it. Roselil has gone home. We are
all going home.

The Trader had it cut up and salted the meat for the winter.

Then she lives on, he says. Does she not, in a way? He looks up at
her as though for confirmation, but she shakes her head.

One day she comes with letters. A ship has arrived. One is from his
father to tell him his mother has passed away.

He puts the letter down. It falls on the floor. My mother is dead,
he says.

She's lucky, says the widow. Dying is not easy.

Yes, it is, he says. Just look at me.

You're not dead. You just smell bad.

Did you take my letters to the Trader and his wife?

I threw them away. You can write letters when you're well.

But I will not be well. I don't want to be well!

It's not for us to decide.

She brings him food, food from the natives with whom she lives, boiled meat, soup, fish. Unfortunately his appetite is ravenous and he cannot abstain from eating. The keg of aquavit is emptying, though as yet it remains half full. Sometimes he lifts it up and dances a few steps with it in the inclining cabin, singing a shanty he learned on his voyage with *Der Frühling*, or one of Brorson's hymns. The air turns chilly; snow intrudes through the timber, ice forms in the cracks of the bulkhead. The widow comes with back issues of the *Christiania-Kureren* and *Kjøbenhavns Posttidende* and together they stuff them into the gaps. She teaches him to keep a train-oil lamp burning by trimming the wick. If he allows it to go out, she pulls his beard and scolds him. When he needs to empty his bowels he climbs down into the hold and squats at the bow. He discharges his filth upon the planks and it seeps away through the cracks. He refrains from ever going ashore. He has made a rule for himself that he will never set foot on land again. He wishes to sail into the sunset as captain of the wrecked *Taasinge Slot*. Until now he has abided by it. He spends most of his time lying in the slanting cot, reading small scraps torn from the *Posttidende*. *Denmark has no other natural wealth than . . . possible perfection! Hippocrates . . . the oldest Danish legislators . . . the country's happiness in sight . . . population of Danish peasantry . . . our number lottery . . . by the new year of 1777 . . . number lottery in Denmark . . . such considerable loss for whoever should gamble . . . state of theology in this country . . .*

He puts on his cassock, which is furry white with mildew, pulls his festering wig down over his forehead and searches for his ruff. But the ruff is gone. He delivers a sermon without it, a sermon of fire and brimstone in the manner of the old pastor at Nakskov before his trembling congregation. His own congregation is humbler and consists of the lice which predominantly inhabit the area of his cuffs, his armpits and the inside and out of his wig, but which nonetheless are many!

The widow comes. What are you doing? She helps him back into the cot.

He passes out, sleeps dreamlessly and arises twelve hours later with a bandage around his head.

You fell, she says.

His body quivers. He eats hard tack soaked in warm aquavit and begins to feel better. He considers his situation. This is not as easy as he thought. Has the ship arrived? he asks.

The ship sailed a long time ago, says the widow. It's winter.

How are things in the colony?

There's a new carpenter and a new cook, she says. And the Trader has written off for a new priest.

Good, he says. Excellent. I have written to Dr Fabricius myself regarding a successor to my position.

He contracts dysentery. The weather is so cold his excrement freezes to his buttocks and thighs, thawing and beginning to exude its stench only when he returns to the cabin. He lies in his cot and hasn't the strength to go into the hold to evacuate his bowels. When eventually he gets to his feet it is too late and he falls back, exhausted, onto the bed.

This is the bottom, he thinks to himself. And about time!

But the bottom is never the bottom. There is always another bottom below it. He descends through nine circles of debasement to debasement that is deeper still. He finds it to be a most satisfying and instructive experience. The widow is with him and observes him from a distance. Then she is there no more. Perhaps he simply imagines her to be there. He lifts up his head and she gives him a little to drink. Aquavit, he groans, give me my aquavit!

There is no more aquavit, she says. You've drunk the whole keg. Now the trouble begins.

Cold, he breathes through chattering teeth. I'm so cold.

I'm washing you, says the widow. You will soon be warm again.

He feels himself turned first one way then another, the wet cloth at his lower regions, the widow's mutterings of annoyance. I am dead, he thinks. She is preparing me for my grave and wrapping me in my shroud. But Purgatory is cold, not at all hot as we learned.

His skin retracts from his bones, which rest hard against the planks of the cot. He can find no respite. He tosses and turns, or else his spirit does, struggling to free itself, while his empty frame remains stiff upon the bunk. He perches attentively on a joist in the ceiling, from where he observes himself lying huddled in his bed, looking up at himself perched on a joist in the ceiling, observing himself lying huddled in his bed. He emits a scarcely human, inorganic stench like waste from a tannery, a pungent chemistry of foulness. He notes how his clothes stick to his skin, the ammonia of his urine burning his thighs. He sees the seeping bedsores, registers the bile that trickles from the corners of his mouth. He senses the way he squirms to be released from his carcass, through such orifices as are amenable. Am I a part of the world or is the world a part of me? When I die, will I then become liquid and be stirred into the great soup of the Unknown? He thanks the Lord for his final days of peace and reconciliation. Then, resolutely, he closes his eyes.

Are you ready now? the widow asks, holding an enormous gold crucifix out in front of him.

Ready for what, my dear? he asks or thinks he asks, squinting his eyes at the crucifix as it swings like a pendulum before him, its glare blinding him.

Ready to leave.

Leave for where? He holds a hand up in front of his face.

For Habakuk and Maria Magdalene, says the widow. The time has come.

What sort of a person are you? he says or thinks he says. Can you not let a dead man lie in peace?

THE TENTH COMMANDMENT

In the Bosom of the Prophets:
Excerpts from the Diary of Morten Falck

(Winter to Summer, 1793)

The Tenth Commandment, as it is most plainly to be taught by a father to his family:
'Thou shalt not covet thy neighbour's wife, nor his man-servant, nor his maid-servant, nor his ox, nor his ass, nor any thing that is thy neighbour's.'
What does this imply?
Answer: That we should fear and love God, so that we may not seduce our neighbour's wife, alienate his domestics or force away from him his cattle; but cause them to remain and do their duty.

Diary, the First Part

. . .

Let there be light

. . .

And darkness

. . .

Who am I?

. . .

I am

Therefore I am God

Therefore God exists!

God's existence is hereby proven

And thereby my own

Give me the widow!

. . .

Mother!

Father!

Sister Kirstine!

?

King Christian VII (and the Crown Prince)!

Jesus Christ!

Our Lord!

I am a question mark in the midst of eternity

Who am I?

. . .

A

B

C

D

M

P

F

Morten

Pedersen

Falck

. . .

I pinch myself

It hurts!

. . .

I am the pen that doth scratch
I am the ink that runneth
The paper that doth absorb
The words
From my hand my spirit
I am the hand that holds the ~~cock~~ pen
I am the spirit that leadeth the hand that holds the pen
I am Morten Pedersen ~~Falck~~

. . .

The passage of light across the floor
The passage of the eye within the socket
The passage of time through a room
One day is seven ells in length
And four ells high

. . .

I am Morten Pedersen Falck
I am Morten Pedersen ~~Falck~~
I am Morten ~~Pedersen Falck~~
I am ~~Morten Pedersen Falck~~
I ~~am Morten Pedersen Falck~~
~~I am Morten Pedersen Falck~~

. . .

The light falls so pleasantly upon the floor
It wanders from wall to wall
My wounds
My legs

My fingers

My ~~member~~ frame

No pain

But lust

No hunger

But thirst

No repentance

But contrition

My front teeth are quite fallen out but for five that dangle like scoundrels
    of the night from a gallows

R.I.P.

Verily I say unto thee

Rise up and go!

I shall not want

Who am I?

The woman comes with my slops

She calls me *Palasi*

Verily I say unto thee, woman, I am priest no more!

I ask for ale

She gives me water

Bright as aquavit

I ask for a kiss

She attends to the warming pan

She takes my night pot

I ask for a smile

She does not smile

Who is she?

She has a comely backside

I must sleep now

. . .

My ejaculations are bloody

Nevertheless, they afford me much enjoyment

. . .

This night my excrement spoke to me in Latin from the malodorous
    depths of the night pot
The eternal tongue
Hoc est Corpus Christi!
It shouted out
This is the body of Christ
Eat me!
This is the blood of Christ
Drink me!
Small wafers it resembled
I laid one upon my tongue
In order to taste it
And receive the salvation
I drank the bitter altar wine
It tasted of urine
Ugh, how vile!

. . .

Music
French horn and lute
Kettledrums!
Blessed tones
The royal musicians play
Master Eckenberg waxes his moustache
And snaps his braces
Performs his somersault
And breaks his neck

. . .

My name is Morten Falck

My arsehole it doth talk
It poureth forth with sweet refrain
Resounding farts without restrain
The Lord's praise it doth sing
With arsehole descant ring

O squelching minor key!
O squeaking major chord!

I have not learned to write down music
Though poet may still be within reach

Such a wretch am I!
Who am I?

. . .

Rain beating hard against the pane
Is winter over?
Will summer soon be here?
The woman who comes here under pretext of tending to my physical
    needs is a thief(ess)
She takes my night pot
And when she brings it back it is empty
Not a drop has she left!
I believe she makes sorcery with it, and enchantments
I scold her on such account
And impress upon her the sacrilege of which she thereby is guilty
My excrement, I tell her, is blessed
It is the body and blood of Christ!
But she pays me no heed
She washes me with the cold water
Without shame she grasps my nakedness
As though it were the shaft of a broom

And washes around it with her cloth
Who art thou, woman?
Who am I?
I was the priest
More I shall not say

. . .

My obituary:
Morten Pedersen Falck
Son of schoolmaster Peder Mortensen, Lier Parish, Diocese of
    Akershus, Norway, born 1731.
And Gundel, née Olavsdatter, Lier Parish, Diocese of Akershus,
    born 1741, died 1791, R.I.P.
Morten Pedersen Falck was born 20 May 1756, a vile Thursday, at the
    schoolmaster's holding by the banks of the Holsfjord, where grows
    a birchwood copse and the life is good.
Christened and led to confirmation in Lier Church by the
    Rev. Mr Clemens.
Latin school at Drammen, graduation with honours.
Theological studies at the University of Copenhagen, 1782–5.
Graduated to the title of Candidatus Theologicus (Third Class), 1785.
Called to the Mission of Greenland, Sukkertoppen Colony, 1787,
    in his 32nd year.
Magister Falck left his home in the Colony last January and has since
    not been seen by any member of its crew. He is therefore presumed
    dead from cold or by drowning.
Loved and missed by his sister Kirstine Gram née Pedersen, Nakskov,
    and by his still living father, the schoolmaster.
Requiescat in Pace.
In Heaven we shall be united!

. . .

The journey here remains as yet all but clear to my memory. My bleating, shrieking, snivelling person was transported over land and water and placed here in the horizontal, being quite without strength and detached from all senses. I recall dreadful visions, white maggots wishing to wriggle into my orifices, small and vile creatures crawling about my body, mice, rats, spiders. It seems to me this continued for some weeks or else an entire year, jolting upon sleds, pitching in the bottom of vessels in choppy waters. Or perhaps merely days. I do not recall it, but see only indirectly images of it, a camera obscura projecting disconnected flashes of memory upon the blurred glass of recollection.

Remember to ask this if ever a person appears with whom one might converse: How long did my journey last? The Lord was in the wilderness for forty days. How long my own cold wandering? But who to ask? There is no one here, only the small woman who silently brings me three meals each day and empties my night pot, whereafter she departs without answering my queries. Perhaps she is deaf, perhaps she is one of the silent keepers of the underworld.

Where is the widow?

Where am I?

I demand to see the widow!

The widow belongs to me!

The widow is to come!

Do I wish to see the widow?

What she has seen, no man ought to allow any woman to see.

She knows me.

I know her not.

And yet I love her.

I think.

Until this hour I have called her only 'the widow'.

What is the widow's name? Remember to ask!

This place is dim, but warm and comfortable. My bed is a soft mattress of straw, my cover reindeer skins sewn together. They are quite alive with vermin, albeit most likely the same creatures as brought here upon my own person and now multiplied in these new preserves. A tallow candle burns upon a small table. Next to it has been placed a Bible, a volume of Pietistic hymns, writing instruments and some sheets of paper of which a dozen already bear the scribble of my handwriting and a number of obscene sketches, though I have no recollection of having either written or drawn. I dip my quill, I put its nib to the hard parchment, I see the ink flow and my hand come trembling to life again. I live!

Lord, have mercy and let me die!

. . .

Alas, my wretched, battered body!

Today I rose from the warmth of my bed and took some small and uncertain steps upon the hard wooden floor. The room in which I have been placed is quite small, smaller than Bertel's front room in the colony as I remember it, and no larger than my bleak habitation on board the *Taasinge Slot*, though more comfortable by far. When my legs become strong enough I shall pace out its measurements, but I believe it to be four paces lengthways and some two and a half in width. To the right of the door is a window, quite impenetrable to the eye, though the light shines through it well. The sun is cast down upon the floor, a field of brightness that wanders from wall to wall, from dawn until dusk, and thus approximately I may judge the time of day, though not the time of year. I hear the lapping of water and pebbles clacking at the changing of the tide. Further away the rush of a river. Now and then voices, albeit distant. I have not yet the courage to put my head outside.

Thus proceed my days: I am awoken after good sleep by the small woman, who brings me a bowl of barley gruel. It is the widow. Now I see it. Only now do I see her.

Remember to ask: From where is this barley acquired that does not taste of mildew and rot? Do they do business with the Trade? If so, it is unlawful business.

When this kindly person has gone, which is to say the widow, at least I think her to be the widow, I sit up in my cot and slurp the gruel. Thereafter I read a little in the two books with which I have been entrusted, though both tire me so immensely that soon I prefer to follow the sun's advancement across the floor. When it has reached the right side of the door, the woman, the widow, returns, now with my mid-day meal, usually boiled meat with hard tack which I chew only with difficulty. I ask her where I am, how long I have been here and whether anyone will come and speak to me, but she offers no reply. When the sun has reached the other wall she brings me supper, usually porridge. I observe the bright square of sunlight wander up the wall to the ceiling joists, there to be extinguished, at which time I light my dip and commit my thoughts to this journal.

All is well.

15 April!
A living human, a person with whom to speak! The widow!

She is here. She enters. She sits down on a chair she has drawn up to the cot. She speaks to me. She tells me of the journey here, which was fraught with difficulties and lasted some score of days on account of ice and bad weather. Moreover, I made matters no easier, she tells me, being quite out of my senses, screaming and behaving like a savage. No, worse than a savage! A man who would lift me up received a punch on the nose by my hand, making his blood squirt, another I kicked in the chest, causing him to lose his breath, and only a dousing with a bucket of cold water could bring him back to his senses. I raged like Samson. And like Samson I had to be bound so as not to injure myself or others. Presently I fell into a state of great feebleness lasting some weeks, in which time I ingested only a little soup and water under protest. Everyone, with the exception of the widow herself, she says with a smile, is astonished that I am still alive, and all consider me to be living testament that the Lord protects His own.

And you? I ask. What do you consider?

It was me who looked after you, she says. Not the Lord.

To this I add no further comment. She wishes to take credit for having saved me. She deserves it. God bless her!

I am at the settlement of the prophets inside the Eternal Fjord, she tells me, though I had already assumed as much.

But why? I ask her.

It was wished, she says.

A priest. Indeed, I understand. They have a priest. Who wished it?

Maria Magdalene, the widow replies.

Habakuk's woman? Can I speak to her?

She will come to you when you're better.

I'm better now. Bring her to me! I wish to speak to her.

The widow says nothing. I take her hand. Dearest, I say.

My name is Lydia. Call me Lydia.

What was your little girl's name?

Her name was Milka, the widow replies curtly. We won't talk about her.

What then is my own name, Lydia?

You are *Palasi*. The priest.

But what is my name? I want to hear you say it.

Palasi!

No! I say. I wish to be *Palasi* no longer. I am Morten Pedersen.

People don't choose their names, says the widow Lydia.

Do people not choose what they wish to be?

You are your name, you are *Palasi*. That's why you're here. No one cares for Morten Pedersen.

She rises. Her visit is over.

Another small woman comes in. I look at her.

You! I say. I know you. You are the cooper's wife. Enike.

She stops. She looks at me. She is one of perhaps several who have cared for me during my infirmity.

How are your children? I ask.

My children are alive and in good health. She speaks her own language, having little command of the Danish, and I must ask her to repeat her words several times over before fully grasping her meaning. My deceased husband left me enough for our keep.

Say my name, I implore.

Palasi, she says.

No, my name is Morten Pedersen. Say it!

My sister wants to speak with *Palasi*, she says.

Who is your sister?

Sofie. Bertel's wife.

Has she been here too, while I have lain here in my weakened state?

She lifts her eyebrows in the affirmative. So three women have attended to me during these weeks and I have made them into one.

Very well, let her come.

And so a third woman presents herself. Sofie. She wishes to hear news of her husband, the catechist. I am aware of neither his business nor his whereabouts, I tell her. I have not seen him in nearly a year.

She shows me her new little boy, born in January, so that I might bless him. A fair child with blue eyes, the image of my dear catechist.

I am no longer *Palasi*, I tell her.

She insists. She holds the child in outstretched arms. I place a hand upon its head and mutter some words. Grateful, she withdraws and turns to leave. But I call her back.

Say my name.

Morten Pedersen, she says.

I thank you, I say. I shall pray for your husband. Go now.

He is alive, she says. I feel that he is alive.

The Lord will protect him, I say.

She leaves.

Boiled meat, from which for lack of capable teeth I must suck the juices and then swallow whole. A cup of cold, fresh spring water.

I ask the widow if the poor, beleaguered *Palasi* might not be given a half pint of ale for his toothache, or better still some aquavit? She pretends not to hear me.

A comely backside. The skin of her bare arms and shoulders as fair as were Madame Kragstedt's, may the Lord have mercy on her.

The widow informs me of the date. Three months have passed. Where were my senses in this time? On the far side of the moon, perhaps, or at the bottom of the sea, like the angakkuqs when summoning the spirits?

17 April

A conversation, committed from memory:

MM: How is Magister Falck feeling now?

MP: Please call me Pedersen, or Morten if you prefer. Falck is now barely acceptable to me. I have forfeited the right to the title of Magister.

MM: You must not shun your responsibility and calling, Magister.

MP: I ask you, please do not address me by that title.

MM: Are you feeling better? Do you have what you need?

MP: I am highly indebted. All I miss is a cup of ale once in a while.

MM: We have no ale. We do not know how to make it and do not purchase it. The same goes for the strong drink that makes the temper flare.

MP: Praiseworthy indeed, Madame. From whom do you purchase your provisions?

MM: We trade with whoever will sell. It is no concern of the Magister's.

MP: I apologize.

MM: Once you are fully recovered I will show you everything and explain how we have organized ourselves here.

MP: So very kind of you. But once it is rumoured within the Colony that its priest of royal sanction and subsidy is being held against his will by false and insubordinate prophets, a delegation will be dispatched here at the double in order to liberate him.

MM: Each day must take care of itself. We place everything in the hands of the Lord.

MP: Moreover, I must warn you, Madame, that a warrant is still outstanding for your arrest and that of your husband. Kragstedt has thus twice the grounds to make a raid upon your settlement and he will do so as soon as the ice is gone from the fjord.

MM: I know of this warrant. We have a copy of it ourselves. What is it they want from us?

MP: I think Professor Rantzau of the Missionskollegium wishes to see you brought to Denmark to be put on trial and sentenced in such manner as may be found appropriate for your offence.

MM: Abduction? They wish to get rid of me and my husband in the expectation that this uprising will end?

MP: I shall not hazard any guess as to the motives of the Powers That Be, but it is by no means unlikely that you are correct, madam.

MM: Why will they not leave us in peace, Magister Falck?

MP: My name is Pedersen. Morten. Greenland is under Danish jurisdiction, you are subjects of King Christian the Seventh, just as I myself, and thereby governed by Danish law.

MM: They say the king is mad.

MP: But the law is not, madam. The law is not mad. We are all Danes equal under the law.

MM: This is not Denmark!

MP: Indeed it is, Madame. This is Denmark!

MM: I am not concerned for my own part, it is my husband's fate I worry about. He is not strong and would not survive a long sea voyage, let alone the air of your country, which they say is full of poisonous vapours and sickness.

MP: Such a death would spare him both trial and imprisonment. It would perhaps be the best outcome.

MM: But we have Magister Falck. If Kragstedt comes to put us in chains we shall not hesitate to make a sacrifice of you!

MP: Alas, dear madam, you do not know Kragstedt. If you did, you would be doing the Trader a great service!

18 April

She is a comely woman, it cannot be denied, and her reason is good. She has a keen eye and unrestrained self-confidence. When she speaks it is always with a smile on her lips and with good humour, as though she finds entertainment in me and my miserable plight, and in the folly of the world *in generalia*. Her husband is said to be a lecher who has slept with more virgins than the prophet Muhammad. In this respect he is neither worse nor better than any Danish man in the country, among them the good Missionary Oxbøl at Holsteinsborg. She informs me he has gone to hunt reindeer in the company of his mistress and that, should I wish it, I may meet with him on his return. Her own thoughts on her husband's infidelity and indecency are kept well hidden, so whether she is angry or sorrowful on account of it is purely a matter of conjecture. Nonetheless, she appears to me to be honest and proper, though I sense she may have something of a temper. Her eyes flashed daggers when I mentioned the warrant and the prospect of their deportation. I do not doubt that she will make good her threat of using me as a shield against the Trader and his officers.

She tells me it was the Missionary Oxbøl who instructed and christened her. He is a good example of the Lord's unsearchable ways, she says with an angry glint in her dark eyes. Thus He can work through even the basest representatives on Earth. She speaks in a jocular tone of the old priest, but has little to say in his favour, which I find quite understandable, judging by what the widow Lydia has related to me about the man and his inclinations towards his female catechumens, and, indeed, any female upon whom his lecherous gaze might fall. It is thus of little consolation, though consolation still, that if possible he is even more unworthy of the vestments than myself, not to speak of his salvation now that his days must be assumed to soon be running out. May the Lord have mercy upon his sinful soul!

19 April

The widow has become a stranger to me, which fact causes me pain, although I cannot ever be said to have known her. She comes and sits with me each day, albeit for a short time only, then goes away again, though not before having reminded me of my pledge and compelling its reiteration. I am to instruct her and lead her to consecration in Christ through the Baptism and confirmation. It is an obsession of hers. I tell her I am no longer to be considered a priest and that any christening or other ecclesiastical ceremony I might perform would be invalid, if not sacrilegious.

Palasi, she says sternly. Remember your pledge. Do your duty!

And I shall do it, indeed, even if it should lead me to my own damnation. It is but a small token in exchange for what she has done.

She asks me about unchristened children and their prospects of salvation. I assume she has her deceased daughter in mind and tell her that small children are unhardened and that the Lord loves them and receives them, though only when they have spent some short time in what is called limbo.

So when I die I will meet her again? she asks.

You will indeed! I reply. If you are christened and then confirmed you will live for evermore together in Paradise.

By this she appears gladdened and contented.

Another matter is that my friend Maria Magdalene moreover wishes me to instruct and christen a large multitude of the natives here at her settlement. All of them feel themselves to be Christian, she explains to me they have received her own and Habakuk's instruction for a number of years and are now eager to be anointed and consecrated unto the Lord by a genuine *palasi*.

I harbour suspicion that this is the true reason for my being brought here.

I am *palasi* no more.

The Magister is soon well enough to go outside, she says with a laugh. My people are looking forward to seeing you again.

Again?

They remember you from the last time you came to see us along with Constable Bjerg, who became so enamoured of one of our girls.

To this I say nothing.

I have never before seen a person with such bright eyes or met a woman of such free and easy mind. Leading her to the confirmation must have been quite a challenge for the good Missionary Oxbøl.

My semen is no longer bloody. A further two teeth lost, molar and incisor.

25 April

For the first time since being brought to this place more dead than alive, I, Morten Pedersen, have been outside in the air.

An inhabitant of the settlement, an inoffensive fellow with the good Christian name of Mathias, though by himself called *Maliarsi*, accompanied me and supported my gait, which as yet is uncertain and most unsteady. The air was thick with chimney smoke from the many inhabited dwellings of the place, and yet delightful to sense. A fresh breeze came off the fjord and, as though I myself were a house with windows thrown open, the air blew straight through my head. Such was the feeling of it. Strongly invigorated thereby, I asked the fellow to lead me up to their church, though the effort quickly proved too strenuous, my breath running short halfway and causing me to sit down directly upon the snow.

They carried me home and put me to bed.

I have a slight sniffle, my feet are cold as ice, my chest chilled, and I am tormented by the most foolish fear of dying, which at one time was the thing I wished for most. But no longer.

All Prayers Day (I think)

How tragic
That life be the fear of death!
And such fear is sinful
And the absence of such fear is likewise a sin
For I was taught both to fear death and to be mindful thereof
Yet suicide is also a sin, one of the greatest
What then should a man do for his salvation?

And what is salvation?
Is it death
Or is it life?
Did the Lord make us that we should die?

With hope of waking again in the morning I retire to sleep.
I had stopped praying, but this evening I make exception and reel off
    my Lord's Prayer.
I feel like Judas

. . .

Febrilia
Coughing badly and spitting mucus
The widow is here
She watches over me
Her eyes do not leave me
She stares at me sideways
Like a black crow on its branch
I love her
But she will not love me
Nor will she let me die!

. . .

Roselil with me this night
Quite exhausted at morning
A small amount of blood gruel by which to be fortified, but then vomited

. . .

the day wanders across the room
seven ells in length
four in width

. . .

spoon food and improvement
yet dreadfully tired

. . .

cast is my frock
I shepherd no more my flock
tra-la-la, tra-la-la . . .
no, a poet I am not!

. . .

1 May

My constitution would seem to be better than I would have thought, for I have survived two attacks upon my life this winter and may thereby once more look forward to further prolongation of my futile destiny. The widow has mixed a concoction of Cochlearia and berries and melted seal blubber, a medication by which the natives have previously fortified me. What is to happen to me when eventually I have fulfilled my pledge and made a good Christian of her? Her twice saving my life is hardly due to personal devotion! I sense in her some antipathy towards me, as indeed towards all Danes. Why then did she take up with Magister Oxbøl? I ask her this and she replies as follows: My humiliation was his humiliation. By lying down on my back and committing the sin, I made him commit a sin many times the greater by lying on top of me, and this was my small revenge.

The woman is a riddle to me. In less enlightened times than these she would surely have been accused of sorcery and thrown upon a pyre.

And yet she is dear to me.

2 May

The prophetess MM honours me with a pleasurable visit. She is an enemy of mine and of the entire Danish presence in this land. This she tells me quite openly. Christ speaks to her in dreams in the night. He says – by her own account! – that this land belongs to the Greenlanders, heathens as well as those christened, and that they should take it back from the thief – i.e., the Dane – who poisons her people with debauchery and filthy lucre. I put it to her that such talk is tantamount to heresy and may send her to the gallows. The Word of the Lord cannot be sent to any hangman, she replies. A brazen woman indeed.

And still we have become good friends. I cannot deny that I think well of her, and she, for her part, clearly enjoys my company. We laugh heartily at each other's errors and cross swords with sarcasm and banter. Her husband is expected here within days. I am somewhat anxious at the prospect.

3 May .

Out of bed to sit in the chair. Dizzy after a short time. Helped back to the cot by the widow.

Does the Magister keep in mind his pledge?

Indeed, he does.

Then she leaves.

4 May

I ask MM: This woman who is called the widow, do you know her?

MM: I have known her for many years. She is the half-sister of the catechist.

I: Yes, I know something of this relation. But what more of her? Why is she troubled so by disquiet and irascible temperament?

MM: She takes after her father, the Missionary Oxbøl.

I: Her father? Missionary Oxbøl?

MM: So you did not know? The same father who begot Bertel, her brother. And the daughter, the little girl who died, was the Missionary's, too. That is why she is so intent upon her christening, Magister Falck, and for that reason you must not deny her. She feels herself sullied, as though by the priest's very excrement, and seeks salvation

that she may die in peace and be reunited with her little daughter, that
both may be cleansed of their incest in Heaven.
This gave me something on which to ponder.
Formed faeces this day.

7 May

Since now finally I am considered restored it has been decided that I am
to be moved into the house in which Habakuk and Maria Magdalene have
their home. They wished not to expend more fuel on a person alone, she
explained, on which matter I expressed my understanding. I live now
in a corner of their room, where privacy is afforded me only by means
of a curtain that may be drawn, but which in no way can exclude the
alarm and disturbance that prevails in such a home. My sleeping place,
a roughly constructed alcove with a straw mattress that nonetheless is
unexceptionably well-filled and clean, fulfils several functions insofar as
it is not only my bed, but also my desk and the place of my daily life.
This accommodation, however, is quite superior seen from the view-
point of my fellow dwellers in the house, who lie side by side, shoulder
to shoulder, and whose most intimate secrets are shared by all and
thereby made the object of much indecent jesting and mirth.

The house is half of peat, half of timber. Its arrangement is much as I
recall the communal dwelling houses of the natives, albeit without the long
crawlspace by which to enter. There is much life and noise from early until
late, crying children and a chatter of men and women talking all at once.
The older children amuse themselves by challenging each other to leap
over the soup cauldron, on occasion upturning it and spilling its contents
onto the floor, whereby much food goes to waste. And yet on such account
there is no corporal discipline nor verbal reproach. Education as to proper
behaviour is a phenomenon unknown to these people, though nonetheless
their children are often charming and inoffensive, quite without the foul
language a city rambler must hear from the street urchins of Copenhagen
or even the offspring of well-situated citizens.

Habakuk has returned from his excursion. He is a good-humoured man, as it transpires, quite tall and well built, clad in tunic and cap and hardly to be distinguished from such servants as are employed by the Trade. And yet he is a man of proper pride and confidence, a self-esteem somewhat less natural than his wife's, and his attitude to me is that of a fine gentleman to a tolerated though quite despicable guest. I find this arrogance and the attendant atmosphere of ill-feeling to be oppressive, and would rather speak to him man to man. However, he seldom deigns to look at me, and when he does it seems only to be with disgust. He is popular with the women of the household, who hang upon his every word and pantingly concur with any utterance that passes his lips.

This communal house is quite colossal, in my estimation thirty ells in length and ten in breadth. A sleeping bench running the length of the long wall opposite my own alcove is inhabited by members of Habakuk's and Maria's families, in all some twenty individuals, adults and children alike. The house is built so as to almost emerge from an earthen slope in the normal Eskimo manner, while its front is comprised of timber beams divided into five windows, so that when approaching from the shore the observer will find it resembles a European colony house, though with only one floor. This mixture may also be perceived in the people themselves, who wear European garments, as well as traditional skins, and use harpoons, bow and arrow and flintlocks for their hunting. Some considerable trade must therefore take place, perhaps with foreign ships that have no qualms about flouting Danish jurisdiction and sovereignty.

At one end of the room is Habakuk's and Maria's chamber, which is to say a large sleeping space separated from the rest of the dwelling by some reindeer skins hanging from a ceiling joist. If any quarrel should arise between the couple on account of his infidelity it must be settled elsewhere. Reindeer skin cannot safeguard the house's occupants against sharing in the joys of marriage and the couple's happiness at being reunited after a successful hunting excursion. This time, however, only a single animal was brought home, to be divided equally between a score of ravenous people hungry for meat, and hardly a week will pass before they must once again make do with the usual seal-blubber soup and spoon food. Nonetheless, they suffer no hardship, in contrast to other outposts of the district.

How long must I remain here?

A singular thought: the majority of the inhabitants of this house and this settlement never pause to ponder this question of how long they must remain here. This is their home, their entire life. A narrow band between the sea and the fell. Though often they will enquire as to conditions in Denmark and Copenhagen – especially curious are the women and older children – they feel not the slightest yearning for other places. To look ahead to a whole life within such a constricted framework: how very odd! And yet it must be happiness of a sort to be at such peace with one's life.

MM informs me that tomorrow I may attend their service.

You mean your witches' sabbath, Madame?

Are you afraid, Magister Falck?

No, I'm not afraid. But don't expect me to take part in your unspeakable indecencies.

Magister Falck, you have my word that we shall behave properly. You have no cause for fear.

I fear not! Be aware, however, that I shall write down everything I observe during your heathen ceremony.

You shall be welcome, Magister. You are hereby appointed to write our chronicles for posterity.

8 May

This service I was obliged to attend was held outdoors in front of their church building while the sun was at its height. Since the snow still lies upon the high ground, the congregation of some one hundred souls had brought with them skins and blankets from their homes, which they placed on the ground and sat upon, young and old alike, slouched in the manner of children with legs stretched out in front of them. Maria Magdalene accompanied me to this battlefield, as I saw it, of heresy and witchcraft, and directed me to a place at which to sit amid the common multitude, albeit slightly aside.

Then Habakuk stepped forth among us, as though conjured from the air, clad in his finest Sunday clothes, i.e., black anorak, breeches of mottled sealskin and kamik boots. He preaches in his own tongue and yet I grasp quite a measure of it, his meaning being aided by gestures and grimaces. I sense my visitations to the savages of the colony now stand me in good stead and I understand more of the language than I had realized.

Habakuk relates a long tale of his hunting excursion and the reason for the poor catch, which seems to have been an unusual occurrence in the wilderness, where he encountered the Devil himself. Already at this point I sensed some considerable unease arise among the congregation: sighs and whimpers passed between them, and one woman emitted a scream and fell into a swoon. Unperturbed, their spiritual leader continued his account of how he came into dispute with Satan and caused him to flee by invoking the weeping wounds of Christ and holding his crucifix in the face of the fiend.

Whether Habakuk really did encounter the Devil is not for me to judge. However, I made note of the fact that Monsieur Lucifer shared an uncanny number of characteristics with my own humble person. The man thus clearly still harbours a grudge against me due to our former controversy in the church, even though it was he whose honour remained intact, a matter he ought rather to recall with contentment.

Fortunately I sensed no ill-feeling towards me on account of these malicious insinuations, all present being far too absorbed in their leader's tale. While I recognized that his narrative was intended to be a parable, it was apparent that his audience took it quite literally. Those seated around him were strongly affected; some began to spring up and down on their posteriors while remaining cross-legged, a quite hazardous activity as they projected themselves almost one ell into the air. Several succumbed to weeping like small children, others mumbled the Lord's Prayer; a young lad chattered in a foreign tongue reminiscent of French. For my own part, I felt a certain commotion of sentiment, due not to Habakuk's sermonizing, but rather to the general mood, and cannot deny that I struggled to restrain my tears. I still feel a lump in my throat while writing this account, but I am not alone, eyes are upon me: I am watched intently from the bench and am ashamed to give in to such an urge.

No matter, after this sermon and an intensity of prayer, likewise led by Habakuk, who it must be said possesses a true gift with words, the crowd rose to its feet and wandered up to the place where a churchyard has been made. Here they stood around the graves, of which there were at least two score, and sang two pretty hymns, one by Pastor Kingo, the other unfamiliar to me, but perhaps penned by Habakuk himself or else his wife.

After these ceremonies were concluded and the congregation dispersed I could not help but notice how smiling and contented they all appeared as they accompanied each other, arm in arm and hand in hand, down to the dwellings. Seldom have I seen such a peaceful and harmonious assembly. Only I walked alone, as if shunned. Perhaps Habakuk's insinuations had been heard and understood, after all. And yet they were nothing but friendly upon my return to the big house. I was astonished to realize that the entire day had passed. Where all these hours had gone, I know not, and I believe I did not sleep.

Perhaps these prophets have not received the truth in its purest Christian form and what is practised here is undoubtedly a mixture of Pietism and heathenism. Yet the Lord may also be among sinners. And He was here today. I sensed Him.

Prayer and asceticism this evening. I decline the soup, although I'm rather tempted by it.

Much farting and laughter among my fellow inhabitants. I feel almost carried back to my passage to this land with the good ship *Der Frühling*.

9 May, morning, the Feast of the Ascension
Not without trepidation do I commit this account. I, Morten Pedersen Falck, do hereby declare that I am of sound mind and that the following is a truthful description of what I saw, in the name of Jesus Christ the Lord.

Upon retiring to bed I promptly fell asleep, though the household about me was quite awake and cheerful and participated merrily in the games put on by Habakuk and his wife for their amusement, such as spillikins and a dance involving all manner of capers and leaping over lamps. I soon slept away from it, only to partake in escapades of my own in dreams, my nightmare presenting me to the Devil, who questioned me upon this and that matter and made obscene and shameless gestures before my face. When I turned away to be free of his dastardly torments he stood immediately before me again and continued his lecherous taunts.

I was awakened abruptly by a tugging at my arm and someone addressing me. It was Habakuk, bent over me and commanding in a loud and fiery voice: Wake up, Priest! Cease your shouting! You're delirious!

I sat up and looked around me at the many faces illuminated by the flickering light of the lamps. I excused my restless sleep with reference to suffering a toothache, which indeed is true.

If you've a bad tooth, then knock it out, said Habakuk.

I thanked him for his advice and said I wished to step outside and get some fresh air.

He stood and watched me as I dressed, whereupon I went out into the night.

Despite Habakuk's animosity, I felt quite light-hearted as I wandered up the slopes behind the settlement. Soon I had gained quite a bit of height and began to sense the cleansing effect of cold air upon my spirit and body.

The churchyard is situated upon a plateau above the church itself, on a ridge that protrudes at right angles from the fell. Here I sat down on a rock to catch my breath and enjoy the still of the night. The sun was up, though hidden behind the high peaks to the north, and the scene was so very much like the earliest dawn at my home of origin, where all as yet were sleeping, even the grouse in the forest and the animals in their stalls, and where the air is as clear and sweet as spring water. I was contented, thereby, and quite awake, not in any way somnolent, and I saw the rippling waves that travelled upon the fjord and the rope that hung down from the little bell in front of the church swayed gently in the breeze.

The settlement of the prophets is situated at a junction of two separate fjords, the Eternal Fjord itself and another which is minor. The peak behind the settlement and the promontory on the other side of this fjord are quite high and pointed, the first approximately a thousand ells tall, judged by my own eye, the other more than double this measure.

I saw a multitude of people, a procession, wandering from a place less than fifty ells up the fell behind me and proceeding as though by a bridge in the air, diagonally upwards towards the high promontory on the other side. They who were close to the ground were still in shade, while those who had reached further up were bathed in the light of the morning sun. All were quite distinct and appeared in no way to be transparent or spectral. It was a procession of tangible individuals. And yet all were dead. Indeed, I knew this to be so, although they in no way appeared to be such, but were vital, cheerful and much as people appear in everyday life.

Alas, what pain for me to see them – and yet such comfort at the same time! I saw my dear mother and several of my deceased relatives, whom I have not seen since childhood. Moreover, which matter struck deeply into my heart, my sister Kirstine, who must therefore have passed away during this last year. Yet the vision is not sorrowful, rather it is a solace and her blessedness shone into my eyes. Furthermore, I saw a number of other acquaintances, among them the cooper Dorph and the carpenter Thomas Møller, whose death I caused, all seemingly in vigour, agile and in good spirits; and also the widow's little girl and Bertel's young son, the studious boy of whom I was so fond. Into the sun wandered Captain Valløe and all his crew, by which I surmise that the *Frühling* has gone down on the return voyage; and in front of them, as though their leader, my friend the ship's boy, who jumped in the sea and drowned. Sad it was to see Miss Schultz's father, the book printer, among them. May the Lord have mercy upon his soul. Yet Miss Schultz herself seemed to be absent. Numerous others I saw, too, who are unfamiliar to me, including a young man in a wig, whose face was gentle and good-humoured; his red cape was of the German cut, and, if I'm not mistaken, it was the Privy Councillor Moltke! It was a quiet procession and the people – that is to say, my mother – appeared not to hear my calling out, no matter how insistent and piercing my voice must have sounded among the fells. I could have gone to the place from which the bridge seemed to emerge, but courage failed me. My father was not among them, though I am unlikely to see him again in this life.

How long I stood and stared at this heavenly procession I know not. It seems to me that perhaps an hour passed. All the time I noticed further acquaintances, old friends from childhood, student comrades, among them my friend Laust; and Mr Egede, who made such effort, albeit in vain, to teach me the Greenlandic affixes. None of this surprised me. I must have been prepared for it without knowing, and merely stood with my arms hanging at my sides and tears running freely down my cheeks without my caring to wipe them away. With peace of mind I left the place and returned to my accommodation in the alcove.

I write these words some few hours after this vision and am as yet highly affected by it, although the sentiment to which it has given rise within me, a feeling of peace and a portent of my own salvation, fulfils me and affords me serenity. However, I must repeatedly turn away from the page and quietly allow my tears to flow. The strangest aspect of it is that I do not feel to have witnessed any supernatural occurrence, nor was the vision in any way distressing. Deeply touched by the sight of my sister once more. But she is dead and blessed, I saw it myself!

Dearest Kirstine, I am no longer fearful of my own demise. May the time be short until we see each other again in the hereafter, where I may greet you with kisses and fond caresses and we may wander together along the shore of Elysium to the gentle whisper of the waves.

15 May

O laughter, this great heathen joy!

Habakuk and Maria Magdalene are my new teachers. Where she is reason, he is practice. He possesses a gift to engender enthusiasm and to jump forward in leaps of religious insight, as I have witnessed on numerous occasions during these days.

No less important is the fact that this great prophet has finally discarded his hostile countenance and has begun to afford me, as priest and Dane, a modicum of gracious kindness. I speculate that his wife has spoken with him, and that he, who like myself is much devoted to her, has resolved to heed her intercession. I sense this relief of the fear by which I was gripped formerly has now sent me to the opposite extreme, causing me to be somewhat obsequious in my behaviour towards him. And yet I have no objection to cowering like a dog, for it is a useful lesson for an old academicus and rationalist such as myself to defer to a man I previously would have considered one of the basest creatures under the sun.

But enough of this!

While I am well aware that a description of the devotions in which Habakuk directs his congregation may appear mirth-provoking, perhaps even repellent to the casual and detached reader, I shall nonetheless commit my observations to this journal and thereby fix in writing these metaphysical ceremonies as I have witnessed them.

It is she who receives the messages from the Lord, for the most part in dreams in which she is placed before Him and He speaks to her. Whatever she is told in these instances she then passes on to her husband, who in turn relates the words to his congregation in the form of sermons. These devotions are held in the early and late hours, on normal days as well as Sundays, depending on the occurrence of the Madame's dreams. People sit close together on the sleeping benches and listen; others soon come milling from without; all are more or less naked as he elaborates to them the joys of Paradise, a place that has much resemblance to this country, with a wealth of seals and reindeer and other prey, yet quite purged of Danes – a primeval Greenland as once it was. Many of the womenfolk are thereby brought to ecstasy and bounce on the spot while seated cross-legged, attaining increasing elevation. At the culmination of this state, the room echoes with squelching breasts and a clamour of rattling voices. There is weeping and laughter, and mucus is slung and spat against the wall of the house to run thickly towards the floor. Thereafter a calmness descends upon the congregation, which Habakuk exploits to bid one of the women to his bed, such behest being without exception happily obeyed, often with the most beatific of smiles. It is then heard that he joins together in flesh with the chosen woman, while his wife remains seated on the bench with her house-dwellers, apparently content and unaffected. She and I are the only ones present who have not removed our clothing and differ thereby from the rest of the congregation. On this account I feel some mutual connection with her, as well as pity, since it must undoubtedly be trying for her to maintain a dignified expression under such circumstances.

Moreover, devotions are performed each Sunday in the church, once again with Habakuk in the role of preacher. The service here consists of questions and answers, whereby Habakuk poses the questions and the rapt congregation replies in an atmosphere of increasing excitement, gradually whipped into a veritable fury of damp-eyed wailing and laughter. However misplaced it may appear, this weeping – and in particular the mirth and merriment that accompanies it – serves strangely to lighten the mood. I, too, partake in it and feel both liberated and gladdened by suddenly giggling without obvious reason, as though I were a demon of Beelzebub.

When this ceremony is over we go up to the churchyard, where we take each other by the hand, dance and sing hymns; for as Habakuk says: We must also be mindful of the dead that they may not be forgotten.

The procession I saw has not shown itself to me again, nor have I endeavoured to seek it out. It was a powerful vision of the kind to which a man should not be exposed too often. However, I have confided the matter to Maria Magdalene, and she smiled and squeezed my hand and said it was good.

I now set to work instructing the unchristened, having first made sure to request and receive Habakuk's permission. He even showed me the kindness of saying that my presence here could be of great assistance to himself and his wife, and also to the population here in general. The widow's dream of finding salvation in baptism will now at long last be fulfilled. She lies with me upon the bench. Habakuk has assured me that it is not a sin, since the Lord sees the human heart and has Himself bequeathed to man the merciful gift of love. In this I believe him and have asked him to marry us, to which he has agreed, even though such a ceremony can only ever be pretence.

The widow's kiss is as sweet as strawberries, and with pursed lips and blushing cheeks she is quite without her usual contrariness. When we entwine behind our curtain we are indeed one flesh! Her gentle breath against my skin when she sleeps. I lie awake and consider her as I write these lines. She is finally mine.

16 May

Today my cassock, my collar and wig were returned to me, all quite ruined, though now repaired and laundered.

Held service in the church today, almost the entire settlement in attendance, inside and out, and I blessed the congregation, christened and unchristened alike. Thereafter we proceeded together to the church-yard and sang two of Kingo's hymns. They rang so finely from the steep fellside.

Habakuk came to me afterwards and thanked me with tears in his eyes and told me he sensed the presence of the Lord. He is indeed an oddly excitable and soulful man, not at all heavy and immoveable as rock, but light and fluttering like a butterfly.

. . .

I am Magister Falck. The people call me *Palasi*.

18 May

A conversation:

MM: Magister Falck, what happens in the view of the Church to the unchristened relatives of the Greenlanders now to be baptized?

Palasi: The unchristened do not belong to the Lord.

MM: So they may not find salvation?

Palasi: If they come to receive instruction, they may be saved.

MM: No, you don't understand, Magister. The unchristened relatives who are dead, what happens to them?

Palasi: It is a shame, but if a person is not christened he may not find salvation, unless he is a small innocent child upon which the Lord shows mercy. If everyone were to be saved regardless of being christened or not, why then should anyone be baptized?

MM: But if they who are now to be christened have no hope of seeing their relatives again in the afterlife, how can this be Christian love?

Palasi: I understand your meaning, dear Maria. But I can do nothing about it.

MM: But if you told them their salvation might lead to that of their loved ones in Heaven? Could you not tell them that, Morten? Recall Paul's First Epistle to the Corinthians: For as in Adam all die, even so in Christ shall all be made alive. This is support for such a solution.

Palasi (long silent): I understand. This is a possible interpretation of the Apostle's words. I think perhaps.

MM: It has been our practice here for some time now. It is why we dance at the graves and in that way we celebrate our dead. Your own eyes have seen their procession cross the fjord into the heavens, Morten. You understand how important it is to remember those who are gone, and to retain hope of seeing them again.

Palasi: You are right. I shall follow your advice and thank you sincerely for it.

MM: You are a good man, Morten Falck.

Her faith is not merely sentiment; she is well-versed in the scriptures and what she preaches is founded thereupon. If I were to stand at St Peter's gate in the company of this woman, I fear he would first admit her and that my own salvation would depend upon whatever recommendation she might care to whisper in his ear.

25 May

Today I was joined to the widow in wedlock. The marriage ceremony was performed by Habakuk in good Christian manner and without the inclusion of any blasphemous antics. The widow plighted her troth to me in front of the church, while the whole settlement looked smilingly upon us. The weather was fine and mild. The bell was rung and must surely have been heard far out over the fjord. Afterwards a festive gathering was held upon the rocks, with salmon to eat.

I am certain the Lord acknowledges this marriage, even though its ceremony was not performed by a member of the ordained clergy.

Since now we are man and wife, Maria has allotted to us a separate house, which is the small dwelling to which I was brought upon my arrival here and in which we are now installed. The widow lies waiting for me in our common bed, to which I may retire without feeling shame towards the Lord or any fellow dweller. I ask her if she feels happiness, but she will not be drawn out. She is a strange woman.

. . .

The same, evening

The widow, my wife, which is to say Lydia, as she has asked me to call her, has shown me her crucifix. It is the same one of solid gold that she held up before me when I lay in my sickbed on the *Taasinge Slot*, but which I then believed to be a fantasy.

She was the thief, not Bertel!

Forgive me, dear friend, wherever you may be.

She had the smith melt the gold and forge this great and heavy cross.

In what coin, I wonder, did the smith demand his payment?

She will say nothing of the matter. Unfortunately, the truth is quite transparent. Most likely he moreover took his share of the gold as additional remuneration, besides the services she rendered him.

But the gold is now once more my own, or rather ours, the crucifix part of our common property, a physical manifestation of our love and alliance.

Trinity tomorrow.

10 June

The instruction of my catechumens proceeds well. The widow is of great help; she is my interpreter and my teacher in the Greenlandic tongue, as well as my devoted wife. With her assistance it is my hope to baptize the first ten within a few weeks, which is not a moment too soon, since before long there will be a deputation from the colony. What will happen then I have no idea, though it will hardly be favourable. Yet if I succeed in finding salvation for these people in baptism I shall not have lived in vain.

A woman who was in the pains of labour wished to see me, believing that she would not survive the birth. I attended to her and performed some examinations of her gravid *interiae et exteriae*, ascertaining that the child was in the transverse position, which I managed to correct. Shortly afterwards she gave birth to a boy and was strong enough to rise and find a solitary place to burn her afterbirth.

This deed of healing has afforded me the reputation of being in more than one sense a man of God. I feel it myself: the Lord was truly with me in this! The child, however, is a result of Habakuk's excesses, and since he did not wish it to be born, much as he undoubtedly wished its unfortunate mother to be taken for good, he has now once more become resentful of my person, a sentiment that would seem reinforced by the increasing favour I now find among the people of the settlement. He has not greeted me since the birth. Yet I am cordial towards him and hope that we may soon be friends as before.

12 June

Two things happened today:

A young man had fallen unconscious; his fellow habitants could not restore him to life and were resigned to lay him in the grave. Yet when I attended him and called upon him loudly and placed my hand upon his feverish brow he immediately woke and asked for water to drink. He is now already much restored.

Moreover: I went up on to the fell in order to pray in solitude and sat beneath a rocky overhang, when a number of boulders fell down around my person, just one of which might easily have killed me. Only by pressing back against the rock did I narrowly avoid being struck. When later today I encountered Habakuk outside my house he glared at me hatefully and his face was clouded.

I confided in the widow and she was at once concerned and fearful. She will speak with Maria Magdalene that she might talk her husband back to his senses.

15 June

Habakuk left this morning without warning, accompanied by a handful of hunters and their women of pleasure, for what is called the Paradise Vale. There he will remain for some time, the widow tells me. Thus, peace and harmony once again prevail in the settlement and I am able to fully devote myself to my work and to my beloved wife.

. . .

She watches the whole night. Only seldom in this recent time have I found her to be asleep when waking up myself.

Dearest, why are you not sleeping?

I'm thinking.

Share your thoughts with me. Am I not your husband?

I want to die.

But, my dearest!

You said I should share my thoughts with you. This is a thought of mine. Now I am sharing it with you.

But why do you want to die?

I've lost everything. I have nothing more to live for.

But, my beloved, what have you lost? You have me.

She says nothing.

She is a stranger to me, another species, a zoological riddle. I fear it was a mistake and a sin that we wedded.

Yet the folds and hiding places of her body are full of sweetness, and when my own body is joined with hers we are one flesh and one species, and I know by the Lord that I love her!

. . .

She asks me about the baptism, how soon it may take place.

It will take place when you are ready to stand before Christ, I reply.

I am ready now!

The day and the time is for me to decide, I tell her. Be patient.

She turns away in fury. Never before have I encountered such haste to become christened.

But Maria Magdalene, too, asks me to fix a date for the ceremony.

The catechumens are eager, she says. They have waited for this for many years, during which, for want of a priest, they have received instruction only from my husband and me.

Why such haste? I enquire.

They yearn for salvation, she replies. They thirst for it. Life is for us uncertain. If you are dead, you cannot be saved through baptism.

I promise her to intensify my instruction and have given my word that the ceremony will take place before the month of July reaches its end.

. . .

July . . .

O, may the summer never reach its close!

The ice drifts past upon the fjord, fracturing and breaking up in the warmth of the sun's rays and in the no less balmy gusts of wind that come sweeping down from the fell. The place is alive with the cries of gulls and children at play. The roofs have been dismantled from the peat houses and the dirt and filth of winter is brushed out through the doorways.

On the flat expanse in front of the church we play a ball game. A seal-skin has been stuffed to form an egg-shaped ball some one ell in length. At each end of the playing area a small cairn of stones has been piled and the object of the game is to topple the cairn with the ball, the method being to run with it under one's arm and to overcome one's opponents. I participate often in this game, and today I succeeded in hitting the cairn and causing it to fall, whereupon I threw my arms triumphantly in the air and ran back to my own camp in jubilation. Unfortunately, I had toppled the wrong cairn and everyone laughed heartily on account of my embarrassing error.

Another game, *the wandering ring*, is a singing game in which a number of participants – men, women and children – form a circle, drawing out between them a long strip of leather on which is threaded a small ring. The person who stands in the middle must guess where the ring will wander, while a taunting rhyme is sung, and where it will stop when the singing comes to an end. Lately I stood for a long time in the middle and tried to ascertain where the ring might be, but was unable, and for this reason I had to remain there while everyone sang and taunted me, though with faces full of kindness and love for their silly *palasi*.

The widow is dearer to me than ever before, and she is happier now, too, I believe. I made her laugh this evening when I said that I would take her back to my own country so that my elderly father might greet his daughter-in-law. She was quite surprised to learn that my father is still alive, and this was most probably the reason for her laughter. She considers me to be an old man, although I am only thirty-seven years and one month.

But still she does not sleep. How long can a person go without sleeping?

. . .

I no longer know what time it is, nor do I care.

Baptized twenty-two of my flock yesterday, among them the widow.

The Lord let the sun shine down upon the ceremony and only a mild wind from the fell was felt. The whole settlement was gathered in front of the church, and the crisp tone of the old ship's bell rang out across the land and sea, and must surely have been heard for miles around. The font was a tin plate and the water in it came from a small tarn at my own direction, since it is found at the place where the deathly procession I witnessed appeared to have its source, for which reason I blessed its waters *in extenso*.

Many come to me to be healed of physical defect and infirmity, now that the Lord has given me this gift. I have become ashamed to think upon the primitive and inferior medical science to which I formerly subscribed and which I practised. How feeble it is compared to the power given by the Lord to he who believes in Him. Thus I say to the cripple: Rise up! And he rises up and walks. And I say to the barren wife: Be now with child, and it occurs. With the blessing of my wife I have already impregnated a number of the settlement's native women – with good result, I am certain.

I have discarded my vestments. During service I wear now only a white tunic, which the widow has sewn according to my instruction. I have thrown away my wig and allow my locks to hang freely about my shoulders, this being of much benefit to them, for they are now more manifold and thicker than since I was a lad with flowing mane, leaping over the rocks at the shore of the Holsfjord. Since my exile upon the *Taasinge Slot* my beard has grown quite without intervention and fringes my chin and mouth, as dark and coarse as sheep's wool. The scurvy by which I was afflicted last year bothers me still, though less so now, which undoubtedly is due to the many physical diversions life with the widow presents to me. I wish to write a thesis on the subject: the detrimental effects of accumulated sexual fluids and suppressed lust. But who would publish such a monograph back home? It would be seen only as a lapsed clergyman's mad fantasies! So much the more fortunate for me that I have made this discovery and found the source of youth before it is too late.

The lice have left me. I commanded them to go, to depart from me in the name of the Lord, and I pointed to the door. They went! My body has in truth become a temple of cleanliness.

Madame Magdalene says likewise that I have become as a young man, and indeed I feel myself to be strong and youthful and in the prime of my manhood, which the widow, my spouse, must also acknowledge at hours both early and late. Life inside the fjord has transformed me. May the Lord be praised! I shall now climb into my bed to lie with my lovely wife and ask her to spread her delectable legs, for these latter words have caused my fluids once more to stream towards their purpose.

. . .

All formerly unchristened are now led to salvation by virtue of instruction and subsequent baptism. In total: 57 adults and 22 children. A number of infants remain, but shall be taken to baptism in proper and orderly manner these coming Sundays, on which occasions those recently baptized shall moreover be confirmed. Thereby this place is quite delivered from heathens and has become an oasis of true Christians in the midst of this savage continent of Greenland!

I thank the Lord each day for having brought me here.

Healed an elderly woman yesterday who suffered from a most dreadful dermatological condition, scabies or scrofulosis. I placed my hand against her brow, without fear of my own contamination thereby, and bade her go to the consecrated tarn upon the fell, there to take off her clothes and wash herself from head to toe, and to pray to the Lord her Saviour. This she did, and returned with the purest and most delicate skin! In the night she came to me and the widow gave up her place beside me, that the woman might express due gratitude for her healing and I bless her reborn *corpus femininum*.

. . .

I grasp the ankle of my spouse with one hand and draw her closer to me in the cot. I look into her eyes: they are dark and indifferent, as though she were a detached observer of this union of our flesh. The sweeping line of her foot is a thing of beauty, its arch is elastic and resilient and rather wrinkled by tiny horizontal grooves, which with bated breath I follow with the tip of my thumb.

Her toes peep up from the ball like friendly guardsmen from behind a breastwork and I kiss them, moistening the pad below the big toe with my saliva, allowing my lips to dwell upon the place, to taste its salty aroma of tanned hide. I look up at her again, an ironic visual comment upon this foot-licking in which I have begun to indulge of late, but she stares distractedly up at the ceiling, scratches her belly with unclean nails and fingers the large crucifix that always hangs upon her breast.

I allow my gaze to wander across her nakedness, holding my breath once more, her fair skin, the round volcanic crater of her navel, the flaccid mounds of her breasts, the deep-red strawberry peaks of the areolae, the raspberry tint of her mouth, the wettened gleam of her teeth – and all of it mine! I may do with it as I please, whenever I want. I wish only to do good by this unity of our flesh. I have no malice! And I tell her as much.

I now permit myself to part her thighs and look upon what they hide, the dizzying depths where opens, with slight reluctance, the other mouth, the manner in which the labia majora, the lips of her sex, stick loosely together, then to release and unfold like a flower receiving the first sun of morning, my face shining upon them, and a low-voiced whimper escapes me at this sight, this moist and red blooming rose, so nearly unendurable in its paining and magnificent splendour. I touch it and feel its suppleness, observe how its hidden muscle fibres make it quiver spasmodically, and I see with contentment and appreciation that it is wet and glistens and is thereby ready to receive my member.

I look at her a third time and now at once she is awakened: her eyes return my gaze.

What is on your mind, dearest? I ask.

Refrain today, she says. I cannot do it today. I don't want to.

Oh, but you can, you shall and you will, I say. We will, and my voice trembles with love and desire. It is lovely and I shall make you content!

No. Not today. It is my daughter's birthday today. Eight years since she came into the world through the hole you so wish to enter. For this reason you must not stick your cock inside me today.

My dear, I say, stiffening in my stiffness, in my satyric curvature upon her. I did not know. Forgive me.

She says nothing. She turns to face the wall. I lie the whole night and listen to her breathing.

. . .

Devotions on the green outside the church. Emotional!

For some time a number of the inhabitants here have spoken of exhuming one of their deceased relatives to see if what is said is correct, which is that the unchristened become saved by virtue of their descendants' salvation. They came to me then with this request, for permission to carry out the enterprise. I conferred with Maria Magdalene, who was at once angered and vexed by the matter and called them ignorant and heretical and was prepared to have the culprits lashed, but after a while she settled and opined that perhaps it was best thus, in the light of day, for otherwise they would do so in the night, when no one could watch them. And thus she allowed it to happen.

A grave was selected and they set about the task with hacks and spades, and within a short time they had dug through the thin covering of earth to the cadaver that lay swathed in skins and which was lifted from the grave at once and placed upon the ground beside it. With caution the skins were unfolded. I stood at the front in order to observe the undertaking and to ensure that no improper conduct occurred with respect to the deceased.

A face then appeared, whole and unscathed, a young woman's, and thereupon her body, as pale and smooth as marble, yet quite without postmortem lividity or any other visible *degeneratia mortis*. Her mother, an elderly wife, kneeled down at her side and burst into tears, whereafter the entire gathering followed suit. I cannot truthfully deny that I, too, felt compelled to stifle a sob. And yet the weeping quickly passed, for the face of the deceased became visibly enlivened, as though awakened by such lamentation, and a smile appeared on her lips, which for some time took on a rosy appearance. We held our breath at this sight, not a word was uttered, and all that could be heard was the wind in the grass. Abruptly the miracle ceased and the young woman slid back into death like a person drowned sliding back into the sea, and her cheeks sank about her cheekbones and became once more ashen and as hard as stone.

I ordered the deceased to be returned to the grave, and after some hesitation the skins were once more folded around her body and she was placed in the position in which she had lain, and earth was thrown on top. Thereafter I said the Lord's Prayer and led the congregation in hymns. They dispersed, moist-eyed and joyful.

Surely there could be no stronger evidence that the Lord is with us here in the Eternal Fjord! Once more I thank Him for having found me worthy to be a part of this!

. . .

Again, during a nightly wandering, I saw the procession of the dead moving along the same path through the air and across the fjord. Moreover, the sound of French horns and drum rolls of numerous kettledrums echoing among the fells. Among the wandering souls was my own self, in my discarded vestments, which fact I noted with peace of mind. I am prepared for the Apocalypse, and for Kragstedt and his men with their blunderbusses and wicked, worldly intent, who soon will come to us under full sail.

My wife received me on my return home. I confided my vision to her and she was most kind. We wept together.

. . .

My wife has disappeared. She has abandoned me!

They tell me she left upon a boat heading out of the fjord, most likely to the colony.

I cannot grasp it and understand neither the widow nor myself. How could I have failed to see it coming?

The widow is to me, and has always been, an enigma. Not long ago she told me she had nothing left to live for. What does she now want at the colony?

I search everywhere, but am unable to find the crucifix. She has stolen my gold for the second time.

. . .

Maria Magdalene believes Habakuk to have taken the widow to Holsteinsborg. This in no way seems to surprise her or make her sorrowful. He fears the inevitable confrontation with His Royal Majesty's representatives in the colony, she says. He could not abide the thought of being arrested and thus has fled to the north. It is but natural.

Natural! But dear Maria, he is your husband!

Habakuk is his own master, she says calmly and quite detached. He does what is best for him. Is that not true of us all?

No. We are Christians!

To which she merely smiles.

But the widow, I say. What does she want at Holsteinsborg?

The ways of the widow are unknowable, she says. Perhaps she is in love with Habakuk. They are old acquaintances, you understand, Magister, from the time she stayed with us some years ago. Besides, she is not well liked by the women here; once they ganged up against her, and even now, with all of us made good Christians, they whisper behind her back.

So this is what she is at! Not only has she broken my trust, abandoned me and robbed me of my gold, she has also betrayed me in the most despicable of ways in order to pursue her base and lecherous desires. Alas, her tears the other night – how false!

We can now only await a flotilla of the Trader's men, armed to the teeth, once rumours of my whereabouts reach beyond the fjord.

Despair and misery are inadequate words to describe the emotions that course through me this night.

Diary, the Second Part

Sukkertoppen Colony
1 August, AD 1793

Again today I stood watching for the ship by which I hope to return home. It did not appear. The Trader believes it will reach us before the end of the month. He is expecting *Der Frühling* once again this year with Captain Valløe at the helm. I have not divulged to him my knowledge about Valløe and his crew. Perhaps I am in doubt as to whether my vision of the spirits was veritable or mere phantasmagoria? In two or three weeks at the most, I shall know.

It has become my habit to clamber up on to this windswept crag that faces the sea and to stand and gaze southwards in the direction in which, hopefully, I shall soon sail. I await reply to my request, written and sent one year ago, to be released from this calling and be replaced by a successor, though at the time I could hardly have predicted the events that have now rendered my departure so imperative. Each day I fear I shall be put in chains, yet I believe the Trader finds amusement and much retribution in allowing me to remain in uncertainty.

· · ·

The diary I kept while at the Eternal Fjord has been lost. I did not leave it behind, despite the chaotic circumstances of my departure. And yet it is nowhere to be found. I hope it is gone, burned or sunk to the bottom of the fjord, that it may not have fallen into the possession of the wrong people. The Trader might find in it an effective means to end me, one that would allow him to complacently wash his hands of me.

· · ·

The full extent of what has happened at the settlement of Igdlut is unknown to me. I hope to receive an epistle from Maria as to the measure of the catastrophe.

I was dragged from sleep in the night, staggered outside and saw the ship at anchor in the bay. The entire settlement was thrown into confusion and uproar. They had armed themselves with the store of rifles, despite Maria Magdalene's urgent calls to remain passive, as good and decent Christians ought. Constable Bjerg could then be seen on the shore, striding back and forth with his sabre like a commandant, and at his side the Trader Kragstedt, he too with sabre, and dressed up like an admiral of the fleet. They beckoned to me and I approached them, although the people wanted to hold me back and stop me leaving.

Palasi, they pleaded, stay with us, do not go!

Maria Magdalene said: Morten, my good friend, do what is right for you to do. Do not fear for us.

And thus I left them. My thought was to bring the Trader and the constable to reason and to mediate between Maria Magdalene and the colony's representatives in good order. Yet, when I came to the shore, rifle shots rang out from the land and from the ship. They were shooting at each other! I cried out that in the name of Jesus they must desist, but the Trader's reply was to put me in chains and ferry me in the rowing boat to the ship, a whaler out of Holsteinsborg. Here, chained to the main mast, all I could do was witness the crime then committed against my beloved companions of Igdlut. A cannon was brought forward and numerous rounds of grapeshot fired towards the land, causing much damage to their dwellings. I saw the people inside them flee in panic to the fells, there to vanish from sight, whereupon the ship's captain sailed ashore with a number of armed seamen and they charged forward with torches and set fire to the dwellings and to our splendid church. When they returned they were well pleased with their work, for most of the settlement and surrounding grass was now ablaze, and not one of their number was harmed. And no knowledge could I gain of the plight of my friends.

In chains I was brought here, though released before our arrival at Sukkertoppen, now to go freely about without notion of what is to happen. Am I to be considered a delinquent or a free man? Will

Kragstedt have me tried and put to the pillory? I am in no doubt that he is within his right to do so.

Such uncertainty is worse than chains and a dungeon!

2 August

My old friend and helper, Bertel, has come back, though not as friend and helper, rather as my enemy and opponent. Where he has been this past year and what has occupied him, he refuses to say. But he has resumed his position of catechist, as I myself carry out the duties of priest in these final days, and we work together and even play an occasional game of chess. Despite his demeanour I am glad that he had not, as many feared, perished, perhaps even by his own hand, for the last that was seen of him he appeared melancholy and withdrawn.

All this pains me. There was a time we got on so well and could almost be considered good friends. But so it is and I shall let it lie. I bless you, dear friend, and wish you well!

4 August

Under cover of night a kayak messenger has delivered to me an epistle from Maria Magdalene. She is well, thank goodness, and in good spirits, though her people are spread to all corners, the settlement charred and all but deserted, and the church quite consumed by fire. Habakuk has returned and she has forgiven him. The woman is foolishly kind! She, if anyone, abides by the Lord's command to forgive not seven times but seventy times seven! He travelled with the widow to Holsteinsborg, as was told to me at the time. There he seems to have delivered her, my illegitimate and faithless wife. What business she might have had at the place, I know not, and Maria's letter says nothing of it. Yet the rumour quickly spread that the priest of Sukkertoppen was now living with the prophets, which fact prompted the colony managers at both Holsteinsborg and Sukkertoppen to join forces and set out upon their destructive and punitive journey into the fjord. Habakuk was committed to the pillory 'to cool off', but someone must have helped him, for in the night he escaped his chains, thereafter to return home *post festum* with his tail between his legs and full of contrition.

The prophetess herself escaped to the fells. Constable Bjerg must yet be a good man, since he gave half an hour of warning before his men set rigorously about the settlement with their torches and grapeshot, whereby one and all were afforded time to flee. One of those from her house, a young lad who threatened one of Kragstedt's constables with a rifle, and perhaps accidentally fired it, was struck by a bullet in the shoulder, but has now all but recovered from his injury. A majority of the settlement's dwellings burned to the ground. The thought of it makes me recall my first sight of the place several years ago, when we came by boat and the smoke of three score chimneys coiled in the air, and young Bjerg so aptly exclaimed that it seemed like an entire peasant village. Most of the settlement's stores were lost to the fire, goods traded from British and other seamen all went up in smoke, and likewise many firearms and much of their gunpowder. And yet not all has perished, their stores of meat survived, and those few remaining have what they need to sustain themselves through this approaching winter.

Maria Magdalene and her unfortunate husband now inhabit a small peat hut at the shore, where they were settled before the reveries gathered momentum. They lack nothing, she assures me with indomitable spirit. Habakuk is, it seems, no longer wanted by the authorities, nor indeed is she. Kragstedt has stated that Dr Rantzau's orders are of no consequence insofar as they are valid only for the Mission, and moreover that he has seen no warrant of arrest. Which is a lie, but let him lie by all means! He is a trader before a commandant and sees advantage in pursuing the matter no further. So be it.

All this I write to Maria Magdalene, the only person besides my deceased sister Kirstine whom I can say to be a true and intimate friend. I enclose with my letter two of my clay pipes, a good portion of tobacco and some tea, and deliver the little bundle to the kayak messenger.

May he return safely!

8 August

Bloody discharge and pains of scurvy. Am quite exhausted. At the place of the prophets my constitution was good, better than since my earliest youth, but now, after only two weeks, the body is once more in rapid decline. Another winter and I shall end beneath soil.

11 August

Still no ship. Autumn's eternal refrain. I clamber upon the rocks and see many things, though never this much-awaited ship.

They say the widow is back! I have yet to see her and have no wish to do so. She must meet her deserved fate alone and I doubt it will be a happy one. They say she again lives with the savages in their peat dwelling. It is as if she were hiding from something. What happened, I wonder, at Holsteinsborg? It seems she makes a living from hunting with bow and arrow, and from fishing in the rivers, though is hardly contented by it – I know her only too well! However, it has become known that she is now a christened woman and, as such, must be assumed to be relatively safe against attack from her own kind.

12 August

She came to me this evening, scratching at my door, whispering that she wished to confess her sins, to cleanse herself of guilt. What shamelessness! Naturally I did not let her in, but stood back from the window, hidden from view, and waited until she went away. She wishes to ingratiate herself by admitting her treachery and thinks that all will be made good by it!

That I could be lured into the mortal sin of leading this warped individual to baptism! It is an act that will haunt me for the rest of my days.

And now I feel a tinge of pain at these harsh words. Only a month ago I considered her to be my wife and kissed her feet in gratitude. Alas, such trickery and pretence. When eventually I am departed from the colony I shall lay down my vestments for good!

Sleepless. Pleased at my dismissal of the widow, no matter how painful. What did she want with me?

Night, 14 August

The widow at my door again. I held it ajar and we spoke through the crack. She informed me of what deed she has committed against her father. Missionary Oxbøl.

May the Lord have mercy on your wretched soul! I told her. I wished at that juncture to close the door, but she jammed her foot inside.

She said that only the gallows now remains, or else suicide, a choice that is entirely her own. If only someone would give her a helping hand, she said, that she might avoid forfeiting her salvation.

That salvation has been forfeited already, I said, with your father's blood on your hands.

You can absolve me of my sins, she said. You told me yourself that confession is the washing away of sin.

I then said the Lord's Prayer, while her foot remained in the door, and through the crack gave her bread and wine in absolution.

Now I can die and see my little girl again, she said. Will you help me with that too, Morten?

Your death is your own business, I said. I will have nothing to do with it.

I am the only person in the colony who knows it was you who set fire to the colony house, she then said. If you won't help me, I'll go to Kragstedt and tell him.

And when I then said nothing, she took my silence to be acceptance and described to me in detail how she would go up on to the cliff to sit down and wait for me, that we might release each other from our mutual bonds.

And thus now my soul has as much need of the Lord's mercy and absolution as the widow's own.

15 August, the Assumption

A visit at long last to Madame Kragstedt, who, it seems, has been waiting for me these past two weeks. She offered me a glass and said: Magister Falck, will you forgive me if I have one myself? Partake as you wish, Madame, I replied kindly, having already heard talk of her present condition. And not one or two, but indeed several did the good lady consume during my time with her, though without it affecting her in any visible manner.

A sorrowful visit.

A no more cheerful visit to the Trader's office this afternoon.

The widow is dead. The Trader informed me of it and looked upon me with an inquisitive smile as he spoke. Though my surprise was, of course, acting – and of the most demanding kind – I nonetheless felt overwhelmed with grief at hearing the words uttered in the small space of the office. As such grief indeed overwhelms me once more as I write! And now there is no reason to play-act, for I am quite solitary.

. . .

They found her at the shore, drowned and badly mutilated, having been dashed against the rocks. This, then, was her fate. I pray that the ship will soon be here with my successor that he may take care of the funeral. I have entered her name in the book of the christened. It is my final kindly nod to the widow. Thereby, she is entitled to a Christian burial. She was an unhappy and deceitful person in need of forgiveness, and that shall be my epitaph for her. My forgiveness she must wait for, as I am not yet ready to bestow it.

. . .

Have received abundant provisions from the Overseer, including one pot and a half of aquavit and good meat.

The widow is here.

All well!

16 August, evening

It is complete. The ship has arrived this midday with my successor, Magister Olaus Landstad of Finnmark, a man of good health and seemingly of solid constitution, with Lapp blood in his veins, I think, which the climate of this land and the Danish living will almost certainly soon put to the test. Which is to say that upon the order of our bishop he is to travel immediately on to Holsteinsborg to succeed the now deceased Missionary Oxbøl. I shall wisely remain silent as to the missionary's demise.

But Sukkertoppen has from this year onward no longer a pastor, and at the resolution of the eminent college none is to be called here again. Magister Landstad has thus a considerably expansive district to frequent, his parish now encompassing both the Holsteinsborg and Sukkertoppen colonies, and I predict that he will hardly be able to conduct regular supervision of it all. Thereby, my friend Maria Magdalene and her faithless husband will, I hope, henceforth enjoy peace in which to live without interference from us Danes. Who knows, perhaps the reveries and notions of liberation will be rekindled and once again ignite the Greenlanders, that they may emerge as a free and independent people!

Magister Landstad has been informed by the Kollegium of these despicable prophets and he questions me eagerly on the matter, promising solemnly that he will make sure their ungodly activities are swiftly brought to an end. I wish him the best of luck!

One of his first duties, however, will be to inter the widow, of which matter I have already informed him. I wish neither to see her nor follow her to the grave!

Alas, it is true! My dear sister is no more; my father informs me of it in his letter. But I saw you, Kirstine, you were one of the saved, and my sorrow will be tinged by the joyous knowledge thereof.

The good ship *Charlotta* sets sail for Bergen in little more than a week. Thereby I will in short time make passage directly to the land of my birth, and hereby I conclude this journal.

Morten Falck
Missionary, Sukkertoppen Mission Station, 1787–93
Departed 24 August 1793

THE ELEVENTH COMMANDMENT

Harpoon

(1791–3)

What does God declare concerning all these commandments?
Answer: He says thus: I the Lord thy God am a jealous God, visiting the
iniquity of the fathers upon the children unto the third and fourth generation
of them that hate me; and shewing mercy unto thousands of them that love
me, and keep my commandments.
What does this imply?
Answer: That God threatens to punish all such as transgress these com-
mandments. We should therefore fear His wrath and not sin against these
commandments. But He promises grace and all blessings to all such as keep
them. We ought, therefore, also to love Him and trust in Him and cheerfully
obey His commandments.

Harpoon!

The hatch is flung open: a red-bearded face appears, roaring.

Look sharp, you two scoundrels, or I'll have the both of you keel-
hauled all the way home to Aberdeen!

Harpoon leaps to his feet. Joe follows him on to the deck. It is pitch-
black; some torches illuminate the foredeck. The moon pitches like the
seasickness towards the horizon in the west, casting darkness rather than
light, and yet causing the sails to appear luminously leaden and grey.
The entire crew is up; they look worn out from the watch and agitated;

they run up and down the ladders, colliding in the confusion, yelling instructions to each other.

Easy now, the captain growls on the bridge.

The first mate stands at the portside bulwark. He endeavours to direct the men.

Joe grunts something in his own language, or perhaps merely grunts.

Harpoon says, Stick to me, Joe.

Aye. The big man puts a hand on his shoulder.

The captain sees them. He beckons. Come here, lads!

They go up on to the foredeck.

He stands with his telescope, though it can be little use in the dark. His clay pipe protrudes from the corner of his mouth, his lip curls around the mouthpiece. But the captain seems happy: his eyes sparkle in the torchlight. He points into the darkness. Harpoon narrows his eyes and stares. He hears rather than sees it, the curve of a back ripping a gash in the waves, the spout projected high into the air. Joe expels some small sounds; he shuffles eagerly on the deck planks.

A bowhead, says the captain, and peers into his telescope, vigilant and yet detached. The Greenland whale. And a splendid one it is. Ready by the boats. We'll have bowhead chops for breakfast.

Ready, the boatswain replies, a low voice beneath the bridge, and the order echoes over the darkened deck behind him.

Ready, lads? the captain enquires. He fixes his eyes on Harpoon and Joe.

Yessir, says Harpoon.

He puts on the greasy, foul-smelling suit. Joe helps him cord it at the neck and hands, checks to make sure it is tight enough. Then the noose is pulled down over his shoulders and fastened around his chest. Joe grasps the other end and tugs. They exchange glances, a faint and knowing smile. Harpoon takes the weapons, a lance fixed upon a long wooden shaft, and a small barbed trident, which he ties to his wrist.

Ready, he says.

Aye, Joe grunts and tugs again on the rope.

The hunt is on. Because of the darkness they delay lowering the rowing boats and try instead to tire the beast by means of the ship itself. Harpoon bides his time. They toy with the whale, or it toys with them, the truth of the matter remains as yet unclear. It arches its back and spouts in anger, dives, surfaces again and thrashes the sea into foam, barging the ship and causing it to shudder.

A playful fella, says the mate in acknowledgement, and the crew laugh tensely.

They stay close to the whale, firing at it with flintlocks, never allowing it peace, hounding it so that it submerges only briefly and with longer intervals between. The sails are set, the ship careens in the seaway, its swallow-tailed flag up above smacking in the darkness, the sea crashing over the deck and retreating again in a rush about the crew's ankles. The mate yells hoarsely and barks out commands; the captain stands and observes, utterly collected.

Get those bloody cloths tightened! the mate bellows.

The crew are at the winches, boot by boot, and tighten with all their might.

Steady, says the captain. His clay pipe is a red, pulsating glow in the murk. His arms are raised slightly at his sides.

A couple of hours pass.

The spout of the whale sounds different; the beast is out of breath and afraid. It is only a pair of ship's lengths ahead and knows it can no longer escape.

Steady now, for God's sake! the mate barks from the rear.

Harpoon looks up at the moon and thinks: Do you see the moon tonight, too, my boy? Do you know which of us will win? The ship or the whale?

Slack the sails, says the captain.

Slack, slack, slack! yells the mate.

Slack those fuckin' sails! a hand echoes.

You hold your filthy tongue and mind your work! the mate barks back at him.

The crew laugh, their teeth and eyes gleam white in the dark.

The sails tug on the screaming winches, they flap in the wind, smacking and cracking like whips. The boom sweeps back and forth across the deck, the crew ducking as one, and then the sails are taut again and the ship leans lazily to port and begins to drift.

Harpoon stands calmly and waits his turn. Joe stands at his side, trembling with excitement and hunger for meat. He feels the heavy hand upon his shoulder.

The captain makes a gesture and in a tone that sounds almost resigned he says: You may lower the boats.

The squeal of the winches is followed by three consecutive splashes as the boats hit the water. The men follow, tumbling over the bulwark and down the ladders. They push off, the oarsmen take the strain, and at once all is still and concentrated. Harpoon stands in the bow of the first boat, the captain's boat. He stares into the darkness; he listens; he breathes in the air. Behind him stands Joe with a firm grip on the line. He feels rather than sees the whale some boat's lengths in front of the stem; he feels the idle vortex made by its tail; he feels the fatigue inside its head, its death wish. He understands this animal. He wishes he could change places with it. He feels how they close in on it with every stroke of the oars, and he counts down, five, four, three, two and flings the harpoon with all his might.

The seamen rest on their oars. They have all heard the harpoon strike, the hollow, satisfying thud of the blade as it tears into skin and flesh, and they keep their distance from the line as it runs from its holder, so as not to be dragged out with it.

Direct hit, says the captain, who is seated in the stern. Haul her in.

Haul her in! the mate yells from one of the other boats.

The boat begins to careen to port, the men lean to starboard; they unwind the line and fold it around the barrel-shaped holder on the floor of the boat.

Here she comes, says the captain. Fire your rifles.

The whale emerges, gasping from its blowhole. From all three boats flintlocks crack, muzzle-flare flashes red and white in the darkness, cascades of blood and blubber spray out in all directions. By the vibrations the line implants to the hull of the boat, the men can feel the beast recoil with every round that strikes it.

Then it is still, yet everyone knows this is the most perilous moment of the hunt; it is during these seconds that the animal decides who is to win, the ship or the whale. Harpoon awaits his order, but the order is unforthcoming.

Now the animal thrashes its tail again; it arches its back, leaps and thrusts itself down into the depths, and the men yell in alarm, Slack! Slack! The line whistles down from the gunwale at an acute angle, a spray of water fanning in its wake.

Just let her go one last time, says the captain calmly. And they allow several hundred fathoms of line to run over the side. Then it is slack once more and the men begin to haul her in.

Harpoon hears the ship behind him, not far away; he hears the keel draw up the sea as it rises, then release and sink into the waves again. They lie on its lee side, sheltered slightly from the seaway. He sees the lanterns swinging in their holders and the figures standing at the bulwark, peering out towards him. He never knows if he will return to them or if the whale will win.

There is not a single command that would make sense at this moment, only a quiet prayer that the line or the harpoon head will not break or the boat be overturned.

The whale appears again, alongside the rowing boat. It emits a hollow groan from its blowhole, and saltwater, slime and blood showers down upon them.

Harpoon!

He has no idea who gives the command, nor does he care. He knows what he must do and the time is now. He stands in the bow and stares into the darkness; he hears the water foam along the flanks of the beast; he tries to ascertain exactly where it lies, listens for the gurgle of its blowhole, and then he hears the captain's inexorable command once more;

he feels the kind yet resolute shove of Joe's hand against his back and he leaps.

He lands not on the whale but in the water alongside it. It thrashes in alarm, lashes its tail and prepares to dive again, an action that must at all costs be prevented. He thrusts the trident into its flank and clambers on to its back. The animal twists and lunges, its tail whips in rage. He gets up on to his knees on the slippery smoothness of its hind and feels for the line, a firm hold, but must cling to the trident. His mouth is full of seawater and blood. He makes his way forward, along the back of the whale, as clumsy as a beached walrus, then rises to his full height amid the frigid spray that issues from the wheezing blowhole; he plunges the harpoon downwards, feels how firmly it lodges in the flesh. He calls back to the boat and they tighten his line.

Now get your Eskimo arse back here! they say.

The whale tries to squirm free. It has been harpooned by all three boats now; the lines slacken, then sing as they tighten, a loud and thrumming vibrato, and Harpoon ducks so as not to get caught up in them and perhaps lose a limb; he is plunged into the water again, has no choice, vanishes below the surface, into the silence of the sea, where sound is woollen and motion is slow and up and down are of no consequence, and there he senses the maelstrom of the whale as it endeavours to rotate around its axis and tear itself free; he hears the stifled shouts of the crew, hears how the whale slams against the boat, causing its wooden frame to groan, then everything slows, he becomes limp and listless, his arms paddle feebly for a moment until he submits, his grip on the trident lost, and he is indifferent.

And then he is on the deck of the ship, heaving and vomiting seawater. Joe is bent over him, untying the line around his chest.

All right?

All right, says Harpoon. Help me out of this suit and bring me my whisky.

†

He is the suicide man who cannot die. Again and again he plunges into the sea from one of the rowing boats belonging to *Henrietta of Aberdeen*, and each time he is resurrected, covered in slime and blood, as on the day he was born. He squirms on the deck, coughing and shivering with cold as the crew laugh at him, prodding him playfully with the toes of their heavy sea boots and call him a bloody devil. Whereupon he is given his whisky and sent to his cot. He knows he is lucky. He was asleep when they found him on the open sea, hunched forward in his kayak; they threw a noose around him and pulled him in. Since then he has plunged into the waters and been dragged up again more times than he cares to recall. It is an arduous business, time and again to expose oneself to death and yet remain alive. The boy died easily. He lay still on his cot and went out like a tallow lamp. Harpoon cannot even catch a cold.

The crew have several names for him. *Harpoon* is for his function on board. *Mutie* is for his silence and reserve. And *Phantom* was given him at the time he was caught in the light of the ship's lantern, drifting upon the sea in his little kayak.

He sleeps below deck with the bearded wild man who is as silent as himself, a man who lets out an occasional grunt of annoyance, now and then perhaps a laugh. His face is kind, his body good and warm to lie up against in the cold of the bow, its planks joined with ice. He sleeps a lot. Days may pass during which nothing happens on deck and the only thing a person can do is to sleep. The captain has some books, but the crew does not read; they consider reading to be a thing for women and landlubbers. Harpoon thinks of his life as a book. It is a book whose script is half erased and whose illustrations are faded and unclear. For each day that passes, and for each time he plunges into the sea, then to be resurrected, more blank pages appear in his book. He staggers about on deck, staring in at the coast without knowing whose coast it is, then returns down below to snuggle up to Joe.

The sea has been rough for some time, but the wind dies down and the sails hang limp while the sea below them swells ominously. In calm, with the ship lying like a dead weight upon the surface, they row about in the boats on the lookout for whales. Harpoon jumps on to the back of them and kills them; he falls in the water, drowns, is resurrected and concludes his job with a glass of whisky. He joins in the work of cutting the blubber and removing the jawbones of the bowhead, and when, on occasion, they catch a sperm whale he puts in his share of effort removing the head from the body and winching it on to the deck, where they puncture the spermaceti organ and tap the wax. They send him into the whale's insides, where he may sit and ponder like Jonah, eventually to emerge with lumps of ambergris, a hard fatty substance secreted in the animal's intestines and destined to perfume the folds of European women's skin and their most intimate places.

The wild man works with him; they are treated as one by the crew, like brothers. But he knows as little about Joe as the rest of the men, and does not understand a word of his language. All he knows is that he can trust him, and that he keeps a tight hold of the rope and hauls him unfailingly back on to deck again. Joe does not take to the water; he is far too big and clumsy, and something about him says he fears it. He is hesitant about entering the boat, and in a strong sea he appears nervous and keeps to the middle of the deck. Harpoon has no idea where he is from. Certainly he is not a Greenlander, nor is he European. His fingers are as soft as silk from the daily work with whale fat; he strokes Harpoon's cheek when they lie down to sleep. Sometimes he whimpers in the night, his legs twitch, he chomps and makes sounds that could be words in his own language, whatever it might be. Harpoon pats him on the arm and speaks soothingly to him; sometimes he says the Lord's Prayer. The wild man sleeps peacefully again.

The captain says he has sailed far and wide during two decades, but never has he seen as many whales as this year. It seems they are sailing in the far north, somewhere between Greenland and America. The ship is quickly fully laden with blubber, ambergris and oil, and it will soon be time to head home to Aberdeen, he says, and there you may all expect a handsome bonus – you as well, Joe and Harpoon. Assuming you want to see Aberdeen? It would certainly like to see you, at any rate. He laughs. You could earn some decent money if put on display in the square.

A storm chases them towards land, where they find shelter from the wind and cast anchor. When they again proceed north, Harpoon spies a number of peat dwellings. Some kayak men follow them, though the captain does not pause to wait. Harpoon stares at the land; he realizes he has been here once, but cannot recall what place it was. It has vanished from the book. He is relieved when the fells sink into the horizon and the only thing to see is the ocean.

Do you know this land, Harpoon? the captain asks.

He shakes his head. The captain studies him with piercing eyes. All right. If that's what you say.

The crew is some one score strong, bearded and red-haired, from the tender-aged ship's boy to the elderly boatswain. They numbered thirty-one on setting sail from Aberdeen a year ago, but several succumbed to the scurvy and fever, and two fell into the sea from the mast. Others have preceded Harpoon; natives picked up along the coast. He has no knowledge of what happened to them. Most likely they drowned or simply turned tail.

The food is plenty and not entirely inedible. Behind them they tow the carcasses of the whales they have butchered, hundreds of lispund of fresh meat, while the inhabitants on the coast die of hunger. Yet some of the meat they keep for themselves; they boil it with onions and cabbage and potatoes, a vegetable Harpoon has never before tasted. Each man receives as much ale as he can drink, moreover a quarter pint of whisky a day, a half pint on days of whale work. Joe receives none. The crew say it doesn't agree with him.

They sail north, pursued by the sun that climbs higher in the sky with each day. Coast comes into view on both sides, the fells are low and uniform, foreign. The men stand about on the deck and stare in at the land; they speak with concern about the captain having got it into his head to find a passage between the continents, the way to China, or perhaps he wishes to reach the North Pole and become celebrated. Or else die. It seems he doesn't find excitement enough in whaling, now he wants to be an explorer and see his name entered in the history books. One of the men says it is because he is loath to return home to his wife in Aberdeen, a raving fury she is, and the other men laugh and spit over the bulwark. And what about you, Harpoon, they say, grinning, have you run away from your woman, too? We all have something we've run away from. Remember that!

Early spring. The earth curtsies to the sun and the horizon is aflare. But *Henrietta of Aberdeen* flees from the sun; she follows the darkness northwards, creaking and aged, and with a crew growing increasingly nervous as to what the captain has in mind. The little Scot has a nose as red as a lantern and a small red beard that points into the air, ever to the north, as does the bowsprit. When he comes on deck the men are subservient and call him *Cap'n*. But when he is out of sight and earshot they curse him and mutter that someone ought to seize his command before they meet an unhappy end. But no one does anything about it and the captain's beard continues to point north. He calls for Harpoon and takes him down into his cabin, where sea charts are spread out over the table. With his clay pipe aglow he points to a place on the chart where the degrees of longitude run as close together as the rigging of a dog sled. He scrutinizes Harpoon questioningly. Speak up, my lad!

Harpoon says, The crew are mutinous, sir.

Who? says the captain. Tell me.

The boatswain, says Harpoon.

The boatswain is lashed to the mast and given a taste of the cat, not enough to hurt him, but more than sufficient to humiliate him. There is peace on board.

They say there's a great maelstrom up there where the land comes to an end, says the captain, and that it sucks all vessels down into the depths. Do you know of it, Harpoon?

I have never heard of such a maelstrom, says Harpoon, and I do not believe it is true.

There's a good lad, says the captain and laughs. I'm glad there's a tongue in your head. You can be of good use to me.

They drop anchor in a bay and row ashore to fetch fresh water, their supply having become greasy and fetid after months at sea. Harpoon goes first, Joe following behind, then the captain and some of the men. The land is as good as snow-free. They come to a small lake that is half covered by winter ice. They fall to their knees and drink.

How odd, they say, that something that does not taste of anything at all can taste so good!

They take off their clothes and jump into the water, dive and thrash, toss lumps of ice at each other and roar. Harpoon and Joe remain on the shore. They sit on the slope and watch the fat, pink men as they dance about, flapping their arms to keep warm, then roll in the heather to dry.

Right, says the captain, we must find another lake. This one is no good any more, now we've polluted it the water's as dirty as what we had to begin with.

Harpoon and Joe explore the area. They come to a slope teeming with hares and Joe comes to life. He kills a dozen by throwing rocks at them. Harpoon hears them fly through the air and the sound of small, shattering skulls. They tie the hind legs of the animals together with twine made of willow and carry them down to the shore, where the men are overjoyed at the prospect of a meal other than whale meat and rancid pork. Beyond a tall ridge they come upon a tarn. Fresh barrels are rolled forward and filled; the old reeking ones are taken apart to be stored. Joe puts his hand on Harpoon's shoulder and points. Halfway up a slope he has noticed some low mounds of peat and stone, and tufts of luscious grass. Dwelling sites. People. They return to the boat.

Well, Mutie, say the men as they ferry the barrels of fresh water back to the ship. Did you and Joe meet your families?

A couple of weeks pass. There are no whales in sight. Joe and Harpoon are put to work tarring the ship. With the rope around his midriff, Harpoon hangs suspended at the side with tar bucket and brush. Joe holds on to the other end. He sees his grinning face up above the bulwark, the limp sails, the tall masts stabbing at the sky above his head.

All right? says Joe.

All right, says Harpoon. Hold tight.

Aye, says Joe.

The tar is burning hot. Harpoon boils it in the galley and is careful not to splash it on his skin. The bucket must not get into the water or the tar will become cold and stiff and lose its ability to penetrate into the planks. One day he stumbles and a dollop of tar spills over the side of the bucket on to Joe's foot. The big man tears off his boot and jigs across the deck, and the men laugh and say what a pretty dance, a man could fall in love. Harpoon gives him his quarter pint of whisky and Joe dances on and howls an unabated monotone lament, until he falls down from exhaustion. Some of the men haul him up to the crow's nest, where he remains to sleep it off. Harpoon climbs up in the night to wake him and helps him down, before he falls out and knocks himself senseless.

One day one of the men shouts and points. They all run to the bulwark and stare. A squadron of kayak men appear between the ice floes. They drift to a halt some boat's lengths from the ship's side and look up to the deck, expectantly. The captain beckons them on board; he orders a ladder to be cast out. The natives climb on to *Henrietta*'s deck. Harpoon stays in the background; he sits on a coil of rope with Joe and smokes his pipe as he considers the savages. They are dark in complexion, their faces and bare arms tattooed, rather tall in height, skin garments festooned with amulets, long hair held in place by pearl-studded straps going under their chins and behind their ears, the same way as some of the natives back home. Harpoon can see that they are not as calm and relaxed as they try to make out. They are alert to danger. He knows they are ready to jump over the side at the slightest sign of hostility. But the captain is composure itself, smiling and kind. It is obvious he is used to the situation, or else he simply possesses a good instinct for dealing with natives.

Harpoon! he calls. Where are you when you're needed? Come here and interpret for me.

He slides down from the coil and approaches.

Ask them if they've anything to sell, says the captain.

He speaks with the men, finding their tongue to be quite understand-able, although their dialect is foreign to him. One of them turns around and whistles sharply with two fingers in his mouth. Shortly afterwards a kone boat appears, rowed by six women. The craft is filled to the rim with narwhal tusks and fox skins. More kayaks approach, some with a female passenger on the deck, her back to the kayak man. The ship's deck is teeming with natives. Now it is the turn of the Europeans to look uneasy. But the captain remains a rock of kindness and composure.

Ask them, he says, if they have traded with ships before.

The natives say ships come every summer.

The captain looks disappointed. Ask them about the sea to the north. How far can one sail?

Far, they answer. Several weeks by kayak. But the ice forms early.

Hm, the captain muses. Ask if one of them will be my pilot.

One of the men agrees to sail north with them. But he wants his wife to go with him. The captain grants his permission.

The savages are very interested in Harpoon. Where does he come from? Where did he learn their language? He tells them he comes from the south, that the land extends further south than can be journeyed in a whole year. He tries to explain to them about the colonies, the houses, the people. They listen and are absorbed.

They say a white man, a king, owns the land. Have you seen this king?

He says there are some people who think the land is theirs, but it is not. They have trading stations, but the land belongs to us.

And you, they say, staring into his face, are you one of us? You sound like us, but look more like one of them.

I am one of you, he says. We are one people. You are my brothers.

†

To everyone's relief the captain changes his mind and gives orders to bear away and follow the western coast south. The information given by the savages has seemingly cured him of his yearning for the North

Pole. Harpoon notes that Joe becomes more restless the further south they sail.

Joe, he says, take it easy. By this time he finds it natural to speak English. Many months have passed since he last spoke a word in Danish.

Week after week they sail with the rocky coast to starboard, towards the sun that moves in a flat curve over the horizon. He sees that Joe keeps a sharp eye on the land. The men say it was near here that Joe joined them. They pull his leg and nudge him with their elbows and say, Hey, Joe, aren't you going ashore to say hello to your mam and dad?

They cast anchor; the rowing boat is lowered. Joe will not go ashore. He hides below deck and pretends to be ill. Harpoon leaves him alone and spends some days on land under the open sky. He wanders across expanses of heather and along the fringe of a forest. So this is a tree, he says to himself and leans back his head. This is what Jonah sat beneath when he was angry with the Lord. The plains rise slowly, gentle hills outlined against a great blue sky. Then at once he is standing on the brink of a vertical drop of several hundred fathoms. Beneath him and in front of him is the sea, pressing against the coast. The difference between the tides is huge, at least ten fathoms. This must be the reason there are no traces of settlements along the coast. The natives here – among them Joe – are inlanders.

He returns to the others. They have made camp by a sizeable river in which they catch salmon that they boil and devour. But the stomach soon tires of such rich fish and after a couple of days they begin to split and salt the salmon and put them in barrels, which they sail out to the ship. Presently, Joe joins them. He sits down in the heather with Harpoon and stares bleakly at the land.

We all have something we're running away from, says Harpoon.

Joe says nothing.

When the first natives appear he hides again. Harpoon can see they are his people: tall, bony men with a loping gait and a tendency to scowl. The captain has been here before and is able to converse with them. They want rifles, he says, but these are poor people, scavengers and ne'er-do-wells with no means of payment. I think it best we make ourselves scarce before we wake up one fine morning with our throats cut and silly grins all over our good Christian faces.

They begin to pack, so as to leave the next day. In the night they keep watch by turn. But none of them sleeps. They lie and listen to the tide and believe they hear the sound of zipping arrows and cries from the forest behind them disguised as bird calls. Nothing happens. But when they go down to the shore in the morning the boat is gone.

The captain orders five of his men into the forest, armed with loaded rifles. Joe goes with them. Harpoon remains behind in the camp, along with the rest of the crew. The day passes without incident. The men return, toss down their rifles and fall exhausted in the heather.

Where's Joe? asks Harpoon.

Your friend Joe has decided to join his own people again, says the captain with a mournful smile. He sends his greeting.

The next morning the boat is returned to the shore and they sail back to the ship. The captain pats Harpoon on the shoulder. We've all got something we're running from, he says. But sooner or later we have to go back. That's how it is.

†

Harpoon!

He stumbles out on to the deck. The boatswain stands with the line. He smiles basely, as though he were about to hang him from the mast.

A right whale, says the boatswain. Make ready, Phantom.

The North Atlantic right whale is the species they catch most. It is a slow swimmer and easy prey; it does not fight as though possessed like some of the other whales, but is as gentle as a milch cow, and, it is said, just as stupid.

The whale is harpooned from the ship's deck entirely without drama; they have it firmly on two lines and it settles itself accommodatingly at the ship's side with a resigned lash of its tail.

Harpoon! yells the mate.

He leaps out and lands on its back, gets to his knees and crawls forward to the blowhole. He plunges the lance into the flesh; it quivers slightly, then settles.

An easy kill, says the mate from the deck. Haul him up, boatswain!

But as he is about to grip the ladder, the boatswain jerks the line at the same time as the whale thrashes one last time, and Harpoon is toppled into the drink. Somehow he finds himself underneath the animal; his hands claw at the cockle shells and tufts of sea grass that stick to the whale's exterior, but he finds no purchase and sinks. As yet he holds his breath, but the water presses down upon his mouth; his lungs strain. Why do I sink? he wonders, and sinks still. Why do I not float to the surface as usual? He realizes something is weighing him down, something in the folds of his suit. He fumbles with the buttons, but his fingers have begun to stiffen and the thirst for air intrudes upon his concentration. He gets a hand inside the collar, then another, and tears it open. He feels inside the sleeve and discovers several flat objects of metal, like beaten plates of lead to the touch. They are sewn inside the hem. A greeting from the boatswain, he manages to think, for having informed on him to the captain. He claws and tears and eventually the material loosens and he is able to remove the weights, to release them and let them descend to the bottom. He must have been propelled backwards, for he feels the rhythmic lashing of the beast's tail, the throes of death, and senses the vibrations from the long lances of the blubber-cutters, who have already set about the catch. If he surfaces now, he reasons, he will risk having his head chopped off or else be cut to pieces. But now it is too late to consider. He obeys the command of his lungs and opens his mouth, feels the rush of saltwater into his lungs. Drowning is not as bad as he thought; in fact, it is not at all unpleasant. His body is as limp and heavy as the lead weights he let drop to the bottom. He feels himself turn slowly backwards and descend. The urge to breathe has quite left him. The sensation is like placing one's head upon a soft silk pillow when most exhausted.

He opens his eyes. Above him rotates a ring of grinning faces with some sky in between. Someone is loosening his lifeline. He turns on to his side and spews seawater and blood.

What a splendid catch! they exclaim, laughing.

The captain takes the boatswain to task. I warn you, Boatswain, any more problems from you and you'll spend the rest of the voyage chained to the mast.

Yessir, says the boatswain. When the captain has gone he bends down over Harpoon, pats him on the cheek and says, That was for ratting on me. But you did well. Now we're quits, so why not be friends? He extends his hand. Harpoon takes it. The boatswain helps him off with his suit and fetches him a half pint of whisky.

†

Halfwit! Numskull! Nitwit! Chump!

The mate is having one of his frequent fits. The deck is covered in whale matter and he has fallen flat on his behind.

Who washed down this deck? the mate howls. Or more to the point, who didn't? I'll personally make sure he gets no bonus and is never hired again!

The men, with their backs turned, shudder with laughter. But all are edgy, all rather on the wrong side of each other. They want to go home to Aberdeen. But the captain has suffered a relapse of his North Pole sickness.

We must stop him, says the boatswain, or he'll sail us right into the maelstrom. And this time you keep your mouth shut, Harpoon.

Aye, says Harpoon.

On the quarterdeck stands the captain. Keep her steady, he says. Due north! His eyes gleam with the madness of midnight sun.

The fan of their wake is red with blood and punctured by partly butchered whale carcasses. The air is filled with the screams of the northern fulmar as they dip down to the carcasses and tear at them with their beaks. They no longer take the blubber, but go directly for the sperm oil, the most valuable of the whale's material, and the scarcest in volume. But if they continue to steer north they will have little to gain from their rich cargo and will be lucky to even survive.

Harpoon!

Another whale, another leap over the side. But the boatswain's hand is firm and Harpoon has found that he can trust him. He hacks a hole in the sperm whale's snout and bucket after bucket of spermaceti is passed over the bulwark. In the hold there is not even room for another barrel stave: now they have begun to collect the filled barrels on the deck, a matter that causes the men concern. They speak of the ship's displacement, that its centre of gravity is too high, that they risk turning over. The schooner draws much water, with a freeboard of only a couple of ells amidships in still weather. The matter is put to the mate, whose response is to have the messenger, one of the elder seamen, bound to the mast and lashed. The next morning it is the mate who stands there bound. He mutters faintly to himself, his shirtfront reddened with the blood that drips from his nose.

I see, says the captain pensively when presented with the sight. And what do you now intend?

We want to go home, says the seaman who was lashed.

Where's your sense of adventure? the captain enquires. Good Scottish seamen you are, one and all, or so I thought. I'm ashamed of you. What would your proud ancestors think!

Sail home or go the same way as your mate here, they say, loosening the man from the mast and tipping him overboard. There is a faint splash and some stifled protest, then silence.

The captain seems unperturbed and merely shakes his head mournfully, while clicking his tongue. We could make history, he says softly, we could sail further north than any ship before us.

There's a reason no ship ever went there before, the seaman says. It could be that ships have no business there.

Cowardly dogs, says the captain with a sigh. If you call yourselves Scotsmen, then from this day on I am no longer a Scot.

Harpoon hears some tumult, a scuffle on the deck. The men converge, then draw back. He sees the captain spreadeagled, with two men on top of him.

Now, says the boatswain, now it's your turn, Harpoon! He hands him the whaler's lance.

What do you want me to do?

Well, take a guess, says the boatswain, and grins.

The men step aside, the boatswain nudges him in the back and he stumbles a couple of steps forward. You're the only man on board who isn't christened. With a Christian man's blood on our hands we're doomed. But you can do it.

No, says Harpoon. I won't. You already have the blood of the mate on your hands.

My friend, says the boatswain in a low voice. Listen well. If you won't do it, they'll kill you, too.

He steps forward to the captain, who is on his back. The writing vanishes from his book, but a new book is in the making, the Book of Harpoon, the nameless heathen. Two men hold the captain down by his shoulders. Now they spring aside. The captain remains flat.

Harpoon, he says, his red beard pointing up at him. Will you let them make a murderer of you, my friend?

He does not reply. He takes another step forward. He points the lance at the captain's stomach.

No, not there, says the captain, not in the stomach. Much pain, a slow death. Further up, my friend. Here.

He moves the point to his chest.

You're a good lad, says the captain. You remind me of my son.

†

The men celebrate down below, blustering the songs of their homeland. Frequently they spill up on to the deck for fistfights, two by two, their knuckles bound with cloth, the others standing in a ring, cheering them on. Harpoon sits on a hatchway and gazes towards the land, the fells that at first are low and uniform, then steep. He tries to establish what feelings he has at the sight.

Hey, Phantom, say the men. Aren't you going home soon?

The boatswain sits down with him. He lights his pipe; they sit a while and smoke.

My good native friend, says the boatswain. Now is the time for you to take your kayak and leave us. If you don't go of your own accord, they'll tip you overboard and this time there'll be no rope around your waist.

Aye, he says.

Go home, says the boatswain. Do what needs to be done. Believe me, it's better than running away. And this comes from a man who has been fleeing for thirty years. Don't forget me now, my friend.

When shortly afterwards he is settled in the kayak they stand at the bulwark and wave. Bye-bye, Harpoon, Mutie, Phantom. Wish us well on our voyage. The good Lord knows we need it!

†

Holsteinsborg, 1793, spring. It is many years since he was here last and the colony has grown considerably, into an entire little town. Many of the houses are of both two and three storeys, staggered up the steep slopes behind the harbour, freshly painted and gleaming with the wealth that whaling has brought to the place. He well understands that Kragstedt has thoughts of something similar at Sukkertoppen. He wanders in and out of the lanes that run between the houses. People take no notice of him. He finds his way to the trading station office and speaks to the Overseer, who makes a quick appraisal of him and takes him on.

He can start right away, the Overseer tells him. Report to the quay-side. He points through the window. The constable there will get him started. Name?

Harpoon hesitates. Jens.

Yes? The Overseer's pen dips in the ink pot and hovers over the page.

Bertelsen.

Settle up once a week with me, Jens Bertelsen. Bed and board is his own matter. He puts the pen back in its holder. Don't just stand there.

He goes down to the harbour. The constable scrutinizes him. Blubber boiling, he says. Come with me.

The blubber house is situated on a promontory outside the colony. It is a two-winged structure, each wing some twenty ells in length. The smoke drifts heavy and fetid out across the fjord from the tall chimney. The constable opens the door and calls inside. A young, bare-chested man comes to receive him and show him the ropes. They do not introduce themselves.

Furnace, says the man. Stoke here. He opens and closes the furnace door. Coal here. Make sure to keep an even temperature. Flues here. Once the blubber's on the boil, you need to tip the kettle to make it run out into the cooling vats. Here. But mind out, it's hot. He laughs and points out a number of scars on his upper body.

They enter the adjoining room. Through holes in the wall, wooden spouts run down to smaller cooling vats in which the blubber oil is left to stand for a few hours while the sediment settles at the bottom. Then it is led off to the next cooling room, where it is poured into flat-bottomed trays and cooled in the draught of the open windows. Eventually it is released through an outlet and siphoned into barrels, ready to be shipped. Questions?

Can I sleep here?

Haven't you any place to live?

I just arrived.

You can sleep in the loft, but I doubt you'll care for it.

Thanks.

He soon finds out it is best to be naked, or as good as. The air is thick with fat and steam, and so hot that he sweats pints in the course of a day. Blubber is brought in from the whole colony: kone boats fully laden; Danish whalers sending in blubber in exchange for lamp oil; natives bringing great piles of cut blubber on litters. The furnace roars all day and all night; he shovels coal and taps the oil. They are a handful of men, all working naked, all losing their footing on the slippery floors, all covered in blubber and soot and resembling the prints of Negro slaves he has seen in the magazines, with great, blinking eyes. Outside, large bays are filled to the brim with unmelted blubber, and more arriving all the time. The foreman harasses them. It is not a job that is ever finished; the purpose of the job is not to drown under yet more work. He finds a good rhythm and sticks to it. If a man is not quick enough to send the melted blubber onwards in the system, the constables will be upon him; and if he is too quick, unmelted blubber enters into the cooling vats and he must start again. To facilitate the process they must clean the copper of impurities six times a day, after which it must be rinsed with water, a highly perilous job, because the vessel is constantly red hot and the water explodes into boiling steam the moment it touches the metal.

The work soon renders him numb and empty. The Book of Bertel is now devoid of script, and the Book of Harpoon has reached its conclusion. He is no longer a narrative, but a man returned to his natural state. He sleeps in the loft above the boiling shop. It is a hot and malodorous place, and the noise from below seems even more deafening than when he is in its midst. And yet he sleeps soundly, naked on the rough planks. Sunday is their day off. He makes himself as clean as he can, and occupies one of the rear benches in the Bertelskirke, bowing his head whenever anyone enters. He recognizes several of the churchgoers and keeps his eye out until eventually he sees her.

She sits on the women's side, small and huddled. He studies her for a long time and she must sense it, for she begins to turn her head and cast glances over her shoulder. When finally their eyes meet, she stiffens. He nods deliberately. She stares at him for a long time.

He rises and leaves. He sits down on the slope below the churchyard and waits, then hears the soft pad of kamik boots behind him.

Bertel, is it you?

He turns his head and smiles over his shoulder. Mother.

I thought you were dead.

I am well. I work for the Trade.

The Trade? she says. Have you been chased from the Mission?

I have taken a break. How is my mother?

Well, she says.

How long have you lived here?

For many years. Ever since we moved from the old colony, I'm sure you remember it. The time your father died.

And the priest, do you see anything of him?

Oh, that was all a long time ago, she says. We are too old now to keep remembering it.

I am not too old, he says. Is he still alive? It was not he who gave the sermon today.

They say he is up at Godhavn, visiting his friend the inspector. Yes, he is alive, the old sinner.

He nods. I will pay him a visit when he comes home.

You do that. But it is by no means certain he will know you. He has become an old man.

Dear Mother, he says, rising to his feet and kissing her.

My sweet Bertel, she replies, and strokes his cheek. Mother's little pastor. You were always my cherished one. I thought you were dead.

I thought so too, he says. But now I feel alive again.

†

He sees the sloop come sailing from the north, its square sail taut in the wind, like a knarr of the Viking age. He has been in the colony for two weeks; soot is etched into his skin; his body is speckled with tiny burns; he has become lean yet strong. He stands in the doorway and takes in the mild sunshine and the cool breeze of the fjord, when he sees the priest clamber on to the quayside. He hurries to put on trousers and a shirt, then goes down to the warehouses. The new arrival straightens his back. He supports himself by a walking stick.

A small man with thin legs, bulging belly and the beginnings of a hunched back, a deformity that pushes his head forward and compels him to look upon the world along the vertical axis, from bottom to top.

Bertel recognizes him immediately, the way he recognizes his own face in a mirror. The pigtail that hangs down over the collar, the mousy grey coat with its small pockets of white napped leather, an abundance of silver buttons and buckles, gold braid that seems almost to spill from the buttonholes. Under the coat, which hangs open at the front, he wears a red suit, buttons sparkling at the fly. Between the breeches and his boots a few inches of chalk-white stocking are visible. Yet the body and the clothing do not match. The garments look like they have been pinned together hastily by a tailor.

He cocks his jutting head to the right and to the left beneath his tricorne hat, fox-like eyes narrowed, as though on his guard. The wooden jetty creaks; it sounds like it might collapse under the priest's misshapen form. He turns stiffly and barks something to the crew. Travelling chests are unloaded onto the quayside; two of the men carry them off. The priest watches them and must twist his entire upper body in order to turn his head, which sits firmly upon its stubby neck like a toad's.

This man with the silver buttons remains standing for a moment, as though his legs are too stiff to move. The wind lifts the tails of his coat. He adjusts his hat, then proceeds unsteadily along the quayside, passing closely by the man with the blackened face who cannot stop looking at him. Peace of God, the priest quacks. He sees that his mouth droops to one side, small and bloodless, pursed into a sour expression. He sees the pale skin and the liver spots, the narrow eyes, the sly look on his face, the crooked matchstick legs that seem to be in peril of breaking under the otherwise inconsiderable weight of the waddling body above them.

Is this how I shall end up looking? Bertel muses.

The next day he hands in his notice and purchases new clothes for his wage, washes himself with soap, a by-product of the blubber-boiling, has his hair cut and is shaved by the colony smith, and approaches one of the town's three catechists.

Nej, says the catechist, addressing him in Danish. Not a chance. Oxbøl will not take on anyone new, at least not a man. This latter comment would seem to be a joke; a grin flashes across the man's face.

But the priest is surely available to speak with? he enquires. If one should have need to confess?

Confession is every Sunday, first public, then personal. But the old missionary hardly works any more. The catechist studies him warily. Does he belong to the parish?

My name is Bertel Jensen. I am a catechist myself. I need to speak to the reverend Pastor concerning a private matter. A matter of the soul.

Your soul is as much a concern of the new priest as of the old one, says the catechist rather more kindly.

The soul in question is that of the Missionary Oxbøl himself.

The man looks at him with a wry smile on his face. In that case you should go to the rectory and ask to speak to him. I cannot help you.

The rectory is a singular, whitewashed building four windows in breadth and boasting two chimneys. A palace. In front of the house stands a flagpole. He pauses and looks up at the flag. It flutters in the wind like a trout wriggling in the current of a stream. The flag is red and white, the flag of the Danes. It feels odd to be here again after so many years.

A young girl opens the door. She leans idly against the frame and looks him up and down with bedchamber eyes. Her long hair hangs loosely down one shoulder. She has been braiding it.

I must speak to the Missionary Oxbøl. *Palasi*. Is he in?

Who should I say is calling? she enquires, studying him still, a calculating look in the face of a small girl.

Bertel Jensen. I am family to the missionary. Tell him I am the son of Martine. He will understand.

Is he expecting you?

I imagine so. I'm sure he has been expecting me for years.

She goes off to find him, leaving the door ajar. He pushes it open and steps inside, stands for a moment in the dark hallway he explored as a boy. Two doors lead off to the rest of the house and a stairway to the first floor. He hesitates, then reaches down and smooths his hand over the wood of the lowermost stairs. He decides on the door to his right.

✝

His memories of his years at Holsteinsborg are few. His mother was taken into the priest's employ at a young age; she prepared meals and cleaned for him. By the time winter came they were living together as man and wife. She had another man, Jens, but the Missionary Oxbøl told her she must choose between them, either the priest or the unchristened hunter. She chose the priest. This she told Bertel many years later.

The priest was a handsome man in those days, she said. And I was young and foolish. But then you came along, my boy, and something good came of it all.

He tries to recall the time he lived at the rectory with his mother and the missionary. These planks and walls and ceilings, each creaking door, the windows offering a singular aspect on the fells. All of these things make it return to him. He used to sit in the kitchen of the missionary's house and read a book his mother had found for him. Always he was afraid the priest would appear. Now and then he would hear his voice from some room in the house, or the sound of the stick he rapped against the wall to summon his servant girl. Then he would know to remain seated and not to go anywhere until she came back.

In the evenings the priest would produce his lute and play and sing. Bertel would sit in a corner of the parlour and make himself invisible, until he was sent out. But his mother was there; it was she for whom he played, for want of a better audience. He still recalls the hesitant twang of the instrument, fingers scraped against the strings, the priest's woolly voice singing the laborious and incomprehensible verses. Bertel never put his hands on the instrument. He knew instinctively he would be punished by the priest's cane.

He remembers an exchange between the priest and his mother, on the other side of a door that stood ajar. He must have been eight or nine.

I am a Christian person.

Indeed. It was I who christened and confirmed you, as I am certain you remember.

Not only have you taken my man away from me and saddled me with a bastard child, you have turned my home into Sodom.

Your home?

No more. I am leaving now.

Then farewell, said the priest. Take your bastard with you.

When Bertel was older he asked her about it and she told him it was because Oxbøl brought home with him the tender young girls who were under his instruction and slept with them. It was a weakness of many priests, not to mention traders, smiths and carpenters, and other good folk besides. It was their distraction in return for working in a land that destroyed their health, and that was why there were so many Greenlanders with pale faces. Like his own.

†

He hears a distant chatter of women's voices, laughter, children crying. It seems to come from all quarters, but the sound is disembodied. There are no women to be seen, no children. It is as if the house has been emptied. Apart from the man in the chair. But even he seems like a ghost.

He looks at him and sees himself, his sister, his son, his niece. The face is freckled, pale and twisted; its eyes stare at him, as blue as water, a mouth that haltingly seeks to form words, perhaps a prayer for help.

Yes? he says and steps another pace forward.

A clock prepares to strike, but makes no further sound, merely ticking, ponderous and uncertain. The ubiquitous women's voices have a calming effect on him. He knows who they are. Family.

The old man groans, a foot scrapes the floor in agitation, his head rocks.

Is there anything I can do to help, Pastor Oxbøl? He stands looking at him. He is beginning to realize what is wrong with the old man.

The priest jumps up and down in his chair, gripping an armrest to support his weight, the knuckles of his left hand whitening. He gobbles madly from the corner of his mouth.

What is the matter with him? Is he ill?

He extends a hand and the old man snatches it. Now they are bound to each other. Oxbøl thrusts himself back into his chair and then appears to relax slightly. A dribble of saliva runs from his mouth to stain the white frill of his shirt.

Do you know who I am, Priest?

Oxbøl looks up at him. His gaze is firm. He seems to be fully aware.

I was one of the children of your parish. I wanted to meet you and see how you are.

A muscle tenses on one side of the priest's face, another relaxes; together they form an expression of what seems to be at once idiocy, doubt and bewilderment. His jaw begins to tremble, tears well in his eyes.

Don't cry, he says and withdraws his hand. Don't be a child.

He does it all the time, a voice says in Greenlandic.

He turns round. A woman has entered the room. Behind her follows the young girl, whose hair is now plaited. He approaches them. The old man's hand reaches out, claw-like, grips his wrist, and when he pulls away the hand and arm follow. The old man sits tilted at an angle and looks like he is about to slide to the floor, yet he does not release his grip.

The woman comes, bends over the priest and pries open his hand.

My name is Bertel Jensen, he says, rubbing his wrist. I come from Sukkertoppen.

The woman considers the old man and lets out a sigh. This is the second time he has been like this. They say the third time is the end. Have you told him who you are?

I told him I was a child of his parish, now come back to look in on him.

A visitor, Lauritz! the woman announces in a loud voice.

The priest gives a start. Tears begin to roll down his cheeks. His eyes dart this way and that.

Take no notice of his crying, it means nothing, the woman says. Or else it means anything at all. He might be glad or disgruntled or hungry. Or he might need the pot. How lucky you are, Lauritz, to have a visitor, she says to him.

The priest's arm twitches and his whole upper body follows suit. Convulsive sobbing contorts his face.

Look how glad he is, says the woman and pats him hard on the cheek.

Well, says Bertel. I'd better leave. I just wanted to see him one last time.

No, stay and eat. There is soup on the stove.

The soup is rich and salty, thickened with oats. He cuts off chunks of seal meat and puts them in his mouth, devouring them with spoonfuls of soup and fresh water. The women and children watch him as he eats. Pale and freckled.

We know who you are, they say. Do you know us?

He nods.

But why have you come?

I wanted to see him one last time.

Did you come to see him die?

I suppose. Why are you all here?

The same reason. If he will die at all. He is strong.

He stays in the priest's house with the women and their children. In the parlour the old man lies in his filthy cot or else sits bound to his chair. He calls for them by beating on the floor with his stick. If he does so too frequently, they take it away from him, in which case he begins to howl or thrash about so violently as to cause himself to fall. Then they give back the stick. Bertel sits with him sometimes. He tells him about the life he has lived; about Sofie, who has gone away; the boy who died; his sister, who cannot find peace in life and who remains unchristened; and about her daughter. The priest appears to understand what he tells him and seems eager to pass comment. Clearly he is unused to remaining silent. Bertel likes to torment him somewhat. I do not believe there to be a single one among your descendants who does not despise you, he says. That is why they are here now. They are waiting for you to die. The priest weeps, his jaw trembles, he rocks backwards and forwards. But his eyes are enraged.

The priest will not die. He regains some of his mobility and begins to rise from the alcove, casting his wet underclothes to the floor and bellowing out for the women to come, as though to make their ears split. They go to him and wash him, scrubbing his body as he stands leaning against the table, putting clean clothes on him. They tie him to the chair with leather straps, so as to prevent him from getting up. Several women must hold him down; he lashes out at them, lunging fists as quick as serpents, but his attendants merely laugh and force him back into the chair. On a couple of occasions he manages to loosen his bindings; they hear a thud as he falls over and find him lying in the middle of the floor, bleeding from a gash in his head, bleating like a goat.

We must do something, they say, looking at Bertel.

Don't look at me, he says.

He is getting lustful again, they say. And he is strong. If first he grabs hold, he will not let go until he has had his way.

The Missionary Oxbøl lies in his alcove and calls out his demands. He wants more and he wants it now! He will not give in. He clamours the whole night, hammering on the walls. His hands find the stool next to the cot: he hurls it across the room and it smashes against the door. One of the women goes in to him and he falls silent.

Bertel's mother, Martine, moves in to the house. She takes on the task of his care. She has a way with him. She feels no hatred towards him and he senses it. He quietens. Bertel does not know what his mother does to settle him, but it is certainly effective.

His sister comes from the Eternal Fjord, where she has been living for some months. There is a radiance about her that startles him. Your old friend Maria Magdalene sends her regards, she tells their father. She would have liked to have been here herself, now that you are about to kick the bucket, but she has more important things to attend to. Later, his mother tells him that his sister has finally been baptized and confirmed by Mr Falck, who has even taken her as his wedded wife.

Now they are gathered. They sit at the deathbed and wait. But the priest grows stronger with each day. He sits tied to his chair and plays chess with Bertel. They can sit for hours with only the chessboard between them.

Check, say the old man from the corner of his mouth. He has begun to utter the occasional word.

Bertel moves his king. Oxbøl's rook approaches. Bertel's knight strikes at his opponent's king and queen.

Check. Five moves, Priest, and it will be mate.

Oxbøl rests a finger upon his king. And topples it. Clever, he hisses in acknowledgement.

Bertel turns the board around and sets up the pieces again. They begin a new game.

The peace lasts a week, until they find Bertel's mother unconscious on the floor of the priest's parlour. She is half-naked, her thighs and back are heavily scratched. The priest pretends to sleep. They see that his fingernails are bloody. They wrap her in a blanket and carry her down to the Trader's house, where she has a small chamber. One of the other women sits with her. In the night, she dies.

See what you have done! they say to the priest. But the priest purses his lips and will not utter a word.

For two days all is quiet. On the third night he begins to pound on the walls and shout.

Let me go to him, his sister says.

No, he replies. I won't have it. He is your own father.

It's the only thing that will quieten him down, you know that. Anyway, it's not that bad.

Bertel goes to him instead and must duck as an object is flung through the air and strikes the wall behind him. The night pot. He can smell its contents of faeces and old man's urine as they run down the wall. His father is already looking for new ammunition. Bertel promptly withdraws.

Mate! his father shrieks.

I told you he would not speak to you, his sister says, and goes to him in her brother's place. At once the commotion abates.

The women begin to bicker, a couple of the children cry. The women chastise Bertel and call him cowardly; one of them waves a red-hot poker in front of him. But if he dies, what are the rest of us to do then? one of them wonders. As long as he is alive we at least have food and shelter for ourselves and our children.

Some noises are heard from the parlour. The women fall silent. Glances are exchanged.

Bertel takes the poker from the fireplace. He goes into the hallway and cautiously opens the door of the parlour.

He sees a reptile with arched back and a tail swishing from side to side. It is pale green. It rears up in the alcove and moves rhythmically, undulating and peristaltic. He sees the muscles of the reptile's back as they tense, sees his sister lie resigned and staring out to the side, the stony look in the reptile's bloodshot eyes, as he cries out: Leave her alone!

The reptile sees the poker with wide and frantic eyes. It opens its jaws mechanically and flicks its forked tongue.

He steps up to the alcove and prods at the reptile's scaled skin with the glowing implement.

The priest screams. His face is contorted with pain and bewilderment. Why? he hisses. I love you both!

His sister yells: Bertel, go away! Don't get involved in this!

But he prods again; the old man screams once more and collapses on to his side.

His sister extricates herself from beneath the weight of his body. Bertel brandishes the poker. She holds him back and twists it from his hand.

Enough! she says. You'll end in the gallows. I won't have such guilt laid upon my shoulders.

The priest lies with his face buried in the pillow. His breathing is erratic. When they turn him over, he stares at them with one eye. The other is closed. His lips move, and his left hand gestures.

What's he doing? says Bertel.

I think he may be blessing us, his sister says.

Bertel attempts to wrest the poker from her hand, but she holds it tight.

No, she says. Give it to me. I shall do what is my right.

And then she lifts the poker and strikes. Bertel sees that the trajectory is well-considered, the delivery is angled so as not to be impaired by the ceiling of the alcove. The weapon is brought down with icy precision. At the same instant, the women spill through the door, the floor is awash with progeny; they cast themselves upon the priest, tearing at him, screaming and flailing, until eventually he slides lifeless from the cot to lie in a heap amid the blood that issues, as though in a flourish, on to the white of the bedclothes.

Those among the women who have children now lift them up and show them the bloodied priest, whose features are no longer recognizable or scarcely human, and they impress upon them the identity of the man and why he is dead, and they tell them that they must never, ever forget this sight, for this is the Devil himself, Lucifer, the Dane, the priest, their father, and now he is gone and will never again do harm to anyone.

PART THREE

The Great Conflagration

(1793–5)

Home

Morten Falck steps on board the good ship *Charlotta* from the rowing boat at Sukkertoppen, casts a final glance towards land and sighs, flops down on to his bunk below deck, digests a number of novels and biographies, rises and goes ashore at Bergen.

24 October 1793, a Thursday: he is standing on the wharf at Bergen. He sees himself in a drawing he might produce: a tall, dark gentleman placed within a converging perspective of houses, fells and drifting clouds, clad in threadbare and unfashionable clothing, transfixed among porters, seamen and travellers, who edge past him rolling barrels, carrying sacks full of grain, flour and coal on their shoulders, pulling horses along by the bit, shouting and remonstrating and altogether knowing who they are, where they come from and where they are going in the short span of time they have at their disposal. Morten Falck is certain of very little beyond the knowledge that he is a stranger and cannot stand here for ever. But where should he go? He has never been to Bergen. This is the first time in six years he has been anywhere comprising more than a couple of hundred people. He feels he has stepped directly into a tempest, a maelstrom of jostling bodies and babbling voices, steaming horses' flanks and wheels that rumble and clatter. Someone shoves him hard in the back, causing him to stumble and fall on one knee. He gets to his feet, apologizes to the furious face that is turned towards him, a red-bearded man with a barrel on his shoulder, and steps around to the other side of

his travelling chest. His stomach complains nervously, a combination of expectation and trepidation as to his usual breakfast of mouldy hard tack and sour ale, the seafarer's staple. His insides yaw and heave in protest at the cobbles after eight weeks of becoming accustomed to the rolling deck. He suppresses a rush of nausea and swallows his saliva.

Where to, master?

Already the porter – a young lad with a broad smile, a nose like a potato and fair hair sticking out like dry straw from under his cap – has a firm grasp on the chest and is, on his own initiative, manhandling it on to his cart.

I need lodgings, Falck says, looking along the wharf at the quaint and uniform fronts of the serving houses that seem alight in the morning sun as it reaches down from the surrounding fells. Puffs of cloud gather and spread, casting restless shadows on the slopes above the town. A place where a poor traveller may rest his head and find a good meal at a fair price, he adds.

Step up, sir, says the lad, with a gesture towards the cart, on which a simple crosspiece does for a seat.

Thank you, my child. I prefer to walk.

The boy grips the handles and sets off.

Indeed, says Morten Falck, who is for a moment hesitant. He finds it difficult to adjust to the sensation of having firm ground beneath his feet; and to the feeling of the breeze as it strokes his cheek, bringing with it the aromas of pine forest, wood smoke, horse dung, cooking smells and the filth and excrement of the street. Terra firma, he says to himself. My own country. My boot now stands upon the same land on which my father treads, if he is still alive. According to the letter that came with the ship by which he now is returned, his father is more or less in the throes of death, which probably means all is as usual and that he is in good health. But in the meantime he might indeed have become properly ill, which cruel fate may befall any hypochondriac. There was something else in the letter that made him anxious, suggestions that *nothing lasts for ever, one has become aged and infirm and misses the engaging chatter of a woman now that my beloved wife, your blessed mother, has departed,* etc. Has his father grown melancholy in his dotage? Or was he trying to tell him something?

The land here is deeply incised by fjords, it has reached out an arm and taken hold of Morten Falck and wrenched him from the claws of the sea. And here he now stands, without any idea of which way is up or down in his life. He will travel east, this much he knows, and by road, if there is one, and if necessary he will go by foot in the manner of the blessed Professor Holberg, a Bergen man by birth, who journeyed in the same way when he was Falck's age. Even though it would surely be quicker to return home by the packet boat. But he has had enough of sailing. No more ships for me, thank you, no more hard tack and oats, or the stench of men and their pent-up desire. The land will embrace him, consume him, with its fair valleys, shady forests and small farms. I shall be bid welcome wherever I go, with a glass of fresh milk and shelter for the night. Of this he has lain and fantasized during the voyage. He has but vague conceptions of the landscapes east of Bergen. There will doubtless be fells and at this time of year most probably snow. Nonetheless, snow is a thing he has grown used to these past years. And everywhere there will be people, countrymen! Indeed, he will go on foot!

Sir? The porter lad stands waiting; he looks back at Falck over his shoulder.

He follows the cart into the town. Soon he finds himself further from the sea than at any time in several years. The weeks on board the *Charlotta* have been peaceful and without event, apart from a single episode off the Cape Farewell, where they narrowly avoided collision with a wreck adrift on the waves. Its upper deck amidships was as yet above water, the masts snapped at the yard, stumps of rope and tattered sails flapping in the wind, from the hold came a foul odour of decay, and the sea around the wreck glistened with train oil. The rough sea gave them no chance of boarding her, and yet they came so close as to make out her name on the side of the bow: *Henrietta of Aberdeen.* The captain made note of it in his log and would inform the shipping company on his return. He believed the vessel to be a Scottish whaler that had made havoc along the coast this past year and which the colony managers had tried unsuccessfully to seize. Morten Falck held a service and prayed for the salvation of the souls who went down with her. The crew of the *Charlotta* were in low spirits for some days following the encounter, which they took to be an omen of ill fortune, and Falck, too, was quite affected by the dismal mood. He saw the face of the widow appear faintly embossed in the darkness between the masts; he awoke in his cot with the feeling of being touched by her putty-like fingers; he heard her voice speak to him, a monotone chunter devoid of recognizable lexis. He was certain she would not allow him to leave the vessel alive.

Now, striding along behind this young porter, whose voice rings out in song, returned to the land of his birth in a town edged by forest and benevolent fells, he gradually awakes from the stupor into which weeks of fatalism had thrown him. He can hardly believe it to be true. Yet the feeling of cobblestones and horse dung beneath his feet tells him it is so. He has come home.

The inn to which he is taken is called The Weary Dragoon. Here he is given a room comprising a chair, a table and an alcove made up with clean linen and deluged with pillows and a thick eiderdown that seem to him like whipped cream, and a mattress so soft he feels as if he floats upon it. Downstairs in the serving house he seats himself at a table and is served teacakes with fresh yellow butter and four soft-boiled eggs. He is offered strong ale, but asks for milk, and the landlady brings him a whole jug. He drinks the fatty emulsion with gusto. She addresses him with a mixture of deference and motherly tenderness, her bosom perilously close to his cheek as she pours the milk for him, a quivering, ample mass, and he senses her warmth and the rank smell of her perspiration. He eats too much and goes to lie down in the soft alcove, where he sleeps until midday. Then a lunch of pea soup with sour cream, yellow-white islands of fat, pancakes folded around satiny sugar and cinnamon, and two varieties of jam. Again, he must retire immediately afterwards. He lies groaning, a cold sweat upon his brow, clutching his stomach and chuckling with disbelief at such a sumptuous meal. Later he rises and wanders about the town, heavy with glucose and fat.

So many people on this autumn day of sunshine in Bergen; so many faces he has never seen, and which he will never see again, or at least not recall. This is something that had all but vanished from his memory: to be surrounded by people about whose lives and vices he is spared the trouble of concerning himself. They are and will remain strangers, dour and inscrutable, and he loves them for the fact that he need never have anything to do with a single one of them.

Later in his room again, floating on his back upon the fluffy luxury of the mattress. He loses himself in the buttery yellow of the descending sun, a rhombus intersected by the cross of the window's muntin on the opposite wall. The figure wanders diagonally upwards to the right, and the more it advances towards the ceiling the more its shadowy crucifix becomes distorted. Its panel turns crimson, eventually matt and colourless, and finally vanishes. He cannot sleep and doesn't care to read. He lies awake, listening to urban sounds, and feels already that he has lived here for a long time.

The widow comes to him in the night. She steals silently beneath his covers, grins suggestively and nestles beside him with a contented sigh. He gets up and tells her to go, but she sleeps as if dead. He tries to push her hair aside to see her face, but no matter how much he grasps it remains concealed, pressed into the plump pillow, her body immovable on the mattress. I have eaten too much, he tells himself, and retires once more, elbowing the widow in annoyance, that she may give him room. In the morning he goes out into town and puts the dream from his mind. On his return he comforts himself with fresh-baked teacakes and eggs. He eats meticulously and without haste, licking his lips, dabbing his mouth with a napkin. For dinner are served thick slices of cold roast in jelly, with carrots, parsnip and kohlrabi, mashed and blended with fresh cream. The landlady hovers about him with her obscenely perspiring bosom and fastidious solicitude; she clucks like a broody hen and presses herself so close he cannot help but feel the warmth that is exuded from her body. He surmises the woman is in need of a husband, or else the one she has is at sea. Perhaps he is the weary dragoon, a fallen or deserted – certainly absent – soldier. He has no idea, nor does he wish to know. He yearns for the fells, away from the lust this woman will surely soon awaken in him, but which until now she has unwittingly kept suppressed by stuffing him with food.

He asks her about the eastbound mail carriage and is told that the route has been discontinued; now only the packet boat goes down the coast and puts in to some of the settlements inside the fjords. But she is willing to make enquiries. If the gentleman really is intent on journeying overland, there is a chance he might be taken up by a private carriage. However, traffic in that direction is rare, she says sceptically. Mostly the land is mountainous and inhospitable. They say the roads are infested with Gypsies and Jewish rabble. I've only ever been as far as Ulrikken myself, and that was far enough, she tells him.

Falck says that his decision is made: he will go by road, irrespective of whatever hindrance it might present. He thanks her for the food, returns to his room and sleeps for the rest of the afternoon.

The good weather does not last; the fells to the east force the moist sea air upwards, where it cools and falls as rain. Yet it is far from cold, even if the wind is bothersome when it sweeps down from the peaks and is funnelled through the streets. His walks along the wharf and among the squares afford him constant, almost incredulous pleasure. To amble, without obligation, without fear of being waylaid by officious colony managers or persistent coopers eager to be married; to wander freely among the crowd, a face like any other. At long last he senses the liberty he has always espoused, the freedom of Rousseau. *Man is born free and everywhere he is in chains!* He has cast away his chains. He has returned home. From street vendors he purchases good autumn apples on which he munches as he goes; he jostles at the stalls with the servant girls and women of the lower classes, bargains and gesticulates, asking questions that give rise to mirth. From foreigners he buys what they refer to as earth apples, tubers that lie baking in small fires or else are fried in pig's fat upon a pan. These were a much-despised food when he was young; now they are commonly eaten, although no self-respecting inn would serve them. When poked from the fire by the ragamuffin merchants, they are put on a plate, split apart and served with a pinch of salt and a good dollop of butter that quickly melts and runs. He dips the pale flesh of the potato in the salty, rather astringent butter and devours it with much enjoyment and an occasional pang of guilty conscience. If his landlady should discover him, he imagines, she would surely be outraged. But his hunger is incessant; it is a hunger accumulated over several years; a room inside him that has stood empty and cold, and which now is being furnished with solid fare, and the three meals a day at The Weary Dragoon are alone insufficient. In a matter of days after his coming ashore, his insides are settled, his diarrhoea has ceased, supplanted by constipation, and he must exert himself to empty his bowels. He senses his girth has increased.

The landlady has spoken with a farmer, who is willing to give him a place on his horse-drawn cart. No other opportunity has been forthcoming and she recommends instead that he take the southbound packet boat that will bring him to Christiania within the fortnight. Or why not stay here in Bergen?

Why not, indeed? But he tells her about his father, who is waiting at the other side of the country, and she understands, sheds a tear and utters something about the love between father and son. There is nothing quite like it. He refrains from comment.

Morten Falck rejoices at the prospect of watching the landscape pass by, inch by inch, from a cart.

Tell the good farmer I shall be delighted.

She slings two large curves of boiled sausage on to his plate. Clear juices ooze from the cut ends. She comes with the bowl of steaming hot mash held against her hip and gives him several dollops. He digs spoonfuls of mashed mountain cranberries from a jar and sets ravenously about his meal.

The Magister will die of hunger before his first day of journeying comes to an end.

He laughs. Madame Therkelsen, I know you will make sure to provide me with a packed lunch for the road.

She withdraws. He can tell by her posture that he has offended her. She already feels she owns a part of me, he thinks to himself. High time I left.

The journey with the farmer is wet and unpleasant. The cart is open and he sits huddled on the seat beside the driver, who utters not a single syllable. A brisk easterly wind buffets his chest and presses the rain into the small openings of his clothing, which he endeavours to keep closed, drawing his coat around him and pulling down his broad-brimmed hat. In the hills they must climb down and walk, when crossing the wetlands, streams and dubious bridges. Several times they must stand in the rain at a ferrying place and wait to be taken across the fjord on a flat-bottomed barge.

They leave Bergen in the final hours of the night and reach their destination, a farmhouse barely visible in the compact darkness, in the early hours of their third day of travel. He has exchanged only the most necessary comments with the farmer along the way, but when they arrive and the wife receives her husband with a kiss, he livens up and shows Falck to a room upstairs. He smiles a lot, speaks softly and with hesitation, and avoids Falck's gaze. The wife serves them cold food. She is a comely woman, risible and chatty. She asks her husband about the journey. Did he sell his wares, how much did he get for the pig, was he cheated? He hands her his purse and she counts the coins, sorting them into rigsdalers, marks and skillings, putting foreign coins aside, then sweeping the money into a coffer before closing it. The farmer asks for aquavit; she fetches a dusty bottle and pours three glasses as heavy as lead and resembling thimbles. They drink. Sweet aquavit, with a bitter taste of almond, and very strong.

Falck senses the warmth return to his body; he becomes animated and tells them about his sea voyage and life among the savages. The wife shudders with rapture. She asks if the savages run about naked and chop off each other's heads; are they to be reckoned as people or are they a sort of animal? She cannot imagine how he could hold prayers for such creatures, let alone christen and confirm them. In her view it amounts to going out into the stables to missionize to the sow, the cows and the colt. What a congregation! She laughs heartily. Once she saw a savage at Bergen. He stood chained in the square and defecated upright like a horse, while rolling his eyes. Such creatures cannot surely be made Christian, she considers. It would be sacrilege.

Falck sleeps until noon the next day. When he gets up he sees that the farm and its fields extend across open land that undulates its way down towards the fjord. And he feels he is home, even if he has yet to arrive. The rain persists, but it is not a rain that lashes and penetrates the seams of his garments, rather it is warm, soft and as tangible as silk, a kindly rain. After a brief walk he returns and knocks on the kitchen door.

The wife greets him. The peace of God to you!

Peace of God, he rejoins.

The gentleman must sit himself down and have something to eat.

He devours a plate of rømmegrøt, while she is busy with her work in the kitchen. He sits and watches her, her quick and practised movements, her strong arms. Somewhere in the house he can hear children arguing and laughing.

Where is your husband? he asks.

Gudmind and our eldest boy have gone into the fells to see to the sheep. He won't be home until evening.

He sits on the bench and studies the simple kitchen. The ceiling is low and supported by thick joists. The fire roars in the stove. The heat makes him feel dozy and yet his mind remains quite clear. Behind him, rain patters against the window. They will be soaked, he says.

Oh, they are used to it. Here it rains most days of the year. We thank the Lord for the rain. But the gentleman had better stay until the weather improves. We can't have him catching his death when he crosses the fells. And we've room enough.

He thanks her. In the afternoon he teaches the children, tests their knowledge of the Bible and offers them a short introduction to the natural sciences. He notes that their knowledge of the proximate environment, plants and animals, nature in general, is quite exact, whereas their conceptions of the wider world are at best medieval.

They laugh when he tells them the Earth is round. We've heard that before, but if it were really round people could only live on top, and the water would run out of the fjord, and then we wouldn't be able to sail or fish.

Their comprehension of the scriptures is at once imperturbably conceited and confused. They seem to believe that the stories of the Bible took place in a recent past inside a neighbouring fjord, and they refer to the apostles and the prophets as though to recently deceased relatives. The local priest would seem to have quite singular methods of rendering theology relevant to his congregation. Perhaps he should have employed some of the same principles in his own work, he muses, but no, the Eskimo are not easily fooled. They would have seen through him right away. He tells the children about the Holy Land, the life and death of the Saviour. They smile overbearingly. Afterwards they ask him again about Greenland and the savages, whether it is true that they go about naked and simply squat down wherever when they need to defecate, and squirt out their young like fish eggs?

He humours them and they nod, reassured that the world accords with their conception of it. He endeavours to go through the alphabet with them, but only the twelve-year-old girl displays any interest in reading. It is a shame, he tells the mother, for she would learn quickly if she went to school. But the mother does not consider it a good thing for girls to read. She herself can write only her name and yet she is happy. Falck resigns himself to this steadfast adherence to stupidity. He tires of the monotony of their cheerfulness, but nonetheless enjoys his time on the idyllic farm by the fjord.

He stays a week. During all this time the sun does not shine once and at no point does he see more of the fells than a few hundred fathoms of their lower slopes. Yet the farmer believes the weather on the whole to be better on the other side, perhaps a week's walking to the east, and offers to take him some miles of the journey. He packs his few belongings, his chest having been sent on by the packet boat, is given cheese and bread by the wife, and bids the children farewell. Their voices ring in his ears as the cart sets out along the road that runs south beside a seemingly endless arm of the fjord. When eventually they reach the final village at the head of the fjord, he climbs down and says his goodbyes to the farmer.

God bless you, Priest, the man says.

He nods and begins to trudge southwards, where the road soon dwindles into a path that follows the course of a river upstream through a valley.

The hike up the fell is uncomplicated, albeit taxing. A few farms lie scattered upon the esker, poor holdings of steeply sloping land bounded by drystone walls, here and there a flock of sheep. The farmers are at work burning off their fields, keeping the flames in check with long rakes, spreading them over the grass, as though painting fire with long brushes, beating them out wherever they seem on the verge of getting out of hand. The seasoned smell of burning grass settles in his nostrils and a small bubble of recollection bursts inside him, dejection, anxiety and excitement in such proportions as he has not felt in twenty years. I was not a happy child, he thinks to himself. I was afraid of dying. This is the first time he has acknowledged the fact. It makes him sorrowful, yet at the same time he feels more at home than ever before. Now I am returned, to these hills and mountains, to this feeling of old. He has not come back in order to be happy, but to be home.

The summery vales are below him, which is to say that he recalls them as such once he is ascended above the treeline, where the wind is as cold as ice. Behind each peak is another; the passes that run between them are sodden and inaccessible, and the wind sweeps right through them. He sticks to the dry slopes, following the empty land between trees and high peaks in order to avoid the freezing wind. His progress is slow, but visibility is good and he makes sure always to have some feature of the landscape by which to keep his bearings, a bend in the fjord further back, two peaks in alignment. By the time darkness falls he is still nowhere near the divide. On this first night he sleeps under the open sky beneath a stunted, though long-whiskered, fir tree whose branches reach to the ground. He manages to light a fire and to boil some gruel in a dented pot from a handful of oats he has with him from the farm. He wraps his blanket around him and settles down for the night, as close to the trunk of the tree as he can get. The widow is there. She sits on her haunches by the fire and prods at the embers, causing sparks to fly into the air. What do you want? he asks, not knowing if she can hear him. You are in my head. Are you the expression of some wish or loss? A fear? We were married and you failed me, then I failed you, and now you are dead. So it is. What has happened cannot be changed.

So what do you want, exactly?

But he knows what she wants; it dawns on him now, lying here in this Norwegian wilderness: she wants him back. That may be, he says to himself, drawing the blanket tighter around his body, though quite out of the question. Then he thinks: But she is not real, she is only a spirit or a nightmare, a product of my own making. Does that mean it is *I* who wants *her* back? The thought terrifies him.

He wakes early, shivering from the cold, and rekindles the fire with his blanket wrapped around him. He heats up the gruel from the evening before and feels his body come alive as the warmth of it spreads inside him. He senses the widow's continued presence, a fug of tanned hide, train-oil lamps and urine tubs. The unbearable heat that bore down on him as he crawled into the communal dwelling house, the laughter that erupted all around, the hospitality of the natives and their merciless arrogance, the way they always descended so relentlessly on his weaknesses. The wind is freezing. He can see that higher up snow is falling, a plume of swirling white coming off the peak like a wagging tail.

He says the Lord's Prayer, gathers his things together and continues on through the valley, which further up becomes a forceable pass that in the course of a few hours leads him into the promised interior. It is not raining, but now and then the dampness condenses into fog or cloud, so dense that he becomes soaked to the skin. He feels as if his very bones are laid open to the cold, that the wind blows right through him. But the effort of walking in such difficult and rocky terrain generates body heat, and as long as he does not succumb to exhaustion, and is compelled to stop and sit down, he retains some measure of warmth.

It is dark by the time he reaches the other side and he is forced to rest high above the treeline in the shelter of an overhanging crag, facing away from the wind. It has begun to snow. Wet flakes swirl around him and melt as they settle on his clothes. He must light a fire of heather, but the plant is wet through and spits and hisses like a fuse. The water is hardly tepid when he gives up and spoons the hard, uncooked oats into his mouth in the hope that a full stomach will give him warmth. But he is freezing and must get to his feet to jump up and down in the dark in order to drive the cold from his body. He lies down and falls into a restless sleep, benumbed and shivering. The widow sits on the bare rock, a short distance away. He asks her to come and warm him, or at least to make herself useful and get the fire going again, but she remains seated with her back to him, staring out into the darkness. It sounds like she is humming or perhaps muttering something to herself.

The next day he has begun to cough; he senses a fever coming on. His thoughts are unclear and he knows he must soon find proper shelter or else he will fall ill. The widow follows him, dragging her feet a few paces behind, a parody of his own fatigue. He is becoming accustomed to her presence. On the ship he was compelled to acknowledge that she did not intend to remain behind in the colony. You seek peace, he thinks to himself. You are like me, you cannot find rest. What can I do for you that would make you willing to return to your grave? He knows the answer. He does not wish to dwell upon it.

The descent is precarious. He has long since lost the path that to begin with was so apparent; now it is erased in the scant vegetation. He finds himself clambering over crags to reach lower climes, only then to be confronted with a sheer drop of some several hundred fathoms. Hours are wasted retreating back over the steep rock to find another way down. By sheer good fortune he reaches the forest before darkness and is able to light a good fire by which to warm himself and make his gruel.

I know what you want, he says. But can't you see that I've come home, that these are my fells, my forest? I know I once promised to take you with me, but now I think you should go home. This is my land, not yours. It is not appropriate for you to follow me like this.

In the afternoon he is lucky to find a track. He tries to judge the position of the sun, though it is concealed by cloud, and elects to go right, where the track appears to slope gently away. It is overgrown; a stone bridge leading over a stream has collapsed without having been repaired and he must wade to his thighs through the icy waters. There are no fresh traces of carriage wheels or other traffic. And yet it is clearly a road and must lead somewhere, probably to another that is more used. The floor of the forest teems with blueberries and mountain cranberries. They have been exposed to frost and have lost their sweetness, but make a welcome supplement to his provisions, which will soon run out. He sleeps among the trees, breaking off branches of foliage on which to lie and cover himself. He is unaware of the cold in the night.

One morning he is woken by some disturbance of the tree under which he lies. He sits up and sees a colossal beast rubbing itself in long rhythmic strokes against the trunk. An elk. It has not seen him, or else it is in such a state of ecstasy and delight at scratching its itch that it does not care. He retreats to a distance, somewhat fearful of the enormous, bony animal, yet also filled with warmth and joy at being in such close proximity to another living creature after almost a week of solitude. Moreover, it has chased away the widow. When finished with its scratching, it stands still and snorts absently. The eye that turns towards Falck rolls slightly in its socket; a tremble runs across the animal's flank, and then it plods off, leaving him even more solitary than before. He is worried about the wolves only when lying down to sleep in the open air, though he has yet to hear their howl. Perhaps the last wolf has been shot here, as in Denmark. In the days that follow, he sees a fox, a deer and a grouse. High in the air, a large bird, presumably an eagle, circles and surveys the area. He is not alone.

His bread is all but gone and the chipwood box given to him by Madame Therkelsen – filled with pickled meat, cheese, sausage, oats and dried peas – will soon be empty. He continues along the same track he has followed for some days; perhaps it leads from a disused mine, he thinks to himself, since it passes no houses or other structures. He decides to ration what provision he has remaining and goes hungry to bed. He is still in the fells, but can tell by the trees, which are taller and less gnarled, that he has descended. The sun has been out and the weather has remained dry since the night it snowed. He is now certain he is going in an easterly direction. In the middle of the day, ten days after saying farewell to the farmer, he spies some clearings upon an esker in the distance. They can be made only by human hand. He feels his heart quicken, then senses that he is not eager to see people again, to hear himself negotiate for shelter and food, to explain where he is from and where he is going. To use their privies, wash in their basins, eat from their plates. To be polite and receive politeness in return. To bring his person and its inexorable smells and sounds into the private domain of others, and to be equally exposed to their own. The triviality of it all. He has felt himself to be in good harmony with his body these past days, passing wind when it suited him, pulling down his breeches to defecate without modesty. But he knows he has begun to smell rather rank and that he has acquired habits approaching base nature, which he must quell if he is to be a guest in someone's house. Preferably he would sleep in the hay of a barn.

There lies a small village at the foot of the esker where he has spotted the clearings in the forest. A handful of houses scattered at each side of the track. The meadows are enclosed by wattle fencing; horses, cows and goats graze peacefully. Some of them lift their heads and watch him as he approaches. A horse whinnies gently, perhaps a kindly welcome, perhaps a warning to its owners. There are no people to be seen.

Among tall weeping birches is a house of two storeys with a dozen shining windows. A manor farm. He crosses the front, where clucking hens disperse with flapping wings, goes up to the front door and knocks. He finds it to be ajar. He remains standing for a moment, then steps inside, hesitantly calling out, though without reply. He ventures further inside, into a kitchen where a pot stands simmering on top of a large stove. It smells of meat and herbs. Beneath the ceiling a cloud of steam has accumulated. On the table are the remains of a meal and some tall glasses with dregs of ale in them. Three plates. He picks up a crust of bread, dabs it quickly in some solidified fat and stuffs it into his mouth.

He hears a woman's voice behind him, swallows and wipes his mouth. He turns round. In front of him stands a tall woman in an apron, her hair tucked into a blue scarf. In one hand she holds a gardening tool, still with clods of soil on it. She looks straight at him and is clearly on her guard, her eyes at once both inhospitable and accommodating, yet quite without indignation at his standing in her kitchen and munching her food.

Would the gentleman be looking for someone?

He clears his throat, in doubt as to whether he will be able to control his voice. I do apologize. The door was open. My name is Morten Falck. Magister Falck, he adds impulsively.

And where on earth has the Magister come from?

From Bergen.

On foot?

Over the fells. He waves his hand in the direction of the forest.

Ah, a wanderer? Somewhere there is laughter in her voice.

For want of a complete answer he changes the subject. Where is this place I have come to, I wonder? he enquires and finds the frivolous, Norwegian Morten Falck he used to know so well to be reunited with him here on the eastern face of the fells.

The place is called Ådalen, she says. Eight Norwegian miles to the east lies Vinje.

Telemarken?

She nods. Where was the Magister thinking of going on foot? She smiles.

He tells her.

Winter will soon be here, says the woman. The summer has been unusually long this year, the harvest has been the best in memory, but the old folk say the winter will be as hard. Not that I credit the old dodderers with any ability to forecast the weather. But that is what they say. She pauses, noting that he has no immediate comment to make. In any circumstance you ought to put off going on until the spring, now that you have negotiated the fells in one piece.

My aged father is waiting for me.

Mr Falck can at least have something to eat. He must be hungry after such a journey. She stifles a smirk, clears the table and puts out some cold remains in front of him. I am cooking a capon, she tells him with a nod towards the pot that stands simmering. I do hope the smell of it does not take away the Magister's appetite.

He is already at work devouring the food.

The woman's name is Gunhild Krøger and she hails from Kristiansand. Her husband, a wealthy farmer, died some years before, leaving her to inherit all that he owned, having no descendants or brothers to carry on the place. Now she runs the farm herself, though on a smaller scale. Much of the land has been leased out, some of the fields lie fallow, the livestock reduced to a small number of milch cows that secure a steady income throughout the year, two hundred sheep providing wool and meat, and a score of hens to supply the household with eggs. Moreover, she grows some barley and has begun to experiment with potatoes.

Falck sets about lending a hand in the running of the farm, in exchange for lodging in one of the widow Krøger's rooms. He helps in the harvesting of winter apples and the last of the beet. He allows the labourer to order him about. There is plenty to be done. He waters the animals, mucks out the stalls, washes the milk basins. He milks the cows and is praised for his good skill. The best time of his day is in the morning when he goes sleepily into the byre with a bucket in each hand and seats himself upon the three-legged stool, leans his brow against the belly of a cow and speaks softly to it, feels the smooth teats slip between his finger and thumb, and hears the pointed, rhythmic jet of milk as it strikes the bottom of the bucket. He eats with the farm folk in the long dining room beyond the kitchen, with Madame Krøger at the head of the table. He gives thanks for their food and the good and decent people chorus, Amen! It is his only task as clergyman. The rest of the time he is allowed to be as unpriestly as he wishes. Madame Krøger asks no questions. No one enquires about Greenland or his past. It does not interest them. He is relieved by the fact, albeit a little disappointed.

In November he goes into the fells with the labourer and some other men, who have been hired for the occasion, to gather and shepherd Madame Krøger's sheep back to the farm. The job takes a week. The young herding girls, who have spent a whole summer in solitude, chirp joyfully at the prospect of returning to their families in the valley. Falck asks one of them if it is not a strain to be isolated for such a long time. There's always company to be had for those who want it, she replies mysteriously. And besides, there's always the animals. One of the girls is clearly pregnant. No one comments upon it.

Madame Krøger confides in him: I suffer dreadfully from cold feet. Sometimes I wish to stick them in the kettle.

Falck makes noises of sympathy.

My blessed husband gave me no children, the Madame continues. He possessed habits which unfortunately rendered it impossible.

He does not enquire into the nature of these habits. Instead he offers to warm her feet and sits down in front of her with them in his lap.

He asks the Madame's age and she says about the same as the Magister's.

Both were born in 1756, she a month earlier than he. He says he feels as though he could be her father. I have travelled far and lived many lives. Madame Krøger's life would appear to have been more stable.

I suppose it seems that way, she says. But like the Magister I feel detached from the person I once was, the carefree, frolicsome girl who went about Kristiansand twirling her skirts. Not much is left of her.

It is evening. The labourer and the maid have retired for the night.

I am not unattractive to you, am I, Magister Falck?

He squeezes her toe. Not at all, Madame Krøger. Why ever would you think such a thing?

Oh, I don't know. It is something a woman may feel when she lacks a man. Uncertainty. You have soft hands, she says. Priestly hands.

Thank you.

I must decide what to do with the young heifer, she says pensively. Is she to be slaughtered or should I bring the neighbour's bull to her?

The bull, he says. Let the poor animal live and have some fun from life.

He goes to her chamber, she raises herself on to her elbows, draws aside the cover and, when he climbs in beside her, she wraps herself around him. She trembles and whimpers and twines her freezing feet in his own.

I will be kind to you, Magister. I just need to warm my feet first.

And then they are together. It soon becomes a habit. Madame Krøger's feet are warmed.

†

The workers know what is going on and it would seem not only that it finds their acceptance, but also that they expect him to settle here permanently. It's no good for women of her age to be alone, says the labourer. They become too exacting. He laughs. He is enjoying his own little adventure with the maid, who has only just been confirmed and is scarcely half his age.

Madame Krøger is a good friend. She asks no questions; she allows him to be without a past and demands of him no future. She laughs when he tries to be funny, though often his wit is feeble. A humourist he is not. She is patient and helpful beneath the covers and she tells him he is a wonderful lover. It prompts him to make greater efforts.

She is not beautiful, yet her face is harmonious and pleasing, her hair long and smooth and very thick. She smells of the day's work, the baking of bread, the boiling of apples, the curdling of milk into whey, examinations of pregnant livestock, the slaughtering of hens, the tending of horses. It reminds him faintly of the urine tubs and blubber pots, while retaining its own distinct character of Norwegian interior. In the evenings she squats down over a bowl and washes herself below, while he stands watching her. He is fond of it. He takes the bowl out and empties it for her when she is done. They retire together.

Life proceeds under these new circumstances. He milks the cows, feeds the hens, argues good-naturedly with the labourer, lends an ear to the maid's concerns and comforts her by telling her that if it feels right, then it is right, and if it does not, it must cease.

It feels right.

Then you have no cause for concern, my child. The Lord sees the purity of your heart.

Will Mr Falck marry us?

I am not a priest, he says. I have cast my vestments.

But the Magister could still marry us, in the name of the Lord?

And so he does, in the finest room of the big house. The labourer and the maid stand holding hands before him; he freshly shaven and lustrous from soap and water, hair wetted and combed, whiskers waxed; she small and demure and very solemn. He performs the ceremony and they make their vows. The Madame has roasted a duck. The groom soaks up the fat from his plate with bread and must subsequently retire to bed with a stomach ache.

I am with child, says the girl.

Indeed, says the Madame. It will be nice with some life in the house.

They drink to her health and congratulate her.

I was born out of wedlock, she says. Such a fate will not befall my own child.

You have a good husband, says Madame Krøger.

†

Sometimes he thinks of his years in Copenhagen. They have come nearer since his leaving Greenland. Who am I, exactly? he wonders. Why do

I feel at home here, among complete strangers? Had I turned left in the forest, where then would I have ended up? Is my life nothing but chance?

He writes to his father and receives a swift reply, only a couple of weeks into the new year. He looks forward to seeing him again, his father writes, if he is still in the land of the living by then. His travelling chest has arrived undamaged; he may come any time he likes. He does not seem to be in any hurry to see me, Falck thinks. His father's letter provides a lengthy account of the infirmities of old age, written in a firm hand, a confident, legible script, encompassing all manner of detail as to his symptoms, the turning blue of his nails, dizziness, chronic fatigue, *aches and pains throughout my entire body*, the usual. *My life is most certainly soon at its end! Alas, to be left alone is the heaviest burden of all!* This persistent mention of being alone. Falck writes back and tells him that he intends to come home in the spring or early summer. His father's complaining has annoyed him. He snaps at the labourer and when the labourer is too cheerful to take notice, he snaps at Madame Krøger. She takes him aside and comforts him.

I wish very much to remain here, he says.

No one is chasing you away, she says.

Snow bending the branches of the trees. Snow piling up on the roof, so that Falck must climb up with the labourer and shovel it away. Snow falling gently, great flakes of it. Snow making the stillness still and the silence nameless. In the new year there is much of it. The wheels of the horse-drawn vehicles are replaced by runners; the horses themselves shod with snow shoes, so as not to sink in the depths. Madame Krøger is as pale as alabaster, though comely. When he lifts up her blouse, her shining breasts appear, two white orbs as firm as hard-boiled eggs. There is little work to do, besides milking the cows and feeding the livestock. And shovelling snow. Sometimes he accompanies Madame Krøger and the labourer on their trips to Vinje with the milk. He wanders about the town, while she takes care of her errands, and feels himself warm amid the snow, feels himself to be as white and still as snow inside.

Through the valley runs a river, in places widening to create a succession of small lakes like pearls on a string. One of these lakes lies below the house. In February, when some light has returned and the icicles hanging from the eaves have yet to start dripping, the labourer clears a circle on the lake, ties skates to his feet and runs upon the ice. Madame Krøger joins him. Falck hears her laughter. He goes to the window and looks out on them. They dance and glide, forwards and back, in figures of eight and other patterns, drawing away from each other, then coming together again. Madame Krøger skates in a long dress, her feet cannot be seen; she floats, keeping her back straight, rather than leaning forward like the labourer, holding her head high, arms behind her back, scarf fluttering behind her. She turns and he can see how the manoeuvre increases her speed; he hears the blades as they cut through the ice, throwing up spray in their wake. The labourer catches up with her, he grasps her left elbow and they glide together in a wide arc, veering off as they near the drift current, where vapour issues from the thin and mushy ice, then return. His arms swing like pendulums; she smooths along, proudly upright. They skate for a long time. The maid comes and stands beside him. They watch them together. He takes her hand and she squeezes it tight. She leans in to him and rests her other hand on her swelling abdomen.

In the stalls he finds an old pair of skis, which he fixes to his boots. It is twenty years since he has last skied, but he still has the knack, he discovers to his delight, and his body remembers how best to fall without hurting himself. He goes up on to the esker and winds his way down through the trees, snow showering from his skis with each twist of his legs, one foot slightly in front of the other, knees bent; he makes fine use of the slender fence post he has taken with him as a ski pole. Madame Krøger comes out and watches him, smiling and nodding appreciatively. He tumbles. She applauds. When he comes in to dinner, ruddy-cheeked and out of breath, eyebrows white with snow, battered by flicking branches and involuntary somersaults, he devours the meal ravenously and drinks a jug of sweet ale. Never in his adult life has he felt so healthy.

But the widow is in the house. Perhaps she has been there all along. Floorboards creak, a door opens and shuts, someone draws breath in a dark cranny. The animals sense her and the maid complains that there is a ghost.

There are no ghosts here, says the Madame. We have never had a single one. Who would it be?

Your blessed husband?

The Madame scolds her. But in the evening she is silent.

He tells her he will be leaving soon.

She nods in the darkness. I know.

She lies on her back, he on his side. His thighs embrace her own; his feet rub warmth into hers beneath the covers. They hold each other's hand.

When will you leave, do you think?

Soon.

Take the skis, then you will arrive sooner. I shall give you a letter to take with you. My husband had relatives and friends further east. They will give you shelter and food.

Early one morning in April he jumps on to the milk cart, clad in the deceased farmer's – the blessed Olav Olavsson's – old wolfskin coat. Madame Krøger hands him the skis and a proper pole.

Farewell, Gunhild Krøger!

Farewell, Morten Falck. Send me word.

†

The labourer drives him to Vinje. They part and the man thanks him for all he has done. On his skis he follows the sled track east. The days have begun to lengthen. The terrain slopes away to his advantage, ever downwards, through curves and bends. The farms and settlements lie close together. He encounters no problems finding accommodation. There is more traffic, more people along the road, pedlars and mongers, knife-grinders and itinerant smiths. Occasionally he accompanies one or another for a couple of days, before parting company again. Some of the way he spends seated upon horse-drawn carriages and sleds. The widow sits jiggling her feet. She follows him in everything he does. I suppose you're happy now, he thinks to himself.

He comes to a village, which may or may not be the one in which he grew up. He looks about. The road is churned up and muddy; he walks at its edge, so as not to get his feet wet in the icy slush. Some men are standing outside the blacksmith's shop. They hold their horses by the bridles and watch him as he approaches. From inside comes the clash of metal against metal and a man is singing. He lifts his hat; the men nod, yet continue to stare at him with suspicion. He cannot see the track that leads to his father's farm and so he continues on out of the village. Only after he has come some way and looks back from upon a ridge does he realize that it is indeed the village of his home. He goes back.

Now he finds the narrow track leading down to the fjord. He passes the schoolhouse, carries on through a wooded area and then comes to a cluster of houses where some boys are at play and cackling hens strut about. A peasant woman he may possibly know empties a bowl through an open door and calls out, though not to him. He comes to an oak tree in which he once climbed; a hilltop with three elms upon it. Now he can see the house. The sun is out; an unseen blackbird sings from some foliage above; the track is almost dry here where the ground falls away, the grass between the wheel tracks is green and tall, the air mild and moist. He has wandered since morning and is hot and thirsty.

The farm appears among the trees: three small, black-painted buildings of timber. He approaches the main house, glances around the yard in which he played as a boy, and only now does it hit him that his mother is dead. Always she has been here, at work in the kitchen, stooped over the flower beds, pottering about in the stables and the barn, in her headscarf and bast shoes, threadbare coat and a dress reaching to the ground, always busy, always in good cheer. As he crosses the yard, she fades away. Now she is gone.

He knocks on the door; a girl comes out. He removes his hat and tells her who he is.

He's around here somewhere, she says. I saw him only a few minutes ago.

The horse is in the pasture, kicking up the snow with its hooves to find grass to eat. He goes up to it. It is a different horse, a mare. The old gelding of which he was always rather frightened is, of course, long dead. The horse looks up for a moment, only to lower its head again, uninterested. His father wrote that he has got rid of much of the live-stock, since being left alone.

He goes into the stable and sees a pair of feet sticking out from one of the stalls. A voice speaks. He recognizes it to be his father's. It sounds muffled.

Here, kitty, come on, the voice says indistinctly.

Falck goes up to the stall.

Father?

Ssh! comes the reply, accompanied by a hand that waves him away.

Falck sees the seat of his father's pants, shiny and pinched, protruding from a hole in the floor. It looks like he has tried to crawl down into the hole and has got stuck.

Do you need any help? Falck enquires, but receives only the same gesture as before, this time followed by an exclamation of annoyance. He stands and waits. He looks around him. The stable seems not to have changed at all. He sees lamps hanging from nails, as they hung twenty years ago, flyspecked now, as then. He sees his own and his sister's names etched into the timber of the stalls. He sees a cracked pane, the glass fractured by his having knocked it with the end of a broom some twenty-five years ago, and he finds himself fearful that his father may have discovered the culprit.

But the voice is mawkish and ghostly now; it beckons from beneath the floorboards. The protruding arse is enlivened. Suddenly, there is activity: his father wriggles and begins to extract himself from the hole, then to appear, beaming with delight, hay and cow dung stuck in his hair, with three kittens squirming in his arms. A black and white farm cat follows him, rubbing itself affectionately against his legs as he gets to his feet.

Ha! he exclaims triumphantly. Gotcha, you little devils!

Falck assimilates the sight of his father, a small, adroit man with white, wavy hair smoothed back from his forehead and fine wrinkles radiating out from the corners of his eyes. His face is tanned, his ears large and jutting, his eyes alert and waggish.

Father.

His father finally removes his gaze from the kittens and looks up at him, studies him intently, head cocked back, as though in wonder or surprise, before speaking.

What happened to your eye, boy?

He reaches a hand up to his bad eye. Oh, nothing much. An accident, that's all.

And your teeth, what happened to them? You've certainly changed, I'll say.

Falck smiles at him. He wants to embrace him, but cannot on account of the kittens. You haven't at all.

We live a quiet life here, his father says. The years pass. Not much happens.

We?

Are you hungry? You must be starving, all that walking. Let's see if Karen has something for us.

He follows his father across the yard and has yet to be welcomed home. He realizes the moment has passed.

The kittens are placed carefully in a haybox that has been made ready for them next to the stove. Their mother lies down beside them and begins to purr as his father tickles her under the chin. He speaks kindly and comfortingly to her.

Will you be staying? he asks.

I don't know. I have no plans in particular.

Did you lose your position? Is that why you're back already?

He explains, while his father scrutinizes him, that he has stepped down quite legitimately and is moreover to receive a small sum each month in allowance. He omits to mention the large debt he has yet to even begin to repay.

We didn't know if you were coming, his father says. We knew nothing. Your letters, we could make head nor tail of them. How long have you been away, anyway?

Eleven years. Six in Greenland.

Well, indeed. Eleven years. It only seems like two since we sent you off. How time flies. His father shakes his head.

Father.

His father calls for the girl. He introduces her. This is Karen. She's been a great help in difficult times. He asks her to bring them some food.

She returns with flat bread and butter and a jug of ale that she pours out into three glasses before seating herself. The ale is fresh; he hears it fizzing in the glasses.

Karen is your new mother, his father says.

Oh, says Falck. He nods to her kindly.

The girl looks down. The cat has jumped into her lap; it narrows its eyes and nudges her hand with the side of its head. Inside in the parlour the big clock ticks.

Falck spreads a thick layer of butter on to his bread and bites off a piece. He sips his ale. He wishes to ask about his mother's final days, but cannot bring himself to, on account of her successor, whose knee rests against his under the table. His father seems cheerful and without cares.

I was saddened to hear of Kirstine's passing away, he says instead.

His father looks up, the ruminating movement of his jaw ceases abruptly. Yes, it was sad, he says curtly.

Do you know the cause of her death?

Her bereaved husband, Mr Gram, wrote to me. You can read his letter, if you like.

Was she ill?

Enough about the dead! his father snaps, his voice tinged with rage.

Your sister rests in consecrated soil, that's good enough for me. Read the letter, but don't mention her name again in this house.

His young stepmother makes up the bed for him in his old room. He lies fully clothed upon it and stares at the ceiling, studies the joists: their veins and grains, he senses with melancholy, gradually become aligned with his recollections. A pocket of time is torn open and empties its contents upon him. He had not thought it would feel like this, had considered it would be pleasant to see it all again. Perhaps he is merely tired.

He unpacks his few belongings from the travelling chest that has been carried up to the loft, books, clothing, a lamp, a candlestick, the chess set and other items from his room in the Mission house. He sniffs at them. They smell of mould and much of his clothing has been ruined by moisture. But they smell of the Mission house, too. He turns a chess piece between his fingers and wonders how Bertel is.

The letter from Mr Gram, his sister's husband, is brief, yet fully informative. An accident with a razor. A great loss of blood. A period of confinement during which there was hope, and yet: *It pleased the Lord thereby, which is His right, to call my beloved home to Him on the night of Christmas Eve, for which reason my yuletide was somewhat unfortunately spent in the company of my aged mother, and we were compelled to tolerate gossip concerning my wife's demise.*

Falck folds the letter and puts it back in the envelope. He places it on his night table. He looks at the envelope lying there. Kirstine is not inside it, and nor is her death. Her death has liberated itself from its report and she has attained salvation. He knows this to be true. Outside it has become evening; the trees catch the last of the sun's amber and the shore of the fjord lies in shadow. He gets up and asks his father if the boat is where it used to be. It is. He goes down and puts it on the water and rows across to the opposite shore where there is still light. He sits in the grass.

Good, he thinks to himself. You did bravely, dear Kirstine. You are in a better place now than we who remain clinging to this life.

†

Since his father retired from the position of schoolmaster, a church warden has been entrusted with the teaching. But he is a sickly and unstable man with a tendency towards hysterical outbursts directed at the boys, and Falck takes on his lessons, albeit without contract of employment. The salary is poor; he has no choice but to remain with his father and his young companion. After a couple of months he confronts the woman and she admits to being pregnant. He puts the matter to his father, who pretends not to have known. You ought at least to show her the courtesy of marrying her, he tells him.

That's easy enough for you to say, you're young. I don't know how much time I've got left, his father says.

All the more reason.

Whatever happens, he is to become an elder brother. He can find within him not a single emotion, not joy, jealousy nor contempt. The disdain of which he makes a display is merely a matter of principle. Yet he must concede that the couple seem to be happy together, despite the forty years that separate them. His father complains of his symptoms and she teases him about it without him taking offence. Falck feels like he is the senior member of the household.

A calling in the Akershus diocese falls vacant. His father talks him into applying. He does not consider himself to be in any position to decline, and moreover he has begun to ponder upon his debt. Thus, he writes to the bishop and asks that he might *look graciously upon a former missionary among savages, who now has returned home to the district of his birth*. He receives in return a rather unkind letter of rejection, one that in no way encourages him to seek other positions. He remains in his father's house, eventually applying formally for the position of school-master. It is the last thing in the world he wants, but he feels certain at least to be offered the job. A new letter of rejection, this time from the prefect's office. Nonetheless, they would like to keep him on until a qualified candidate presents himself. His humiliation is there to be read in black and white and is made no less by his having no alternative but to remain in the job. He requests tamely that he might move in to the rooms above the schoolroom, but this request is also denied. The accommodation is for the schoolmaster alone. But then the old church warden, who has been living in the school's annexe, passes away, and he now has a place of his own, a door he can close behind him.

Winter comes. His accommodation is freezing cold. The children he teaches are unwilling and contrary, sly and malicious. Waiting in the little schoolroom in the mornings, he is gripped by terror at the sound of their approaching footsteps. The months pass.

In April, almost a year after his leaving the farm at Ådalen, which now seems to him to be a paradise of human closeness, friendship and female devotion, he receives a letter from Madame Krøger. It relates all manner of events to him. She has been compelled to employ new people now the labourer and the maid have taken on their own smallholding. The birth passed off without drama, mother and child are well. She mentions the cows by name, not as cows, but rather as old friends, which of them have calved, which have been slaughtered, which have been covered by the bull. She tells of the cockerel that lay dead one morning, pecked to death by the hens, those faithless creatures. *A wolf has wreaked havoc in our district, or perhaps a dog, though my little lambs have so far been left untouched. Increasingly I sense the evening of life to be at my door, a dark and sombre guest, Morten, who comes and seats himself at the table, notwithstanding that no one has invited him. One feels lonely and longs for a friend. Oh, Morten, you know you have a home here, if you should feel so inclined. We were such good friends.*

Shaken, he puts down the letter. He had considered Madame Krøger to be inexhaustible, self-supporting, refined and wholly independent, particularly of stray clergy. A woman who was the measure of any man, and yet would remain a woman through and through. That was what he admired about her. And now she comes almost crawling on her knees to him!

He sits down immediately to pen a reply. But what to write? What do I want? he asks himself, chewing on the quill. Why does it feel so impossible to return to Madame Krøger and lie down to rest between her thighs and breasts?

He writes a few sentences. They are insincere and falsely sympathetic, and yet he genuinely feels compassion for her. Why is it so? Does the hand know something I do not? Can the pen read thoughts to which I myself have no access? Hastily, he scribbles the letter, as neutral in tone as possible, informing her that he is well and in good cheer and devoted to another. The lies are easier to write than the truth.

I cannot go back, he tells himself. I can only go forward, in a ceaseless circle, and may hope only that when the circle is complete and the motion halts I shall have arrived at the place that is best for me.

He puts the cork back in the ink pot, sprinkles sand on the paper, wipes the pen and seals the letter. Then he goes to the mail station and sends it by the westbound carriage.

His work at the school goes on. He knows he must do something, but has no idea what. Perhaps what needs to be done will do itself. Perhaps time will do the job for him. He pins his faith on time, the dogged rotation of the globe and the relentless advance of all things. Nothing continues to be the same. Time is a fall, one plunges and plummets, and sooner or later one is sure to collide with one thing or another.

The sun burns away the snow from the branches of the trees, buds appear. He goes out on to the ice and jigs for trout. When spring comes he puts out nets from the rowing boat. He fries the fish or boils them, eating them with kohlrabi or potatoes and thick dollops of butter that melt and dissolve into the flesh. He becomes fat from the same fare and from sitting down all day, fat and without cheer. To climb up the hill from the shore makes him breathless. Sometimes he goes to his father's house and sits for a while, listening to the old man's wretched lamentations about this or that ailment.

You're a physician of a kind, his father says. Can't you tell me once and for all what is wrong with me?

He looks like he would rather eat his words when Falck tells him to take off his clothes and get on the cot. But he does as he is instructed. He lies on his back and looks up at him.

Where does it hurt?

Here. And there. Everywhere, in fact.

Falck presses his hands against his father's abdomen, he jabs his fingers under the ribs, taps his chest, listens to his heartbeat, strikes the joints of his elbow and knee with a small hammer, peers into his mouth, eyes and ears, presses on the glands of his throat, tells him to stand up and walk a few paces across the floor and back.

Father, you are in good health.

His father seems disappointed. But why does it hurt, then? Sometimes I wake up screaming from the pain. And my hand, my hand is lifeless, it prickles, look at the way it's hanging down. He holds it up for his son to see.

It's nothing, Father. A bit of rheumatism, that's all, making the hand go to sleep. It is only to be expected at your age.

His father shakes his head and puts on his clothes. One of these days I'll go to Christiania and find a proper physician who can tell me what's wrong.

Falck asks to hold the little child. Karen brings him to him. The boy chuckles and flaps his hands with vigour on seeing his thirty-seven-year-older brother. How lively he is, Falck comments.

The boy's mother sits watching them. You ought to get married yourself and start a family, she says.

Who would want such an old man?

I know someone who would, she says. Should I ask her to come?

He hands the boy back to her. As he is leaving he hears his father say to Karen: I think he grieves in secret after being betrothed up there. I've asked him about it, but he won't speak of it.

He does not dwell upon his past in Greenland, though seemingly it would dwell upon him. The eye of a savage keeps watch on him through a crack in the unnaturally blue sky; he senses the smell of urine tubs and naked bodies seeping out over the well-kept and excessively green grass. The yellow sun, the white clouds, the sharply outlined fells seem anything but real. He is dreaming this place, or else it is dreaming him.

He asks one of the more diligent boys to read aloud. David, Psalm 23 and onwards, he instructs. The boy commences, his bright voice enunciating the familiar verses: *The Lord is my shepherd, I shall not want*. Falck's mind begins to wander. The widow is there, of course, seated over by the stove. Then speak to me, he commands. Say something! Tell me what you want. *He leadeth me beside the still waters, He restoreth my soul*. And yet he knows what she wants. She wants him back, like Madame Krøger, like Madame Therkelsen, Madame Kragstedt and Miss Schultz, all of them laying claim to him. *Yea, though I walk through the valley of the shadow of death, I will fear no evil*. He cannot recall the widow's features. Always her back is turned on him. He tries to picture her face. He remembers her naked body, even in the minutest detail, a freckle, a wrinkle, the thin, red skin of her knuckles. *Thou preparest a table before me in the presence of mine enemies*. But her face has faded away. If he forces himself to recall it, he sees only ordinary features that could belong to anyone. He can picture Maria Magdalene quite clearly. A light object strikes him and catches in his hair. Absently, he brushes it away. He wonders if he might write to Maria Magdalene and whether such a letter would ever reach its destination. But she is in one place, he in another, and all that needs to be conquered is distance. *Thou anointest my head with oil, my cup runneth over*. He recalls how she recited this very verse. It was one of her favourite scriptures. That must be why he thinks of it. No, he remembers now, he has asked one of the boys to read it aloud. He sighs and wakes up to chaos, to crusts of bread flying through the air, pellets of paper, even shoes have been turned into projectiles amid a commotion of jeering and laughter. The boy at the front reads on, unperturbed. *Surely, goodness and mercy shall follow me all the days of my life and I will dwell in the house of the Lord for ever*.

Quiet! he yells, leaping to his feet and striking the nearest available boy blindly on the cheek, unfortunately the one who was reading aloud, the best behaved of them all, whose voice thereby halts abruptly, accompanied by a startled rubbing of the afflicted cheek. The boy glances up at Falck with a forlorn look in his eyes. The room is now silent. The boy clears his throat. The reading continues. *The earth is the Lord's, and the fullness thereof; the world, and they that dwell therein.*

Rather unburdened by his outburst, despite the wrong boy having borne the brunt, he closes the school after lessons are over. But the crack in the sky is there still as he returns home, the eye observing him, the sense of everything's unreality. He thinks he hears a heathen chuckle somewhere far off, mingling with the echo of the Psalms of David.

†

He begins to drink. The urge has accumulated within him like water behind a dam; now he opens the sluices, and his mouth, and tilts the bottle towards the ceiling. He buys aquavit at the blacksmith's in the village, the place where melancholy men stand and lurk, their hands on the bridles of their horses. It tastes of raw spirits and of the myrtle that is supposed to conceal the fact, but does not. It makes him feel worse than ever before, and yet he is afflicted in a way that is new to him and he is appreciative of the variety it lends to his existence. He arranges his furniture so as to remind him of his room in the Mission house in the colony: the table in the middle of the floor, bedstead in the alcove by the wall. In the bed the widow lies and waits for him.

For a week he drinks with purpose and feels himself descend into familiar despondency and inertia. He falls asleep, slumped over the table, crosses the yard to the schoolroom and sleeps on at his desk, bombarded by pellets of paper. Eventually, he cannot be bothered to even get up in the mornings and remains flat out in his bed. The boys come and knock on his door. Magister! they shout. He stays put. Karen comes and attends to him. She scolds him, she kisses his cheek and helps him out of the alcove, and he lacks the strength to protest. She shaves him, gives him clean clothes, makes him porridge and sits with him to eat it. Yet another woman who takes pity on him. What is it with these women? What is it that attracts them to a man lying at the bottom of his own debasement?

If your father won't marry me, you can have me instead, she says.

You are an odd one, he says. Over her shoulder he can see the widow seated, combing her long hair with the bone of a reindeer jaw.

He resumes his work, unable to face the nuisance and melodrama of dying as slowly as someone his age must surely be expected to die. He teaches, he walks in the forests and along the shore, ruminating. The fullness of time, he ponders, what is that? Does time fill me up or do I fill time? Am I he who drinks or he who is being drunk, and can anything be done to stop it?

Time is a dam, filling up with the trivialities of the schoolmaster's life, which Morten Falck leads among the gentle hills of Lier parish. The dam of time swells; its waters grow deeper and deeper; years cover the bottom, months accumulate on top, weeks, days, minutes batter the bulwark as Morten Falck ambles, and the sun's lever sweeps through the sprouting forests, drawing the chlorophyll from the ground and up into the treetops that they may bulge with life.

The dam of time bursts. He goes to his father, requests and receives a loan, and time gushes out. Its force snatches him up and whisks him away; he is standing on the deck of the packet boat that plies the route between Christiania and Copenhagen; a country sinks into the sea behind him, another appears ahead. The deck rolls, he stands firm, an exclamation mark or rather a question mark, but yet standing. The sun shines, rain falls, night falls, daylight returns, the sun shines. He drinks sour ale and eats mouldy hard tack. He feels utterly at home.

Copenhagen

From the roadstead he is ferried through the forest of masts to the yellow toll house that is the Toldboden. He sits in the stern and stares at the city in front of him, sees the smoke of the glue factories, the distilleries and breweries, the textile factories and tanneries, and some thirty thousand fires, hearths and stoves within and without the ramparts. It is as if the smoke is stuck between the steeples. He hears the harsh, rhythmic clatter of the steam engine on the Holmen, and senses the smell of the gutter, the rotting food and filthy canals. He recalls the smell that greeted him when crawling inside the communal dwelling houses of the colony, and he feels the same twinge of excitement now as he clambers on to the quayside. May, 1795. The sun bearing down upon the royal city, upon the charred remains of Christiansborg, which burned to the ground the year before, upon the verdigris of the mansion house roofs, and upon Morten Falck. He is thirty-nine years old.

He rents a room in a tall white house on the corner of Skvaldergården and Størrestræde, some few steps from the Holmens Kirke. All day long he hears the punching of the steam engine, the infernal contraption, to use its popular name. From Gammel Strand he can look across to the ruins of the former palace and is shocked to see how the blaze has decimated a structure everyone believed would stand for ever. A mountain of stone consumed like tinder. How was it possible? Not only the palace, but its whole concept, gone up in smoke. If it can burn, then anything can. Nothing is safe any more. He remembers the magnificence of the baroque facade, the great number of its windows, and the clock facing the palace square, whose bell so crisply struck the hour.

A copperplate engraver from Ditmarsken, one Jacobus Buntzen, who rents accommodation in the same building, has produced an engraving of the fire, which he shows to him. Monsieur Buntzen reveals himself to be an obliging man, some few years younger than Falck, and often he invites him in to his fine rooms on the first floor, where he listens with interest to Falck's stories of his years in Greenland.

And it is the Magister's intention to return to that country?

It is the only place I can exist.

Let me show you something, Magister Falck. The engraver clearly feels at home in the rooms of his landlord, an examining magistrate of the Stocks House Commission at present residing in the provinces, to whom Falck, with his ever-latent feelings of guilt, to his relief has yet to be introduced. Buntzen ushers him in to a large room whose walls are covered with black-and-white and coloured engravings, many of which depict scenes of torture and dismemberment, the breaking of bodies on the wheel, the crushing of bones, public whippings and other sophisticated means of achieving confession. The gallery is off-limits to the women of the house, servants naturally excepted, the engraver informs him reassuringly. The esteemed magistrate is a sworn adherent of the purifying powers of torture, he explains with a touch of sarcasm of which Falck does not fail to take note. He finds the inspiration and strength to carry out his duty in this room, he has told me.

I see, says Falck tamely.

Come, let me show you something else, Mr Falck. He places a hand on Falck's shoulder and leads him on to another room. The walls here are plastered with more or less obscene engravings, mainly scenes from the colonies, purporting to be anthropological studies. Slave women copulating with goats and bulls, or with well-endowed men; a black woman whipped until she bleeds, the penis of a bewigged man in her mouth; another strung up by her feet, as yet seemingly alive, while a squirming foetus is removed through a hole in her abdomen. The smile on the engraver's face is wide and innocent.

Note the pleasure in the faces of these women, Buntzen says, his voice now thick with sarcasm. This is how men, certain men, wish their inclinations to be considered, as imparting pleasure to their victims and therefore essentially as something good, whereby they are conveniently relieved of their guilt.

Falck says nothing. The engraver leads him over to a depiction of two people clad in garments of skin. Two Greenlanders, he sees at once, one armed with a harpoon, the other with a bow and arrow. Their faces are framed by the hoods of their anoraks. There is nothing offensive about the picture and yet apparently it has been classified as unfit for the female eye.

This one is by my own hand, Buntzen explains, copied from an old oil painting. I believe the poor savages it portrays were abducted and brought to this country in Egede's day.

Falck leans forward and narrows his bad eye in order to study the detail. The two natives stare blankly ahead in such a way as hardly to meet the gaze of the beholder at all, though they would appear to be looking straight at the artist. There is something strangely absent about them, something secretive, which perhaps was the intention, and yet he recognizes this haze of indifference behind which the Eskimo will often retreat. Behind the two figures the artist has placed an inscrutable darkness. For some reason it is this dense, heathen darkness that Falck finds most moving. In such darkness I lived for six years, he thinks to himself, in its midst.

The engraver studies him. I hope the Magister is not ill at ease?

No, he says. Not at all.

Do you like the work?

Oh, he says, I find it quite marvellous. These people. I am. They are. My friends. What a disgrace that they should be consigned to this abominable room!

The engraver looks at him kindly. Falck laughs and dabs his eyes with his handkerchief.

I think I need something with which to fortify myself, he says. If Monsieur Buntzen would care to keep me company, I should like to offer him a glass.

The engraver pats him on the back. They retire to a serving house and have rather too much too drink. There is a musician with a lute, and the engraver turns out to possess a decent tenor and an extensive repertoire of languishing German ballads.

Copenhagen at night is a restless place. Nightmen clatter with their carts, students bellow out their songs, militia fire their guns in the air, cannon salute at odd times, street-door hags call out hoarsely for custom, bottles chink as they skate across the cobbles. He lies listening to the heavy-booted steps of the watchman, the sound of the mace striking the ground, his rusty voice, full of drunken piety: *Take ye heed, watch and pray, for ye know not when the time is.*

He writes a lengthy letter to the Missionskollegium and requests a meeting. A couple of days later he is summoned by messenger to appear in person at the office of one Mr Friedrich. Professor Rantzau, to whom he addressed his reports from Sukkertoppen, has retired from his position and now lives somewhere in Jutland. Mr Friedrich is accommodating, though highly formal in his greeting. He is shown a chair. Friedrich seats himself behind a desk, resting his hand ponderously upon a thick bundle of documents held together by string. Falck stares at the bundle. He knows what it contains, besides his general correspondence with the college. His diary. Pornographic drawings of the widow. His account of his religious crisis. His unlawful nuptials to the widow. Everything. The past. Morten Falck in his entirety. His heart sinks and he realizes that he will never be permitted to return to Greenland, nor, in all likelihood, to ever again carry out the work of a priest.

I have not yet had the opportunity of going through the Magister's papers, Mr Friedrich says.

Falck swallows. He briefly considers snatching the documents and running away with them.

I shall study them carefully within the next few days before addressing his application.

Falck nods. Is there any calling vacant in the country at present?

One, says Friedrich, and drums his fingers on the pile. Though our number of missionaries has been drastically reduced. It is by no means out of the question. The Magister has previously been incumbent in Greenland and it must be assumed gained much useful experience there, even if he did return prematurely. What was the reason for that, exactly?

My father called me home, he lies. My poor mother and my only sister passed away within a short time of each other. He was despairing. I could not fail him.

I see. Hm. Indeed. Magister Falck must be aware that if he should go back he should be prepared for the eventuality that the term of his employment will extend to the remainder of his lifetime.

I understand and am quite prepared. I see missionary work as my calling and destiny.

Does the Magister have kin, besides his father, who I presume is somewhat advanced in years?

No others, Mr Friedrich. I am alone.

Very well. Appear here in person on Monday. I shall read his dossier, and by then we shall be that much the wiser.

Mr Friedrich shakes his hand and shows him out. Falck casts a parting glance back at the desk, on which lie his life's most intimate and shameful contents, ready to be perused by the morally elevated and scarcely broad-minded Mr Friedrich. He has no choice but to go away and leave it behind. Empty of thought, he wanders home along the canal.

†

Tuesday, the second of June. He bucks himself up to visit his former sweetheart, Miss Schultz.

The engraver is well acquainted with the printer Schultz, with whom he has collaborated on several occasions. Sadly, however, the printer himself is no longer among the living, though a Madame Schultz remains, and as far as he knows, their three daughters have all married. Falck summons his courage and approaches the printer's house in Nørregade, where he lived for five years. He looks up at the window on the first floor where his room used to be and has to leap aside to avoid being run down by a carriage that comes rumbling through the gateway. He enters the yard.

The tree is still there and the bench, but the young daughters are gone. A couple of the printers sit puffing on bulldog pipes on the bench. He nods to them, their faces unfamiliar. He goes out on to the street again, to the main entrance on Studiestræde, where he climbs the step and knocks on the front door. A maid ushers him in. He waits in the hall, while she goes inside to announce him.

The Madame is pleased to receive the Magister, she says on her return.

He feels his throat constrict as he is led through the apartment to an open door leading to the drawing room. The widow Schultz looks up from a game of patience. She sweeps the playing cards together and puts them aside.

Mr Falck, she says, smiling. Do come in. Forgive me for not coming to receive you in person. I'm afraid I'm rather poor on my legs. She beckons him towards her.

Falck relaxes. The matter would seem to be proceeding more felicitously then he had imagined. He crosses the cluttered, dimly lit room from whose walls the family's forebears stare from gilded frames, and approaches the chair in which the Madame is seated. She grasps his hand, drawing him towards her, and looks up at him with a dowager's graceful smile.

Oh, how familiar!

And Madame Schultz has hardly changed at all. He bows and kisses her cheek. He studies her for a moment. Something is not right, he thinks.

The Madame calls for the maid, who enters, carrying a tray on which stand a bottle and two small glasses. Do sit down, Morten Falck. Let us have a cosy chat, the two of us. I hope you are in no hurry?

He draws up a chair and seats himself. He realizes he is still holding the woman's hand and that he has no desire to release it. He keeps staring at her.

I have the entire day, Madame Schultz.

They talk for a number of hours. Outside, a passing downpour lashes against the windows for some minutes. Madame Schultz invites him to stay for dinner. They enjoy a portion of salted goose meat with curly kale at the long dining table, together with the maid, who goes back and forth to serve. He tells her all manner of things and she listens attentively. He would like to enquire about Abelone and how she fares, but senses that the Madame takes it for granted that he is already informed of her destiny and on that account he cannot bring himself to ask. He has a nagging feeling that something is amiss.

Does the Magister recall our outing to the Dyrehaven?

As though it were yesterday, Madame.

Was it not on that occasion that the Magister and our dear Abelone became enchanted with each other? She smiles wistfully. I spoke to my sister of it.

Your sister?

The first Madame Schultz. My sister died of the fever some five years ago. Her bereaved husband, the printer, was kind enough to marry me and we enjoyed a few short years of happiness before he departed.

Falck senses himself gaping.

Oh, the lady in front of him exclaims. You thought I was the former Madame Schultz?

Yes.

Do you not remember me at all, Magister? I do resemble my sister, I believe, but she was rather taller than me. I was on the outing, too. I too remember it like it was yesterday.

On his return to his lodging he bumps into Buntzen in the doorway.

The engraver puzzles over his countenance. Mr Falck, you look like you've seen a ghost.

I asked someone's forgiveness for a sin of old and was absolved by the wrong person, Falck says. He goes up the stairs to his room and flops down on his bed, where, after a short time, he falls asleep.

The next day he receives a message that bewilders him somewhat. The sender is a Professor Hendrik Støvring of Lille Kannikestræde. *Dear Magister Falck, If the Magister should be inclined and have the occasion, he is hereby invited to an informal luncheon at the home of the undersigned and his wife, Friday 5th at 12 a.m. We both look forward to the Magister's company and to hearing of his many adventures among the heathens. Faithfully, Hendrik Støvring, Dr. Phil., & spouse.*

The letter is clearly penned in a woman's hand, rather than by the Professor himself. He recognizes the ethereal, feminine style, an echo of Madame Kragstedt's numerous letters and messages to him in the colony. Moreover, the notepaper is perfumed with lavender. Aha, he says to himself, recalling the gift he once made to Abelone of a flacon of lavender scent. It must be she. Madame Støvring, the professor's wife! So she did indeed recover from what happened between us.

He confides in Buntzen and shows him the invitation. My clothes are old and ragged, he says. Would you be able to lend me a coat, Monsieur Buntzen, or perhaps tell me where I might rent a suit for small coin?

The engraver steps back and looks him up and down. We seem to be of much the same height and stature, he says. Come with me.

When Falck makes his way through the city that Friday morning he is resplendent in clean and pleasantly smelling clothes, which to anyone's eye would appear new. He has long since discarded his wig, now threadbare and rotten. Moreover, wigs and all that goes with them have fallen out of fashion. It is the French Revolution in Denmark: off with their wigs! His hair has been cut short and he has retained a suggestion of mutton-chop whiskers, a revolutionary style, according to the engraver, who has found much enjoyment in orchestrating his transformation. *Sehr altmodisch*, distinctly modern, but be careful not to tangle with the police, Mr Falck, for they will suspect you of being a French or Swedish spy. The blue coat is short and fashionable, as simple as it is elegant. He leaves it open in the brash and relaxed style of the day, which is really just a matter of allowing the flamboyant silver buttons of the trouser fly to be visible.

He walks through Øster Kvarter, the worst slum of the city, pursued by a cloud of intensely perfumed fragrance. His appearance is to his liking; he avoids being spattered by the carriage wheels as they plough through the gutter or by the contents of buckets emptied from windows. He edges his way through the prostitutes and privy councillors, soldiers, officers and foul-smelling peasants, freed Negro slaves, and even a chained bear driven along with a pointed stick by an inebriated cripple in carnival garb. He feels uplifted; his suit lends him a sense of control, of power, of being able to steer his life. From the doorways prostitutes whistle at him and he cannot help but feel foolishly proud that they find him worthy of their attention and acknowledgement. He wonders how Miss Schultz, now Madame Støvring, has been treated by the years. Will she be a girl, a woman or a Madame? Will she allow me to kiss her cheek? Will I dare? Will it be appropriate? Has she invited me to show me the person she has become or to exact vengeance upon me?

On Ulfeldts Plads he pauses at the monument of infamy and wipes his brow with Buntzen's handkerchief, studies the fine, now sweat-stained monogram, and puts it back in his pocket. He observes two wild bushmen displayed on the square, a man and a woman, barely clad. For a handsome sum, members of the public may accompany the couple into a wooden shed and, according to the whip-brandishing keeper, who speaks an odd mixture of German and Italian, witness *delicatissime inklinaziones, eine naturwissenshaftlige illustrazione in natura!* Falck tries to summon some form of Christian sympathy for the hapless couple, but finds it hard, for they stand there, giggling and scratching their groins, and are obviously rather well-oiled, as indeed is the man with the whip, so that all he is capable of feeling is abhorrence.

Sir, you will burn in hell! he snarls at the man, receiving a sheepish, sickly grin and an outstretched hand in return.

Ja, mein Herr. Some copper, *mein Herr, di soldi, per gli poveri barbari, für die hungrigen Barbaren. Lieber Herr, signore. Prego.*

He tosses the man a coin.

The oriels of Lille Kannikestræde and the half-timbered facades lean over the street that lies in half-light, though a brisk easterly wind has swept all cloud from the sky. He finds the house and is admitted. Madame Støvring receives him in a salon that looks like a waiting room, in which all the furniture is placed up against the walls. She beams with joy at the sight of him, takes both his hands and squeezes tightly.

Morten Falck, she says.

Madame Støvring.

Oh, surely there is no need for formality, Magister?

No. Of course not. Abelone.

But I am not Abelone. Do you not recognize me, Morten Falck?

He feels a twinge in his abdomen. Again, he has mistaken two sisters.

Forgive me, he mumbles. Filippa?

Cathrine, she says. I quite understand you have us mixed up. It was all such a long time ago.

She is the youngest sister. The last time he saw her she was a gangling twelve-year-old with spindly arms and wide, innocent eyes. Now she has put on flesh, her cheeks have become full, slanting her eyes ever so slightly; the line of her neck and shoulder is curved and soft, her skin appears fresh and healthy. Her hair is put up, simply yet elegantly, her cosmetics are discreet, barely noticeable, her dress uniformly turquoise in colour, light and relaxed. A summer dress. Her arms are bare and rounded; they look strong. She wears no jewellery. She looks exactly like his recollection of Abelone. He finds it eerie.

How you stare, Morten Falck, she says with a laugh.

You look enchanting, Mrs Støvring. Cathrine.

No, *you* look enchanting, Morten Falck.

Borrowed plumes, I'm afraid. He smooths a hand down the cloth of his coat.

Did you know that all three of us were rather in love with you back then?

Really? All three? With me?

We drew lots for you, Morten Falck. The truth of the matter is that I won. It was just a game, of course. We were but foolish young girls.

And your sister? he enquires with caution.

Filippa has moved to Elsinore, she says, misunderstanding his intention, perhaps on purpose. She is married and has two children. Can you imagine? She giggles.

No, he says, hardly at all. He has only a very vague recollection of the middle sister, a daisy on the lawn of Kongens Have.

But tell me now, what on earth has happened to you? She steps up to him and peers at his eye, puts her hand to his cheek.

Oh, nothing much. He withdraws slightly. The other one works perfectly well. My sight is impeccable.

Did you clash with the natives?

Not at all. The natives are decent folk. We Europeans could learn much from them.

But are they not heathens?

All the more woeful that we are the more ignorant.

She smiles. For a few seconds nothing is said. She breaks the silence: But how selfish and thoughtless of me! You wish to say hello to Abelone, of course. She drags him along. You must meet my husband, too. Hendrik, she says as they enter the dining room, this is Mr Falck, whom I have been telling you about.

A thickset man with dark, curly hair and a moist pout, his ponderous cheeks penned in by a high, starched collar, turns towards them from the window at which he has been standing. He steps forward a few measured paces and greets his guest formally in a thin and tinny voice. He draws out a chair for his wife; they seat themselves at the table. A double-leaved door opens; tureens and steaming bowls are carried in. A haggard, elderly looking woman then enters; she nods in greeting, lifts the hem of her voluminous dress, which looks as if it weighs more than the body it encloses, and sits down to eat.

Falck stares at the woman.

Cathrine speaks to her in a loud voice. Abelone, won't you say hello to our guest?

The woman looks up from her plate. Her eyes meet Falck's without sign of recognition.

It's Magister Falck, Cathrine all but shouts from her place. Your old friend, the theologian, the one who rented a room from our father. He has come to see you.

Good afternoon, the woman says. An honour.

Falck nods stiffly. He cannot help but stare. It is she, he sees it now. Her decrepit features have already caused his recollection of the young Abelone's to fade. She has died before his eyes.

My sister-in-law has been quite ill, Professor Støvring explains in a low voice. Apoplexy, a stroke. She very nearly succumbed. We are very fortunate to have our dear Abelone with us, are we not, Cathrine? He places a hand on his wife's arm.

Don't you recognize Mr Falck? Abelone's sister persists.

An honour, Abelone repeats. She sounds like a mechanical bird opening its beak to faintly croak.

She is in some pain, Cathrine says regretfully. She must remember to take her medicine or else she becomes terribly unsettled and may even begin to wander in the streets. Apart from that, she is quite restored.

Falck recognizes the catatonic lethargy brought about by opium: the expressionless face, the distant gaze, movements as though made by a puppeteer. She lifts her spoon to her mouth and slurps her soup, then spoons up some more and slurps again.

They speak of events in France. Falck has neglected to keep abreast of developments and the professor is guarded in his comments. The Cabinet and the entire government, indeed the country as a whole, is imbued with paranoia and the fear of revolution, he says. The censor watches over the shoulder of those who write. Whatever a man might think on the matter, he does wise to keep it to himself. And the Magister should be careful not to be caught out in such costume after dark, he adds. He risks being arrested for espionage.

He explains that he has borrowed his suit from a friend and that as soon as he has returned home he will change into his old clothes again. He asks the professor cautiously whether he believes the revolution will spread to the Nordic countries.

Hendrik cannot conceive it will come to that in Denmark, Cathrine interjects. He considers the Danes to lend themselves poorly to revolution. Is that not so, my dear?

A steaming hot roast is brought in. The meat is apportioned on to the plates. Cutlery scrapes against porcelain, to suppressed sounds of chewing and swallowing.

Professor Støvring speaks: The Danish people are too humorously inclined to chop off each other's heads. His sombre tone makes Falck uncertain as to whether he believes this to be a good or a bad thing.

They put down their knives and forks and pause respectfully while Abelone, at the head of the table, presses a large silk scarf to her face and expels some stifled sobs. Her shoulders tremble.

The professor looks across at her with an expression of resignation and lets out a sigh. Give your sister a glass of water, he says.

Cathrine pours her a glass. Abelone drinks. Falck sees the quiver of her jaw. Presently, they continue eating.

The professor mutters something to his wife in German. His tone suggests reproach. Falck is unable to catch what he says.

Their plates are removed; they start on the fish, a fried whole carp. Cathrine smiles at him across the table; they toast, and he endeavours to smile back.

Life is not always easy, says the professor.

Falck glances up at him, unsure whether he has been addressed. No, indeed, he says. So very true, Professor.

These are uncertain times, Støvring says. Who knows what may happen? I recommend, Magister, that you return to Greenland as quickly as possible. It would seem to be the safest place for a European at present.

That is indeed my wish, says Falck.

Over dessert the mood is more buoyant. The professor enquires about Greenland and his experiences there. He tries his best to answer in a way the professor might understand. It seems Støvring has drawn up a list of questions he now follows in turn. After ten questions and answers he wipes his mouth and gets up from the table.

Now, if Mr Falck will excuse me. My day is far from over. I have a lecture to deliver at two o'clock, after which I am to meet with the cabinet secretary. He turns his attention to his wife. I may be late home, dear. Very interesting to meet you, Magister Falck. Perhaps we shall see each other again. All of a sudden he seems enlivened.

Falck rises and shakes Støvring's extended hand. I hope so, my learned Professor.

The Magister must come and see us again, Støvring says, almost heartily. You must tell us more about what you have seen. It is all most fascinating.

He pecks his wife on the cheek, walks the few paces to the door, swivels and bows stiffly before leaving the room. Abelone gets to her feet as though on command; she pushes back her chair, mumbles something incomprehensible and withdraws.

Remember to take your medicine, Cathrine tells her. You know how poorly you are when you forget. I shall look in on you later, my dear.

It's so very sad, says Cathrine once they are alone. But she is alive and that's the important thing.

The image of Miss Schultz chasing ahead of him across a meadow appears in his mind's eye, his forcing her to the ground, her laughter as she turns and pulls up her dress. Is this the sin that led to her illness, the things they did in his room above the printing shop? It is a question to which no answer will ever be revealed to him. He feels the urge to ask someone's forgiveness, Cathrine's perhaps, but knows it would be inappropriate.

†

As he walks home he hears the fire bells toll. Some members of the fire brigade come running past. He asks, but no one knows where the blaze is. On Amager Torv he can see black smoke billowing into the sky from behind the Holmens Kirke and he crosses over to the palace square to better observe the extinguishing. He is relieved to discover that the fire seems to be on the Holmen, apparently in one of the great storehouses and some good distance from human habitation. Those who stand gathered with him believe the cause to be that new and infernal contraption, the steam engine.

The weather is glorious, the city resplendent in sunshine. People stroll, arm in arm, horse-drawn carriages clatter noisily by, fishwives monger, fruit pedlars push along their carts and the city's hordes of unemployed soldiers drift aimlessly about, many of them obliviously drunk.

Falck walks out to Christianshavn, crossing the Knippelsbro to see the square in front of the orphanage again, where Master Eckenberg once held court. When later he returns to the palace square, black smoke is pouring over the roof of the Admiralty, and soldiers and seamen mill at the entry to Gammelholm. A large crowd has gathered on the square to watch the blaze. They say it is the stockpile of pit coal that is alight and makes the smoke so black; it is evident from the suffocating smell. He hears indignant comments about the chief fire officer having left for the country and being uncontactable, and the Admiralty on the Holmen refusing to admit the civilian fire brigade into their restricted area, insisting that the work of extinguishing is a matter for the Navy. How typical of such bigwigs! The tone is animated and sarcastic, the mood bordering on frivolous. What burns is ship timbers and coal, nothing for an ordinary Copenhagener to be concerned about. But what a spectacle it will be when the roof collapses on the main store and the fire is infused with oxygen!

Messengers arrive in carriages from the royal household's summer residence at Frederiksberg, where the sight of such ominous plumes above the city rooftops seems to have given rise to concern. But late in the afternoon the smoke subsides, and with a sense of disappointment and anti-climax Falck supposes the blaze to be extinguished. The crowds disperse, strolling at a time of day at which strolling does not occur; Vimmelskaftet and Amager Torv are cauldrons of people like himself, who feel displaced from their usual rhythm and faintly hope that something will still happen.

And yet an indistinct inkling, or perhaps the persistent flow of uniformed men towards the Holmen, prompts him to go back to the palace square. He sees that the smoke has not diminished at all, on the contrary, it has spread, though now much lighter in colour than before and thereby from a distance all but invisible in the sun. Nearly all the windows and roof hatches of the Admiralty are wide open; rope and canvas are thrown from them and carried down to boats moored at the quay. Papers scatter into the air, naval documents to be saved from the flames, but the wind stirs them up and casts them about, while the heat causes them to combust and burn up in mid-flight; they dance in the air like flaming butterflies and are snatched by the easterly wind to drift in across the city. From the Admiral of the Fleet's residence furniture is lowered to the street and ferried away in boats by the canal. Falck sees able seamen and soldiers forming human chains, passing along leather buckets filled with water, while others struggle in vain to make an old fire hydrant work. And then, for the first time, he sees flames. On top of one of the buildings of the main store a wooden statue of Neptune flares. Within minutes most of the store is engulfed and the men on the ground beat a hasty retreat. Falck is aware of a low and disquieting rumble, like the rolling of thunder, and feels a rush of wild excitement as he realizes that the fire is anything but under control. He senses a quite identical sentiment ripple through the crowd that surrounds him: laughter, tears and curses. Imagine if the whole city were to burn!

A careening carriage comes clattering at speed along Gammel Strand. It pulls in and draws to a halt in front of the church, where rescued rope and canvas lie piled in colossal, untidy heaps. Four footmen leap to the ground, the door is opened and a murmur of excitement runs through the crowd, followed by cheers as a slender, uniformed figure steps from the vehicle. Falck recognizes Denmark's regent, the Crown Prince

Frederik, and feels the same surge of elation as the rest of the onlookers. He joins in the cheering.

The Crown Prince hesitates, seemingly in doubt as to whether to direct his attention to the fire on one side or to his jubilant subjects on the other. A man comes running, halts abruptly and salutes. The Crown Prince follows on his heels; they disappear behind the church. The roar of the blaze intensifies. Falck hears the unambiguous, irascible crackle of burning wood. Narrowing his eyes, he sees the rain of sparks. All around him, talk is of the wind. It is brisk and from the south-east. The blaze may jump!

When the Crown Prince returns, now at a trot, he is again met by a clamour of cheers. Falck's voice is among them. Without pause, the regent climbs into the carriage, which takes off at a gallop along Holmens Kanal in the direction of Amalienborg Palace.

So much for his holiday, someone comments.

Those overfed privy councillors had best get their fat bellies moving and do something! another says.

What, those lackeys of the Germans? They'd rather see the city burn than neglect their puddings and pies.

Our beloved Crown Prince will know what to do. We must trust in him.

The blaze spreads quickly across Gammelholm. Roofs collapse, causing a build-up of pressure inside the buildings that blows the windows from their frames; shards of glass rain down, sparks fountain over the rooftops, house by house bursting into flames, combusting either spontaneously or by contact. Falck realizes it is but a matter of time before Skvaldergården's surrounding district will be consumed. He hurries home across Holmens Bro to find the street engulfed by smoke, its inhabitants in the process of rescuing furniture and belongings. It dawns on him that a number of the adjacent houses are already aflame. The blinding sun has obscured the fact.

The house in which he lodges is in turmoil. Outside number twelve the engraver stands directing men who are busy carrying out furniture and loading it on to a farmer's cart. A message has been sent to the magistrate at his country home.

You'd better hurry! Buntzen says. Grab your things and get to safety! Falck sees that his friend, too, is in the grip of the general frenzied derangement. He speaks animatedly to the driver, an Amager peasant, slaps him chummily on the back, echoes the man's dialect and instructs him to hasten to the agreed place and then come back immediately. The man demands payment in advance; Buntzen produces a leather purse and tosses it to him. Its coins are examined one by one. Eventually, the man climbs up on to the box and shows his worn-out horses the whip.

Buntzen, who besides his work as an engraver is also a correspondent of the *Kjøbenhavns Danske Posttidende*, is well-informed as to what is happening; he has boys running messages for him; they appear continually with reports of new developments. The blaze is under control on the Holmen and now confined to the main store, he says, an impressive feat indeed for a band of drunken soldiers. But the fire has jumped, disaster is imminent and the wind only makes matters worse. The Crown Prince has convened a meeting of his cabinet to consider which way the flames will be blown. Buntzen laughs frantically and looks at Falck with a fixed smile on his face. This will be bad, Magister.

But the fire brigade, Falck says. Surely they will be able to carry out their work here?

Let us hope for the best, says Buntzen. The city is as dry as straw, it won't take much. He puts a friendly hand on Falck's shoulder. Let us place our faith in God!

He climbs the stairs to collect his belongings. The smoke is hardly visible and yet his eyes smart. Entering his small chamber, he hears cries from further up, followed by the sound of running footsteps echoing round the staircase. He pokes his head out to see what is going on.

The house is on fire! cries a man coming down the stairs with a pair of boots in his hands and the front flap of his breeches hanging down. Hurry, man! The roof is ablaze!

He leaves his chest where it is, finds his sack, fills it hastily with whatever is within reach, swings it over his shoulder and lugs it down to the street. The houses of Skvaldergården have regurgitated their inhabitants. They stand with heads leaned back, staring up. The flames are easily seen now. A deep, angry rumble has filled the air and seems to be approaching. It feels like the city's whole foundation trembles.

He looks around for Monsieur Buntzen, but cannot see him anywhere. He runs down to Gammel Strand and is almost struck by a cart laden with bundles of documents and stuffed animals. The whole of Copenhagen is on the streets. People lugging chairs, chests, hatboxes, dressmaking dummies clad in finery, busts, cats, clocks, porcelain bowls. Shouts rain down upon hackney carriages that clatter by without stopping. He goes back to number twelve and sees Buntzen emerge on to the street.

Mr Falck, would you do me a great favour?

Of course, Monsieur Buntzen.

Take this painting and look after it for me. He gestures towards a full-sized portrait leaning against the wall. Allow me to introduce the Duke of Augustenborg.

Where should I take it? Falck asks.

Oh, where indeed? Somewhere not on fire. To the palace square, perhaps. I hear it is safe there, the palace having burned down last year. I'll come and look for you later this evening and relieve you of it.

Falck considers the canvas. It depicts a man in dress uniform, staring at the beholder with the full disdain of authority, one hand resting on his sabre, in the other a Bible.

The painting belongs to His Grace himself, Buntzen explains. He has already paid me a considerable sum to produce an engraving of it in copper. I should rather not see it lost.

But the cart? Would that not be better?

The cart will not be back. I was only lucky to get the most valuable items away. Unfortunately, I forgot all about the Duke's portrait here. Perhaps secretly I wish it to be lost. The engraver laughs hysterically again.

I shall take care of it, Falck promises.

Excellent. And now you must go. May God be with you! See you later!

The smoke from the rooftops settles, dense and suffocating, seeping towards the canal. The street is filled with stacked furniture and house-hold items waiting to be removed to safety, and Falck cannot help but think of the inferno of burning bureaus, settees, chests of drawers, clavi-chords, eiderdowns and linen to which the street will be reduced by evening, if it is not all gone. The residents continue to carry things out of their buildings, though it is clearer now that their efforts are in vain. The gentlemen of the houses amble back and forth and converse with one another, smoking on their long-stemmed pipes. The women scold their children, who chase barrel hoops across the cobblestones with long sticks. Each time a hoop is about to lose momentum, a child's stick whips it on again. There is no despair, no weeping, only this strangely hectic and high-spirited excitement that Falck also feels.

He lifts up the sack by its strap and swings it over his shoulder again, picks up the Duke of Augustenborg and carries him off in the direction of Gammel Strand. Here the crowds are much greater than only an hour ago. A deluge of lost souls, forced to acknowledge they are homeless, moves towards Holmens Bro to cross to the safety of the palace square. Falck keeps the Duke to the inside on his left, but is constantly shoved from the pavement by people jostling past, the canvas obscuring his view; and it seems that the further one gets from the house fronts, the greater the risk of being mangled beneath the thundering, iron-bound wheels of the horse-drawn vehicles. A hackney carriage comes hurtling towards the flow of refugees. They shout out to the driver, endeavour to stop the horses by snatching at their bridles, but at least two men are dragged under the vehicle. Falck cannot see what becomes of them. The carriage is halted, the horses rear up, whinnying and kicking their hooves wildly in the air, foam slobbering from their muzzles. The crowd that surrounds the carriage clamours at the box, setting about the driver, who flails his whip to no avail. The rabble drag him on to the cobbles. He vanishes in the throng. Falck hears him cry out and then cease. The horses rear up again, two by two, they roll their eyes, the carriage overturns and is dragged along. Someone is inside. Whoever it is screams heart-rendingly, a woman. Falck recognizes Abelone Schultz. Her dress is in tatters, her hair pulled loose; she resembles a lunatic. People point and snigger at her exposed crinoline, her soiled underskirts and distorted face. Falck wants to help her, but is hampered by the Duke. After a moment he sees her carried helplessly away by the current of the crowd. I can do nothing, he tells himself. He ducks behind his painting, peeps out over the Duke and sees Abelone flapping her arms and wailing. On the corner ahead of her a carriage pulls up with armed guards at its rear. The door is flung open with a bang and a voice calls out: Miss Schultz! She staggers towards it; a hand is extended and she is pulled inside. There is a spatter of applause, then booing and a hail of caustic oaths as the vehicle draws away. Shaken, yet relieved, Falck continues his crablike passage along the house fronts towards Holmens Bro, accompanied by the Duke.

On Gammel Strand the smoke is oppressive. Above him the rooftops are ablaze and he is frightened that timber beams or roofing tiles will fall on his head. But he remains calm, pressing ahead, step by step, and when the crush becomes too great he stands still and waits. Eventually he reaches the bridge. He can see that the church is as yet untouched, although the Admiralty facade is on fire and engulfed by flames. Even the bulwark of Holmens Kanal burns right down to the water. But it is clear that the wind carries the fire and its sparks away from the church and to the city. Soldiers and able seamen are still organized in human chains; tall ladders have been leaned against the walls of the church; the brigades pass along leather buckets filled with water from the canal, which are then emptied from the ladders on to the church roof and cast down to be returned to the beginning of the line. Some harangue them angrily and say they should look after people's homes instead. God can take care of His own house! Others more faithful shout down the protesters or else attack them with sticks or bare knuckles. Falck sees a gaggle of fishwives chase a man into the canal; they stand mocking him as he drowns, only then to see him hauled into a passing boat.

Falck lifts the Duke above his head and pushes along through the crowd as it makes its way across the bridge. He barely avoids collision with two men carrying a steaming pot of soup between them. Many have food with them, which would seem to be the most sensible thing to salvage from the flames. A wife carries a roast goose in her apron; a baker lugs along a sack of freshly baked *kringler* and offers them for sale at twice the normal price. He is ridiculed for it by the throng; they threaten to throw his pastries in the canal and send him the same way if he cannot show some public spirit. Halfway across the bridge he notices a procurer, easily recognizable in foppish garb, driving a flock of grotesquely painted women in front of him, some of them bearing furniture, others great bundles of linen, one with a slopping bowl of punch. The man, who would seem to be in his fifties, looks pleased with himself; he walks with a steaming cup of punch in his hand and lifts his tricorne hat right and left in greeting. Around him, people snigger and pass derisive comment. They call him *Professor*. Will the learned professor now deliver his lectures in God's open air? Is the professor driving his cattle to pasture? The 'professor' grins and nods.

Falck crosses on to the square, where the crowds have flattened the fence that enclosed the palace ruins and have surged in to the site itself. There is room here. Falck breathes easier. People have gathered in groups. They sit about on the ground, eating and drinking, where the cobbles have long since been removed. There is music. Stalls are being set up. A festive market atmosphere arises. A tent camp has already been established, where once was a palace. Cooking odours waft from improvised kitchens; people help each other clamber up into the gaping cornices of what remains of the palace walls. A calm has descended here; it is as though daily life has simply carried on, or else a new one has begun. Women sit sewing, boys chase their eternal hoops, girls skip and play tag or hopscotch. The men are few. Most are probably involved in extinguishing the fire. Falck is seized by restlessness. He wishes to be a good example of the civic spirit himself, to engage in saving his city. But the Duke of Augustenborg taps him commandingly on the shoulder and reminds him of his presence. He regrets having taken responsibility for the painting, and is annoyed by the idiotic Duke standing there, indifferent to the blaze, resplendent in his crosses and ribbons and stars, clutching his insignia, the Bible and his sabre, which fact seems to Falck to be additionally objectionable, a picture of all that is wrong with the German nobility. He is inclined to leave the Duke to his own devices, to tell him to go to hell. But he has promised Buntzen to look after him, and so he will. His Grace is leaned up against a lamp standard. Falck has dumped his sack on the ground and stands looking over to Gammel Strand, where the hordes press their way forward at a snail's pace.

The Admiralty is still burning, as is at least a third of the district facing the Holmen. The fine white house in which he and Buntzen lived is in flames. He hopes everyone got out in time. He thinks of the two rooms with their unpleasant engravings of torture. And the two natives with their empty eyes. He wonders if anyone might have saved them. Further along the street, towards Kongens Nytorv, he can see tiny figures at work on the rooftops, tacking ship's sails on to them to be soaked by the fire pumps below. It would appear to be effective prevention against the flames and he cannot fathom why the method was not put to use before the blaze spread to the city.

A man addresses him. Sir, is this not the Duke of Augustenborg?

Indeed, yes, he replies without seeing who has spoken.

Ah, my old friend, says the man, who now steps up to the canvas. Promise me you will take good care of this portrait. He is a noble man and a loyal friend.

Falck stiffens when he sees who has spoken to him. The Crown Prince himself, on foot, with five escorts to ensure his safety.

The regent's face lights up; he turns again to Falck. You must be the Assessor Biering.

No, your Royal Highness. My name is Falck. Magister Falck.

Is there anything I can do for you, honourable Assessor? He comes closer, closer than Falck finds comfortable; a tall and graceful man, who, like everyone else, has been gripped by the madness of the fire and there is no knowing what he might do next. Falck withdraws slightly; the Crown Prince hesitates and looks at him enquiringly with watery eyes. Perhaps he is mad like his father, Falck thinks.

Falck stutters a reply without any idea of what he is trying to say, then says: What can *I* do for *you*, your royal highness?

Be brave, Assessor, says the Crown Prince, with a pat on his arm, and then something else that is drowned out by the commotion of collapsing buildings, whinnying horses and shouting.

Falck bows as deeply as he can; the regent swivels on his heels and marches off in the direction of Amager Torv.

Falck stands for some time and wonders if he has comported himself appropriately towards His Royal Highness and whether he ought to have said more and been more accommodating. Perhaps he should have taken the opportunity to attract favourable notice, something that might have stood him in good stead with the Missionskollegium. But now it is too late.

The fire brigade is on its way at long last. Pipes are fed into the canal, the pumps are manned. The feeble jets that reach halfway up the facades fail to convince.

And yet the fire does not seem to have spread further. Mainly it is the districts closest to the Holmen that are afflicted. The fire has consumed itself, he hears someone say. No, the wind has blown it out, another opines. Falck feels an urge to tell them that their conjecture is incorrect and foolish, yet he is still buoyant and elated by the general mood around him. He no longer wishes to see the city burn; this will suffice. And on Monday, in three days' time, he is to appear in person at the Missions-kollegium to receive his assessment regarding renewed service in the Greenland Mission. Moreover, he must work out an agreement with the Royal Greenland Trade concerning his debt, for fear that he should end up in the gaol. For the first time in years he gives thought to how he might solve his problems. For too long he has allowed matters to remain unattended. Mr Friedrich's bundle of documents, annual reports,

Kragstedt's statements on his conduct as missionary, will hardly be laudatory. And then the reports from his own hand, whose contents he barely recalls, but which most likely are gibberish with much invoking of trumpets and hymns, and probably a great deal about Rousseau, not exactly a favoured name in Denmark at present. All is there, he thinks, on Friedrich's desk, and he shrinks at the thought of them poring over the documents and assessing his character, perhaps even at that very moment. He realizes the verdict may be quite as destructive to his reputation as the fire is to the houses on the other side of the canal. But he can do something about it, he can put forward arguments, refer to his enmity with Kragstedt, reject the diary as a forgery.

He is torn from his thoughts. All around him people huddle together and point. He sees smoke rising from the Nikolaj Kirke, though it cannot be said whether it comes from the church itself or from buildings in the vicinity. The church is in no danger, someone says. It survived the fire of '28 and will surely survive today: the pumps are better and more numerous now.

It is as if the words themselves trigger what happens next, like some sarcastic retort. Falck sees flames lick the steeple, hardly visible in the blinding sunlight, and yet there is no doubt now that the church is burning. Nikolaj Kirke is the people's church, the Copenhageners' own, not the Navy's like Holmens Kirke, which has escaped the blaze. It is a church the people use, a home from home, a haven of respect and hope in the midst of the misery of the surrounding streets. And now it is aflame. For the first time he senses terror in those around him.

May the Lord have mercy on us! Please, not Sankt Nikolaj!

The flames in the lantern wave near-invisibly, calamitously; they leap to the church roof and crawl up the great spire. Black smoke plumes out and the steeple is engulfed. People stand close and stare silently and incredulously at the ancient Gothic church where many of them have been christened, confirmed and married. Some endeavour to call out to the fire brigade to save their church, but it has enough on its hands trying to rescue the houses along Gammel Strand. And then a pump is dispatched. New water pipes are rigged together, the pump is manned, bucket brigades are organized, and the men who remain on the palace square, Falck being one, run across and join them. The Duke must look after himself, along with his sack of belongings.

It is soon apparent that the church cannot be saved. The steeple is too tall to be reached by the hoses, moreover the stairs inside the tower are blocked by flame. Falck joins a bucket brigade; he is deployed to the entrance of Vingårdsstræde, where he receives slopping leather buckets from the man on his right and passes them to the man on his left. He has no idea what happens to the water at the end of the chain, whether it is hurled directly at the church's structure or is filling a pump. But they are short of buckets, there is a long interval between each, the water in the canal is not reaching the blaze, and the men become increasingly frustrated at standing there to no avail. We might just as easily piss on it, one of them says. It is indeed a dreadful state of affairs, for water is available in copious amounts only a few paces from where they stand. But no fire pump, no bucket brigade can make use of it in time.

Then comes a deep rumble of collapsing beams, and the shower of sparks that ensues chases Falck and the other men out on to Amager Torv, and from there they watch as the steeple of the Nikolaj Kirke tips over. They hear the onlookers scream by the palace ruin: Jesus Christ! Falck stares in dread. The steeple wobbles and gives way; seeming almost to nod a greeting to the throng that stands and gapes, it sways, then topples lazily onto the houses of Store Kirkestræde. Sparks shoot into the sky as the flaming spire with its contents of burning timber crashes down. They rain upon a large area like some apocalyptic display of pyrotechnics, mirrored in the palace canal. Guttering, mostly of wood, ignites and bursts into flame; the blaze spreads to the roofs, timber frames, window frames; it works its way down through the staircases, floor by floor, until the houses collapse under their own weight. Øster Kvarter burns to the ground in its entirety. The conflagration conquers new territories: it lays the slums to ruin and reaches almost to Kongens Nytorv; there, however, to change its mind, halted by bucket-wielding citizens keeping doused their makeshift barriers of canvas, it halts at

Østergade, jumping instead nonchalantly to its left, a westerly turn, nudged along by the wind from the east, now to leap from roof to roof.

A man wails: What are we to think of our Lord now? He allows His house to burn, yet spares the Comedy House!

The city is an anthill prodded by boys with sticks. Streets as yet untouched by fire or smoke are blocked by carriages, many of them in flames, their panic-stricken horses unable to go forward or back. He sees men hacking at one of the beasts with an axe. At the Knippelsbro there is an exodus towards Christianshavn; fire pumps stand abandoned everywhere he looks, some of them on fire; carriages and carts lie overturned with broken axles, or else aflame. No one is concerned any longer with putting out the fire, only with saving themselves. Now and then shots ring out. It is rumoured that the rabble has taken up arms and will storm the palace of Amalienborg, that the guard is shooting at random, that the ammunition depot has ignited, that the Swedes are coming to seize the city and slaughter its inhabitants.

Falck returns to the palace square. The Duke is where he left him and he is met by his reproving stare. But his sack of belongings is gone. No matter. There was not a single thing in it that he could not do without. He lifts the canvas by its frame to take it with him out of the city. Then he puts it back. He looks down at himself. He is still in Buntzen's fine suit, now filthy with soot and soaking wet. Nonetheless, it lends him as yet the self-confidence of an elegant gentleman. It is a feeling that instils in him an odd sense of loyalty to the Duke. He must save his portrait! The wind is still in the south-east, the sensible course would seemingly be to cross the Knippelsbro to Christianshavn. But if the wind turns he risks becoming trapped there, along with thousands of homeless undesirables from the slum of the incinerated Øster Kvarter. It seems safer to proceed along the outer boundary of the blaze in the same direction as the wind. Thus, he will arrive at Vesterport or Nørreport and thereby escape into the countryside.

He follows Frederiksholms Kanal, where the crews of the vessels moored there are busy taking down the masts, so as to come under the bridges and out of the city. The wind whistles through the palace ruin, tugging violently at his canvas; he must struggle no matter how he carries it. There are fewer people here; horses released from their carriages canter about or stand nibbling grass at the verges. He sees the carcass of one in the canal, only its back protruding from the water, its fanning mane floating gently on the surface, the animal still in its harness. In several places the water is all but obliterated by documents from the Admiralty. Falck wonders what they might contain and how great a loss they might be now that they have been destroyed by fire and water. He finds it hard to imagine they can be of any real value. There are no bodies in the canal, only the horse, which surprises him. Here it was in his student days that he salvaged corpses for the surgical academy on Norgesgade. Then there was never a shortage of candidates for the scalpel. The fire would appear to have stimulated the survival instinct, breaking the popular habit of expiring.

He comes to Rådhusstræde and goes left around the Rådhus, past the Vajsenhus and the Missionskollegium, where a gentleman in a cassock paces back and forth in front of the church, looking anxiously up and down the street.

Mr Friedrich? Falck enquires, putting down the Duke.

The man glances at him absently. Tell me, when will that carriage be here? he barks angrily.

What carriage? Falck asks.

We need a carriage immediately. Our entire archive, the library, irreplaceable, all will be lost if the fire should reach us here. How dare they leave me in the lurch like this? It's a scandal, malevolence of the highest degree. I shall make certain those responsible will receive their due reward in court. Who are you? He turns his gaze to Falck, his eyes wandering up and down his apparel.

My name is Morten Falck, Magister. We have met. I am at Mr Friedrich's service, if he should require my assistance.

The city is burning to the ground, it is the will of the Lord, Friedrich says. All will be destroyed, all! We are all of us damned. This is our revolution. The fire of the streets of Paris has reached us. But the documents must be saved, the documents are our history, our common memory. Can the Magister find a carriage?

I shall try, he tells him. If you would take care of this painting that is in my keeping.

He leaves the Duke and runs up to Gammel Torv. He relishes having his hands free once more. He is hungry. It will soon be dark. The square is peaceful and calm, almost devoid of people; there are lights in the windows, somewhere someone is playing a piano, the fountain splashes soporifically. Men enter and exit the Rådhus, where a dim light shines from a pair of lamps on the ground floor. The clock in the tower says almost eleven-thirty. He buys some spiced pastries from a woman and stuffs them ravenously into his mouth. A platoon of soldiers marches in the direction of Vimmelskaftet. There are no carriages in sight. He hears the noise of the fire; it sounds as if it is approaching, yet there is hardly any smoke in the air. He feels calm here. Most likely the fire is going out, he thinks to himself.

He follows the soldiers. On Vimmelskaftet the traffic is busier, and on Amager Torv mad confusion prevails once again. People lug whatever they have been able to take with them from their homes. A woman carries a birdcage, its occupant, a parrot, clearly dead or unconscious. Another drags her children; a third is on her knees praying, her little boy kicking her furiously. A gentleman endeavours to sell his furniture, which stands in a disorganized pile in the middle of the street. A chiffonier! he cries despairingly, clawing at Falck's shoulder. The man stands raving, Look, fine little drawers and cupboards, press here and *voila*, a secret compartment! He breaks into shrill laughter. Only five rigsdalers. No thank you, says Falck. Four rigsdalers? He wrenches away. A dressing table! the man shouts out behind him, an embroidered footstool! A bargain! You'll come to regret it, sir, mark my words!

The gutters of the fine commercial houses on the right of the square are alight; furniture and other contents rain down from the windows. There are many horse-drawn carts, some fully laden, though guarded by soldiers with raised sabres; the horses rear up and are unmanageable. Falck notes that most vehicles proceed along Naboløs, presumably towards Købmagergade and Nørreport. He sees some tumult on the side of the street that is burning, where a few fire pumps squirt feeble jets on to the facades of buildings whose insides are disintegrating in flame. A group of traders and small shopkeepers appropriate the pumps and drag them over to the other side of the street, where they proceed to douse their own houses and businesses as yet unreached by the blaze.

Falck catches sight of the Crown Prince on the square. An officer stands calmly addressing him; he points his sabre towards the houses. The Crown Prince nods and says something in reply, gesticulating as he speaks. The officer salutes. A house in Store Kannikestræde collapses, a cloud of dust and smoke propelled into the air. The Crown Prince seems to notice something on the cobblestones; he bends down and picks it up. A coin. He holds it up in front of him, as pleased as a little boy, and turns it between his fingers. It glints in the light of the burning buildings. He stops a young woman with two children in tow and presents it to her. She stares at him in terror; he makes a dismissive gesture of his hand as though to say, My dear woman, it is nothing, then returns to his officer to resume their discussion. Everywhere, people are falling over themselves when they realize the identity of the tall man in uniform; a fine gentleman approaches in a series of bows, a wheedling smile turning the corners of his mouth. But the Crown Prince does not heed him. He has seen a man who at the last moment managed to avoid being run down by a carriage; he darts forward and helps him to his feet. He speaks to him with a look of concern, brushes the dirt from his coat. His escorts stand back and observe, exchange weary looks. The addled victim assures his rescuer that he is unharmed. The Crown Prince takes his hand and shakes it. And with that he proceeds away, calmly and with what to Falck seems to be a contented smile, in the direction of Østergade.

Falck has dismissed all thought of the Duke of Augustenborg and his promise to Mr Friedrich and plunges into the work of extinguishing the blaze, or rather into the saving of the northern side of Vimmelskaftet, which so far has been spared. Dousing the buildings that have yet to succumb and leaving those that are ablaze to their inevitable fate has shown to be a good strategy. Falck appropriates a leather bucket and runs down to the canal, where an able seaman hands him a full one in return for his empty. He scuttles back to Vimmelskaftet with its contents sloshing and empties it into the tank of one of the pumps, then hurries back with it to the canal. Though this shuttle service between the canal and the square is quite without system, he feels it is meaningful. Hundreds of men and older boys are involved in this transport of water, criss-crossing in all directions, each and every one with his own idea as to what must be done, and yet their efforts are all too slow, the buckets are too few, and the pumps are empty most of the time. Then some tipcarts appear with great stacks of buckets; the crowd erupts into a cheer and within a moment the buckets are in use. The fire gains ground on the southern side of Vimmelskaftet, the wind nudging it along, step by step, but the northern side would seem to be safe. The hours pass. It is well into the night. Falck is beyond exhaustion; his legs carry him and he follows as though in some all-too-lifelike dream. Around him the city burns; he is in its midst, emptying every fifth bucket over himself before returning to the flaming street. Barrels of fresh water are rolled forth and turned upright, their lids are broken up and people flock to quench their thirst. The mood has turned from panic and confusion to cheerful discipline; it is clear that the work of extinguishing is running well, despite every difficulty. But the fire blazes throughout Læderstræde and out to the canal; it lights up the sky and its sparks rain down upon the throngs and burn holes in their clothes. Everywhere there are rats fleeing from burning or flooded basements; they rise up on their hind legs, sniffing the air to take stock, before scurrying across the street in the direction of the churchyard. A brood of old wives, apparently gripped by gambling fever, storm the lottery outlet and snatch what tickets they can find. Others plunder coffee and aquavit. Some of the thieves are caught, beaten with sticks and thrown into the canal. A hackney carriage appears out of nowhere on Vimmelskaftet. Falck hears the driver offer transport for the sum of twenty-five rigsdalers. People snort with outrage and shower him with oaths, yet he insists on his price. The horse rears up; someone grasps its bridle and is lifted into the air. The rabble are upon the vehicle in an instant, thrashing out at the driver, who attempts to defend himself with his whip, only then to leap to the pavement and flee up a side street. The horse rears again; it drags the men along who endeavour to hold it back. After a moment it comes to a halt and is still. A blow is delivered to its forehead and when it collapses to the ground they unhitch it from the harness and use the carriage to carry water.

The fire stops when it reaches the almshouse opposite the Helligånds-kirke, popularly called the Cloister. The female residents, women of the nobility who have come down in the world, sink to their knees on the cobbles and pray. Falck watches incredulously as the blaze yields, sparing the Cloister, while the houses around it go up in flame and are laid to ruin. Dear Lord, Falck says to himself, forgive my miserable sins. I have doubted! Later, the fire seizes the building's basement and the place burns down like all the others in the row.

Shop signs ignite, gilded or painted script advertising *Gentlemen's Clothing*, *Watch-maker*, *Portrait-painter* and *Apothecary* bubbles and sizzles away. The copper plates of the book printers' shops, their edifying monographs, travel descriptions with coloured illustrations of bushmen, unicorns and Cyclops, romantic tales, broadsheet verse and royal decrees melt in the storerooms and curl into small blobs of metal; oil paintings flare and are gone; cabinets of curiosities collected over a hundred and fifty years combust in seconds or else are dispatched through windows and smashed to pieces on the cobblestones; wardrobes of gilded gowns, embroidered, saffron-tainted blouses, brocade slippers perfumed by the feet of fine ladies, cotton undergarments with foul-smelling stains of perspiration, menstruation towels hung out to dry, horsehair wigs, leather coats, ladies' bustles, all succumb to the flames; libraries of magnificent hand-written, pre-Gutenberg editions feed the blaze still further; anatomical preparations and prepared corpses go up in smoke; brooches of gold, silver buckles and thousands of items of jewellery melt and are reduced to droplets of precious metal under collapsed timber; boiling tar drips from the roofs; documents whirl to the skies in flame and descend to earth as flakes of soot; window panes are transformed into a caramel mass that seeps from the frames; stairways collapse with a rhythmically syncopated groan; bottles of distilled alcohol burst like small bubbles of fire on the shelves of the apothecaries; barrels of ethyl spirit spontaneously combust, sending cold, blue balls of flame out through the windows of the basements. The building that houses the synagogue on Læderstræde crumbles to the ground; outside the street is impassable. The fire jumps across Hyskenstræde. It sweeps across the city and continues west.

Back on Nytorv, Falck encounters inmates of the debtors' prison bound together at the wrists in a long chain, on their way to the gaol at Christianshavn. They look pale and starved; they blink their eyes and stare, horrified and incredulous, at the burning buildings.

The Rådhus is not aflame, but now as he stands by the fountain in the middle of the square he can see that its fate is sealed. The blaze roars from the windows of Rådhusstræde, and the easterly wind, which seems almost to have increased, sends showers of sparks, near-invisible in the sunlight, across the square to the buildings on the other side. Those who live in the direction of the wind gradually realize that the flames will not stop until they reach the ramparts. The streets are cluttered with stacks of furniture, some alight, some destroyed by water from the fire pumps or because they have been roughly evacuated through windows. But there are all manner of horse-drawn vehicles; it seems the drivers of the hackney carriages have finally mustered some public spirit; even peasants from distant villages, Dragør, Sundbyerne, Kastrup, have come to help and transport goods and belongings without payment. Most probably it has dawned on them that they are quite as dependent upon the city as those who live in it. Long columns of vehicles laden with furniture and other items are on their way out to the ramparts or else to Amager.

In front of the Missionskollegium he finds the Duke where he left him. The same mood of exodus as everywhere else. He sees desks and chairs from the schoolroom have been carried out, furniture from the teachers' residences and offices. He recognizes several items. The doors of the main entrance have been removed and leaned up against the wall. Documents are scattered over the steps and in the street, papers dancing in the air, some of them stuck in gutters and cornices. Falck stares at them. Somewhere among them is his name, letters he has sent, letters he is ashamed to have written, ashamed that others have read, letters written to him, his despicable diary. He wonders if Friedrich had the chance to read it all. Perhaps he put it aside to read on Saturday or Sunday, perhaps it has been brought to safety elsewhere in the city. Bundled leather files are put on to a cart. They are marked with journal numbers. He helps hand them up to the man on the cart, who piles them high and secures them with straps before driving off with them. People shake their heads. Such labour, and all for the sake of papers! Can it be true that the scribblings of priests are more important than so much else? Falck watches the cart as it disappears from sight along Frederiksberggade. Friedrich is nowhere to be seen.

He leaves the Duke once more and goes back to Gammel Torv. He wants to see the magical moment when the fire will jump. He ought to hurry out of the city and ensure the safety of the portrait. But he cannot tear himself away. The clock in the tower of the Rådhus issues a few hesitant chimes. The striking train is in need of winding, but the whole building has been evacuated and this is perhaps its final hour. Three o'clock. It occurs to him that it is mid-afternoon. But what day? Saturday? He has no idea what to do. What is his duty as a citizen? To bring the Duke to safety or to attend to the living? He is indebted to the engraver and moreover is fond of him and would like to do him a service. If he leaves the city with the portrait, he will have done something good and another person will be grateful to him. If he remains to join in the work of saving the city, his efforts will probably make little difference. But the civic spirit is important, too. This is my city, he thinks to himself.

He sits at the railing of the fountain. It is still working, splashing away without regard. People scurry about: a platoon of soldiers marches purposefully in one direction, then a command is barked and they turn and march in another. A fine gentleman stands and stares forlornly at a burning carriage; a girl attempts to jump over the iron railing, her dress gets stuck and he is afforded a glimpse of becoming ankle; a wife fries pancakes over an open fire. He buys one and sits munching it. The easiest thing is to do nothing, he muses.

Musical instruments are being thrown from a high window on the corner of Vestergade. He sees them hit the cobbles and hears them shatter into pieces, a stifled acoustic disintegration that identifies each instrument by turn. Drums, French horn, violins, timpani, even a small and delicate spinet goes the same way. The madness ceases. People gather at the debris, pick up some of the items in their hands, pluck a string, blow into a horn. Then someone shouts: a thin male at the window above. Falck sees his glaring eyes, the twist of his face. He holds a bottle in one hand and steadies himself against the window sill with the other. His upper body leans perilously towards the pavement below. People in the street cry out to him: In the name of Jesus, man! They reach up their arms towards him. Don't jump, dear friend, come down from there! The man grimaces; he utters something that is drowned out by the noise, then throws his bottle into the sky; it descends in an arc and explodes against the cobbles. He is gone from the window. The gutters of the house have begun to burn. Shortly afterwards he appears in the doorway, playing a violin. It sounds unlike proper music, more a kind of melodious twitch.

He approaches the fountain where Falck is seated. Falck notices something familiar about him and is himself recognized immediately. The young man's face lights up.

Your Reverence. Long time no see.

You? Falck exclaims, recoiling.

Your humble servant, he says, with a courteous bow.

Parallel worlds collide and entangle inside Falck's head, mingling improperly and disagreeably.

The hermaphrodite sticks the violin under his chin and plays a trill. Then he puts it down and looks at Falck with mournful eyes. Everything's gone, he says. The music has stopped.

I know you, Falck says after a while.

Of course you do! We made each other's acquaintance one night many years ago. I owe you five marks, Priest. You rendered me the service you'd paid me to perform. He puts his hand in his pocket and produces a leather pouch. He tosses it to Falck, who catches it in the air.

You are a musician now?

Yes, I'm a musician. He picks on the strings of his violin. I was put in charge of the orchestra's instruments. But now it's all too late. Too late, too late. He places the violin under his chin again and walks off in the direction of Vestergade as he plays. Goodbye, Priest! he calls out. Falck watches the young man until he is gone. Or the young woman, he thinks to himself, calling to mind her grotesque and inadmissibly muddled gender lying naked in the shed at the ramparts. He realizes he still holds the leather pouch in his hand. He looks inside. It is heavy with coins, a small fortune. He recalls his last encounter with the boy at the Dyrehavsbakken, when he stood and watched him emptying people's pockets and refrained from giving him away. He stuffs the purse into his pocket. He will give the money to someone in need, he resolves, someone suffering on account of this catastrophe.

The fire jumps. A flight of stairs collapses on Rådhusstræde; windows and doors spew dust and smoke; and a horse panics, wrenches itself free and gallops away in the direction of Nørregade. The roof of the Rådhus is ablaze, the fire is at the clock tower, beams and rafters and gutters in its grip. The square is teeming with people. They stop what they are doing and stare up at the building.

About bloody time, they say.

The Rådhus clock strikes the half-hour agonizingly slowly. The onlookers jeer, clap and whistle. Falck loosens his collar, the heat is stifling. He remembers the Duke and runs back to the Missionskollegium. The portrait is where he left it, the building shuttered and abandoned. The fire reaches out from the Rådhus and will ignite the college's gutters. He picks up the painting and makes his way towards the perimeter.

A wide corridor of the city is alight now. Falck stands on the rampart with a good view of the blaze. On each side of the corridor the fire brigade battles to save the adjoining houses by putting wet canvas around them and keeping them doused with the fire pumps. Accidents are many. He watches them happen or hears of them, and he sees the results. Men who fall from rooftops, women trampled by horses or crowds, children trapped inside labyrinthine buildings; cowering in a loft when the roof collapses, many are struck by falling tiles and timber; some exploit the situation to stick a dagger into an old enemy; the militia opens fire at the slightest provocation, shooting at thieves or suspected thieves, and if they escape the rain of bullets they are beaten to death by the rabble or chased into the canal, where people in heavily laden boats seek to drown them with their oars to stop them from clinging to the gunwale and capsizing them. Hordes of drunks risk summary justice to steal kegs of aquavit, breaking them open to drink themselves senseless. When the fire comes, the kegs explode, blue beacons scattered about the streets.

It seems half the city has gathered on the ramparts. They have dragged furniture and mattresses with them, armchairs, chaises longues, tables and benches. Peasants and citizens, women in tight crinoline and servant girls in airy shifts, officers and enlisted men; the fire is democratic: all are homeless and sit now in splintered, water-damaged furniture, or else they break it into pieces to throw on the campfires. There is music and singing; alehouse keepers have rolled along their barrels and set up serving places in tents or under treetops; goats, pigs and hens are slaughtered and roasted on the spit, sizzling and crackling above the flames. Beneath the ramparts some men butcher a horse with axes and lug a hindquarter to one of the fires. Falck sees that the leather bit is still between its teeth. The air is thick with the smells of cooking and excrement. From the trees children stare down at him. All the time he hears the blaze as it tears down buildings and causes panes to explode. He listens to the music and the singing on the rampart. He sits by a campfire where a great hunk of meat turns above the flame. A kind soul offers him a slice. He takes it, along with some bread, and eats. He drinks fresh fruit wine and feels his strength draining away. The last thing he sees before he falls asleep is the Duke of Augustenborg leaning against a tree, looking down at him disapprovingly. The widow is there. She has snuggled up and lies spooned against his back. He is glad of her company.

†

It must be Sunday. Carrying the Duke, he proceeds down Vimmelskaftet in the direction of Amager Torv. A pack of dogs comes hurtling towards him in tight formation. He jumps aside, holding the Duke in front of him. They pass without taking any notice, like a sled team. It is becoming light.

He turns around. He has no idea where to go. All is quiet. He walks back to Gammel Torv and sees that the Rådhus lies in ruins. The Vajsenhus and the Missionskollegium have also burnt down, as have the majority of houses surrounding Nytorv. As he makes his way towards Lille Kannikestræde the bells begin to peal from the churches that have survived, calling the faithful to Sunday service. It looks like it will be a fine day.

He stops outside number twelve, puts down the Duke and raps on the door with the knocker. A maid opens it a slight crack. He says his name. He is not immediately admitted, but must stand and wait in the street while she announces him to the lady of the house. He has not encountered a single watchman on his way and he has heard tell that the city swarms with prisoners who have absconded while taking part in the work of extinguishing the blaze. The residents are wary.

The door opens. Cathrine stands in front of him. She stares at him without recognition, then suddenly her face lights up.

What on earth happened to you, Morten Falck?

I have been to war with the Swede.

She lets him in.

My lodgings were in one of the houses that are no more, he explains apologetically. I have lost everything.

But not your life! she says. We were so worried about you. There were all sorts of rumours. I didn't dare go out.

I am quite unharmed. He realizes that she is standing with her hand against his chest. He takes it and kisses it, presses it to his cheek. She strokes his hair. He succumbs to tears.

She instructs the servants to make up a bed for him in one of the rooms and to prepare a bath. His ruined clothes cannot be used again; he must borrow from the professor.

He cannot let go of her hand, but clutches it in his own. There is something I must say, he says.

There is plenty of time for that. Now you must take a bath and get some rest.

I must ask your forgiveness, he says. Can you forgive me? On behalf of your sister?

Oh, Morten. It has all been forgotten, such a long time ago. My sister is beyond such thoughts now. She suffers not.

No, but perhaps I do. He who fails another fails first and foremost himself. Especially if, as I, he has entered into covenant with the Lord. This fire. So much has happened these last days. It feels like a dream. I have discovered there must have been something wrong with me all these years. I have not been a good person, Cathrine. I have committed many wicked deeds. Now I must ask forgiveness.

She stands quite motionless and stares at him. Her eyes are blue, her mouth hints at thoughts and emotions he is unable to determine. You are not a bad person, Morten Falck, and it is very arrogant of you to think that you should be so much more exceptional and abominable than the rest of us.

No, indeed. Yes. I suppose. Now you have made me confused. But you must forgive me, do you hear?

†

Some days pass. He resides with the professor, consumes three meals a day, strolls in Rosenborg Have with Cathrine on his arm. One day they take a carriage into the country, to the house where Buntzen has taken up residence, and deliver the undamaged portrait of the Duke. Abelone is with them. The sun shines on her face; she seems to savour the warmth and light. The engraver invites them to stay for lunch. He instructs the staff to set a table in the garden. They eat a roast marinated in honey. For dessert they pluck strawberries in the vegetable garden and eat them with cream and syrup. They spend a whole day in the engraver's garden. In the evening they drive back into the city. Falck senses he has begun to have feelings for Cathrine, feelings he perhaps ought not to harbour, or which were better directed towards Abelone. He tells her this and she is kind and understanding, but afterwards there is a distance between them, which he knows he must accept. The widow waits for him. He knows it.

Much of what happened during the two days and nights the fire raged feels unreal to him, not least his encounter with the hermaphrodite. But the heavy leather purse reminds him that it was real enough. He spends some of the money on a new cassock and ruff collar, some books and other items to replace what he had in his sack. He does not purchase a wig. The day of the wig is over, a new century is just around the corner. He still has a great deal of money left. Some of it he keeps, the rest he puts in the collection box of Vor Frue Kirke.

At the Missionskollegium he meets with Mr Friedrich, who recalls their encounter during the blaze, a chance occurrence that turns out to Falck's advantage. Shortly after they parted, a carriage came and Friedrich seems to believe it was at Falck's behest. Much of the furnishings and the archive were saved, Friedrich tells him. But alas, everything is in chaos. We should like to have had the opportunity to ponder the Magister's references and credentials, but it will take months to restore order to the archive. And, of course, some considerable part of it has been lost.

Quite, says Falck. Does this mean the Mission will not employ me?

We have a vacant calling at Holsteinsborg, Friedrich says. Our Magister Landstad there has regrettably come to grief. If Magister Falck is willing to accept the position, then it is his.

He accepts and yet remains anxious that his papers might suddenly turn up. But nothing is forthcoming. He continues to put off approaching the Trade as regards his debt. When finally he does, he is told the office has no record of any sum of debt to the trading station at Sukkertoppen and that a large number of documents were lost in the fire. And with that the matter is closed.

†

10 August 1795, Laurentiusdag, the Feast of St Lawrence. Morten Falck bids farewell to Professor Støvring and his wife. He takes Abelone's hand and kisses it. She smiles, an elevated, angelic smile, then withdraws her hand from his. The professor has arranged a carriage. He arrives at the Toldboden in the late morning and steps down into a boat that rows him out to the hooker, the *Hans Egede*. The sky is overcast; around him rigging and sails snap in the wind. He boards the ship by the ladder, swings his legs over the bulwark and puts his feet on the deck. The captain welcomes him aboard.

It's late in the year for a passage to Greenland, the captain says. We must expect bad weather.

I'm used to bad weather, says Falck, and smiles. I look forward to it.

Well, then, I think the Magister will have much to enjoy in the weeks ahead, says the captain with a laugh.

Falck goes below and installs himself in his cabin.

EPILOGUE

The Graves

(14 August 1815)

The fog lies densely in the fjord, though it is well into morning. I am seated on the stern thwart and recall the first time I sailed here. Then, too, the fog lay thick.

The kayak man is a mixture from the colony. They say he is the son of the former Trader Kragstedt, who returned home, following the death of his wife. Indeed, there is some resemblance. Most of them are gone now, returned home or dead. These are new times. Hammer, the smith, is still alive, though has been compelled to relinquish the tool after which he is named. He has become pious in his old age; an abiding inclination to absorb himself in the scriptures has taken possession of him, which I find praiseworthy, albeit rather comical. The present colony manager is Rasmus Bjerg, a man of substance who is kindly disposed to the Mission and moreover a friend of the Greenlander. It must be a lonely life for someone like him. He came to the country when quite young; now he is ageing and grey and has neither wife nor so much as an illegitimate child to keep him company. No one else is left from that time. Apart from myself.

The boy says something from the thwart in the bow and I am torn from my thoughts.

This Habakuk, he does not seem to be keen on visitors, he says with a grin. He has sent the fog out, so that we cannot come and disturb him.

The fog is often thick here, I tell him. It has nothing to do with Habakuk, my friend.

Is it true he was a sorcerer and could conjure?

That is just talk. You should not believe such tales.

How do you know? I see he is rather offended at having been cut down to size.

I knew him.

He looks at me with wide eyes. You knew Habakuk?

He even held you in his arms when you were a baby. It is not that long since he lived. He was a tall man. And a skilled orator. Highly devout and saintly deep down. He could spellbind a crowd when he spoke. Of course, he had his good and bad sides like everyone else. There was no more to it than that. Actually, it was his wife Maria Magdalene who was behind it all. She had the brains. But they are dead and gone now, both of them.

People say they walk again.

That is just superstition. You should not be afraid of it.

I'm not afraid, he says, insulted.

We rock gently back and forth in time with the oars. The oarswomen look constantly back over their shoulders and keep the kayak man in sight. We stay close to the shore. Directly above us is the sun and a blue sky and yet the fog is at all sides, dense and dullish silver. It is indeed all very portentous and I am compelled to reproach myself, as I have reproached the boy, for being superstitious.

The kayak man says something and points. We are here!

The women hold their oars aloft. We glide into a bay. A raven caws from the esker. None of us speaks. The raven caws again.

Diavalu, one of the women says. They laugh nervously.

Presently we jump out and pull up the boat. A handful of people come down to the shore and help. Welcome, priest! *Palasi tikilluarit!* I recognize one of the men: Habakuk's and Maria Magdalene's son Detlef, who shot his sister in the eye with an arrow and thereby caused her death. Now he is middle-aged with children and grandchildren, a renowned hunter, yet light of skin. Another one! We are shown to the family's house and fed soup. In return we give them tea brought from the colony. I offer my excuses before the food makes me drowsy and lethargic. I wish to go up and see the old settlement, I tell them. Afterwards, there will be devotions.

There is hardly anything left to see, says Detlef. It was an unusual place to live, Priest.

Indeed, I reply. They were unusual people. They tried to do things differently.

Yes, and look where it got them, he says scornfully. We Greenlanders belong by the fjord, not in the fells like ravens and foxes. It's important we don't forget it.

I am an old man now, yet still adroit. My joints are hardly stiff. I ask my boy to come with me. We clamber up through the thick vegetation that lines the shore and emerge almost immediately above the fog. I stop halfway up the slope. The boy halts at my side. We look up at the plateaus that unfold between the rock.

Was it here? the boy asks.

Yes, it was here.

It's a splendid place.

Yes, I know of no other like it. It is so magnificent. In such a place a man feels close to God, don't you think?

I do, he says, gazing upwards with an obliging smile.

We stand for a while and enjoy the sun. Then we continue the ascent; he goes first, his steps light and springy.

By the time we reach the uppermost plateau the fog has been sucked from the fjord and we can see the little cluster of peat dwellings where smoke coils from the chimneys, and the inhabitants themselves as they help the oarswomen and the kayak man carry our pack up the slope. I have told them it is best to camp above the fjord, so as to avoid the fog in the late and early hours, and it would seem they have heeded my advice, though it is against their nature to dwell away from the shore.

Twenty years ago two hundred people lived here, I tell the boy.

And now nothing is left, he says.

I'm sure there will be something. All we have to do is find it. Come.

We pass a couple of dilapidated peat houses and the remains of the great oven in which they smoked their salmon. Otherwise, only some patterns in the light-coloured moss show where the dwellings stood.

While the boy explores, I sit down on a rock to catch my breath. I am in my fifties now, an old man, though sound in wind and limb. My wife and children and children's children keep me in vigour, I suppose. The Lord has blessed me. The boy has a wife himself and three healthy offspring of his own already. So I am rich in joys as well as worries. And yet I remember to thank the Lord for each day. I live in a healthy manner, drinking no other alcohol than the colony's fresh ale, and I stay well away from the Trade's mouldy meat. The parishioners of the colony, also children of a kind, who come to confess their sins or simply to talk with their priest, play their own part in keeping my mind fresh.

New times indeed. Following the unrest in Denmark, the war with the English and the state bankruptcy, Greenland had to look after itself. In many ways it was good for us. We learned to stand on our own feet. The clergy dwindled in number, some died, others were fortunate enough to find passage home. In these present years I am the only working priest along the entire coast between Godthåb and Jakobshavn. Oddly enough, such isolation has led the Mission to flourish and prompted many Greenlanders to move to the colonies to be christened and to sing their beloved hymns in the church each Sunday. I have myself composed a couple of them – this said in all modesty. I have developed quite a knack with the lute, an instrument I inherited from an old missionary at Holsteinsborg. Of him, the less said the better!

Following the deaths of Maria Magdalene and Habakuk, the people lost interest in religious reveries. Habakuk died in 1798, she four years later. May the Lord have mercy upon their souls. The settlement here has lain abandoned for twenty years. Everything usable – or nearly everything – has been carried down to the dwellings at the shore.

I take the boy over to the graves. There are no names on them, but

I know who lies beneath. I tell him about each in turn. I think he is incredulous that I am old enough to have met them.

My ancient father, he quips.

Here lies Habakuk, I tell him, and here Maria Magdalene. The graves are untouched; few people come here and those who do are mindful not to disturb the peace of the dead. Habakuk's reputation still lives and I consider it will continue to do so for a long time yet. I stick the toe of my boot under one of the flat stones, lifting it slightly and allowing it to fall again with a thud. The boy jumps. They can't hurt you, I tell him and chuckle. There's no need to be afraid.

I'm not afraid of the dead, he replies, disgruntled.

I ruffle his hair. He laughs and flaps away my hand.

He is grown now and has become a man. We work together in the Mission. He doesn't like me still calling him a boy. He says he wants to be a ship's captain, but he knows my hope is for him to be ordained as a priest like myself. A bright capacity would be wasted if he were to sail the seven seas. Besides, I would die of loneliness. He is my best friend.

It takes a while for us to find the last of the graves. They lie up on the esker, high above the tableland, on a plateau of the fell commanding a view to the east, west and south. Three together.

The boy flops down in the grass. He lights his pipe and puffs. Who lies here?

Old friends, I tell him.

There are no coffins in the soil, only three bodies wrapped in linen, two of them at each other's side, the third and smallest at a right angle at their feet. The grass around the gravestones is tall; it bends in the wind that comes sweeping from the fell. Rosebay grows at the place and small, hardy bunches of violet flowers, whose name escapes me in my old age. I pull away some tufts and the inscriptions are revealed.

I remember him, the boy says, smoothing his hand over the stone. He was kind and gave me books. Did you lay him to rest, Father?

Yes, I laid all three in the ground, though they died at different times. I felt they should lie together. But go now, let me sit here a while on my own. There is something I must repay. Afterwards I shall tell you the whole story. I think the time is right for you to hear it.

I watch him as he canters down to the tableland below. The further away he gets, the smaller he becomes and the more he looks like the boy I brought up with concern and love. The whole story? I wonder. No, perhaps not the whole story. Some of it must follow me to the grave. But the Lord knows the truth. He knows me and has blessed me. He is full of forgiveness to whoever prays for it.

I went to the smith, old Niels Hammer, to have the stones hewn and the inscriptions cut. He grumbled about the many words. I am a smith, he complained, not a book printer! And yet he carried out the work and I managed to ensure it was done without mistakes of spelling. I know something about the smith, as I know things about most people. On the other hand, he knows something about me. He it was who received the gold and forged from it a crucifix.

My hand is curled around its cross as I sit here at the graves on the south-facing slope. Gold washed from a river in the north. It feels warm and heavy in my hand. It is hard to give up. And yet I take it from around my neck and feel its familiar weight vanish from my chest. I have worn it for twenty years. I place it between the two graves where it belongs. It is a relief to be unburdened of it. On top of it I lay some stones, forming a kind of bridge between the graves. I brush away the dust from my hands and kneel in the heather. I say the Lord's Prayer. I bless the graves. It is quiet here. Lichen grows in the cracks of the gravestones, but the inscriptions can still be distinguished, tainted green on grey slabs of stone:

HERE LIES THE BODY OF

MR MORTEN PEDERSEN FALCK

BORN 20 MAY 1756

DIED 12 MAY 1807

Grey of Age, Toil and Endeavour in the Name of God
Depart in Peace, faithful Friend

And on the other:

LYDIA PEDERSEN FALCK

ARNARULUNNGUAQ

CHRISTENED JENSEN

Here laid to Rest

By her Brother Bertel Jensen

Ordained Priest of Sukkertoppen Colony

Author's Afterword

This novel is a fantasy, constructed around events that took place more than two hundred years ago. Events occurring in the novel did not necessarily occur in reality, or else they did so in another place at another time, in a different sequence, with different people and in different weather. The characters are my own inventions, although some really did exist. Who can truly know a person, not least someone who, for instance, died in 1802? I have allowed myself to hazard a guess.

The famine that is mentioned may be historically correct, but if so it is unrecorded. Several periods did occur in which the hunting failed – periods of 'two winters without summer' – and these most certainly were the cause of great hardship in eighteenth-century Greenland. In some cases, nine tenths of the population of an area perished due to epidemics and hunger. Nonetheless, colony people were little concerned as to whether those in the outlying district lived or died, so accounts of these times of scarcity are sporadic.

I have tried to recreate actual places, times and incidents as exactly as possible: Sukkertoppen (1785–93), Copenhagen (1782–87), the great fire of 1795, and so on. Frequent use has been made of eye-witness accounts, though these have been tailored at my own discretion. The physical reality that my fictional characters inhabit, however, is authentic only to the extent that I have been able – or considered it suitable – to make it.

I owe the novel's title to the writer and historian Mads Lidegaard, a true friend of Greenland. His Danish account of the prophets' rise and fall can be accessed online and may be compared to my own. Pastor Hother Ostermann's more than one hundred biographies of Danes and Norwegians in Greenland up until 1814 have been an invaluable source. Clergymen with a love of writing have always been numerous, in Greenland as elsewhere. We are deeply indebted to them, because without them we would have nothing but ledgers. That said, they are by no means always impartial. Finn Gad, the author of a three-volume history of Greenland, may be a lesser writer, but he is to be praised for his sober and detailed work, even if it may seem dull in comparison. Of the Greenlandic writers, mention must be made of the catechist Peter Gundel, whose book *Jeg danser af glæde* (I Dance with Joy) provides insight into the plight of an intelligent and gifted Greenlander afflicted by illness in an isolated settlement during colonial days, though much later than the events described here.

It is said that the prophetess Maria Magdalene's correspondence with the priest, apparently a rather thick bundle, perished when it was used to light a fire in an emergency. Most likely it was cold and perhaps their letters saved a life. But in the flames were lost what to all intents and purposes was the only historical, handwritten document penned by a Greenlander in the eighteenth century. Sad, but all the more fortunate for me, because it left me free to use my imagination.

Acknowledgements

The Danish Arts Foundation, for its three-year grant; the Council of Danish Artists (and Jens and Lise on the island of Hirsholm), for allowing me to stay in their Artists' Residence; the Cultural Foundation Denmark-Greenland, for financially supporting a research journey to Maniitsoq and the Eternal Fjord in August 2010; Tea Dahl Christensen, Director (until 2011), Maniitsoq Museum; Peter Henningsen, Director, Frilandsmuseet; Søren Rud, Senior Lecturer, The SAXO Institute, University of Copenhagen; Simon Pasternak, Senior Editor, Gyldendal; Johannes Riis, Literary Director, Gyldendal; Jon Kyst, Akademisk Rejsebureau; Inge Kyst; Bodil Kyst; Bente Hauptmann; Aviaaja Kleist Burkal; Staffan Söderberg; Elsebeth Schiller; Tage Schjøtt, Saga Maps; Aalipaaraq Kreutzmann; Benny Vadmand, hypnotist.